The Portable Thomas Wolfe

A partial list of other volumes in the
Viking Portable Library
appears at the end of the book.

The Portable

THOMAS WOLFE

Edited by Maxwell Geismar

NEW YORK : THE VIKING PRESS

1946

CONTENTS

From Death to Morning

The Hills Beyond

country two miles from my home town where people waited for the streetcar."

It is the care that went into the planes and surfaces of Wolfe's work—the tactile areas—that makes it an inhabitable literary world, just as it was the continuous rehearsal of his experience in his own mind—and the slow discovery of the underlying substratum of meaning —that made it, finally, a durable world. He wrote in the large, to be sure. But what is chiefly responsible for the notion of Wolfe as a quantitative writer is, I think, a sort of quantitative reading of him. And, faced by these increasingly massive blocks of material, these steadily accumulating blue and red volumes, 6 by 8 inches, 500 words per page, 900 pages per volume, each volume somehow seeming much heavier than the last, it is probably difficult not to read him in a 6-by-8-inch way. Yet in such an episode as that of Starwick in Europe, which is probably the best single episode in Wolfe's work and which comes at the end of his best and also his biggest volume, you may suddenly realize the kind of craftsmanship that has gone into the hundreds of scenes within scenes which form the whole panorama of this world.

Wolfe may have been thinking of something like this when he remonstrated with Scott Fitzgerald, who had suggested more Flaubert and less Zola in the younger writer's work:

You have had to work and sweat blood yourself and you know what it is like to try to write a living word or create a living thing. So don't talk this foolish stuff to me about exuberance or being a conscious artist or not bringing things into emotional relief, or any of the rest of it. . . . The little fellows who don't know may picture a man as a great "exuberant" six-foot-six clodhopper straight out of nature who bites off half a plug of apple tobacco, tilts the corn liquor jug and lets half of it gurgle down his throat, wipes off his mouth with the back of one hairy paw, jumps three feet in the air and clacks his heels together four times before he hits the floor again and yells, "Whoopee, boys, I'm a rootin, tootin, shootin son of a gun from Buncombe County—out of my way now, here I come!"—and then wads up three hundred thousand words or so, hurls it at a blank page, puts covers on it and says, "Here's my book!" Now, Scott, the boys who write book reviews in New York may think it's done that way; but the man who wrote *Tender Is the Night* knows better. You know you never did it that way, you know I never did, you know that no one else who ever wrote a line worth reading ever did. . . . I want to be a better artist. I want to be a more selective artist. I want to be a more restrained artist. I want to use such talents as I have, control such forces as I may own, direct such energy as I may use more cleanly, more surely and to better purpose. But Flaubert me no Flauberts, Bovary me no Bovarys, Zola me no Zolas. And exuberance me no exuberances.[1]

And perhaps also these selections from Wolfe, standing on their own, will dispose of some other current notions about his writing.

The simplest thing to do with some of these statements is to admit them. Was he an heir to the Southern rhetoricians, a pet of poeticizers and an easy prey for choral arrangements? Yes, naked and alone, he came into that agrarian society of Shakespearian Festivals and Stedman's Selections. But notice also, a little later, the Wolfe of a trip North in *Of Time and the River*—the Wolfe of Shakespearian take-offs, of a low and gaudy native humor. Was he, again, in his youth, a prime case of the Rural Romanticist—of the *Weltschmerz* of the Hinterland? Yes, but even then he was writing chiefly of other twisted rural souls; he soon wrote of Harvard aristocrats, Boston hoodlums, the Park Avenue *bourgeoisie*. Caught up in the web of cosmopolitan sophistication,

---

[1] *Quoted from a letter to Fitzgerald, published in The Crack-Up (New Directions, 1945).*

was he also reminiscent, in opening accents at once credulous and bigoted, of the familiar, even the stereotyped Provincial in the Magic City—a semitropical cousin of Dreiser's in our letters, and sometimes almost equally "flaccid and elephantine," as Henry Mencken noted in respect to Wolfe's literary ancestor? Yet, as early as his second novel, he had summarized the whole vexing cultural issue of Eastern ease and grace in, for example, that fabulous Castle on the Hudson; or in those "French" writers, Feuillet, Capus, Courteline and René Bazin; or merely in his suggestion to the critics of sexual activity in America that, even in Boston, on the Esplanade, at nighttime, in the hot and sultry month of August, the noise of the kissing was like the noise the wind makes through a leafy grove—and that they were still selling cradles down in Georgia. At this point, too, he began to see the Enfabled Rock, with all its enchantment and all its bitterness, a little more clearly than Scott Fitzgerald himself, say, had ever seen his Lost City. During the course of the 1930's, in fact, Wolfe took on a cultural as well as a personal perspective that was not entirely granted to some of the more typical literary figures of the 1920's. It is even possible that this writer, heavy-handed as he seemed among the whole group of deft and delicate American moderns, was the one who changed most sharply and surely. At any rate the rebellious and introverted mind becomes one of the most acute and entertaining social commentators of the decade—and a prime chronicler of the national mind in the epoch of the bust and the hangover.

Yes; still—wasn't he finally, as was announced by some of our more consistently disappointed students of the Literary Craft—wasn't he, after all, a, so to speak, *professional* believer, an optimist, a happy vulgarian among the disenchanted professors, and the blind Yea-

Sayer of contemporary Belles Lettres? Well, he was also, as you might note for the record, a Yea-Sayer whose constant companions were despair and disease, whose closest friend was death; a poet of springtime in the hearts of men who was well acquainted with autumn and its shriveled forms; a seeker of sensuous beauty who had met "the sickening and abominable end of flesh"; a lover of all life who felt himself "life's monstrous outcast"; a naïve and resplendent enthusiast, in short, who came trailing visions of the abyss.

As a matter of fact these visions—of guilt and of horror; and these recurrent fears that he would "strangle like a mad dog in the tunnel's dark"—are at the center of Wolfe's work, and we ought to look into them in order to understand him.

II

In some ways, too, he was an unduly sensitive and difficult young man.

Probably that outsized carcass, nature's gift to him, was the initial factor. "The really important thing—the *truly* autobiographical thing," Wolfe wrote in respect to his later, "objective" novels, "was the fact of physical variation: to create a figure who would illustrate that variation and all the great human experiences that attend it." In any case this is a persistent theme in Wolfe's work from one of the earliest short stories, "No Cure for It," whose youthful hero resembles a monkey, to "Gulliver" itself, whose mature hero laments the accident of birth that had imprisoned a spirit "fierce and proud and swift as flight" in such a grotesque tenement.

But the fact of physical variation was complicated by the fact of physical disease. Some of the most remarkable passages in Wolfe's first novel deal with this, and Eugene

Gant grows up under its shadow: the early sickness of his brother Grover, the final sickness of Ben, the cancerous infection of Gant himself which almost seems to grow and spread as the novel grows and spreads—this interminable diseased growth that outlasts the first novel and spreads well into the second, with the father's black arterial death blood flowing out over these pages just as the son's life blood went into them. *Look Homeward, Angel* is first and foremost a study of the distorted and dissolving body.

> I give thanks for every dirty lust and hunger that crawled through the polluted blood of my noble ancestors. I give thanks for every scrofulous token that may ever come upon me. I give thanks for the love and mercy that kneaded me over the washtub the day before my birth. I give thanks for the country slut who nursed me and let my dirty bandage fester across my navel. . . . By God, I shall spend the rest of my life getting my heart back, healing and forgetting every scar you put upon me when I was a child.

Yet the festering Gant of the novel is balanced by Eliza Gant and her almost equally cancerous spiritual sickness—her insensate passion for property.

> Mama, Mama, in God's name, what is it? What do you want? Are you going to strangle and drown us all? Don't you own enough? Do you want more string? Do you want more bottles? . . . Don't you own enough? Do you want the town? What is it?

On this note the early Wolfean hero leaves the "rich and mysterious South"—this barren spiritual wilderness, as Eugene Gant then believes, with its cheap mythology, its swarming superstitions, its "hostile and murderous entrenchment against all new life."

Wolfe himself, however, was not so easily rid of his Southern associations—and obligations. He was supported by his family during the early years of his Northern education, and the sense of debt to a society he had apparently repudiated forms a recurrent and uneasy motif in his letters home.[1] As early as 1917, at Chapel Hill, he noted that expenses were much higher. "I try to pay up every check I get and then, naturally, go broke . . . . However, I'm as economical as possible"—a refrain, with its element of truth and its element of absurdity, that is to echo through these letters for the next twenty years. "Do you want me home?" Wolfe again wrote to Julia Elizabeth Wolfe in 1919:

> If so, let me know immediately. I shall need money—a considerable sum. Your last check—$25—did not cover my debts as my room and board were $30 alone and I also had books equipment etc. So there is debt of approx. $15 on last month together with $30 for this month. . . . I'll need $70. Sorry bill is this large. If you think best I stay here deduct expense home and send rest. Pardon my lack of enthusiasm but I'm all in and must go to an English conference with my professor.

From now on, however, Wolfe wrote from Harvard in 1921, he really would practice strict economy.

> I know I have wasted some money, which has worried me considerably, and which I will try to profit by. The rest of the family hold it against me, I know, that I have been to school so much and spent so much, and there is much truth in what they are saying about me. . . . I am in a delicate, trying position before you and the family [he said again in the same year] and I am trying to meet and solve the problem as honestly and courageously as I can. Of one thing I earnestly entreat you never to doubt: That is the sense of gratitude and loyalty I feel to you and Papa. That is stronger now in me than it ever was, stronger than, when as a little boy, we

---

[1] Thomas Wolfe's Letters to His Mother, edited by John S. Terry (New York: Charles Scribner's Sons, 1945) is an invaluable source book of the writer's earlier years, and I have drawn heavily upon it for the biographical account that follows. A Note on Thomas Wolfe, by Edward Aswell (Harper & Bros., 1941), is also informative and interesting.

occupied the same room, stronger than when you took me on your trips to Florida and elsewhere. When I retire at night, when I wake in the morning I am conscious of the weight of my gratitude; it is the spur that drives me on.

And this was all in a sense true. He had gone north in the face of the family's suspicion and hostility. He intended to become a writer in the face of their belief that a writer was a man "like Lord Byron or Lord Tennyson or Longfellow or Percy Bysshe Shelley"—a man who was far away from them. Moreover, he had given up a respectable teaching job in Asheville to become such a man—and meanwhile to live off the family's bounty—and he had made this decision in the face of William Oliver Wolfe's mortal sickness. ("While I am absent Papa may die. I foresee these consequences. Do you think they have not been gouged in my very soul?") And the relationship with Julia Wolfe was a delicate one.

For, whether consciously or not, it was part of the mother's natural instinct, if not altogether to her natural interest, to continue to tie the son down; her gesture of generosity, in supporting the young Wolfe, was also an act of domination. While, on the other side of the partnership, by thus allowing himself to be supported—and over this period Wolfe seems curiously and even wilfully unself-sufficient—the son may have been deliberately allowing himself to remain in this childhood pattern. It is possible that the very forms of Wolfe's opposition to the pattern—he is always losing Julia's checks or overdrawing her account—that these obvious gestures of revolt were also designed to keep himself penniless and dependent. It was only later, with the *Angel,* and with Julia still supporting him, that he was able to free himself by destroying her—and by destroying her, created her.

But even on the partial level of human behavior which people, quite wisely, prefer to take for the whole, it is difficult to feel a perpetual gratitude toward a ceaseless benefactor. And particularly, say, when the bene- factor is buying real estate in Miami, and when one, from the provinces, in the midst of the Boston blue bloods, is using one's vest to patch one's trousers. (Later, the ragged young Wolfe, venturing down to interview a Broadway theatrical producer in respect to his new play, was given two five-dollar bills as a handout.) In any case, the expressions of indebtedness in these letters become a little stylized, while the accents of bitterness become sharper. "You are the only one who ever writes me from home now," Wolfe wrote to his mother in 1921, "and you have about deserted me."

Two weeks from today I will be twenty-one years old— legally the beginning of manhood. If the time has come for me to go out on my own, so be it, but please try not to treat me with the indifference that has characterized your cor- respondence, or lack of it, for the last year. You would not be intentionally guilty of cruelty to me but unintentionally you have been. Uncle Henry says it is a family trait to forget once out of sight—but how in God's name can I believe you would forget me in a year's time?

You didn't want me at home [he added], you said nothing about my returning and I shall see that your desires and those of the family are satisfied.

This increasing bitterness extended from his family to his friends.

As a matter of fact I almost have an aversion—natural or unnatural, to seeing any of my old friends—unless, by God, I know they are friends whether you bloom, or if you wither . . . . I couldn't stand Asheville now—I couldn't stand the silly little grins on the silly little drugstore faces. I couldn't stand the silly little questions of "What're you doing now?" —And the silly little "oh" and the silly little silence that follows when you say you are writing—as if they could know

—stupid little vermin as they are—the tragedy, and the heartbreak, and the travail of mind and spirit—that has kept me ragged.

And it was a bitterness that extended from his family and friends to his work itself:

To Langner's credit he did not ask me to retract a thing—I can keep all this—all he wants is a shorter, simpler play. Well, I will take one more chance and give him what he wants, in spite of the fact that Professor Baker will throw up his hands and say that I have "prostituted my art," and so on, when I see him. Well, "my art" has kept me ragged and driven me half mad;—I will see now if prostitution can put a few decent garments on my back and keep me housed. My good friends, Professor Baker included, have told me for years now of "my great talent," "my artistry," and so on—they have told me it would be a terrible thing for me to do anything else but write. They have said, "You have it—it's bound to come"—but not once has anyone given me advice on the simple little matter of keeping the breath of life in my body until the miracle does happen. That I can write better plays than most of those on Broadway I have no doubt—God help me if I can't—but to write such filthy, sexy twaddle, rot, and bunkum as this, I must cast all conscience to the winds. Well, I can and will do even that, for *money, money, money.*

Although there was now a question as to whether he could do even that. "My life being so up in the air, I find it hard to accomplish anything I want to write."

In part at least Wolfe had dug himself into this hole, too. Were his present fears somewhat extreme? His earlier hopes had been ever more so. He had worked with Frederick Koch and the Carolina Playmakers at Chapel Hill. He had gone on to the celebrated George Pierce Baker and The 47 Workshop at Cambridge, and there, grooming himself for the stage, along with the young Phillip Barry, he had almost persuaded himself that his early play, *The Mountaineers,* was going to be another *You and I.*

For a one-act play it is somewhat long, and will stand condensation and polishing, but it is the real thing and deals
with a great tragedy. . . . It's the best play that has been
written here this year simply because I have burned with
eagerness and desire to have the truth out.

Well, a score of young provincials, watching the lights
of Boston and New York, have written such letters home
from the time of Royall Tyler, and there is also unconscious comedy in Wolfe's detailed summary of his
next and even better play—and of an earlier Eugene
who is "wild with grief" as he bids farewell to a rotting
Southern aristocracy. "Master of Oakmont. Master of a
ruined kingdom, and a rotting Mansion— What a farce!
Lord of Misrule."

A similarly youthful tone, at once intense and inflated,
marks the "destiny" letter which Wolfe sent home two
years later, in 1923:

The plays I am going to write may not be suited to the
tender bellies of old maids, sweet young girls, or Baptist
Ministers but they will be true and honest and courageous,
and the rest doesn't matter. If my play goes on I want you
to be prepared for execrations upon my head. I have stepped
on toes right and left—I spared Boston with its nigger-senti-
mentalists no more than the South, which I love, but which
I am nevertheless pounding. I am not interested in writing
what our pot-bellied member of the Rotary and Kiwanis call
a "good show"—I want to know life and understand it and
interpret it without fear or favor. This, I feel, is a man's work
and worthy of a man's dignity. For life is not made up of
sugary, sticky, sickening Edgar A. Guest sentimentality, it is
not made up of dishonest optimism, God is *not* always in his
Heaven, all is *not* always right with the world. It is not all
bad, but it is not all good, it is not all ugly, but it is not all
beautiful, it is life, life, life—the only thing that matters. It
is savage, cruel, kind, noble, passionate, selfish, generous,
stupid, ugly, beautiful, painful, joyous,—it is all these, and
more, and it's all these I want to know and, by God, I shall,
though they crucify me for it. I will go to the ends of the

earth to find it, to understand it, I will know this country
when I am through as I know the palm of my hand, and I
will put it on paper and make it true and beautiful.

But there is also a new note. Did this early Wolfe, like
any Lardnerian song writer from Schenectady, consider
himself "inevitable"? Did he earnestly believe that "the
only thing that can stop me now is insanity, disease, or
death"—and go on, innocently, to proclaim that "I
never forget; I have never forgotten"? He had nevertheless become aware of something which Lardner's para-
noiac yokels never quite realized: that he who is inevitable is the victim of his inevitability—trapped and
bound by even the most beneficent sense of destiny.
"That is what my life means to me: I am at the mercy
of this thing and I will do it or die." Already he had
plunged himself into that involved and interminable
evocation of his own life and backgrounds, that tortuous
American remembrance of things past which formed the
core of his work—and already disease and death formed
the medium of approach, so to speak—the opaque psy-
chological liquid through which he swam.

For as early as 1920, too, while he was still at Chapel
Hill, Wolfe had developed a heavy cold which hung
on persistently.

The thing got down into my chest and a week or two
ago, I began to cough—at first a dry cough—then a rattling,
tearing sort of cough, full of phlegm. I became worried. My
right lung was sore. Of course I had to be out in all kinds of
weather, and this didn't help. One night I started coughing
here, in my room, and I put my handkerchief to my mouth.
When I drew it away there was a tiny spot of blood on it. I
was half sick with horror and I tried not to think of it.
Thereafter when I coughed I kept my mouth closed and
coughed in my throat. I swallowed pneumonia salve at night
in huge balls, and rubbed my chest with the stuff. I ate
cough drops.

And, remembering as he did his early family background—and his brother Ben had died of pneumonia—it is no wonder that the impoverished country man kept track of his health with an almost neurasthenic solicitude. "The meanest, most persistent cold I ever had," he wrote from Boston at "Xmas time," in 1923, "is slowly breaking up." He was "all nerves" in New York the year after, and had lost fifteen pounds during the summer. While he was teaching at New York University he noted that his eyes had gone bad. "I hope it is the cold, I don't know."—"I haven't wasted time by sleeping," he wrote again, "I am worked to a frazzle, and my left eye went bad about ten days ago." And his physical ailments, as Wolfe knew, were accentuated by his working habits —that is, by the fits of nervous frenzy and the spells of nervous exhaustion that followed each other during his work days, by his increasing sense of being deserted and alone ("I suppose I am one of the loneliest people in the world"), and by the dreams of time and guilt which now began to mark his nights: by all these symptoms of the heightened physical and spiritual intensity which had now become his normal routine. And now, too, as Julia Wolfe continued patiently and inexorably to accumulate her plots in Miami, the earlier accents of filial bitterness become those of exasperation, and almost of renunciation.

"I have no belief in your property or in anyone's property any more," Wolfe wrote from England in 1926. "I have no hope or belief or expectancy of getting anything from it now or hereafter—and he who ceases to hope or believe ceases to desire." "Money in our family," he said two months later, "has been a deadly poison—for it you have lost comfort, peace, and in the end, money itself; it has been a breeder of suspicion, of jealousy, of falsehood among brother and sister." His own life at home had ceased to be possible, he said the next year, and it had taken him twenty-seven years to rise above the hatreds of his childhood and the ugly and rancorous feeling which had existed in the family during his youth. "The next time we get hold of money let's put it in the bank, or on our back, or in our bellies—where it will do some good."

Yet, with this condemnation of his Southern home, there was no fond acceptance of his Northern life either. If the earlier Wolfe had displayed a certain impatience with Asheville's "little vermin" who awaited the proof of his dramatic talent; if what had actually stopped him at this point was not disease or death but the Theatre Guild, which had rejected his play; and if consequently these Northern intellectuals too, and indeed the entire Enfabled Rock, the whole glamorous pageantry of "that distant Babylon, cloud-capped and rosy-hued there in the smoke of his imagination," had turned stale and bitter for the provincial aspirant—now he had even more to say on the subject. Was his strongest impression of the Northern metropolis that of "thousands of inferior people undeveloped physically, dwarfed mentally"—from whom would grow the America of tomorrow, the hope of the world, which it was impossible to regard without a sinking of the heart? The nation itself now seemed compounded of such people, or of overgrown and ill-bred children, insolent to everything but money, servile, boastful and cowardly. "That, I am sorry to say, is my free opinion of this noble land—the amalgamated Boosters, Kiwanians, Lions, and, in general, the Federated Half Breeds of the World." If he remained in it at all, said this morose and peevish Wolfe, it was simply because other countries were not much better off—"the rabble everywhere is much the same—loud, ignorant, and cheap"—and when their leaders were not fools they were rascals. Furthermore, while he lived in New York, it was not for the sake of the hundred million who surrounded him, and whom he ignored unless they began to blow their bad breath and their superstitions in his face, but because New York was the money center and there was still a great deal of money in him:

I am sure I could make it out of advertising, the movies, or some form of publicity (fat, juicy, sugar-coated lies for our great Boob Public to swallow). I know a great deal about some things (not as much, it is true, as most of my fellow country men who know almost everything), but I have read and studied much and observed abundantly. Perhaps I shall end up by persuading the morons that the way to live forty years longer is to eat yeast every day, or to keep the voice beautiful by smoking Lucky Strikes. There is no limit apparently to what they are willing to believe, if you say it to them long enough.

Now, in fact, these accents of provincial superstition and arrogance, of vindictive envy and blind hatred, reach their climax in the young Wolfe. But now, of course, he was in the very midst of the first of that series of profound and agonizing creative struggles—those traumas of articulation—which marked, which actually *were*, his life. He was writing the *Angel*.

III

What was remarkable, moreover, was not that the young Wolfe was the sort of person he seemed to be —but that he wasn't.

For in a sense it seemed that almost everything around him—his origins, his temperament, the particular pattern his life fell into—conspired to make him into this sort of bigoted provincial; the real fascination of his story is by what sort of spiritual jujitsu he managed to slip out of fortune's iron collar—though perhaps that is the fascination of human life itself, and magic is its true medium, and in the realm of the psyche a Houdini is a piker.

What was a fact, anyhow, was that Wolfe's work was both a resolution to and at least a partial triumph over these native maladies and phobias—over his resemblance to Œdipus and his attachment to Mammon; over his romantic infatuation for and subsequent disenchantment with the Enfabled Rock; over that lingering but still very powerful tradition—and particularly for this child of Julia's "Old Kentucky Home" in North Carolina—of Southern gentility; over his aversion to the "Federated Half Breeds" of the world and his infatuation with Fame and the Fair Medusa; and even over his initial handicap, that huge and hypersensitive body which, just as it brought home to Wolfe the infinite extent of human stupidity, very early showed to him "the barren unity of life." This wound, too, became another entrance to experience, and similarly, through his work, built in spite of and outside of Time, he trapped and made a friend of his last enemy also. What was remarkable was that this harsh and arrogant young man, whose proudest claim was that he had never forgotten, that he never forgot, *did* forget.

The resolution was not always quite complete, of course. The broken accents of superstition are likely to recur in Wolfe's weaker passages up to the end, just as his troubles did not quite stop with the publication of *Look Homeward, Angel*—just as, in fact, they seemed to be starting all over again. Like Bunyan's Pilgrim, Wolfe took quite a while to arrive at the Celestial City, and like Dante's he seemed, for a time, to be merely moving from the simpler to the more involved circles of Life in the Inferno. The six years between the *Angel* and *Of Time and the River*, the years from 1929 to 1935, are

almost the most involved and the most interesting years
of Wolfe's career; during this period he passed from an
apprentice to a craftsman and from revolt to "discovery,"
and the account of this process which is contained in
The Story of a Novel forms a particularly illuminating
diary of the writer in America.

Some of these tortures were self-inflicted again—it
would be difficult to prove how many of them are not
—and sometimes it seemed that when Wolfe, like God,
did not have any troubles he was forced to invent them.
Perhaps it was inevitable that the gas heater in his New
York apartment would leak—but was it inevitable that,
waking up steadily with a headache, he should never
guess it was leaking? In Paris, down again with "a terrific cold in the foggy weather," he entrusted his manuscript to a perverse *concierge,* and it was Wolfe who
ended up in a French jail for abusing a French citizen.
In Germany, in the midst of those jolly Beer Festivals
which appealed so bluntly to his nether soul, he was
beaten up and landed in a jolly German hospital. Some
years after his first novel Wolfe is still patching up his
old clothes—"I had really got to the point where I felt
disgraced every time I appeared in public"—and still
working "ten, twelve and fourteen hours a day here" for
weeks on end, with his back up to the wall. And when
he had finally surmounted the almost insuperable hurdle
of his second novel, why, of all the literary agents in
New York, did Wolfe pick a young man who was as
temperamental as himself? In the lawsuit which followed, and which dragged on endlessly, with its lurid
charges and counter-charges threatening whatever peace
of mind Wolfe might have achieved, lay the final stroke
of this ludicrous and sometimes almost heartbreaking
drama of the country man and the arts: a drama, really,
which has in it all the elements of a crossroads tragedy,

and the central figures of which might appear as the Hillbilly and the Furies. For this indigenous Orestes certainly had a touch of the Doppus in him—this local Faustus was a kinsman of Peter Schlemiel.

But maybe it was also this fundamental innocence that made Wolfe what he was—a believer in humanity who wore down even his own lawyers—and these continual afflictions that kept his head bowed when it might have been turned. For there was no doubt as to the attraction of the New York society Wolfe describes in *The Web and the Rock*—and from Howells in Boston to Cather in Chicago not many of our literary pilgrims have described it more vividly. After his arrival, moreover, Wolfe *was* a sort of literary sensation; surrounded as he was by his circles of aesthetic admirers, owning the deep friendship of his two celebrated artistic friends, he might well call this his "Magic Year." So the Retreat to Brooklyn—the deliberate self-immolation and the return to darkness and anonymity; the halting efforts of the hillman to comprehend the urban Brooklyn character and to penetrate the barbaric Brooklyn accents; the final conviction of this night-prowler among desolate alleys that here was his second and in a sense even his true home—all this was a strategic move of the highest order. And, just as Wolfe came to settle here, so, too, for all his earlier exasperation, it was his continuing bond with his first home and with the hill people themselves—his recurrent complaint in the very arms of the Fair Medusa that he was "still very homesick and lonely"—that helped him equally to preserve a sort of balance on the pavements of the metropolis.

Were these country people among the benighted citizenry of what Henry Mencken had just called the Sahara of the Bozart—and, proud possessors of a low cunning, not altogether unrelated to William Faulkner's later Bundrens and Snopeses? They were also enigmatic, not without resources, full of tricks as well as quirks— like Dashiell Hammett's Continental Op, they sometimes took pleasure in playing the other half of a half-wit. "*Esse Quam Videri.*" Did Julia Wolfe herself, for example, show a certain maternal naïveté, according to the most enlightened modern standards, in her claim that her prodigy had slept with her "until he was a great big boy"—and did she, further, go on to relate a number of outrageous anecdotes about her boy's nursing habits? (By these same modern standards, she was no doubt compensating, through this maternal possessiveness, for a wandering and rhetorical husband.) Yet there was nothing untoward here in her mind; while we would do well to keep in our minds the physical frankness of these somewhat non-puritanical and almost pre-Victorian mountaineers—and to notice also their more intimate contact with the Negro spirit. If Calvin and Knox finally reached these Southern hills too, they had arrived, so to speak, through the courtesy of Drake and Frobisher (and Thomas Otway was as likely to be known in these regions as Alfred Tennyson), and there was still that little detour through darkest Africa.

There was another interesting Southern strain here which affected Faulkner and Caldwell as well as Wolfe, and which the more cultivated Southern writers—the "superior" people—neglected at their own risk. There was, in these hill people with their involved family histories and their back-country rituals, their abundant hospitality and their endless talking, their mountain laughter and their clinging legends of sin and bloodshed, a strain that probably comes closest, among all our rich regional strains, to what we have labeled the "Russian" soul: I mean, of course, merely the human soul, though at once more deeply enslaved and freer, a soul, as it were, in fetters and in ecstasy. And there is also a mountain mixture here that is not so noticeable in the Mississippi deltas or in the Georgia pinelands—of primitive myth *and* equalitarian enlightenment; of voodoo and the bill of rights.

"You belong to North Carolina," William Oliver Wolfe had told his son when Tom wanted to go to the University of Virginia. "And you must go to Chapel Hill. And that's a good school." And so it was. For, while the hill people were suspicious of "culture," they were not altogether averse to "learning"—Julia Wolfe kept a sharp eye on her boy's Northern extravagances, but she also bought a set of the Harvard Classics which her boy was reading. The Civil War, too, was part of their public consciousness as well as of their tribal memory; they had attended every presidential inauguration since McKinley, and every World's Fair. It was at St. Louis that Grover Cleveland Wolfe died of typhoid—his twin, the Ben of the novels, was Benjamin Harrison Wolfe—and Tom himself bought a low-rate ticket to Chicago in 1934. "I've done what all the rest of you have done and came to see the Fair." Although, during his apprenticeship, Wolfe had suffered the indignity of depending on these hill people for his financial support, it was also true that they *did* support him. And though, in his maturity, he had the shrewdness to draw upon them for the substance of his writing—for his mental capital—it was also true that he was less professionally and more directly and humanly involved with them.

"If people at home think they find some reference to themselves and to Asheville in this story," he wrote about his last novel, "I hope they will feel this time that both my head and my heart are in the right place and that I have written as one of them." And the town's indignation over his first novel had at first shocked and then embittered Wolfe[1] precisely because he had always, at heart, felt himself "one of them"—because the relationship of the writer and his people concerned Wolfe as it had not always concerned the aesthetic rebels of the 1920's and as it would not always concern the social revolutionaries of the 1930's. You might almost say, in fact, that in Wolfe's work the American people came back into the American novel. At least, for all his hyperbole, he is the first major novelist of the '30's to depict American family life in relatively normal terms—he may even be, coming on the heels of Fitzgerald, Hemingway and Dos Passos, the first novelist to depict family life at all. To some degree Wolfe marks the return of the "invisible roof" that Sherwood Anderson felt had once extended over the Ohio towns at the turn of the century: a roof that has hardly spread itself over contemporary letters.

And one, perhaps, in spite of all our technological additions, that seems hardly large enough to house both General Motors and the UAW. But in a more immediate sense it was surely there for Tom Wolfe. "There are only fifteen hundred people in Zebulon County," says the narrator in "The Return of the Prodigal," "and we're all related somehow." "I would just like, for example," Wolfe wrote his mother, "to get a list of the twenty children or more that your grandfather had by his two marriages and what happened to them and where they settled and what parts of the country they move to, and so forth." There were some lively relatives in Boston (the Bascom Pentlands of *Time and the River*), there were Westalls and Penlands in Oregon, and through all

---

[1] There are interesting accounts of Asheville and the Angel in both The Story of a Novel and You Can't Go Home Again, and this whole issue is a crucial one in Wolfe's mature thinking.

these numerous Eastern and Western towns he would be almost sure, sooner or later, to run across a wandering uncle, an eccentric aunt, a long-lost cousin. Perhaps it was just this sense of kinfolk, extending over the width of a continent and across the span of the Republic's history, that gave Wolfe so sure a sense of his country; that allowed him, the awkward provincial that he seemed, to move through the metropolitan salons with a sort of ease that a Dreiser or a Sinclair Lewis, for example, could never quite manage (for there might well be some forgotten Westall or Penland ensconced in these chambers also)—and that, when Mrs. Jack's World went up in the blaze of '29, enabled Wolfe to understand the Brooklyn scene as well. For wasn't even the "pavement cypher," the "dweller in mean streets," the "C. Green" of *You Can't Go Home Again,* who finally makes his little impression upon an impersonalized urban society by splashing his blood and bones upon an American sidewalk from an open window twelve floors up in a luxurious American hotel—wasn't even this anonymous and starving Brooklynite a sort of kinsman, too?

At any rate, just as Wolfe's first novel had marked a shift in that literary tide, always flowing east in the munificent '20's, from the middle-western towns to Chicago, from Chicago to New York, and from New York to London, Paris and Capri—so, by the time of his last novel, Wolfe had come to occupy a special position among that new Younger Generation which came of age in the economic distress of the '30's. Did the Chicago novelist, James T. Farrell, take Wolfe to task for his burgeoning style during those lean years?—And use such a Wolfean phrase as "in the green heart of June" as an example of sucking a dry lemon? Still, whatever the diction, and there was something in this sermon that recalled the pot and the kettle, it was precisely the green heart of June that was lacking in Farrell himself and in the majority of his colleagues of social crisis—these new urban writers who seemed in many ways so closely identified with the machine civilization they were attacking. It was possible, too, that on the Chicago West Side—along those wide industrial thoroughfares that ran, as Sherwood Anderson noticed, "on and on forever, out of nowhere into nothing"—that there, there had never been a month of June. So it was, after all, the whole web of Wolfe's agrarian origins—his entire and immediate and intense sense of the rich and varied nature of places, persons and things—that allowed him to place the crack-up of contemporary city culture within a wider framework of values.

During these years there was blind anger in Wolfe's work also—those familiar accents of indignation and bewilderment that mark the writing of the period.

Everywhere around me, during those years [Wolfe says] I saw the evidence of an incalculable ruin and suffering. My own people, the members of my own family, had been ruined, had lost all the material wealth and accumulation of a lifetime in what was called the "depression." And that universal calamity had somehow struck the life of almost everyone I knew.

And prowling in his endless quest through the great web and jungle of the city, he saw and felt the full weight of the calamity:

I saw acts of sickening violence and cruelty, the menace of brute privilege, a cruel and corrupt authority trampling ruthlessly below its feet the lives of the poor, the weak, the wretched, and defenseless of the earth.
And the staggering impact of this black picture of man's inhumanity to his fellow man, the unending repercussions

of these scenes of suffering, violence, oppression, hunger, cold, and filth and poverty going on unheeded in a world in which the rich were still rotten with their wealth left a scar upon my life, a conviction in my soul which I shall never lose.

But just as Wolfe had escaped from the neo-Menckenian twaddle of the "mob" and the "aliens" who comprised the "Federated Half Breeds"—and as he had watched the more sophisticated members of the Lost Generation perform "as if there really were a new and desolate race of youth"—so he now escaped from the melodramatic and moralistic elements that marked the typical social novelists of the period. He succumbed, moreover, to neither of the two ideological extremes that ran through the literary thinking of the 1930's—neither to a complete and blank personal despair nor to a sweet and childlike trust in the revolutionary utopia—but merely to a reasonable belief in the fortitude of man: "his ability to suffer and somehow to survive."

For a somewhat verbose young man, Wolfe expressed a similar notion with a curious simplicity just before his death[1]—in those final letters written to the "Fox":

Your own philosophy has led you to accept the order of things as they are because you have no hope of changing them; and if you could change them, you feel that any other order would be just as bad. In everlasting terms—those of eternity—you and the Preacher may be right: for there is no greater wisdom than the wisdom of Ecclesiastes, no acceptance finally so true as the stern fatalism of the rock. Man was born to live, to suffer, and to die, and what befalls him is a tragic lot. There is no denying this in the final end. *But we must, dear Fox, deny it all along the way.*

---

[1] In July 1938, after having delivered a new manuscript of more than a million words, Wolfe became ill with pneumonia. He died that September, at the age of thirty-eight.

Where were the provincial accents now? You *could* say he had gained a sort of rationale for that earlier lyricism on the "promise" of America.

And everywhere, through the immortal dark, something moving in the night, and something stirring in the hearts of men, and something crying in their wild, unuttered blood, the wild unuttered tongues of its huge prophecies—so soon the morning, soon the morning: O America.

At least that celebrated Wolfean door, that long-sought-for door, opened out now not merely upon a personal exit but on a communal vista. And just as Wolfe had joined that whole earlier pilgrimage of East and West in our literature—that long quest of our hinterland Jasons for the Gilded Fleece—so now he linked himself to that later sequence of writers who saw the Magic City no longer as the center of ease and grace but as the symbol of industrial conquest.—The symbol, I mean, of that whole new mechanized and standardized social arrangement whose triumph was complete when Woolworths came to Winesburg, and whose typical human products—the pavement cypher and the man-swarm atom—were separated by our historical tradition but *not* by our technological progress from what Wolfe, for all his love of the German people, had very early felt to be "the beast with the swine-face and the quenchless thirst."

Yes, Wolfe also remained at times the black and bitter Yea-Sayer of the new novelists of social crisis. And the fears and hatreds that still marked his work, the dark Faustian frenzies, the sense of disease and the almost morbid apprehensiveness of time's passing—these, too, were in the end a little more than strictly personal. With his corrosive doubts as to our future as well as his lyrical hope for the wild unuttered tongues of our huge prophecies, he belongs among those other artists in the national letters—from Melville and Whitman to Dreiser and Sherwood Anderson himself: those who were expansive by nature and constrained by necessity.

MAXWELL GEISMAR

Harrison, N. Y.
January 1946

THE NOVELS

THE NOVELS

Look Homeward, Angel

ARTEMIDORUS, FAREWELL

Editor's Preface

ALTHOUGH the hero changes his name in mid-stream, in one sense Wolfe's four big novels are actually one novel, with a beginning, a middle and an end.

Look Homeward, Angel (1929) traces the early life of this Southern hero. *Of Time and the River* (1935) follows his Northern adventures—at Harvard and the "School for Utility Cultures" in downtown Manhattan —and his European experiences in London and Paris. *The Web and the Rock* (1939) continues with his first success as a writer and his reception into the circles of distinguished New York society—that life of wealth and culture . . . "so beautiful and right and good," toward which, as the young Wolfe says, all the myriads of the earth aspire. *You Can't Go Home Again* (1940) concludes with the hero's rejection of this society, his retreat to Brooklyn, his return home in the midst of the economic crisis, and his final summary of his own life and values up to that point.

II

The selection from *Look Homeward, Angel* deals with Eugene Gant's adolescence from the time he leaves for college to the moment of his decision to leave the

South. It is from the third part of the novel. The earlier parts have described the married life of Oliver and Eliza Gant, the lives of the other children—Helen, Luke, Steve and Ben himself—and the town life of Altamont.

Because it expresses the moods of a young man's rebellion, and speaks so directly to all sorts of young people, the *Angel* will very probably continue to be Wolfe's best-known novel, though it probably isn't his best novel. Yet the central study of the Gant family and of Oliver and Eliza's mutual disintegration—the father because he has lost any fixed purpose in life, and the mother because she has sacrificed her life to an inadequate purpose—is certainly a remarkable achievement. And Wolfe's first view of the Southern scene in general, impassioned and ingenuous as it is, has the virtue of also being direct—whereas maturity is in part at least the art of being oblique.

The author's note and the celebrated prefatory passage of *Look Homeward, Angel* are also printed here.

LOOK HOMEWARD, ANGEL

TO THE READER

This is a first book, and in it the author has written of experience which is now far and lost, but which was once part of the fabric of his life. If any reader, therefore, should say that the book is "autobiographical" the writer has no answer for him: it seems to him that all serious work in fiction is autobiographical—that, for instance, a more autobiographical work than Gulliver's Travels *cannot easily be imagined.*

This note, however, is addressed principally to those persons whom the writer may have known in the period covered by these pages. To these persons, he would say what he believes they understand already: that this book was written in innocence and nakedness of spirit, and that the writer's main concern was to give fullness, life, and intensity to the actions and people in the book he was creating. Now that it is to be published, he would insist that this book is a fiction, and that he meditated no man's portrait here.

But we are the sum of all the moments of our lives— all that is ours is in them: we cannot escape or conceal it. If the writer has used the clay of life to make his book, he has only used what all men must, what none can keep from using. Fiction is not fact, but fiction is fact selected and understood, fiction is fact arranged and charged with purpose. Dr. Johnson remarked that a man would turn over half a library to make a single book: in the same way, a novelist may turn over half the people in a town to make a single figure in his novel. This is not the whole method but the writer believes it illustrates the whole method in a book that is written from a middle distance and is without rancor or bitter intention.

Artemidorus, Farewell

. . . a stone, a leaf, an unfound door; of a stone, a leaf, a door. And of all the forgotten faces.

Naked and alone we came into exile. In her dark womb we did not know our mother's face; from the prison of her flesh have we come into the unspeakable and incommunicable prison of this earth.

Which of us has known his brother? Which of us has looked into his father's heart? Which of us has not remained forever prison-pent? Which of us is not forever a stranger and alone?

O waste of loss, in the hot mazes, lost, among bright stars on this most weary unbright cinder, lost! Remembering speechlessly we seek the great forgotten language, the lost lane-end into heaven, a stone, a leaf, an unfound door. Where? When?

O lost, and by the wind grieved, ghost, come back again.

I

EUGENE was not quite sixteen years old when he was sent away to the university. He was, at the time, over six feet and three inches tall, and weighed perhaps 130 pounds. He had been sick very little in his life, but his rapid growth had eaten sharply at his strength: he was full of a wild energy of mind and body that devoured him and left him exhausted. He tired very quickly.

He was a child when he went away: he was a child who had looked much on pain and evil, and remained a fantasist of the Ideal. Walled up in his great city of visions, his tongue had learned to mock, his lip to sneer, but the harsh rasp of the world had worn no grooving in the secret life. Again and again he had been bogged in the grey slough of factuality. His cruel eyes had missed the meaning of no gesture, his packed and bitter heart had sweltered in him like a hot ingot, but all his hard wisdom melted at the glow of his imagination. He was not a child when he reflected, but when he dreamt, he was; and it was the child and dreamer that governed his belief. He belonged, perhaps, to an older and simpler race of men: he belonged with the Mythmakers. For him, the sun was a lordly lamp to light him on his grand adventuring. He believed in brave heroic lives. He believed in the fine flowers of tenderness and gentleness he had little known. He believed in beauty and in order, and that he would wreak out their mighty forms upon the distressful chaos of his life. He believed in love, and in the goodness and glory of women. He believed in valiance, and he hoped that, like Socrates, he would do nothing mean or common in the hour of danger. He exulted in his youth, and he believed that he could never die.

Four years later, when he was graduated, he had passed his adolescence, the kiss of love and death burned on his lips, and he was still a child.

When it was at last plain that Gant's will was on this inflexible, Margaret Leonard had said, quietly:

"Well, then, go your ways, boy. Go your ways. God bless you."

She looked a moment at his long thin figure and turned to John Dorsey Leonard with wet eyes:

"Do you remember that shaver in knee-pants who came to us four years ago? Can you believe it?"

John Dorsey Leonard laughed quietly, with weary gentle relaxation.

"What do you know about it?" he said.

When Margaret turned to him again her voice, low and gentle, was charged with the greatest passion he had ever heard in it.

"You are taking a part of our heart with you, boy. Do you know that?"

She took his trembling hand gently between her own lean fingers. He lowered his head and closed his eyelids tightly.

"Eugene," she continued, "we could not love you more if you were our own child. We wanted to keep you with us for another year, but since that cannot be, we are sending you out with our hopes pinned to you. Oh, boy, you are fine. There is no atom in you that is not fine. A glory and a chrism of bright genius rest upon you. God bless you: the world is yours."

The proud words of love and glory sank like music to his heart, evoking their bright pictures of triumph, and piercing him with the bitter shame of his concealed desires. Love bade him enter, but his soul drew back, guilty of dust and sin.

He tore his hand from her grasp, clinching, with the strangled cry of an animal, his convulsive throat.

"I can't!" he choked. "You mustn't think——" He could not go on; his life groped blindly to confessional.

Later, after he left her, her light kiss upon his cheek, the first she had ever given him, burned like a ring of fire.

That summer he was closer to Ben than ever before. They occupied the same room at Woodson Street. Luke had returned to the Westinghouse plant at Pittsburgh after Helen's marriage.

Gant still occupied his sitting room, but the rest of

the house he had rented to a sprightly grey-haired widow of forty. She looked after them beautifully, but she served Ben with an especial tenderness. At night, on the cool veranda, Eugene would find them below the ripening clusters, hear the quiet note of his brother's voice, his laugh, see the slow red arc of his cigarette in darkness.

The quiet one was more quiet and morose than he had ever been before: he stalked through the house scowling ferociously. All his conversation with Eliza was short and bitterly scornful; with Gant he spoke hardly at all. They had never talked together. Their eyes never met —a great shame, the shame of father and son, that mystery that goes down beyond motherhood, beyond life, that mysterious shame that seals the lips of all men, and lives in their hearts, had silenced them.

But to Eugene, Ben talked more freely than ever before. As they sat upon their beds at night, reading and smoking before they slept, all of the pain and bitterness of Benjamin Gant's life burst out in violent denunciation. He began to speak with slow, sullen difficulty, halting over his words as he did when he read, but speaking more rapidly as his quiet voice became more passionate.

"I suppose they've told you how poor they are?" he began, tossing his cigarette away.

"Well," said Eugene, "I've got to go easy. I mustn't waste my money."

"Ah-h!" said Ben, making an ugly face. He laughed silently, with a thin and bitter contortion of his lips.

"Papa said that a lot of boys pay their own way through college by waiting on tables and so on. Perhaps I can do something like that."

Ben turned over on his side until he faced his brother, propping himself on his thin hairy forearm.

"Now listen, 'Gene," he said sternly, "don't be a damned little fool, do you hear? You take every damn cent you can get out of them," he added savagely.

"Well, I appreciate what they're doing. I'm getting a lot more than the rest of you had. They're doing a lot for me," said the boy.

"For *you*, you little idiot!" said Ben, scowling at him in disgust. "They're doing it all for themselves. Don't let them get away with that. They think you'll make good and bring a lot of credit to them some day. They're rushing you into it two years too soon, as it is. No, you take everything you can get. The rest of us never had anything, but I want to see you get all that's coming to you. My God!" he cried furiously. "Their money's doing no one any good rotting in the damned bank, is it? No, 'Gene, get all you can. When you get down there, if you find you need more to hold your own with the other boys, make the old man give it to you. You've never had a chance to hold your head up in your own home town, so make the most of your chances when you get away."

He lighted a cigarette and smoked in bitter silence for a moment.

"To hell with it all!" he said. "What in God's name are we living for!"

Eugene's first year at the university was filled for him with loneliness, pain, and failure. Within three weeks of his matriculation, he had been made the dupe of a half-dozen classic jokes, his ignorance of all campus tradition had been exploited, his gullibility was a by-word. He was the greenest of all green freshmen, past and present: he had listened attentively to a sermon in chapel by a sophomore with false whiskers; he had prepared studiously for an examination on the contents of the college catalogue; and he had been guilty of the inexcusable blunder of making a speech of acceptance on his election, with fifty others, to the literary society.

And these buffooneries—a little cruel, but only with the cruelty of vacant laughter, and a part of the schedule of rough humor in an American college—salty, extravagant, and national—opened deep wounds in him, which his companions hardly suspected. He was conspicuous at once not only because of his blunders, but also because of his young wild child's face, and his great raw length of body, with the bounding scissor legs. The undergraduates passed him in grinning clusters: he saluted them obediently, but with a sick heart. And the smug smiling faces of his own classmen, the wiser Freshmen, complacently guiltless of his own mistakes, touched him at moments with insane fury.

"Smile and smile and s-mile—damn you!" he cursed through his grating teeth. For the first time in his life he began to dislike whatever fits too snugly in a measure. He began to dislike and envy the inconspicuous mold of general nature—the multitudinous arms, legs, hands, feet, and figures that are comfortably shaped for ready-made garments. And the prettily regular, wherever he found it, he hated—the vacantly handsome young men, with shining hair, evenly parted in the middle, with sure strong middling limbs meant to go gracefully on dance floors. He longed to see them commit some awkward blunder—to trip and sprawl, to be flatulent, to lose a strategic button in mixed company, to be unconscious of a hanging shirt-tail while with a pretty girl. But they made no mistakes.

As he walked across the campus, he heard his name called mockingly from a dozen of the impartial windows, he heard the hidden laughter, and he ground his teeth. And at night, he stiffened with shame in his dark bed,

ripping the sheet between his fingers as, with the un-
balanced vision, the swollen egotism of the introvert,
the picture of a crowded student room, filled with the
grinning historians of his exploits, burned in his brain.
He strangled his fierce cry with a taloned hand. He
wanted to blot out the shameful moment, unweave the
loom. It seemed to him that his ruin was final, that he
had stamped the beginning of his university life with
folly that would never be forgotten, and that the best
he could do would be to seek out obscurity for the next
four years. He saw himself in his clown's trappings and
thought of his former vision of success and honor with
a lacerating self-contempt.

There was no one to whom he could turn: he had no
friends. His conception of university life was a romantic
blur, evoked from his reading and tempered with
memories of Stover at Yale, Young Fred Fearnot, and
jolly youths with affectionate linked arms, bawling out
a cheer-song. No one had given him even the rudimentary data of the somewhat rudimentary life of an American university. He had not been warned of the general
taboos. Thus, he had come greenly on his new life, un-
prepared, as he came ever thereafter on all new life, save
for his opium visions of himself a stranger in Arcadia.

He was alone. He was desperately lonely.

But the university was a charming, an unforgettable
place. It was situated in the little village of Pulpit Hill,
in the central midland of the big state. Students came
and departed by motor from the dreary tobacco town of
Exeter, twelve miles away: the countryside was raw,
powerful, and ugly, a rolling land of field, wood, and
hollow; but the university itself was buried in a pastoral
wilderness, on a long tabling butte which rose steeply
above the country. One burst suddenly, at the hilltop, on
the end of the straggling village street, flanked by faculty

houses, and winding a mile in to the town center and the university. The central campus sloped back and up over a broad area of rich turf, groved with magnificent ancient trees. A quadrangle of post-Revolutionary buildings of weathered brick bounded the upper end: other newer buildings, in the modern bad manner (the Pedagogic Neo-Greeky), were scattered around beyond the central design: beyond, there was a thickly forested wilderness. There was still a good flavor of the wilderness about the place—one felt its remoteness, its isolated charm. It seemed to Eugene like a provincial outpost of great Rome: the wilderness crept up to it like a beast.

Its great poverty, its century-long struggle in the forest, had given the university a sweetness and a beauty it was later to forfeit. It had the fine authority of provincialism—the provincialism of an older South. Nothing mattered but the state: the state was a mighty empire, a rich kingdom—there was, beyond, a remote and semibarbaric world.

Few of the university's sons had been distinguished in the nation's life—there had been an obscure President of the United States, and a few Cabinet members, but few had sought such distinction: it was glory enough to be a great man in one's state. Nothing beyond mattered very much.

In this pastoral setting a young man was enabled to loaf comfortably and delightfully through four luxurious and indolent years. There was, God knows, seclusion enough for monastic scholarship, but the rare romantic quality of the atmosphere, the prodigal opulence of springtime, thick with flowers and drenched in a fragrant warmth of green shimmering light, quenched pretty thoroughly any incipient rash of bookishness. Instead, they loafed and invited their souls or, with great energy and enthusiasm, promoted the affairs of glee clubs, athletic teams, class politics, fraternities, debating societies, and dramatic clubs. And they talked—always they talked, under the trees, against the ivied walls, assembled in their rooms, they talked—in limp sprawls— incessant, charming, empty Southern talk; they talked with a large easy fluency about God, the Devil, and philosophy, the girls, politics, athletics, fraternities, and the girls— My God! how they talked!

"Observe," lisped Mr. Torrington, the old Rhodes Scholar (Pulpit Hill and Merton, '14), "observe how skillfully he holds suspense until the very end. Observe with what consummate art he builds up his climax, keeping his meaning hidden until the very last word." Further, in fact.

At last, thought Eugene, I am getting an education. This must be good writing, because it seems so very dull. When it hurts, the dentist says, it does you good. Democracy must be real, because it is so very earnest. It must be a certainty, because it is so elegantly embalmed in this marble mausoleum of language. Essays For College Men—Woodrow Wilson, Lord Bryce, and Dean Briggs.

But there was no word here of the loud raucous voice of America, political conventions and the Big Brass Band, Tweed, Tammany, the Big Stick, lynching bees and black barbecue parties, the Boston Irish, and the damnable machinations of the Pope as exposed by the *Babylon Hollow Trumpet* (Dem.), the rape of the Belgian virgins, rum, oil, Wall Street, and Mexico.

All that, Mr. Torrington would have said, was temporary and accidental. It was unsound.

Mr. Torrington smiled moistly at Eugene and urged him tenderly into a chair drawn intimately to his desk.

"Mr.—? Mr.—?—" he said, fumbling at his index cards.

"Gant," said Eugene.

"Ah, yes—Mr. Gant," he smiled his contrition. "Now —about your outside reading?" he began.

But what, thought Eugene, about my inside reading?

Did he like to read? Ah—that was good. He was so glad to hear it. The true university in these days, said Carlyle (he did hope Eugene like rugged old Thomas), was a collection of books.

"Yes, sir," said Eugene.

That, it seemed to him, was the Oxford Plan. Oh, yes—he had been there, three years, in fact. His mild eye kindled. To loaf along the High on a warm spring day, stopping to examine in the bookseller's windows the treasures that might be had for so little. Then to Buol's or to a friend's room for tea, or for a walk in the meadows or Magdalen gardens, or to look down into the quad, at the gay pageant of youth below. Ah—ah! A great place? Well—he'd hardly say that. It all depended what one meant by a great place. Half the looseness in thought—unfortunately, he fancied, more prevalent among American than among English youth—came from an indefinite exuberance of ill-defined speech.

"Yes, sir," said Eugene.

A great place? Well, he'd scarcely say that. The expression was typically American. Butter-lipped, he turned on the boy a smile of soft unfriendliness:

"It kills," he observed, "a man's useless enthusiasms."

Eugene whitened a little.

"That's fine," he said.

Now—let him see. Did he like plays—the modern drama? Excellent. They were doing some very interesting things in the modern drama. Barrie—oh, a charming fellow! What was that? Shaw!

"Yes, sir," said Eugene. "I've read all the others. There's a new book out."

"Oh, but really! My dear boy!" said Mr. Torrington with gentle amazement. He shrugged his shoulders and became politely indifferent. Very well, if he liked. Of course, he thought it rather a pity to waste one's time so when they were really doing some first-rate things. That was *just* the trouble, however. The appeal of a man like that was mainly to the unformed taste, the uncritical judgment. He had a flashy attraction for the immature. Oh, yes! Undoubtedly an amusing fellow. Clever—yes, but hardly significant. And—didn't he think—a trifle noisy? Or had he noticed that? Yes—there was to be sure an amusing Celtic strain, not without charm, but unsound. He was not in line with the best modern thought.

"I'll take the Barrie," said Eugene.

Yes, he rather thought that would be better.

"Well, good day. Mr.—Mr.—?—?" he smiled, fumbling again with his cards.

"Gant."

Oh, yes, to be sure—Gant. He held out his plump limp hand. He did hope Mr. Gant would call on him. Perhaps he'd be able to advise him on some of the little problems that, he knew, were constantly cropping up during the first year. Above all, he mustn't get discouraged.

"Yes, sir," said Eugene, backing feverishly to the door. When he felt the open space behind him, he fell through it, and vanished.

Anyway, he thought grimly, I've read all the damned Barries. I'll write the damned report for him, and damned well read what I damn well please.

God save our King and Queen!

He had courses besides in Chemistry, Mathematics, Greek, and Latin.

He worked hard and with interest at his Latin. His instructor was a tall shaven man, with a yellow saturnine face. He parted his scant hair cleverly in such a way as to suggest horns. His lips were always twisted in a satanic smile, his eyes gleamed sideward with heavy malicious humor. Eugene had great hopes of him. When the boy arrived, panting and breakfastless, a moment after the class had settled to order, the satanic professor would greet him with elaborate irony: "Ah, there, Brother Gant! Just in time for church again. Have you slept well?"

The class roared its appreciation of these subtleties. And later, in an expectant pause, he would deepen his arched brows portentously, stare up mockingly under his bushy eyebrows at his expectant audience, and say, in a deep sardonic voice:

"And now, I am going to request Brother Gant to favor us with one of his polished and scholarly translations."

These heavy jibes were hard to bear because, of all the class, two dozen or more, Brother Gant was the only one to prepare his work without the aid of a printed translation. He worked hard on Livy and Tacitus, going over the lesson several times until he had dug out a smooth and competent reading of his own. This he was stupid enough to deliver in downright fashion, without hesitation, or a skillfully affected doubt here and there. For his pains and honesty he was handsomely rewarded by the Amateur Diabolist. The lean smile would deepen as the boy read, the man would lift his eyes significantly to the grinning class, and when it was over, he would say:

"Bravo, Brother Gant! Excellent! Splendid! You are

riding a good pony—but a little too smoothly, my boy. You ride a little too well."

The class sniggered heavily.

When he could stand it no longer, he sought the man out one day after the class.

"See here, sir! See here!" he began in a voice choking with fury and exasperation. "Sir—I assure you—" he thought of all the grinning apes in the class, palming off profitably their stolen translations, and he could not go on.

The Devil's Disciple was not a bad man: he was only, like most men who pride themselves on their astuteness, a foolish one.

"Nonsense, Mr. Gant," said he kindly. "You don't think you can fool me on a translation, do you? It's all right with me, you know," he continued, grinning. "If you'd rather ride a pony than do your own work, I'll give you a passing grade—so long as you do it well."

"But—" Eugene began explosively.

"But I think it's a pity, Mr. Gant," said the professor, gravely, "that you're willing to slide along this way. See here, my boy, you're capable of doing first-rate work. I can see that. Why don't you make an effort? Why don't you buckle down and really study, after this?"

Eugene stared at the man, with tears of anger in his eyes. He sputtered but could not speak. But suddenly, as he looked down into the knowing leer, the perfect and preposterous injustice of the thing—like a caricature—overcame him: he burst into an explosive laugh of rage and amusement which the teacher, no doubt, accepted as confession.

"Well, what do you say?" he asked. "Will you try?"

"All right! Yes!" the boy yelled. "I'll try it."

He bought at once a copy of the translation used by

the class. Thereafter, when he read, faltering prettily here and there over a phrase, until his instructor should come to his aid, the satanic professor listened gravely and attentively, nodding his head in approval from time to time, and saying, with great satisfaction, when he had finished: "Good, Mr. Gant. Very good. That shows what a little real work will do."

And privately, he would say: "You see the difference, don't you? I knew at once when you stopped using that pony. Your translation is not so smooth, but it's your own now. You're doing good work, my boy, and you're getting something out of it. It's worth it, isn't it?"

"Yes," said Eugene gratefully, "it certainly is——"

By far the most distinguished of his teachers this first year was Mr. Edward Pettigrew ("Buck") Benson, the Greek professor. Buck Benson was a little man in the middle forties, a bachelor, somewhat dandified, but old-fashioned, in his dress. He wore wing collars, large plump cravats, and suède-topped shoes. His hair was thick, heavily greyed, beautifully kept. His face was courteously pugnacious, fierce, with large yellow bulging eyeballs, and several bulldog pleatings around the mouth. It was an altogether handsome ugliness.

His voice was low, lazy, pleasant, with an indolent drawl, but without changing its pace or its inflection he could flay a victim with as cruel a tongue as ever wagged, and in the next moment wipe out hostility, restore affection, heal all wounds by the same agency. His charm was enormous. Among the students he was the subject for comical speculation——in their myths, they made of him a passionate and sophisticated lover, and his midget cycle car, which bounded like an overgrown toy around the campus, the scene of many romantic seductions.

He was a good Grecian—an elegant indolent scholar. Under his instruction Eugene began to read Homer. The boy knew little grammar—he had learned little at Leonard's—but, since he had had the bad judgment to begin Greek under someone other than Buck Benson, Buck Benson thought he knew even less than he did. He studied desperately, but the bitter dyspeptic gaze of the elegant little man frightened him into halting, timorous, clumsy performances. And as he proceeded, with thumping heart and tremulous voice, Buck Benson's manner would become more and more weary, until finally, dropping his book, he would drawl:

"Mister Gant, you make me so damned mad I could throw you out the window."

But, on the examination, he gave an excellent performance, and translated from sight beautifully. He was saved. Buck Benson commended his paper publicly with lazy astonishment, and gave him a fair grade. Thereafter, they slipped quickly into an easier relation: by spring, he was reading Euripides with some confidence.

But that which remained most vividly, later, in the drowning years which cover away so much of beauty, was the vast sea-surge of Homer which beat in his brain, his blood, his pulses, as did the sea-sound in Gant's parlor shells, when first he heard it to the slowly pacing feet and the hexametrical drawl of Buck Benson, the lost last weary son of Hellas.

Dwaney de clangay genett, argereoyo beeoyo—above the whistle's shriek, the harsh scream of the wheel, the riveter's tattoo, the vast long music endures, and ever shall. What dissonance can quench it? What jangling violence can disturb or conquer it—entombed in our flesh when we were young, remembered like "the apple tree, the singing, and the gold"?

II

Before his first year was ended, the boy had changed his lodging four or five times. He finished the year living alone in a big bare carpetless room—an existence rare at Pulpit Hill, where the students, with very few exceptions, lived two or three to a room. In that room began a physical isolation, hard enough to bear at first, which later became indispensable to him, mind and body.

He had come to Pulpit Hill with Hugh Barton, who met him at Exeter and drove him over in the big roadster. After his registration, he had secured lodging quickly at the house of an Altamont widow whose son was a student. Hugh Barton looked relieved and departed, hoping to reach home and his bride by nightfall.

With fine enthusiasm, but poor judgment, Eugene paid the widow two months in advance. Her name was Bradley: she was a flabby petulant woman with a white face and heart disease. But her food was excellent. Mrs. Bradley's student son answered to his initial letters— "G. T." G. T. Bradley, a member of the sophomore class, was a surly scowling youth of nineteen—a mixture, in equal parts, of servility and insolence. His chief, but thwarted, ambition was to be elected to membership in a fraternity. Having failed to win recognition by the exercise of his natural talents, he was driven by an extraordinary obsession that fame and glory would come to him if he were known as the slave-driver of a number of Freshmen.

But these tactics, tried on Eugene, produced at once defiance and resentment. Their hostility was bitter: G. T. set himself to thwart and ruin the beginnings of the boy's university life. He trapped him into public blunders, and solicited audiences to witness his humiliation; he wheedled his confidence, and betrayed it. But there is a final mockery, an ultimate treachery that betrays us into shame: our capacity for villainy, like all our other capacities, is so small. The day came when Eugene was free from bondage. He was free to leave the widow's house of sorrow. G. T. approached him, scowling, diffidently.

"I hear you're leaving us, 'Gene," he said.

"Yes," said Eugene.

"Is it because of the way I've acted?"

"Yes," said Eugene.

"You take things too seriously, 'Gene," he said.

"Yes," said Eugene.

"I don't want you to go having hard feelings, 'Gene. Let's shake hands and be friends."

He thrust his hand out stiffly. Eugene looked at the hard weak face, the furtive, unhappy eyes casting about for something they might call their own. The thick black hair was plastered stiff with grease; he saw white points of dandruff at the roots. There was an odor of talcum powder. He had been borne and nourished in the body of his white-faced mother—for what? To lap the scornful stroking fingers of position; to fawn miserably before an emblem. Eugene had a moment of nausea.

"Let's shake hands, 'Gene," said the boy once more, waggling his outthrust fingers.

"No," said Eugene.

"You don't hate me, do you?" whined G. T.

"No," said Eugene.

He had a moment of pity, of sickness. He forgave because it was necessary to forget.

Eugene lived in a small world, but its ruins for him were actual. His misfortunes were trifling, but their effect upon his spirit was deep and calamitous. He withdrew deeply and scornfully into his cell. He was friendless, whipped with scorn and pride. He set his face blindly against all the common united life around him.

It was during this bitter and desperate autumn that Eugene first met Jim Trivett.

Jim Trivett, the son of a rich tobacco farmer in the eastern part of the state, was a good-tempered young tough of twenty years. He was a strong, rather foul-looking boy, with a coarse protruding mouth, full-meated and slightly ajar, constantly rayed with a faint loose smile and blotted at the corner with a brown smear of tobacco juice. He had bad teeth. His hair was light-brown, dry, and unruly: it stuck out in large untidy mats. He was dressed in the last cheap extreme of the dreadful fashion of the time: skin-tight trousers that ended an inch above his oxford shoes exposing an inch of clocked hose, a bobtailed coat belted in across his kidneys, large striped collars of silk. Under his coat he wore a big sweater with high-school numerals.

Jim Trivett lived with several other students from his community in a lodging-house near Mrs. Bradley's but closer to the west gate of the university. There were four young men banded together for security and companionship in two untidy rooms heated to a baking dryness by small cast-iron stoves. They made constant preparations for study, but they never studied: one would enter sternly, announcing that he had "a hell of a day tomorrow," and begin the most minute preparations for a long contest with his books: he would sharpen his pencils carefully and deliberately, adjust his lamp, replenish the red-hot stove, move his chair, put on an eyeshade, clean his pipe, stuff it carefully with tobacco, light, relight, and empty it, then, with an expression of profound relief, hear a rapping on his door.

"Come in the house, Goddamn it!" he would roar hospitably.

"Hello, 'Gene! Pull up a chair, son, and sit down," said Tom Grant. He was a thickly built boy, gaudily dressed; he had a low forehead, black hair, and a kind, stupid, indolent temper.

"Have you been working?"

"Hell, yes!" shouted Jim Trivett. "I've been working like a son-of-a-bitch."

"God!" said Tom Grant, turning slowly to look at him. "Boy, you're going to choke to death on one of those some day." He shook his head slowly and sadly, then continued with a rough laugh: "If old man Trivett knew what you were doing with his money, damn if he wouldn't bust a gut."

"'Gene!" said Jim Trivett, "what the hell do you know about this damned English, anyway?"

"What he doesn't know about it," said Tom Grant, "you could write out on the back of a postage stamp. Old man Sanford thinks you're hell, 'Gene."

"I thought you had Torrington," said Jim Trivett.

"No," said Eugene, "I wasn't English enough. Young and crude. I changed, thank God! What is it you want, Jim?" he asked.

"I've got a long paper to write. I don't know what to write about," said Jim Trivett.

"What do you want me to do? Write it for you?"

"Yes," said Jim Trivett.

"Write your own damn paper," said Eugene with mimic toughness, "I won't do it for you. I'll help you if I can."

"When are you going to let Hard Boy take you to Exeter?" said Tom Grant, winking at Jim Trivett.

Eugene flushed, making a defensive answer.

"I'm ready to go any time he is," he said uneasily.

"Look here, Legs!" said Jim Trivett, grinning loosely. "Do you really want to go with me or are you just bluffing?"

"I'll go with you! I've told you I'd go with you!" Eugene said angrily. He trembled a little.

Tom Grant grinned slyly at Jim Trivett.

"It'll make a man of you, 'Gene," he said. "Boy, it'll sure put hair on your chest." He laughed, not loudly, but uncontrollably, shaking his head as at some secret thought.

Jim Trivett's loose smile widened. He spat into the woodbox.

"Gawd!" he said. "They'll think spring is here when they see old Legs. They'll need a stepladder to git at him."

Tom Grant was shaken with hard fat laughter.

"They sure God will!" he said.

"Well, what about it, 'Gene?" Jim Trivett demanded suddenly. "Is it a go? Saturday?"

"Suits me!" said Eugene.

When he had gone, they grinned thirstily at each other for a moment, the pleased corrupters of chastity.

"Pshaw!" said Tom Gant. "You oughtn't to do that, Hard Boy. You're leading the boy astray."

"It's not going to hurt him," said Jim Trivett. "It'll be good for him."

He wiped his mouth with the back of his hand, grinning.

"Wait a minute!" whispered Jim Trivett. "I think this is the place."

They had turned away from the center of the dreary tobacco town. For a quarter of an hour they had walked briskly through drab autumnal streets, descending finally a long rutted hill that led them past a thinning squalor of cheap houses, almost to the outskirts. It was three weeks before Christmas: the foggy air was full of chill menace. There was a brooding quietness, broken by far, small sounds. They turned into a sordid little road, unpaved, littered on both sides with Negro shacks and the dwellings of poor whites. It was a world of rickets. The road was unlighted. Their feet stirred dryly through fallen leaves.

They paused before a two-story frame house. A lamp burned dimly behind lowered yellow shades, casting a murky pollen out upon the smoky air.

"Wait a minute," said Jim Trivett, in a low voice, "I'll find out."

They heard scuffling steps through the leaves. In a moment a Negro man prowled up.

"Hello, John," said Jim Trivett, almost inaudibly.

"Evenin', boss!" the Negro answered wearily, but in the same tone.

"We're looking for Lily Jones's house," said Jim Trivett. "Is this it?"

"Yes, suh," said the Negro, "dis is it."

Eugene leaned against a tree, listening to their quiet conspiratorial talk. The night, vast and listening, gathered about him its evil attentive consciousness. His lips were cold and trembled. He thrust a cigarette between them and, shivering, turned up the thick collar of his overcoat.

"Does Miss Lily know you're comin'?" the Negro asked.

"No," said Jim Trivett. "Do you know her?"

"Yes, suh," said the Negro. "I'll go up dar wid yo'."

Eugene waited in the shadow of the tree while the two men went up to the house. They avoided the front veranda, and went around to the side. The Negro rapped gently at a latticed door. There were always latticed doors. Why?

He waited, saying farewell to himself. He stood over his life, he felt, with lifted assassin blade. He was mired to his neck, inextricably, in complication. There was no escape.

There had been a faint closed noise from the house: voices and laughter, and the cracked hoarse tone of an old phonograph. The sound stopped quickly as the Negro rapped: the shabby house seemed to listen. In a moment, a hinge creaked stealthily: he caught the low startled blur of a woman's voice. Who is it? Who?

In another moment, Jim Trivett returned to him, and said quietly:

"It's all right, 'Gene. Come on."

He slipped a coin into the Negro's hand, thanking him. Eugene looked for a moment into the black broad friendliness of the man's face. He had a flash of warmth through his cold limbs. The black bawd had done his work eagerly and kindly: over their bought unlovely loves lay the warm shadow of his affection.

They ascended the path quietly and, mounting two or three steps, went in under the latticed door. A woman stood beside it, holding it open. When they had entered, she closed it securely. Then they crossed the little porch and entered the house.

They found themselves in a little hall which cleft the width of the house. A smoky lamp, wicked low, cast its dim circle into the dark. An uncarpeted stair mounted to the second floor. There were two doors both to left and right, and an accordion hat-rack, on which hung a man's battered felt hat.

Jim Trivett embraced the woman immediately, grinning, and fumbling in her breast.

"Hello, Lily," he said.

"Gawd!" She smiled crudely, and continued to peer at Eugene, curious at what the maw of night had thrown in to her. Then, turning to Jim Trivett with a coarse laugh, she said:

"Lord a' mercy! Any woman that gits him will have to cut off some of them legs."

"I'd like to see him with Thelma," said Jim Trivett, grinning.

Lily Jones laughed hoarsely. The door to the right opened and Thelma, a small woman, slightly built, came out, followed by high empty yokel laughter. Jim Trivett embraced her affectionately.

"My Gawd!" said Thelma, in a tinny voice. "What've we got here?" She thrust out her sharp wrenny face, and studied Eugene insolently.

"I brought you a new beau, Thelma," said Jim Trivett.

"Ain't he the lankiest feller you ever seen?" said Lily Jones impersonally. "How tall are you, son?" she added, addressing him in a kind drawl.

He winced a little.

"I don't know," he said. "I think about six three."

"He's more than that!" said Thelma positively. "He's seven foot tall or I'm a liar."

"He hasn't measured since last week," said Jim Trivett. "He can't be sure about it."

"He's young, too," said Lily, staring at him intently. "How old are you, son?"

Eugene turned his pallid face away, indefinitely.

"Why," he croaked, "I'm about——"

"He's going on eighteen," said Jim Trivett loyally. "Don't you worry about him. Old Legs knows all the ropes, all right. He's a bearcat. I wouldn't kid you. He's been there."

"He don't look that old," said Lily doubtfully. "I wouldn't call him more'n fifteen, to look at his face. Ain't he got a little face, though?" she demanded in a slow puzzled voice.

"It's the only one I've got," said Eugene angrily. "Sorry I can't change it for a larger one."

"It looks so funny stickin' way up there above you," she went on patiently.

Thelma nudged her sharply.

"That's because he's got a big frame," she said. "Legs is all right. When he begins to fill out an' put some meat on them bones he's goin' to make a big man. You'll be a heartbreaker sure, Legs," she said harshly, taking his cold hand and squeezing it. In him the ghost, his stranger, turned grievously away. O God! I shall remember, he thought.

"Well," said Jim Trivett, "let's git goin'." He embraced Thelma again. They fumbled amorously.

"You go on upstairs, son," said Lily. "I'll be up in a minute. The door's open."

"See you later, 'Gene," said Jim Trivett. "Stay with them, son."

He hugged the boy roughly with one arm, and went into the room to the left with Thelma.

Eugene mounted the creaking stairs slowly and entered the room with the open door. A hot mass of coals glowed flamelessly in the hearth. He took off his hat and overcoat and threw them across a wooden bed. Then he sat down tensely in a rocker and leaned forward, holding his trembling fingers to the heat. There was no light save that of the coals; but, by their dim steady glow, he could make out the old and ugly wallpaper, stained with long streaks of water rust, and scaling, in dry tattered scrolls, here and there. He sat quietly, bent forward, but he shook violently, as with an ague, from time to time. Why am I here? This is not I, he thought.

Presently he heard the woman's slow heavy tread upon the stairs: she entered in a swimming tide of light, bearing a lamp before her. She put the lamp down on a table and turned the wick. He could see her now more plainly. Lily was a middle-aged country woman, with a broad heavy figure, unhealthily soft. Her smooth peasant face was mapped with fine little traceries of wrinkles at the corners of mouth and eyes, as if she had worked much in the sun. She had black hair, coarse and abundant. She was whitely plastered with talcum powder. She was dressed shapelessly in a fresh loose dress of gingham, unbelted. She was dressed like a housewife, but she conceded to her profession stockings of red silk, and slippers of red felt, rimmed with fur, in which she walked with a flat-footed tread.

The woman fastened the door, and returned to the hearth where the boy was now standing. He embraced her with feverish desire, fondling her with his long nervous hands. Indecisively, he sat in the rocker and drew her down clumsily on his knee. She yielded her kisses with the coy and frigid modesty of the provincial harlot, turning her mouth away. She shivered as his cold hands touched her.

"You're cold as ice, son," she said. "What's the matter?"

She chafed him with rough embarrassed professionalism. In a moment she rose impatiently.

"Let's git started," she said. "Where's my money?"

He thrust two crumpled bills into her hand.

Then he lay down beside her. He trembled, unnerved and impotent. Passion was extinct in him.

The massed coals caved in the hearth. The lost bright wonder died.

When he went downstairs, he found Jim Trivett waiting in the hall, holding Thelma by the hand. Lily led
them out quietly, after peering through the lattice into
the fog, and listening for a moment.

"Be quiet," she whispered, "there's a man across the
street. They've been watching us lately."

"Come again, Slats," Thelma murmured, pressing his
hand.

They went out softly, treading gently until they
reached the road. The fog had thickened: the air was
saturated with fine stinging moisture.

At the corner, in the glare of the street-lamp, Jim
Trivett released his breath with loud relief, and stepped
forward boldly.

"Damn!" he said. "I thought you were never coming.
What were you trying to do with the woman, Legs?"
Then, noting the boy's face, he added quickly, with
warm concern: "What's the matter, 'Gene? Don't you
feel good?"

"Wait a minute!" said Eugene thickly. "Be all right!"

He went to the curb, and vomited into the gutter.
Then he straightened, mopping his mouth with a
handkerchief.

"How do you feel?" asked Jim Trivett. "Better?"

"Yes," said Eugene, "I'm all right now."

"Why didn't you tell me you were sick?" said Jim
Trivett chidingly.

"It came on all of a sudden," said Eugene. He added
presently: "I think it was something I ate at that damn
Greek's tonight."

"I felt all right," said Jim Trivett. "A cup of coffee
will fix you up," he added with cheerful conviction.

They mounted the hill slowly. The light from winking corner lamps fell with a livid stare across the fronts
of the squalid houses.

"Jim," said Eugene, after a moment's pause.

"Yes. What is it?"

"Don't say anything about my getting sick," he said awkwardly.

Surprised, Jim Trivett stared at him.

"Why not? There's nothing in that," he said. "Pshaw, boy, anyone's likely to get sick."

"Yes, I know. But I'd rather you wouldn't."

"Oh, all right. I won't. Why should I?" said Jim Trivett.

Eugene was haunted by his own lost ghost: he knew it to be irrecoverable. For three days he avoided everyone: the brand of his sin, he felt, was on him. He was published by every gesture, by every word. His manner grew more defiant, his greeting to life more unfriendly. He clung more closely to Jim Trivett, drawing a sad pleasure from his coarse loyal praise. His unappeased desire began to burn anew: it conquered his bodily disgust and made new pictures. At the end of the week he went again, alone, to Exeter. No more of him, he felt, could be lost. This time he sought out Thelma.

When he went home for Christmas, his loins were black with vermin. The great body of the state lay like a barren giant below the leaden reek of the skies. The train roared on across the vast lift of the Piedmont: at night, as he lay in his berth, in a diseased coma, it crawled up into the great fortress of the hills. Dimly, he saw their wintry bulk, with its bleak foresting. Below a trestle, silent as a dream, a white rope of water coiled between its frozen banks. His sick heart lifted in the haunting eternity of the hills. He was hillborn. But at dawn, as he came from the cars with the band of returning students, his depression revived. The huddle of cheap buildings at the station seemed meaner and nearer than ever before. The hills, above the station flats, with their cheap propped houses, had the unnatural closeness of a vision. The silent Square seemed to have rushed together during his absence, and as he left the car and descended the street to Dixieland, it was as if he devoured toy-town distances with a giant's stride.

The Christmas was grey and chill. Helen was not there to give it warmth. Gant and Eliza felt the depression of her absence. Ben came and went like a ghost. Luke was not coming home. And he himself was sick with shame and loss.

He did not know where to turn. He paced his chill room at night, muttering, until Eliza's troubled face appeared above her wrapper. His father was gentler, older than he had ever seen him: his pain had returned on him. He was absent and sorrowful. He talked perfunctorily with his son about college. Speech choked in Eugene's throat. He stammered a few answers and fled from the house and the vacant fear in Gant's eyes. He walked prodigiously, day and night, in an effort to command his own fear. He believed himself to be rotting with a leprosy. And there was nothing to do but rot. There was no cure. For such had been the instruction of the moralists of his youth.

He walked with aimless desperation, unable to quiet for a moment his restless limbs. He went up on the eastern hills that rose behind Niggertown. A winter's sun labored through the mist. Low on the meadows, and high on the hills, the sunlight lay on the earth like milk.

He stood looking. A shaft of hope cut through the blackness of his spirit. "I will go to my brother," he thought.

He found Ben still in bed at Woodson Street, smoking. He closed the door, then spun wildly about as if caged.

"In God's name!" Ben cried angrily. "Have you gone crazy? What's wrong with you?"

"I'm—I'm sick!" he gasped.

"What's the matter? Where've you been?" asked Ben sharply. He sat up in bed.

"I've been with a woman," said Eugene.

"Sit down, 'Gene," said Ben quietly, after a moment. "Don't be a little idiot. You're not going to die, you know. When did this happen?"

The boy blurted out his confession.

Ben got up and put on his clothes.

"Come on," said he, "we'll go to see McGuire."

As they walked townward, he tried to talk, explaining himself in babbling incoherent spurts.

"It was like this," he began, "if I had known, but at that time I didn't—of course I know it was my own fault for——"

"Oh, for God's sake!" said Ben impatiently. "Dry up! I don't want to hear about it. I'm not your damned Guardian Angel."

The news was comforting. So many people, after our fall from grace, are.

They mounted to the wide dark corridor of the Doctors' and Surgeons', with its sharp excitement of medical smells. McGuire's anteroom was empty. Ben rapped at the inner door. McGuire opened it: he pulled away the wet cigarette that was plastered on his heavy lip, to greet them.

"Hello, Ben. Hello, son!" he barked, seeing Eugene. "When'd you get back?"

"He thinks he's dying of galloping consumption, McGuire," said Ben, with a jerk of the head. "You may be able to do something to prolong his life."

"What's the matter, son?" said McGuire.

Eugene gulped dryly, craning his livid face.

"If you don't mind," he croaked. "See you alone." He turned desperately upon his brother. "You stay here. Don't want you with me."

"I don't want to go with you," said Ben surlily. "I've got troubles enough of my own."

Eugene followed McGuire's burly figure into the office; McGuire closed the door, and sat down heavily at his littered desk.

"Sit down, son," he commanded, "and tell me about it." He lit a cigarette and stuck it deftly on his sag wet lip. He glanced keenly at the boy, noting his contorted face.

"Take your time, son," he said kindly, "and control yourself. Whatever it is, it's probably not as bad as you think."

"It was this way," Eugene began in a low voice. "I've made a mistake. I know that. I'm willing to take my medicine. I'm not making any excuses for what has happened," his voice rose sharply; he got halfway out of his chair, and began to pound fiercely upon the untidy desk. "I'm putting the blame on no one. Do you understand that?"

McGuire turned a bloated bewildered face slowly upon his patient. His wet cigarette sagged comically from his half-opened mouth.

"Do I understand what?" he said. "See here, 'Gene: what the hell are you driving at? I'm no Sherlock Holmes, you know. I'm your doctor. Spit it out."

The boy answered with a bitter writhen face.

"What I've done," he said dramatically, "thousands have done. Oh, I know they may pretend not to. But they do! You're a doctor—you know that. People high-up in society, too. I'm one of the unlucky ones. I got caught. Why am I any worse than they are? Why—" he continued rhetorically.

"I think I catch your drift," said McGuire dryly. "Let's have a look, son."

Eugene obeyed feverishly, still declaiming.

"Why should I bear the stigma for what others get away with? Hypocrites—a crowd of damned, dirty, whining hypocrites, that's what they are. The Double Standard! Hah! Where's the justice, where's the honor of that? Why should I be blamed for what people in High Society——"

McGuire lifted his big head from its critical stare, and barked comically.

"Who's blaming you? You don't think you're the first one who ever had this sort of trouble, do you? There's nothing wrong with you, anyway."

"Can—can you cure me?" Eugene asked.

"No. You're incurable, son!" said McGuire. He scrawled a few hieroglyphics on a prescription pad. "Give this to the druggist," he said, "and be a little more careful hereafter of the company you keep. People in High Society, eh?" he grinned. "So that's where you've been?"

The great weight of blood and tears had lifted completely out of the boy's heart, leaving him dizzily buoyant, wild, half-conscious only of his rushing words.

He opened the door and went into the outer room. Ben got up quickly and nervously.

"Well," he said, "how much longer has he got to live?" Seriously, in a low voice, he added: "There's nothing wrong with him, is there?"

"No," said McGuire, "I think he's a little off his nut. But, then, you all are."

When they came out on the street again, Ben said: "Have you had anything to eat?"

"No," said Eugene.

"When did you eat last?"

"Sometime yesterday," said Eugene. "I don't remember."

"You damned fool!" Ben muttered. "Come on—let's eat."

The idea became very attractive. The world was washed pleasantly in the milky winter sunshine. The town, under the stimulus of the holidays and the returning students, had wakened momentarily from its winter torpor: warm brisk currents of life seethed over the pavements. He walked along at Ben's side with a great bounding stride, unable to govern the expanding joy that rose yeastily in him. Finally, as he turned in on the busy avenue, he could restrain himself no longer: he leaped high in the air, with a yelp of ecstasy:

"Squee-ee!"

"You little idiot!" Ben cried sharply. "Are you crazy!"

He scowled fiercely, then turned to the roaring passers-by, with a thin smile.

"Hang onto him, Ben!" yelled Jim Pollock. He was a deadly little man, waxen and smiling under a black mustache, the chief compositor, a Socialist.

"If you cut off his damned big feet," said Ben, "he'd go up like a balloon."

They went into the big new lunchroom and sat at one of the tables.

"What's yours?" said the waiter.

"A cup of coffee and a piece of mince pie," said Ben.

"I'll take the same," said Eugene.

"Eat!" said Ben fiercely. "Eat!"

Eugene studied the card thoughtfully.

"Bring me some veal cutlets breaded with tomato sauce," he said, "with a side-order of hash-brown potatoes, a dish of creamed carrots and peas, and a plate of hot biscuits. Also a cup of coffee."

Eugene got back his heart again. He got it back fiercely and carelessly, with an eldritch wildness. During the remainder of his holiday, he plunged recklessly through the lively crowds, looking boldly but without insolence at the women and young girls. They grew unexpectedly out of the waste drear winter like splendid flowers. He was eager and alone. Fear is a dragon that lives among crowds—and in armies. It lives hardly with men who are alone. He felt released—beyond the last hedge of desperation.

Freed and alone, he looked with a boding detachment at all the possessed and possessing world about him. Life hung for his picking fingers like a strange and bitter fruit. *They*—the great clan huddled there behind the stockade for warmth and safety—could hunt him down some day and put him to death: he thought they would.

But he was not now afraid—he was content, if only the struggle might be fruitful. He looked among the crowds printed with the mark of his danger, seeking that which he might desire and take.

He went back to the university sealed up against the taunts of the young men: in the hot green Pullman they pressed about him with thronging jibe, but they fell back sharply, as fiercely he met them, with constraint.

There came and sat beside him Tom French, his handsome face vested in the hard insolence of money. He was followed by his court jester, Roy Duncan, the slave with the high hard cackle.

"Hello, Gant," said Tom French harshly. "Been to Exeter lately?" Scowling, he winked at grinning Roy.

"Yes," said Eugene, "I've been there lately, and I'm on my way there now. What's it to you, French?"

Discomfited by this hard defiance, the rich man's son drew back.

"We hear you're stepping out among them, 'Gene," said Roy Duncan, cackling.

"Who's we?" said Eugene. "Who's them?"

"They say," said Tom French, "that you're as pure as the flowing sewer."

"If I need cleaning," said Eugene, "I can always use the Gold Dust Twins, can't I? French and Duncan, the Gold Dust Twins—who never do any work."

The cluster of grinning students, the young impartial brutes who had gathered above them on the seats back and front, laughed loudly.

"That's right! That's right! Talk to them, 'Gene!" said Zeno Cochran, softly. He was a tall lad of twenty, slender and powerful, with the grace of a running horse. He had punted against the wind for eighty yards in the Yale Bowl. He was a handsome fellow, soft-spoken and kindly, with the fearless gentleness of the athlete.

Confused and angry, with sullen boastfulness, Tom French said:

"Nobody has anything on me. I've been too slick for them. Nobody knows anything about me."

"You mean," said Eugene, "that everyone knows all about you, and nobody wants to know anything about you."

The crowd laughed.

"Wow!" said Jimmy Revell.

"What about that, Tom?" he asked challengingly. He was very small and plump, the son of a carpenter, offensively worthy, working his way through college by various schemes. He was a "kidder," an egger-on, finding

excuse for his vulgarity and malice in a false and loud
good humor.

Eugene turned quietly on Tom French. "Stop it!" he
said. "Don't go on because the others are listening. I
don't think it's funny. I don't like it. I don't like you. I
want you to leave me alone now. Do you hear?"

"Come on," said Roy Duncan, rising, "leave him alone,
Tom. He can't take a joke. He takes things too seriously."

They left him. Unperturbed, relieved, he turned his
face toward the vast bleak earth, grey and hoary in the
iron grip of winter.

Winter ended. The sleety frozen earth began to soften
under thaw and the rain. The town and campus paths
were dreary trenches of mud and slime. The cold rain
fell: the grass shot up in green wet patches. He hurtled
down the campus lanes, bounding along like a kangaroo,
leaping high at the lower boughs to clip a budding twig
with his teeth. He cried loudly in his throat—a whinny-
ing squeal—the centaur-cry of man or beast, trying to
unburden its overladen heart in one blast of pain and joy
and passion. At other times he slouched by, depressed by
an unaccountable burden of weariness and dejection.

He lost count of the hours—he had no sense of time—
no regular periods for sleep, work, or recreation,
although he attended his classes faithfully, and ate with
fair regularity by compulsion of dining-hall or boardinghouse schedules. The food was abundant, coarse, greasily
and badly cooked. It was very cheap: at the college
commons, twelve dollars a month; at the boardinghouses,
fifteen. He ate at the commons for a month: his interest
in food was too profound and too intelligent to stand it
longer. The commons was housed in a large bleak building of white brick. It was called officially Stiggins Hall,

but, in the more descriptive epithet of the students—The Sty.

He went to see Helen and Hugh Barton several times. They lived thirty-five miles away at Sydney, the state capital. It was a town of thirty thousand people, sleepy, with quiet leafy pavements, and a capitol Square in the center, with radial streets. At the head of the main street, across from the capitol, a brown weathered building of lichened stone, was a cheap hotel—the largest and most notorious brothel in town. There were also three denominational colleges for young women.

The Bartons had rented quarters in an old house on the street above the Governor's Mansion. They lived in three or four rooms on the ground floor.

It was to Sydney that Gant had come, a young man, from Baltimore, on his slow drift to the South. It was in Sydney that he had first started business for himself and conceived, from the loss of his first investments, his hatred of property. It was in Sydney that he had met and wedded the sainted Cynthia, the tubercular spinstress who had died within two years of their marriage.

Their father's great ghost haunted them: it brooded over the town, above the scouring oblivion of the years that wipes all trace of us away.

Together, they hunted down into the mean streets, until they stood at length before a dreary shop on the skirts of the Negro district.

"This must be it," she said. "His shop stood here. It's gone now."

She was silent a moment. "Poor old Papa." She turned her wet eyes away.

There was no mark of his great hand on this bleak world. No vines grew round the houses. That part of him which had lived here was buried—buried with a dead woman below the long grey tide of the years. They stood quietly, frightened, in that strange place, waiting to hear the summons of his voice, with expectant unbelief, as someone looking for the god in Brooklyn.

In April the nation declared war on Germany. Before the month was out, all the young men at Pulpit Hill who were eligible—those who were twenty-one—were going into service. At the gymnasium he watched the doctors examine them, envying them the careless innocence with which they stripped themselves naked. They threw off their clothes in indifferent heaps and stood, laughing and certain, before the doctors. They were clean-limbed, sound and white of tooth, graceful and fast in their movements. The fraternity men joined first—those merry and extravagant snobs of whom he had never known, but who now represented for him the highest reach of urbane and aristocratic life. He had seen them, happy and idle, on the wide verandas of their chapter houses—those temples where the last and awful rites of initiation were administered. He had seen them, always together, and from the herd of the uninitiated always apart, laughing over their mail at the post office, or gambling for "black cows" at the drugstore. And, with a stab of failure, with regret, with pain at his social deficiency, he had watched their hot campaigns for the favor of some desirable freshman—someone vastly more elegant than himself, someone with blood and with money. They were only the sons of the little rich men, the lords of the village and county, but as he saw them go so surely, with such laughing unconstraint, in well-cut clothes, well-groomed, well-brushed, among the crowd of humbler students, who stiffened awkwardly with peasant hostility and constraint—they were the flower of chivalry, the sons of the mansion house. They were Sydney, Raleigh, Nash. And now, like gentlemen, they were going to war.

The gymnasium was thick with the smell of steam and of sweating men coming in to the showers from the playing fields. Washed, with opened shirt, Eugene walked slowly away into the green budding shade of the campus, companioned by an acquaintance, Ralph Hendrix.

"Look!" said Ralph Hendrix, in a low angry tone. "Look at that, will you!" He nodded towards a group of students ahead. "That little Horse's Neck is booting the Dekes all over the campus."

Eugene looked, then turned to examine the bitter common face beside him. Every Saturday night, after the meeting of the literary society, Ralph Hendrix went to the drugstore and bought two cheap cigars. He had bent narrow shoulders, a white knobby face, and a low forehead. He spoke in a monotonous painful drawl. His father was foreman in a cotton mill.

"They're all Horses' Necks," he said. "They can go to hell before I'll boot to get in."

"Yes," said Eugene.

But he wanted to get in. He wanted to be urbane and careless. He wanted to wear well-cut clothes. He wanted to be a gentleman. He wanted to go to war.

On the central campus, several students who had been approved by the examining board, descended from the old dormitories, bearing packed valises. They turned down under the trees, walking towards the village street. From time to time they threw up an arm in farewell.

"So long, boys! See you in Berlin." The shining and dividing sea was closer and not so wide.

He read a great deal—but at random, for pleasure. He read Defoe, Smollet, Sterne, and Fielding—the fine salt of the English novel lost, during the reign of the Widow of Windsor, beneath an ocean of tea and molasses. He read the tales of Boccaccio, and all that remained of a tattered copy of the *Heptameron*. At Buck Benson's suggestion, he read Murray's *Euripides* (at the time he was reading the Greek text of the *Alcestis*—noblest and loveliest of all the myths of Love and Death). He saw the grandeur of the *Prometheus* fable—but the fable moved him more than the play of Æschylus. In fact, Æschylus he found sublime—and dull: he could not understand his great reputation. Rather—he could. He was Literature—a writer of masterpieces. He was almost as great a bore as Cicero—that windy old moralist who came out so boldly in favor of Old Age and Friendship. Sophocles was an imperial poet—he spoke like God among flashes of lightning: the *Œdipus Rex* is not only one of the greatest plays in the world, it is one of the greatest stories. This story—perfect, inevitable, and fabulous—wreaked upon him the nightmare coincidence of Destiny. It held him birdlike before its great snake-eye of wisdom and horror. And Euripides (whatever the disparagement of pedantry) he thought one of the greatest lyrical singers in all poetry.

He liked all weird fable and wild invention, in prose or verse, from the *Golden Ass* to Samuel Taylor Coleridge, the chief prince of the moon and magic. But he liked the fabulous wherever he found it, and for whatever purpose.

The best fabulists have often been the greatest satirists: satire (as with Aristophanes, Voltaire, and Swift) is a high and subtle art, quite beyond the barn-yard snipings and wholesale geese-slaughterings of the present degenerate age. Great satire needs the sustenance of great fable. Swift's power of invention is incomparable: there's no better fabulist in the world.

He read Poe's stories, *Frankenstein,* and the plays of
Lord Dunsany. He read *Sir Gawayne and the Grene
Knight* and the *Book of Tobit.* He did not want his ghosts
and marvels explained. Magic was magic. He wanted old
ghosts—not Indian ghosts, but ghosts in armor, the
spirits of old kings, and pillioned ladies with high coned
hats. Then, for the first time, he thought of the lonely
earth he dwelt on. Suddenly, it was strange to him that
he should read Euripides there in the wilderness.

Around him lay the village; beyond, the ugly rolling
land, sparse with cheap farmhouses; beyond all this,
America—more land, more wooden houses, more towns,
hard and raw and ugly. He was reading Euripides, and
all around him a world of white and black was eating
fried food. He was reading of ancient sorceries and old
ghosts, but did an old ghost ever come to haunt this
land? The ghost of Hamlet's Father, in Connecticut,

> . . . . . . I am thy father's spirit,
> Doomed for a certain term to walk the night
> Between Bloomington and Portland, Maine.

He felt suddenly the devastating impermanence of the
nation. Only the earth endured—the gigantic American
earth, bearing upon its awful breast a world of flimsy
rickets. Only the earth endured—this broad terrific earth
that had no ghosts to haunt it. Stogged in the desert,
half-broken and overthrown, among the columns of lost
temples strewn, there was no ruined image of Menkaura,
there was no alabaster head of Akhnaton. Nothing had
been done in stone. Only this earth endured, upon whose
lonely breast he read Euripides. Within its hills he had
been held a prisoner; upon its plain he walked, alone, a
stranger.

O God! O God! We have been an exile in another land
and a stranger in our own. The mountains were our

masters: they went home to our eye and our heart before
we came to five. Whatever we can do or say must be
forever hillbound. Our senses have been fed by our terrific land; our blood has learned to run to the imperial
pulse of America which, leaving, we can never lose and
never forget. We walked along a road in Cumberland,
and stooped, because the sky hung down so low; and
when we ran away from London, we went by little rivers
in a land just big enough. And nowhere that we went
was far: the earth and the sky were close and near. And
the old hunger returned—the terrible and obscure
hunger that haunts and hurts Americans, and that makes
us exiles at home and strangers wherever we go.

Eliza visited Helen in Sydney in the spring. The girl
was quieter, sadder, more thoughtful than she had ever
been. She was subdued by the new life: chastened by her
obscurity. She missed Gant more than she would confess.
She missed the mountain town.

"What do you have to pay for this place?" said Eliza,
looking around critically.

"Fifty dollars a month," said Helen.

"Furnished?"

"No, we had to buy furniture."

"I tell you what, that's pretty high," said Eliza, "just
for downstairs. I believe rents are lower at home."

"Yes, I know it's high," said Helen. "But, good
heavens, Mama! Do you realize that this is the best
neighborhood in town? We're only two blocks from the
Governor's Mansion, you know. Mrs. Mathews is no common boardinghouse keeper, I can assure you! No sir!"
she exclaimed, laughing. "She's a real swell—goes to all
the big functions and gets in the papers all the time. You
know Hugh and I have got to try to keep up appear-
ances. He's a young man just starting out here."

"Yes. I know," Eliza agreed thoughtfully. "How's he been doing?"

"O'Toole says he's the best agent he's got," said Helen. "Hugh's all right. We could get along together anywhere, as long as there's no damned family about. It makes me furious at times to see him slaving to feather O'Toole's pockets. He works like a dog. You know, O'Toole gets a commission on every sale he makes. And Mrs. O'T. and those two girls ride around in a big car and never turn their hands over. They're Catholics, you know, but they get to go everywhere."

"I tell you what," said Eliza with a timid half-serious smile, "it might not be a bad idea if Hugh became his own boss. There's no use doing it all for the other fellow. Say, child!" she exclaimed, "why wouldn't it be a good idea if he tried to get the Altamont agency? I don't believe that fellow they've got is much account. He could get it without trying."

There was a pause.

"We've been thinking of that," the girl admitted slowly. "Hugh has written in to the main office. Anyway," she said a moment later, "he'd be his own boss. That's something."

"Well," said Eliza slowly, "I don't know but what it'd be a good idea. If he works hard there's no reason why he shouldn't build a good business up. Your papa's been complaining here lately about his trouble. He'd be glad to have you back." She shook her head slowly for a moment. "Child! they didn't do him a bit of good, up there. It's all come back."

They drove over to Pulpit Hill at Easter for a two days' visit. Eliza took him to Exeter and bought him a suit of clothes.

"I don't like those skimpy trousers," she told the salesman. "I want something that makes him look more of a man."

When he was newly dressed, she puckered her lips, smiling, and said:

"Spruce up, boy! Throw your shoulders back! That's one thing about your father—he carries himself straight as an arrow. If you go all humped over like that, you'll have lung trouble before you're twenty-five."

"I want you to meet my mother," he said awkwardly to Mr. Joseph Ballantyne, a smooth pink young man who had been elected president of the Freshman class.

"You're a good smart-looking fellow," said Eliza, smiling, "I'll make a trade with you. If you drum up some boarders for me among your friends here in this part of the state, I'll throw in your board free. Here are some of my cards," she added, opening her purse. "You might hand a few of them out, if you get a chance, and say a good word for Dixieland in the Land of the Sky."

"Yes, ma'am," said Mr. Ballantyne, in a slow surprised voice, "I certainly will."

Eugene turned a hot distressed face toward Helen. She laughed huskily, ironically, then turning to the boy, said:

"You're welcome at any time, Mr. Ballantyne, boarders or not. We'll always find a place for you."

When they were alone, in answer to his stammering and confused protests, she said with an annoyed grin:

"Yes, I know. It's pretty bad. But you're away from it most of the time. You're the lucky one. You see what I've had to listen to, the last week, don't you? You see, don't you?"

When he went home at the end of the year, late in May, he found that Helen and Hugh Barton had preceded him. They were living with Gant, at Woodson

Street. Hugh Barton had secured the Altamont agency.

The town and the nation boiled with patriotic frenzy —violent, in a chaotic sprawl, to little purpose. The spawn of Attila must be crushed ("exterminated," said the Reverend Mr. Smallwood) by the sons of freedom. There were loans, bond issues, speech-making, a talk of drafts, and a thin trickle of Yankees into France. Pershing arrived in Paris and said, "Lafayette, we are here!" but the French were still looking. Ben went up before the enlistment board and was rejected. "Lungs—weak!" they said quite definitely. "No—not tubercular. A tendency. Underweight." He cursed. His face was a little more like a blade—thinner, greyer. The cleft of his scowl was deeper. He seemed more alone.

Eugene came up into the hills again and found them in their rich young summer glory. Dixieland was partly filled by paying guests. More arrived.

Eugene was sixteen years old. He was a College Man. He walked among the gay crowd of afternoon with a sense of elation, answering the hearty greetings with joy, warming to its thoughtless bombast.

"They tell me you're batting a thousand down there, son," yelled Mr. Wood, the plump young pharmacist, who had been told nothing at all. "That's right, boy! Go get 'em." The man passed forward cheerfully, up the prosperous glade of his store. Fans droned.

After all, Eugene thought, he had not done so badly. He had felt his first wounds. He had not been broken. He had seen love's bitter mystery. He had lived alone.

III

There was at Dixieland a girl named Laura James. She was twenty-one years old. She looked younger. She was there when he came back.

Laura was a slender girl, of medium height, but looking taller than she was. She was very firmly molded: she seemed fresh and washed and clean. She had thick hair, very straight and blonde, combed in a flat bracelet around her small head. Her face was white, with small freckles. Her eyes were soft, candid, cat-green. Her nose was a little too large for her face: it was tilted. She was not pretty. She dressed very simply and elegantly in short plaid skirts and waists of knitted silk.

She was the only young person at Dixieland. Eugene spoke to her with timid hauteur. He thought her plain and dull. But he began to sit with her on the porch at night. Somehow, he began to love her.

He did not know that he loved her. He talked to her arrogantly and boastfully as they sat in the wooden porch swing. But he breathed the clean perfume of her marvelous young body. He was trapped in the tender cruelty of her clear green eyes, caught in the subtle net of her smile.

Laura James lived in the eastern part of the state, far east even of Pulpit Hill, in a little town built on a salt river of the great coastal plain. Her father was a wealthy merchant—a wholesale provisioner. The girl was an only child: she spent extravagantly.

Eugene sat on the porch rail one evening and talked to her. Before, he had only nodded, or spoken stiffly a word or two. They began haltingly, aware painfully of gaps in their conversation.

"You're from Little Richmond, aren't you?" he said.

"Yes," said Laura James, "do you know anyone from there?"

"Yes," said he, "I know John Bynum and a boy named Ficklen. They're from Little Richmond, aren't they?"

"Oh, Dave Ficklen! Do you know him? Yes. They both go to Pulpit Hill. Do you go there?"

"Yes," he said, "that's where I knew them."

"Do you know the two Barlow boys? They're Sigma Nus," said Laura James.

He had seen them. They were great swells, football men.

"Yes, I know them," he said, "Roy Barlow and Jack Barlow."

"Do you know 'Snooks' Warren? He's a Kappa Sig."

"Yes. They call them Keg Squeezers," said Eugene.

"What fraternity are you?" said Laura James.

"I'm not any," he said painfully. "I was just a Freshman this year."

"Some of the best friends I have never joined fraternities," said Laura James.

They met more and more frequently, without arrangement, until by silent consent they met every night upon the porch. Sometimes they walked along the cool dark streets. Sometimes he squired her clumsily through the town, to the movies, and later, with the uneasy pugnacity of youth, past the loafing cluster at Wood's. Often he took her to Woodson Street, where Helen secured for him the cool privacy of the veranda. She was very fond of Laura James.

"She's a nice girl. A lovely girl. I like her. She's not going to take any beauty prizes, is she?" She laughed with a trace of good-natured ridicule.

He was displeased.

"She looks all right," he said. "She's not as ugly as you make out."

But she *was* ugly—with a clean lovely ugliness. Her face was freckled lightly, over her nose and mouth: her features were eager, unconscious, turned upward in irregular pertness. But she was exquisitely made and exquisitely kept: she had the firm young line of spring, budding, slender, virginal. She was like something swift, with wings, which hovers in a wood—among the feathery trees suspected, but uncaught, unseen.

He tried to live before her in armor. He showed off before her. Perhaps, he thought, if he were splendid enough, she would not see the ugly disorder and meanness of the world he dwelt in.

Across the street, on the wide lawn of the Brunswick —the big brick gabled house that Eliza once had coveted —Mr. Pratt, who crawled in that mean world in which only a boardinghouse husband can exist, was watering wide green spaces of lawn with a hose. The flashing water motes gleamed in the red glare of sunset. The red light fell across the shaven pinched face. It glittered on the buckles of his arm-bands. Across the walk, on the other lobe of grass, several men and women were playing croquet. There was laughter on the vine-hid porch. Next door, at the Belton, the boarders were assembled on the long porch in bright hash-house chatter. The comedian of the Dixie Ramblers arrived with two chorus girls. He was a little man, with the face of a weasel and no upper teeth. He wore a straw hat with a striped band, and a blue shirt and collar. The boarders gathered in around him. In a moment there was shrill laughter.

Julius Arthur sped swiftly down the hill, driving his father home. He grinned squintily and flung his arm up in careless greeting. The prosperous lawyer twisted a plump Van Dyked face on a wry neck curiously. Unsmiling, he passed.

A Negress in the Brunswick struck on the several bells of a Japanese gong. There was a scramble of feet on the porch; the croquet players dropped their mallets and walked rapidly towards the house. Pratt wound his hose over a wooden reel.

A slow bell-clapper in the Belton sent the guests in a

scrambling drive for the doors. In a moment there was a clatter of heavy plates and a loud foody noise. The guests on the porch at Dixieland rocked more rapidly, with low mutters of discontent.

Eugene talked to Laura in thickening dusk, sheeting his pain in pride and indifference. Eliza's face, a white blur in the dark, came up behind the screen.

"Come on out, Mrs. Gant, and get a breath of fresh air," said Laura James.

"Why, no-o, child. I can't now. Who's that with you?" she cried, obviously flustered. She opened the door. "Huh? Heh? Have you seen 'Gene? Is it 'Gene?"

"Yes," he said. "What's the matter?"

"Come here a minute, boy," she said.

He went into the hall.

"What is it?" he asked.

"Why, son, what in the world! I don't know. You'll have to do something," she whispered, twisting her hands together.

"What is it, Mama? What are you talking about?" he cried irritably.

"Why—Jannadeau's just called up. Your papa's on a rampage again and he's coming this way. Child! There's no telling what he'll do. I've all these people in the house. He'll ruin us." She wept. "Go and try to stop him. Head him off if you can. Take him to Woodson Street."

He got his hat quickly and ran through the door.

"Where are you going?" asked Laura James. "Are you going off without supper?"

"I've got to go to town," he said. "I won't be long. Will you wait for me?"

"Yes," she said.

He leaped down on the walk just as his father lurched in from the street by the high obscuring hedge that shut the house from the spacious yard of the attorney Hall.

Gant reeled destructively, across a border of lilies, onto the lawn, and strode for the veranda. He stumbled, cursing, on the bottom step and plunged forward in a sprawl upon the porch. The boy jumped for him, and half-dragged, half-lifted his great drunken body erect. The boarders shrank into a huddle with a quick scattering of chairs: he greeted them with a laugh of howling contempt.

"Are you there? I say, are you there? The lowest of the low—boardinghouse swine! Merciful God! What a travesty! A travesty on Nature! That it should come to this!"

He burst into a long peal of maniacal laughter.

"Papa! Come on!" said Eugene in a low voice. He took his father cautiously by the sleeve. Gant flung him half across the porch with a gesture of his hand. As he stepped in again swiftly, his father struck at him with a flailing arm. He evaded the great mowing fist without trouble, and caught the falling body, swung from its own pivot, in his arms. Then quickly, before Gant could recover, holding him from behind, he rushed him towards the door. The boarders scattered away like sparrows. But Laura James was at the screen before him: she flung it open.

"Get away! Get away!" he cried, full of shame and anger. "You stay out of this." For a moment he despised her for seeing his hurt.

"Oh, let me help you, my dear," Laura James whispered. Her eyes were wet, but she was not afraid.

Father and son plunged chaotically down the wide dark hall, Eliza, weeping and making gestures, just before them.

"Take him in here, boy. Take him in here," she whispered, motioning to a large bedroom on the upper side of the house. Eugene propelled his father through a blind passage of bathroom, and pushed him over on the creaking width of an iron bed.

"You damned scoundrel!" Gant yelled, again trying to reap him down with the long arm, "let me up or I'll kill you!"

"For God's sake, Papa," he implored angrily, "try to quiet down. Everyone in town can hear you."

"To hell with them!" Gant roared. "Mountain Grills— all of them, fattening upon my heart's-blood. They have done me to death, as sure as there's a God in heaven."

Eliza appeared in the door, her face contorted by weeping.

"Son, can't you do something to stop him?" she said. "He'll ruin us all. He'll drive everyone away."

Gant struggled to stand erect when he saw her. Her white face stirred him to insanity.

"There it is! There! There! Do you see! The fiend-face I know so well, gloating upon my misery. Look at it! Look! Do you see its smile of evil cunning? Greeley, Will, the Hog, the Old Major! The Tax Collector will get it all, and I shall die in the gutter!"

"If it hadn't been for me," Eliza began, stung to retaliation, "you'd have died there long ago."

"Mama, for God's sake!" the boy cried. "Don't stand there talking to him! Can't you see what it does to him! Do something, in heaven's name! Get Helen! Where is she?"

"I'll make an end to it all!" Gant yelled, staggering erect. "I'll do for us both now."

Eliza vanished.

"Yes, sir, Papa. It's going to be all right," Eugene began soothingly, pushing him back on the bed again. He dropped quickly to his knees, and began to draw off one of Gant's soft tongueless shoes, muttering reassurances all the time: "Yes, sir. We'll get you some good hot soup and put you to bed in a jiffy. Everything's going to be all right." The shoe came off in his hand and, aided by the furious thrust of his father's foot, he went sprawling back.

Gant got to his feet again and, taking a farewell kick at his fallen son, lunged towards the door. Eugene scrambled up quickly, and leaped after him. The two men fell heavily into the roughly grained plaster of the wall. Gant cursed, flailing about clumsily at his tormentor. Helen came in.

"Baby!" Gant wept, "they're trying to kill me. O Jesus, do something to save me, or I perish."

"You get back in that bed," she commanded sharply, "or I'll knock your head off."

Very obediently he suffered himself to be led back to bed and undressed. In a few minutes she was sitting beside him with a bowl of smoking soup. He grinned sheepishly as she spooned it into his opened mouth. She laughed—almost happily—thinking of the lost and irrevocable years. Suddenly, before he slept, he lifted himself strongly from the pillows that propped him, and, with staring eyes, called out in savage terror:

"Is it a cancer? I say, is it a cancer?"

"Hush!" she cried. "No. Of course not! Don't be foolish."

He fell back exhausted, with eyes closed. But they knew that it was. He had never been told. The terrible name of his malady was never uttered save by him. And in his heart he knew—what they all knew and never spoke of before him—that it was, it was a cancer. All day, with fear-stark eyes, Gant had sat, like a broken statue, among his marbles, drinking. It was a cancer.

The boy's right hand bled very badly across the wrist, where his father's weight had ground it into the wall.

"Go wash it off," said Helen. "I'll tie it up for you."

He went into the dark bathroom and held his hand under a jet of lukewarm water. A very quiet despair was in his heart, a weary peace that brooded too upon the house of death and tumult, that flowed, like a soft exploring wind, through its dark halls, bathing all things quietly with peace and weariness. The boarders had fled like silly sheep to the two houses across the street: they had eaten there, they were clustered there upon the porches, whispering. And their going brought him peace and freedom, as if his limbs had been freed from a shackling weight. Eliza, amid the slow smoke of the kitchen, wept more quietly over the waste of supper; he saw the black mournful calm of the Negress's face. He walked slowly up the dark hall, with a handkerchief tied loosely round his wound. He felt suddenly the peace that comes with despair. The sword that pierces very deep had fared through the folds of his poor armor of pride. The steel had shared his side, had bitten to his heart. But under his armor he had found himself. No more than himself could be known. No more than himself could be given. What he was—he was: evasion and pretense could not add to his sum. With all his heart he was glad.

By the door, in the darkness, he found Laura James.

"I thought you had gone with the others," he said.

"No," said Laura James. "How is your father?"

"He's all right now. He's gone to sleep," he answered. "Have you had anything to eat?"

"No," she said, "I didn't want it."

"I'll bring you something from the kitchen," he said. "There's plenty there." In a moment he added: "I'm sorry, Laura."

"What are you sorry for?" she asked.

He leaned against the wall limply, drained of his strength at her touch.

"Eugene. My dear," she said. She pulled his drooping face down to her lips and kissed him. "My sweet, my darling, don't look like that."

All his resistance melted from him. He seized her small hands, crushing them in his hot fingers, and devouring them with kisses.

"My dear Laura! My dear Laura!" he said in a choking voice. "My sweet, my beautiful Laura! My lovely Laura. I love you, I love you." The words rushed from his heart, incoherent, unashamed, foaming through the broken levees of pride and silence. They clung together in the dark, with their wet faces pressed mouth to mouth. Her perfume went drunkenly to his brain; her touch upon him shot through his limbs a glow of magic; he felt the pressure of her narrow breasts, eager and lithe, against him with a sense of fear—as if he had dishonored her—with a sickening remembrance of his defilement.

He held between his hands her elegant small head, so gloriously wound with its thick bracelet of fine blonde hair, and spoke the words he had never spoken—the words of confession, filled with love and humility.

"Don't go! Don't go! Please don't go!" he begged. "Don't leave, dear. Please!"

"Hush!" she whispered. "I won't go! I love you, my dear."

She saw his hand, wrapped in its bloody bandage: she nursed it gently with soft little cries of tenderness. She fetched a bottle of iodine from her room and painted the stinging cut with a brush. She wrapped it with clean strips of fine white cloth, torn from an old waist, scented with a faint and subtle perfume.

Then they sat upon the wooden swing. The house seemed to sleep in darkness. Helen and Eliza came presently from its very quiet depth.

"How's your hand, 'Gene?" Helen asked.

"It's all right," he said.

"Let me see! O-ho, you've got a nurse now, haven't you?" she said, with a good laugh.

"What's that? What's that? Hurt his hand? How'd you do that? Why, here—say—I've got the very thing for it, son," said Eliza, trying to bustle off in all directions.

"Oh, it's all right now, Mama. It's been fixed," he said wearily, reflecting that she had the very things always too late. He looked at Helen, grinning:

"God bless our Happy Home!" he said.

"Poor old Laura!" she laughed, and hugged the girl roughly with one hand. "It's too bad you have to be dragged into it."

"That's all right," said Laura. "I feel like one of the family now, anyhow."

"He needn't think he can carry on like this," said Eliza resentfully. "I'm not going to put up with it any longer."

"Oh, forget about it!" said Helen wearily. "Good heavens, Mama. Papa's a sick man. Can't you realize that?"

"Pshaw!" said Eliza scornfully. "I don't believe there's a thing in the world wrong with him but that vile licker. All his trouble comes from that."

"Oh—how ridiculous! How ridiculous! You can't tell me!" Helen exclaimed angrily.

"Let's talk about the weather," said Eugene.

Then they all sat quietly, letting the darkness soak into them. Finally Helen and Eliza went back into the house: Eliza went unwillingly, at the girl's insistence, casting back the doubtful glimmer of her face upon the boy and girl.

The wasting helve of the moon rode into heaven over the bulk of the hills. There was a smell of wet grass and lilac, and the vast brooding symphony of the million-noted little night things, rising and falling in a constant ululation, and inhabiting the heart with steady unconscious certitude. The pallid light drowned out the stars, it lay like silence on the earth, it dripped through the leafy web of the young maples, printing the earth with swarming moths of elvish light.

Eugene and Laura sat with joined hands in the slowly creaking swing. Her touch shot through him like a train of fire: as he put his arm around her shoulders and drew her over to him, his fingers touched the live firm cup of her breast. He jerked his hand away, as if he had been stung, muttering an apology. Whenever she touched him, his flesh got numb and weak. She was a virgin, crisp like celery—his heart shrank away from the pollution of his touch upon her. It seemed to him that he was much the older, although he was sixteen, and she twenty-one. He felt the age of his loneliness and his dark perception. He felt the grey wisdom of sin—a waste desert, but seen and known. When he held her hand, he felt as if he had already seduced her. She lifted her lovely face to him, pert and ugly as a boy's; it was inhabited by a true and steadfast decency, and his eyes were wet. All the young beauty in the world dwelt for him in that face that had kept wonder, that had kept innocency, that had lived in such immortal blindness to the terror and foulness of the world. He came to her, like a creature who had traveled its life through dark space, for a moment of peace and conviction on some lonely planet, where now he stood, in the vast enchanted plain of moonlight, with moonlight falling on the moonflower of her face. For if a man should dream of heaven and, waking, find within his hand a flower as token that he had really been there— what then, what then?

"Eugene," she said presently, "how old are you?"

His vision thickened with his pulse. In a moment he answered with terrible difficulty.

"I'm—just sixteen."

"Oh, you child!" she cried. "I thought you were more than that!"

"I'm—old for my age," he muttered. "How old are you?"

"I'm twenty-one," she said. "Isn't it a pity?"

"There's not much difference," he said. "I can't see that it matters."

"Oh, my dear," she said. "It does! It matters so much!"

And he knew that it did—how much he did not know. But he had his moment. He was not afraid of pain, he was not afraid of loss. He cared nothing for the practical need of the world. He dared to say the strange and marvelous thing that had bloomed so darkly in him.

"Laura," he said, hearing his low voice sound over the great plain of the moon, "let's always love each other as we do now. Let's never get married. I want you to wait for me and to love me forever. I am going all over the world. I shall go away for years at a time; I shall became famous, but I shall always come back to you. You shall live in a house away in the mountains, you shall wait for me, and keep yourself for me. Will you?" he said, asking for her life as calmly as for an hour of her time.

"Yes, dear," said Laura in the moonlight. "I will wait for you forever."

She was buried in his flesh. She throbbed in the beat of his pulses. She was wine in his blood, a music in his heart.

"He has no consideration for you or anyone else," Hugh Barton growled. He had returned late from work at his office, to take Helen home. "If he can't do better than this, we'll find a house of our own. I'm not going to have you get down sick on account of him."

"Forget about it," Helen said. "He's getting old."

They came out on the veranda.

"Come down tomorrow, honey," she said to Eugene. "I'll give you a real feed. Laura, you come too. It's not always like this, you know." She laughed, fondling the girl with a big hand.

They coasted away downhill.

"What a lovely girl your sister is," said Laura James. "Aren't you simply crazy about her?"

Eugene made no answer for a moment.

"Yes," he said.

"She is about you. Anyone can see that," said Laura.

In the darkness he caught at his throat.

"Yes," he said.

The moon quartered gently across heaven. Eliza came out again, timidly, hesitantly.

"Who's there? Who's there?" she spoke into the darkness. "Where's 'Gene? Oh! I didn't know! Are you there, son?" She knew very well.

"Yes," he said.

"Why don't you sit down, Mrs. Gant?" asked Laura. "I don't see how you stand that hot kitchen all day long. You must be worn out."

"I tell you what!" said Eliza, peering dimly at the sky. "It's a fine night, isn't it? As the fellow says, a night for lovers." She laughed uncertainly, then stood for a moment in thought.

"Son," she said in a troubled voice, "why don't you go to bed and get some sleep? It's not good for you staying up till all hours like this."

"That's where I should be," said Laura James, rising.

"Yes, child," said Eliza. "Go get your beauty sleep. As the saying goes, early to bed and early to rise——"

"Let's all go, then. Let's all go!" said Eugene impatiently and angrily, wondering if she must always be the last one awake in that house.

"Why, law, no!" said Eliza. "I can't, boy. I've all those things to iron."

Beside him, Laura gave his hand a quiet squeeze, and rose. Bitterly, he watched his loss.

"Good night, all. Good night, Mrs. Gant."

"Good night, child."

When she had gone, Eliza sat down beside him, with a sigh of weariness.

"I tell you what," she said. "That feels good. I wish I had as much time as some folks, and could sit out here enjoying the air." In the darkness, he knew her puckering lips were trying to smile.

"Hm!" she said, and caught his hand in her rough palm. "Has my baby gone and got him a girl?"

"What of it? What if it were true?" he said angrily. "Haven't I a right as much as anyone?"

"Pshaw!" said Eliza. "You're too young to think of them. I wouldn't pay any attention to them, if I were you. Most of them haven't an idea in the world except going out to parties and having a good time. I don't want my boy to waste his time on them."

He felt her earnestness beneath her awkward banter. He struggled in a chaos of confused fury, trying for silence. At last he spoke in a low voice, filled with his passion:

"We've got to have something, Mama. We've got to have something, you know. We can't go on always alone —alone."

It was dark. No one could see. He let the gates swing open. He wept.

"I know!" Eliza agreed hastily. "I'm not saying——"

"My God, my God, where are we going? What's it all

about? He's dying—can't you see it? Don't you know it? Look at his life. Look at yours. No light, no love, no comfort—nothing." His voice rose frantically: he beat on his ribs like a drum. "Mama, Mama, in God's name, what is it? What do you want? Are you going to strangle and drown us all? Don't you own enough? Do you want more string? Do you want more bottles? By God, I'll go around collecting them if you say so." His voice had risen almost to a scream. "But tell me what you want. Don't you own enough? Do you want the town? What is it?"

"Why, I don't know what you're talking about, boy," said Eliza angrily. "If I hadn't tried to accumulate a little property none of you would have had a roof to call your own, for your papa, I can assure you, would have squandered everything."

"A roof to call our own!" he yelled, with a crazy laugh. "Good God, we haven't a bed to call our own. We haven't a room to call our own. We have not a quilt to call our own that might not be taken from us to warm the mob that rocks upon this porch and grumbles."

"Now, you may sneer at the boarders all you like—" Eliza began sternly.

"No," he said. "I can't. There's not breath or strength enough in me to sneer at them all I like."

Eliza began to weep.

"I've done the best I could!" she said. "I'd have given you a home if I could. I'd have put up with anything after Grover's death, but he never gave me a moment's peace. Nobody knows what I've been through. Nobody knows, child. Nobody knows."

He saw her face in the moonlight, contorted by an ugly grimace of sorrow. What she said, he knew, was fair and honest. He was touched deeply.

"It's all right, Mama," he said painfully. "Forget about it! I know."

She seized his hand almost gratefully and laid her white face, still twisted with her grief, against his shoulder. It was the gesture of a child: a gesture that asked for love, pity, and tenderness. It tore up great roots in him, bloodily.

"Don't!" he said. "Don't, Mama! Please!"

"Nobody knows," said Eliza. "Nobody knows. I need someone too. I've had a hard life, son, full of pain and trouble." Slowly, like a child again, she wiped her wet weak eyes with the back of her hand.

"Ah," he thought, as his heart twisted in him full of wild pain and regret, "she will be dead some day and I shall always remember this. Always this. This."

They were silent a moment. He held her rough hand tightly, and kissed her.

"Well," Eliza began, full of cheerful prophecy, "I tell you what: I'm not going to spend my life slaving away here for a lot of boarders. They needn't think it. I'm going to set back and take things as easy as any of them." She winked knowingly at him. "When you come home next time, you may find me living in a big house in Doak Park. I've got the lot—the best lot out there for view and location, far better than the one W. J. Bryan has. I made the trade with old Dr. Doak himself, the other day. Look here! What about it!" She laughed. "He said, 'Mrs. Gant, I can't trust any of my agents with you. If I'm to make anything on this deal, I've got to look out. You're the sharpest trader in this town.' 'Why, pshaw! Doctor,' I said (I never let on I believed him or anything), 'all I want is a fair return on my investment. I believe in everyone making his profit and giving the other fellow a chance. Keep the ball a-rolling!' I said, laughing as big as you please. 'Why, Mrs. Gant!' he said—" She was off on a lengthy divagation, recording with an absorbed gusto the interminable minutiae of her transaction with the worthy Quinine King, with the attendant phenomena, during the time, of birds, bees, flowers, sun, clouds, dogs, cows, and people. She was pleased. She was happy.

Presently, returning to an abrupt reflective pause, she said: "Well, I may do it. I want a place where my children can come to see me and bring their friends, when they come home."

"Yes," he said, "yes. That would be nice. You mustn't work all your life."

He was pleased at her happy fable: for a moment he almost believed in a miracle of redemption, although the story was an old one to him.

"I hope you do," he said. "It would be nice. . . . Go on to bed now, why don't you, Mama? It's getting late." He rose. "I'm going now."

"Yes, son," she said, getting up. "You ought to. Well, good night." They kissed with a love, for the time, washed clean of bitterness. Eliza went before him into the dark house.

But before he went to bed, he descended to the kitchen for matches. She was still there, beyond the long littered table, at her ironing board, flanked by two big piles of laundry. At his accusing glance she said hastily:

"I'm a-going. Right away. I just wanted to finish up these towels."

He rounded the table, before he left, to kiss her again. She fished into a button box on the sewing machine and dug out the stub of a pencil. Gripping it firmly above an old envelope, she scrawled out on the ironing board a rough mapping. Her mind was still lulled in its project.

"Here, you see," she began, "is Sunset Avenue, coming

up the hill. This is Doak Place, running off here at right angles. Now this corner lot here belongs to Dick Webster; and right here above it, at the very top is——"

Is, he thought, staring with dull interest, the place where the Buried Treasure lies. Ten paces N.N.E. from the Big Rock, at the roots of the Old Oak Tree. He went off into his delightful fantasy while she talked. What if there *was* a buried treasure on one of Eliza's lots? If she kept on buying, there might very well be. Or why not an oil well? Or a coal mine? These famous mountains were full (they said) of minerals. 150 Bbl. a day right in the backyard. How much would that be? At $3.00 a Bbl., there would be over $50.00 a day for everyone in the family. The world is ours!

"You see, don't you?" she smiled triumphantly. "And right there is where I shall build. That lot will bring twice its present value in five years."

"Yes," he said, kissing her. "Good night, Mama. For God's sake, go to bed and get some sleep."

"Good night, son," said Eliza.

He went out and began to mount the dark stairs. Benjamin Gant, entering at this moment, stumbled across a mission chair in the hall. He cursed fiercely, and struck at the chair with his hand. Damn it! Oh, damn it! Mrs. Pert whispered a warning behind him, with a fuzzy laugh. Eugene paused, then mounted softly the carpeted stair, so that he would not be heard, entering the sleeping porch at the top of the landing on which he slept.

He did not turn on the light, because he disliked seeing the raw blistered varnish of the dresser and the bent white iron of the bed. It sagged, and the light was dim— he hated dim lights, and the large moths, flapping blindly around on their dusty wings. He undressed in the moon. The moonlight fell upon the earth like a magic unearthly dawn. It wiped away all rawness, it hid all sores. It gave all common and familiar things—the sagging drift of the barn, the raw shed of the creamery, the rich curve of the lawyer's crab-apple trees—a uniform bloom of wonder. He lighted a cigarette, watching its red glowing suspiration in the mirror, and leaned upon the rail of his porch, looking out. Presently, he grew aware that Laura James, eight feet away, was watching him. The moonlight fell upon them, bathing their flesh in a green pallor, and steeping them in its silence. Their faces were blocked in miraculous darkness, out of which, seeing but unseen, their bright eyes lived. They gazed at each other in that elfin light, without speaking. In the room below them, the light crawled to his father's bed, swam up the cover, and opened across his face, thrust sharply upward. The air of the night, the air of the hills, fell on the boy's bare flesh like a sluice of clear water. His toes curled in to grip wet grasses.

On the landing, he heard Mrs. Pert go softly up to bed, fumbling with blind care at the walls. Doors creaked and clicked. The house grew solidly into quiet, like a stone beneath the moon. They looked, waiting for a spell and the conquest of time. Then she spoke to him—her whisper of his name was only a guess at sound. He threw his leg across the rail, and thrust his long body over space to the sill of her window, stretching out like a cat. She drew her breath in sharply, and cried out softly, "No! No!" but she caught his arms upon the sills and held him as he twisted in.

Then they held each other tightly in their cool young arms, and kissed many times with young lips and faces. All her hair fell down about her like thick corn-silk, in a sweet loose wantonness. Her straight dainty legs were clad in snug little green bloomers, gathered in by an elastic above the knee.

They were locked limb to limb: he kissed the smooth sheen of her arms and shoulders—the passion that numbed his limbs was governed by a religious ecstasy. He wanted to hold her, and go away by himself to think about her.

He stooped, thrusting his arm under her knees, and lifted her up exultantly. She looked at him frightened, holding him more tightly.

"What are you doing?" she whispered. "Don't hurt me."

"I won't hurt you, my dear," he said. "I'm going to put you to bed. Yes. I'm going to put you to bed. Do you hear?" He felt he must cry out in his throat for joy.

He carried her over and laid her on the bed. Then he knelt beside her, putting his arm beneath her and gathering her to him.

"Good night, my dear. Kiss me good night. Do you love me?"

"Yes." She kissed him. "Good night, my darling. Don't go back by the window. You may fall."

But he went, as he came, reaching through the moonlight exultantly like a cat. For a long time he lay awake, in a quiet delirium, his heart thudding fiercely against his ribs. Sleep crept across his senses with goose-soft warmth: the young leaves of the maples rustled, a cock sounded his distant elfin minstrelsy, the ghost of a dog howled. He slept.

He awoke with a high hot sun beating in on his face through the porch awnings. He hated to awake in sunlight. Some day he would sleep in a great room that was always cool and dark. There would be trees and vines at his windows, or the scooped-out lift of the hill. His clothing was wet with night-damp as he dressed. When he went downstairs he found Gant rocking miserably upon the porch, his hand gripped over a walking stick.

"Good morning," he said. "How do you feel?"

His father cast his uneasy flickering eyes on him, and groaned.

"Merciful God! I'm being punished for my sins."

"You'll feel better in a little," said Eugene. "Did you eat anything?"

"It stuck in my throat," said Gant, who had eaten heartily. "I couldn't swallow a bite. How's your hand, son?" he asked very humbly.

"Oh, it's all right," said Eugene quickly. "Who told you about my hand?"

"She said I had hurt your hand," said Gant sorrowfully.

"Ah-h!" said the boy angrily. "No. I wasn't hurt."

Gant leaned to the side and, without looking, clumsily patted his son's uninjured hand.

"I'm sorry for what I've done," he said. "I'm a sick man. Do you need money?"

"No," said Eugene, embarrassed. "I have all I need."

"Come to the office today, and I'll give you something," said Gant. "Poor child, I suppose you're hard up."

But instead, he waited until Laura James returned from her morning visit to the city's bathing pool. She came with her bathing suit in one hand, and several small packages in the other. More arrived by Negro carriers. She paid and signed.

"You must have a lot of money, Laura," he said. "You do this every day, don't you?"

"Daddy gets after me about it," she admitted, "but I love to buy clothes. I spend all my money on clothes."

"What are you going to do now?"

"Nothing—whatever you like. It's a lovely day to do something, isn't it?"

"It's a lovely day to do nothing. Would you like to go off somewhere, Laura?"

"I'd love to go off somewhere with you," said Laura James.

"That is the idea, my girl. That is the idea," he said exultantly, in throaty and exuberant burlesque. "We will go off somewhere alone—we will take along something to eat," he said lusciously.

Laura went to her room and put on a pair of sturdy little slippers. Eugene went into the kitchen.

"Have you a shoebox?" he asked Eliza.

"What do you want that for?" she said suspiciously.

"I'm going to the bank," he said ironically. "I wanted something to carry my money in." But immediately he added roughly:

"I'm going on a picnic."

"Huh? Hah? What's that you say?" said Eliza. "A picnic? Who are you going with? That girl?"

"No," he said heavily, "with President Wilson, the King of England, and Dr. Doak. We're going to have lemonade—I've promised to bring the lemons."

"I'll vow, boy!" said Eliza fretfully. "I don't like it —your running off this way when I need you. I wanted you to make a deposit for me, and the telephone people will disconnect me if I don't send them the money today."

"Oh, Mama! For God's sake!" he cried annoyed. "You always need me when I want to go somewhere. Let them wait! They can wait a day."

"It's overdue," she said. "Well, here you are. I wish I had time to go off on picnics." She fished a shoebox out of a pile of magazines and newspapers that littered the top of a low cupboard.

"Have you got anything to eat?"

"We'll get it," he said, and departed.

They went down the hill, and paused at the musty little grocery around the corner on Woodson Street, where they bought crackers, peanut butter, currant jelly, bottled pickles, and a big slice of rich yellow cheese. The grocer was an old Jew who muttered jargon into a rabbi's beard as if saying a spell against Dybbuks. The boy looked closely to see if his hands touched the food. They were not clean.

On their way up the hill, they stopped for a few minutes at Gant's. They found Helen and Ben in the dining room. Ben was eating breakfast, bending, as usual, with scowling attention, over his coffee, turning from eggs and bacon almost with disgust. Helen insisted on contributing boiled eggs and sandwiches to their provision: the two women went back into the kitchen. Eugene sat at table with Ben, drinking coffee.

"O-oh my God!" Ben said at length, yawning wearily. He lighted a cigarette. "How's the Old Man this morning?"

"He's all right, I think. Said he couldn't eat breakfast."

"Did he say anything to the boarders?"

"'You damned scoundrels! You dirty Mountain Grills! Whee——!' That was all."

Ben snickered quietly.

"Did he hurt your hand? Let's see."

"No. You can't see anything. It's not hurt," said Eugene, lifting his bandaged wrist.

"He didn't hit you, did he?" asked Ben sternly.

"Oh, no. Of course not. He was just drunk. He was sorry about it this morning."

"Yes," said Ben, "he's always sorry about it—after he's raised all the hell he can." He drank deeply at his cigarette, inhaling the smoke as if in the grip of a powerful drug.

"How'd you get along at college this year, 'Gene?" he asked presently.

"I passed my work. I made fair grades—if that's what you mean? I did better—this spring," he added, with some difficulty. "It was hard getting started—at the beginning."

"You mean last fall?"

Eugene nodded.

"What was the matter?" said Ben, scowling at him. "Did the other boys make fun of you?"

"Yes," said Eugene, in a low voice.

"Why did they? You mean they didn't think you were good enough for them? Did they look down on you? Was that it?" said Ben savagely.

"No," said Eugene, very red in the face. "No. That had nothing to do with it. I look funny, I suppose. I looked funny to them."

"What do you mean you look funny?" said Ben pugnaciously. "There's nothing wrong with you, you know, if you didn't go around looking like a bum. In God's name," he exclaimed angrily, "when did you get that hair cut last? What do you think you are: the Wild Man from Borneo?"

"I don't like barbers!" Eugene burst out furiously. "That's why! I don't want them to go sticking their damned dirty fingers in my mouth. Whose business is it, if I never get my hair cut?"

"A man is judged by his appearance today," said Ben sententiously. "I was reading an article by a big businessman in the *Post* the other day. He says he always looks at a man's shoes before he gives him a job."

He spoke seriously, haltingly, in the same way that he read, without genuine conviction. Eugene writhed to hear his fierce condor prattle this stale hash of the canny millionaires, like any obedient parrot in a teller's cage.

Ben's voice had a dull flat quality as he uttered these admirable opinions: he seemed to grope behind it all for some answer, with hurt puzzled eyes. As he faltered along, with scowling intensity, through a success-sermon, there was something poignantly moving in his effort: it was the effort of his strange and lonely spirit to find some entrance into life—to find success, position, companionship. And it was as if, spelling the words out with his mouth, a settler in the Bronx from the fat Lombard plain, should try to unriddle the new world by deciphering the World Almanac, or as if some woodsman, trapped by the winter, and wasted by an obscure and terrible disease, should hunt its symptoms and its cure in a book of Household Remedies.

"Did the Old Man send you enough money to get along on?" Ben asked. "Were you able to hold your own with the other boys? He can afford it, you know. Don't let him stint you. Make him give it to you, 'Gene."

"I had plenty," said Eugene, "all that I needed."

"This is the time you need it—not later," said Ben. "Make him put you through college. This is an age of specialization. They're looking for college-trained men."

"Yes," said Eugene. He spoke obediently, indifferently, the hard bright mail of his mind undinted by the jargon: within, the Other One, who had no speech, saw.

"So get your education," said Ben, scowling vaguely. "All the Big Men—Ford, Edison, Rockefeller—whether they had it or not, say it's a good thing."

"Why didn't you go yourself?" said Eugene curiously.

"I didn't have anyone to tell me," said Ben. "Besides, you don't think the Old Man would give me anything, do you?" He laughed cynically. "It's too late now."

He was silent a moment; he smoked.

"You didn't know I was taking a course in advertising, did you?" he asked, grinning.

"No. Where?"

"Through the Correspondence School," said Ben. "I get my lessons every week. I don't know"—he laughed diffidently—"I must be good at it. I make the highest grades they have—98 or 100 every time. I get a diploma, if I finish the course."

A blinding mist swam across the younger brother's eyes. He did not know why. A convulsive knot gathered in his throat. He bent his head quickly and fumbled for his cigarettes. In a moment he said:

"I'm glad you're doing it. I hope you finish, Ben."

"You know," Ben said seriously, "they've turned out some Big Men. I'll show you the testimonials sometime. Men who started with nothing: now they're holding down big jobs."

"I hope you do," said Eugene.

"So, you see you're not the only College Man around here," said Ben with a grin. In a moment, he went on gravely: "You're the last hope, 'Gene. Go on and finish up, if you have to steal the money. The rest of us will never amount to a damn. Try to make something out of yourself. Hold your head up! You're as good as any of them—a damn sight better than these little pimps about town." He became very fierce; he was very excited. He got up suddenly from the table. "Don't let them laugh at you! By God, we're as good as they are. If any of them laughs at you again, pick up the first damn thing you get your hand on and knock him down. Do you hear?" In his fierce excitement he snatched up the heavy carving steel from the table and brandished it.

"Yes," said Eugene awkwardly. "I think it's going to be all right now. I didn't know how to do at first."

"I hope you have sense enough now to leave those old hookers alone?" said Ben very sternly. Eugene made no answer. "You can't do that and be anything, you know.

And you're likely to catch everything. This looks like a nice girl," he said quietly, after a pause. "For heaven's sake, fix yourself up and try to keep fairly clean. Women notice that, you know. Look after your fingernails, and keep your clothes pressed. Have you any money?"

"All I need," said Eugene, looking nervously towards the kitchen. "Don't, for God's sake!"

"Put it in your pocket, you little fool," Ben said angrily, thrusting a bill into his hand. "You've got to have some money. Keep it until you need it."

Helen came out on the high front porch with them as they departed. As usual, she had added a double heaping measure to what they needed. There was another shoebox stuffed with sandwiches, boiled eggs, and fudge.

She stood on the high step-edge, with a cloth wound over her head, her gaunt arms, pitted with old scars, akimbo. A warm sunny odor of nasturtiums, loamy earth, and honeysuckle washed round them its hot spermy waves.

"O-ho! A-ha!" she winked comically. "I know something! I'm not as blind as you think, you know——" She nodded with significant jocularity, her big smiling face drenched in the curious radiance and purity that occasionally dwelt so beautifully there. He thought always, when he saw her thus, of a sky washed after rain, of wide crystalline distances, cool and clean.

With a rough snigger she prodded him in the ribs:

"Ain't love grand! Ha-ha-ha-ha! Look at his face, Laura." She drew the girl close to her in a generous hug, laughing, oh, with laughing pity, and as they mounted the hill, she stood there, in the sunlight, her mouth slightly open, smiling, touched with radiance, beauty, and wonder.

They mounted slowly towards the eastern edge of

town, by the long upward sweep of Academy Street, which bordered the Negro settlement sprawled below it. At the end of Academy Street, the hill loomed abruptly; a sinuous road, well paved, curved up along the hillside to the right. They turned into this road, mounting now along the eastern edge of Niggertown. The settlement fell sharply away below them, rushing down along a series of long clay streets. There were a few frame houses by the roadside: the dwellings of Negroes and poor white people, but these became sparser as they mounted. They walked at a leisurely pace up the cool road speckled with little dancing patches of light that filtered through the arching trees and shaded on the left by the dense massed foliage of the hill. Out of this green loveliness loomed the huge raw turret of a cement reservoir: it was streaked and blotted coolly with water marks. Eugene felt thirsty. Further along, the escape from a smaller reservoir roared from a pipe in a foaming hawser, as thick as a man's body.

They climbed sharply up, along a rocky trail, avoiding the last long corkscrew of the road, and stood in the gap, at the road's summit. They were only a few hundred feet above the town: it lay before them with the sharp nearness of a Sienese picture, at once close and far. On the highest ground, he saw the solid masonry of the Square, blocked cleanly out in light and shadow, and a crawling toy that was a car, and men no bigger than sparrows. And about the Square was the treeless brick jungle of business—cheap, ragged, and ugly, and beyond all this, in indefinite patches, the houses where all the people lived, with little bright raw ulcers of suburbia further off, and the healing and concealing grace of fair massed trees. And below him, weltering up from the hollow along the flanks and shoulders of the hill, was Niggertown. There seemed to be a kind of center at the Square, where all the cars crawled in and waited, yet there was no purpose anywhere.

But the hills were lordly, with a plan. Westward, they widened into the sun, soaring up from buttressing shoulders. The town was thrown up on the plateau like an encampment: there was nothing below him that could resist time. There was no idea. Below him, in a cup, he felt that all life was held: he saw it as might one of the old schoolmen writing in monkish Latin a Theater of Human Life; or like Peter Breughel, in one of his swarming pictures. It seemed to him suddenly that he had not come up on the hill from the town, but that he had come out of the wilderness like a beast, and was staring now with steady beast-eye at this little huddle of wood and mortar which the wilderness must one day repossess, devour, cover over.

The seventh from the top was Troy—but Helen had lived there; and so the German dug it up.

They turned from the railing, with recovered wind, and walked through the gap, under Philip Roseberry's great arched bridge. To the left, on the summit, the rich Jew had his castle, his stables, his horses, his cows, and his daughters. As they went under the shadow of the bridge Eugene lifted his head and shouted. His voice bounded against the arch like a stone. They passed under and stood on the other side of the gap, looking from the road's edge down into the cove. But they could not yet see the cove, save for green glimmers. The hillside was thickly wooded, the road wound down its side in a white perpetual corkscrew. But they could look across at the fair wild hills on the other side of the cove, cleared halfway up their flanks with ample field and fenced meadow, and forested above with a billowing sea of greenery.

The day was like gold and sapphires: there was a

swift flash and sparkle, intangible and multifarious, like sunlight on roughened water, all over the land. A rich warm wind was blowing, turning all the leaves back the same way, and making mellow music through all the lute-strings of flower and grass and fruit. The wind moaned, not with the mad fiend-voice of winter in harsh boughs, but like a fruitful woman, deep-breasted, great, full of love and wisdom; like Demeter unseen and hunting through the world. A dog bayed faintly in the cove, his howl spent and broken by the wind. A cowbell tinkled gustily. In the thick wood below them the rich notes of birds fell from their throats, straight down, like nuggets. A woodpecker drummed on the dry unbarked bole of a blasted chestnut-tree. The blue gulf of the sky was spread with light massy clouds: they cruised like swift galleons, tacking across the hills before the wind, and darkening the trees below with their floating shadows.

The boy grew blind with love and desire: the cup of his heart was glutted with all this wonder. It overcame and weakened him. He grasped the girl's cool fingers. They stood leg to leg, riven into each other's flesh. Then they left the road, cutting down across its loops along steep wooded paths. The wood was a vast green church; the bird cries fell like plums. A great butterfly, with wings of blue velvet streaked with gold and scarlet markings, fluttered heavily before them in freckled sunlight, tottering to rest finally upon a spray of dogwood. There were light skimming noises in the dense undergrowth to either side, the swift bullet-shadows of birds. A garter snake, greener than wet moss, as long as a shoelace and no thicker than a woman's little finger, shot across the path, its tiny eyes bright with terror, its small forked tongue playing from its mouth like an electric spark. Laura cried out, drawing back in sharp terror;

at her cry he snatched up a stone in a wild lust to kill the tiny creature that shot at them, through its coils, the old snake-fear, touching them with beauty, with horror, with something supernatural. But the snake glided away into the undergrowth and, with a feeling of strong shame, he threw the stone away. "They won't hurt you," he said.

At length, they came out above the cove, at a forking of the road. They turned left, to the north, towards the upper and smaller end. To the south, the cove widened out in a rich little Eden of farm and pasture. Small houses dotted the land, there were green meadows and a glint of water. Fields of young green wheat bent rhythmically under the wind; the young corn stood waist-high, with light clashing blades. The chimneys of Rheinhart's house showed above its obscuring grove of maples; the fat dairy cows grazed slowly across the wide pastures. And farther below, half tree-and-shrub-hidden, lay the rich acres of Judge Webster Tayloe. The road was thickly coated with white dust; it dipped down and ran through a little brook. They crossed over on white rocks, strewn across its bed. Several ducks, scarcely disturbed by their crossing, waddled up out of the clear water and regarded them gravely, like little children in white choir aprons. A young country fellow clattered by them in a buggy filled with empty milk cans. He grinned with a cordial red face, saluting them with a slow gesture, and leaving behind an odor of milk and sweat and butter. A woman, in a field above them, stared curiously with shaded eyes. In another field, a man was mowing with a scythe, moving into the grass like a god upon his enemies, with a reaping hook of light.

They left the road near the head of the cove, advancing over the fields on rising ground to the wooded cup of the hills. There was a powerful masculine stench of broad dock-leaves, a hot weedy odor. They moved over a pathless field, knee-high in a dry stubbly waste, gathering on their clothes clusters of brown cockle burrs. All the field was sown with hot odorous daisies. Then they entered the wood again, mounting until they came to an island of tender grass, by a little brook that fell down from the green hill along a rocky ferny bed in bright cascades.

"Let's stop here," said Eugene. The grass was thick with dandelions: their poignant and wordless odor studded the earth with yellow magic. They were like gnomes and elves, and tiny witchcraft in flower and acorn.

Laura and Eugene lay upon their backs, looking up through the high green shimmer of leaves at the Caribbean sky, with all its fleet of cloudy ships. The water of the brook made a noise like silence. The town behind the hill lay in another unthinkable world. They forgot its pain and conflict.

"What time is it?" Eugene asked. For they had come to a place where no time was. Laura held up her exquisite wrist, and looked at her watch.

"Why!" she exclaimed, surprised. "It's only half-past twelve!"

But he scarcely heard her.

"What do I care what time it is!" he said huskily, and he seized the lovely hand, bound with its silken watch-cord, and kissed it. Her long cool fingers closed around his own; she drew his face down to her mouth.

They lay there, locked together, upon that magic carpet, in that paradise. Her grey eyes were deeper and clearer than a pool of clear water; he kissed the little freckles on her rare skin; he gazed reverently at the snub tilt of her nose; he watched the mirrored dance of the sparkling water over her face. All of that magic world—flower and field and sky and hill, and all the sweet woodland cries, sound and sight and odor— grew into him, one voice in his heart, one tongue in his brain, harmonious, radiant, and whole—a single passionate lyrical noise.

"My dear! Darling! Do you remember last night?" he asked fondly, as if recalling some event of her childhood.

"Yes," she gathered her arms tightly about his neck, "why do you think I could forget it?"

"Do you remember what I said—what I asked you to do?" he insisted eagerly.

"Oh, what are we going to do? What are we going to do?" she moaned, turning her head to the side and flinging an arm across her eyes.

"What is it? What's the matter? Dear!"

"Eugene—my dear, you're only a child. I'm so old —a grown woman."

"You're only twenty-one," he said. "There's only five years' difference. That's nothing."

"Oh!" she said. "You don't know what you're saying. It's all the difference in the world."

"When I'm twenty, you'll be twenty-five. When I'm twenty-six, you'll be thirty-one. When I'm forty-eight, you'll be fifty-three. What's that?" he said contemptuously. "Nothing."

"Everything," she said, "everything. If I were sixteen, and you twenty-one it would be nothing. But you're a boy and I'm a woman. When you're a young man I'll be an old maid; when you grow old I shall be dying. How do you know where you'll be, what you'll be doing five years from now?" she continued in a moment. "You're only a boy—you've just started college. You have no plans yet. You don't know what you're going to do."

"Yes, I do!" he yelled furiously. "I'm going to be a lawyer. That's what they're sending me for. I'm going to be a lawyer, and I'm going into politics. Perhaps," he added with gloomy pleasure, "you'll be sorry then, after I make a name for myself." With bitter joy he foresaw his lonely celebrity. The Governor's Mansion. Forty rooms. Alone. Alone.

"You're going to be a lawyer," said Laura, "and you're going everywhere in the world, and I'm to wait for you, and never get married. You poor kid!" She laughed softly. "You don't know what you're going to do."

He turned a face of misery on her; brightness dropped from the sun.

"You don't care?" he choked. "You don't care?" He bent his head to hide his wet eyes.

"Oh, my dear," she said, "I do care. But people don't live like that. It's like a story. Don't you know that I'm a grown woman? At my age, dear, most girls have begun to think of getting married. What—what if I had begun to think of it, too?"

"Married!" The word came from him in a huge gasp of horror as if she had mentioned the abominable, proposed the unspeakable. Then, having heard the monstrous suggestion, he immediately accepted it as a fact. He was like that.

"So! That's it!" he said furiously. "You're going to get married, eh? You have fellows, have you? You go out with them, do you? You've known it all the time, and you've tried to fool me."

Nakedly, with breast bare to horror, he scourged himself, knowing in the moment that the nightmare cruelty of life is not in the remote and fantastic, but in the probable—the horror of love, loss, marriage, the ninety seconds treason in the dark.

"You have fellows—you let them feel you. They feel

your legs, they play with your breasts, they—" His voice became inaudible through strangulation.

"No. No, my dear. I haven't said so," she rose swiftly to a sitting position, taking his hands. "But there's nothing unusual about getting married, you know. Most people do. Oh, my dear! Don't look like that! Nothing has happened. Nothing! Nothing!"

He seized her fiercely, unable to speak. Then he buried his face in her neck.

"Laura! My dear! My sweet! Don't leave me alone! I've been alone! I've always been alone!"

"It's what you want, dear. It's what you'll always want. You couldn't stand anything else. You'd get so tired of me. You'll forget this ever happened. You'll forget me. You'll forget—forget."

"Forget! I'll never forget! I won't live long enough."

"And I'll never love anyone else! I'll never leave you! I'll wait for you forever! Oh, my child, my child!"

They clung together in that bright moment of wonder, there on the magic island, where the world was quiet, believing all they said. And who shall say —whatever disenchantment follows—that we ever forget magic, or that we can ever betray, on this leaden earth, the apple tree, the singing, and the gold? Far out beyond that timeless valley, a train, on the rails for the East, wailed back its ghostly cry: life, like a fume of painted smoke, a broken wrack of cloud, drifted away. Their world was a singing voice again: they were young and they could never die. This would endure.

He kissed her on her splendid eyes; he grew into her young Mænad's body, his heart numbed deliciously against the pressure of her narrow breasts. She was as lithe and yielding to his sustaining hand as a willow rod—she was bird-swift, more elusive in repose than the dancing water-motes upon her face. He held her tightly lest she grow into the tree again, or be gone amid the wood like smoke.

Come up into the hills, O my young love. Return! O lost, and by the wind grieved, ghost, come back again, as first I knew you in the timeless valley, where we shall feel ourselves anew, bedded on magic in the month of June. There was a place where all the sun went glistering in your hair, and from the hill we could have put a finger on a star. Where is the day that melted into one rich noise? Where the music of your flesh, the rhyme of your teeth, the dainty languor of your legs, your small firm arms, your slender fingers, to be bitten like an apple, and the little cherry-teats of your white breasts? And where are all the tiny wires of finespun maidenhair? Quick are the mouths of earth, and quick the teeth that fed upon this loveliness. You who were made for music, will hear music no more: in your dark house the winds are silent. Ghost, ghost, come back from that marriage that we did not foresee, return not into life, but into magic, where we have never died, into the enchanted wood, where we still lie, strewn on the grass. Come up into the hills, O my young love: return. O lost, and by the wind grieved, ghost, come back again.

IV

One day, when June was coming to its end, Laura James said to him:

"I shall have to go home next week." Then, seeing his stricken face, she added, "But only for a few days—not more than a week."

"But why? The summer's only started. You will burn up down there."

"Yes. It's silly, I know. But my people expect me

for the Fourth of July. You know, we have an enormous
family—hundreds of aunts, cousins, and in-laws. We
have a family re-union every year—a great barbecue
and picnic. I hate it. But they'd never forgive me if I
didn't come."

Frightened, he looked at her for a moment.

"Laura! You're coming back, aren't you?" he said
quietly.

"Yes, of course," she said. "Be quiet."

He was trembling violently; he was afraid to question her more closely.

"Be quiet," she whispered, "quiet!" She put her arms
around him.

He went with her to the station on a hot midafter-
noon. There was a smell of melted tar in the streets.
She held his hand beside her in the rattling trolley,
squeezing his fingers to give him comfort, and whispering from time to time:

"In a week! Only a week, dear."

"I don't see the need," he muttered. "It's over 400
miles. Just for a few days."

He passed the old one-legged gateman on the station
platform very easily, carrying her baggage. Then he
sat beside her in the close green heat of the Pullman
until the train should go. A little electric fan droned
uselessly above the aisle; a prim young lady whom he
knew, arranged herself amid the bright new leather of
her bags. She returned his greeting elegantly, with a
shade of refined hauteur, then looked out the window
again, grimacing eloquently at her parents who gazed
at her raptly from the platform. Several prosperous
merchants went down the aisle in expensive tan shoes
that creaked under the fan's drone.

"Not going to leave us, are you, Mr. Morris?"

"Hello, Jim. No, I'm running up to Richmond for a few days." But even the grey weather of their lives could not deaden the excitement of that hot chariot to the East.

" 'Board!"

He got up trembling.

"In a few days, dear." She looked up, taking his hand in her small gloved palms.

"You will write as soon as you get there? Please!"

"Yes. Tomorrow—at once."

He bent down suddenly and whispered, "Laura—you will come back. You will come back!"

She turned her face away and wept bitterly. He sat beside her once more; she clasped him tightly as if he had been a child.

"My dear, my dear! Don't forget me ever!"

"Never. Come back. Come back."

The salt print of her kiss was on his mouth, his face, his eyes. It was, he knew, the guttering candle-end of time. The train was in motion. He leaped blindly up the passage with a cry in his throat.

"Come back again!"

But he knew. Her cry followed him, as if he had torn something from her grasp.

Within three days he had his letter. On four sheets of paper, bordered with victorious little American flags, this:

MY DEAR:

I got home at half-past one, just too tired to move. I couldn't sleep on the train at all last night, it seemed to get hotter all the way down. I was so blue when I got here, I almost cried. Little Richmond is too ghastly for words—everything burned up and everyone gone away to the mountains or the sea. How can I ever stand it even for a week! [Good! he thought. If the weather holds, she will come back all the sooner.] It would be heaven now to get one breath of mountain air. Could you find your way back to our place in the valley again? ["Yes, even if I were blind," he thought.] Will you promise to look after your hand until it gets well? I worried so after you had gone, because I forgot to change the bandage yesterday. Daddy was glad to see me: he said he was not going to let me go again but, don't worry, I'll have my own way in the end. I always do. I don't know anyone at home any more—all of the boys have enlisted or gone to work in the shipyards at Norfolk. Most of the girls I know are getting married, or married already. That leaves only the kids. [He winced. "As old as I am, maybe older."] Give my love to Mrs. Barton, and tell your mother I said she must not work so hard in that hot kitchen. And all the little cross-marks at the bottom are for you. Try to guess what they are.

                                                              LAURA.

He read her prosy letter with rigid face, devouring the words more hungrily than if they had been lyrical song. She would come back! She would come back! Soon.

There was another page. Weakened and relaxed from his excitement, he looked at it. There he found, almost illegibly written, but at last in her own speech, as if leaping out from the careful aimlessness of her letter, this note:

                                                          July 4.

Richard came yesterday. He is twenty-five, works in Norfolk. I've been engaged to him almost a year. We're going off quietly to Norfolk tomorrow and get married. My dear! My dear! I couldn't tell you! I tried to, but couldn't. I didn't want to lie. Everything else was true. I meant all I said. If you hadn't been so young, but what's the use of saying that? Try to forgive me, but please don't forget me. Good-by and God bless you. Oh, my darling, it was heaven! I shall never forget you.

When he had finished the letter, he reread it, slowly and carefully. Then he folded it, put it in his inner breast pocket, and leaving Dixieland, walked for forty minutes, until he came up in the gap over the town again. It was sunset. The sun's vast rim, blood-red, rested upon the western earth, in a great field of murky pollen. It sank beyond the western ranges. The clear sweet air was washed with gold and pearl. The vast hills melted into purple solitudes: they were like Canaan and rich grapes. The motors of cove people toiled up around the horseshoe of the road. Dusk came. The bright winking lights in the town went up. Darkness melted over the town like dew: it washed out all the day's distress, the harsh confusions. Low wailing sounds came faintly up from Niggertown.

And above him the proud stars flashed into heaven: there was one, so rich and low, that he could have picked it, if he had climbed the hill beyond the Jew's great house. One, like a lamp, hung low above the heads of men returning home. (O Hesperus, you bring us all good things.) One had flashed out the light that winked on him the night that Ruth lay at the feet of Boaz; and one on Queen Isolt; and one on Corinth and on Troy. It was night, vast brooding night, the mother of loneliness, that washes our stains away. He was washed in the great river of night, in the Ganges tides of redemption. His bitter wound was for the moment healed in him: he turned his face upward to the proud and tender stars, which made him a god and a grain of dust, the brother of eternal beauty and the son of death—alone, alone.

"Ha-ha-ha-ha-ha!" Helen laughed huskily, prodding him in the ribs. "Your girl went and got married, didn't she? She fooled you. You got left."

"Wh-a-a-a-t!" said Eliza banteringly, "has my boy been—as the fellow says" (she sniggered behind her hand) "has my boy been a-courtin'?" She puckered her lips in playful reproach.

"Oh, for God's sake," he muttered angrily. "What fellow says!"

His scowl broke into an angry grin as he caught his sister's eye. They laughed.

"Well, 'Gene," said the girl seriously, "forget about it. You're only a kid yet. Laura is a grown woman."

"Why, son," said Eliza with a touch of malice, "that girl was fooling you all the time. She was just leading you on."

"Oh, stop it, please."

"Cheer up!" said Helen heartily. "Your time's coming. You'll forget her in a week. There are plenty more, you know. This is puppy love. Show her that you're a good sport. You ought to write her a letter of congratulation."

"Why, yes," said Eliza, "I'd make a big joke of it all. I wouldn't let on to her that it affected me. I'd write her just as big as you please and laugh about the whole thing. I'd show them! That's what I'd——"

"Oh, for God's sake!" he groaned, starting up. "Leave me alone, won't you?"

He left the house.

But he wrote the letter. And the moment after the lid of the mail-box clanged over it, he was writhen by shame. For it was a proud and boastful letter, salted with scatterings of Greek, Latin, and English verse, quotable scraps, wrenched into the text without propriety, without accuracy, without anything but his pitiful and obvious desire to show her his weight in the point of his wit, the depth of his learning. She would be sorry when she knew her loss! But, for a moment at the end, his fiercely beating heart stormed through:

. . . and I hope he's worth having you—he can't deserve you, Laura; no one can. But if he knows what he has, that's something. How lucky he is! You're right about me—I'm too young. I'd cut off my hand now for eight or ten years more. God bless and keep you, my dear, dear Laura.

Something in me wants to burst. It keeps trying to, but it won't, it never has. O God! If it only would! I shall never forget you. I'm lost now and I'll never find the way again. In God's name write me a line when you get this. Tell me what your name is now—you never have. Tell me where you're going to live. Don't let me go entirely, I beg of you, don't leave me alone.

He sent the letter to the address she had given him—to her father's house. Week melted into week: his life mounted day by day in a terrible tension to the delivery of the mail, morning and afternoon, fell then into a miasmic swamp when no word came. July ended. The summer waned. She did not write.

Upon the darkening porch, awaiting food, the boarders rocked, oh, rocked with laughter.

The boarders said: "Eugene's lost his girl. He doesn't know what to do, he's lost his girl."

"Well, well! Did the Old Boy lose his girl?"

The little fat girl, the daughter of one of the two fat sisters whose husbands were hotel clerks in Charleston, skipped to and from him, in slow May dance, with fat calves twinkling brownly above her socks.

"Lost his girl! Lost his girl! Eugene, Eugene, has lost his girl."

The fat little girl skipped back to her fat mother for approbation: they regarded each other with complacent smiles loosely netted in their full-meated mouths.

"Don't let them kid you, big boy. What's the matter: did soneone get your girl?" asked Mr. Hake, the flour salesman. He was a dapper young man of twenty-six years, who smoked large cigars; he had a tapering face, and a high domy head, bald on top, fringed sparsely with fine blond hair. His mother, a large grass-widow near fifty, with the powerful craggy face of an Indian, a large mass of dyed yellow hair, and a coarse smile, full of gold and heartiness, rocked mightily, laughing with hoarse compassion:

"Git another girl, 'Gene. Why, law! I'd not let it bother me two minutes." He always expected her to spit, emphatically, with gusto, after speaking.

"You should worry, boy. You should *worry!*" said Mr. Farrel, of Miami, the dancing instructor. "Women are like streetcars: if you miss one, there's another along in fifteen minutes. Ain't that right, lady?" he said pertly, turning to Miss Clark, of Valdosta, Georgia, for whom it had been uttered. She answered with a throaty confused twiddle-giggle of laughter. "Oh, aren't men the awfullest——"

Leaning upon the porch rail in the thickening dusk, Mr. Jake Clapp, a well-to-do widower from Old Hominy, pursued his stealthy courtship of Miss Florry Mangle, the trained nurse. Her limp face made a white blot in the darkness; she spoke in a tired whine:

"I thought she was too old for him when I saw her. 'Gene's only a kid. He's taken it hard, you can tell by looking at him how miserable he is. He's going to get sick if he keeps on at this rate. He's thin as a bone. He hardly eats a bite. People get run down like that and catch the first disease that comes along——"

Her melancholy whine continued as Jake's stealthy thigh fumbled against her. She kept her arms carefully folded across her sagging breasts.

In the grey darkness, the boy turned his starved face on them. His dirty clothes lapped round his scarecrow body: his eyes burned like a cat's in the dark, his hair fell over his forehead in a matted net.

"He'll git over it," said Jake Clapp, in a precise country drawl, streaked with a note of bawdry. "Every boy has got to go through the Calf-Love stage. When I was about 'Gene's age——" He pressed his hard thigh gently against Florry, grinning widely and thinly with a few gold teeth. He was a tall solid man, with a hard precise face, lewdly decorous, and slanting Mongol eyes. His head was bald and knobby.

"He'd better watch out," whined Florry sadly. "I know what I'm talking about. That boy's not strong—he has no business to go prowling around to all hours the way he does. He's on the verge of——"

Eugene rocked gently on his feet, staring at the boarders with a steady hate. Suddenly he snarled like a wild beast, and started down the porch, unable to speak, reeling, but snarling again and again his choking and insane fury.

"Miss Brown" meanwhile sat primly at the end of the porch, a little apart from the others. From the dark sun-parlor at the side came swiftly the tall elegant figure of Miss Irene Mallard, twenty-eight, of Tampa, Florida. She caught him at the step edge, and pulled him round sharply, gripping his arms lightly with her cool long fingers.

"Where are you going, 'Gene?" she said quietly. Her eyes of light violet were a little tired. There was a faint exquisite perfume of rosewater.

"Leave me alone!" he muttered.

"You can't go on like this," she said in a low tone. "She's not worth it—none of them are. Pull yourself together."

"Leave me alone!" he said furiously. "I know what

I'm doing!" He wrenched away violently, and leaped down into the yard, plunging around the house in a staggering run.

"Ben!" said Irene Mallard sharply.

Ben rose from the dark porch swing where he had been sitting with Mrs. Pert.

"See if you can't do something to stop him," said Irene Mallard.

"He's crazy," Ben muttered. "Which way did he go?"

"By there—around the house. Go quick!"

Ben went swiftly down the shallow steps and loped back over the lawn. The yard sloped sharply down: the gaunt back of Dixieland was propped upon a dozen rotting columns of whitewashed brick, fourteen feet high. In the dim light, by one of these slender piers, already mined with crumbling ruins of wet brick, the scarecrow crouched, toiling with the thin grapevine of his arms against the temple.

"I will kill you, House," he gasped. "Vile and accursed House, I will tear you down. I will bring you down upon the whores and boarders. I will wreck you, House."

Another convulsion of his shoulders brought down a sprinkling rain of dust and rubble.

"I will make you fall down on all the people in you, House," he said.

"Fool!" cried Ben, leaping upon him, "what are you trying to do?" He caught the boy's arms from behind and dragged him back. "Do you think you can bring her back to you by wrecking the house? Are there no other women in the world, that you should let one get the best of you like this?"

"Let me go! Let me go!" said Eugene. "What does it matter to you?"

"Don't think, fool, that I care," said Ben fiercely.

"You're hurting no one but yourself. Do you think you'll hurt the boarders by pulling the house down on your own head? Do you think, idiot, that anyone cares if you kill yourself?" He shook the boy. "No. No. I don't care what you do, you know. I simply want to save the family the trouble and expense of burying you."

With a great cry of rage and bafflement Eugene tried to free himself. But the older brother held on as desperately as the Old Man of the Sea. Then, with a great effort of his hands and shoulders, the boy lifted his captor off the ground, and dashed him back against the white brick wall of the cellar. Ben collapsed, releasing him, with a fit of dry coughing, holding his hand against his thin breast.

"Don't be a fool," he gasped.

"Did I hurt you?" said Eugene dully.

"No. Go into the house and wash yourself. You ought to comb your hair once or twice a week, you know. You can't go around like a wild man. Get something to eat. Have you any money?"

"Yes—I have enough."

"Are you all right now?"

"Yes—don't talk about it, please."

"I don't want to talk about it, fool. I want you to learn a little sense," said Ben. He straightened, brushing his whitened coat. In a moment, he went on quietly: "To hell with them, 'Gene. To hell with them all. Don't let them worry you. Get all that you can. Don't give a damn for anything. Nothing gives a damn for you. To hell with it all! To hell with it! There are a lot of bad days. There are a lot of good ones. You'll forget. There are a lot of days. Let it go."

"Yes," said Eugene wearily, "let it go. It's all right now. I'm too tired. When you get tired you don't care, do you? I'm too tired to care. I'll never care any more.

I'm too tired. The men in France get tired and don't care. If a man came and pointed a gun at me now, I wouldn't be scared. I'm too tired." He began to laugh, loosely, with a sense of delicious relief. "I don't care for anyone or anything. I've always been afraid of everything, but when I got tired I didn't care. That's how I shall get over everything. I shall get tired."

Ben lighted a cigarette.

"That's better," he said. "Let's get something to eat." He smiled thinly. "Come along, Samson."

They walked out slowly around the house.

He washed himself, and ate a hearty meal. The boarders finished, and wandered off into the darkness variously—some to the band-concert on the Square, some to the moving pictures, some for walks through the town. When he had fed he went out on the porch. It was dark and almost empty save where, at the side, Mrs. Selborne sat in the swing with a wealthy lumber man from Tennessee. Her low rich laughter bubbled up softly from the vat of the dark. "Miss Brown" rocked quietly and decorously by herself. She was a heavily built and quietly dressed woman of thirty-nine years, touched with that slightly comic primness—that careful gentility—that marks the conduct of the prostitute incognito. She was being very refined. She was a perfect lady and would, if aroused, assert the fact.

"Miss Brown" lived, she said, in Indianapolis. She was not ugly: her face was simply permeated with the implacable dullness of the Mid-Westerner. In spite of the lewdness of her wide thin mouth, her look was smug. She had a fair mass of indifferent brown hair, rather small brown eyes, and a smooth russet skin.

"Pshaw!" said Eliza. "I don't believe her name's 'Miss Brown' any more than mine is."

There had been rain. The night was cool and black; the flower bed before the house was wet, with a smell of geraniums and drenched pansies. He lighted a cigarette, sitting upon the rail. "Miss Brown" rocked.

"It's turned off cool," she said. "That little bit of rain has done a lot of good, hasn't it?"

"Yes, it was hot," he said. "I hate hot weather."

"I can't stand it either," she said. "That's why I go away every summer. Out my way we catch it. You folks here don't know what hot weather is."

"You're from Milwaukee, aren't you?"

"Indianapolis."

"I knew it was somewhere out there. Is it a big place?" he asked curiously.

"Yes. You could put Altamont in one corner of it and never miss it."

"How big is it?" he said eagerly. "How many people have you there?"

"I don't know exactly—over three hundred thousand with the suburbs."

He reflected with greedy satisfaction.

"Is it pretty? Are there a lot of pretty houses and fine buildings?"

"Yes—I think so," she said reflectively. "It's a nice homelike place."

"What are the people like? What do they do? Are they rich?"

"Why—yes. It's a business and manufacturing place. There are a lot of rich people."

"I suppose they live in big houses and ride around in big cars, eh?" he demanded. Then, without waiting for a reply, he went on: "Do they have good things to eat? What?"

She laughed awkwardly, puzzled and confused.

"Why, yes. There's a great deal of German cooking. Do you like German cooking?"

"Beer!" he muttered lusciously. "Beer—eh? You make it out there?"

"Yes." She laughed, with a voluptuous note in her voice. "I believe you're a bad boy, Eugene."

"And what about the theaters and libraries? You have lots of shows, don't you?"

"Yes. A lot of good shows come to Indianapolis. All the big hits in New York and Chicago."

"And a library—you have a big one, eh?"

"Yes. We have a nice library."

"How many books has it?"

"Oh, I can't say as to that. But it's a good big library."

"Over 100,000 books, do you suppose? They wouldn't have half a million, would they?" He did not wait for an answer, he was talking to himself. "No, of course not. How many books can you take out at a time? What?"

The great shadow of his hunger bent over her; he rushed out of himself, devouring her with his questions.

"What are the girls like? Are they blonde or brunette? What?"

"Why, we have both kinds—more dark than fair, I should say." She looked through the darkness at him, grinning.

"Are they pretty?"

"Well! I can't say. You'll have to draw your own conclusions, Eugene. I'm one of them, you know." She looked at him with demure lewdness, offering herself for inspection. Then, with a laugh of teasing reproof, she said: "I believe you're a bad boy, Eugene. I believe you're a bad boy."

He lighted another cigarette feverishly.

"I'd give anything for a smoke," muttered "Miss

Brown." "I don't suppose I could here?" She looked round her.

"Why not?" he said impatiently. "There's no one to see you. It's dark. What does it matter anyway?"

Little electric currents of excitement played up his spine.

"I believe I will," she whispered. "Have you got a cigarette?"

He gave her his package; she stood up to receive the flame he nursed in his cupped hands. She leaned her heavy body against him as, with puckered face and closed eyes, she held her cigarette to the fire. She grasped his shaking hands to steady the light, holding them for a moment after.

"What," said "Miss Brown," with a cunning smile, "what if your mother should see us? You'd catch it!"

"She'll not see us," he said. "Besides," he added generously, "why shouldn't women smoke the same as men? There's no harm in it."

"Yes," said "Miss Brown," "I believe in being broad-minded about these things, too."

But he grinned in the dark, because the woman had revealed herself with a cigarette. It was a sign—the sign of the province, the sign unmistakable of debauchery.

Then, when he laid his hands upon her, she came very passively into his embrace as he sat before her on the rail.

"Eugene! Eugene!" she said in mocking reproof.

"Where is your room?" he said.

She told him.

Later, Eliza came suddenly and silently out upon them, on one of her swift raids from the kitchen.

"Who's there? Who's there?" she said, peering into the gloom suspiciously. "Huh? Hah? Where's Eugene?

Has anyone seen Eugene?" She knew very well he was there.

"Yes, here I am," he said. "What do you want?"

"Oh! Who's that with you? Hah?"

"'Miss Brown' is with me."

"Won't you come out and sit down, Mrs. Gant?" said "Miss Brown." "You must be tired and hot."

"Oh!" said Eliza awkwardly, "is that you, 'Miss Brown'? I couldn't see who it was." She switched on the dim porch light. "It's mighty dark out here. Someone coming up those steps might fall and break a leg. I tell you what," she continued conversationally, "this air feels good. I wish I could let everything go and just enjoy myself."

She continued in amiable monologue for another half-hour, her eyes probing about swiftly all the time at the two dark figures before her. Then hesitantly, by awkward talkative stages, she went into the house again.

"Son," she said before she went, troubled, "it's getting late. You'd better go to bed. That's where we all ought to be."

"Miss Brown" assented gracefully and moved towards the door.

"I'm going now. I feel tired. Good night, all."

He sat quietly on the rail, smoking, listening to the noises in the house. It went to sleep. He went back and found Eliza preparing to retire to her little cell.

"Son!" she said, in a low voice, after shaking her puckered face reproachfully for a moment, "I tell you what—I don't like it. It doesn't look right—your sitting out alone with that woman. She's old enough to be your mother."

"She's *your* boarder, isn't she?" he said roughly, "not mine. I didn't bring her here."

"There's one thing sure," said Eliza, wounded. "You

don't catch me associating with them. I hold up my head as high as anyone." She smiled at him bitterly.

"Well, good night, Mama," he said, ashamed and hurt. "Let's forget about them for a while. What does it matter?"

"Be a good boy," said Eliza timidly. "I want you to be a good boy, son."

There was a sense of guilt in her manner, a note of regret and contrition.

"Don't worry!" he said, turning away suddenly, wrenched bitterly, as he always was, by a sense of the childlike innocence and steadfastness that lay at the bottom of her life. "It's not your fault if I'm not. I shan't blame you. Good night."

The kitchen light went out; he heard his mother's door click gently. Through the dark house a shaft of air blew coolly. Slowly, with thudding heart, he began to mount the stairs.

But on that dark stair, his foot-falls numbed in the heavy carpet, he came squarely upon a woman's body that, by its fragrance, like magnolia, he knew was that of Mrs. Selborne. They held each other sharply by the arms, discovered, with caught breath. She bent towards him: a few strands of her blonde hair brushed his face, leaving it aflame.

"Hush-h!" she whispered.

So they paused there, holding each other, breast to breast, the only time that they had ever touched. Then, with their dark wisdom of each other confirmed, they parted, each a sharer in the other's life, to meet thereafter before the world with calm untelling eyes.

He groped softly back along the dark corridor until he came to the door of "Miss Brown's" room. It was slightly ajar. He went in.

She took all his medals, all that he had won at Leonard's school—the one for debating, the one for declaiming, the one in bronze for William Shakespeare. W. S. 1616–1916—Done for a Ducat!

He had no money to give her: she did not want much —a coin or two at a time. It was, she said, not the money: it was the principle of the thing. He saw the justice of her argument.

"For," said she, "if I wanted money, I wouldn't fool with you. Somebody tries to get me to go out every day. One of the richest men in this town (old man Tyson) has been after me ever since I came. He's offered me ten dollars if I'll go out in his car with him. I don't need your money. But you've got to give me something. I don't care how little it is. I wouldn't feel decent unless you did. I'm not one of your little Society Chippies that you see every day uptown. I've too much self-respect for that."

So, in lieu of money, he gave her his medals as pledges.

"If you don't redeem them," said "Miss Brown," "I'll give them to my own son when I go home."

"Have you a son?"

"Yes. He's eighteen years old. He's almost as tall as you are and twice as broad. All the girls are mad about him."

He turned his head away sharply, whitening with a sense of nausea and horror, feeling in him an incestuous pollution.

"That's enough, now," said "Miss Brown" with authority. "Go to your room and get some sleep."

But, unlike the first one in the tobacco town, she never called him "son."

> Poor Butterfly, for her heart was break-king,
> Poor Butterfly, for she loved him so-o——

Miss Irene Mallard changed the needle of the little phonograph in the sun-parlor, and reversed the well-worn record. Then as with stately emphasis, the opening measure of *Katinka* paced out, she waited for him, erect, smiling, slender, beautiful, with long lovely hands held up like wings to his embrace. She was teaching him to dance. Laura James had danced beautifully: it had maddened him to see her poised in the arms of a young man dancing. Now, clumsily, he moved off on a conscientious left foot, counting to himself. One, two, three, four! Irene Mallard slipped and veered to his awkward pressure, as bodiless as a fume of smoke. Her left hand rested on his bony shoulder lightly as a bird: her cool fingers were threaded into his hot sawing palm.

She had thick hair of an oaken color, evenly parted in the middle; her skin was pearl-pale, and transparently delicate; her jaw was long, full, and sensuous—her face was like that of one of the pre-Raphaelite women. She carried her tall graceful body with beautiful erectness, but with the slightly worn sensuousness of fragility and weariness: her lovely eyes were violet, always a little tired, but full of slow surprise and tenderness. She was like a Luini madonna, mixed of holiness and seduction, the world and heaven. He held her with reverent care, as one who would not come too near, who would not break a sacred image. Her exquisite and subtle perfume stole through him like a strange whisper, pagan and divine. He was afraid to touch her—and his hot palm sweated to her fingers.

Sometimes she coughed gently, smiling, holding a small crumpled handkerchief, edged with blue, before her mouth.

She had come to the hills not because of her own health, but because of her mother's, a woman of sixty-five, rustily dressed, with the petulant hang-dog face of age and sickness. The old woman suffered from asthma and heart disease. They had come from Florida. Irene Mallard was a very capable business woman; she was the chief bookkeeper of one of the Altamont banks. Every evening Randolph Gudger, the bank president, telephoned her.

Irene Mallard pressed her palm across the mouthpiece of the telephone, smiling at Eugene ironically, and rolling her eyes entreatingly aloft.

Sometimes Randolph Gudger drove by and asked her to go with him. The boy went sulkily away until the rich man should leave: the banker looked bitterly after him.

"He wants me to marry him, 'Gene," said Irene Mallard. "What am I going to do?"

"He's old enough to be your grandfather," said Eugene. "He has no hair on the top of his head; his teeth are false, and I don't know what-all!" he said resentfully.

"He's a rich man, 'Gene," said Irene, smiling. "Don't forget that."

"Go on, then! Go on!" he cried furiously. "Yes—go ahead. Marry him. It's the right thing for you. Sell yourself. He's an old man!" he said melodramatically. Randolph Gudger was almost forty-five.

But they danced there slowly in a grey light of dusk that was like pain and beauty; like the lost light undersea, in which his life, a lost merman, swam, remembering exile. And as they danced she, whom he dared not touch, yielded her body unto him, whispering softly to his ear, pressing with slender fingers his hot hand. And she, whom he would not touch, lay there, like a sheaf of grain, in the crook of his arm, token of the world's remedy—the refuge from the one lost face out of all the faces, the anodyne against the wound named Laura—a thousand flitting shapes of beauty to bring him comfort and delight. The great pageantry of pain and pride and death hung through the dusk its awful vision, touching his sorrow with a lonely joy. He had lost; but all pilgrimage across the world was loss: a moment of cleaving, a moment of taking away, the thousand phantom shapes that beaconed, and the high impassionate grief of stars.

It was dark. Irene Mallard took him by the hand and led him out on the porch.

"Sit down here a moment, 'Gene. I want to talk to you." Her voice was serious, low-pitched. He sat beside her in the swing, obediently, with the sense of an impending lecture.

"I've been watching you these last few days," said Irene Mallard. "I know what's been going on."

"What do you mean?" he said thickly, with thudding pulses.

"You know what I mean," said Irene Mallard sternly. "Now you're too fine a boy, 'Gene, to waste yourself on that Woman. Anyone can see what she is. Mother and I have both talked about it. A woman like that can ruin a young boy like you. You've got to stop it."

"How did you know about it?" he muttered. He was frightened and ashamed. She took his trembling hand and held it between her cool palms until he grew quieter. But he drew no closer to her: he halted, afraid, before her loveliness. As with Laura James, she seemed too high for his passion. He was afraid of her flesh; he was not afraid of "Miss Brown's." But now he was tired of the woman and didn't know how he could pay her. She had all his medals.

All through the waning summer he walked with Irene Mallard. They walked at night through the cool streets filled with the rustle of tired leaves. They went together to the hotel roof and danced; later "Pap" Rheinhart, kind and awkward and shy, and smelling of his horse, came to their little table, sitting and drinking with them. He had spent the years since Leonard's at a military school, trying to straighten the wry twist of his neck. But he remained the same as ever—quizzical, dry, and humorous. Eugene looked at that good shy face, remembering the lost years, the lost faces. And there was sorrow in his heart for what would come no more. August ended.

September came, full of departing wings. The world was full of departures. It had heard the drums. The young men were going to the war. Ben had been rejected again in the draft. Now he was preparing to drift off in search of employment in other towns. Luke had given up his employment in a war-munitions factory at Dayton, Ohio, and had enlisted in the Navy. He had come home on a short leave before his departure for the training school at Newport, Rhode Island. The street roared as he came down at his vulgar wide-legged stride, in flapping blues, his face all on the grin, thick curls of his unruly hair coiling below the band of his hat. He was the cartoon of a gob.

"Luke!" shouted Mr. Fawcett, the land-auctioneer, pulling him in from the street to Wood's pharmacy. "By God, son, you've done your bit. I'm going to set you up. What are you going to have?"

"Make it a dope," said Luke. "Colonel, yours truly!" He lifted the frosty glass in a violently palsied hand, and stood posed before the grinning counter. "F-f-f-Forty years ago," he began, in a hoarse voice, "I might have

refused, but now I can't, G-G-G-God help me! I
c-c-c-c-can't!"

Gant's sickness had returned on him with increased
virulence. His face was haggard and yellow: a tottering
weakness crept into his limbs. It was decided that he
must go again to Baltimore. Helen would go with him.

"Mr. Gant," said Eliza persuasively, "why don't you
just give up everything and settle down to take things
easy the rest of your days? You don't feel good enough to
tend to business any more; if I were you, I'd retire. We
could get $20,000 for your shop without any trouble
——— If I had that much money to work with, I'd show
them a thing or two." She nodded pertly with a smart
wink. "I could turn it over two or three times within two
years' time. You've got to trade quick to keep the ball
a-rolling. That's the way it's done."

"Merciful God!" he groaned. "That's my last refuge on
earth. Woman, have you no mercy? I beg of you, leave
me to die in peace: it won't be long now. You can do
what you please with it after I'm gone, but give me a
little peace now. In the name of Jesus, I ask it!" He
sniffled affectedly.

"Pshaw!" said Eliza, thinking no doubt to encourage
him. "There's nothing wrong with you. Half of it's only
imagination."

He groaned, turning his head away.

Summer died upon the hills. There was a hue, barely
guessed, upon the foliage, of red rust. The streets at
night were filled with sad lispings: all through the night,
upon his porch, as in a coma, he heard the strange noise
of autumn. And all the people who had given the town
its light thronging gaiety were vanished strangely over-

night. They had gone back into the vast South again.
The solemn tension of the war gathered about the
nation. A twilight of grim effort hovered around him,
above him. He felt the death of joy; but the groping
within him of wonder, of glory. Out of the huge sprawl
of its first delirium, the nation was beginning to articulate the engines of war—engines to mill and print out
hatred and falsehood, engines to pump up glory, engines
to manacle and crush opposition, engines to drill and
regiment men.

But something of true wonder had come upon the land
—the flares and rockets of the battlefields cast their light
across the plains as well. Young men from Kansas were
going to die in Picardy. In some foreign earth lay the
iron, as yet unmolded, that was to slay them. The
strangeness of death and destiny was legible upon lives
and faces which held no strangeness of their own. For,
it is the union of the ordinary and the miraculous that
makes wonder.

Luke had gone away to the training school at Newport. Ben went to Baltimore with Helen and Gant, who,
before entering the hospital again for radium treatment,
had gone on a violent and unruly spree which had compelled their rapid transference from one hotel to another
and had finally brought Gant moaning to his bed, hurling against God the anathemas that should have been
saved for huge riotings in raw oysters washed down
chaotically with beer and whisky. They all drank a great
deal: Gant's excesses, however, reduced the girl to a
state of angry frenzy, and Ben to one of scowling and
cursing disgust.

"You damned old man!" cried Helen, seizing and
shaking his passive shoulders as he lay reeking and
sodden on an untidy bed. "I could wear you out! You're

not sick; I've wasted my life nursing you, and you're not as sick as I am! You'll be here long after I'm gone, you selfish old man! It makes me furious!"

"Why, baby!" he roared, with a vast gesture of his arms, "God bless you, I couldn't do without you."

"Don't 'baby' me!" she cried.

But she held his hand next day as they rode out to the hospital, held it as, quaking, he turned for an instant and looked sadly at the city stretched behind and below him.

"I was a boy here," he muttered.

"Don't worry," she said, "we're going to make you well again. Why! You'll be a boy again!"

Hand in hand they entered the lobby where, flanked with death and terror and the busy matter-of-factness of the nurses and the hundred flitting shapes of the quiet men with the grey faces and gimlet eyes who walk so surely in among the broken lives—with arms proposed in an attitude of enormous mercy—many times bigger than Gant's largest angel—is an image of gentle Jesus.

Eugene went to see the Leonards several times. Margaret looked thin and ill, but the great light in her seemed on this account to burn more brightly. Never before had he been so aware of her enormous tranquil patience, the great health of her spirit. All of his sin, all of his pain, all the vexed weariness of his soul were washed away in that deep radiance: the tumult and evil of life dropped from him its foul and ragged cloak. He seemed to be clothed anew in garments of seamless light.

But he could confess little that lay on his heart: he talked freely of his work at the university, he talked of little else. His heart was packed with its burden for confessional, but he knew he could not speak, that she would not understand. She was too wise for anything but faith. Once, desperately, he tried to tell her of Laura: he blurted out a confession awkwardly in a few words. Before he had finished she began to laugh.

"Mr. Leonard!" she called. "Imagine this rascal with a girl! Pshaw, boy! You don't know what love is. Get along with you. There'll be time enough to think of that ten years from now." She laughed tenderly to herself, with absent misty gaze.

"Old 'Gene with a girl! Pity the poor girl! Ah, Lord, boy! That's a long way off for you. Thank your stars!"

He bent his head sharply, and closed his eyes. O! My lovely Saint! he thought. How close you have been to me, if anyone. How I have cut my brain open for you to see, and would my heart, if I had dared, and how alone I am, and always have been.

He walked through the streets at night with Irene Mallard; the town was thinned and saddened by departures. A few people hurried past, as if driven along by the brief pouncing gusts of wind. He was held in the lure of her subtle weariness: she gave him comfort and he never touched her. But he unpacked the burden of his heart, trembling and passionate. She sat beside him and stroked his hand. It seemed to him that he never knew her until he remembered her years later.

The house was almost empty. At night Eliza packed his trunk carefully, counting the ironed shirts and mended socks with satisfaction.

"Now, you have plenty of good warm clothes, son. Try to take care of them." She put Gant's check in his inner pocket and fastened it with a safety pin.

"Keep a sharp eye on your money, boy. You never know who you'll run up with on a train."

He dawdled nervously towards the door, wishing to melt away, not end in leavetaking.

"It does seem you might spend one night at home with your mother," she said querulously. Her eyes grew misty at once, her lips began to work tremulously in a bitter self-pitying smile. "I tell you what! It looks mighty funny, doesn't it? You can't stay with me five minutes any more without wanting to be up and off with the first woman that comes along. It's all right! It's all right. I'm not complaining. It seems as if all I was fit for is to cook and sew and get you ready to go off." She burst volubly into tears. "It seems that that's the only use you have for me. I've hardly laid eyes on you all summer."

"No," he said bitterly, "you've been too busy looking after the boarders. Don't think, Mama, that you can work on my feelings here at the last minute," he cried, already deeply worked-on. "It's easy to cry. But I was here all the time if you had had time for me. Oh, for God's sake! Let's make an end to this! Aren't things bad enough without it? Why must you act this way whenever I go off? Do you want to make me as miserable as you can?"

"Well, I tell you," said Eliza hopefully, becoming dry-eyed at once, "if I make a couple of deals and everything goes well, you may find me waiting for you in a big fine house when you come back next spring. I've got the lot picked out. I was thinking about it the other day," she went on, giving him a bright and knowing nod.

"Ah-h!" He made a strangling noise in his throat and tore at his collar. "In God's name! Please!" There was a silence.

"Well," said Eliza gravely, plucking at her chin, "I want you to be a good boy and study hard, son. Take care of your money—I want you to have plenty of good food and warm clothes—but you mustn't be extravagant, boy. This sickness of your papa's has cost a lot of money. Everything is going out and nothing's coming in. Nobody knows where the next dollar's coming from. So you've got to watch out."

Again silence fell. She had said her say; she had come as close as she could, but suddenly she felt speechless, shut out, barred from the bitter and lonely secrecy of his life.

"I hate to see you go, son," she said quietly, with a deep and indefinable sadness.

He cast his arms up suddenly in a tortured incomplete gesture.

"What does it matter! O God, what does it matter!"

Eliza's eyes filled with tears of real pain. She grasped his hand and held it.

"Try to be happy, son," she wept, "try to be a little more happy. Poor child! Poor child! Nobody ever knew you. Before you were born——" she shook her head slowly, speaking in a voice that was drowned and husky with her tears. Then, huskily, clearing her throat, she repeated, "Before you were born——"

v

When he returned to the university for his second year, he found the place adjusted soberly to war. It seemed quieter, sadder—the number of students was smaller and they were younger. The older ones had gone to war. The others were in a state of wild, but subdued, restlessness. They were careless of colleges, careers, successes—the war had thrilled them with its triumphing *Now*. Of what use Tomorrow! Of what use all labor for Tomorrow! The big guns had blown all spun schemes to fragments: they hailed the end of all planned work with a fierce, a secret joy. The business of education went on half-heartedly, with an abstracted look: in the classroom, their eyes were vague upon the book, but their ears cocked attentively for alarums and excursions without.

Eugene began the year earnestly as roommate of a young man who had been the best student in the Altamont High School. His name was Bob Sterling. Bob Sterling was nineteen years old, the son of a widow. He was of middling height, always very neatly and soberly dressed; there was nothing conspicuous about him. For this reason, he could laugh good-naturedly, a little smugly, at whatever was conspicuous. He had a good mind—bright, attentive, studious, unmarked by originality or inventiveness. He had a time for everything: he apportioned a certain time for the preparation of each lesson, and went over it three times, mumbling rapidly to himself. He sent his laundry out every Monday. When in merry company he laughed heartily and enjoyed himself, but he always kept track of the time. Presently, he would look at his watch, saying: "Well, this is all very nice, but it's getting no work done," and he would go.

Everyone said he had a bright future. He remonstrated with Eugene, with good-natured seriousness, about his habits. He ought not to throw his clothes around. He ought not to let his shirts and drawers accumulate in a dirty pile. He ought to have a regular time for doing each lesson; he ought to live by regular hours.

They lived in a private dwelling on the edge of the campus, in a large bright room decorated with a great number of college pennants, all of which belonged to Bob Sterling.

Bob Sterling had heart disease. He stood on the landing, gasping, when he had climbed the stairs. Eugene opened the door for him. Bob Sterling's pleasant face was dead white, spotted by pale freckles. His lips chattered and turned blue.

"What is it, Bob? How do you feel?" said Eugene.

"Come here," said Bob Sterling with a grin. "Put your head down here." He took Eugene's head and placed it against his heart. The great pump beat slowly and irregularly, with a hissing respiration.

"Good God!" cried Eugene.

"Do you hear it?" said Bob Sterling, beginning to laugh. Then he went into the room, chafing his dry hands briskly.

But he fell sick and could not attend classes. He was taken to the College Infirmary, where he lay for several weeks, apparently not very ill, but with lips constantly blue, a slow pulse, and a subnormal temperature. Nothing could be done about it.

His mother came and took him home. Eugene wrote him regularly twice a week, getting in return short but cheerful messages. Then one day he died.

Two weeks later the widow returned to gather together the boy's belongings. Silently she collected the clothing that no one would ever wear. She was a stout woman in her forties. Eugene took all the pennants from the wall and folded them. She packed them in a valise and turned to go.

"Here's another," said Eugene.

She burst suddenly into tears and seized his hand.

"He was so brave," she said, "so brave. Those last days—I had not meant to—— Your letters made him so happy."

"She's alone now," Eugene thought.

"I cannot stay here," he thought, "where he has been. We were here together. Always I should see him on the

landing, with the hissing valve and the blue lips, or hear
him mumbling his lessons. Then, at night, the óther cot
would be empty. I think I shall room alone hereafter."

But he roomed the remainder of the term in one of the
dormitories. He had two roommates—one, an Altamont
young man who answered to the name of L. K. Duncan
(the "L" stood for Lawrence, but everyone called him
"Elk") and the other, the son of an Episcopal minister,
Harold Gay. Both were several years older than Eugene:
Elk Duncan was twenty-four, and Harold Gay, twenty-
two. But it is doubtful whether a more precious congress
of freaks had ever before gathered in two small rooms,
one of which they used as a "study."

Elk Duncan was the son of an Altamont attorney, a
small Democratic politician, mighty in county affairs.
Elk Duncan was tall—an inch or two over six feet—and
incredibly thin, or rather narrow. He was already a little
bald, he had a high prominent forehead, and large pale
bulging eyes: from that point his long pale face sloped
backward to his chin. His shoulders were a trifle bowed
and very narrow; the rest of his body had the symmetry
of a lead pencil. He always dressed very foppishly, in
tight suits of blue flannel, with high stiff collars, fat
silken cravats, and colored silk handkerchiefs. He was a
student in the Law School, but he spent a large part of
his time, industriously, in avoiding study.

The younger students—particularly the Freshmen—
gathered around him after meals with mouths slightly
ajar, feeding upon his words like manna, and hungrily
demanding more, the wilder his fable became. His
posture towards life was very much that of the barker
of a carnival side-show: loquacious, patronizing, and
cynical.

The other roommate, Harold Gay, was a good soul, no

older than a child. He wore spectacles, which gave the only glister to the dull greyness of his face; he was plain and ugly without any distinction: he had been puzzled so long by at least four-fifths of the phenomena of existence that he no longer made any effort to comprehend them. Instead, he concealed his shyness and bewilderment under a braying laugh that echoed at all the wrong places, and a silly grin full of an absurd and devilish knowingness. His association with Elk Duncan was one of the proud summits of his life: he weltered in the purple calcium which bathed that worthy, he smoked cigarettes with a debauched leer, and cursed loudly and uneasily with the accent of a depraved clergyman.

"Harold! Harold!" said Elk Duncan reprovingly. "Damn, son! You're getting hard! If you go on like this, you'll begin to chew gum, and fritter away your Sunday-school money at the movies. Think of the rest of us, please. 'Gene here's only a young boy, as pure as a barnyard privy, and, as for me, I've always moved in the best circles, and associated with only the highest class of bartenders and ladylike streetwalkers. What would your father say if he could hear you? Don't you know he'd be shocked? He'd cut off your cigarette money, son."

"I don't give a damn what he'd do, Elk, nor you either!" said Harold toughly, grinning. "So, what the hell!" he roared as loudly as he could. There was an answering howl from the windows of the whole dormitory—cries of "Go to hell!" "Cut it out!" and ironical cheers, at which he was pleased.

The scattered family drew together again at Christmas. A sense of impending dissolution, of loss and death, brought them back. The surgeon at Baltimore had given no hope. He had, rather, confirmed Gant's death-warrant.

"Then how long can he live?" asked Helen.

He shrugged his shoulders. "My dear girl!" he said. "I have no idea. The man's a miracle. Do you know that he's Exhibit A here? Every surgeon in the place has had a look. How long can he last? I'll swear to nothing—I no longer have any idea. When your father left here, the first time, after his operation, I never expected to see him again. I doubted if he would last the winter through. But he's back again. He may be back many times."

"Can you help him at all? Do you think the radium does any good?"

"I can give him relief for a time. I can even check the growth of the disease for a time. Beyond that, I can do nothing. But his vitality is enormous. He is a creaking gate which hangs by one hinge—but which hangs, nevertheless."

Thus, she had brought him home, the shadow of his death suspended over them like a Damocles sword. Fear prowled softly through their brains on leopard feet. The girl lived in a condition of repressed hysteria: it had its outburst daily at Eliza's or in her own home. Hugh Barton had purchased a house to which he had taken her.

"You'll get no peace," he said, "as long as you're near them. That's what's wrong with you now."

She had frequent periods of sickness. She went constantly to the doctors for treatment and advice. Sometimes she went to the hospital for several days. Her illness manifested itself in various ways—sometimes in a terrible mastoid pain, sometimes in nervous exhaustion, sometimes in an hysterical collapse in which she laughed and wept by turns, and which was governed partly by Gant's illness and a morbid despair over her failure to bear a child. She drank stealthily at all times—she drank in nibbling draughts for stimulus, never enough for drunkenness. She drank vile liquids—seeking only the effect of alcohol and getting at it in strange ways through a dozen abominations called "tonics" and "extracts." Almost deliberately she ruined her taste for the better sort of potable liquors, concealing from herself, under the convenient labelings of physic, the ugly crawling hunger in her blood. This self-deception was characteristic of her. Her life expressed itself through a series of deceptions—of symbols: her dislikes, affections, grievances, brandishing every cause but the real one.

But, unless actually bedridden, she was never absent from her father for many hours. The shadow of his death lay over their lives. They shuddered below its horror; its protracted menace, its unsearchable enigma, deprived them of dignity and courage. They were dominated by the weary and degrading egotism of life, which is blandly philosophical over the death of the alien, but sees in its own the corruption of natural law. It was as hard for them to think of Gant's death as of God's death: it was a great deal harder, because he was more real to them than God, he was more immortal than God, he was God.

This hideous twilight into which their lives had passed froze Eugene with its terror, and choked him with fury. He would grow enraged after reading a letter from home and pound the grained plaster of the dormitory wall until his knuckles were bloody. They have taken his courage away! he thought. They have made a whining coward out of him! No, and if I die, no damned family about. Blowing their messy breaths in your face! Snuffling down their messy noses at you! Gathering around you till you can't breathe. Telling you how well you're looking with hearty smiles, and boo-hooing behind your back. O messy, messy, messy death! Shall we never be alone? Shall we never live alone, think alone, live in a house by ourselves alone? Ah! but I shall! I shall! Alone, alone, and far away, with falling rain. Then, bursting suddenly into the study, he found Elk Duncan, with unaccustomed eye bent dully upon a page of Torts, a bright bird held by the stare of that hypnotic snake, the law.

"Are we to die like rats?" he said. "Are we to smother in a hole?"

"Damn!" said Elk Duncan, folding the big calfskin and cowering defensively behind it.

"Yes, that's right, that's right! Calm yourself. You are Napoleon Bonaparte and I'm your old friend, Oliver Cromwell. Harold!" he called. "Help! He killed the keeper and got out."

"'Gene!" yelled Harold Gay, hurling a thick volume from him under the spell of Elk's great names. "What do you know about history? Who signed Magna Charta, eh?"

"It wasn't signed," said Eugene. "The King didn't know how to write, so they mimeographed it."

"Correct!" roared Harold Gay. "Who was Æthelred the Unready?"

"He was the son of Cynewulf the Silly and Undine the Unwashed," said Eugene.

"On his Uncle Jasper's side," said Elk Duncan, "he was related to Paul the Poxy and Genevieve the Ungenerous."

"He was excommunicated by the Pope in a Bull of the year 903, but he refused to be cowed," said Eugene.

"Instead, he called together all the local clergy, including the Archbishop of Canterbury, Dr. Gay, who was elected Pope," said Elk Duncan. "This caused a great schism in the Church."

"But as usual, God was on the side of the greatest number of canons," said Eugene. "Later on, the family migrated to California, and made its fortune in the Gold Rush of '49."

"You boys are too good for me!" yelled Harold Gay, getting up abruptly. "Come on! Who's going to the Pic?"

The Pic was the only purchasable entertainment that the village afforded steadily. It was a moving-picture theater, inhabited nightly by a howling tribe of students who rushed down aisles, paved with peanut shells, through a shrapnel fire of flying goobers, devoting themselves studiously for the remainder of the evening to the unhappy heads and necks of Freshmen, and less attentively, but with roars of applause, indignation, or advice, to the poor flicker-dance of puppets that wavered its way illegibly across the worn and pleated screen. A weary but industrious young woman with a scrawny neck thumped almost constantly at a battered piano. If she was idle for five minutes, the whole pack howled ironically, demanding: "Music, Myrtle! Music!"

It was necessary to speak to everyone. If one spoke to everyone, one was "democratic"; if one did not, one was a snob, and got few votes. The appraisal of personality, like all other appraisal with them, was coarse and blunt. They were suspicious of all eminence. They had a hard peasant hostility to the unusual. A man was brilliant? Was there a bright sparkle to him? Bad, bad! He was not safe; he was not sound. The place was a democratic microcosmos—seething with political interests: national, regional, collegiate.

The campus had its candidates, its managers, its bosses, its machines, as had the state. A youngster developed in college the political craft he was later to exert in Party affairs. The son of a politician was schooled by his crafty sire before the down was off his cheeks: at sixteen, his life had been plotted ahead to the governorship, or to the proud dignities of a Congressman. The boy came deliberately to the university to bait and set his first traps; deliberately he made those friendships that were most likely to benefit him later. By his junior year, if he was successful, he had a political manager, who engineered his campus ambitions; he moved with circumspection, and spoke with a trace of pomp nicely weighed with cordiality:

"Ah, there, gentlemen." "Gentlemen, how are you?" "A nice day, gentlemen."

The vast champaign of the world stretched out its limitless wonder, but few were seduced away from the fortress of the state, few ever heard the distant reverberation of an idea. They could get no greater glory for themselves than a seat in the Senate, and the way to glory—the way to all power, highness, and distinction whatsoever—was through the law, a string tie, and a hat. Hence politics, law schools, debating societies, and speechmaking. The applause of listening senates to command.

The yokels, of course, were in the saddle—they composed nine-tenths of the student body: the proud titles were in their gift, and they took good care that their world should be kept safe for yokelry and the homespun virtues. Usually, these dignities—the presidencies of student bodies, classes, Y.M.C.A.'s, and the managerships of athletic teams—were given to some honest serf who had established his greatness behind a plow before working in the college commons, or to some industrious hack who had shown a satisfactory mediocrity in all directions. Such an industrious hack was called an "all-round man." He was safe, sound, and reliable. He would never get notions. He was the fine flower of university training. He was a football scrub, and a respectable scholar in all subjects. He was a universal Two Man. He always got Two on everything, except Moral Character, where he shone with a superlative Oneness. If he did not go into the law or the ministry, he was appointed a Rhodes Scholar.

In this strange place Eugene flourished amazingly. He was outside the pale of popular jealousies: it was quite obvious that he was not safe, that he was not sound, that decidedly he was an irregular person. He could never be an all-round man. Obviously, he would never be governor. Obviously, he would never be a politician, because he said funny things. He was not the man to lead a class or say a prayer; he was a man for curious enterprise. Well, thought they benevolently, we need some such. We are not all made for weighty business.

He was happier than he had ever been in his life, and more careless. His physical loneliness was more complete and more delightful. His escape from the bleak horror of disease and hysteria and death impending, that hung above his crouched family, left him with a sense of aerial buoyancy, drunken freedom. He had come to the place alone, without companions. He had no connections. He had, even now, not one close friend. And this isolation was in his favor. Everyone knew him at sight; everyone called him by name, and spoke to him kindly. He was not disliked. He was happy, full of expansive joy, he greeted everyone with enthusiastic gusto. He had a vast tenderness, an affection for the whole marvelous and unvisited earth, that blinded his eyes. He was closer to a feeling of brotherhood than he had ever been, and more alone. He was filled with a divine indifference for all appearance. Joy ran like a great wine through his young expanding limbs; he bounded down the paths with wild cries in his throat, leaping for life like an apple, trying to focus the blind desire that swept him apart, to melt down to a bullet all of his formless passion, and so, slay death, slay love.

He began to join. He joined everything. He had never "belonged" to any group before, but now all groups were beckoning him. He had without much trouble won a place for himself on the staff of the college paper and the magazine. The small beginning trickle of distinctions widened into a gushet. It began to sprinkle, then it rained. He was initiated into literary fraternities, dramatic fraternities, theatrical fraternities, speaking fraternities, journalistic fraternities, and in the spring into a social fraternity. He joined enthusiastically, submitted with fanatical glee to the hard mauling of the initiations, and went about lame and sore, more pleased than a child or a savage, with colored ribbons in his coat lapel, and a waistcoat plastered with pins, badges, symbols, and Greek letterings.

But not without labor had his titles come. The early autumn was lusterless and slack: he could not come from the shadow of Laura. She haunted him. When he went home at Christmas, he found the hills bleak and close, and the town mean and cramped in the grim stinginess of winter. There was a ludicrous, a desperate gaiety in the family.

"Well!" said Eliza sorrowfully, as she peered above the stove, "let's all try to be happy this time and enjoy a quiet Christmas. You never know! You never know!" She shook her head, unable to continue. Her eyes were wet. "It may be the last time we're all together. The old trouble! The old trouble!" she said hoarsely, turning to him.

"What old trouble?" he said angrily. "Good God, why are you so mysterious?"

"My heart!" she whispered, with a brave smile. "I've said nothing to anyone. But last week—I thought I was gone." This was delivered in a boding whisper.

"Oh, my God!" he groaned. "You'll be here when the rest of us are rotten."

Helen burst into a raucous angry laugh, looking at his sullen face, and prodding him roughly with her big fingers.

"K-K-K-K-K-K-K! Did you ever know it to fail? Did you? If you come to her with one of your kidneys gone, she's always got something worse the matter with her. No, sir! I've never known it to fail!"

"You may laugh! You may laugh!" said Eliza with a smile of watery bitterness. "But I may not be here to laugh at much longer."

"Good heavens, Mama!" the girl cried irritably. "There's nothing wrong with you. You're not the sick one! Papa's the sick one. He's the one that needs attention. Can't you realize that—he's dying. He may not last the winter out. I'm the sick one! You'll be here long after we're both gone."

"You never know," said Eliza mysteriously. "You never know who'll be the first one to go. Only last week, there was Mr. Cosgrave, as fine a looking man as——"

"They're off!" Eugene screamed with a crazy laugh, stamping up and down the kitchen in a frenzy. "By God! They're off!"

At this moment, one of the aged harpies, of whom the house always sheltered two or three during the grim winter, lurched from the hall back into the door space. She was a large raw-boned hag, a confirmed drug-eater, who moved by a violent and dissonant jerking of her gaunt limbs, pawing abruptly at the air with a gnarled hand.

"Mrs. Gant," said she, writhing her loose grey lips horribly before she could speak. "Did I get a letter? Have you seen him?"

"Seen who? Go on!" said Eliza fretfully. "I don't know what you're talking about, and I don't believe you do, either."

Smiling hideously at them all, and pawing the air, the monster got under way again, disappearing like an old wagon with loose wheels. Helen began to laugh, hoarsely, as Eugene's face hung forward with mouth half-open in an expression of sullen stupefaction. Eliza laughed, too, slily, rubbing her nosewing with a finger.

"I'll vow!" she said. "I believe she's crazy. She takes dope of some sort—that's certain. It makes my flesh crawl when she comes around."

"Then why do you keep her in the house?" said Helen resentfully. "Good heavens, Mama! You could get rid of her if you wanted to. Poor old 'Gene!" she said, beginning to laugh again. "You always catch it, don't you?"

"The time draws near the birth of Christ," said he piously.

She laughed; then, with abstracted eyes, plucked vaguely at her large chin.

His father spent most of the day staring vacantly into the parlor fire. Miss Florry Mangle, the nurse, gave him the morbid comfort of her silence: she rocked incessantly before the fire, thirty heel-taps to the minute, with arms tight-folded on her limp breasts. Occasionally she talked of death and disease. Gant had aged and wasted shockingly. His heavy clothes wound round his feeble shanks: his face was waxen and transparent—it was like a great beak. He looked clean and fragile. The cancer, Eugene thought, flowered in him like some terrible but beautiful plant. His mind was very clear, not doting, but sad and old. He spoke little, with almost comical gentleness, but he ceased to listen almost as soon as one answered.

"How have you been, son?" he asked. "Are you getting along all right?"

"Yes. I am a reporter on the paper now; I may be managing editor next year. I have been elected to several organizations," he went on eagerly, glad of the rare chance to speak to one of them about his life. But when he looked up again, his father's stare was fixed sadly in the fire. The boy stopped in confusion, pierced with a bitter pain.

"That's good," said Gant, hearing him speak no more. "Be a good boy, son. We're proud of you."

Ben came home two days before Christmas: he prowled through the house like a familiar ghost. He had left the town early in the autumn, after his return from Baltimore. For three months he had wandered alone through the South, selling to the merchants in small towns space for advertisements upon laundry cards. How well this curious business succeeded he did not say: he was scrupulously neat, but threadbare and haggard, and more fiercely secretive than ever. He had found employment at length upon a newspaper in a rich tobacco town of the Piedmont. He was going there after Christmas.

He had come to them, as always, bearing gifts.

Luke came in from the naval school at Newport, on Christmas eve. They heard his sonorous tenor shouting

greetings to people in the street; he entered the house
upon a blast of air. Everyone began to grin.

"Well, here we are! The Admiral's back! Papa, how's
the boy! Well, for God's sake!" he cried, embracing
Gant, and slapping his back. "I thought I was coming to
see a sick man! You're looking like the flowers that bloom
in the spring."

"Pretty well, my boy. How are you?" said Gant, with
a pleased grin.

"Couldn't be better, Colonel. 'Gene, how are you, Old
Scout? Good!" he said, without waiting for an answer.
"Well, well, if it isn't Old Baldy," he cried, pumping
Ben's hand. "I didn't know whether you'd be here or not.
Mama, old girl," he said, as he embraced her, "how're
they going? Still hitting on all six. Fine!" he yelled, be-
fore anyone could reply to anything.

"Why, son—what on earth!" cried Eliza, stepping
back to look at him. "What have you done to yourself?
You walk as if you are lame."

He laughed idiotically at sight of her troubled face
and prodded her.

"Whah—whah! I got torpedoed by a submarine," he
said. "Oh, it's nothing," he added modestly. "I gave a
little skin to help out a fellow in the electrical school."

"What!" Eliza screamed. "How much did you give?"

"Oh, only a little six-inch strip," he said carelessly.
"The boy was badly burned: a bunch of us got together
and chipped in with a little hide."

"Mercy!" said Eliza. "You'll be lame for life. It's a
wonder you can walk."

"He always thinks of others—that boy!" said Gant
proudly. "He'd give you his heart's-blood."

The sailor had secured an extra valise, and stocked it
on the way home with a great variety of beverages for

his father. There were several bottles of Scotch and rye whiskies, two of gin, one of rum, and one each of port and sherry wine.

Everyone grew mildly convivial before the evening meal.

"Let's give the poor kid a drink," said Helen. "It won't hurt him."

"What! My ba-a-by! Why, son, you wouldn't drink, would you?" Eliza said playfully.

"Wouldn't he!" said Helen, prodding him. "Ho! ho! ho!"

She poured him out a stiff draught of Scotch whisky.

"There!" she said cheerfully. "That's not going to hurt him."

"Son," said Eliza gravely, balancing her wine glass, "I don't want you ever to acquire a taste for it." She was still loyal to the doctrine of the good Major.

"No," said Gant. "It'll ruin you quicker than anything in the world, if you do."

"You're a goner, boy, if that stuff ever gets you," said Luke. "Take a fool's advice."

They lavished fair warnings on him as he lifted his glass. He choked as the fiery stuff caught in his young throat, stopping his breath for a moment and making him tearful. He had drunk a few times before—minute quantities that his sister had given him at Woodson Street. Once, with Jim Trivett, he had fancied himself tipsy.

When they had eaten, they drank again. He was allowed a small one. Then they all departed for town to complete their belated shopping. He was left alone in the house.

What he had drunk beat pleasantly through his veins in warm pulses, bathing the tips of ragged nerves, giving to him a feeling of power and tranquillity he had never known. Presently, he went to the pantry where the liquor was stored. He took a water tumbler and filled it experimentally with equal portions of whisky, gin, and rum. Then, seating himself at the kitchen table, he began to drink the mixture slowly.

The terrible draught smote him with the speed and power of a man's fist. He was made instantly drunken, and he knew instantly why men drank. It was, he knew, one of the great moments in his life—he lay, greedily watching the mastery of the grape over his virgin flesh, like a girl for the first time in the embrace of her lover. And suddenly, he knew how completely he was his father's son—how completely, and with what added power and exquisite refinement of sensation, was he Gantian. He exulted in the great length of his limbs and his body, through which the mighty liquor could better work its wizardry. In all the earth there was no other like him, no other fitted to be so sublimely and magnificently drunken. It was greater than all the music he had ever heard; it was as great as the highest poetry. Why had he never been told? Why had no one ever written adequately about it? Why, when it was possible to buy a god in a bottle, and drink him off, and become a god oneself, were men not forever drunken?

He had a moment of great wonder—the magnificent wonder with which we discover the simple and unspeakable things that lie buried and known, but unconfessed, in us. So might a man feel if he wakened after death and found himself in Heaven.

Then a divine paralysis crept through his flesh. His limbs were numb; his tongue thickened until he could not bend it to the cunning sounds of words. He spoke aloud, repeating difficult phrases over and over, filled with wild laughter and delight at his effort. Behind his drunken body his brain hung poised like a falcon, looking on him with scorn, with tenderness, looking on all laughter with grief and pity. There lay in him something that could not be seen and could not be touched, which was above and beyond him—an eye within an eye, a brain above a brain, the Stranger that dwelt in him and regarded him and was him, and that he did not know. But, thought he, I am alone now in this house; if I can come to know him, I will.

He got up, and reeled out of the alien presences of light and warmth in the kitchen; he went out into the hall where a dim light burned and the high walls gave back their grave-damp chill. This, he thought, is the house.

He sat down upon the hard mission settle, and listened to the cold drip of silence. This is the house in which I have been an exile. There is a stranger in the house, and there's a stranger in me.

O house of Admetus, in whom (although I was a god) I have endured so many things. Now, house, I am not afraid. No ghost need fear come by me. If there's a door in silence, let it open. My silence can be greater than your own. And you who are in me, and who I am, come forth beyond this quiet shell of flesh that makes no posture to deny you. There is none to look at us: O come, my brother and my lord, with unbent face. If I had 40,000 years, I should give all but the ninety last to silence. I should grow to the earth like a hill or a rock. Unweave the fabric of nights and days; unwind my life back to my birth; subtract me into nakedness again, and build me back with all the sums I have not counted. Or let me look upon the living face of darkness; let me hear the terrible sentence of your voice.

There was nothing but the living silence of the house: no doors were opened.

Presently, he got up and left the house. He wore no

hat or coat; he could not find them. The night was blanketed in a thick steam of mist: sounds came faintly and cheerfully. Already the earth was full of Christmas. He remembered that he had bought no gifts. He had a few dollars in his pocket; before the shops closed he must get presents for the family. Bareheaded he set off for the town. He knew that he was drunk and that he staggered; but he believed that with care and control he could hide his state from anyone who saw him. He straddled the line that ran down the middle of the concrete sidewalk, keeping his eyes fixed on it and coming back to it quickly when he lurched away from it. When he got into the town the streets were thronged with late shoppers. An air of completion was on everything. The people were streaming home to Christmas. He plunged down from the Square into the narrow avenue, going in among the staring passers-by. He kept his eye hotly on the line before him. He did not know where to go. He did not know what to buy.

As he reached the entrance to Wood's pharmacy, a shout of laughter went up from the lounging beaux. The next instant he was staring into the friendly grinning faces of Julius Arthur and Van Yeats.

"Where the hell do you think you're going?" said Julius Arthur.

He tried to explain; a thick jargon broke from his lips.

"He's cock-eyed drunk," said Van Yeats.

"You look out for him, Van," said Julius. "Get him in a doorway, so none of his folks will see him. I'll get the car."

Van Yeats propped him carefully against the wall; Julius Arthur ran swiftly into Church Street, and drew up in a moment at the curb. Eugene had a vast inclination to slump carelessly upon the nearest support. He placed his arms around their shoulders and collapsed. They wedged him between them on the front seat; somewhere bells were ringing.

"Ding-dong!" he said, very cheerfully. "Cris-muss!"

They answered with a wild yell of laughter.

The house was still empty when they came to it. They got him out of the car, and staggered up the steps with him. He was sorry enough that their fellowship was broken.

"Where's your room, 'Gene?" said Julius Arthur, panting, as they entered the hall.

"This one's as good as any," said Van Yeats.

The door of the front bedroom, opposite the parlor, was open. They took him in and put him on the bed.

"Let's take off his shoes," said Julius Arthur. They unlaced them and pulled them off.

"Is there anything else you want, son?" said Julius.

He tried to tell them to undress him, put him below the covers, and close the door, in order to conceal his defection from his family, but he had lost the power of speech. After looking and grinning at him for a moment, they went out without closing the door.

When they had gone he lay upon the bed, unable to move. He had no sense of time, but his mind worked very clearly. He knew that he should rise, fasten the door, and undress. But he was paralyzed.

Presently the Gants came home. Eliza alone was still in town, pondering over gifts. It was after eleven o'clock. Gant, his daughter, and his two sons came into the room and stared at him. When they spoke to him, he burred helplessly.

"Speak! Speak!" yelled Luke, rushing at him and choking him vigorously. "Are you dumb, idiot?"

I shall remember that, he thought.

"Have you no pride? Have you no honor? Has it come to this?" the sailor roared dramatically, striding around the room.

Doesn't he think he's hell, though? Eugene thought. He could not fashion words, but he could make sounds, ironically, in the rhythm of his brother's moralizing. "Tuh-tuh-tuh-tuh! Tuh-tuh-tuh-tuh! Tuh-tuh-tuh-tuh!" he said, with accurate mimicry. Helen, loosening his collar, bent over him laughing. Ben grinned swiftly under a cleft scowl.

Have you no this? Have you no that? Have you no this? Have you no that?—he was cradled in their rhythm. No, ma'am. We've run out of honor today, but we have a nice fresh lot of self-respect.

"Ah, be quiet," Ben muttered. "No one's dead, you know."

"Go heat some water," said Gant professionally. "He's got to get it off his stomach." He no longer seemed old. His life in a marvelous instant came from its wasting shadow; it took on a hale sinew of health and action.

"Save the fireworks," said Helen to Luke, as she left the room. "Close the door. For heaven's sake, try to keep it from Mama, if you can."

This is a great moral issue, thought Eugene. He began to feel sick.

Helen returned in a very few minutes with a kettle of hot water, a glass, and a box of soda. Gant fed him the solution mercilessly until he began to vomit. At the summit of his convulsion Eliza appeared. He lifted his sick head dumbly from the bowl, and saw her white face at the door, and her weak brown eyes, that could take on so much sharpness and sparkle when her suspicion was awakened.

"Hah? Huh? What is it?" said Eliza.

But she knew, of course, instantly, what it was.

"What say?" she asked sharply. No one had said anything. He grinned feebly at her, tickled, above his nausea and grief, at the palpable assumption of blind innocence which always heralded her discoveries. Seeing her thus, they all laughed.

"Oh, my Lord!" said Helen. "Here she is. We were hoping you wouldn't get here till it was over. Come and look at your Baby," she said, with a good-humored snicker, keeping his head comfortably supported on the palm of her hand.

"How do you feel now, son?" Gant asked kindly.

"Better," he mumbled, discovering, with some elation, that his vocal paralysis was not permanent.

"Well, you see!" Helen began, kindly enough, but with a brooding satisfaction. "It only goes to show we're all alike. We all like it. It's in our blood."

"That awful curse!" Eliza said. "I had hoped that I might have one son who might escape it. It seems," she said, bursting into tears, "as if a Judgment were on us. The sins of the fathers——"

"Oh! for heaven's sake!" Helen cried angrily. "Stop it! It's not going to kill him: he'll learn a lesson from it."

Gant gnawed his thin lip, and wetted his great thumb in the old manner.

"You might know," he said, "that I'd get the blame for it. Yes—if one of them broke a leg it would be the same."

"There's one thing sure!" said Eliza. "None of them ever got it from my side of the house. Say what you will, his grandfather, Major Pentland, never in his life allowed a drop in his house."

"Major Pentland be damned!" said Gant. "If you'd depended on him for anything you'd have gone hungry."

Certainly, thought Eugene, you'd have gone thirsty.

"Forget it!" said Helen. "It's Christmas. Let's try to have a little peace and quiet once a year."

When they had left him, the boy tried to picture them lulled in the dulcet tranquillity they so often invoked. Its effects, he thought, would be more disastrous than any amount of warfare.

In the darkness, everything around and within him, swam hideously. But presently he slid down into a pit of distressed sleep.

Everyone had agreed on a studious forgiveness. They stepped with obtrusive care around his fault, filled pleasantly with Christmas and mercy. Ben scowled at him quite naturally, Helen grinned and prodded him, Eliza and Luke surrendered themselves to sweetness, sorrow, and silence. Their forgiveness made a loud noise in his ears.

During the morning his father asked him to come for a walk. Gant was embarrassed and hang-dog: a duty of gentle admonishment devolved upon him—he had been counselled to it by Helen and Eliza. Now, no man in his time could carry on in the big, bow-wow style better than Gant, but none was less fitted to scatter the blossoms of sweetness and light. His wrath was sudden, his invective sprang from the moment, but he had for this occasion no thunderbolts in his quiver, and no relish for the business before him. He had a feeling of personal guilt; he felt like a magistrate fining for intoxication a culprit with whom he has been on a spree the night before. Besides—what if the Bacchic strain in him had been passed on to his son?

They walked on in silence across the Square, by the rimmed fountain. Gant cleared his throat nervously several times.

"Son," said he presently, "I hope you'll take last night as a warning. It would be a terrible thing if you let whisky get the best of you. I'm not going to speak harshly to you about it: I hope you'll learn a lesson by it. You had better be dead than become a drunkard."

There! He was glad it was over.

"I will!" Eugene said. He was filled with gratitude and relief. How good everyone was. He wanted to make passionate avowals, great promises. He tried to speak. But he couldn't. There was too much to be said.

But they had their Christmas, beginning thus with parental advice and continuing through all the acts of contrition, love, and decorum. They put on, over their savage lives, the raiment of society, going diligently through the forms and conventions, and thinking, "now, we are like all other families"; but they were timid and shy and stiff, like rustics dressed in evening clothes.

But they could not keep silence. They were not ungenerous or mean: they were simply not bred to any restraint. Helen veered in the wind of hysteria, the strong uncertain tides of her temperament. At times when, before her own fire, her vitality sank, and she heard the long howl of the wind outside, she almost hated Eugene.

"It's ridiculous!" she said to Luke. "His behaving like this. He's only a kid—he's had everything, we've had nothing! You see what it's come to, don't you?"

"His college education has ruined him," said the sailor, not unhappy that his candle might burn more brightly in a naughty world.

"Why don't you speak to her?" she said irritably. "She may listen to you—she won't to me! Tell her so! You've seen how she's rubbed it into poor old papa, haven't you? Do you think that old man—sick as he is—is to blame? 'Gene's not a Gant, anyway. He takes after her side of the house. He's queer—like all of them! *We're* Gants!" she said with a bitter emphasis.

"There was always some excuse for Papa," said the sailor. "He's had a lot to put up with." All his convictions in family affairs had been previously signed with her approval.

"I wish you'd tell her that. With all his moping into books, he's no better than we are. If he thinks he's going to lord it over me, he's mistaken."

"I'd like to see him try it when I'm around," said Luke grimly.

The boy was doing a multiple penance—he had committed his first great wrong in being at once so remote from them and so near to them. His present trouble was aggravated by the cross-complication of Eliza's thrusts at his father, and the latent but constantly awakening antagonism of mother and daughter. In addition, he bore directly Eliza's nagging and carping attack. All this he was prepared for—it was the weather of his mother's nature (she was as fond of him as of any of them, he thought), and the hostility of Helen and Luke was something implacable, unconscious, fundamental, that grew out of the structure of their lives. He was of them, he was recognizably marked, but he was not with them, nor like them. He had been baffled for years by the passionate enigma of their dislike—their tenders of warmth and affection, when they came, were strange to him: he accepted them gratefully and with a surprise he did not wholly conceal. Otherwise, he had grown into a shell of sullenness and quiet: he spoke little in the house.

He was wearing ragged from the affair and its consequences. He felt that he was being unfairly dealt with, but as the hammering went on he drew his head bullishly down and held his tongue, counting the hours until his holiday should end. He turned silently to Ben —he should have turned nowhere. But the trusted brother, frayed and bitter on his own accord, scowled bitterly, and gave him the harsh weight of his tongue. This finally was unendurable. He felt betrayed—utterly turned against and set upon.

The outbreak came three nights before his departure as he stood, tense and stolid, in the parlor. For almost an hour, in a savage monotone, Ben had tried deliberately, it seemed, to goad him to an attack. He had listened without a word, smothering in pain and fury, and enraging by his silence the older brother who was finding a vent for his own alien frustration.

"—and don't stand there scowling at me, you little thug. I'm telling you for your own good. I'm only trying to keep you from being a jailbird, you know."

"The trouble with you," said Luke, "is that you have no appreciation for what's been done for you. Everything's been done for you, and you haven't sense enough to appreciate it. Your college education has ruined you."

The boy turned slowly on Ben.

"All right, Ben," he muttered. "That's enough, now. I don't care what he says, but I've had enough of it from you."

This was the admission the older one had wanted. They were all in very chafed and ugly temper.

"Don't talk back to me, you little fool, or I'll bat your brains out."

The boy sprang at his brother like a cat, with a snarling cry. He bore him backward to the floor as if he were a child, laying him down gently and kneeling above him, because he had been instantly shocked by the fragility of his opponent and the ease of his advantage. He struggled with such mixed rage and shame as those who try quietly to endure the tantrum of a trying brat. As he knelt above Ben, holding his arms pinned, Luke fell heavily on his back, uttering excited cries, strangling him with one arm and cuffing awkwardly with the other.

"All right, B-B-Ben," he chattered, "you grab his legs."

A free scrimmage upon the floor followed, with such a clatter of upset scuttles, fire-irons, and chairs, that Eliza was brought at a fast gallop from the kitchen.

"Mercy!" she shrieked, as she reached the door. "They'll kill him!"

But, although being subdued—in the proud language of an older South "defeated, sir, but never beaten"— Eugene was doing very well for his age, and continued to chill the spines of his enemies with strange noises in his larynx, even after they had all clambered panting to their feet.

"I f-f-f-fink he's gone crazy," said Luke. "He j-j-jumped on us without a word of warning."

The hero replied to this with a drunken roll of the head, a furious dilation of the nostrils, and another horrible noise in his throat.

"What's to become of us!" wept Eliza. "When brother strikes brother, it seems that the smash-up has come." She lifted the padded arm chair, and placed it on its legs again.

When he could speak, Eugene said quietly, to control the trembling of his voice:

"I'm sorry I jumped on you, Ben. You," he said to the excited sailor, "jumped on my back like a coward. But I'm sorry for what's happened. I'm sorry for what I did the other night and now. I said so, and you wouldn't leave me alone. You've tried to drive me crazy with your talk. And I didn't," he choked, "I didn't think you'd turn against me as you have. I know what the others are like—they hate me!"

"Hate you!" cried Luke excitedly. "For G-g-god's sake! You talk like a fool. We're only trying to help you, for your own good. Why should we hate you!"

"Yes, you hate me," Eugene said, "and you're ashamed to admit it. I don't know why you should, but you do. You wouldn't ever admit anything like that, but it's the truth. You're afraid of the right words. But it's been different with you," he said, turning to Ben. "We've been like brothers—and now, you've gone over against me."

"Ah!" Ben muttered, turning away nervously. "You're crazy. I don't know what you're talking about!" He lighted a cigarette, holding the match in a hand that trembled.

But although the boy had used a child's speech of woe and resentment, they knew there was a core of truth in what he had said.

"Children, children!" said Eliza sadly. "We must try to love one another. Let's try to get along together this Christmas—what time's left. It may be the last one we'll ever have together." She began to weep: "I've had such a hard life," she said, "it's been strife and turmoil all the way. It does seem I deserve a little peace and happiness now."

They were touched with the old bitter shame: they dared not look at one another. But they were awed and made quiet by the vast riddle of pain and confusion that scarred their lives.

"No one, 'Gene," Luke began quietly, "has turned against you. We want to help you—to see you amount to something. You're the last chance—if booze gets you the way it has the rest of us, you're done for."

The boy felt very tired; his voice was flat and low. He began to speak with the bluntness of despair: what he said had undebatable finality.

"And how are you going to keep booze from getting me, Luke?" he said. "By jumping on my back and trying to strangle me? That's on a level with every other effort you've ever made to know me."

"Oh," said Luke ironically, "you don't think we understand you?"

"No," Eugene said quietly. "I don't think you do. You know nothing whatever about me. I know nothing about you—or any of you. I have lived here with you for seventeen years and I'm a stranger. In all that time have you ever talked to me like a brother? Have you ever told me anything of yourself? Have you ever tried to be a friend or a companion to me?"

"I don't know what you want," Luke answered, "but I thought I was acting for the best. As to telling you about myself, what do you want to know?"

"Well," said Eugene slowly, "you're six years older than I am: you've been away to school, you've worked in big cities, and you are now enlisted in the United States Navy. Why do you always act like God Almighty," he continued with rankling bitterness. "I know what sailors do! You're no better than I am! What about liquor? What about women?"

"That's no way to talk before your mother," said Luke sternly.

"No, son," said Eliza in a troubled voice. "I don't like that way of talking."

"Then I won't talk like that," Eugene said. "But I had expected you to say that. We do not want to be told what we know. We do not want to call things by their names, although we're willing to call one another bad ones. We call meanness nobility and hatred honor. The way to make yourself a hero is to make me out a scoundrel. You won't admit that either, but it's true. Well, then, Luke, we won't talk of the ladies, black or white, you may or may not know, because it would make you uncomfortable. Instead, you can keep on being God and I'll listen to your advice, like a little boy in Sunday school. But I'd rather read the Ten Commandments where it's written down shorter and better."

"Son," said Eliza again with her ancient look of trouble and frustration, "we must try to get on together."

"No," he said. "Alone. I have done an apprenticeship here with you for seventeen years, but it is coming to an end. I know now that I shall escape; I know that I have been guilty of no great crime against you, and I am no longer afraid of you."

"Why, boy!" said Eliza. "We've done all we could for you. What crime have we accused you of?"

"Of breathing your air, of eating your food, of living under your roof, of having your life and your blood in my veins, of accepting your sacrifice and privation, and of being ungrateful for it all."

"We should all be thankful for what we have," said Luke sententiously. "Many a fellow would give his right eye for the chance you've been given."

"I've been given nothing!" said Eugene, his voice mounting with a husky flame of passion. "I'll go bent over no longer in this house. What chance I have I've made for myself in spite of you all, and over your opposition. You sent me away to the university when you could do nothing else, when it would have been a crying disgrace to you among the people in this town if you hadn't. You sent me off after the Leonards had cried me up for three years, and then you sent me a year too soon—before I was sixteen—with a box of sandwiches, two suits of clothes, and instructions to be a good boy."

"They sent you some money, too," said Luke. "Don't forget that."

"I'd be the only one who would, if I did," the boy

answered. "For that is really what is behind everything, isn't it? My crime the other night was not in getting drunk, but in getting drunk without any money of my own. If I did badly at the university with money of my own, you'd dare say nothing, but if I do well on money you gave me, I must still be reminded of your goodness and my unworthiness."

"Why, son!" said Eliza diplomatically, "no one has a word to say against the way you've done your work. We're very proud of you."

"You needn't be," he said sullenly. "I've wasted a great deal of time and some money. But I've had something out of it—more than most—I've done as much work for my wages as you deserve. I've given you a fair value for your money; I thank you for nothing."

"What's that! What's that!" said Eliza sharply.

"I said I thank you for nothing, but I take that back."

"That's better!" said Luke.

"Yes, I have a great deal to give thanks for," said Eugene. "I give thanks for every dirty lust and hunger that crawled through the polluted blood of my noble ancestors. I give thanks for every scrofulous token that may ever come upon me. I give thanks for the love and mercy that kneaded me over the washtub the day before my birth. I give thanks for the country slut who nursed me and let my dirty bandage fester across my navel. I give thanks for every blow and curse I had from any of you during my childhood, for every dirty cell you ever gave me to sleep in, for the ten million hours of cruelty or indifference, and the thirty minutes of cheap advice."

"Unnatural!" Eliza whispered. "Unnatural son! You will be punished if there's a just God in heaven."

"Oh, there is! I'm sure there is!" cried Eugene. "Because I have been punished. By God, I shall spend the rest of my life getting my heart back, healing and forgetting every scar you put upon me when I was a child. The first move I ever made, after the cradle, was to crawl for the door, and every move I have made since has been an effort to escape. And now at last I am free from you all, although you may hold me for a few years more. If I am not free, I am at least locked up in my own prison, but I shall get me some beauty, I shall get me some order out of this jungle of my life: I shall find my way out of it yet, though it take me twenty years more —alone."

"Alone?" said Eliza, with the old suspicion. "Where are you going?"

"Ah," he said, "you were not looking, were you? I've gone."

VI

During the few remaining days of his holiday, he stayed almost entirely away from the house, coming for a brief and mumbled meal, and late at night, for bed. He waited for departure as a prisoner for release. The dolorous prelude to a journey—the wet platform eyes, the sudden radiation of hectic warmth, the declarations of love at sound of the whistle—left him this time unmoved. The tear-ducts, he was beginning to discover, had, like sweat-glands, dermic foundations, and were easily brought to a salty sparkle at mere sight of a locomotive. He had, therefore, the somewhat detached composure of a gentleman on his way to a comfortable week end, who stands in a noisy crowd, waiting for the ferry.

He gave benediction to the words in which he had so happily defined his position as wage-earner. They stated and confirmed an attitude, and in some measure protected him against the constant betrayals of sentiment.

During the spring he worked stupendously at joining activities, knowing that here was coin whose ring they could hear. He wrote conscientiously each item of his distinctions; his name found its way back more than once to the indulgent Altamont papers. Gant kept the clippings proudly, and gave public readings when he could.

The boy had two short awkward letters from Ben, who was now stationed one hundred miles away, in the tobacco town. At Easter, Eugene visited him, staying at his lodgings, where again his unerring destiny had thrown him into the welcoming arms of a grey-haired widow. She was under fifty—a handsome silly woman, who prodded and teased him as she would an adored child. She addressed him—with a loose giggle—as "Old Curly-Head," at which he fetched out his usual disgusted plea to his Maker. "O my God! Listen to this!" She had reverted to an astonishing romping girlhood, and would exercise her playfulness by leaping suddenly upon Old Curly-Head, dealing him a stiff dig in the ribs, and skipping away with a triumphant "Hah! Got you that time!"

There was forever in that town a smell of raw tobacco, biting the nostrils with its acrid pungency: it smote the stranger coming from the train, but all the people in the town denied it, saying: "No; there is no smell at all." And within a day the stranger too could smell it no more.

On Easter morning he arose in the blue light and went with the other pilgrims to the Moravian cemetery.

"You ought to see it," Ben said. "It's a famous custom: people come from everywhere." But the older brother did not go. Behind massed bands of horns, the trumpeting blare of trombones, the big crowds moved into the strange burial ground where all the stones lay flat upon

the graves—symbol, it was said, of all-leveling Death.
But as the horns blared, the old ghoul-fantasy of death
returned, the grave slabs made him think of tablecloths:
he felt as if he were taking part in some obscene feast.

Spring was coming on again across the earth like a
light sparkle of water-spray: all of the men who had
died were making their strange and lovely return in
blossom and flower. Ben walked along the streets of the
tobacco town looking like asphodel. It was strange to
find a ghost there in that place: his ancient soul prowled
wearily by the cheap familiar brick and all the young
façades.

There was a Square on high ground; in the center a
courthouse. Cars were parked in close lines. Young
men loitered in the drugstore.

How real it is, Eugene thought. It is like something
we have always known about and do not need to see.
The town would not have seemed strange to Thomas
Aquinas—but he to the town.

Ben prowled along, greeting the merchants with a
grave scowl, leaning his skull against their round skulls
of practicality, across their counters—a phantom soliciting advertisement in a quiet monotone.

"This is my kid brother, Mr. Fulton."

"Hello, son! Dogged if they don't grow tall 'uns up
there, Ben. Well, if you're like Old Ben, young fellow,
we won't kick. We think a lot of him here."

That's like thinking well of Balder, in Connecticut,
Eugene thought.

"I have only been here three months," said Ben,
resting in bed on his elbow and smoking a cigarette.
"But I know all the leading businessmen already. I'm
well thought of here." He glanced at his brother quickly
and grinned, with a shy charm of rare confession. But

his fierce eyes were desperate and lonely. Hill-haunted? For—home? He smoked.

"You see, they think well of you, once you get away from your people. You'll never have a chance at home, 'Gene. They'll ruin everything for you. For heaven's sake, get away when you can.—What's the matter with you? Why are you looking at me like that?" he said sharply, alarmed at the set stare of the boy's face. In a moment he said: "They'll spoil your life. Can't you forget about her?"

"No," said Eugene. In a moment he added: "She's kept coming back all spring."

He twisted his throat with a wild cry.

The spring advanced with a mounting hum of war. The older students fell out quietly and drifted away to enlistments. The younger strained tensely, waiting. The war brought them no sorrow: it was a pageant which might, they felt, pluck them instantly into glory. The country flowed with milk and honey. There were strange rumors of a land of Eldorado to the north, amid the war industry of the Virginia coast. Some of the students had been there, the year before: they brought back stories of princely wages. One could earn twelve dollars a day, with no experience. One could assume the duties of a carpenter, with only a hammer, a saw, and a square. No questions were asked.

War is not death to young men; war is life. The earth had never worn raiment of such color as it did that year. The war seemed to unearth pockets of ore that had never been known in the nation: there was a vast unfolding and exposure of wealth and power. And somehow—this imperial wealth, this display of power in men and money, was blended into a lyrical music. In Eugene's mind, wealth and love and glory melted into

a symphonic noise: the age of myth and miracle had
come upon the world again. All things were possible.

He went home stretched like a bowstring and announced his intention of going away into Virginia. There
was protest, but not loud enough to impede him. Eliza's
mind was fastened on real-estate and the summer trade.
Gant stared into the darkness at his life. Helen laughed
at him and scolded him; then fell to plucking at her
chin, absently.

"Can't do without her? You can't fool me! No, sir. I
know why you want to go," she said jocularly. "She's a
married woman now: she may have a baby, for all you
know. You've no right to go after her."

Then abruptly, she said:

"Well, let him go if he wants to. It looks silly to me,
but he's got to decide for himself."

He got twenty-five dollars from his father—enough
to pay his railway fare to Norfolk and leave him a few
dollars.

"Mark my words," said Gant. "You'll be back in a
week's time. It's a wild-goose chase you're going on."

He went.

All through the night he drew towards her across
Virginia, propped on his elbow in the berth and staring
bewitched upon the great romantic country clumped
with dreaming woodlands and white as a weird dawn
beneath the blazing moonlight.

Early in the morning he came to Richmond. He had
to change trains; there was a wait. He went out from
the station and walked up the hill towards the fine old
State House drenched cleanly in the young morning
light. He ate breakfast at a lunchroom on Broad Street,
filled already with men going to their work. This casual
and brief contact with their lives, achieved after his

lonely and magnificent approach through the night, thrilled him by its very casualness. All the little ticking sounds of a city beginning its day, the strange familiarity of voices in an alien place, heard curiously after the thunder of the wheels, seemed magical and unreal. The city had no existence save that which he conferred on it: he wondered how it had lived before he came, how it would live after he left. He looked at all the men, feeding with eyes that held yet the vast moon-meadows of the night and the cool green width of the earth. They were like men in a zoo; he gazed at them, looking for all the little particular markings of the town, the fine mapping upon their limbs and faces of their own little cosmos. And the great hunger for voyages rose up in him—to come always, as now at dawn, into strange cities, striding in among them, and sitting with them unknown, like a god in exile, stored with the enormous vision of the earth.

The counterman yawned and turned the crackling pages of a morning paper. That was strange.

Cars clanked by, beginning to work through the town. Merchants lowered their awnings; he left them as their day began.

An hour later he was riding for the sea. Eighty miles away lay the sea and Laura. She slept unwitting of the devouring wheels that brought him to her. He looked at the aqueous blue sky whitened with little clouds, and at the land wooded with pines and indefinable tokens of the marshes and bright salt.

The train drew under the boat-shed at Newport News. The terrific locomotive, as beautiful as any ship, breathed with unlaborious fatigue at the rail-head. There, by lapping water, she came to rest, like a completed destiny.

The little boat lay waiting at the dock. Within a few

minutes he had left the hot murky smell of the shed and was cruising out into the blue water of the Roads. A great light wind swept over the water, making a singing noise through the tackle of the little boat, making a music and a glory in his heart. He drove along the little decks at a bounding stride, lunging past the staring people, with wild noises in his throat. The lean destroyers, the bright mad camouflage of the freighters and the transports, the lazy red whirl of a propeller, half-submerged, and the light winy sparkle of the waves fused to a single radiance and filled him with glory. He cried back into the throat of the enormous wind, and his eyes were wet.

Upon the decks of the boats, clean little figures in white moved about; under the bulging counter of a huge Frenchman young naked men were swimming. They come from France, he thought, and it is strange that they should be here.

Oh, the wonder, the magic and the loss! His life was like a great wave breaking in the lonely sea; his hungry shoulder found no barriers—he smote his strength at nothing, and was lost and scattered like a wrack of mist. But he believed that this supreme ecstasy which mastered him and made him drunken might some day fuse its enormous light into a single articulation. He was Phaeton with the terrible horses of the sun: he believed that his life might pulse constantly at its longest stroke, achieve an eternal summit.

The hot Virginias broiled under the fierce blue oven of the sky, but in the Roads the ships rocked in the freshening breeze of war and glory.

Eugene remained in the furnace of Norfolk for four days, until his money was gone. He watched it go without fear, with a sharp quickening of his pulses, tasting the keen pleasure of his loneliness and the unknown turnings of his life. He sensed the throbbing antennæ of the world: life purred like a hidden dynamo, with the vast excitement of ten thousand glorious threats. He might do all, dare all, become all. The far and the mighty was near him, around him, above him. There was no great bridge to span, no hard summit to win. From obscurity, hunger, loneliness, he might be lifted in a moment into power, glory, love. The transport loading at the docks might bear him war-ward, love-ward, fame-ward Wednesday night.

He walked by lapping water through the dark. He heard its green wet slap against the crusted pier-piles: he drank its strong cod scent, and watched the loading of great boats drenched in blazing light as they weltered slowly down into the water. And the night was loud with the rumble of huge cranes, the sudden loose rattle of the donkey-engines, the cries of the overseers, and the incessant rumbling trucks of stevedores within the pier.

His imperial country, for the first time, was gathering the huge thrust of her might. The air was charged with murderous exuberance, rioting and corrupt extravagance.

Through the hot streets of that town seethed the toughs, the crooks, the vagabonds of a nation—Chicago gunmen, bad niggers from Texas, Bowery bums, pale Jews with soft palms, from the shops of the city, Swedes from the Middle West, Irish from New England, mountaineers from Tennessee and North Carolina, whores, in shoals and droves, from everywhere. For these the war was a fat enormous goose raining its golden eggs upon them. There was no thought or belief in any future. There was only the triumphant *Now*. There was no life beyond the moment. There was only an insane flux and reflux of getting and spending.

Young men from Georgia farms came, in the evenings, from their work on piers, in camps, in shipyards, to dress up in their peacock plumage. And at night, hard and brown and lean of hand and face, they stood along the curbing in $18 tan leathers, $80 suits, and $8 silk shirts striped with broad alternating bands of red and blue. They were carpenters, masons, gang overseers, or said they were: they were paid $10, $12, $14, $18 a day.

They shifted, veered from camp to camp, worked for a month, loafed opulently for a week, enjoying the brief bought loves of girls they met upon the ocean beach or in a brothel.

Strapping black buck-niggers, with gorilla arms and the black paws of panthers, earned $60 a week as stevedores, and spent it on a mulatto girl in a single evening of red riot.

And more quietly, soberly, in this crowd, moved the older thriftier workmen: the true carpenters, the true masons, the true mechanics—the canny Scotch-Irish of North Carolina, the fishermen of the Virginia coast, the careful peasantry of the Middle West, who had come to earn, to save, to profit from the war.

Everywhere amid this swarming crowd gleamed the bright raiment of blood and glory: the sailors thronged the streets in flapping blues and spotless whites—brown, tough, and clean. The marines strode by in arrogant twos, stiff as rods in the loud pomp of chevrons and striped trousers. Commanders grey and grim, hardhanded C. P. O.'s, and elegant young ensigns out of college, with something blonde and fluffy at their side, went by among the red cap-buttons of French matelots, or the swagger sea-wise port of the Englishmen.

Through this crowd, with matted uncut hair that fell into his eyes, that shot its spirals through the rents of his old green hat, that curled a thick scroll up his dirty neck, Eugene plunged with hot devouring eyes— soaked in his sweat by day, sharp and stale by night.

In this great camp of vagrant floaters he lost himself: he came home into this world from loneliness. The hunger for voyages, the hunger that haunts Americans, who are a nomad race, was half-assuaged here in this maelstrom of the war.

He lost himself in the crowd. He lost count of the days. His little store of money melted. He moved from a cheap hotel, loud at night with the noise of harlotry, to a little attic room in a lodging-house, an oven of hot pine and tarred roof; he moved from the lodging-house to a fifty-cent cot in the Y. M. C. A., where, returning night by night, he paid his fee, and slept in a room with forty snoring sailors.

Finally, his money gone, he slept, until driven out, in all-night lunchrooms; upon the Portsmouth ferry; and over lapping water on a rotting pier.

By night he prowled about among the Negroes; he listened to their rich proposed seductions; he went where the sailors went, down Church Street, where the women were. He prowled the night with young beast-lust, his thin boy-body stale with sweat, his hot eyes burning through the dark.

He grew hungry for food. His money was gone. But there was a hunger and thirst in him that could not be fed. Over the chaos of his brain hung the shadow of Laura James. Her shadow hung above the town, above all life. It had brought him here; his heart was swollen with pain and pride; he would not go to find her.

He was obsessed with the notion that he would find her in the crowd, upon the street, around the corner. He would not speak to her if he met her. He would go proudly and indifferently by. He would not see her.

She would see him. She would see him at some heroic moment, just as he was receiving the love and respect of beautiful women. She would speak to him; he would not speak to her. She would be stricken; she would be beaten down; she would cry to him for love and mercy.

Thus, unclean, unkempt, clothed in rags and hunger and madness, he saw himself victorious, heroic and beautiful. He was mad with his obsession. He thought he saw Laura on the streets a dozen times a day: his heart turned rotten; he did not know what he should do or say, whether to run or remain. He brooded for hours over her address in the telephone directory; sitting by the phone, he trembled with excitement because its awful magic could be sounded at a gesture, because within a minute he could be with her, voice to voice.

He hunted out her home. She was living in an old frame house far out from the center of the town. He stalked carefully about the neighborhood, keeping a block away from the house at all times, observing it obliquely, laterally, from front and back, with stealthy eye and a smothering thud of the heart, but never passing before it, never coming directly to it.

He was foul and dirty. The soles of his shoes wore through: his calloused feet beat against hot pavements. He stank.

At length, he tried to get work. Work there was in great abundance—but the princely wages of which he had been told were hard to find. He could not swear he was a carpenter, a mason. He was a dirty boy, and looked it. He was afraid. He went to the Navy Yard at Portsmouth, the Naval Base at Norfolk, the Bush Terminal—everywhere there was work, abundant work —hard labor that paid four dollars a day. This he would gladly have taken; but he found that he could not have his wages until after the second week, and that one week's pay would be withheld to tide him over in illness, trouble, or departure.

And he had no money left.

He went to a Jew and pawned the watch Eliza had given him upon his birthday. He got five dollars on it. Then he went by boat once more to Newport News, and by trolley up the coast to Hampton. He had heard, in the thronging rumor of Norfolk, that there was work upon the flying field, and that the worker was fed and housed upon the field, at company expense.

In the little employment shack at the end of the long bridge that led across into the field, he was signed on as a laborer and searched by the sentry, who made him open his valise. Then he labored across the bridge, kneeing his heavy bag, which bulged with his soiled and disorderly belongings, before him.

He staggered at length into the rude company office and sought out the superintendent, a man in the thirties, shaven, pale, weary, who wore a blue eyeshade, armbands, and talked with a limp cigarette plastered on his lip.

Eugene thrust out his employment slip in shaking fingers. The man looked briefly at it.

"College boy, aren't you, son?" he said, glancing at Eugene.

"Yes, sir," said Eugene.

"Did you ever do day labor before?" said the man.

"No, sir," said Eugene.

"How old are you, son?" the man asked.

Eugene was silent for a moment. "I'm—nineteen," he said at length, wondering, since he had lied, why he had not had courage to say twenty.

The superintendent grinned wearily.

"It's hard work, son," the man said. "You'll be among the wops and the Swedes and the hunkies. You'll live in the same bunkhouse, you'll eat with them. They don't smell nice, son."

"I have no money," said Eugene. "I'll work hard. I won't get sick. Give me the job. Please!"

"No," said the man. "No, I won't do that."

Eugene turned blindly away.

"I tell you what I'll do," said the superintendent. "I'll give you a job as a checker. You'll be with the office force. That's where you belong. You'll live with them in their own bunkhouse. They're nice fellows," he said elegantly, "college fellows, like yourself."

"Thank you," said Eugene, clenching his fingers, with husky emotion. "Thank you."

"The checker we've got is quitting," said the superintendent. "You'll go to the stables with him in the morning to get your horse."

"H-h-h-horse?" said Eugene.

"You'll have a horse," said the superintendent, "to ride around on."

With strong bowel-excitement Eugene began to think of the horse, with joy, with fear. He turned to go. He could not bear to talk of money.

"H-h-how much—?" he finally croaked, feeling that he must. Business.

"I'll give you $80 a month to begin with," said the manager with a touch of magnificence. "If you make good, I'll give you a hundred."

"And my keep?" whispered Eugene.

"Sure!" said the manager. "That's thrown in."

Eugene reeled away with his valise, and with a head full of exploding rockets.

These months, although filled with terror and hunger, must be passed in rapid summary, with bare mention of the men and actions that a lost boy knew. They belong to a story of escape and wandering—valuable here to indicate the initiation to the voyage this life will make. They are a prelude to exile, and into their nightmare chaos no other purpose may be read than the blind groping of a soul towards freedom and isolation.

Eugene worked upon the flying field for a month. Three times a day he rode around the field to check the numbers of two dozen gangs who were engaged in the work of grading, leveling, blasting from the spongy earth the ragged stumps of trees and filling interminably, ceaselessly, like the weary and fruitless labor of a nightmare, the marshy earth-craters, which drank their shoveled toil without end. The gangs were of all races and conditions: Portugee niggers, ebony-black, faithful and childlike, who welcomed him with great toothy grins, each pointing to his big white pin, on which was printed his number, crying out in strange outlandish voices, "feefety-nine, nine-net-ty seex," and so on; Bowery bums, in greasy serge and battered derbies, toying distastefully with pick-handles that shredded their dirty uncalloused palms—their hard evil faces, with their smudge of beard, were like things corrupt, green-yellow, that grow under barrels. And there were also drawling fishermen from the Virginia coast, huge gorilla niggers from Georgia and the lower South, Italians, Swedes, Irishmen—part of the huge compost of America.

He came to know them and their overseers—tough reckless men, grey-haired and lustful, full of swift action and coarse humor.

Stuck like a jigging doll upon the horse, whom he feared, he rode, staring into heaven, sometimes almost unconscious of the great engine expanding and contracting below him with a brown sensual rhythm. The bird-men filled the blue Virginia weather with the great drone of the Liberties.

At length, hungry again for the ships and faces, he left his work and spent his earnings in a week of gaudy riot in Norfolk and on the Virginia beaches. Almost penniless again, with only the savage kaleidoscope of a thousand streets, a million lights, the blazing confusion and the strident noise of carnival, he returned to Newport News in search of employment, accompanied by another youth from Altamont, likewise a thriftless adventurer in war-work, whom he had found upon the beach. This worthy, whose name was Sinker Jordan, was three years older than Eugene. He was a handsome reckless boy, small in stature, and limping from an injury he had received in a football game. His character was weak and volatile—he hated effort, and was obstinate only in cursing ill-fortune.

The two young men had a few dollars between them. They pooled their resources, and, with wild optimism, purchased from a pawnbroker in Newport News the rudiments of carpenter's equipment—hammers, saws, and T-squares. They went inland fifteen or twenty miles to a dreary government camp sweltering in the Virginia pines. They were refused employment here and in black dejection returned in the afternoon to the town they had left so hopefully in the morning. Before sundown they had secured employment in the Shipbuilding Yards, but they had been discharged five minutes after they reported for work, when they confessed to a grinning foreman in a room full of wood-shavings and quietly slatting belts, that they had no knowledge of the intensely special carpentry of ship's carving. Nor (they might have added) of any other.

They were quite moneyless now, and once on the street again, Sinker Jordan had hurled upon the pavement the fatal tools, cursing savagely the folly that threatened now to keep them hungry. Eugene picked the tools up, and took them back to the imperturbable Uncle, who repurchased them for only a few dollars less than the sum they had paid him in the morning.

Thus the day. They found a lodging in a dingy house where, as an appropriate climax to his folly, Sinker Jordan surrendered their remaining capital into the greedy palm of the landlady—and a real lady too, she admitted. But, having previously eaten, they had all the hope of a full belly and their youth—they slept, Sinker without care and without effort.

Eugene was early up at dawn, and after futile efforts to waken the luxuriously somnolent Sinker, he was off to the dingy yellow piers along the waterfront, which were stored with munitions for the war. After a morning tramping up and down the dusty road outside the guarded enclosures, he had obtained employment for himself and Sinker from the chief checker, a nervous ugly man, swollen with petty tyranny. He had gimlet eyes, glittering below spectacles, and hard muscular jaws that writhed constantly.

Eugene went to work at seven the next morning—Sinker, a day or two later, only when his last small coin had vanished. Eugene screwed up his pride and borrowed a few dollars from one of the other checkers. On this he and Sinker lived meagerly until pay-day—which was only a few days off. This money slipped quickly through their careless fingers. Down to a few coins again, with the next pay-day almost two weeks off, Sinker gambled at dice with the checkers, behind the great fortress of sacked oats upon the pier—lost, won, lost, rose penniless and cursing God. Eugene knelt beside the checkers, with his last half-dollar in his palm, heedless of Sinker's bitter taunt. He had never thrown dice before: naturally, he won—$8.50. He rose exultantly from their profane surprise, and took Sinker to dinner at the best hotel.

A day or two later, he went behind the oats again, gambled with his last dollar—and lost.

He began to starve. Day crawled into weary day. The fierce eye of July beat down upon the pier with a straight insufferable glare. The boats and trains slid in and out, crammed to the teeth with munitions—with food for the soldiers. The hot grainy air on the pier swam before his eyes speckled with dancing patches, and he made weary tallies on a sheet as the big black stevedores swarmed past him with their trucks. Sinker Jordan cadged small sums from the other checkers, and lived miserably on bottled pop and cheese at a little grocery across the road from the pier. Eugene was unable to beg or borrow. Partly from pride, but more from the powerful brooding inertia of his temper, which more and more was governing his will to act, he found himself unable to speak. Each day he said: "I shall speak to one of them today. I shall say that I must eat, and that I have no money." But when he tried to speak he could not.

As they grew more efficient in their work they were called back, after the day's end, for work at night. This extra work, with its time-and-half pay, he would otherwise have been glad to get, but stumbling from exhaustion, the command to return was horrible. For several days now he had not been home to the dingy little room which he shared with Sinker Jordan. At the end of his day's work, he would climb to a little oasis in the enormous wall of sacked oats and sink into exhausted sleep, with the rattling of cranes and winches, the steady rumble of the trucks, and the remote baying of boats anchored in the stream—mixing in a strange faint symphony in his ears.

And he lay there, with the fading glimmer of the world about him, as the war mounted to its climax of blood and passion during that terrible month. He lay there, like his own ghost, thinking with pain, with grief, of all the million towns and faces he had not known. He was the atom for which all life had been a plot—Cæsar had died and a nameless wife of Babylon, and somewhere here, upon this marvelous dying flesh, his myriad brain, their mark, their spirit, rested.

And he thought of the strange lost faces he had known, the lonely figures of his family, damned in chaos, each chained to a destiny of ruin and loss— Gant, a fallen Titan, staring down enormous vistas of the Past, indifferent to the world about him; Eliza, beetle-wise, involved in blind accretions; Helen, child-less, pathless, furious—a great wave breaking on the barren waste; and finally, Ben—the ghost, the stranger, prowling at this moment in another town, going up and down the thousand streets of life, and finding no doors.

But the next day, on the pier, Eugene was weaker than ever. He sat sprawled upon a throne of plump fat sacks, with blurred eyes watching the loading of the bags at the spout, marking raggedly his tally upon the sheet as the stevedores plunged in and out. The terrible heat steamed through the grainy pollen of the air: he moved each limb with forethought, picking it up and placing it as if it were a detached object.

At the end of the day he was asked to return for nightwork. He listened, swaying on his feet, to the far-sounding voice of the chief checker.

The supper hour came, upon the heated pier, with the sudden noise of silence. There were small completed noises up and down the enormous shed: a faint drumming of footfalls of workers walking towards the entrance, a slap of water at the ship's hull, a noise from the bridge.

Eugene went behind the oat pile and climbed blindly up until he reached his little fortress at the top. The world ebbed from his fading sense: all sound grew fainter, more far. Presently, he thought, when I have rested here, I shall get up and go down to work. It has been a hot day. I am tired. But when he tried to move he could not. His will struggled against the imponderable lead of his flesh, stirring helplessly like a man in a cage. He thought quietly, with relief, with tranquil joy, "They will not find me here. I cannot move. It is over. If I had thought of this long ago, I would have been afraid. But I'm not, now. Here—upon the oat pile—doing my bit—for Democracy. I'll begin to stink. They'll find me then."

Life glimmered away out of his weary eyes. He lay half-conscious, sprawled upon the oats. He thought of the horse.

In this way the young checker, who had loaned him money, found him. The checker knelt above him, supporting Eugene's head with one hand, and putting a bottle of raw hard liquor to his mouth with the other. When the boy had revived somewhat, the checker helped him to descend the pile and walked slowly with him up the long wooden platform of the pier.

They went across the road to a little grocery-store. The checker ordered a bottle of milk, a box of cracker and a big block of cheese. As Eugene ate, the tears began to flow down his grimy face, dredging dirty gullies on his skin. They were tears of hunger and weakness: he could not restrain them.

The checker stood over him watchfully, with a kindly troubled stare. He was a young man with a lantern jaw, and a thin dish face: he wore scholarly spectacles, and smoked a pipe reflectively.

"Why didn't you tell me, boy? I'd have let you have the money," he said.

"I—don't—know," said Eugene, between bites of cheese. "Couldn't."

With the checker's loan of five dollars he and Sinker Jordan lived until pay-day. Then, after dining together on four pounds of steak, Sinker Jordan departed for Altamont and the enjoyment of an inheritance which had fallen due a few days before, on his twenty-first birthday. Eugene stayed on.

He was like a man who had died, and had been reborn. All that had gone before lived in a ghostly world. He thought of his family, of Ben, of Laura James, as if they were ghosts. The world itself turned ghost. All through that month of August, while the war marched to its ending, he looked upon its dying carnival. Nothing seemed any longer hard and hot and raw and new. Everything was old. Everything was dying. A vast aerial music, forever far-faint, like the language of his forgotten world, sounded in his ears. He had known birth. He had known pain and love. He had known hunger. Almost he had known death.

At night, when he was not called back for work he rode by trolley to one of the Virginia beaches. But the only sound that was real, that was near and present, was the sound in his heart, in his brain, of the everlasting

sea. He turned his face towards it: behind him, the
cheap million lights of the concessionaires, the clatter,
the racket, the confetti, the shrill blare of the saxophones,
all the harsh joyless noise of his country, was softened,
was made sad, far, and phantom. The wheeling merry-
go-round, the blaring dance-orchestra, played *K-K-K-
Katy, Beautiful Katy, Poor Little Buttercup*, and *Just a
Baby's Prayer at Twilight*.

And that cheap music turned elfin and lovely: it was
mixed into magic—it became a part of the romantic and
lovely Virginias, of the surge of the sea, as it rolled in
from the eternal dark, across the beach, and of his own
magnificent sorrow—his triumphant loneliness after pain
and love and hunger.

His face was thin and bright as a blade, below the
great curling shock of his hair; his body as lean as a
starved cat's; his eyes bright and fierce.

"O sea!" he thought, "I am the hill-born, the prison-
pent, the ghost, the stranger, and I walk here at your
side. O sea, I am lonely like you, I am strange and far
like you, I am sorrowful like you; my brain, my heart,
my life, like yours, have touched strange shores. You
are like a woman lying below yourself on the coral floor.
You are an immense and fruitful woman with vast thighs
and a great thick mop of curling woman's hair floating
like green moss above your belly. And you will bring me
to the happy land, you will wash me to glory in bright
ships."

There by the sea of the dark Virginias, he thought of
the forgotten faces, of all the million patterns of himself,
the ghost of his lost flesh. The child that heard Swain's
cow, the lost boy in the Ozarks, the carrier of news
among the blacks, and the boy who went in by the lattice
with Jim Trivett. And the waitress, and Ben, and Laura?
Dead, too? Where? How? Why? Why has the web been

woven? Why do we die so many deaths? How came I
here beside the sea? O lost, O far and lonely, where?

Sometimes, as he walked back among the dancers, a
scarecrow in flapping rags, he looked and saw himself
among them. He seemed to be two people: he constantly
saw himself with dark bent face sitting upon the top rail
of a fence, watching himself go by with a bright herd
of young people. He saw himself among the crowds,
several inches shorter than he was, fitting comfortably
into a world where everything was big enough for him.

And while he stared and saw himself beloved and admitted, he heard them laugh: he felt suddenly the hard
white ring of their faces about him, and he plunged
away, with cursing mouth.

O my sweet bitches! My fine cheap sluts! You little
crawling itch of twiddlers: you will snigger at me! At
me! At me! (He beat his hands against his ribs.) You
will mock at me, with your drugstore pimps, your
Jazz-bo apes, your gorilla gobs, you cute little side-porch
chippies! What do you understand? The lust of a goat,
the stink of your kind—that does for you, my girls. And
yet you laugh at me! Ah, but I'll tell you why you laugh:
you are afraid of me because I am not like the others.
You hate me because I do not belong. You see I am finer
and greater than anyone you know: you cannot reach me
and you hate me. That's it! The ethereal (yet manly)
beauty of my features, by boyish charm (for I am Just a
Boy) blended with the tragic wisdom of my eyes (as old
as life and filled with the brooding tragedy of the ages),
the sensitive and delicate flicker of my mouth, and my
marvelous dark face blooming inward on strange loveliness like a flower—all this you want to kill because you
cannot touch it. Ah me! (Thinking of his strange beauty,

his eyes grew moist with love and glory, and he was forced to blow his nose.) Ah, but She will know. The love of a lady. Proudly, with misty eyes, he saw her standing beside him against the rabble: her elegant small head, wound with a bracelet of bright hair, against his shoulder, and with two splendid pearls in her ears. Dearest! Dearest! We stand here on a star. We are beyond them now. Behold! They shrink, they fade, they pass—victorious, enduring, marvelous love, my dearest, we remain.

Brooding thus on the vision of his own beauty, stirred by his own heroic music, with misty eyes, he would pass over into the forbidden settlement, with its vigilant patrols of naval and military police on the watch for their own, and prowl softly down a dark little street to a dingy frame house with drawn blinds, where dwelt a love that for three dollars could be bought and clothed with his own fable. Her name was Stella Blake. She was never in a hurry.

With her lived a young corn-haired girl of twenty years whose family lived in Pulpit Hill. Sometimes he went to see her.

Twice a week the troops went through. They stood densely in brown and weary thousands on the pier while a council of officers, tabled at the gangways, went through their clearance papers. Then, each below the sweating torture of his pack, they were filed from the hot furnace of the pier into the hotter prison of the ship. The great ships, with their motley jagged patches of deception, waited in the stream: they slid in and out in unending squadrons.

Sometimes the troops were black—labor regiments from Georgia and Alabama; big gorilla bucks from Texas. They gleamed with sweat and huge rich laughter:

they were obedient as children and called their cursing officers "boss."

"And don't you call me 'boss' again, you bastards!" screamed a young Tennessee lieutenant, who had gone slowly insane during the moving, as he nursed his charges through hell. They grinned at him cheerfully, with affection, like good obedient children, as he stamped, raving, up and down the pier. From time to time they goaded him into a new frenzy with complaints about lost hats, bayonets, small arms, and papers. Somehow he found things for them; somehow he cursed his way through, keeping them in order. They grinned affectionately, therefore, and called him boss.

"And what in Jesus' name have you done now?" he yelled, as a huge black sergeant with several enlisted men, who had gathered at the examiner's table, burst suddenly into loud roars of grief.

The fiery lieutenant rushed at the table, cursing.

The sergeant and several enlisted men, all Texas darkies, had come away from camp without a clean bill of health: they were venereals and had not been cured.

"Boss," blubbered the big black sergeant, "we wants to go to France. We don't want to git lef' in dis Gawd-damn hole."

(Nor do I blame them, thought Eugene.)

"I'll kill you! So help me God, I'll kill you!" screamed the officer, hurling his trim cap upon the ground and stamping upon it. But, a moment later, with a medical officer he was leading them away for examination behind the great wall of sacked oats. Five minutes later they emerged. The Negroes were cavorting with joy: they pressed around their fierce commander, seizing and kissing his hand, fawning upon him, adoring him.

"You see," said the dish-faced checker, while he and Eugene watched, "that's what it takes to hold a crowd of niggers. You can't be nice to 'em. They'd do anything for that guy."

"He would for them," said Eugene.

These Negroes, he thought, who came from Africa, were sold at the block in Louisiana, and live in Texas, are now on their way to France.

Mr. Finch, the chief checker with the ugly slit eyes, approached Eugene with a smile of false warmth. His grey jaws worked.

"I've got a job for you, Gant," he said. "Double-time pay. I want you to get in on some of the easy money."

"What is it?" said Eugene.

"They're loading this ship with big stuff," said Mr. Finch. "They're taking her out into the stream to get it on. I want you to go out with her. They'll take you off in a tug tonight."

The dish-faced checker, when jubilantly he told him of his appointment, said:

"They asked me to go, but I wouldn't."

"Why not?" said Eugene.

"I don't want the money bad enough. They're loading her with T. N. T. and nitro-glycerin. The niggers play baseball with those cases. If they ever drop one, they'll bring you home in a bucket."

"It's all in the day's work," said Eugene dramatically. This was danger, war. He was definitely in on it, risking his hide for Democracy. He was thrilled.

When the big freighter slid away from the pier, he stood in the bow with spread legs, darting his eyes about with fierce eagle glances. The iron decks blistered his feet through the thin soles of his shoes. He did not mind. He was the captain.

She anchored seaward down the Roads, and the great barges were nosed in by the tugs. All through the day, under a broiling sun, they loaded her from the rocking barges: her huge yellow booms swung up and down; by nightfall she rode deeply in the water, packed to her throat with shells and powder, and bearing on the hot plates of her deck 1200 grisly tons of field artillery.

Eugene stood with fierce appraising eyes, walking about the guns with a sense of authority, jotting down numbers, items, pieces. From time to time he thrust a handful of moist scrap-tobacco into his mouth, and chewed with an air of relish. He spat hot sizzling gobs upon the iron deck. "God!" thought he. "This is man's work. Heave-ho, ye black devils! There's a war on!" He spat.

The tug came at nightfall and took him off. He sat apart from the stevedores, trying to fancy the boat had come for him alone. The lights went twinkling up the far Virginia shores. He spat into the swirling waters.

When the trains slid in and out, the stevedores raised the wooden bridges that spanned the tracks. Foot by foot, with rhythmic pull and halt, the gangs tugged at the ropes, singing, under the direction of their leader, their song of love and labor:

"Jelly Roll! (Heh!) Je-e-elly Roll."

They were great black men, each with his kept woman. They earned fifty or sixty dollars a week.

Once or twice again, in the dying summer, Eugene went to Norfolk. He saw the sailor, but he no longer tried to see Laura. She seemed far and lost.

He had not written home all summer. He found a letter from Gant, written in his father's Gothic sprawl— a sick and feeble letter, written sorrowfully and far away. O lost! Eliza, in the rush and business of the summer trade, had added a few practical lines. Save his money. Get plenty of good food. Keep well. Be a good boy.

The boy was a lean column of brown skin and bone. He had lost over thirty pounds during the summer: he was over six foot four and weighed little more than one hundred and thirty pounds.

The sailor was shocked at his emaciation, and bullied him with blustering reproof:

"Why didn't you t-t-tell me where you were, idiot? I'd have sent you money. For G-g-god's sake! Come on and eat!" They ate.

The summer waned. When September came, Eugene quit his work and, after a luxurious day or two in Norfolk, started homeward. But, at Richmond, where there was a wait of three hours between trains, he changed his plans suddenly and went to a good hotel.

He was touched with pride and victory. In his pockets he had $130 that he had won hardily by his own toil. He had lived alone, he had known pain and hunger, he had survived. The old hunger for voyages fed at his heart. He thrilled to the glory of the secret life. The fear of the crowd, a distrust and hatred of group life, a horror of all bonds that tied him to the terrible family of the earth, called up again the vast Utopia of his loneliness. To go alone, as he had gone, into strange cities; to meet strange people and to pass again before they could know him; to wander, like his own legend, across the earth—it seemed to him there could be no better thing than that.

He thought of his own family with fear, almost with hatred. "My God! Am I never to be free?" he thought. "What have I done to deserve this slavery? Suppose—suppose I were in China, or in Africa, or at the South Pole. I should always be afraid of his dying while I was away." (He twisted his neck as he thought of it.) "And how they would rub it in to me if I were not there!

Enjoying yourself in China," they would say, "while your father was dying. Unnatural son! Yes, but curse them! Why should I be there? Can they not die alone? Alone! O God, is there no freedom on this earth?"

With quick horror, he saw that such freedom lay a weary world away, and could be bought by such enduring courage as few men have.

He stayed in Richmond several days, living sumptuously in the splendid hotel, eating from silver dishes in the grill, and roaming pleasantly through the wide streets of the romantic old town, to which he had come once as a Freshman at Thanksgiving, when the university's team had played Virginia there. He spent three days trying to seduce a waitress in an ice-cream and candy store: he lured her finally to a curtained booth in a chop-suey restaurant, only to have his efforts fail when the elaborate meal he had arranged for with the Chinaman aroused her distaste because it had onions in it.

Before he went home he wrote an enormous letter to Laura James at Norfolk, a pitiable and boasting letter which rose at its end to an insane crow: "I was there all summer and I never looked you up. You were not decent enough to answer my letters; I saw no reason why I should bother with you any more. Besides, the world is full of women; I got my share and more this summer."

He mailed the letter, with a sense of malevolent triumph. But the moment the iron lid of the box clanged over it, his face was contorted by shame and remorse: he lay awake, writhing as he recalled the schoolboy folly of it. She had beaten him again.

VII

Eugene returned to Altamont two weeks before the term began at Pulpit Hill. The town and the nation

seethed in the yeasty ferment of war. The country was
turning into one huge camp. The colleges and universities were being converted into training camps for
officers. Everyone was "doing his bit."

It had been a poor season for tourists. Eugene found
Dixieland almost deserted, save for a glum handful of
regular or semiregular guests. Mrs. Pert was there, sweet,
gentle, a trifle more fuzzy than usual. Miss Newton, a
wrenny and neurotic old maid, with asthma, who had
gradually become Eliza's unofficial assistant in the man-
agement of the house, was there. Miss Malone, the gaunt
drug-eater with the loose grey lips, was there. Fowler, a
civil engineer with blond hair and a red face, who came
and departed quietly, leaving a sodden stench of corn
whisky in his wake, was there. Gant, who had now
moved definitely from the house on Woodson Street,
which he had rented, to a big back room at Eliza's, was
there—a little more waxen, a little more petulant, a little
feebler than he had been before. And Ben was there.

He had been home for a week or two when Eugene
arrived. He had been rejected again by both army and
navy examining boards, he had been rejected as unfit in
the draft; he had left his work suddenly in the tobacco
town and come quietly and sullenly home. He was
thinner and more like old ivory than ever. He prowled
softly about the house, smoking innumerable cigarettes,
cursing in brief snarling fury, touched with despair and
futility. His old surly scowl was gone, his old angry mutter; his soft contemptuous laugh, touched with so much
hidden tenderness, had given way to a contained but
savage madness.

During the brief two weeks that Eugene remained at
home before departing again for Pulpit Hill, he shared
with Ben a little room and sleeping porch upstairs. And
the quiet one talked—talked himself from a low fierce

mutter into a howling anathema of bitterness and hate that carried his voice, high and passionate, across all the sleeping world of night and rustling autumn.

"What have you been doing to yourself, you little fool?" he began, looking at the boy's starved ribs. "You look like a scarecrow."

"I'm all right," said Eugene. "I wasn't eating for a while. But I didn't write them," he added proudly. "They thought I couldn't hold out by myself. But I did. I didn't ask for help. And I came home with my own money. See?" He thrust his hand into his pocket and pulled out his soiled roll of banknotes, boastfully displaying it.

"Who wants to see your lousy little money?" Ben yelled furiously. "Fool! You come back, looking like a dead man, as if you'd done something to be proud of. What've you done? What've you done except make a monkey of yourself?"

"I've paid my own way," Eugene cried resentfully, stung and wounded. "That's what I've done."

"Ah-h," said Ben, with an ugly sneer, "you little fool! That's what they've been after! Do you think you've put anything over on them? Do you? Do you think they give a damn whether you die or not, as long as you save them expense? What are you bragging about? Don't brag until you've got something out of them."

Propped on his arm, he smoked deeply, in bitter silence, for a moment. Then more quietly, he continued.

"No, 'Gene. Get it out of them any way you can. Make them give it to you. Beg it, take it, steal it—only get it somehow. If you don't, they'll let it rot. Get it, and get away from them. Go away and don't come back. To hell with them!" he yelled.

Eliza, who had come softly upstairs to put out the lights, and had been standing for a moment outside the door, rapped gently and entered. Clothed in a tattered old sweater and indefinable under-lappings, she stood for a moment with folded hands, peering in on them with a white troubled face.

"Children," she said, pursing her lips reproachfully, and shaking her head, "it's time everyone was in bed. You're keeping the whole house awake with your talk."

"Ah-h," said Ben with an ugly laugh, "to hell with them."

"I'll vow, child!" she said fretfully, "you'll break us up. Have you got that porch light on, too?" Her eyes probed about suspiciously. "What on earth do you mean by burning up all that electricity!"

"Oh, listen to this, won't you?" said Ben, jerking his head upward with a jeering laugh.

"I can't afford to pay all these bills," said Eliza angrily, with a smart shake of her head. "And you needn't think I can. I'm not going to put up with it. It's up to us all to economize."

"Oh, for God's sake!" Ben jeered. "Economize! What for? So you can give it all away to Old Man Doak for one of his lots?"

"Now, you needn't get on your high horse," said Eliza. "You're not the one who has to pay the bills. If you did, you'd laugh out of the other side of your mouth. I don't like any such talk. You've squandered every penny you've earned because you've never known the value of a dollar."

"Ah-h!" he said. "The value of a dollar! By God, I know the value of a dollar better than you do. I've had a little something out of mine, at any rate. What have you had out of yours? I'd like to know that. What the hell's good has it ever been to anyone? Will you tell me that?" he yelled.

"You may sneer all you like," said Eliza sternly, "but

if it hadn't been for your papa and me accumulating a little property, you'd never have had a roof to call your own. And this is the thanks I get for all my drudgery in my old age," she said, bursting into tears. "Ingratitude! Ingratitude!"

"Ingratitude!" he sneered. "What's there to be grateful for? You don't think I'm grateful to you or the old man for anything, do you? What have you ever given me? You let me go to hell from the time I was twelve years old. No one has ever given me a damned nickel since then. Look at your kid here. You've let him run around the country like a crazy man. Did you think enough of him this summer to send him a postcard? Did you know where he was? Did you give a damn, as long as there was fifty cents to be made out of your lousy boarders?"

"Ingratitude!" she whispered huskily, with a boding shake of the head. "A day of reckoning cometh."

"Oh, for God's sake!" he said, with a contemptuous laugh. He smoked for a moment. Then he went on quietly:

"No, Mama. You've done very little to make us grateful to you. The rest of us ran around wild and the kid grew up here among the dope-fiends and streetwalkers. You've pinched every penny and put all you've had into real-estate which has done no one any good. So don't wonder if your kids aren't grateful to you."

"Any son who will talk that way to his mother," said Eliza with rankling bitterness, "is bound to come to a bad end. Wait and see!"

"The hell you say!" he sneered. They stared at each other with hard bitter eyes. He turned away in a moment, scowling with savage annoyance, but stabbed already with fierce regret.

"All right! Go on, for heaven's sake! Leave us alone! I don't want you around!" He lit a cigarette to show his indifference. The lean white fingers trembled, and the flame went out.

"Let's stop it!" said Eugene wearily. "Let's stop it! None of us is going to change! Nothing's going to get any better. We're all going to be the same. We've said all this before. So, for God's sake, let's stop it! Mama, go to bed, please. Let's all go to bed and forget about it." He went to her, and with a strong sense of shame, kissed her.

"Well, good night, son," said Eliza slowly, with gravity. "If I were you I'd put the light out now and turn in. Get a good night's sleep, boy. You mustn't neglect your health."

She kissed him, and went away without another glance at the older boy. He did not look at her. They were parted by hard and bitter strife.

After a moment, when she had gone, Ben said without anger:

"I've had nothing out of life. I've been a failure. I've stayed here with them until I'm done for. My lungs are going: they won't even take a chance on me for the Army. They won't even give the Germans a chance to shoot at me. I've never made good at anything. By God!" he said, in a mounting blaze of passion. "What's it all about? Can you figure it out, 'Gene? Is it really so, or is somebody playing a joke on us? Maybe we're dreaming all this. Do you think so?"

"Yes," said Eugene, "I do. But I wish they'd wake us up." He was silent, brooding over his thin bare body, bent forward on the bed for a moment. "Maybe," he said slowly, "maybe—there's nothing, nobody to wake."

"To hell with it all!" said Ben. "I wish it were over."

Eugene returned to Pulpit Hill in a fever of war excitement. The university had been turned into an armed camp. Young men who were eighteen years old were being admitted into the officers' training corps. But he was not yet eighteen. His birthday was two weeks off. In vain he implored the tolerance of the examining board. What did two weeks matter? Could he get in as soon as his birthday arrived? They told him he could not. What, then, could he do? They told him that he must wait until there was another draft. How long would that be? Only two or three months, they assured him. His wilted hope revived. He chafed impatiently. All was not lost.

By Christmas, with fair luck, he might be eligible for service in khaki: by spring, if God was good, all the proud privileges of trench-lice, mustard gas, spattered brains, punctured lungs, ripped guts, asphyxiation, mud, and gangrene, might be his. Over the rim of the earth he heard the glorious stamp of the feet, the fierce sweet song of the horns. With a tender smile of love for his dear self, he saw himself wearing the eagles of a colonel on his gallant young shoulders. He saw himself as Ace Gant, the falcon of the skies, with 63 Huns to his credit by his nineteenth year. He saw himself walking up the Champs-Élysées, with a handsome powdering of grey hair above his temples, a left forearm of the finest cork, and the luscious young widow of a French marshal at his side. For the first time he saw the romantic charm of mutilation. The perfect and unblemished heroes of his childhood now seemed cheap to him—fit only to illustrate advertisements for collars and toothpaste. He longed for that subtle distinction, that air of having lived and suffered that could only be attained by a wooden leg, a rebuilt nose, or the seared scar of a bullet across his temple.

Meanwhile, he fed voraciously, and drank gallons of water in an effort to increase his poundage. He weighed himself a half-dozen times a day. He even made some effort at systematic exercise: swinging his arms, bending from his hips, and so on.

And he talked about his problem with the professors. Gravely, earnestly, he wrestled with his soul, mouthing with gusto the inspiring jargon of the crusade. For the present, said the professors, was his Place not Here? Did his Conscience tell him that he Had to go? If it did, they said gravely, they would say nothing more. But had he considered the Larger Issues?

"Is not," said the Acting Dean persuasively, "is not this your Sector? Is your own Front Line not here on the campus? Is it not here that you must Go Over The Top? Oh, I know," he went on with a smile of quiet pain, "I know it would be easier to go. I have had to fight that battle myself. But we are all part of the Army now; we are all enlisted in the Service of Liberty. We are all Mobilized for Truth. And each must Do His Bit where it will count for most."

"Yes," said Eugene, with a pale tortured face, "I know. I know it's wrong. But oh, sir—when I think of those murderous beasts, when I think of how they have menaced All that we Hold Dear, when I think of Little Belgium, and then of My Own Mother, My Own Sister——" He turned away, clenching his hands, madly in love with himself.

"Yes, yes," said the Acting Dean gently, "for boys with a spirit like yours it's not easy."

"Oh, sir, it's hard!" cried Eugene passionately. "I tell you it's hard."

"We must endure," said the Dean quietly. "We must be tempered in the fire. The Future of Mankind hangs in the balance."

Deeply stirred they stood together for a moment, drenched in the radiant beauty of their heroic souls.

Eugene was managing editor of the college paper. But, since the editor was enlisted in the corps, the entire work of publication fell to the boy. Everyone was in the Army. With the exception of a few dozen ratty Freshmen, a few cripples, and himself, everyone, it seemed, was in the Army. All of his fraternity brothers, all of his college mates, who had not previously enlisted, and many young men who had never before thought of college, were in the Army. "Pap" Rheinhart, George Graves, Julius Arthur—who had experienced brief and somewhat unfortunate careers at other universities, and a host of young Altamonters who had never known a campus before, were all enlisted now in the Student's Army.

During the first days, in the confusion of the new order, Eugene saw a great deal of them. Then, as the cogs of the machine began to grind more smoothly, and the university was converted into a big army post, with its punctual monotony of drilling, eating, studying, inspection, sleeping, he found himself detached, alone, occupying a position of unique and isolated authority.

He Carried On. He Held High the Torch. He Did His Bit. He was editor, reporter, censor, factotum of the paper. He wrote the news. He wrote the editorials. He seared them with flaming words. He extolled the crusade. He was possessed of the inspiration for murder.

He came and he went as he chose. When the barracks went dark at night, he prowled the campus, contemptuous of the electric flash and the muttered apologies of the officious shavetails. He roomed in the village with a tall cadaver, a gaunt medical student with hollow cheeks and a pigeon-breast, named Heston. Three or four times a week he was driven over the rutted highway to Exeter where, in a little print shop, he drank the good warm smell of ink and steel.

Later, he prowled up the dreary main street of the town as the lights went up, ate at the Greek's, flirted with a few stray furtive women until the place went dead at ten o'clock, and came back through the dark country-side in a public-service car beside a drunken old walrus who drove like a demon, and whose name was "Soak" Young.

October began, and a season of small cold rain. The earth was a sodden reek of mud and rotten leaves. The trees dripped wearily and incessantly. His eighteenth birthday came, and he turned again, with a quivering tension, towards the war.

He got a brief sick letter from his father; a few pages, practical, concrete with her blunt pungent expression, from Eliza:

Daisy has been here with all her tribe. She went home two days ago, leaving Caroline and Richard. They have all been down sick with the flu. We've had a siege of it here. Everyone has had it, and you never know who's going to be next. It seems to get the big strong ones first. Mr. Hanby, the Methodist minister, died last week. Pneumonia set in. He was a fine healthy man in the prime of life. The doctors said he was gone from the start. Helen has been laid up for several days. Says it's her old kidney trouble. They had McGuire in Thursday night. But they can't fool me, no matter what they say. Son, I hope you will never surrender to that awful craving. It has been the curse of my life. Your papa seems to go along about the same as usual. He eats well, and gets lots of sleep. I can't notice any change in him from a year ago. He may be here long after some of the rest of us are under the sod. Ben is still here. He mopes around the house all day and complains of having no appetite. I think he needs to get to work again doing something that will take his mind off himself. There are only a few people left in the house. Mrs. Pert and Miss Newton hang on as usual. The Crosbys have gone back to Miami. If it gets much colder here I'll just pack up and go too. I guess I must be getting old. I can't stand the cold the way I could when I was young. I want you to buy yourself a good warm overcoat before the winter sets in. You must also eat plenty of good substantial food. Don't squander your money but . . .

He heard nothing more for several weeks. Then, one drizzling evening at six o'clock, when he returned to the room that he occupied with Heston, he found a telegram. It read: "Come home at once. Ben has pneumonia. Mother."

VIII

There was no train until the next day. Heston quieted him during the evening with a stiff drink of gin manufactured from alcohol taken from the medical laboratory. Eugene was silent and babbled incoherently by starts: he asked the medical student a hundred questions about the progress and action of the disease.

"If it were double pneumonia she would have said so. Doesn't it seem that way to you? Hey?" he demanded feverishly.

"I should think so," said Heston. He was a kind and quiet boy.

Eugene went to Exeter the next morning to catch the train. All through a dreary grey afternoon it pounded across the sodden state. Then, there was a change and a terrible wait of several hours at a junction. Finally, as dark came, he was being borne again towards the hills.

Within his berth he lay with hot sleepless eyes, staring out at the black mass of the earth, the bulk of the hills. Finally, in the hours after midnight, he dropped into a nervous doze. He was wakened by the clatter of the trucks as they began to enter the Altamont yards. Dazed, half-dressed, he was roused by the grinding halt, and a moment later was looking out through the curtains into the grave faces of Luke and Hugh Barton.

"Ben's very sick," said Hugh Barton.

Eugene pulled on his shoes and dropped to the floor, stuffing his collar and tie into a coat pocket.

"Let's go," he said. "I'm ready."

They went softly down the aisle, amid the long dark snores of the sleepers. As they walked through the empty station towards Hugh Barton's car, Eugene said to the sailor:

"When did you get home, Luke?"

"I came in last night," he said. "I've been here only a few hours."

It was half-past three in the morning. The ugly station settlement lay fixed and horrible, like something in a dream. His strange and sudden return to it heightened his feeling of unreality. In one of the cars lined at the station curbing, the driver lay huddled below his blanket. In the Greek's lunchroom a man sat sprawled face downward on the counter. The lights were dull and weary: a few burned with slow lust in the cheap station-hotels.

Hugh Barton, who had always been a cautious driver, shot away with a savage grinding of gears. They roared townward through the rickety slums at fifty miles an hour.

"I'm afraid B-B-B-Ben is one sick boy," Luke began.

"How did it happen?" Eugene asked. "Tell me."

He had taken influenza, they told Eugene, from one of Daisy's children. He had moped about, ill and feverish, for a day or two, without going to bed.

"In that G-g-g-god-damn cold barn," Luke burst out. "If that boy dies it's because he c-c-c-couldn't keep warm."

"Never mind about that now," Eugene cried irritably, "go on."

Finally he had gone to bed, and Mrs. Pert had nursed him for a day or two.

"She was the only one who d-d-d-did a damn' thing for him," said the sailor. Eliza, at length, had called in Cardiac.

"The d-d-damned old quack," Luke stuttered.

"Never mind! Never mind!" Eugene yelled. "Why dig it up now? Get on with it!"

After a day or two, he had grown apparently convalescent, and Cardiac told him he might get up if he liked. He got up and moped about the house for a day, in a cursing rage, but the next day he lay a-bed, with a high fever. Coker at length had been called in, two days before——

"That's what they should have done at the start," growled Hugh Barton over his wheel.

"Never mind!" screamed Eugene. "Get on with it."

And Ben had been desperately ill, with pneumonia in both lungs, for over a day. The sad prophetic story, a brief and terrible summary of the waste, the tardiness, and the ruin of their lives, silenced them for a moment with its inexorable sense of tragedy. They had nothing to say.

The powerful car roared up into the chill dead Square. The feeling of unreality grew upon the boy. He sought for his life, for the bright lost years, in this mean cramped huddle of brick and stone. "Ben and I, here by the City Hall, the Bank, the grocery store," he thought. "Why here? In Gath or Ispahan. In Corinth or Byzantium. Not here. It is not real."

A moment later, the big car sloped to a halt at the curb, in front of Dixieland. A light burned dimly in the hall, evoking for him chill memories of damp and gloom. A warmer light burned in the parlor, painting the lowered shade of the tall window a warm and mellow orange.

"Ben's in that room upstairs," Luke whispered, "where the light is."

Eugene looked up with cold dry lips to the bleak front room upstairs, with its ugly Victorian bay window. It was next to the sleeping porch where, but three weeks before, Ben had hurled into the darkness his savage curse at life. The light in the sickroom burned grayly, bringing to him its grim vision of struggle and naked terror.

The three men went softly up the walk and entered the house. There was a faint clatter from the kitchen, and voices.

"Papa's in here," said Luke.

Eugene entered the parlor and found Gant seated alone before a bright coal-fire. He looked up dully and vaguely as his son entered.

"Hello, Papa," said Eugene, going to him.

"Hello, son," said Gant. He kissed the boy with his bristling cropped mustache. His thin lip began to tremble petulantly.

"Have you heard about your brother?" he snuffled. "To think that this should be put upon me, old and sick as I am. O Jesus, it's fearful——"

Helen came in from the kitchen.

"Hello, Slats," she said, heartily embracing him. "How are you, honey? He's grown four inches more since he went away," she jeered, sniggering. "Well, 'Gene, cheer up! Don't look so blue. While there's life there's hope. He's not gone yet, you know." She burst into tears, hoarse, unstrung, hysterical.

"To think that this must come upon me," Gant sniffled, responding mechanically to her grief, as he rocked back and forth on his cane and stared into the fire. "Oh, boo-hoo-hoo! What have I done that God should——"

"You shut up!" she cried, turning upon him in a blaze of fury. "Shut your mouth this minute. I don't want to hear any more from you! I've given my life to you! Everything's been done for you, and you'll be here when we're all gone. You're not the one who's sick." Her feeling towards him had, for the moment, gone rancorous and bitter.

"Where's Mama?" Eugene asked.

"She's back in the kitchen," Helen said. "I'd go back and say hello before you see Ben if I were you." In a low brooding tone, she continued: "Well, forget about it. It can't be helped now."

He found Eliza busy over several bright bubbling pots of water on the gas stove. She bustled awkwardly about, and looked surprised and confused when she saw him.

"Why, what on earth, boy! When'd you get in?"

He embraced her. But beneath her matter-of-factness, he saw the terror in her heart: her dull black eyes glinted with bright knives of fear.

"How's Ben, Mama?" he asked quietly.

"Why-y," she pursed her lips reflectively, "I was just saying to Doctor Coker before you came in. 'Look here,' I said. 'I tell you what, I don't believe he's half as bad off as he looks. Now, if only we can hold on till morning, I believe there's going to be a change for the better.'"

"Mama, in heaven's name!" Helen burst out furiously. "How can you bear to talk like that? Don't you know that Ben's condition is critical? Are you never going to wake up?"

Her voice had its old cracked note of hysteria.

"Now, I tell you, son," said Eliza, with a white tremulous smile, "when you go in there to see him, don't make out as if you knew he was sick. If I were you, I'd make a big joke of it all. I'd laugh just as big as you please and say, 'See here, I thought I was coming to see a sick man.

Why, pshaw!' (I'd say) 'there's nothing wrong with you. Half of it's only imagination!'"

"Oh, Mama! for Christ's sake!" said Eugene frantically. "For Christ's sake!"

He turned away, sick at heart, and caught at his throat with his fingers.

Then he went softly upstairs with Luke and Helen, approaching the sickroom with a shriveled heart and limbs which had gone cold and bloodless. They paused for a moment, whispering, before he entered. The wretched conspiracy in the face of death filled him with horror.

"N-n-n-now, I wouldn't stay but a m-m-m-minute," whispered Luke. "It m-m-might make him nervous."

Eugene, bracing himself, followed Helen blindly into the room.

"Look who's come to see you," her voice came heartily. "It's Highpockets."

For a moment Eugene could see nothing, for dizziness and fear. Then, in the grey shaded light of the room, he descried Bessie Gant, the nurse, and the long yellow skull's-head of Coker, smiling wearily at him, with big stained teeth, over a long chewed cigar. Then, under the terrible light which fell directly and brutally upon the bed alone, he saw Ben. And in that moment of searing recognition he saw, what they had all seen, that Ben was dying.

Ben's long thin body lay three-quarters covered by the bedding; its gaunt outline was bitterly twisted below the covers, in an attitude of struggle and torture. It seemed not to belong to him, it was somehow distorted and detached as if it belonged to a beheaded criminal. And the sallow yellow of his face had turned grey: out of this granite tint of death, lit by two red flags of fever, the stiff black furze of a three-day beard was growing. The beard was somehow horrible; it recalled the corrupt vitality of hair, which can grow from a rotting corpse. And Ben's thin lips were lifted, in a constant grimace of torture and strangulation, above his white somehow dead-looking teeth, as inch by inch he gasped a thread of air into his lungs.

And the sound of this gasping—loud, hoarse, rapid, unbelievable, filling the room, and orchestrating every moment in it—gave to the scene its final note of horror.

Ben lay upon the bed below them, drenched in light, like some enormous insect on a naturalist's table, fighting, while they looked at him, to save with his poor wasted body the life that no one could save for him. It was monstrous, brutal.

As Eugene approached, Ben's fear-bright eyes rested upon the younger brother for the first time and bodilessly, without support, he lifted his tortured lungs from the pillow, seizing the boy's wrist fiercely in the hot white circle of his hands, and gasping in strong terror like a child: "Why have you come? Why have you come home, 'Gene?"

The boy stood white and dumb for a moment, while swarming pity and horror rose in him.

"They gave us a vacation, Ben," he said presently. "They had to close down on account of the flu."

Then he turned away suddenly into the black murk, sick with his poor lie, and unable longer to face the fear in Ben's grey eyes.

"All right, 'Gene," said Bessie Gant, with an air of authority. "Get out of here—you and Helen both. I've got one crazy Gant to look after already. I don't want two more in here." She spoke harshly, with an unpleasant laugh.

She was a thin woman of thirty-eight years, the wife of Gant's nephew, Gilbert. She was of mountain stock: she was coarse, hard, and vulgar, with little pity in her, and a cold lust for the miseries of sickness and death. These inhumanities she cloaked with her professionalism, saying:

"If I gave way to my feelings, where would the patient be?"

When they got out into the hall again, Eugene said angrily to Helen:

"Why have you got that death's-head here? How can he get well, with her around? I don't like her!"

"Say what you like—she's a good nurse." Then, in a low voice, she said: "What do you think?"

He turned away, with a convulsive gesture. She burst into tears, and seized his hand.

Luke was teetering about restlessly, breathing stertorously and smoking a cigarette, and Eliza, working her lips, stood with an attentive ear cocked to the door of the sickroom. She was holding a useless kettle of hot water.

"Huh? Hah? What say?" asked Eliza, before anyone had said anything. "How is he?" Her eyes darted about at them.

"Get away! Get away! Get away!" Eugene muttered savagely. His voice rose. "Can't you get away?"

He was infuriated by the sailor's loud nervous breathing, his large awkward feet. He was angered still more by Eliza's useless kettle, her futile hovering, her "huh?" and "hah?"

"Can't you see he's fighting for his breath? Do you want to strangle him? It's messy! Messy! Do you hear?" His voice rose again.

The ugliness and discomfort of the death choked him; and the swarming family, whispering outside the door, pottering uselessly around, feeding with its terrible hunger for death on Ben's strangulation, made him mad with alternate fits of rage and pity.

Indecisively, after a moment, they went downstairs, still listening for sounds in the sickroom.

"Well, I tell you," Eliza began hopefully. "I have a feeling, I don't know what you'd call it——" She looked about awkwardly and found herself deserted. Then she went back to her boiling pots and pans.

Helen, with contorted face, drew him aside, and spoke to him in whispered hysteria, in the front hall.

"Did you see that sweater she's wearing? Did you see it? It's filthy!" Her voice sank to a brooding whisper. "Did you know that he can't bear to look at her? She came into the room yesterday, and he grew perfectly sick. He turned his head away and said 'Oh, Helen, for God's sake, take her out of here.' You hear that, don't you? Do you hear? He can't stand to have her come near him. He doesn't want her in the room."

"Stop! Stop! For God's sake, stop!" Eugene said, clawing at his throat.

The girl was for the moment insane with hatred and hysteria.

"It may be a terrible thing to say, but if he dies I shall hate her. Do you think I can forget the way she's acted? Do you?" Her voice rose almost to a scream. "She's let him die here before her very eyes. Why, only day before yesterday, when his temperature was 104, she was talking to Old Doctor Doak about a lot. Did you know that?"

"Forget about it!" he said frantically. "She'll always be like that! It's not her fault. Can't you see that? O God, how horrible! How horrible!"

"Poor old Mama!" said Helen, beginning to weep. "She'll never get over this. She's scared to death! Did you see her eyes? She knows, of course she knows!"

Then suddenly, with mad brooding face, she said:

"Sometimes I think I hate her! I really think I hate her." She plucked at her large chin, absently. "Well, we mustn't talk like this," she said. "It's not right. Cheer up. We're all tired and nervous. I believe he's going to get all right yet."

Day came grey and chill, with a drear reek of murk and fog. Eliza bustled about eagerly, pathetically busy, preparing breakfast. Once she hurried awkwardly upstairs with a kettle of water, and stood for a second at the door as Bessie Gant opened it, peering in at the terrible bed, with her white puckered face. Bessie Gant blocked her further entrance, and closed the door rudely. Eliza went away making flustered apologies.

For what the girl had said was true, and Eliza knew it. She was not wanted in the sickroom; the dying boy did not want to see her. She had seen him turn his head wearily away when she had gone in. Behind her white face dwelt this horror, but she made no confession, no complaint. She bustled around doing useless things with an eager matter-of-factness. And Eugene, choked with exasperation at one moment, because of her heavy optimism, was blind with pity the next when he saw the terrible fear and pain in her dull black eyes. He rushed towards her suddenly, as she stood above the hot stove, and seized her rough worn hand, kissing it and babbling helplessly.

"Oh, Mama! Mama! It's all right! It's all right! It's all right."

And Eliza, stripped suddenly of her pretenses, clung to him, burying her white face in his coat sleeve, weeping bitterly, helplessly, grievously, for the sad waste of the irrevocable years—the immortal hours of love that might never be relived, the great evil of forgetfulness and indifference that could never be righted now. Like a child she was grateful for his caress, and his heart twisted in him like a wild and broken thing, and he kept mumbling:

"It's all right! It's all right! It's all right!"—knowing that it was not, could never be, all right.

"If I had known. Child, if I had known," she wept, as she had wept long before at Grover's death.

"Brace up!" he said. "He'll pull through yet. The worst is over."

"Well, I tell you," said Eliza, drying her eyes at once, "I believe it is. I believe he passed the turning-point last night. I was saying to Bessie——"

The light grew. Day came, bringing hope. They sat down to breakfast in the kitchen, drawing encouragement from every scrap of cheer doctor or nurse would give them. Coker departed, noncommittally optimistic. Bessie Gant came down to breakfast and was professionally encouraging.

"If I can keep his damn family out of the room, he may have some chance of getting well."

They laughed hysterically, gratefully, pleased with the woman's abuse.

"How is he this morning?" said Eliza. "Do you notice any improvement?"

"His temperature is lower, if that's what you mean."

They knew that a lower temperature in the morning was a fact of no great significance, but they took nourishment from it: their diseased emotion fed upon it—they had soared in a moment to a peak of hopefulness.

"And he's got a good heart," said Bessie Gant. "If that holds out, and he keeps fighting, he'll pull through."

"D-d-don't worry about his f-f-fighting," said Luke, in a rush of eulogy. "That b-b-boy'll fight as long as he's g-g-got a breath left in him."

"Why, yes," Eliza began, "I remember when he was a child of seven—I know I was standing on the porch one day—the reason I remember is Old Mr. Buckner had just come by with some butter and eggs your papa had——"

"O my God!" groaned Helen, with a loose grin. "Now we'll get it."

"Whah—whah!" Luke chortled crazily, prodding Eliza in the ribs.

"I'll vow, boy!" said Eliza angrily. "You act like an idiot. I'd be ashamed!"

"Whah—whah—whah!"

Helen sniggered, nudging Eugene.

"Isn't he crazy, though? Tuh-tuh-tuh-tuh-tuh." Then, with wet eyes, she drew Eugene roughly into her big bony embrace.

"Poor old 'Gene. You always got on together, didn't you? You'll feel it more than any of us."

"He's not b-b-buried yet," Luke cried heartily. "That boy may be here when the rest of us are pushing d-d-daisies."

"Where's Mrs. Pert?" said Eugene. "Is she in the house?"

A strained and bitter silence fell upon them.

"I ordered her out," said Eliza grimly, after a moment. "I told her exactly what she was—a whore." She spoke with the old stern judiciousness, but in a moment her face began to work and she burst into tears. "If it hadn't been for that woman I believe he'd be well and strong today. I'll vow I do!"

"Mama, in heaven's name!" Helen burst out furiously. "How dare you say a thing like that? She was the only friend he had: when he was taken sick she nursed him hand and foot. Why, the idea! The idea!" she panted in her indignation. "If it hadn't been for Mrs. Pert he'd have been dead by now. Nobody else did anything for him. You were willing enough, I notice, to keep her here and take her money until he got sick. No, sir!" she declared with emphasis. "Personally, I like her. I'm not going to cut her now."

"It's a d-d-d-damn shame!" said Luke, stanch to his goddess. "If it hadn't been for Mrs. P-P-P-Pert and you, Ben would be S. O. L. Nobody else around here gave a damn. If he d-d-d-dies, it's because he didn't get the proper care when it would have done him some good. There's always been too d-d-damn much thought of saving a nickel, and too d-d-damn little about flesh and blood!"

"Well, forget about it!" said Helen wearily. "There's one thing sure: I've done everything I could. I haven't been to bed for two days. Whatever happens, I'll have no regrets on that score." Her voice was filled with a brooding ugly satisfaction.

"I know you haven't! I know that!" The sailor turned to Eugene in his excitement, gesticulating. "That g-g-girl's worked her fingers to the bone. If it hadn't been for her——" His eyes got wet; he turned his head away and blew his nose.

"Oh, for Christ's sake!" Eugene yelled, springing up from the table. "Stop it, won't you! Let's wait till later."

In this way, the terrible hours of the morning lengthened out, while they spent themselves trying to escape from the tragic net of frustration and loss in which they were caught. Their spirits soared to brief moments of insane joy and exultancy, and plunged into black pits of despair and hysteria. Eliza alone seemed consistently hopeful. Trembling with exacerbated nerves, the sailor and Eugene paced the lower hall, smoking incessant cigarettes, bristling as they approached each other, ironically polite when their bodies touched. Gant dozed in the parlor or in his own room, waking and sleeping by starts, moaning petulantly, detached, vaguely aware only of the meaning of events, and resentful because of the sudden indifference to him. Helen went in and out of the sickroom constantly, dominating the dying boy by the power of her vitality, infusing him with moments of hope and confidence. But when she came out, her hearty cheerfulness was supplanted by the strained blur of hysteria; she wept, laughed, brooded, loved, and hated by turns.

Eliza went only once into the room. She intruded with a hot-water bag, timidly, awkwardly, like a child, devouring Ben's face with her dull black eyes. But when above the loud labor of his breath his bright eyes rested on her, his clawed white fingers tightened their grip in the sheets, and he gasped strongly, as if in terror:

"Get out! Out! Don't want you."

Eliza left the room. As she walked she stumbled a little, as if her feet were numb and dead. Her white face had an ashen tinge, and her dull eyes had grown bright and staring. As the door closed behind her, she leaned against the wall and put one hand across her face. Then, in a moment, she went down to her pots again.

Frantically, angrily, with twitching limbs they demanded calm and steady nerves from one another; they insisted that they keep away from the sickroom——but, as if drawn by some terrible magnet, they found themselves again and again outside the door, listening, on tiptoe, with caught breath, with an insatiate thirst for horror, to the hoarse noise of his gasping as he strove to force air down into his strangled and cemented lungs. And eagerly, jealously, they sought entrance to the room, waiting their turn for carrying water, towels, supplies.

Mrs. Pert, from her refuge in the boardinghouse across the street, called Helen on the phone each half-hour, and the girl talked to her while Eliza came from the kitchen into the hall, and stood, hands folded, lips pursed, with eyes that sparkled with her hate.

The girl cried and laughed as she talked.

"Well . . . that's all right, Fatty. . . . You know how I feel about it. . . . I've always said that if he had one true friend in the world, it's you . . . and don't think we're *all* ungrateful for what you've done. . . ."

During the pauses, Eugene could hear the voice of the other woman across the wires, sobbing.

And Eliza said, grimly: "If she calls up again you let me talk to her. I'll fix her!"

"Good heavens, Mama!" Helen cried angrily. "You've done enough already. You drove her out of the house when she'd done more for him than all his family put together." Her big strained features worked convulsively. "Why, it's ridiculous!"

Within Eugene, as he paced restlessly up and down the hall or prowled through the house a-search for some entrance he had never found, a bright and stricken thing kept twisting about like a trapped bird. This bright thing, the core of him, his Stranger, kept twisting its head about, unable to look at horror, until at length it gazed steadfastly, as if under a dreadful hypnosis, into the eyes of death and darkness. And his soul plunged downward, drowning in that deep pit: he felt that he could never again escape from this smothering flood of pain and ugliness, from the eclipsing horror and pity of it all. And as he walked, he twisted his own neck about, and beat the air with his arm like a wing, as if he had received a blow in his kidneys. He felt that he might be clean and free if he could only escape into a single burning passion—hard, and hot, and glittering —of love, hatred, terror, or disgust. But he was caught, he was strangling, in the web of futility—there was no moment of hate that was not touched by a dozen shafts of pity: impotently, he wanted to seize them, cuff them, shake them, as one might a trying brat, and at the same time to caress them, love them, comfort them.

As he thought of the dying boy upstairs, the messy ugliness of it—as they stood whimpering by while he strangled—choked him with fury and horror. The old fantasy of his childhood came back to him: he remembered his hatred of the semi-private bathroom, his messy discomfort while he sat at stool and stared at the tub filled with dirty wash, sloppily puffed and ballooned by cold grey soapy water. He thought of this as Ben lay dying.

Their hopes revived strongly in the forenoon when word came to them that the patient's temperature was lower, his pulse stronger, the congestion of the lungs slightly relieved. But at one o'clock, after a fit of coughing, he grew delirious, his temperature mounted, he had increasing difficulty in getting his breath. Eugene and Luke raced to Wood's pharmacy in Hugh Barton's car, for an oxygen tank. When they returned, Ben had almost choked to death.

Quickly they carried the tank into the room, and placed it near his head. Bessie Gant seized the cone, and started to put it over Ben's mouth, commanding him to breathe it in. He fought it away tigerishly: curtly the nurse commanded Eugene to seize his hands.

Eugene gripped Ben's hot wrists: his heart turned rotten. Ben rose wildly from his pillows, wrenching like a child to get his hands free, gasping horribly, his eyes wild with terror:

"No! No! 'Gene! 'Gene! No! No!"

Eugene caved in, releasing him and turning away, white-faced, from the accusing fear of the bright dying eyes. Others held him: he was given temporary relief. Then he became delirious again.

By four o'clock it was apparent that death was near. Ben had brief periods of consciousness, unconsciousness, and delirium—but most of the time he was delirious. His breathing was easier, he hummed snatches of popular songs, some old and forgotten, called up now from the lost and secret adyts of his childhood; but always he returned, in his quiet humming voice, to a popular song of wartime—cheap, sentimental, but now tragically moving: "Just a Baby's Prayer at Twilight":

> . . . when lights are low.
> Poor baby's years

Helen entered the darkening room.

> Are filled with tears.

The fear had gone out of his eyes: above his gasping he looked gravely at her, scowling, with the old puzzled child's stare. Then, in a moment of fluttering consciousness, he recognized her. He grinned beautifully, with the thin swift flicker of his mouth.

"Hello, Helen! It's Helen!" he cried eagerly.

She came from the room with a writhen and contorted face, holding the sobs that shook her until she was halfway down the stairs.

As darkness came upon the grey wet day, the family gathered in the parlor, in the last terrible congress before death, silent, waiting. Gant rocked petulantly, spitting into the fire, making a weak whining moan from time to time. One by one, at intervals, they left the room, mounting the stairs softly, and listening outside the door of the sickroom. And they heard Ben, as, with

incessant humming repetition, like a child, he sang his
song:

> There's a mother there at twilight
> Who's glad to know——

Eliza sat stolidly, hands folded, before the parlor
fire. Her dead white face had a curious carven look; the
inflexible solidity of madness.

"Well," she said at length, slowly, "you never know.
Perhaps this is the crisis. Perhaps——" Her face hardened into granite again. She said no more.

Coker came in and went at once, without speaking, to
the sickroom. Shortly before nine o'clock Bessie Gant
came down.

"All right," she said quietly. "You had all better come
up now. This is the end."

Eliza got up and marched out of the room with a
stolid face. Helen followed her: she was panting with
hysteria, and had begun to wring her big hands.

"Now, get hold of yourself, Helen," said Bessie Gant
warningly. "This is no time to let yourself go."

Eliza went steadily upstairs, making no noise. But, as
she neared the room, she paused, as if listening for
sounds within. Faintly, in the silence, they heard Ben's
song. And suddenly, casting away all pretense, Eliza
staggered, and fell against the wall, turning her face into
her hand, with a terrible wrenched cry:

"O God! If I had known! If I had known!"

Then, weeping with bitter unrestraint, with the contorted and ugly grimace of sorrow, mother and daughter
embraced each other. In a moment they composed
themselves, and quietly entered the room.

Eugene and Luke pulled Gant to his feet and supported him up the stairs. He sprawled upon them,
moaning in long quivering exhalations.

"Mer-ci-ful God! That I should have to bear this in my old age. That I should——"

"Papa! For God's sake!" Eugene cried sharply. "Pull yourself together! It's Ben who's dying—not us! Let's try to behave decently to him for once."

This served to quiet Gant for a moment. But as he entered the room, and saw Ben lying in the semiconscious coma that precedes death, the fear of his own death overcame him, and he began to moan again. They seated him in a chair, at the foot of the bed, and he rocked back and forth, weeping:

"O Jesus! I can't bear it! Why must you put this upon me? I'm old and sick, and I don't know where the money's to come from. How are we ever going to face this fearful and croo-el winter? It'll cost a thousand dollars before we're through burying him, and I don't know where the money's to come from." He wept affectedly with sniffling sobs.

"Hush! hush!" cried Helen, rushing at him. In her furious anger, she seized him and shook him. "You damned old man, you, I could kill you! How dare you talk like that when your son's dying? I've wasted six years of my life nursing you, and you'll be the last one to go!" In her blazing anger, she turned accusingly on Eliza:

"You've done this to him. You're the one that's responsible. If you hadn't pinched every penny he'd never have been like this. Yes, and Ben would be here, too!" She panted for breath for a moment. Eliza made no answer. She did not hear her.

"After this, I'm through! I've been looking for you to die—and Ben's the one who has to go." Her voice rose to a scream of exasperation. She shook Gant again. "Never again! Do you hear that, you selfish old man?

You've had everything—Ben's had nothing. And now he's the one to go. I hate you!"

"Helen! Helen!" said Bessie Gant quietly. "Remember where you are."

"Yes, that means a lot to us," Eugene muttered bitterly.

Then, over the ugly clamor of their dissension, over the rasp and snarl of their nerves, they heard the low mutter of Ben's expiring breath. The light had been re-shaded: he lay, like his own shadow, in all his fierce grey lonely beauty. And as they looked and saw his bright eyes already blurred with death, and saw the feeble beating flutter of his poor thin breast, the strange wonder, the dark rich miracle of his life surged over them its enormous loveliness. They grew quiet and calm, they plunged below all the splintered wreckage of their lives, they drew together in a superb communion of love and valiance, beyond horror and confusion, beyond death.

And Eugene's eyes grew blind with love and wonder: an enormous organ-music sounded in his heart, he possessed them for a moment, he was a part of their loveliness, his life soared magnificently out of the slough of pain and ugliness. He thought:

"That was not all! That really was not all!"

Helen turned quietly to Coker, who was standing in shadow by the window, chewing upon his long unlighted cigar.

"Is there nothing more you can do? Have you tried everything? I mean—*everything?*"

Her voice was prayerful and low. Coker turned towards her slowly, taking the cigar between his big stained fingers. Then, gently, with his weary yellow smile, he answered: "Everything. Not all the king's horses, not all the doctors and nurses in the world, can help him now."

"How long have you known this?" she said.

"For two days," he answered. "From the beginning." He was silent for a moment. "For ten years!" he went on with growing energy. "Since I first saw him, at three in the morning, in the Greasy Spoon, with a doughnut in one hand and a cigarette in the other. My dear, dear girl," he said gently as she tried to speak, "we can't turn back the days that have gone. We can't turn life back to the hours when our lungs were sound, our blood hot, our bodies young. We are a flash of fire—a brain, a heart, a spirit. And we are three-cents-worth of lime and iron—which we cannot get back."

He picked up his greasy black slouch hat, and jammed it carelessly upon his head. Then he fumbled for a match and lit the chewed cigar.

"Has everything been done?" she said again. "I want to know! Is there anything left worth trying?"

He made a weary gesture of his arms.

"My dear girl!" he said. "He's drowning! Drowning!"

She stood frozen with the horror of his pronouncement.

Coker looked for a moment more at the grey twisted shadow on the bed. Then, quietly, sadly, with tenderness and tired wonder, he said: "Old Ben. When shall we see *his* like again?"

Then he went quietly out, the long cigar clamped firmly in his mouth.

In a moment, Bessie Gant, breaking harshly in upon their silence with ugly and triumphant matter-of-factness, said: "Well, it will be a relief to get this over. I'd rather be called into forty outside cases than one in which any of these damn relations are concerned. I'm dead for sleep."

Helen turned quietly upon her.

"Leave the room!" she said. "This is our affair now. We have the right to be left alone."

Surprised, Bessie Gant stared at her for a moment with an angry, resentful face. Then she left the room.

The only sound in the room now was the low rattling mutter of Ben's breath. He no longer gasped; he no longer gave signs of consciousness or struggle. His eyes were almost closed; their grey flicker was dulled, coated with the sheen of insensibility and death. He lay quietly upon his back, very straight, without sign of pain, and with a curious upturned thrust of his sharp thin face. His mouth was firmly shut. Already, save for the feeble mutter of his breath, he seemed to be dead—he seemed detached, no part of the ugly mechanism of that sound which came to remind them of the terrible chemistry of flesh, to mock at illusion, at all belief in the strange passage and continuance of life.

He was dead, save for the slow running down of the worn-out machine, save for that dreadful mutter within him of which he was no part. He was dead.

But in their enormous silence wonder grew. They remembered the strange flitting loneliness of his life, they thought of a thousand forgotten acts and moments—and always there was something that now seemed unearthly and strange: he walked through their lives like a shadow—they looked now upon his grey deserted shell with a thrill of awful recognition, as one who remembers a forgotten and enchanted word, or as men who look upon a corpse and see for the first time a departed god.

Luke, who had been standing at the foot of the bed, now turned to Eugene nervously, stammering in an unreal whisper of wonder and disbelief:

"I g-g-g-guess Ben's gone."

Gant had grown very quiet: he sat in the darkness at the foot of the bed, leaning forward upon his cane, escaped from the revery of his own approaching death, into the wasteland of the past, blazing back sadly and poignantly the trail across the lost years that led to the birth of his strange son.

Helen sat facing the bed, in the darkness near the windows. Her eyes rested not on Ben but on her mother's face. All by unspoken consent stood back in the shadows and let Eliza repossess the flesh to which she had given life.

And Eliza, now that he could deny her no longer, now that his fierce bright eyes could no longer turn from her in pain and aversion, sat near his head beside him, clutching his cold hand between her rough worn palms.

She did not seem conscious of the life around her. She seemed under a powerful hypnosis: she sat very stiff and erect in her chair, her white face set stonily, her dull black eyes fixed upon the grey cold face.

They sat waiting. Midnight came. A cock crew. Eugene went quietly to a window and stood looking out. The great beast of night prowled softly about the house. The walls, the windows seemed to bend inward from the thrusting pressure of the dark. The low noise in the wasted body seemed almost to have stopped. It came infrequently, almost inaudibly, with a faint fluttering respiration.

Helen made a sign to Gant and Luke. They rose and went quietly out. At the door she paused, and beckoned to Eugene. He went to her.

"You stay here with her," she said. "You're her youngest. When it's over come and tell us."

He nodded, and closed the door behind her. When they had gone, he waited, listening for a moment. Then he went to where Eliza was sitting. He bent over her.

"Mama!" he whispered. "Mama!"

She gave no sign that she had heard him. Her face did not move; she did not turn her eyes from their fixed stare.

"Mama!" he said more loudly. "Mama!"

He touched her. She made no response.

"Mama! Mama!"

She sat there stiffly and primly like a little child.

Swarming pity rose in him. Gently, desperately, he tried to detach her fingers from Ben's hand. Her rough clasp on the cold hand tightened. Then, slowly, stonily, from right to left, without expression, she shook her head.

He fell back, beaten, weeping, before that implacable gesture. Suddenly, with horror, he saw that she was watching her own death, that the unloosening grip of her hand on Ben's hand was an act of union with her own flesh, that, for her, Ben was not dying—but that a part of *her*, of *her* life, *her* blood, *her* body, was dying. Part of her, the younger, the lovelier, the better part, coined in her flesh, borne and nourished and begun with so much pain there twenty-six years before, and forgotten since, was dying.

Eugene stumbled to the other side of the bed and fell upon his knees. He began to pray. He did not believe in God, nor in Heaven or Hell, but he was afraid they might be true. He did not believe in angels with soft faces and bright wings, but he believed in the dark spirits that hovered above the heads of lonely men. He did not believe in devils or angels, but he believed in Ben's bright demon to whom he had seen him speak so many times.

Eugene did not believe in these things, but he was afraid they might be true. He was afraid that Ben would get lost again. He felt that no one but he could pray for Ben now: that the dark union of their spirits made only *his* prayers valid. All that he had read in books, all the tranquil wisdom he had professed so glibly in his philosophy course, and the great names of Plato and Plotinus, of Spinoza and Immanuel Kant, of Hegel and Descartes, left him now, under the mastering surge of his wild Celtic superstition. He felt that he must pray frantically as long as the little ebbing flicker of breath remained in his brother's body.

So, with insane sing-song repetition, he began to mutter over and over again: "Whoever You Are, be good to Ben tonight. Show him the way . . . Whoever You Are, be good to Ben tonight. Show him the way . . ." He lost count of the minutes, the hours: he heard only the feeble rattle of dying breath, and his wild synchronic prayer.

Light faded from his brain, and consciousness. Fatigue and powerful nervous depletion conquered him. He sprawled out on the floor, with his arms pillowed on the bed, muttering drowsily. Eliza, unmoving, sat across the bed, holding Ben's hand. Eugene, mumbling, sank into an uneasy sleep.

He awoke suddenly, conscious that he had slept, with a sharp quickening of horror. He was afraid that the little fluttering breath had now ceased entirely, that the effect of his prayer was lost. The body on the bed was almost rigid: there was no sound. Then, unevenly, without rhythm, there was a faint mutter of breath. He knew it was the end. He rose quickly and ran to the door. Across the hall, in a cold bedroom, on two wide beds, Gant, Luke, and Helen lay exhausted.

"Come," cried Eugene. "He's going now."

They came quickly into the room. Eliza sat unmoving, oblivious of them. As they entered the room, they heard, like a faint expiring sigh, the final movement of breath.

The rattling in the wasted body, which seemed for hours to have given over to death all of life that is worth saving, had now ceased. The body appeared to grow rigid before them. Slowly, after a moment, Eliza withdrew her hands. But suddenly, marvelously, as if his resurrection and rebirth had come upon him, Ben drew upon the air in a long and powerful respiration; his grey eyes opened. Filled with a terrible vision of all life in the one moment, he seemed to rise forward bodilessly from his pillows without support—a flame, a light, a glory—joined at length in death to the dark spirit who had brooded upon each footstep of his lonely adventure on earth; and, casting the fierce sword of his glance with utter and final comprehension upon the room haunted with its grey pageantry of cheap loves and dull consciences and on all those uncertain mummers of waste and confusion fading now from the bright window of his eyes, he passed instantly, scornful and unafraid, as he had lived, into the shades of death.

We can believe in the nothingness of life, we can believe in the nothingness of death and of life after death —but who can believe in the nothingness of Ben? Like Apollo, who did his penance to the high god in the sad house of King Admetus, he came, a god with broken feet, into the grey hovel of this world. And he lived here a stranger, trying to recapture the music of the lost world, trying to recall the great forgotten language, the lost faces, the stone, the leaf, the door.

O Artemidorus, farewell!

Of Time and the River

JASON'S VOYAGE

Editor's Preface

EUGENE GANT goes to Harvard, and in Boston he starts his first restless exploration of the metropolis, which, says Wolfe, had stunned him with its huge and instant shock.

He is invited to join Professor Hatcher's celebrated course for dramatists, and there he meets Francis Starwick—"that rare and tragically gifted creature who was one of the most extraordinary figures of his generation." Starwick is not altogether convincing in this role —he seems more like any number of young Middle Westerners who attempt to forget their origins by acquiring an accent. Yet, to the eager provincial, he may be the personification of Eastern grace and sophistication.

However, Oliver Gant has been dying of cancer. He is a big and enduring sort of man and takes a long time to die—the pages that deal with him are among the most memorable in Wolfe's work. Afterward Eugene moves on to the School for Utility Cultures and there, among his students, he first meets his "little Jews"— those Jews who become the bane and the conscience of his days, and the final test of his stature. Just as these lower New York City scenes are the prelude to Wolfe's later portraits of upper-class New York society, so the Hudson Valley aristocrats of *Of Time and the River*—

Joel and Rosalind Pierce—lead into the European adventures.

The conflict of Europe and America—of East and West—is actually the unifying theme of the novel, and the alternation of rich and poor stratas of society in the novel is the structural device Wolfe uses to build up this central theme. Furthermore, both the increasing sharpness of Wolfe's view of experience and the brilliance with which these areas of experience are described make *Of Time and the River* his best work. If anything is the matter with it, it is only that there is a good deal of a very good thing.

The selection that follows is from Book V of the novel. It deals with the climax of Eugene Gant's European travels—his final recognition of Starwick's nature, and his return, from this Eastern eminence, to the American earth.

The legend Wolfe uses here is that of Jason's Voyage, but it could just as well have been the Ascent of Icarus.

OF TIME AND THE RIVER

Jason's Voyage

I

ABOUT four o'clock on the afternoon of New Year's Eve, 1924, as Eugene was entering the Louvre, he met Starwick. Starwick was elegantly dressed, as always, in casual, beautifully tailored, brown tweed garments. He still carried a cane and twirled it indolently as he came down the steps. He was the same old picture of bored, languorous, almost feminine grace, but instead of a shirt he was wearing a Russian blouse of soft blue wool which snuggled around his neck in voluptuous folds and had a kind of diamond-shaped design of crimson threads along the band.

For a moment, halfway down the grey stone steps, worn and hollowed as ancient European steps are worn and hollowed by the soft incessant eternity of feet, as the other people thronged past him, he paused, his pleasant ruddy face and cleft chin turned vaguely up towards those soft skies of time, already fading swiftly with the early wintry light.

As always, Frank looked magnificent, and with his Russian blouse, and the expression of inscrutable sorrow on his face, more mysterious and romantic than ever. Even in this foreign scene, he seemed to take possession of his surroundings with a lordly air. So far from looking like an alien, a foreigner, or a common tourist, Frank seemed to belong to the scene more than anybody there.

237

It was as if something very frail and rare and exquisite and weary of the world—Alfred de Musset or George Moore, or the young Oscar, or Verlaine—had just come out of the Louvre, and it all seemed to belong to him.

The enormous central court of the Louvre, the soaring wings of that tremendous and graceful monument, the planned vistas of the Tuileries before him, fading into the mist-hazed air and the soft greying light—the whole tremendous scene, with all its space and strength and hauntingly aerial grace—at once as strong as ancient battlemented time, and as delicate and haunting as music on a spinet—swept together in a harmonious movement of spaciousness and majesty and graceful loveliness to form a background for the glamorous personality of Francis Starwick.

Even as he stood there, the rare and solitary distinction of his person was evident as it had never been before. People were streaming out of the museum and down the steps past him—for already it was the closing hour—and as they went by they all looked common, shabby, and drearily prosaic by comparison. A middle-aged Frenchman of the middle class, a chubby, ruddy figure of a man, dressed in cloth of the hard, ugly, ill-cut black that this class of Frenchmen wears, came by quickly with his wife, his daughter, and his son. The man was driven along by the incessant, hot sugar of that energy which drives the race and which, with its unvaried repetition of oaths, ejaculations, denials, affirmations, and exactitudes, lavished at every minute upon the most trivial episodes of life, can become more drearily tedious than the most banal monotone. Compared with Starwick, his figure was thick, blunt, common in its clumsy shapelessness, and his wife had the same common, swarthy, blunted look. An American came down the steps with his wife: he was neatly dressed in the ugly light-greyish clothes that so many Americans wear, his wife was also neatly turned out with the tedious and metallic stylishness of American apparel. They had the naked, inept, and uneasy look of tourists, everything about them seemed troubled and alien to the scene, even to the breezy quality of the air, and the soft thick skies about them. When they had descended the steps, they paused a moment in a worried and undecided way, the man pulled at his watch and peered at it with his meager prognathous face, and then said nasally:

"Well, we told them we'd be there at four-thirty. It's about that now."

All of these people, young and old, French, American, or of whatever nationality, looked dreary, dull and common, and uneasily out of place, when compared with Starwick.

After a moment's shock of stunned surprise, a drunken surge of impossible joy, Eugene ran towards him shouting, "Frank!"

Starwick turned, with a startled look upon his face: in a moment the two young men were shaking hands frantically, almost hugging each other in their excitement, both blurting out at once a torrent of words which neither heard. Finally, when they had grown quieter, Eugene found himself saying:

"But where the hell have you been, Frank? I wrote you twice: didn't you get any of my letters?—what happened to you?—where were you?—did you go down to the South of France to stay with Egan, as you said you would?"

"Ace," said Starwick—his voice had the same, strangely mannered, unearthly quality it had always had, only it was more mysterious and secretive than ever before—"Ace, I have been there."

"But why——?" the other began, "why aren't you
——?" He paused, looking at Starwick with a startled
glance. "What happened, Frank?"

For, by his few quiet and noncommittal words, Starwick had managed to convey perfectly the sense of
sorrow and tragedy—of a grief so great it could not be
spoken, a hurt so deep it could not be told. His whole
personality was now pervaded mysteriously by this air
of quiet, speechless, and incommunicable sorrow; he
looked at the other youth with the eyes of Lazarus returned from the tomb, and that glance said more eloquently than any words could ever do that he now knew
and understood things which no other mortal man could
ever know or understand.

"I should prefer not to talk about it," he said very
quietly, and by these words Eugene understood that
some tragic and unutterable event had now irrevocably
sundered Starwick from Egan—though what that event
might be, he saw it was not given him to know.

Immediately, however, in his old, casual, and engaging fashion, speaking between lips that barely moved,
Starwick said:

"Look! What are you doing now? Is there any place
you have to go?"

"No. I was just going in here. But I suppose it's too
late now, anyway."

At this moment, indeed, they could hear the bells ringing in the museum, and the voices of the guards, crying
impatiently:

"On ferme! On ferme, messieurs!"—and the people
began to pour out in streams.

"Ace," said Starwick, "they're closing now. Besides,"
he added wearily, "I shouldn't think it would matter to
you, anyway. . . . God!" he cried suddenly, in a high,
almost womanish accent of passionate conviction, "what

junk! What mountains and oceans of junk! And so bad!"
he cried passionately, in his strange, unearthly tone. "So
incredibly and impossibly bad. In that whole place
there are just three things worth seeing—but *they!*"—his
voice was high again with passionate excitement—"*they*
are *unspeakably* beautiful, Eugene! God!" he cried, high
and passionate again, "how *beautiful* they are! How
utterly, impossibly beautiful!" Then with a resumption
of his quiet, matter-of-fact tone he said, "You must come
here with me sometime. I will show them to you.
. . . Look!" he said, in his casual tone again, "will you
come to the Régence with me and have a drink?"

The whole earth seemed to come to life at once. Now
that Starwick was here, this unfamiliar world, in whose
alien life he had struggled like a drowning swimmer,
became in a moment wonderful and good. The feeling of
numb, nameless terror, rootless desolation, the intolerable sick anguish of homelessness, insecurity, and homesickness, against which he had fought since coming to
Paris, and which he had been ashamed and afraid to
admit, was now instantly banished. Even the strange
dark faces of the French as they streamed past no longer
seemed strange, but friendly and familiar, and the moist
and languorous air, the soft thick greyness of the skies
which had seemed to press down on his naked sides, to
permeate his houseless soul like a palpable and viscous
substance of numb terror and despair, were now impregnated with all the vital energies of living, with the
intoxication of an unspeakable, nameless, infinitely
strange and various joy. As they walked across the vast
court of the Louvre towards the great arched gateway
and all the brilliant traffic of the streets, the enormous
dynamic murmur of the mysterious city came to him and
stirred his entrails with the sensual premonitions of unknown, glamorous, and seductive pleasure. Even the

little taxis, boring past with wasplike speed across the
great space of the Louvre and through the sounding
arches, now contributed to this sense of excitement,
luxury, and joy. The shrill and irritating horns sounded
constantly through the humid air, and filled his heart
with thoughts of New Year: already the whole city
seemed astir, alive now with the great carnival of New
Year's Eve.

At the Régence, they found a table on the terrace of
the old café where Napoleon had played dominoes, and
among the gay clatter of the crowd of waning afternoon,
they drank brandy, talked passionately and with almost
delirious happiness, drank brandy again, and watched
the swarming and beautiful life upon the pavements and
at the crowded tables all around them.

The streams of traffic up and down the whole Avenue
de l'Opéra and the Place de la Comédie Française, the
delicate, plain, and beautiful façade of the Comédie
across the Square from them, the statue of frail De
Musset, half-fainting backward in the arms of his re-
storing muse—all this seemed not only part of him, but
now that Starwick was here, to gain an enormous enhancement and enchantment, to be the total perfume of
an incredibly good and lovely and seductive life, the
whole of which, in all its infinite ramifications, seemed to
be distilled into his blood like a rare liquor, and to belong
to him. And so they drank and talked and drank until
full dark had come, and tears stood in their eyes, and
the brandy saucers were racked up eight deep upon
their table.

Then, gloriously sad and happy and exultantly triumphant, and full of nameless joy and evil, they stepped
into one of the shrill, exciting little taxis, and were
charioted swiftly up that thronging noble street, until

the great soaring masses of the Opéra stood before them and the Café de la Paix was at one side.

And they were young, all-conquering and exultant, and all the magic life of strange million-footed Paris belonged to them, and all its strange and evil fragrance burned fierce and secret in their veins, and they knew that they were young and that they would never die, that it was New Year's Eve in Paris, and that that magic city had been created for them. By this time they had between them about 400 francs.

Then followed the huge kaleidoscope of night: at one o'clock, leaving a café, they got into a taxi, and vociferously demanded of the ruddy driver, in French made eloquently confident by alcohol and joy, that they be taken to the resorts most frequented by "nos frères—vous comprenez—les honnêtes hommes—les ouvriers."

He smilingly assented, and from that time on until dawn they made a madman's round of little vile cafés, so mazed, so numerous, so inextricably confused in the vast weblike slum and jungle of nocturnal Paris, that later they could never thread their way back through that labyrinth of crooked alleyways, and drunkenness and confusion. Their driver took them to a region which they later thought was somewhere in that ancient, foul, and tangled quarter between the Boulevard de Sébastopol and Les Halles. And all that night from one o'clock to dawn, they threaded noxious alleys, beside the shuttered façades, of ancient, evil, cronelike houses, and stopped at every blaze of garish light to enter dirty little dives, where sullen, evil-visaged men surveyed them sullenly over bistro bars, and gave them with a slimy hand cheap vile cognac in greasy little glasses. In these places there was always the evil, swelling, fatly unctuous and seductive music of accordians, the hoarse bravos of applause.

Here one bought metal slugs, a dozen for five francs, and gave them to sluttish sirens with no upper teeth for the favor of a dance; and here also there were many soldiers, Colonial Negroes, black as ebony, were most in favor; and here were men with caps and scarves and evil, furtive eyes, who watched them steadily.

From place to place, from dive to dive, all through that huge and noxious labyrinth of night, their wild debauch wore on. And presently they noticed that wherever they went, two gendarmes followed them, stood quietly at the bar, and courteously and genially took the drinks they always bought for them, and were always there when they entered the next place. And the ruddy and good-natured taxi-man was always there as well, and he too always drank with them, and always said, with robust satisfaction: "Mais, oui! Parbleu! A votre santé, messieurs!"

The grey haggard light of daybreak showed the cold grey waters of the Seine, ancient, narrowed, flowing on between huge stone walls, the haggard steep façades of the old shuttered houses in the Latin Quarter, the narrow angularity of the silent streets. In Montparnasse, they got out at the corner of the Boulevard Edgar Quinet, and demanded the reckoning. All that remained to them was less than fifty francs; they took it all, the soiled and nibbled little five-franc notes, the coppery one- and two-franc pieces, the ten- and twenty-five- and fifty-centime pieces, and poured it into his hands, and stood there, guilty, silent, and ashamed before his astonished and reproachful face, because he had stood by them well and loyally all through that blind kaleidoscope of night, and it was New Year's Eve, and they were drunk and gay, and, he had thought, rich Americans, and he had hired for, earned, expected, more.

"It's all we have," they said.

That ruddy robust man then did something that is
perhaps rare in the annals of French taxidom, and which
they never forgot.

After an astonished moment, while he looked at the
little wad of bills and coins in his broad palm, he suddenly laughed loud and cheerfully, tossed the little wad
of money in the air and caught it as it fell, stripped off a
five-franc note and pocketed the rest, handed the five-
franc note to Starwick, and said cheerfully——

"It's all right! You two boys take this and buy yourselves some breakfast to sober up on. Happy New Year!"
—and with a friendly farewell wave of the hand, drove
off.

They had delicious morning crescent rolls, fresh baked
and crusty, and thick rich chocolate, at a little bakery in
the Boulevard Edgar Quinet, next to Starwick's quarters.
He was living in a studio, loaned to him, he said, by "two
friends," whom he did not name, and who were "out of
town for the holidays."

The studio was one of a row of similar buildings all
fronting on a little enclosed alleyway. One entered from
a street through a gate set in the wall: one rang a bell,
and presently la concierge pressed a button which released the door. Inside, it was very quiet and still and
grey with the grey morning light of New Year's Day.
And all the city was shut out. Then they entered Starwick's studio: in the grey light a big room with a slanting roof of grey glazed glass emerged: around the walls
were paintings, the limbs and fragments of unfinished
sculptures, a few chairs and tables, and a couch bed. At
the back there was a balcony, and steps ascending to it:
here too there was a cot, and Starwick told Eugène he
could sleep up there.

Both young men were groggy with weariness and the
night's debauch: in the cold grey light, life looked black

and ugly, they were exhausted and ashamed. Starwick lay down upon the couch and went to sleep; Eugene ascended to the balcony, pulled off his clothes and tossed them in a heap, and fell into the deep drugged sleep of drunkenness and exhaustion.

He slept till noon; and was awakened by the sound of steps below, the opening and closing of the door, and suddenly a woman's voice, light, gay, authoritative, and incisive:

"Darling, we're back again!" the gay, light voice cried out. "Welcome to our city! Happy New Year," she went on more quietly, and with a note of tender intimacy. "How have you been?"

He heard Starwick's quiet voice as it answered her, and presently the low, brief, and almost sullen tones of another woman. Starwick called sleepily up to Eugene, telling him to dress at once and come down: when he got downstairs, Starwick and the two women were waiting for him.

The one with the light, gay, incisive voice greeted him warmly and cordially, and made him feel instantly at home. She seemed to be the older of the two, and yet there was not much difference in their ages. The other woman shook hands with him almost curtly, and muttered a few words of greeting. She was a big dark-haired New England sort of girl; she wore dark, drab, rusty-looking clothes, and her face had a sullen, almost heavy cast to it. While Starwick, and the other woman, whose name was Elinor, rattled gaily on together, the dark girl sat sullenly and awkwardly in her chair, and said nothing. Once or twice they spoke to her: she had a way of answering with a few curt sullen words and a short angry laugh, which went as quickly as it came, and left her face heavy and sullen again. But the moment she laughed, Eugene noticed that her mouth was very red and sweet, her teeth beautifully white, and for a moment the girl's sullen face was illuminated by a radiant tender loveliness. He heard Frank call her Ann: Starwick seemed to want to tease her, and when he spoke to her there was a little burble of malicious laughter in his voice. Turning to Eugene, his pleasant face reddening and the burble of malicious laughter playing in his throat, Frank said:

"She is *very* beautiful. You'd never think it, but she really *is*, you know."

Ann muttered something short and angry, and, her face flushing, she laughed her short sudden laugh of anger and exasperation. And as she did so, her face came alive at once with its radiant loveliness, and he saw that what Starwick said of her was true.

II

That was a fine life that he had that year. He lived in a little hotel in the rue des Beaux Arts. He had a good room there which cost him twelve francs a day. It was a good hotel, and was the place where Oscar Wilde had died. When anyone wanted to see the celebrated death-room, he would ask to see "le chambre de Monsieur Veeld," and Monsieur Gely, the proprietor, or one of his buxom daughters, would willingly show it.

At nine o'clock in the morning the maid would come in with chocolate or coffee, bread and jam and butter, which was included in the price of the room. She put it down on a little cabinet beside his bed, which had a door and a chamber pot inside. After she went out he would get up and move it to the table, and drink the chocolate and eat some bread and jam. Then he would go back to bed and sleep until noon and sometimes later: at one o'clock, Starwick and the two women would come to take him to lunch. If they did not come, they would send him a *pneumatique* telling him where to meet them. They went to a great many different places, but the lunch was always good. Sometimes they would send a *pneumatique* telling him to meet them at the Dome or the Rotonde. When he got there, they would be sitting at a table on the terrace, and already very gay. Starwick would have a stack of saucers racked up before him on the table. On each saucer would be a numeral which said 3:50, or 5:00, or 6:00, or 7:50 francs, depending on what he had been drinking.

Usually it was cognac, but sometimes Starwick would greet him with a burble of laughter, saying in his sensuous and voluptuous voice: "Did you ever drink Amer Picon?"

"No," he would say.

"Well," said Starwick, "you ought to try it. You really ought, you know." And the soft burble would come welling up out of his throat again, and Elinor, looking at him tenderly, smiling, would say:

"Francis! You idiot! Leave the child alone!"

Then they would go to lunch. Sometimes they went to a place near by called Henriettes which Elinor had known about when she was an ambulance driver in the war. Again, they would cross the river and eat at Prunier's, Weber's, the Café Régence, Fouquet's, or at a place halfway up the hill in Montmartre, which was in a Square called the Place des Martyrs, and which was called L'Ecrevisse, probably because of a little shellfish which they sold there, and which was a specialty. That was a fine place: they always ate out on the terrace where they could see everything that was going on in the little Square, and Elinor, who had known the place for years, said how lovely it would be in spring.

Often they would eat at little places, which were not

very expensive and which Elinor also knew about. She
knew about everything: there was nothing about Paris
she did not know. Elinor did the talking, rattling off her
French like a native—or, anyway, like a native of Boston
who speaks French well—trippingly off the tongue,
getting the same intonations and gestures the French got,
when she argued with them, saying:

"Mais non—mais non mais non mais non mais non
mais non!" so rapidly that we could hardly follow her,
and she could say: "Oui. C'est ça!—Mais parfaitement!
—Entendu! . . . Formidable!" etc., in the same way a
Frenchman could.

Yet there was a trace of gaiety and humor in everything she said and did. She had "the light touch" about
everything, and understood just how it was with the
French. Her attitude towards them was very much the
manner of a mature and sophisticated person with a
race of clamoring children. She never grew tired of observing and pointing out their quaint and curious ways:
if the jolly proprietor of a restaurant came to the table
and proudly tried to speak to them his garbled English,
she would shake her head sharply, with a little smile,
biting her lower lip as she did so, and saying with a
light and tender humor:

"Oh, nice! . . . He wants to speak his English! . . .
Isn't he a dear? . . . No, no," she would say quickly if
anyone attempted to answer him in French. "Please let
him go ahead—poor dear! He's so proud of it!"

And again she would shake her head, biting her lower
lip, with a tender wondering little smile, as she said so,
and "Yes!" Francis would say enthusiastically and with
a look of direct, serious, and almost sorrowful earnestness. "And how grand the man is about it—how simple
and grand in the way he does it! . . . Did you notice
the way he used his hand—I mean like someone in a

painting by Cimabue—it really is, you know," he said earnestly. "The centuries of living and tradition that have gone into a single gesture—and he's quite unconscious of it. It's grand—I mean like someone in a painting by Cimabue—it really is, you know," he said with the sad, serious look of utter earnestness. "It's really *quite* incredible."

"Quite," said Elinor, who with a whimsical little smile had been looking at a waiter with sprouting mustaches, as he bent with prayerful reverence, stirring the ingredients in a salad bowl—"Oh, Francis, darling, look—" she whispered, nodding towards the man. "Don't you *love* it? . . . Don't you simply *adore* the way they do it! . . . I *mean*, you know! Now where? Where?" she cried, with a gesture of complete surrender—*"where* could you find anything like that in America? . . . I mean, you simply couldn't find it—that's all."

"Quite!" said Francis concisely. And turning to Eugene, he would say with that impressive air of absolute sad earnestness, "And it's really *most* important. It really is, you know. It's astonishing to see what they can put into a single gesture. I mean—the Whole Thing's there. It really is."

"Francis!" Elinor would say, looking at him with her gay and tender little smile, and biting her lip as she did so—"You *kid*, you! I *mean!*——"

Suddenly she put her hand strongly before her eyes, bent her head, and was rigid in a moment of powerful and secret emotion. In a moment, however, she would look up, wet-eyed, suddenly thrust her arm across the table at Eugene, and, putting her hand on his arm with a slight gallant movement, say quietly:

"Oh, I'm sorry—you poor child! . . . After all, there's no reason why you should have to go through all this. . . . I mean, darling," she explained gently, "I have an

adorable kid at home just four years old—sometimes
something happens to make me think of him—you
understand, don't you?"

"Yes," he said.

"Good," she said briskly and decisively, with a swift
and gallant smile, as she patted his arm again. "I knew
you would!"

She had left her husband and child in Boston, she had
come here to join Francis, fatality was in the air, but
she was always brave and gallant about it. As Francis
would say to Eugene as they sat drinking alone in a
café:

"It's *mad*—Boston! . . . Perfectly *mad*—Boston! . . .
I mean, the kind of thing they do when they ride a horse
up the steps of the State House. . . . I mean, perfectly
grand, you know," he cried with high enthusiasm. "They
stop at nothing. It's simply *swell*—it really is, you know."

Everyone was being very brave and gallant and stopping at nothing, and the French were charming, charming, and Paris gave them just the background that they
needed. It was a fine life.

Elinor took charge of everything. She took charge of
the money, the making of plans, the driving of bargains
with avaricious and shrewd-witted Frenchmen, and the
ordering of food in restaurants.

"It's really astonishing, you know," said Starwick,
"the way she walks in everywhere and has the whole
place at her feet in four minutes. . . . Really, Gene,
you should have been with us this afternoon when she
made arrangements with the man at the motor agency
in the Champs Elysées for renting the car. . . . Really,
I felt quite sorry for him before the thing was over. . . .
He kept casting those knowing and rather *bitter* glances
of reproach at me," said Starwick, with his burble of

soft laughter, "as if he thought I had betrayed him by not coming to his assistance. . . . There was something *very* cruel about it . . . like a great cat, playing with a mouse . . . there really was, you know," said Starwick earnestly. "She can be completely without pity when she gets that way," he added. "She really can, you know . . . which makes it all the more astonishing—I mean, when you consider what she really is—the way she let me go to sleep on her shoulder the night we were coming back from Rheims, and I was so horribly drunk and got so disgustingly sick," he said with a simple, touching earnestness. "I mean, the *compassion* of it— it was *quite* like that Chinese goddess of the Infinite Compassion, they have in Boston—it *really* was, you know. It's quite astonishing," he said earnestly, "when you consider her background, the kind of people that she came from—it really *is*, you know . . . she's a grand person, simply terrific . . . it's utterly *mad*— Boston . . . it really is."

Certainly it was very pleasant to be in the hands of such a captain. Elinor got things done with a beautiful, serene assurance that made everything seem easy. There was no difficulty of custom or language, no weird mystery and complication of traffic, trade, and commerce, so maddening and incomprehensible to most Americans, that Elinor did not understand perfectly. Sometimes she would just shake her head and bite her lip, smiling. Sometimes she would laugh with rich astonishment, and say: "*Perfectly* insane, of course— but then, that's the way the poor dears are, and you can't change them. . . . I *know!* I *know!* . . . It's quite incredible, but they'll *always* be that way, and we've simply got to make the best of it."

She was a heavily built woman about thirty years old who seemed older than she was. She dressed very plainly

nd wore a rather old hat with a cockade, which gave
er a look of eighteenth-century gallantry. And the impression of maturity was increased by her heavy and
unyouthful figure, and the strong authority of her face
which, in spite of her good-humored, gay, and whimsical
mile, her light Bostonian air of raillery, indicated the
controlled tension and restraint of nerves of a person of
tubborn and resolute will who is resolved always to act
with aristocratic grace and courage.

In spite of her heavy figure, her rough and rather
unhealthy-looking skin, she was a distinguished-looking
woman, and in her smile, her tone, her play of wit, and
even in the swift spitefulness and violence which could
lash out and strike and be gone before its victim had a
chance to retort or defend himself, she was thoroughly
feminine. And yet the woman made no appeal at all to
sensual desire: although she had left her husband and
child to follow Starwick to France, and was thought by
her own family to have become his mistress, it was impossible to imagine her in such a role. And for this
eason, perhaps, there was something ugly, dark, and
inister in their relation, which Eugene felt strongly but
could not define. He felt that Elinor was lacking in the
attraction or desire of the sensual woman as Starwick
eemed to be lacking in the lust of the sensual man, and
here was therefore something in their relation that came
rom the dark, the murky swampfires of emotion, some-
hing poisonous, perverse and evil, and full of death.

Just the same, it was fine to be with Elinor when she
was gay and deft and charming, and enormously assured,
and taking charge of things. At these times, everything
n life seemed simple, smooth, and easy; there were no
dreary complications, the whole world became an enormous oyster ready to be opened, Paris an enormous
reasure-hoard of unceasing pleasure and delight. It was

good to be with her in a restaurant, and to let her do the ordering.

"Now, children," she would say in her crisp, gay, and yet authoritative tone, staring at the menu with a little frowning smile of studious yet whimsical concentration, "the rest of you can order what you like, but Mother's going to start with fish and a bottle of Vouvray—I seem to remember that it's very good here—Le Vouvray est bon ici, n'est-ce pas?" she said turning to the waiter.

"Mais, oui, madame!" he said with just the right kind of earnest enthusiasm, "C'est une spécialité."

"Bon," she said crisply. "Alors, une bouteille du Vouvray pour commencer—does that go for the rest of you, mes enfants?" she said, looking around her. They nodded their agreement.

"Bon—bon, madame," the waiter said, nodding his vigorous approval, as he put the order down. "Vous serez bien content avec le Vouvray—et puis?"—He looked at her with suave respectful inquiry. "Pour manger?"

"Pour moi," said Elinor, "le poisson—le filet de sole—n'est-ce pas—Marguery?"

"Bon, bon," he said with enthusiastic approval, writing it down. "Un filet de sole—Marguery—pour Madame—et pour Monsieur?" he said, turning suavely to Eugene.

"La même chose," said that linguist recklessly and even as the waiter was nodding enthusiastically, and saying:

"Bon. Bon—parfaitement! La même chose pour monsieur," and writing it down, the others had begun to laugh at him. Starwick with his bubbling laugh, Elinor with her gay little smile of raillery and even Ann, the dark and sullen beauty of her face suddenly luminous with a short and almost angry laugh as she said:

"He hasn't said his other word yet—why don't you tell him that you want some 'mawndiawnts'"—ironically she imitated his pronunciation of the word.

"What's wrong with 'mendiants'?" he said, scowling at her. "What's the joke?"

"Nothing," said Starwick bubbling with laughter. "They're very good. They really are, you know," he said earnestly. "Only we've been wondering if you wouldn't learn another word some day and order something else."

"I know lots of other words," he said angrily. "Only, how am I ever going to get a chance to use them when the rest of you make fun of me every time I open my mouth? I don't see what the great joke is," he said resentfully. "These French people understand what I want to say," he said. "Ecoute, garçon," he said appealingly to the attentive and smiling waiter.—"Vous pouvez comprendre——"

"Cawmprawndre," said Ann mockingly.

"Vous pouvez comprendre—ce-que-je-veux-dire," he blundered on painfully.

"Mais, oui, monsieur!" the waiter cried with a beautiful reassuring smile. "Parfaitement. Vous parlez très bien. Vous êtes ici à Paris depuis longtemps?"

"Depuis six semaines," he said proudly.

The waiter lifted arms and eyebrows eloquent with astounded disbelief.

"Mais c'est merveilleux!" the waiter cried, and as the others jeered Eugene said with bitter sarcasm:

"Everyone can't be a fine old French scholar the way you are; after all, I'm not traveled like the rest of you—I've never had your opportunities. And even after six weeks here there are still a few words in the French language that I don't know. . . . But I'm going to speak the ones I do know," he said defiantly, "and no one's going to stop me."

"Of course you are, darling!" Elinor said quickly and smoothly, putting her hand out on his arm with a swift movement. "Don't let them tease you! . . . I think it's mean of you," she said reproachfully. "Let the poor dear speak his French if he wants to—I think it's sweet."

He looked at her with a flushed and angry face while Starwick bubbled with laughter, tried to think of something to say in reply, but, as always, she was too quick for him, and before he could think of something apt and telling, she had flashed off as light and quick as a rapier blade:

"—Now, children," she was studying the card again— "what shall it be after the fish—who wants meat?"

"No fish for me," said Ann, looking sullenly at the menu. "I'll take"—suddenly her dark, sullen, and nobly beautiful face was transfigured by her short and almost angry laugh again—"I'll take an 'awmlet,'" she said sarcastically, looking at Eugene.

"Well, take your 'awmlet,'" he muttered. "Only don't say it that way."

"Pas de poisson," she said quietly to the waiter. "I want an omelet."

"Bon, bon," he nodded vigorously and wrote. "Une omelette pour Madame. Et puis après——?" he said inquiringly.

"Rien," she said.

He looked slightly surprised and hurt, but in a moment, turning to Eugene, said:

"Et pour monsieur?—Après le poisson?"

"Donnez-moi un Chateaubriand garni," he said.

And again Ann, whose head had been turned sullenly down towards the card, looked up suddenly and laughed with that short and almost angry laugh that seemed to illuminate with accumulating but instant radiance all of the dark and noble beauty of her face.

"God!" she said. "I knew it!—If it's not mendiants, it's Chateaubriand garni."

"Don't forget the Nuits St. George," said Starwick with his bubbling laugh. "That's still to come."

"When he gets through," she said, "there won't be a steak or raisin left in France."

And she looked at Eugene for a moment, her face of noble and tender beauty transfigured by its radiant smile. But almost immediately, she dropped her head again in its customary expression that was heavy and almost sullen, and that suggested something dumb, furious, and silent locked up in her, for which she could find no release.

He looked at her for a moment with scowling, half-resentful eyes, and all of a sudden, flesh, blood, and brain, and heart, and spirit, his life went numb with love for her.

"And now, my children," Elinor was saying gaily, as she looked at the menu, "what kind of salad is it going —" She looked up swiftly and caught Starwick's eye, and instantly their gaze turned upon their two companions. The young woman was still staring down with her sullen, dark, and dumbly silent look, and the boy was devouring her with a look from which the world was lost, and which had no place in it for time or memory.

Dark Helen in my heart forever burning.

"L'écrevisse," Eugene said, staring at the menu. "What does that mean, Elinor?"

"Well, darling, I'll tell you," she said with a grave light gaiety of tone, "an écrevisse is a kind of crawfish they have over here—a delicious little crab—but *much, much* better than anything we have."

"Then the name of the place really means *The Crab?*" he asked.

"*Stop* him!" she shrieked faintly. "You barbarian, you!" she went on with mild reproach. "It's not at *all* the same."

"It's really not, you know," said Starwick, turning to him seriously. "The whole quality of the thing is different. It really is. . . . Isn't it astonishing," he went on with an air of quiet frankness, "the genius they have for names? I mean, even in the simplest words they manage to get the whole spirit of the race. I mean, this Square here, even," he gestured briefly, "La Place des Martyrs. The whole thing's there. It's really quite incredible, when you think of it," he said somewhat mysteriously. "It really is."

"Quite!" said Elinor. "And, oh, my children, if it were only spring and I could take you down the Seine to an adorable place called La Pèche Miraculeuse."

"What does that mean, Elinor?" Eugene asked again.

"Well, darling," she said with an air of patient resignation, "if you *must* have a translation I suppose you'd call it *The Miraculous Catch*—a fishing catch, you know. Only it *doesn't* mean that. It would be sacrilege to call it that. It means *La Pèche Miraculeuse* and nothing else—it's *quite* untranslatable—it really is."

"*Yes*," cried Starwick enthusiastically, "and even their simplest names—their names of streets and towns and places: L'Etoile, for example—how grand and simple that is!" he said quietly, "and how perfect—the whole design and spatial grandeur of the thing is in it," he concluded earnestly. "It really is, you know."

"Oh, absolutely!" Elinor agreed. "You couldn't call it *The Star,* you know. That means nothing. But *L'Etoile* is perfect—it simply *couldn't* be anything else."

"*Quite!*" Starwick said concisely, and then, turning to Eugene with his air of sad instructive earnestness, he continued: "And that woman at Le Jockey Club last

night—the one who sang the songs—you know?" he
said with grave malicious inquiry, his voice trembling a
little and his face flushing as he spoke, "the one you
kept wanting to find out about—what she was saying?"
Quiet ruddy laughter shook him.

"*Perfectly* vile, of course!" cried Elinor with gay
horror. "And all the time, poor dear, he kept wanting to
know what it meant. . . . I was going to throw something at you if you kept on—if I'd had to translate *that*
I think I should simply have passed out on the spot——"

"I know," said Starwick, burbling with laughter. "I
caught the look in your eye—it was really *quite* murderous! And *terribly* amusing!" he added. Turning to his
friend, he went on seriously: "But really, Gene, it *is*
rather stupid to keep asking for the meaning of everything. It *is*, you know. And it's so extraordinary," he said
protestingly, "that a person of your quality—your *kind*
of understanding—should be so dull about it! It really
is."

"Why?" the other said bluntly, and rather sullenly.
"What's wrong with wanting to find out what's being
said when you don't understand the language? If I don't
ask, how am I going to find out?"

"But not at *all!*" Starwick protested impatiently.
"That's not the point at all: you can find out nothing
that way. Really you can't," he said reproachfully. "The
whole point about that song last night was not the
words—the meaning of the thing. If you tried to translate it into English, you'd lose the spirit of the whole
thing. Don't you see," he went on earnestly, "it's not the
meaning of the thing—you can't translate a thing like
that, you really can't—if you tried to translate it, you'd
have nothing but a filthy and disgusting jingle——"

"But so long as it's French it's beautiful?" the other
said sarcastically.

"But *quite!*" said Starwick impatiently. "And it's very stupid of you not to understand that, Gene. It really is. The whole spirit and quality of the thing is *so* French— so *utterly* French!" he said in a high and rather woman-ish tone, "that the moment you translate it you lose everything. . . . There's nothing disgusting about the song in French—the words mean nothing, you pay no attention to the words; the extraordinary thing is that you forget the words. . . . It's the whole design of the thing, the *tone*, the *quality*. . . . In a way," he added deeply, "the thing has an *enormous* innocence— it really has, you know. . . . And it's so disappointing that you fail to see this. . . . Really, Gene, these ques-tions you keep asking about names and meanings are becoming tiresome. They really are. . . . And all these books you keep buying and trying to translate with the help of a dictionary . . . as if you're ever going to understand anything—I mean, *really* understand," he said profoundly, "in that way."

"You may get to understand the language that way," the other said.

"But not at *all!*" cried Starwick. "That's just the point —you really find out nothing: you miss the whole spirit of the thing—just as you missed the spirit of that song, and just as you missed the point when you asked Elinor to translate La Pèche Miraculeuse for you. . . . It's extraordinary that you fail to see this. . . . The next thing you know," he concluded sarcastically, a burble of malicious laughter appearing as he spoke, "you will have enrolled for a course of lessons"—he choked suddenly, his ruddy face flushing deeply with his merriment— "for a course of lectures at the Berlitz language school."

"Oh, but he's entirely capable of it!" cried Elinor, with gay conviction. "I wouldn't put it past him for a moment. . . . My *dear*," she said drolly, turning towards him, "I have never known such a glutton for knowledge. It's simply amazing. . . . Why, the child wants to know the meaning of everything!" she said with an astonished look about her. "The confidence he has in my knowledge is rather touching—it really is —and I'm so unworthy of it, darling," she said a trifle maliciously. "I don't deserve it at all!"

"I'm sorry if I've bored you with a lot of questions, Elinor," he said.

"But you *haven't!*" she protested. "Darling, you *haven't* for a moment! I *love* to answer them! It's only that I feel so—so *incompetent*. . . . But listen, Gene," she went on coaxingly, "couldn't you try to forget it for a while—just sort of forget all about these words and meanings and enter into the spirit of the thing? . . . Couldn't you, dear?" she said gently, and even as he looked at her with a flushed face, unable to find a ready answer to her deft irony, she put her hand out swiftly, patted him on the arm, and nodding her head with an air of swift satisfied finality, said:

"Good! I knew you would! . . . He's really a darling when he wants to be, isn't he?"

Starwick burbled with malicious laughter at sight of Eugene's glowering and resentful face; then went on seriously:

"—But their genius for names is quite astonishing!— I mean, even in the names of their towns you get the whole thing. . . . What could be more like Paris," he said quietly, "than the name of Paris? . . . The whole quality of the place is in the name. Or Dijon, for example. Or Rheims. Or Carcassonne. The whole spirit of Provence is in the word: what name could more perfectly express Arles than the name it has? It gives you the whole place, its life, its people, its peculiar fragrance. . . . And how different we are from them in that respect. . . . I mean," his voice rose on a note of passionate conviction, "you could almost say that the whole difference between us—the thing we lack, the thing they have—the whole thing that is wrong with us, is evident in our names. . . . It really is, you know," he said earnestly, turning towards his friend again. "The whole thing's most important. . . . How harsh and meaningless most names in America are, Eugene," he went on quietly. "Like addresses printed on a thousand envelopes at once by a stamping machine—labels by which a place may be identified but without meaning. . . . Tell me," he said quietly, after a brief pause, "what was the name of that little village your father came from? You told me one time—I remember because the whole thing I'm talking about—the thing that's wrong with us—was in that name. What was it?"

"Brant's Mill," the other young man answered.

"Quite!" said Starwick with weary concision. "A man named Brant had a mill, and so they called the place Brant's Mill."

"What's wrong with that?"

"Oh, nothing, I suppose," said Starwick quietly. "The whole thing's quite perfect. . . . *Brant's* Mill," there was a note of bitterness in his voice and he made the name almost deliberately rasping as he pronounced it. "It's a name—something to call a place by—if you write it on a letter it will get there. . . . I suppose that's what a name is for. . . . Gettysburg—I suppose a man named Gettys had a house or a farm, and so they named the town after him. . . . And your mother? What was the name of the place she came from?"

"It was a place called Yancey County."

"Quite," said Starwick as before. "And the name of the town?"

"There wasn't any town, Frank. It was a kind of cross-roads settlement called the Forks of Ivy."

"No!" Elinor's light Bostonian accent of astounded merriment rang gaily forth. "Not *really!* You *know* it wasn't!"

"But not at *all!*" said Starwick in a tone of mild and serious disagreement. "The Forks of Ivy is not bad. It's really surprisingly good, when you consider most of the other names. It even has," he paused, and considered carefully, "a kind of quality. . . . But Yancey——" He paused again, the burble of sudden laughter came welling up, and for a moment his pleasant ruddy face was flushed with laughter. "*Ya-a-ancey* County"—with deliberate malice he brought the word out in a rasping countrified tone—"God!" he said frankly, turning to the other boy, "isn't it awful! . . . How harsh! How stupid! How banal! . . . And what are some of the names, where you come from, Gene?" he went on quietly after a brief pause. "I'm sure you haven't yet done your worst," he said. "There must be others just as sweet as Ya-a-ancey."

"Well, yes," the boy said, grinning, "we've got some good ones: there's Sandy Mush, and Hooper's Bald, and Little Hominy. And we have names like Beaverdam and Balsam, and Chimney Rock and Craggy and Pisgah and the Rat. We have names like Old Fort, Hickory, and Bryson City; we have Clingman's Dome and Little Switzerland; we have Paint Rock and Saluda Mountain and the Frying Pan Gap——"

"Stop!" shrieked Elinor, covering her ears with her shocked fingers. "The Frying Pan Gap! Oh, but that's *horrible!*"

"But how perfect!" Starwick quietly replied. "The whole thing's there. And in the great and noble region

where I come from"—the note of weary bitterness in his
tone grew deeper—"out where the tall caw-r-n grows
we have Keokuk and Cairo and Peoria." He paused, his
grave eyes fixed in a serious and reflective stare: for a
moment his pleasant ruddy face was contorted by the
old bestial grimace of anguish and confusion. When he
spoke again, his voice was weary with a quiet bitterness
of scorn. "I was born," he said, "in the great and noble
town of Bloomington but"—the note of savage irony
deepened—"at a very tender age I was taken to Moline.
And now, thank God, I am in Paris"; he was silent a
moment longer, and then continued in a quiet and almost
lifeless tone: "Paris, Dijon, Provence, Arles . . . Yancey,
Brant's Mill, Bloomington." He turned his quiet eyes
upon the other boy. "You see what I mean, don't you?
The whole thing's there."

"Yes," the boy replied, "I guess you're right."

III

They were sitting at a table in one of the night places
of Montmartre. The place was close and hot, full of gilt
and glitter, heavy with that unwholesome and seductive
fragrance of the night that comes from perfumery, wine,
brandy, and the erotic intoxication of a nighttime
pleasure place. Over everything there was a bright yet
golden blaze of light that wrought on all it touched—
gilt, tinsel, table linen, the natural hue and coloring of
the people, the faces of men, and the flesh of the women
—an evil but strangely thrilling transformation.

The orchestra had just finished playing a piece that
everyone in Paris was singing that year. It was a gay
jigging little tune that Mistinguette had made famous;
its name was *Ça, c'est Paris*, and one heard it everywhere. One heard lonely wayfarers whistling it as they

walked home late at night through the silent narrow streets of the Latin Quarter, and one heard it hummed by taxi-drivers, waiters, and by women in cafés. It was played constantly to the tune of flutes and violins by dance orchestras in the night-clubs of Montmartre and Montparnasse. And, accompanied by the swelling rhythms of the accordion, one heard it at big dance-halls like the Bal Bullier, and in the little dives and stews and café-brothel-dancing places along noisome alleyways near the markets and the Boulevard de Sébastopol.

In spite of its gay jigging lilt, that tune had a kind of mournful fatality. It was one of those songs which seem to evoke perfectly—it is impossible to know why—the whole color, life, and fragrance of a place and time as nothing else on earth can do. For the boy, that song would haunt him ever after with the image of Paris and of his life that year, with the memory of Starwick, Elinor, and Ann.

The song had for him the fatality of something price-less, irrecoverably lost, full of that bitter joy and anguish we can feel at twenty-four, when the knowledge of man's brevity first comes to us, when we first know ruin and defeat, when we first understand what we have never known before: that for us, as for every other man alive, all passes, all is lost, all melts before our grasp like smoke; when we know that the moment of beauty carries in it the seeds of its own instant death, that love is gone almost before we have it, that youth is gone before we know it, and that, like every other man, we must grow old and die.

The orchestra had finished playing this tune, and the dancers were going to their tables from the polished little square of floor; in a moment Starwick called the leader of the orchestra over to the table and asked him to play

Starwick's favorite song. This was a piece called *My Chile Bon Bon;* it was not new, Starwick had first heard it several years before in Boston, but like the other piece this tune was pregnant with the mournful fatality of a place and period; in its grotesque words and haunting melody there was the sense of something irrevocable, an utter surrender and a deliberate loss, a consciousness of doom. These two pieces together evoked the whole image and quality of that year, and of the life of these four people: for Starwick, in fact, this *Chile Bon Bon* song somehow perfectly expressed the complete fatality that had now seized his life, the sensual inertia of his will.

The orchestra leader nodded smilingly when Starwick asked him to play the song, went back and conferred with his musicians for a moment, and, himself taking up a violin, began to play. As the orchestra played, the leader walked towards their table, and, bending and swaying with the infinite ductile grace which a violin seems to give to all its performers, he stood facing the two women, seeming to offer up the wailing, hauntingly mournful and exciting music as a kind of devotion to their loveliness.

Elinor, tapping the tune out with her fingers on the tablecloth, hummed the words lightly, absently, under her breath; Ann sat quietly, darkly, sullenly attentive; Starwick, at one end of the table, sat turned away, his legs indolently crossed, his ruddy face flushed with emotion, his eyes fixed in a blind stare, and a little wet.

Once, while the piece was being played, Starwick's pleasant ruddy face was contorted again by the old bestial grimace of nameless anguish and bewilderment which Eugene had seen so many times before, and in which the sense of tragic defeat, frustration, the premonition of impending ruin, was legible.

When the orchestra leader had finished with the tune, Starwick turned wearily, thrust his arm indolently across the table towards Ann and, wiggling his fingers languidly and a trifle impatiently, said quietly:

"Give me some money."

She flushed a little, opened her purse, and said sullenly:

"How much do you want?"

The weary impatience of his manner became more evident, he wiggled his languid fingers in a more peremptory command, and, burbling a little with laughter at sight of her sullen face, he said in a low tone of avaricious humor:

"Give, give, give. . . . Money, money, money," he said in a low gloating tone, and burbled again, with a rich welling of humor, as he looked at her.

Red in the face, she flung a wad of bank notes down upon the table with almost vicious force, he accepted them languidly, stripped off 300 franc notes and handed them indolently to the orchestra leader, who responded with a bow eloquent with adoration; and then, without pausing to count them, Starwick thrust the remainder carelessly in his pocket.

"Ann!" he said reproachfully. "I am *very* hurt!" He paused a moment; the flow and burble of soft laughter came quickly, flushing his ruddy face, and he continued as before, with a mock gravity of reproachful humor.

"I had hoped"—his shoulders trembled slightly—"that by this time your *finer* nature"—he trembled again with secret merriment—"your *finer* nature would be ready to reveal itself."

"My finer nature be damned!" Ann said angrily. "Whether you like it or not, I think it's disgraceful the way you fling money around! Three hundred francs to a man for playing that damned song! And you've done the same thing at least a dozen times! God, I'm sick of hearing about your *Chile Bon Bon!*" she concluded bitterly. "I wish the damned thing had never been written."

"Ann!" again the soft mockery of sounded reproach. "And this is the way you repay us, after all we've done for you! It's not that I'm angry but I'm *very, very* hurt," he said gently. "I really am, you know."

"Ah-h!" She made a sudden exasperated movement as if she was going to push the table away from her and get up, and then said with angry warning: "Now, look here, Frank, don't you start that again about how much you've done for me. Done for me!" she said furiously. "Done for me!" She laughed, short and hard, with angry exasperation, and was unable to find words to continue.

Starwick's burble of soft laughter answered her:

"I *know!*" he said, his face reddening a little as he spoke. "But, after all, you *are* a little *tight,* Ann." His shoulders trembled slightly, and his ruddy face grew deeper with its hue of humor. "I think," he said gently, and paused again, trembling with quiet laughter, "I think it may be what is known as the Beacon Hill influence. And really," he continued seriously, looking at her with grave eyes, "you really ought to try to get it out of you."

"Now, Frank," cried Ann angrily, half rising from the table, "if you start that again about my being stingy ——" She sat down again abruptly, and burst out with bitter resentment, "I'm not stingy and you know it! . . . It's not that I mind spending the money, giving it to you when I've got it. . . . It's only that I think everyone ought to try to bear his own share. . . . If you think that's my New England stinginess you're welcome to your opinion. . . . But I've always felt that way and always will! . . . Stingy!" she muttered, "I'm not. . . . I'm just tired of being the goat all the time. . . . It seems

to me the rest of you ought to share in the expense sometime!"

"But not at *all!*" cried Starwick in a tone of astonished
protest. "I can't see that that makes the *slightest* difference," he went on gently. "After all, Ann, it's not as
if we were four old maids from Boston doing the grand
tour and putting down every cent we spend in a mutual
account book," he said a trifle sarcastically. "It's not that
kind of thing at all. When four people know each other
the way we do, the last thing in the world that could
possibly be of value is money. What belongs to one
belongs to all. Really," he said a trifle impatiently, "I
should think you'd understand that. It's *quite* astonishing
to see a person of your quality with such a material—
rather *grasping*—view of money. I shouldn't think it
would make the *slightest* difference to you. You really
ought to get it out of your system, Ann," he said quietly.
"You really must. Because you *are* a *grand* person—you
really are, you know."

She flushed, and then muttered sullenly:

"Ah! Grand person my eye! I've heard all that before!
You can't get around it that way!"

"But you *are!*" he said, with earnest insistence. "You
are a *very* grand person—that's what makes the whole
thing such a pity."

She flushed again, and then sat staring at the table
in sullen embarrassment.

"And, Ann," said Starwick gently, beginning to burble
with his soft flow of wicked laughter, "you are really
very beautiful in that red dress"—his sensuous mannered tone trembled again with its burble of wicked
humor—"and *very* seductive—and *very*—" his shoulders
trembled and his face trembled as he spoke—"you are
really *quite* voluptuous," he said with sensual relish, and
suddenly choked with laughter. When he had composed

himself, he turned his still laughter-reddened face to-wards Eugene, and said earnestly: "It's *quite* astonish-ing! She really is, you know! She's *gloriously* beautiful!"

"Frank!" she looked at him for a moment with an ex-pression of baffled exasperation. Then, suddenly she laughed her short and angry laugh: "God!" she cried sarcastically. "It's a high price to pay for compliments, isn't it?"

But that laugh, short and angry as it was, had made radiant, as it always did, her dark and noble beauty. Instantly her face had been lifted, transfigured from its customary expression of dark and almost heavy sullen-ness, her cheeks, which in repose had the pendulous sagging quality of a plump child, were suffused with rose, her sweet red mouth and white teeth suddenly shone with a radiant and lovely smile, and Eugene noticed now, as he had begun to notice, that her grey eyes when she looked at Starwick were no longer hard and angry, but smoky, luminous with a depthless tender-ness.

"You *are*," Starwick concluded quietly, seriously, his pleasant face still a trifle flushed with laughter. "You are one of the most *gloriously* beautiful creatures that ever lived."

What he said was the simple truth. The girl's beauty that night was almost unbelievable. She had put on a new evening dress which had been made for her by a famous designer. The dress was a glorious red, that seemed almost to float with an aerial buoyancy of filmy gauze; no dress in the world could have suited her dark beauty, or revealed the noble proportions of her figure half so well. Her hair, which was black, coarse, and fragrant, was parted simply in the middle: Eugene noted that there were already a few streaks of coarse grey in it but her face had the dignity of her grand and honest character—the sullen plumpness of a child and the radiant sudden sweetness and happiness of her smile, combined.

And in every other respect, Ann showed this strange and lovely union of delicacy and grandeur, of the child and the woman. Her hands were long, brown, and narrow, the fingers long and delicate, the bones as fine and small as a bird's, and yet they were strong, sensitive, able-looking hands as well. Her arms were long and slender, as firm and delicate as a young girl's, but Eugene noted that her breasts were not round and firm, but the long heavy sloping breasts of a big woman. When she got up to dance with Starwick she topped him by a head, and yet, radiant with a joy and happiness she had never known before, she seemed to float there in his arms, an Amazonian figure, great of thigh and limb and breast, and a creature of a loveliness as delicate and radiant as a child's.

They danced superbly together: in deference to Starwick, the orchestra played his *Chile Bon Bon* song again; when they returned to the table Starwick's ruddy face was flushed with the emotion the song always aroused in him, his eyes looked wet, and in a high, passionate, almost womanish tone, he cried to Eugene:

"God! Isn't it grand! Isn't it simply superb! It's one of the great songs of the world, it really is, you know! The thing has the same quality as a great primitive—the same quality as a primitive Apollo or Cimabue's Madonna, in the Louvre. Christ!" he cried in a high womanish tone, "the whole thing's there—it really is! I think it's the greatest song that was ever written!"

He poured out a glass of champagne, cold and sparkling, and drank it thirstily, his eyes wet, his face flushed deeply with his feeling.

IV

In the dull grey light of the short and swiftly waning winter's day, the two young men were leaving the museum, to spend the rest of the afternoon, until the time of their appointed meeting with the women, in drink and talk at one of the innumerable and seductive cafés of the magic city. Outside the Louvre, they hailed a taxi and were driven swiftly over one of the bridges of the Seine, through the narrow streets of the Latin Quarter, and at length stopped and got out before La Closerie des Lilas, where they were to meet the two women later on.

They spent the remainder of the afternoon in the chill wintry air of the terrace, warm with drink, with argument or discussion, and with the gaiety of life and voices of people all around them, the pageant of life that passed forever on the street before them—all that priceless, rare, and uncostly pleasure and excitement of café life which seemed unbelievable and magical to these two young Americans. The dull grey air, which was at once chill and wintry, and yet languorous, filled them with the sense of some powerful, strange, and inhuman excitement that was impending for them.

And the bright gaiety of the colors, the constant flash and play of life about them and along the pavements, the smell and potent intoxication of the cognac, gave them the sensation of a whole world given over without reserve or shame to pleasure. All these elements, together with that incomparable fusion of odors—at once corrupt and sensual, subtle and obscene—which exudes from the very texture of the Paris life—odors which it is impossible to define exactly, but which seem in the dull wintry air to be compacted of the smells of costly perfumes, of wine, beer, brandy, and of the acrid and nostalgic fumes of French tobacco, of roasted chestnuts, black French coffee, mysterious liquors of a hundred brilliant and intoxicating colors, and the luxurious flesh of scented women—smote the two young men instantly with the sensual impact of this strange and fascinating world.

But in spite of all the magic of the scene, and the assurance and security which Starwick's presence always gave to him, the ghost of the old unquiet doubt would not wholly be laid at rest, the ache of the old hunger stirred in Eugene. Why was he here now? Why had he come? The lack of purpose in this present life, the dozing indolence of this existence in which no one worked, in which they sat constantly at tables in a café, and ate and drank and talked, and moved on to sit at other tables, other cafés—and, most of all, the strange dull faces of the Frenchmen, the strange and alien life of this magic city which was so seductive but so unalterably foreign to all that he had ever known—all this had now begun to weigh inexplicably upon a troubled spirit, to revive again the old feelings of naked homelessness, to stir in him the nameless sense of shame and guilt which an American feels at a life of indolence and pleasure, which is part of the very chemistry of his blood, and which he can never root out of him. And feeling the obscure but powerful insistence of these troubled thoughts within his mind, he turned suddenly to Starwick, and, without a word of explanation, said:

"But do you really feel at home here?"

"What do you mean by 'feeling at home'?"

"Well, I mean don't you ever feel out of place here? Don't you ever feel as if you didn't belong to this life— that you are a foreigner?"

"But not at all!" said Starwick, a trifle impatiently. "On the contrary, I think it is the first time in my life that I have *not* felt like a foreigner. I never felt at home in the

Middle West where I was born; I hated the place from my earliest childhood, I always felt out of place there, and wanted to get away from it. But I felt instantly at home in Paris from the moment I got here—I am far closer to this life than to any other life I've ever known, for the first time in my life I feel thoroughly at home."

"And you don't mind being a foreigner?"

"But of course not!" Starwick said curtly. "Besides, I am *not* a foreigner. You can only be foreign in a place that is foreign to you. This place is not."

"But, after all, Frank, you are not a Frenchman. You are an American."

"Not at all," Starwick answered concisely. "I am an American only by the accident of birth; by spirit, temperament, inclination, I have always been a European."

"And you mean you could continue to lead this kind of life without ever growing tired of it?"

"What do you mean by this kind of life?" said Starwick.

His friend nodded towards the crowded and noisy terrace of the café.

"I mean sitting around at café's all day long, going to night-clubs—eating, drinking, sitting—moving on from one place to another—spending your life that way?"

"Do you think it's such a bad way to spend your life?" said Starwick quietly. He turned, regarding his friend with serious eyes. "Don't you find it very amusing?"

"Yes, Frank, for a time. But after a while, don't you think you'd get tired of it?"

"No more tired," said Starwick, "than I would of going to an office day after day at nine o'clock and coming away at five, doing useless and dreary work that someone else could do as well. On the contrary—this kind of life"—he nodded towards the crowded tables—"seems to me much more interesting and amusing."

"But how can you feel that you belong to it?" the other said. "I should think that would make a difference to you. It does to me—the feeling that I am a stranger here, that this is not my life, that I know none of these people."

"Are you getting ready to tell me now that an American never really gets to know any French people?" said Starwick, repeating the banal phrase with a quiet sarcasm that brought a flush to the other's face.

"Well, it's not likely that he will, from what I've heard."

Starwick cast a weary look around him at the chattering group of people at the other tables.

"God!" he said quietly. "I shouldn't think he'd want to. I imagine most of them are about as dull a lot as you could find."

"If you feel that way about them, what is the great attraction Paris holds for you? How can you possibly feel that way about the people and still say you feel at home here?"

"Because Paris belongs to the world—to Europe—more than it belongs to France. One does not come here because he wants to know the French: he comes because he can find here the most pleasant, graceful, and civilized life on earth."

"Yes, but there are other things that may be more important than leading a graceful and pleasant life."

"What, for instance?" said Starwick, looking at him.

"Getting your work done is one of them. For you, I should think that would be a great deal more important."

Starwick was again silent; the old bestial grimace, image of an unutterable anguish and confusion in his soul, for a moment contorted his pleasant ruddy face, developed, passed, was gone; he said quietly and with the infinite weariness of despair that had now become the image of his life:

"Getting my work done! My God, as if it mattered."

"There was a time when you thought it did, Frank."

"Yes, there was a time when I did think so," he said lifelessly.

"And now you no longer feel that way about it?"

Starwick was silent; when he spoke again, it was not to answer directly.

"Always the old unquiet heart," he said wearily and sadly; he turned and looked silently at his friend for a moment. "Why? Since I first knew you, you have been like that, Eugene—wanting to devour the earth, lashing your soul to frenzy in this useless, hopeless, and impossible search for knowledge."

"Why useless or hopeless, Frank?"

"Because it is a kind of madness in you that grows worse all the time; because you cannot cure it, or ever satisfy this hunger of yours while you have it; because it will exhaust you, break your heart, and drive you mad; and because, even if you could gratify this impossible desire to absorb the whole sum of recorded knowledge and experience in the world, you would gain nothing by it."

"There I can't agree with you."

"Do you really think," said Starwick wearily, "that if you could achieve this hopeless ambition of reading all the books that were ever printed—of knowing all the people—seeing all the places—that you would be any better off than you now are? Now, day after day, you go prowling up and down along the book-stalls on the Seine, pawing through tons of junk and rubbish until your very heart is sick with weariness and confusion. When you are not with us, you sit alone in a café with a dictionary beside you trying to decipher the meaning of some useless and meaningless book. You no longer enjoy what you read, because you are tortured by a consciousness of the vast number of books you have not read; you go to the museums—to the Louvre—and you no longer enjoy the pictures, because you torture your brain and exhaust your energy in a foolish effort to see and remember all of them. You no longer enjoy the crowd, you go out on the streets of Paris, you sit here in this crowded café—and instead of taking pleasure in all this gaiety and life about you, you are tortured by the thought that you know none of these people, that you know nothing about their lives, that there are four million people here in Paris and you do not know a dozen of them. . . . Eugene, Eugene," he said sadly, "this thing in you is growing worse all the time; if you do not master it, it is a disease that will some day drive you mad and destroy you."

"And yet, Frank, many people on this earth have had the same disease. Because of it, in order to get knowledge, Doctor Faust sold his soul to the devil."

"Alas," said Starwick, "where is the devil?" In a moment he continued quietly, as before: "Do you think that you will really gain in wisdom if you read a million books? Do you think you will find out more about life if you know a million people rather than yourself? Do you think you will get more pleasure from a thousand women than from two or three—see more if you go to a hundred countries instead of six? And finally, do you think you'll get more happiness from life by 'getting your work done' than by doing nothing? My God, Eugene"—his voice was weary with the resigned fatality of despair that had now corrupted him—"you still feel that it is important that you 'do your work,' as you call it, but what will it matter if you do or don't? You want to lead the artist's life, to do the artist's work, to create out of the artist's materials—what will it matter in the end if you do this, or nothing?"

"You did not always feel so, Frank."

"No," said Starwick wearily, "there was a time when I felt differently. There was a time when I felt that the artist's life was the finest life on earth—the only life I would care to lead."

"And now?"

"Now—nothing—nothing," he spoke so quietly that his words were scarcely audible. "It no longer matters. . . . I go to the Louvre and look at that colossal mountain of junk—up and down those endless corridors hung with the dull or worthless work of thousands of dead men who once felt as I did—that they must create, express the image of their soul—that art and the artist's life were all that mattered. Now they are dead, their dreary works have been left behind as a kind of useless relic of their agony: in that whole gigantic storage-plant of worthless art—there are just three pictures I should have cared to paint—and I know it's not in me to paint any of them. I thought I wanted to write plays, but now I feel the same about that, too; among all the thousands of plays I have read or seen, I doubt that there are a dozen which I should have cared to write—and I know now that I could have written none of them. . . . What does it matter? Why do you goad your spirit and exhaust your mind with these frantic efforts, these useless desires to add another book or play to the mountains of books and plays that have already been written? Why should we break our hearts to add to that immense accumulation of dull, fair, or trivial work that has already been done?" He was silent a moment longer, and then the color in his ruddy face deepening with excitement, he said in a high, passionate tone: "What is great—what is priceless—what we would give our lives to do—is so impossible—so utterly, damnably impossible! And if we can never do the best—then why do anything?"

For a moment, there returned to the other a memory

of the moonlit streets of Cambridge, and of a night when
Starwick, drunk with wine and the generous and extravagant enthusiasm of youth, had turned to him and in
a voice that rung along the sleeping street, had called
him a mighty poet. And he remembered how his own
heart had beat hot with hope and joy at the sound of
those proud and foolish words, and how he had grasped
Starwick's hand and wrung it with a hard grip of passionate conviction, and told Frank what he believed at
that moment with all the ardor of his heart—that Starwick was the greatest young man of his time and generation.

And remembering now those two drunk and happy
boys who stood there in the moon-still streets, and spoke
to each other the compact of their devotion and belief,
he wanted to ask Frank if this weary acquiescence in
defeat, that had now become the very color of his life,
was a better thing than the proud and foolish vision of a
boy.

But he said nothing, and after a moment's silence,
Starwick looked at his watch and called the waiter, saying that it was already time for their meeting with the
two women at a café in Montparnasse. Therefore, they
paid the bill, and departed; but what Frank had said to
him that day would live in his memory in years to come.
For in Frank's words were implicit every element of the
resignation, despair, and growing inertia and apathy of
his will.

v

The relations between these four people had now been
strained to the breaking point. That month of debauch
had exacted a stern tribute from them. Their exhausted
bodies and frayed nerves cried out for rest, a period of
curative repose when the well of their drained energy

could be filled up again. But, like creatures hopelessly addicted to a drug, they could not break the bonds of this tyranny of pleasure which held them. Starwick seemed to be completely enslaved by this senseless and furious quest, this frantic seeking after new sensations, this hopeless pursuit of a happiness, a fulfilment, that they never found. He seemed unable or unwilling to break the evil spell. Rather, as if a poisonous hunger was feeding on his vitals—a hunger that grew constantly from the food it fed upon, and that could not be assuaged by any means—the evil inertia of his will, the ugly impassivity of his resignation became every day more marked.

Of all of them, he alone preserved the appearance of calm. And that cold, impassive calm was maddening: he met the storms of anger, protests, reproaches, and persuasions of the others with an air of sad humility, a kind of sorrowful acceptance, a quiet agreement to every accusation or indictment, a grand manner of sweet, sorrowful contrition that was more hateful than any deliberate insult could have been. For behind this impenetrable armor of humility, this air of mysterious fatality, there was evident a hateful arrogance which said that words were useless because no words could express the fatal wisdom of his soul, and which, with a stubborn and abominable perversity, seemed deliberately resolved on ruin.

His conduct became daily more absurd, extravagant, ridiculous. He was acting like a melodramatic fool, but it was impossible to laugh at his folly because of the desperate fatality that attended it. He did unbelievable things, contrived unbelievable situations that seemed fitting only in a world of opera but were shamefully unreal and unnecessary in the real one. What was really shameful and unworthy in his conduct was this—his fatality served no purpose, his reckless and deliberate pursuit of danger did no good except to dignify the melodramatic unreality of a comic-opera situation with the realities of blood and death.

He was constantly and deliberately involving himself and others in these ridiculous but perilous situations. One night, in one of the Montmartre resorts, he had a quarrel with a man that would have been farcical save for the ugly consequences it produced, the painful and shameful memory it would later evoke. The man, an unpleasant, wizened-looking little Frenchman, a creature of the night, with obscene eyes, a yellowed skin, and a pointed beard half covering the features of a rodent, had not been able to keep his ugly eyes off Ann, had measured the noble proportions of her beauty with a kind of foul leering appraisal that had in it something almost as palpable and sensual as a naked touch, and now, as the orchestra struck up another tune, he approached the table, bowed, and asked her, courteously enough, for a dance.

Ann reddened furiously in the face, looked down sullenly at the tablecloth and, before she was able to think of a reply, Starwick said:

"Mademoiselle does not care to dance. Please go away."

The cold arrogance of Starwick's tone, and his curt dismissal, enraged the Frenchman. When he replied, his lips were bared in an ugly smile that showed unpleasant fangs of yellowed teeth; he said:

"Is the lady not allowed to speak for herself?—Is Monsieur perhaps her guardian?"

"Will you please go away now?" Starwick said again, with a cold and weary impassivity. "You are boring us."

"But, it's marvelous!" The little Frenchman cast back

his yellowed face and bared his fangs in a laugh of envenomed mockery. "It's Monsieur D'Artagnan come to life again, and a lady so shy and modest that she can't speak for herself! But, it's superb!" he cried again, and with an ironic bow, concluded: "Monsieur, with all my heart I thank you for this wonderful diversion! You are very droll!"

Starwick's reply to this was to pick up the seltzer bottle on the table and, without for a moment altering his air of cold impassivity, to squirt the siphon straight in the little Frenchman's yellow face.

In a moment, the place was a seething maelstrom of excitement. People all over sprang up from their tables, the dancers stopped dancing, the orchestra stopped with a crash, and the proprietor and the waiter came towards them on the run.

In a moment, they were surrounded by an excited group of gesticulating, chattering people, all trying to talk at once. Starwick was standing up now, facing his antagonist, cold and impassive save for a deeper flush of excitement on his ruddy face. As for the little Frenchman, the look of murderous hatred on his face was horrible. Without stopping to dry his dripping face with the napkin which an excited and persuasive waiter was offering him, he thrust aside the manager, who was trying to restrain him, and coming close to Starwick, snarled:

"Your name, monsieur! I demand to know your name. My representatives will call upon you in the morning."

"Good," said Starwick coldly. "I shall wait for them. Monsieur shall have whatever satisfaction he desires."

And taking a card from his purse, he wrote the studio address below his name and gave it to the man.

"Ah, good!" the Frenchman cried harshly, glancing at it. "Until tomorrow!"

And calling for his bill, and silent to all the apologies and cajoleries of the proprietor, he departed.

"But, Frank, darling!" Elinor cried, when they had seated themselves again. "What do you intend to do? Surely you're not going to——" She did not finish, but stared at him with a troubled and astonished face.

"Yes," said Starwick coldly and quietly. "He has asked me to fight a duel, and if he wants it, I shall meet him."

"Oh, but don't be absurd!" cried Elinor with an impatient laugh. "What on earth do you know about fighting duels! My poor child, how can you be so ridiculous! This is the twentieth century, darling. Don't you know that people don't act that way any more?"

"Quite!" said Starwick, with a stony calm. "Nevertheless, I shall meet him if he wants me to." He looked at her with quiet eyes for a moment, and then said gravely: "I've *got* to do that. I really have, you know."

"Got to!" Elinor cried impatiently. "Why, the child is *mad!*" Her tone immediately became crisp, incisive, authoritative: she began to speak to him quietly, kindly, but in a peremptory tone, as one might speak to a child:

"Francis," she said quietly. "Listen to me! Don't be an idiot! What does it matter about that wretched little man? It's all over now! A duel! Good heavens! Don't be such a child! Who ever heard of such a thing?"

His face reddened a little from her ridicule, but he answered, in a cold impassive tone:

"Quite! Nevertheless, I shall meet him if he wants it!"

"Meet him!" Elinor cried again. "Oh, Francis, how can you be so stupid! Meet him with what?"

"With whatever weapon he wants to use," Starwick replied. "Pistols or swords—it doesn't matter!"

"Pistols or swords!" Elinor shrieked faintly, and began to laugh. "Why, you idiot, what do you know about

pistols or swords? You've never had a sword in your hand
in your life—and as for pistols, you wouldn't even know
how to point the thing and press the trigger!"

"It doesn't matter," he said in a very quiet and fatal
way. "I shall fire into the air."

In spite of the ridiculous and melodramatic quality of
these foolish words, no one laughed. They saw suddenly
what fatal consequences this farcical situation might
have, and having felt the desperation of his soul—that
terrible despair which now seemed to be driving him
on to seek ruin everywhere—they knew he would do
exactly as he said, if given the opportunity.

Elinor started to go: she beckoned to a waiter and
called for the bill, and said persuasively:

"Come on! Let's get out of this place! You've had too
much to drink! I think your head needs clearing—a
little fresh air will do you good. You'll feel different
about all this tomorrow!"

"But not at all!" he said patiently, and then, as she
started to get up: "Will you please sit down. We're not
going yet."

"But why, darling? Aren't you ready? Haven't you
raised enough hell for one evening—or do you want to
fight a duel with someone else? Besides, I do think you
might think of Ann. I know she's wanted to go for some
time."

"But why?" he said, turning to Ann with an air of fine
surprise. "Aren't you enjoying yourself? It's a very good
place, and the music is awfully good—it really is, you
know."

"Oh, charming, charming!" she muttered sarcastically.
She had been staring at the tablecloth sullenly, with a
flaming face, ever since the quarrel had begun, and now
looking up suddenly, with a short and angry laugh, she
said:

"God! I don't know whether to walk out of here or *crawl!* I feel all—*undressed!*"

At these words, his face really did flush crimson with embarrassment. He looked at her for a moment, and then said sharply, with a note of stern reproof and anger in his voice:

"Ann! It's *very* bad and *very* wrong—and—and—very *mean* of you to talk like that."

"That's how I feel," she muttered.

"Then," he said quietly, but with two deep and angry spots of color flaming in his cheeks, "I'm *thoroughly* ashamed of you. It's *quite* unworthy of you. At a time like this, a person of your quality has got to show more" —he paused, choosing the word carefully—"more *fiber.* You really must, you know!"

"Oh, fiber my eye!" she flared up, looking at him with flushed, lovely and angry eyes. "You don't lack fiber simply because you don't want to be made a fool of! Frank, you make me tired, the way you talk! Everywhere we go now someone's always showing 'fiber'—and everyone is having a rotten, awful time. For God's sake, let's not talk so much about showing fiber and let's try to enjoy ourselves and get some pleasure and some happiness from life, and act like decent, natural people for a change. I had looked forward so much to coming on this trip with Elinor—and now——" Tears of anger and disappointment glittered in her eyes, she looked down at the table sullenly in an effort to conceal them, and then muttered: "Playing the fool and making scenes and starting rows everywhere we go! Getting into trouble everywhere, making people hate us, never having any fun! Squirting siphons at some wretched little man——" She made a sudden impulsive gesture of disgust and turned away. "God! It makes me sick!"

"I'm sorry to know you feel that way," he said quietly.

"I'll try to see it doesn't happen again—but, after all, Ann—the reason it did happen is because I like you so *very* much, and have so much respect for you and won't stand for anyone insulting you!"

"Ah-h! Insulting me!" she said angrily. "Good heavens, Francis, do you think I need protection from a wretched little man like that? When I've been a nurse, and had to go alone to every rotten slum in Boston, and learned to handle people twice his size! Protect me!" she said bitterly. "Thank you for nothing! I didn't come over here to be protected—I don't need it. I can take care of myself. Just try to act and feel like a decent human being—let's try to be friends together and to show some consideration for each other—and don't worry about protecting me!"

VI

Eugene slept little that night. The quarrel in the night-club and its consequences seemed fantastic, incredible, like a nightmare. At daybreak he got up and went to the window and stared out at the grey light just breaking on the roofs and chimney pots of Paris. The old buildings emerged haggard, pale, lemony, with all the wonderful, homely practicality of dawn and morning, and looking at them, Montmartre, the blaze of lights, the music and the drunken voices, and the quarrel with the Frenchman—the whole strange and evil chemistry of night—seemed farther away, more unreal and dreamlike than ever. Could it have happened? Had Starwick really been challenged to a duel? Was he going through with it?

He got up and dressed, and with dry lips and a strange, numb lightness in his limbs, descended to the street and hailed a passing taxi in the rue Bonaparte. The sounds of morning, shutters being rolled up, scrub-women and maids down on their knees at entrances, shops being opened—all this made the night before seem more unreal than ever.

When he got to the studio he found everybody up. Ann was already at work making coffee, scrambling eggs for breakfast. Elinor was just combing up her hair, Starwick was in the balcony and had not yet come down. Elinor kept talking as she arranged her hair, and from the balcony Starwick answered her:

"But Frank!" she was saying, "you know you wouldn't be fool enough to do such a thing! Surely you don't mean you intend to go through with it?"

"Ace," he said coldly from above, "I do mean to. Quite!"

"But—oh! Don't be an ass!" she cried impatiently. Turning to Ann, with a little, frowning smile, she bit her lips, and shaking her head slightly, cried in an astounded tone:

"Isn't it *incredible!* Did you ever hear of such an *insane* thing in all your life!"

But in the set of her jaw, the faint smile around the corner of her mouth, there was the look of grim decision they had all seen before.

As Eugene entered, Ann turned from the stove, and spoon in hand, stood looking at him sullenly for a moment. Suddenly she laughed her short and angry laugh, and turned away towards Elinor, saying:

"God! Here's the second! Don't they make a pair!"

"But my *dear!*" cried Elinor with a light, gay malice. "Where is the top hat? Where are the striped trousers and the morning coat? Where is the dueling case with the revolvers? . . . All right, Monsieur D'Artagnan," she called up towards the balcony ironically. "Your friend, Monsieur Porthos, has arrived . . . and break-

fast is ready, darling! What's that they say about an
army?" she innocently inquired. "That it ought not to
fight on an empty stomach? . . . Ahem!" she cleared her
throat. "Will Monsieur D'Artagnan condescend to have
the company of two frail women for breakfast on the
morning of the great affair . . . or does Monsieur prefer
to be left alone with his devoted second to discuss—
ahem! ahem! . . . the final arrangements?"

Starwick made no reply, until he had come down the
steps:

"You can stay, if you want to," he said indifferently. "I
shall have nothing to say to them anyway." Turning to
Eugene, he said with magnificent, bored weariness:
"Find out what they want. Let me know what they want
to do."

"B—but, what do you want me to say to them, Frank?
What shall I tell them?"

"Anything," said Starwick indifferently. "Anything
you like. Say that I will meet him anywhere—on any
terms—whatever they like. Let them settle it their own
way."

He picked up a spoon and started to eat his orange.

"Oh, Frank, you idiot!" cried Elinor, seizing him by
the hair, and shaking his head. "Don't be stupid! You
know you're not going on with this farce!"

He lifted quiet, wearily patient eyes and looked at her:

"Sorry!" he said. "But I've *got* to. If that's what he
wants, I really must. I owe the man that much—I really
do, you know!"

Breakfast then proceeded in a painful and uneasy
silence, broken only by Elinor's malicious thrusts, and
maintained by Starwick's weary and impassive calm.

At ten o'clock, there were steps along the alleyway
outside, some one mounted the stoop, and the studio bell
jangled. The two women exchanged uneasy looks, Star-

wick got up quietly and turned away, and in a moment
Elinor called out sharply: "Entrez."

The door opened and a man entered the room. He
wore striped trousers that were in need of pressing, a
frayed and worn-looking frock coat, and he carried a
briefcase under his arm. He was bald, sallow, about
forty-five years old, and had a little mustache and furtive
eyes. He looked at each person in the room quickly,
sharply, and then said inquiringly:

"Monsieur Star-*week?*"

"Ace," said Starwick quietly, and turned.

"Ah, bon!" the little Frenchman said briskly, and
smiled, showing yellow fangs of teeth. He had been bent
slightly forward, holding his briefcase with thin, eager
fingers, as he waited. Now he came forward swiftly, took
a card out of his wallet, and presenting it to Starwick
with something of a flourish, said:

"Monsieur, permettez-moi. Ma carte."

Starwick glanced at the card indifferently, and was
about to put it down upon the table when the little
Frenchman interrupted him. Stretching out his thin and
rather grimy hand, he said courteously yet eagerly:

"S'il vous plaît, monsieur!"—took the card again, and
put it back into his wallet.

Starwick indicated a chair and said:

"Won't you sit down?"

From that time on, the conversation proceeded in
mutilated French and English. The little Frenchman sat
down, hitched up his striped trousers carefully and with
his arched fingers poised upon his bony knees, bent
forward and, with another ingratiating and somewhat
repulsive smile, said:

"Monsieur Star-week ees Américain, n'est-ce pas?"

"Ace," said Starwick.

"And was at Le Rat Mort last night?"

"Ace," said Starwick again.

"Et Monsieur?" He nodded inquiringly towards Eugene, "vas also zere?"

"Ace," Starwick answered.

"Et Mademoiselle . . . et Mademoiselle," he turned with courteous inquiry towards the two young women— "zey vere also zere?"

"Ace," said Starwick as before.

"Ah, bon!" the little Frenchman cried, nodding his head vigorously, and with an air of complete satisfaction. Then, rubbing his bony little hands together dryly and briskly, he took up his thin and battered old briefcase, which he had been holding firmly between his knees, swiftly unfastened the straps and unlatched it, and took out a few sheets of flaming, yellow paper covered with notations in a fine, minute hand:

"Monsieur"—he began, clearing his throat, and rattling the flimsy sheets impressively—"Monsieur, I s'ink"—he looked up at Starwick ingratiatingly, but with an air of sly insinuation—"Monsieur, I s'ink, perhaps, vas"—he shrugged his shoulders slightly, with an air of deprecation—"Monsieur vas—drink-*ing?*"

Starwick made no answer for a moment: his face reddened, he inclined his head, and said coldly, but unconcedingly:

"Oui! C'est ça, monsieur!"

"Ah-h!" the little Frenchman cried again with a dry little cackle of satisfaction, "an' ven one drink— espeecial*ee*, monsieur, ven ve are yong," he laughed ingratiatingly again, "he sometime do an' say some t'ings zat he regret—eh?"

"But of course!" cried Elinor at this point, quickly, impatiently, eagerly. "That's just the point! Frank was drinking—the whole thing happened like a flash—it's all over now—we're sorry—everyone is sorry:—it was a regrettable mistake—we're sorry for it—we apologize!"

"But not at all!" cried Starwick reddening angrily, and looking resentfully towards Elinor. "Not at all! I do *not* agree with you!"

"Oh, Frank, you idiot, be quiet! Let me handle this," she cried. Turning to the little Frenchman, she said swiftly, smoothly, with all her coaxing and formidable persuasiveness:

"Monsieur, what can we do to remedy this regrettable mistake?"

"Comment?" said the Frenchman, in a puzzled tone.

"Monsieur Starwick," Elinor went on with coaxing persuasion, "Monsieur Starwick—comme vous voyez, monsieur—est très jeune. Il a toutes les fautes de la jeunesse. Mais il est aussi un homme de grand esprit; de grand talent. Il a le tempérament d'un artiste: d'un homme de génie. Comme un Français, monsieur, vous," she went on flatteringly, "*vous* connaissez cette espèce d'hommes. Vous savez qu'ils ne sont pas toujours responsables de leurs actes. C'est comme ça avec Monsieur Starwick. Il est de bon cœur, de bon volonté: il est honnête, généreux et sincère, mais il est aussi plein de tempérament—impulsif:—il manque de jugement. Hier soir nous avons tous—comme on dit—fait la noce ensemble. Monsieur Starwick a bu beaucoup—a bu trop—et il a été coupable d'une chose regrettable. Mais aujourd'hui il se repent très sincèrement de sa conduite.

"Il vous offre ses apologies les plus profondes. Il a déjà souffert assez. Dans ces circonstances, monsieur," she concluded, with an air of charming persuasiveness, "on peut excuser le jeune homme, n'est-ce pas?—on peut pardonner une faute si honnêtement et sincèrement regrettée."

And she paused, smiling at him with an air of hopeful finality, as if to say: "There! You agree with me, don't you? I knew you would!"

But the Frenchman was not to be so easily persuaded. Waving thin fingers sideways in the air, and shaking his head without conviction, he laughed a dry, dubious laugh, and said:

"Ah-h! I don't know—mademoiselle! Zese apologies!" —again he waved thin dubious fingers—"eet ees all ver-ree well to meck apologies bot ze—vat you say?— ze dom-mage!—ze dom-mage is done. . . . Monsieur," he said gravely, turning to Starwick, "you have been coupable of a ver-ree gret offense. Ze—ze—vay you say?— *ze assault,* monsieur—ze assault ees 'ere in France—une chose très sérieuse! Vous comprenez?"

"Ace," said Starwick coldly.

"Mon client," the little Frenchman cleared his throat portentously—"mon client, Monsieur Reynal, 'as been terriblement blessé—insulté! monsieur!" he cried sharply. "Eet ees necessaree zu meck des réparations, n'est-ce pas?"

"Ace," said Starwick coldly. "Whatever reparation you desire."

The Frenchman stared at him a moment in an astonished way and then, in an excited and eager tone, cried:

"Ah, bon! Zen you agree?"

"Perfectly," said Starwick.

"Bon! Bon!" the little man said eagerly, rubbing his hands together with greedy satisfaction. "Monsieur est sage—ees, vat you say?—ees ver-ree wise. Monsieur est Américain—n'est-ce pas?—un étranger—comme vous, mademoiselle . . . et vous, monsieur . . . et vous, mademoiselle—you are 'ere zu meck ze tour—zu be libre—free—n'est-ce pas—zu avoid ze complications——"

"But," said Elinor, in a bewildered tone, "what is—I don't understand——"

"Alors," the Frenchman said, "eet ees bettaire to avoid ze complications—oui! Ah," he said, with an arching glance at Starwick, "mais Monsieur est sage . . . est très, très sage! C'est toujours mieux de faire des réparations . . . et éviter les conséquences plus sérieuses."

"But!" cried Elinor again, her astonishment growing, "I don't understand. What reparations are you talking about?"

"Zese, madame!" the Frenchman said, and coughing portentously, he rattled the flimsy sheets of paper in his hand, held them up before his eyes, and began to read:

"Pour l'endommagement d'un veston du soir—trois cents francs!"

"What? *What?*" said Elinor in a small, chilled tone. "For—*what?*"

"Mais, oui, madame!" the Frenchman now cried passionately, for the first time rising to the heights of moral indignation, "un veston du soir complet—ruiné, madame!—*complètement, absolument* ruiné! . . . Trois cents francs, monsieur," he said cunningly, turning to Starwick, "c'est pas cher! . . . Pour moi, oui!—c'est cher—mais pour vous—ah-h!"—he waved his dirty fingers and laughed with scornful deprecation—"c'est rien! Rien du tout." He rattled the flimsy paper in his hands, cleared his throat, and went on:

"Pour l'endommagement d'une chemise—une chemise, n'est-ce pas, du soir?"—he looked up inquiringly —"cinquante francs——"

"But this," gasped Elinor, "this is——" She looked at Starwick with an astounded face. Starwick said nothing.

"Pour l'angoisse mentale," the Frenchman continued.

"What?" Elinor gasped and looked at Ann. "What did he say?"

"Mental anguish," Ann answered curtly. "All right," she turned to the Frenchman, "how much is the mental anguish?"

"C'est cinq cent francs, mademoiselle."

"But this man?" cried Elinor, turning to Ann with an air of astounded enlightenment, "this man is——"

"He's a shyster lawyer, yes!" Ann said bitterly. "Couldn't you see it from the first?"

"Ah, mademoiselle," the Frenchman began with a re-proachful grimace, and a little, deprecating movement of his fingers, "you are——"

"How much?" Ann answered in her level, toneless French. "How much do you want?"

"Vous comprenez, mademoiselle——"

"How much?" she said harshly. "How much do you want?"

His furtive eyes gleamed with a sudden fox-glint of eager greed.

"Mille francs!" he said eagerly. "Mille francs pour tout ensemble! . . . Pour vous, mademoiselle"—he laughed again with scornful deprecation as he waved his grimy fingers—"c'est rien—pour moi——"

She got up abruptly, went over to the shelf that ran around the wall and got her purse. She opened it, took out a roll of bills, and coming back tossed them on the table before him.

"But, mademoiselle," he stammered, unable to believe his good luck, his eyes glued upon the roll of bills in a stare of hypnotic fascination.

"Give me a receipt," she said.

"Comment?" he looked puzzled for a moment, then cried, "Ah-h! Un reçu! Mais oui, mais oui, mademoiselle! Tout de suite!"

Trembling with frantic haste, he scrawled out a receipt on a sheet of yellow paper, gave it to her, clutched the banknotes with a trembling claw, and stuffed them in his wallet.

"Now get out," said Ann.

"Mademoiselle?" he scrambled hastily to his feet, clutched his briefcase and his hat, and looked nervously at her. "Vous dites?"

"Get out of here," she said, and began to move slowly towards him.

He scrambled for the door like a frightened cat, stammering:

"Mais oui . . . mais parfaitement . . . mais——"
He almost stumbled going down the steps, glancing back with nervous apprehension as he went. She shut the door behind him, came back, sat down in her chair, and stared sullenly at her plate, saying nothing. Starwick was crimson in the face, but did not look at anyone and did not speak. Elinor was busy with her napkin: she had lifted it to her face and was holding it firmly across her mouth. From time to time her breast and stomach and her heavy shoulders trembled in a kind of shuddering convulsion, smothered and explosive snorts and gasps came from her.

It got too much for her: they heard a faint, choked shriek, she rose and rushed blindly across the room, entered the bathroom and slammed the door behind her. And then they heard peal after peal of laughter, shrieks and whoops and yells of it, and finally a dead silence, broken at times by exhausted gasps. Ann continued to look sullenly and miserably at her plate. As for Starwick, he sat there wearily detached, impassive, magnificent as always, but his face had the hue and color of boiled lobster.

VII

One night, in a small bar or *bistro* upon the hill of Montmartre, Starwick met a young Frenchman who was to become the companion of his adventures in many strange and devious ways thereafter. It was about four o'clock in the morning: after the usual nightly circuit of the gilded pleasure resorts, cafés, and more unsavory dives and stews of the district, Starwick had become very drunk and unruly, had quarreled with Elinor and Ann when they tried to take him home, and since that time had been wandering aimlessly through the district, going from one cheap bar to another.

The women hung on doggedly: Starwick had refused to let them accompany him, and they had asked Eugene to stay with him and try to keep him out of trouble. Eugene, in fact, was only less drunk than his companion, but fortified by that sense of pride and duty which a trust imposed by two lovely women can give a young man, he hung on, keeping pace with Starwick, drink for drink, until the whole night fused into a drunken blur, a rout of evil faces, the whole to be remembered later as jags of splintered light upon a chain of darkness, as flying images, fixed, instant, and intolerably bright, in the great blank of memory. And out of all these blazing pictures of the night and the wild reel of their debauch, one would remain forever after, to haunt his vision mournfully. It was the memory—or rather the *consciousness*—of the two women, Ann and Elinor, waiting in the dark, following the blind weave of their drunken path, all through the mad kaleidoscope of night, never approaching them, but always there. He had not seemed to look at them, to notice them, and yet later he had always known that they were there. And the memory fused to one final mournful image that was to return a thousand times to haunt him in the years to come. He and Starwick had come out of one of the bars that broke the darkness of the long steep hill, and were reeling down past shuttered stores and old dark houses towards the invitation of another blaze of light.

Suddenly he knew that Ann and Elinor were behind them. For a moment he turned, and saw the two women pacing slowly after them, alone, patient, curiously enduring. The image of that long silent street of night, walled steeply with old houses and shuttered shops, and of the figures of these two women pacing slowly behind them, in the darkness, seemed in later years to bear the sorrowful legend of what their lives—of what so much of life—was to become. And for this reason it burned forever in his memory with a mournful, dark, and haunting radiance, became in fact, detached from names and personalities and identic histories—became something essential, everlasting, and immutable in life. It was an image of fruitless love and lost devotion, of a love that would never come to anything, and of beautiful life that must be ruinously consumed in barren adoration of a lost soul, a cold and unresponding heart. And it was all wrought mournfully there into the scheme of night, made legible in the quiet and gracious loveliness of these two women, so strong, so patient, and so infinitely loyal, pacing slowly down behind two drunken boys in the slant steep street and emptiness of night.

Suddenly the image blazed to the structure of hard actuality: another bar, and all around hoarse laughter, high sanguinary voices, a sudden scheme of faces scarred with night, and livid with night's radiance—whores, taxidrivers, Negroes, and those other nameless unmistakable ones—who come from somewhere—God knows where—and who live somehow—God knows how—and who recede again at morning into unknown cells—but who live here only, brief as moths, and baleful as a serpent's eye, in the unwholesome chemistry of night.

He found himself leaning heavily on the zinc counter of the bar, staring at a pair of whited, flabby-looking arms, the soiled apron and shirt, the soiled nighttime face and dark, mistrustful eyes of night's soiled barman. The blur of hoarse voices, shouts and oaths and laughter fused around him, and suddenly beside him he heard Starwick's voice, drunken, quiet, and immensely still:

"Monsieur," it said—its very stillness cut like a knife through all the fog of sound about him—"monsieur, du feu, s'il vous plaît."

"But sairtainlee, monsieur," a droll and pleasant-sounding voice said quietly. "W'y not?"

He turned and saw Starwick, a cigarette between his lips, bending awkwardly to get the light from a proffered cigarette which a young Frenchman was holding carefully for him. At last he got it; puffing awkwardly, and straightening, he slightly raised his hat in salutation, and said with drunken gravity:

"Merci. Vous êtes bien gentil."

"But," said the young Frenchman again, drolly, and with a slight shrug of his shoulder, "not at all! Eet ees noz-zing!"

And as Starwick started to look at him with grave drunken eyes, the Frenchman returned his look with a glance that was perfectly composed, friendly, good-humored, and drolly inquiring.

"Monsieur?" he said courteously, as Starwick continued to look at him.

"I think," said Starwick slowly, with the strangely mannered and almost womanish intonation of his voice, "I think I like you *very* much. You are *very* kind, and *very* generous, and altogether a *very* grand person. I am *enormously* grateful to you."

"But," the Frenchman said, with droll surprise, and a slight astonished movement of his shoulders, "I 'ave done noz-zing! You ask for du feu—a light—and I geev to you. I am glad eef you like—bot"—again he shrugged his shoulders with a cynical but immensely engaging humor—"eet ees not so ver-ree grand."

He was a young man, not more than thirty years old, somewhat above the middle height, with a thin, nervously active figure, and thin, pointedly Gallic features. It was a pleasant, most engaging face, full of a sharply cynical intelligence; the thin mouth was alive with humor—with the witty and politely cynical disbelief of his race, and his tone, his manner—everything about him—was eloquent with this racial quality of disbelief, a quality that was perfectly courteous, that would raise its pointed eyebrows and say politely, "You s'ink so"— but that accepted without assent, was politely noncommittal without agreement.

He was dressed as many young Frenchmen of that period dressed—a style that served to combine the sinister toughness of the Apache with a rather gaudy and cheap enhancement of the current fashions. His clothes were neat but cheaply made; he wore a felt hat with a wide brim, creased, French fashion, up the sides, an overcoat with padded shoulders, cut in sharply at the waist, his trousers had a short and skimpy look, and barely covered the tops of his shoes. He wore spats, and a rather loud-colored scarf which he knotted loosely, cravat-fashion, and which thus concealed his collar and his shirt. Finally, when he smoked a cigarette, he drew the smoke in slowly, languorously, knowingly, with lidded eyes, and a cruel and bitter convulsion of his thin lips that gave his sharp face a sinister Apache expression.

Starwick was now crying out in a high drunken tone of passionate assurance:

"But yes! Yes! Yes!—You are a *grand* person—a *swell* person—I like you *enormously*. . . ."

"I am glad," said the Frenchman politely, with another almost imperceptible movement of the shoulders.

"But yes! You are my friend!" Starwick cried in a high passionate tone. "I like you—you must drink with me."

"Eef you like—of course!" the Frenchman politely agreed. Turning to the soiled barman who continued to look at them with dark mistrustful eyes, he said, in a hard, sharp voice, "Une fine. . . . And you, monsieur?" he turned inquiringly towards Eugene, "I s'ink you have another drink?"

"No, not know." His glass was not yet empty. "We—we have both already had something to drink."

"I can see," the Frenchman said politely, but with a swift flicker of cynical mirth across his thin mouth, that needed no translation. Raising his glass, he said courteously:

"À votre santé, messieurs," and drank.

"Look!" cried Starwick. "You are our friend now, and you must call us by our names. My name is Frank; his is Eugene—what is yours?"

"My name ees Alec," said the young Frenchman smiling. "Zat ees w'at zey call me."

"But it's perfect!" Starwick cried enthusiastically. "It's a *swell* name—a *wonderful* name! Alec!—Ecoute!" he said to the soiled barman with the ugly eye, "Jub pawnse qu'il faut—encore du cognac," he said drunkenly, making a confused and maudlin gesture with his arm. "Encore du cognac, s'il vous plaît!" And as the barman silently and sullenly filled the three glasses from a bottle on the bar, Starwick turned to Alec, shouting with dangerous hilarity: "Cognac forever, Alec!—Cognac for you and me and all of us forever!—Nothing but drunkenness—glorious drunkenness—divine poetic drunkenness forever!"

"Eef you like," said Alec, with a polite and acquiescent shrug. He raised his glass and drank.

It was four o'clock when they left the place. Arm in arm they reeled out into the street, Starwick holding onto Alec for support, and shouting drunkenly:

"Nous sommes des amis!—Nous sommes des amis éternels! Mais oui! Mais oui!"

The whole dark and silent street rang and echoed with his drunken outcry. "Alec et moi—nous sommes des frères—nous sommes des artistes! Nothing shall part us! Non—jamais! Jamais!"

A taxi, which had been waiting in the darkness several doors away, now drove up swiftly and stopped before them at the curb. Ann and Elinor were inside: Elinor opened the door and spoke gently:

"Frank, get in the taxi now, we're going home."

"Mais jamais! Jamais!" Starwick yelled hysterically. "I go nowhere without Alec!—We are brothers—friends —he has a poet's soul."

"Frank, don't be an idiot!" Elinor spoke quietly, but with crisp authority. "You're drunk; get in the taxi; we're going home."

"Mais oui!" he shouted. "Je suis ivre! I am drunk! I will always be drunk—nothing but drunkenness forever for Alec and me!"

"Listen!" Elinor spoke quietly, pleasantly to the Frenchman. "Won't you go away, please, and leave him now?" He is drunk, he does not know what he is doing, he really must go home now."

"But, of course, madame," said Alec courteously, "I go now." He turned to Starwick and spoke quietly, with his thin, engaging smile: "I s'ink, Frank, eet ees bettaire eef you go home now, non?"

"But no! But no!" cried Starwick passionately. "I will go nowhere without Alec. . . . Alec!" he cried, clutching him with drunken desperation. "You cannot go! You must not go! You cannot leave me!"

"Tomorrow, perhaps," said Alec, smiling. "Ees eet not bettaire eef we go togezzer tomorrow?—I s'ink zen you feel motch bettaire."

"No! No! Starwick cried obstinately. "Now! Now! Alec, you cannot leave me! We are brothers, we must tell each other everything. . . . You must show me all you know, all you have seen—you must teach me to smoke opium—take me where the opium smokers go— Alec! Alec! J'ai la nostalgie pour la boue . . ."

"Oh, Frank, quit talking like a drunken idiot! Get in the car, we're going home . . ."

"But no! But no!" Starwick raved on in his high drunken voice. "Alec and I are going on together—he has promised to take me to the places that he knows— to show me the dark mysteries—the lower depths . . ."

"Oh, Frank, for God's sake get in the car; you're making a damned fool of yourself!"

"But no! I will not go without Alec—he must come with us—he is going to show me . . ."

"But I show you, Frank," said Alec smoothly. "Tonight, non!" He spoke firmly, waved a hand. "Eet ees impossible. I wet 'ere for someone. I must meet, I 'ave engagement—yes. Tomorrow, eef you like, I meet you 'ere! Tonight, non!" His voice was harsh, sharp with irrevocable refusal. "I cannot. Eet ees impossible."

By dint of infinite prayers and persuasions, and by Alec's promises that he would meet him next day to take him on a tour of "the lower depths," they finally got Starwick into the taxi. All the way down the hill, however, as the taxi sped across Paris, through the darkened silent streets, and across the Seine into the Latin Quarter, Starwick raved on madly about his eternal friendship with Alec, from whom he could never

more be parted. The taxi turned swiftly into the dark
and empty little rue des Beaux Arts and halted before
Eugene's hotel. The two women waited in nervous and
impatient haste for Eugene to get out, Elinor giving his
arm a swift squeeze and saying:

"Good night, darling. We'll see you tomorrow morning. Don't forget our trip to Rheims."

When he got out, however, Starwick followed him,
and began to run drunkenly towards the corner, smashing at the shutters of the shops with his cane and screaming at the top of his voice:

"Alec! Alec! Où est Alec? Alec! Alec! Mon ami Alec!
Où êtes-vous?"

Eugene ran after Starwick and caught him just as he
was disappearing around the corner into the rue Bonaparte, headed for the Seine. By main strength and pleading he brought him back, and managed to get him into
the taxi again, which had followed his pursuit in swift
watchful reverse. He slammed the door upon that raving
madman, and as the taxi drove off, he heard, through a
fog of drunkenness, Elinor's swift, "Thank you, darling.
You behaved magnificently—tomorrow—" and Starwick raving:

"Alec! Alec! Where is Alec?"

They sped off up the silent empty street, a narrow
ribbon lit sparsely by a few lamps, and walled steeply
with its high old shuttered houses. Eugene walked back
to his hotel, rang the night bell, and was let in. As he
stumbled up the circuitous and perilous ascent of five
flights, he caught a moment's glimpse of the little concierge and his wife, startled from their distressful sleep,
clutching each other together in a protective embrace,
as they peered out at him from the miserable little alcove
where they slept—a moment's vision of their pale,
meager faces and frightened eyes.

He climbed the winding flights of stairs, and let himself into his room, switching on the light, and flinging himself down upon the bed immediately in a stupor of drunken exhaustion.

It seemed to him he had not lain there five minutes before he heard Starwick smashing at the street door below, and shouting drunkenly his own name and that of Alec. In another minute he heard Starwick stumbling up the stairs; he went to the door, opened it, and caught him just as he came stumbling in. Starwick was raving, demented, no longer conscious of his acts: he began to smash and beat at the bed with his stick, crying:

"There!—And there!—And there!—Out, out, damned spot, and make an end to you. . . . The stranger—the one I never knew—the stranger you have become—out! Out! Out!"

Turning to Eugene then, he peered at him with drunken bloodshot eyes, and said:

"Who are you?—Are you the stranger?—Are you the one I never knew?—Or are you . . . ?" His voice trailed off feebly, and he sank down into a chair, sobbing drunkenly.

And getting to his feet at length, he looked about him wildly, smote the bed again with his stick, and cried out loudly:

"Where is Eugene? Where is the Eugene that I knew? —Where?—Where?—Where?" He staggered to the door and flung it open, screaming: "Alec! Where are you?"

He reeled out into the hall, and for a moment hung dangerously against the stair rail, peering drunkenly down into the dizzy pit five flights below. Eugene ran after him, seized him by the arm, and together they fell or reeled to the bottom. It was a journey as distorted

and demented as a dream—a descent to be remembered
later as a kind of corkscrew nightmare, broken by blind
lurchings into a creaking rail, by the rattling of Starwick's
stick upon the banisters, by blind sprawls and stum-
blings, and by blobs and blurs of frightened faces at each
landing, where Monsieur Gely's more sober patrons
waited in breath-caught silence at their open doors.
They reached the bottom finally amid such universal
thanksgiving, such prayers for their safety, as Gely's
hotel had never known before.

A vast sigh, a huge and single respiration of relief
rustled up the steep dark pit of the winding stairs. But
another peril lay before them. At the foot of the stairs
there stood a monstrous five-foot vase which, by its
luster and the loving care with which it was polished
every day by Marie, the maid, must have been the pride
of the establishment. Starwick reeled blindly against it
as he went past, the thing rocked sickeningly, and even
as it tottered slowly over, Eugene heard Madame Gely's
gasp of terror, heard her low, "Mon Dieu! Ça tombe, ça
tombe!" and a loud united "Ah-h-h!" of thankfulness
as he caught it in his hands, and gently, safely, with
such inner triumph as a man may feel who leaps through
space and lands safely hanging to a flying trapeze, restored it to its former position. As he looked up he saw
old Gely and his wife peering from their quarters with
fat perturbed faces, and the little concierge and his
wife still clutched together, peering through their curtains in a covert of bright frightened eyes.

They got out into the street at last. In the rue Bonaparte they stopped a taxi drilling through. When they
reached Montmartre again the night was breaking in
grey light behind the church of Sacré Cœur. After further drinks of strong bad cognac, they piled out of the

place into another taxi, and went hurtling back through Paris. By the time they arrived at the studio full light had come.

The women were waiting up for them. Starwick mumbled something and, holding his hand over his mouth, rushed across the room into the bathroom and vomited. When he was empty, he staggered out, reeled towards the couch where Ann slept, and toppled on it, and was instantly sunk in senseless sleep.

Elinor regarded him for a while with an air at once contemplative and amused. "And now," she said cheerfully, "to awake the Sleeping Beauty from his nap." She smiled her fine bright smile, but the lines about her mouth were grimly set, and her eyes were hard. She approached the couch, and looking down upon Starwick's prostrate and bedraggled form, she said sweetly: "Get up, darling. It's breakfast time."

He groaned feebly, and rolled over on his side.

"Up, up, up, my lamb!" Her tone was dulcet, but the hand that grasped his collar and pulled him to a sitting position was by no means gentle. "We are waiting for you, darling. The day's at morn, the hour draws close, it's almost time. Remember, dear, we're starting out for Rheims at nine o'clock."

"O God!" groaned Starwick wretchedly. "Don't ask me to do that! Anything, anything but that. I can't! I'll go anywhere with you if you just leave me alone until tomorrow." He flopped back on the bed again.

"Sorry, precious," she said in a light and cheerful tone, as hard as granite, "but it's too late now! You should have thought of that before. Our plans are made, we're going—and *you*," suddenly her voice hardened formidably, "*you're* coming with us." She looked at him a moment longer with hard eyes, bent and grasped him by the collar, and roughly jerked him up to a sitting position again.

"Francis," she said sternly, "pull yourself together now and get up! We're going to have no more of this nonsense!"

He groaned feebly, and staggered to his feet. He seemed to be on the verge of collapse, his appearance was so pitiable that Ann, coming from the bathroom at this moment, flushed with hot sympathy as she saw him, and cried out angrily, accusingly, to Elinor:

"Oh, leave him alone! Let him sleep if he wants to. Can't you see he is half dead? Why should we drag him along to Rheims if he doesn't feel like going? We can put the trip off until tomorrow, anyway. What does it matter when we go?"

Elinor smiled firmly and shook her head with a short inflexible movement. "No, sir," she said quietly. "Nothing is going to be put off. We are going today, as we planned. And Mr. Starwick is going with us! He may go willingly or against his will, he may be conscious or unconscious when he gets there, but, alive or dead, he's going!"

At these unhappy tidings, Starwick groaned miserably again. She turned to him and, her voice deepening to the authority of indignation, she said:

"Frank! You've *got* to see this through! There's no getting out of it now! If you don't feel well, that's just too bad—but you've got to see this thing through anyway! You've known about this trip for the past week— if you chose to spend last night making the rounds of every joint in Montmartre you've no one to blame for it but yourself! But you've *got* to go. You're not going to let us down this time!"

And steeled and wakened by the challenge of her

tone—that challenge which one meets so often in people who have let their whole life go to hell, and lacking stamina for life's larger consequences insist on it for trivialities—he raised his head, looked at her with angry, bloodshot eyes, and said quietly:

"Very well, I'll go. But I resent your asking it *very* much!"

"All right, my dear," she said quietly. "If you resent it, you resent it—and that's that! Only, when you make a promise to your friends they expect you to live up to it."

"Ace," said Starwick coldly. "Quite."

"And now," she spoke more kindly, "why don't you go into the bathroom, Frank, and straighten up a bit? A little cold water across your head and shoulders would do you no end of good." She turned to Ann and said quietly: "Did you finish in there?"

"Yes," said Ann curtly, "it's all right now. I've cleaned it up." For a minute she stared sullenly at the older woman, and suddenly burst into her short and angry laugh:

"God!" she said, with a rich, abrupt, and beautifully coarse humanity. "I never saw the like of it in my life! I don't see where he put it all!" Her voice trembled with a full, rich, infuriated kind of humor. "Everything was there!" she cried, "except the kitchen sink!"

Starwick flushed deeply, and looking at her, said, quietly, gravely: "I'm sorry, Ann. I'm *terribly, terribly* sorry!"

"Oh, it's all right," she said shortly, yet with a kind of tenderness. "I'm used to it. Don't forget that I served three years' training in a hospital once. You get so you don't notice those things."

"You are a *very* swell person," he said slowly and distinctly. "I'm *terribly* grateful."

She flushed, and turned away, saying curtly: "Sit down, Frank. You'll feel better when you have some coffee. I'm making it now." And in her silent and competent way she set to work.

In these few commonplace words, all that was strong, grand, and tender in Ann's soul and character was somehow made evident. Brusque and matter-of-fact as her words had been when she referred to the disgusting task just performed, their very curtness, and the rich and coarse humanity of her sudden angry laugh, had revealed a spirit of noble tenderness and strength, a spirit so strong and sweet and full of love that it had risen triumphant not only over the stale, dead, and snobbish little world from which she came, but also over the squeamishness which such a task would have aroused in most of the people who made up that world.

To Starwick, she symbolized certain divinities known to his art and his experience: Maya, or one of the great Earth-Mothers of the ancients, or the goddess of Compassionate Mercy of the Chinese, to whom he often likened her.

But to the other youth, her divinity was less mythical, more racial and mundane. She seemed to fulfill in part his vision of the grand America, to make palpable the female quality of that fortunate, good, and happy life of which he had dreamed since childhood—to evoke the structure of that enchanted life of which every American has dreamed as a child. It is a life that seems forever just a hand's-breadth off and instantly to be grasped and made our own, the moment that we find the word to utter it, the key to open it. It is a world distilled of our own blood and earth, and qualified by all our million lights and weathers, and we know that it will be noble, intolerably strange and lovely, when we find it. Finally, she was the incarnation of all the secret beauty of New England, the other side of man's dark heart, the buried loveliness that all men long for.

VIII

The car which they had chartered for a four months' tour was brought around from a garage at nine o'clock. A few minutes later they were on their way to Rheims.

Elinor drove; Eugene sat beside her; Ann and Starwick were in the rear seat. The car was a good one—a Panhard—and Elinor drove swiftly, beautifully, with magnificent competence, as she did all things, getting ahead of everybody else, besting even the swerve of the taxi-drivers in their wasplike flight, and doing it all with such smooth ease that no one noticed it.

They seemed to get through the great dense web, the monumental complication of central Paris by a kind of magic. As always, Elinor communicated to everyone and everything the superb confidence of her authority. In her presence, and under her governance, the strange and alien world about them became instantly familiar as the Main Street of one's native town, making even the bewildering and intricate confusion of its swarming mass wonderfully natural and easy to be grasped. Paris, in fact, under the transforming magic of this woman's touch, became curiously American, the enchantment beautifully like Eugene's own far-off visions as a child.

It was astounding. The whole city had suddenly taken on the clear and unperplexing porportions of a map— of one of those beautifully simple and comforting maps which are sold to tourists, in which everything is charming, colorful, and cosy as a toy, and where everything that need be known—all the celebrated "points of interest"—the Eiffel Tower, the Madeleine, and Notre

Dame, the Trocadéro, and the Arc de Triomphe, are pictured charmingly, in vivid colors.

Paris, in fact, had this morning become a brilliant, lovely, flashing toy. It was a toy which had been miraculously created for the enjoyment of brilliant, knowing, and sophisticated Americans like Elinor and himself. It was a toy which could be instantly understood, preserved, and enjoyed, a toy that they could play with to their hearts' content, a toy which need confuse and puzzle none of them for a moment, particularly since Elinor was there to explain the toy and make it go.

It was incredible. Gone was all the blind confusion, the sick despair, the empty desolation of his first month in Paris. Gone was the old blind and baffled struggle against the staggering mass and number of a world too infinitely complex to be comprehended, too strange and alien to be understood. Gone were all the old sensations of the drowning horror, the feeling of atomic desolation as he blindly prowled the streets among alien and uncountable hordes of strange dark faces, the sensation of being an eyeless grope-thing that crawled and scuttled blindly on the sea-depths of some terrible oceanic world of whose dimensions, structure, quality, and purpose it could know nothing. Gone were all those feelings of strife, profitless, strange, and impotent futility—those struggles that racked the living sinews of man's life and soul with quivering exhaustion and with sick despair, the hideous feeling of being emptied out in planetary vacancy, of losing all the high hope of the spirit's purpose, the heart's integrity—of being exploded, emptied out and dissipated into hideous, hopeless nothingness where all the spirit of man's courage turned dead and rotten as a last year's apple, and all his sounding plans of work and greatness seemed feebler than the scratchings of a

dog upon a wall—a horror that can seize a man in the
great jungle of an unknown city and a swarming street
and that is far more terrible than the unknown mystery
of any Amazonian jungle of the earth could be.

It was all gone now—the devouring hunger, and the
drowning horror, and the blind confusion of the old,
swarm-haunted mind of man—the fruitless struggle of
the Faustian life—and in its place he had the glittering
toy, the toy of legend and enchantment and of quick
possession.

The French, they were a charming race—so gay, so
light, and so incorrigible—so childlike and so like a
race of charming toys.

Elinor made their relation to all these good people
swarming in the streets around them wonderfully easy,
clear, and agreeable. There was nothing strange about
them, their ways were unpredictable, since they were
French, but they were perfectly understandable. Her
attitude, expressed in a rapid, gay, and half-abstracted
chatter—a kind of running commentary on the life
around her as she drove—made the whole thing plain.
They were a quaint lot, a droll lot, an incomparable lot
—they were charming, amazing, irresponsible, a race
of toys and children—they were "French."

"All right, my dear," she would murmur to herself
as a fat taxi-driver snaked recklessly in ahead of her and
came to a triumphant stop, "have it your own way, my
darling—have it your own way—I shan't argue with
you—God!" she would cry, throwing her head back
with a sudden rich burst of laughter, "look at the old
boy with the whiskers over there at the table—did you
see him twirl his gay mustachios and roll his roguish
eyes at that girl as she went by? *Simply* incredible!" she
cried with another laugh, and bit her lips, and shook her
head in fine astonishment. "Thank you!" she murmured

politely, as the gendarme shrilled upon his whistle and
beckoned with his small white club. "Monsieur l'Agent,
vous êtes bien gentil", as she smoothly shifted gears
and shot past him.

In this wonderful and intoxicating way all of Paris
defiled past them like a great glittering toy, a splendid
map of rich, luxurious shops and great cafés, an ani-
mated and beautiful design of a million gay and fascinating people, all bent on pleasure, all filled with joy,
all with something so vivid, bright, particular, and incomparable about them that the whole vast pattern
resolved itself into a thousand charming and brilliant
pictures, each wonderful and unforgettable, and all
fitting instantly into the single structure, the simple and
magnificent clarity of the whole design.

They swept through the huge central web of Paris,
and were passing through the great shabby complication
of the Eastern Quarters, the ragged, ugly sprawl of
the suburbs.

And now, swift as dreams, it seemed, they were out
in open country, speeding along roads shaded by tall
rows of poplars, under a sky of humid grey, whitened
with a milky and soul-troubling light.

Elinor was very gay, mercurial, full of sudden spontaneous laughter, snatches of song, deep gravity, swift
inexplicable delight. Ann maintained a sullen silence.
As for Starwick, he seemed on the verge of collapse all
the time. At Château-Thierry he announced that he
could go no farther; they stopped, got him into a little
café, and fortified him with some brandy. He sank into
a stupor of exhaustion, from which they could not rouse
him. To all their persuasions and entreaties he just shook
his head and mumbled wearily:

"I can't!—Leave me here!—I can't go on!"

Three hours passed in this way before they succeeded

in reviving him, getting him out of the café—or estaminet—and into the car again. Ann's face was flushed with resentful anger. She burst out furiously:

"You had no right to make him come along on this trip! You knew he couldn't make it; he's dead on his feet. I think we ought to take him back to Paris now."

"Sorry, my dear," said Elinor crisply, with a fine bright smile, "but there'll be no turning back! We're going on!"

"Frank can't go on!" Ann cried angrily. "You know he can't! I think it's a rotten shame for you to insist on this when you see what shape he's in."

"Nevertheless, we're going on," said Elinor with grim cheerfulness. "And Mr. Starwick is going with us. He'll see it through now to the bitter end. And if he dies upon the way, we'll give him a soldier's burial here upon the field of honor. . . . Allons, mes enfants! Avancez!" And humming gaily and lightly the tune of Malbrouck, she shifted gears and sent the car smoothly, swiftly forward again.

It was a horrible journey. One of those experiences which, by the grim and hopeless protraction of their suffering, leave their nightmare image indelibly upon the memories of everyone who has experiencd them. The grey light of the short winter's day was already waning rapidly when they drove out of Château-Thierry. As they approached Rheims, dark had almost come, the lights of the town had begun to twinkle, sparsely, with provincial dismalness, in the distance. No one knew the purpose of their visit; no one knew what the trip was for, what they were coming to see—no one had inquired.

It was almost dark when they entered the town. Elinor drove immediately to the cathedral, halted the car, and got out.

"Voilà, mes amis!" she said ironically. "We are here!"

And she made a magnificent flourishing gesture towards the great ruined mass, which, in the last faint grey light of day, was dimly visible as a gigantic soaring monument of shattering arches and demolished buttresses, a lacework of terrific stone looped ruggedly with splinters of faint light, the demolished façades of old saints and kings and shell-torn towers—the twilit ruins of a twilight world.

"Magnificent!" cried Elinor enthusiastically. "Superb! —Frank! Frank! You must get out and feast your eyes upon this noble monument! I have heard you speak so often of its beauty. . . . But, my dear, you *must!*" she said, answering with fine persuasion his feeble and dispirited groan. "You'd never forgive yourself, or me either, if you knew you'd come the whole way to Rheims without a single look at its cathedral."

And, despite his wearily mumbled protests, she took him by the arm and pulled him from the car. Then, for a moment, as he stared drunkenly, with blind, unseeing eyes, at the great grey twilit shape, she propped him up and held him between herself and Eugene.

Then they all got back into the car, and she drove them to the best café, the best hotel in town. Starwick almost collapsed getting out of the car. His knees buckled under him, and he would have fallen if Ann had not caught him, put her arm around him, and held him up. His condition was pitiable. He could no longer hold his head up; it lolled and wobbled drunkenly on his neck like a flower too heavy for its heavy stalk. His eyes were glazed and leaden, and as they started into the café, he had to be held up. He lifted his feet and dragged them after him like leaden weights. The café was a large and splendid one. They found a table to one side. Starwick staggered towards the cushioned seat against the wall and immediately collapsed. From that time on, he was never wholly conscious. Ann sat down beside him, put her arm around him and supported him. He sank against her shoulder like a child. The girl's face was flushed with anger, she stared at Elinor with resentful eyes, but by no word or gesture did Elinor show that she noticed anything amiss either in Ann's or Starwick's behavior.

Rather, she chatted gaily to Eugene, she kept up a witty and high-spirited discourse with everyone around her, she had never been more mercurial, quick, gay and charming than she was that evening. And announcing gaily that she was the hostess that was "giving the party," she ordered lavishly—a delicious meal, with champagne from the celebrated cellars of the establishment. And everyone, spurred to hunger by the cold air and their long journey, ate heartily—everyone save Ann who ate little and sat in angry silence, with one arm around Starwick's shoulders, and Starwick, who could not be roused from his deep stupor to eat anything.

It was after nine o'clock before they got up to go. Elinor paid the bill, and still chatting as gaily and as lightly as if the whole wretched expedition had brought nothing but unqualified joy to all her guests, started for the door. Starwick had to be half-carried, half dragged out by Ann and Eugene, under the prayerful guidance of several deeply troubled waiters. They put him in the car and got in themselves. Elinor looking around lightly, and crying out cheerfully: "Are we ready children?" started the motor for the long drive back to Paris.

That was a hideous and unforgettable journey. Before they were done with it, they thought that it would never end. Under the protraction of its ghastly horror time lengthened out interminably, unbelievably, into centuries. It seemed to them at last that they would never arrive, that they were rolling through a spaceless vacancy without progression, that they were hung there in the horrible ethers of some planetary emptiness where their wheels spun futilely and forever in moveless movement, unsilent silence, changeless change.

From the very beginning they did not know where they were going. By the time they got out of Rheims they were completely lost. It was a cold night, late in February; a thick foglike mist that grew steadily more impenetrable as the night wore on, had come down and blanketed the earth in white invisibility. And through this mist there were diffused two elements: the weird radiance of a submerged moon which gave to the sea of fog through which they groped, the appearance of an endless sea of milk, and the bitter clutch of a stealthy, raw, and cruelly penetrating cold which crept into man's flesh and numbed him to the bone of misery.

All through that ghastly and interminable night, they groped their way across France in the milky ocean of antarctic fog. It seemed to them that they had traveled hundreds of miles, that Paris had long since been passed, lost, forgotten in the fog, that they were approaching the outer suburbs of Lyons or Bordeaux, that presently they would see the comforting lights of the English Channel, or that they had turned northwards, had crossed Belgium, and soon would strike the Rhine.

From time to time the road wound through the ghostly street of some old village; the white walls of village houses rose sheer and blank beside the road, sheeted in phantasmal mist like ghosts, and with no sound within. Then they would be groping their way out through the open countryside again—but where or in what country, no one knew, none dared to say—and suddenly, low and level, beside them to the left, they would see the moon. It would suddenly emerge in some blind hole that opened in that wall of fog, and it was such a moon as no man living ever saw before. It was an old, mad, ruined crater of a moon, an ancient, worn, and demented thing that smoldered red like an expiring coal, and that was like the old ruined moon of a fantastic dream. It hung there on their left, just at the edge of a low ridge of hills, and it was so low, so level, and so ghostly-near, it seemed to them that they could touch it.

Towards midnight they groped their way into a whited ghostly phantom of a town which Elinor at length, with the sudden recognition of a person who revisits some old scene of childhood, discovered to be Soissons. She had known the town well during the war: the ambulance unit, in which she had been for eighteen months a driver, had been stationed here. Starwick was half conscious, huddled into Ann's shoulder on the dark rear seat. He groaned pitiably and said that he could go no farther, that they must stop. They found a hotel café that was still open and half-carried, half-dragged him in. They got brandy for him, they tried to revive him; he looked like a dead man and said that he could go no farther, that they must leave him there. And for the first time Elinor's grave tone showed concern and sharp anxiety, for the first time her hard eye softened into care. She remained firm; gently, obdurately, she refused him. He collapsed again into unconsciousness; she turned her worried eyes upon the others and said quietly:

"We can't leave him here. We've got to get him back to Paris somehow."

After two ghastly hours in which they tried to revive

him, persuade him to gird up his fainting limbs for final
effort, they got him back into the car. Ann covered him
with blankets and held him to her for the remainder of
the night, as a mother might hold a child. In the faint
ghost-gleam of light her face shone dark and somber,
her eyes were dark, moveless, looking straight ahead.

Armed with instructions from an anxious waiter, they
set out again on the presumptive road to Paris. The interminable night wore on; the white blanket of the fog
grew thicker, they passed through more ghost villages,
sheer and sudden as a dream, sheeted in the strange
numb silence of that ghostly nightmare of a fog. The
old red crater of the moon vanished in a ruined helve
at length behind a rise of earth. They could no longer
see anything, the road before was utterly blotted out,
the car lights burned against an impenetrable white
wall, they groped their way in utter blindness, they
crawled at a snail's pace.

Finally, they felt their way along, inch by inch and
foot by foot. Eugene stood on the runningboard of the
car, peering blindly into that blank wall of fog, trying
only to define the edges of the road. The bitter penetra-
tion of raw cold struck through the fog and pierced
them like a nail. From time to time Elinor stopped the
car, while he stepped down and stamped numb feet
upon the road, swung frozen arms, and lustily blew
warmth back into numb fingers. Then that infinite groping patience of snail's progress would begin again.

Somewhere, somehow, through that blind sea of fog,
there was a sense of morning in the air. The ghosts of
towns and villages grew more frequent—the towns
were larger now, occasionally Elinor bumped over
phantom curbs before the warning shouts of her lookout could prevent her. Twice they banged into trees

along unknown pavements. There was a car-track now, the bump of cobbles, the sense of greater complications in the world about them.

Suddenly, they heard the most thrilling and evocative of all earth's sounds at morning—the lonely clopping of shod hooves upon the cobbles. In the dim and ghostly sheeting of that light, they saw the horse, the market cart balanced between its two high creaking wheels, laden with sweet clean green-and-gold of carrot bunches, each neatly trimmed as a bouquet.

They could discern the faint ghost-glimmer of the driver's face, the big slow-footed animal, dappled grey, and clopping steadily towards the central markets.

They were entering Paris, and the fog was lifting. In its huge shroud of mist dispersing, the old buildings of the city, emerged ghostly, haggard, pallidly nascent in the dim grey light. A man was walking rapidly along a terraced pavement, with bent head, hands thrust in pockets—the figure of the worker since the world began. They saw at morning, in grey waking light, a waiter, his apron ends tucked up, lifting racked chairs from the tables of a café, and on light mapled fronts of bars and shops, the signs *Bière—Pâtisserie— Tabac*. Suddenly, the huge winged masses of the Louvre swept upon them, and it was grey light now, and Eugene heard Elinor's low, fervent, "Thank God!"

And now the bridge, the Seine again, the frontal blank of the old buildings on the quays, faced haggardly towards light, the narrow lane of the rue Bonaparte, and in the silent empty street at length, his own hotel.

They said good-by quickly, hurriedly, abstractedly, as he got out; and drove away. The women were thinking of nothing, no one now, but Starwick, life's fortunate darling, the rare, the precious, the all-favored one. In the grey light, unconscious, completely swaddled in the heavy rugs, Starwick still lay pillowed on Ann's shoulder.

IX

All day Eugene slept the dreamless, soundless sleep of a man who has been drugged. When he awoke, night had come again. And this concatenation of night to night, of dreamless and exhausted sleep upon the strange terrific nightmare of the night before, the swift kaleidoscope of moving action which had filled his life for the past two days, now gave to that recent period a haunting and disturbing distance, and to the events that had gone before the sad finality of irrevocable time. Suddenly he felt as if his life with Ann, Elinor, and Starwick was finished, done; for some strangely troubling reason he could not define, he felt that he would never see them again.

He got up, dressed, and went downstairs. He saw old Gely and his wife, his daughters, Marie the maid, and the little concierge: it seemed to him that they looked at him strangely, curiously, with some sorrowful sad knowledge in their eyes, and a nameless numb excitement gripped him, dulled his heart. He felt the nameless apprehension that he always felt—that perhaps all men feel—when they have been away a day or two. It was a premonition of bad news, of some unknown misfortune: he wanted to ask them if someone had come for him—without knowing who could come—if they had a message for him—not knowing who might send him one—an almost feverish energy to demand that they tell him at once what unknown calamity had befallen him in his absence. But he said nothing, but still haunted by what he thought was the strange and troubling look in their eyes—a look he had often thought he observed in people, which seemed to tell of a secret knowledge, an inhuman chemistry, a communion in men's lives to which his own life was a stranger—he hurried out into the street.

Outside the streets were wet with mist, the old cobbles shone with a dull wet gleam, through the mist the lamps burned dimly, and through the fog he heard the swift and unseen passing of the taxi-cabs, the shrill tooting of their little horns.

Yet everything was ghostlike and phantasmal—the streets of Paris had the unfamiliar reality of streets that one revisits after many years of absence, or walks again after the confinement of a long and serious illness.

He ate at a little restaurant in the rue de la Seine, and troubled by the dismal lights, the high old houses, and the empty streets of the Latin Quarter sounding only with the brief passage of some furious little taxi drilling through those narrow lanes towards the bridge of the Seine and the great blaze and gaiety of night, he finally forsook that dark quarter, which seemed to be the image of the unquiet loneliness that beset him, and crossing the bridge, he spent the remainder of the evening reading in one of the cafés near Les Magasins du Louvre.

The next morning when he awoke, a *pneumatique* was waiting for him. It was from Elinor, and read:

"Darling, where are you? Are you still recovering from the great debauch, or have you given us the go-by, or what? The suspense is awful—won't you say it ain't so, and come to lunch with us today at half-past twelve? We'll be waiting for you at the studio.—Elinor"—Below this, in a round and almost childish hand, was written: "We want to see you. We missed you yesterday.—Ann."

He read this brief and casual little note over again

and again, he laughed exultantly, and smote his fist into the air, and read again. All of the old impossible joy was revived in him. He looked about the room and found everything in it good and homely. He went to the window and looked out: a lemony sunlight was falling on the old pale walls and roofs and chimney pots of Paris: everything sparkled with health and hope and work and morning—and all because two girls from Boston in New England had written him a note.

He held the flimsy paper of the *pneumatique* tenderly, as if it were a sacred parchment too old and precious for rough handling; he even lifted it to his nose and smelled it. It seemed to him that all the subtle, sensuous femininity of the two women was in it—the seductive and thrilling fragrance, impalpable and glorious as the fragrance of a flower, which their lives seemed to irradiate and to give to everything, to everyone they touched, a sense of triumph, joy, and tenderness. He read the one blunt line that Ann had written him as if it were poetry of haunting magic: the level, blunt, and toneless inflexibility of her voice sounded in the line as if she had spoken, he read into her simple words a thousand buried meanings—the tenderness of a profound, simple, and inarticulate spirit, whose feelings were too deep for language, who had no words for them.

When he got to the studio he found the two women waiting, but Starwick was not there. Ann was quietly, bluntly matter-of-fact as usual; Elinor almost hilariously gay, but beneath her gaiety he sensed at once a deep and worried perturbation, a worn anxiety that shone nakedly from her troubled eyes.

They told him that on their return from Rheims, Starwick had left the studio to meet Alec and had not been seen since. No word from him had they had that night or the day before, and now, on the second day since his disappearance, their anxiety was evident.

But during lunch—they ate at a small restaurant in the neighborhood, near the Montparnasse railway station—Elinor kept up a gay and rapid conversation, and persisted in speaking of Starwick's disappearance as a great lark—the kind of thing to be expected from him.

"*Perfectly* insane, of course!" she cried, with a gay laugh. "But then, it's typical of him: it's just the kind of thing that kind would do. Oh, he'll turn up, of course," she said, with quiet confidence, "he'll turn up in a day or two, after some wild adventure that no one in the world but Francis Starwick could have had. . . . I *mean!*" she cried, "picking that Frenchman—Alec—up the way he did the other night. *Utterly* mad, of course!" she said gaily. "But then, there you *are!* It wouldn't be Frank if he didn't!"

"I see nothing very funny about it," said Ann bluntly. "It looks like a pretty rotten mess to me. We know nothing at all about that Frenchman—who he is, what he does; we don't even know his name. For all you know he may be one of the worst thugs or criminals in Paris."

"Oh, I know, my dear—but don't be absurd!" Elinor protested. "The man's all right—Frank's always picking up these people—it always turns out all right in the end —oh, but of course!" she cried, as if dispelling a troubling thought from her mind, "of course it will! It's too ridiculous to allow yourself to be upset like this!"

But in spite of her vigorous assurance, her eyes were full of care, and of something painful and baffled, an almost naked anguish.

He left them after lunch, promising to meet them again for dinner. Starwick had not come back. When they had finished dinner, the two women went back to the studio to wait for Starwick's possible return, and Eugene went to look for him in Montmartre, promising to let them know at once if he found Starwick or got news of him. When he got to Montmartre, he made a round first of all the resorts which Starwick had liked best and frequented most, as Eugene remembered them, of course; but no one had seen him since they had last been there all together. Finally, he went to the bistro in the rue Montmartre, where they had first encountered Alec, and asked the soiled barman with the dark mistrustful eye, if he had seen either Alec or Starwick in the past three days. The man eyed him suspiciously for a moment before answering. Then he surlily replied that he had seen neither of them. In spite of the man's denial, he stayed on, drinking one cognac after another at the bar, while it filled up, ebbed and flowed, with the mysterious rout and rabble of the night. He waited until four o'clock in the morning: neither Starwick nor Alec had appeared. He got into a taxi and was driven back across Paris to Montparnasse. When he got to the studio, the two women were still awake, waiting, and he gave them his disappointing news. Then he departed, promising to return at noon.

All through that day they waited: the apprehension of the two women was now painfully evident, and Ann spoke bluntly of calling in the police. Towards six o'clock that evening, while they were engaged in vigorous debate concerning their course of action, there were steps along the alleyway outside, and Starwick entered the studio, followed by the Frenchman, Alec.

Starwick was in excellent spirits, his eyes were clear, his ruddy face looked fresh, and had a healthy glow. In response to all their excited greetings and inquiries, he laughed gleefully, teasingly, and refused to answer.

When they tried to find out from Alec where Starwick had been, he too smiled an engaging but malicious smile, shrugged his shoulders politely, and said: "I do not know, I s'ink he tells you if he v'ants—if not!" again he smiled, and shrugged politely. And this moody and secretive silence was never broken. Starwick never told them where he had been. Once or twice, during dinner, which was an hilarious one, he made casual and mysteriously hinting references to Brussels, but, in response to all of Elinor's deft, ironic cross-examination, he only laughed his burbling laugh, and refused to answer.

And she, finally defeated, laughed suddenly, a laugh of rich astonishment, crying: "*Perfectly* insane, of course! But then, what did I tell you? It's just the sort of thing that Frank *would* do!"

But, in spite of all her high light spirits, her gay swift laughter, her distinguished ease, there was in the woman's eyes something the boy had never seen before: a horrible, baffled anguish of torment and frustration. And although her manner towards the Frenchman, Alec, was gracious, gay, and charming—although she now accepted him as "one of us," and frequently said with warm enthusiasm that he was "a *perfectly* swell person—I like him *so* much!" there was often something in her eyes when she looked at him that it was not good to see.

Alec was their guest, and Starwick's constant companion, everywhere they went thereafter. And everywhere, in every way, he proved himself to be a droll, kind, courteous, witty, and urbanely cynical person: a man of charming and engaging qualities, and delightful company. They never asked his name, nor inquired about his birth, his family, or his occupation. They seemed to accept his curious fellowship with Starwick as a matter of course: they took him on their daily round of cafés, restaurants, night-clubs, and resorts, as if he were a life-long friend of the family. And he accepted all their favors gracefully, politely, with wit and grace and charm, with a natural and distinguished dignity and ease. He, too, never asked disturbing questions; he was a diplomat by nature, a superb tactician from his birth. Nevertheless, the puzzled, doubting, and inquiring expression in his eyes grew deeper day by day; his tongue was eloquently silent, but the question in his puzzled eyes could not be hidden, and constantly sought speech.

As for Eugene, he now felt for the first time an ugly, disquieting doubt: suddenly he remembered many things—words and phrases and allusions, swift, casual darts and flashes of memory that went all the way back to the Cambridge years, that had long since been forgotten—but that now returned to fill his mind. And sometimes when he looked at Starwick, he had the weird and unpleasant sensation of looking at some one he had never seen before.

X

At the last moment, when it seemed that the argosy of their battered friendship was bound to sink, it was Elinor who saved it again. Ann, in a state of sullen fury, had announced that she was sailing for home the next week; Eugene, that he was going South to "some quiet little place where"—so did his mind comfortably phrase it— "he could settle down and write." As for Starwick, he remained coldly, wearily, sorrowfully impassive; he accepted this bitter dissolution of their plans with a weary resignation at once sad and yet profoundly indifferent; his own plans were more wrapped in a mantle of mysterious and tragic secretiveness than ever before. And seeing the desperate state which their affairs had come to, and that she could not look for help from these three gloomy secessionists, Elinor instantly took charge of things again, and became the woman who had driven an ambulance in the war.

"Listen, my darlings," she said with a sweet, crisp frivolity, that was as fine, as friendly, as comforting, and as instantly authoritative as the words of a capable mother to her contrary children—"no one is going away; no one is going back home; no one is going anywhere except on the wonderful trip we've planned from the beginning. We're going to start out next week, Ann and I will do the driving, you two boys can loaf and invite your souls to your hearts' content, and when you see a place that looks like a good place to work in, we'll stop and stay until you're tired of working. Then we'll go on again."

"Where?" said Starwick in a dead and toneless voice. "Go on where?"

"Why, my dear child!" Elinor cried in a gay tone. "Anywhere! Wherever you like! That's the beauty of it! We're not going to be bound down by any program, any schedule: we shall stay where we like, and go anywhere our sweet selves desire.

"I thought, however," she continued in a more matter-of-fact way, "that we would go first to Chartres and then on to Touraine, stopping off at Orléans or Blois or Tours —anywhere we like, and staying as long as we care to. After that, we could do the Pyrenees and all that part of France: we might stop a few days at Biarritz and then strike off into the Basque country. I know *incredible* little places we could stop at."

"Could we see Spain?" asked Starwick, for the first time with a note of interest in his voice.

"But, of *course!*" she cried. "My dear child, we can see anything, everything, go anywhere your heart desires. That's the beauty of the whole arrangement. If you feel like writing, if you want to run down to Spain to get a little writing done—why, presto! chango! Alacazam!" she said gaily, snapping her fingers, "the thing is done! There's nothing simpler!"

For a moment, no one spoke. They all sat entranced in a kind of unwilling but magical spell of wonder and delight. Elinor, with her power to make everything seem delightfully easy, and magically simple and exciting, had clothed that fantastic program with all the garments of naturalness and reason. Everything now seemed not only possible, but beautifully, persuasively practicable—even that ludicrous project of "running down to Spain to do a little writing," that hopeless delusion of "stopping off and working, anywhere you like, until you are ready to go on again"—she gave to the whole impossible adventure not only the thrilling colors of sensuous delight and happiness, but also the conviction of a serious purpose, a reasonable design.

And in a moment, Starwick, rousing himself from his abstracted and fascinated reverie, turned to Eugene and, with the old gleeful burble of laughter in his throat, remarked simply in his strangely fibered voice:

"It sounds swell, doesn't it?"

And Ann, whose sullen, baffled look had more and more been tempered by an expression of unwilling interest, now laughed her sudden angry laugh, and said:

"It *would* be swell if everyone would only act like decent human beings for a change!"

In spite of her angry words, her face had a tender, radiant look of joy and happiness as she spoke, and it seemed that all her hope and belief had returned to her.

"But of course!" Elinor answered instantly, and with complete conviction. "And that's just exactly how everyone *is* going to act! Eugene will be all right," she cried, "the moment that we get out of Paris! You'll see! We've

gone at a perfectly *killing* pace this last month or two!
No one in the world could stand it! Eugene is tired, our
nerves are all on edge, we're worn out by staying up all
night, and drinking, and flying about from one place to
another—but a day or two of rest will fix all that. . . .
And that, my children, is just exactly what we're going
to do—now—at once!" She spoke firmly, kindly, with
authority. "We're getting out of Paris today!"

"Where?" said Starwick. "Where are we going?"

"We're all going out to St. Germain-en-Laye to rest
up for a day or two before we leave. We'll stay at your
pension, Francis, and you can pack your things while
we're out there, because you won't be going back again.
After that we'll come back to Paris to spend the night—
we won't stay here over a day at the outside: Ann and
I will clear our things out of the Studio, and Eugene
can get packed up at his hotel—that should mean, let's
see—" she tapped her lips lightly with thoughtful fingers
—"we should be packed up and ready to start Monday
morning, at the latest."

"Hadn't I better stay in town and do my packing
now?" Eugene suggested.

"Darling," said Elinor softly, with a tender and seductive humor, putting her fingers on his arm, "you'll do
nothing of the sort! You're driving out with us this afternoon! We all love you so much that we're going to take
no chance on losing you at the last minute!"

And for a moment, the strange and almost noble
dignity of Elinor's face was troubled by a faint smile of
pleasant, tender radiance, the image of the immensely
feminine, gracious, and lovely spirit which almost grotesquely seemed to animate her large and heavy body.

Thus, under the benevolent and comforting dictator-
ship of this capable woman, hope had been restored to

them, and in gay spirits, shouting and laughing and singing, feeling an impossible happiness when they thought
of the wonderful adventure before them, they drove out
to St. Germain-en-Laye that afternoon. The late sun was
slanting rapidly towards evening when they arrived:
they left their car before an old café near the railway
station, and for an hour walked together through the
vast aisles of the forest, the stately, sorrowful design of
that great planted forest, so different from anything in
America, so different from the rude, wild sweep and
savage lyricism of our terrific earth, and so haunted by
the spell of time. It was the forest which Henry IV had
known so well, and which, in its noble planted colonnades, suggested an architecture of nature that was like
a cathedral, evoked a sense of time that was ancient,
stately, classical, full of sorrow and a tragical joy, and
haunted forever by the pacings of noble men and women
now long dead.

When they came out of the forest at the closing hour
—for in this country, in this ancient noble place, even
the forests were controlled, and closed and opened by
the measurements of mortal time—the old red sun of
waning day had almost gone.

For a time, they stood on the great sheer butte of St.
Germain, and looked across the space that intervened
between themselves and Paris. Below them in the valley,
the Seine wound snakewise through a series of silvery
silent loops, and beyond, across the fields and forests
and villages, already melting swiftly into night, and
twinkling with a diamond dust of lights, they saw the
huge and smoking substance that was Paris, a design of
elfin towers and ancient buildings and vast inhuman
distances, an architecture of enchantment, smoky, lovely
as a dream, seeming to be upborne, to be sustained, to
float there like the vision of an impossible and unap-

proachable loveliness, out of a huge opalescent mist. It was a land of far Cockaigne, forever threaded by the eternity of its silver, silent river; a city of enfabled walls, like Carcassonne, and never to be reached or known.

And while they looked it seemed to them that they heard the huge, seductive, drowsy murmur of that magic and eternal city—a murmur which seemed to resume into itself all of the grief, the joy, the sorrow, the ambitions, hopes, despairs, defeats, and loves of humanity. And though all life was mixed and intermingled in that distant, drowsy sound, it was itself detached, remote, eternal and undying as the voice of time. And it hovered there forever in the timeless skies of that elfin city, and was eternally the same, no matter what men lived or died.

They turned, and went into the old café near the station for an apéritif before dinner. It was one of those old, pleasantly faded cafés that one finds in little French towns. The place had the comfortable look and feel of an old shoe: the old, worn leather cushions, the chairs and tables, the mirrors in their frames of faded gilt, the old stained woods conveyed a general air of use, of peace, of homely shabby comfort, which suggested the schedule of generations of quiet people who had come here as part of the ordered ritual of a day, and which was so different from the feverish pulse, the sensual flash and glitter of the cafés of Paris. The noble peace and dignity of the great forest, and the magic vision of the time-enchanted city in the evening light, the silver, shining loops of its eternal river, still haunted their spirits, and filled their hearts with wonder and a tranquil joy. And the old café seemed to possess them, to make them its own, with its homely comfort: it was one of those places that one thinks of at once, instinctively, by a powerful intuition, as being a "good" place, and yet they could not have said why. As they came in, the proprietor smiled and spoke to them in a quiet, casual, and friendly manner as if he had always known them and, in a moment, when they were seated in the comfortable old leathers against the wall, their waiter came, and smilingly waited for their order. He was one of those waiters that one often sees abroad: an old man with a sharp, worn face, full of quiet humor and intelligence, an old, thin figure worn in service, but still spry and agile, a decent "family man" with wife and children, a man seasoned in humanity, whose years of service upon thousands of people had given him a character that was wise, good, honest, gentle, and a trifle equivocal. Each ordered an apéritif, the two women a cassis-vermouth, the two young men, Pernod: they talked quietly, happily, and with the weary, friendly understanding that people have when all their passion of desire and grief and conflict is past. The world that they had lived in for the last two months— that world of night and Paris and debauch—seemed like an evil dream, and the way before them now looked clear and plain.

When they left the café, full dark had come: they got in the car and drove to the pension at the other end of town, where Elinor had already engaged rooms for all of them. It now turned out that Elinor had taken rooms for Starwick at this pension three months before, upon his arrival in Paris, but after the first two weeks he had not lived in them, although most of his clothing, books, and other belongings were still there. It was one more of his costly, wrong, and tragically futile efforts to find a place—some impossibly fortunate and favorable place that never would be found—where he could "settle down and get his writing done."

When the four friends got to the pension, dinner had already begun. A table had been reserved for them, and as they entered the dining-room, everyone stopped eating—two dozen pairs of old dead eyes were turned mistrustfully upon the young people, and in a moment, all over the room, at every table, the old heads bent together eagerly in conspiratorial secrecy, a low greedy whispering went up.

Starwick and Elinor were apparently already well and unfavorably known to the old pensionnaires. The moment they entered, in the vast and sibilant whispering that went around the room, envenomed fragments of conversation could be heard:

"Ah, c'est lui! . . . Et la dame aussi! . . . Ils sont revenus ensemble. . . . Mais, oui, oui!" At the next table to them an old hag with piled masses of dyed reddish hair, dressed in an old-fashioned dress bedecked with a thousand little gauds, peered at them for a moment with an expression of venomous and greedy curiosity, and then, leaning half across the table towards an old man with a swollen apoplectic face and thick white mustaches, and a little wizened old hag with the beady eyes of a reptile—possibly his wife—she hissed:

"Mais oui! . . . Oui! . . . C'est lui, le jeune Américain! . . . Personne ici ne l'a pas vu depuis trois mois." The old man here muttered something in a choked and phlegmy sort of voice, and the old parrot-visaged hag straightened, struck her bony hand sharply on the table, and cried out in a comical booming note:

"Mais justement! . . . Justement! . . . C'est comme vous voyez!" . . . Here she lowered her voice again, and peering around craftily at Elinor and Frank, who were shaking with laughter, she muttered hoarsely:

"Il n'est pas son mari! . . . Il est beaucoup plus jeune. . . . Mais non, mais non, mais non, mais non, mais non!" she cried with a rapid and violent impatience as the old man muttered out a question to her greedy ear.—"Elle est déjà mariée! . . . Oui! Oui!" This last was boomed out positively, with an indignant glance at Elinor. "Mais justement! Justement! . . . C'est comme vous voyez!"

That night Elinor was instant, swift, and happy as a flash of light. There was nothing that she did not seem to apprehend immediately, to interpret instantly, to understand before a word could be spoken, and to translate at once into a mercurial hilarity which swept everyone along with it, and made all share instantly in its wild swift gaiety, even when it would have been impossible to say why one was gay. The soup was served: it was a brown disquieting liquid in which were floating slices of some troubling and unknown tissue—a whitish substance of an obscenely porous texture. It was probably tripe: Eugene stared at it with a sullen and suspicious face, and as he looked up, Elinor rocked back in her chair with a gust of wild hilarity, placed her fingers across her mouth and laughed a rich and sudden laugh. Then, before he could speak, she placed light fingers swiftly on his arm, and said swiftly, gravely, in a tone of commiserating consent:

"Yes, I know, darling! I quite agree with you!"

"What is it?" he said dumbly, in a bewildered tone. "It looks like——"

"Exactly! Exactly!" Elinor cried at once, before he could finish, and was swept by that wild light gale of merriment again. "That's exactly what it looks like— and don't say another word! We all agree with you!" She looked drolly at the uneasy liquid in the soup-plate, and then said, firmly and positively: "No, I think not! . . . If you don't mind, I'd rather not!"—and then seeing his face again, was rocked with rude and sudden laughter. "God!" she cried. "Isn't it marvelous! Will you look at the poor kid's face!" And put light fingers gravely, swiftly, tenderly upon his arm again.

The great wave of this infectious gaiety swept them along: it was a wonderful meal. Starwick's burble of gleeful, rich, humorous and suggestive laughter was heard again; Ann laughed her short and sudden laugh, but her face was radiant, happy, lovelier than it had ever been, everything seemed wonderfully good and pleasant to them. Elinor called the waitress and quietly sent the troubling soup away, but the rest of the meal was excellent, and they made a banquet of it with two bottles of the best Sauterne the pension afforded. Their hilarity was touched somewhat by the scornful patronage of bright young people among their dowdy elders, and yet they did not intend to be unkind: the whole place seemed to them a museum of grotesque relics put there for their amusement, they were determined to make a wonderful occasion of it, the suspicious eyes, greedy whisperings and conferring heads of the old people set them off in gales of laughter, and Elinor, after a glance around and a sudden peal of full rich laughter, would stifle her merriment with her fingers, and say:

"Isn't it marvelous! . . . God! Isn't it wonderful! . . . Could anyone have imagined it! . . . Frank. . . . Frank!" she said quietly in a small stifled tone, "will you *look!* . . . Will you *kindly* take one look at the old girl with the dyed hair and all the thingumajigs, at the next table. . . . And the major! . . . And oh! If looks could *kill!* The things they are saying about *us!* . . . I'm sure they think we're *all* living in sin together. . . . Such *goings* on!" she cried with a gay pretense of horror. "Such open barefaced goings on, my friends, right in the face of decent people! . . . Now, is that terrible or not,

Monsieur Duval, I ask you! . . . Darling," she said,
turning to Starwick, and speaking in a tone of droll reproach, "don't you feel a sense of guilt? . . . Do you
intend to do the right thing by a girl or not? . . . Are
you going to make an honest woman of me, or aren't
you? . . . Come on, now, darling," she said coaxingly,
bending a little towards him, "set my tortured heart at
rest! Just tell me that you intend to do the right thing
by me! Won't you?" she coaxed.

"Quite!" said Starwick, his ruddy face reddening with
laughter as he spoke. "But what"—the burble of gleeful
and malicious laughter began to play in his throat as he
spoke—"just what is the right thing? . . . Do you
mean?"—he trembled a little with soundless laughter,
and then went on in a gravely earnest but uncertain
tone—"do you mean that you want to live?"—he arched
his eyebrows meaningly, and then said in a tone of droll
impossibly vulgar insinuation—"you know what I mean
—*really* live, you know?"

"Frank!" she shrieked, and rocked back in her chair,
covering her mouth with her fingers. "But not at *all*,
darling," she went on with her former ironic seriousness.
"You're talking to an innocent maid from Boston, Mass.,
who doesn't know what you *mean*—you *beast!*" she
cried. "Don't you know we Boston girls cannot begin
to really live until you make an honest woman of us
first?"

"In that case," Starwick said quietly, his face reddening again with laughter, "I should think we could begin
to live at once. It seems to me that another man has
already taken care of making you an honest woman!"

"God!" shrieked Elinor, falling back in her chair
with another burst of rich and sudden laughter. "Poor
Harold! . . . I had forgotten him! . . . That's all this

place needs to make it perfect—Harold walking in right now to glare at us over the tops of his horn-rimmed spectacles——"

"Yes," said Starwick, "and your father and mother bringing up the rear and regarding me"—he choked—"with very *bitter* looks—you know," he said, turning to Eugene, "they feel *quite* bitterly towards me—they really do, you know. It's obvious," he said, "that they regard me as an unprincipled seducer who has defiled," his voice trembled uncertainly again, "who has defiled the virtue of their only *darter!*" he brought this word out with a droll and luscious nasality that made them howl with laughter.

"But really," he went on seriously, turning to Elinor as he wiped his laughter-reddened face with a handkerchief, "I'm sure that's how they feel about it. When your mother and father came to the Studio the other day and found me there"—Elinor's parents were at that time in Paris—"your father *glared* at me in much the same way that Cotton Mather would look at Casanova. But *quite!* He really did, you know. I'm sure he thought you had become my concubine."

"But, darling," Elinor replied, in her playful coaxing tone, "can't I be your concubine? . . . Oh, how *mean* you are!" she said reproachfully. "I do *so* want to be somebody's concubine." She turned to Eugene protestingly. "Now is that mean or not, I ask you! Here I am, a perfectly good well-meaning female thirty years old, brought up in Boston all my life, and with the best advantages. I've been a good girl all my life and tried to do the best I could for everyone, but try as I will," she sighed, "no one will help me out in my life-long ambition to be somebody's concubine. Now is that fair or not—I ask you!"

"But not at all!" said Starwick reprovingly. "Before

you can realize your ambition you've got to go out first
and get yourself a reputation! . . . And," he added,
with a swift exuberant glance at the crafty whispering
old heads and faces all around them, "I think you're
getting one very fast."

They went upstairs immediately to the rooms that
Elinor had engaged. Starwick had two comfortable big
rooms in one wing of the pension; in his living room a
comfortable wood fire had been laid and was crackling
away lustily. Elinor had taken a small bedroom for
Eugene, and a larger room for herself and Ann. In Ann's
room, a good wood fire was also burning cheerfully.
Elinor and Starwick obviously wanted to be alone to talk
together—they conveyed this by a kind of mysterious
more-to-this-than-meets-the-eye quietness that had been
frequent with them during all these weeks. They announced that they were going for a walk.

XI

When they had gone, Eugene went to Ann's door and
knocked. She showed no surprise at seeing him, but
stood aside sullenly until he had come in, and then closed
the door behind him. Then she went back, sat down in a
chair before the fire, and leaned forward upon her knees,
and for some time stared dumbly and sullenly into the
crackling flames.

"Where are the others?" she said presently. "Have
they gone out?"

"Yes," he said. "They went for a walk. They said
they'd be gone about an hour."

"Yes," she said cynically, "and they thought it would
be good for me if you and I were left alone for a while.
I'm such a grand person that something just *has* to be
done for me. God!" she concluded bitterly, "I'm getting

tired of having people do me good! I'm fed up with it!"

He made no reply to this and she said nothing more. Her big body supported by her elbows, she continued to lean forward and stare sullenly into the flames.

He had taken a seat in another chair, and at length the silence, and his position in the chair, and the girl's sullen expression became painfully awkward, unhappy, and embarrassing. He got up abruptly, took a pillow from the bed, threw it upon the floor, and lay down flat beside her chair, stretched out comfortably with his head to the dancing flames. The feel of the fire, its snap and crackle, the soft flare and fall of burned wood ash, and the resinous piny smell, together with the broad old wooden planking of the floor, the silence of the house and the feel of numb silent night outside, something homelike in the look of the room—these things, together with Ann's big New England body leaned forward towards the fire, the sullen speechless integrity of her grand and lovely face, and the smell of her, which was the smell of a big healthy woman warmed by fire—all of these things filled his senses with something immensely strong, pleasant, and familiar, something latent in man's blood, which he had not felt in many years, and that now was quiet but powerfully reawakened. It filled his heart, his blood, his senses with peace and certitude, with drowsy sensual joy, and with the powerful awakening of an old perception, like the rediscovery of an ancient faith, that the sensuous integument of life was everywhere the same, that the lives of people in this little town in France were the same as the lives of people in the town he came from, the same as the lives of people everywhere on earth. And after all the dark and alien world of night, of Paris, and another continent, which he had known now for several months, this rediscovery of the buried life, the fundamental structure of the great family of earth to which all men belong, filled him with a quiet certitude and joy.

Ann did not move; bent forward, leaning on her knees, she continued to stare into the fire, and looking up at her warm, dark, sullen face, he fell asleep—into a sleep which, after all the frenzy and exhaustion of the last weeks, was as deep and soundless as if he were drugged.

How long he lay asleep there on the floor he did not know. But he was wakened by the sound of her voice— a sullen monotone that spoke his name—that spoke his name quietly with a toneless, brooding insistence and that at first he thought he must have dreamed. It was repeated, again and again, quietly, insistently, without change or variation until he knew there was no doubt of it, that he no longer was asleep. And with something slow and strange and numb beating through him like a mighty pulse, he opened his eyes and looked up into her face. She had bent forward still more and was looking down at him with a kind of slow, brooding intensity, her face smoldering and drowsy as a flower. And even as he looked at her, she returned his look with that drowsy, brooding stare, and again, without inflection, spoke his name.

He sat up like a flash and put his arms around her. He was beside her on his knees and he hugged her to him in a grip of speechless, impossible desire: he kissed her on the face and neck, again and again; her face was warm with the fire, her skin as soft and smooth as velvet; he kissed her again and again on the face, clumsily, thickly, with that wild, impossible desire, and with a horrible feeling of guilt and shame. He wanted to kiss her on the mouth, and he did not dare to do it: all the time that he kept kissing her and hugging her to him with a clumsy, crushing grip, he wanted her more than he had ever wanted any woman in his life, and at the same time he felt a horrible profanity in his touch, as if he were violating a Vestal virgin, trying to rape a nun.

And he did not know why he felt this way, the reason for these senseless feelings of guilt and shame and profanation. He had been with so many whores, and casual loose promiscuous women, that he would have thought it easy to make love to this big, clumsy, sullen-looking girl, but now all he could do was to hug her to him in an awkward grip, to mutter foolishly at her, and to kiss her warm sullen face again and again.

He tried to put his clumsy hand upon her breast, but the feeling of shame and profanation swept over him, and he could not keep it there. He put his hand upon her knee, and thrust it under the skirt: the warm flesh of her leg stung him like an electric shock and he jerked his hand away. And all the time the girl did nothing, made no attempt to resist or push him away, just yielded with a dumb sullen passiveness to his embraces, her face smoldering with a slow sullen passion that he could not fathom or define. He did not know why she had wakened him, why she had called his name, what meaning, what emotion lay behind her brooding look, her dumb and sullen passiveness, whether she yielded herself willingly to him or not.

He did not know why he should have this sense of shame and guilt and profanation when he touched her. It may have come from an intrinsic nobility and grandeur in her person and in her character that made physical familiarity almost unthinkable; it may even have come in part from a feeling of social and class inferiority —a feeling which may be base and shameful, but to which young men are fiercely sensitive—the feeling which all Americans know and have felt cruelly, even those who scornfully deny that it exists and yet have themselves done most to foster it. Certainly he had at times been bitterly conscious of the girl's "exclusiveness" —the fact that she was a member of "an old Boston family"—a wealthy, guarded, and powerfully entrenched group; he knew that a beautiful and desirable woman like Ann would have had many opportunities to pick and choose among wealthy men of her own class, and that he himself was just the son of a workingman.

But most of all, he knew that, more than anything else, the thing that checked him now, that overpowered him with its loveliness, that filled his heart with longing and impossible desire, and at the same moment kept him from possession—was the passionate and bitter enigma of that strange and lovely thing which had shaped itself into his life and could never be lost, could never be forgotten, and was never to be known: the thing he knew by these two words—"New England."

And as the knowledge came to him he felt the greatest love and hatred for this thing that he had ever known. A kind of wild cursing anger, a choking expletive of frustration and despair possessed him. He took her by the arms and jerked her to her feet, and cursed her bitterly. And she came dumbly, passively, sullenly as before, neither yielding nor resisting, as he shook her, hugged her, cursed her incoherently in that frenzy of desire and frustrate shame:

"Look here," he panted thickly, shaking her. "Say something! . . . Do something! . . . Don't stand there like a God-damned wooden Indian! . . . Who the hell do you think you are, anyway? . . . Why are you any better than anyone else? . . . Ann! Ann! Look at me! . . . Speak! What is it? . . . Oh, God-damn you!" he said with a savagely unconscious humor that neither of them noticed, "but I love you! . . . Oh, you big, dumb, beautiful Boston bitch," he panted amorously, "just turn your

face to me—and look at me—and by God! I will! I will!"
he muttered savagely, and for the first time, and with a
kind of desperation, kissed her on the mouth, and glared
around him like a madman and, without knowing what
he was doing, began to haul and drag her along towards
the bed, muttering, "By God, I'll do it!—Oh, you sweet,
dumb, lovely trollop of a Back Bay—Ann!" he cried
exultantly. "Oh, by God, I'll thaw you out, I'll melt your
ice, my girl—by God, I'll open you!—Is it her arm,
now?" he began gloatingly, and lifted her long arm with
a kind of slow, rending ecstasy and bit into her shoulder
haunch, "or her neck, or her warm face and sullen
mouth, or the good smell of her, or that lovely belly,
darling—that white, lovely, fruitful Boston belly," he
gloated, "good for about a dozen babies, isn't it?—or the
big hips and swelling thighs, the long haunch from waist
to knee—oh, you fertile, dumb, unplowed plantation of
a woman—but *I'll* plant you!" he yelled exultantly—
"and the big, dumb eyes of her, and her long hands and
slender fingers—how did you ever get such slender,
graceful hands, you delicate, big—here! give me the
hands now—and all the fine, long lady-fingers"—he
said with gentle, murderous desire, and suddenly felt
the girl's long fingers trembling on his arm, took them in
his hands and felt them there, and all her big, slow body
trembling in his grasp, and was suddenly pierced with
a wild and nameless feeling of pity and regret.

"Oh, Ann, don't," he said, and seized her hand, and
held it prayerfully. "Don't look like that—don't be afraid
—oh, look here!" he said desperately again, and put his
arms around her trembling shoulders and began to pat
her soothingly. "Please don't act like that—don't
tremble so—don't be afraid of me!—Oh, Ann, please
don't look at me that way—I didn't mean it—I'm so

God-damned sorry, Ann—Ah-h! it's going to be all right!
It's going to be all right! I swear it's going to be all
right!" he stammered foolishly, and took her hand, and
pleaded with her, not knowing what he was saying, and
sick with guilt and shame and horror at the profanation
of his act.

Her breath was fluttering, coming uncertainly, panting
short and quick and breathless like a frightened child;
this and her slender hands, her long trembling fingers,
the sight of her hands so strangely, beautifully delicate
for such a big woman, filled him with an unspeakable
anguish of remorse. She began to speak, a breathless,
panting, desperate kind of speech, and he found himself
desperately agreeing with everything she said, even
though he did not hear or understand half of it!

". . . Mustn't stay here," she panted. "Let's get out
of here . . . go somewhere . . . anywhere . . . I've
got to talk to you. . . . Something I've got to tell you!"
she panted desperately. ". . . You don't understand
. . . awful, horrible mistake!" she muttered. ". . . Got
to tell you, now! . . . Come on! Let's go."

"Oh, yes—sure—anywhere, Ann. Wherever you say,"
he agreed eagerly to everything she said: they put on
their hats and coats with trembling haste, and were preparing to leave just as Starwick and Elinor returned.

Starwick asked them where they were going: they
said they were going for a walk. He said, "Oh!" noncommittally. Both he and Elinor observed their flushed,
excited manner, and trembling haste, with a curious and
rather perturbed look, but said nothing more, and they
departed.

The pension was silent: everyone had already gone
to bed, and when they got out into the street, it was the
same. It was a night of still, cold frost, and everywhere

around them there were the strange, living presences of silence and of sleep. The houses had the closed, shuttered, and attentive secrecy that houses in a small French town have at night, no one else seemed to be abroad: they strode rapidly along in the direction of the railway station, saying nothing for a time, their feet sounding sharply on the frozen ground as they walked.

At length, beneath one of the sparse, infrequent street lamps, Ann paused, turned to him, and in a rapid, excited tone which was so different from her usual sullen curtness, began to speak:

"Look here!" she said, "we've got to forget about all that tonight—about everything that happened! . . . It was my fault," she muttered, with a kind of dumb, spinsterly agony of conscience which, in its evocation of the straight innocence and integrity of her kind and person, was somehow pitiably moving. "I didn't mean to lead you on," she said naïvely. "I shouldn't have let you get started."

"Oh, Ann," he said, "you didn't do anything! It wasn't your fault! You couldn't help it—I was the one who started it."

"No. No," she muttered, with a kind of sullen, miserable doggedness. "It was all my fault. . . . Could have stopped it." She turned abruptly, miserably, and began to stride on again.

"But, Ann," he began, with a kind of desperate persuasiveness, as he caught up with her, "don't take it this way. . . . Don't worry about it like this! . . . We didn't do anything bad, honestly we didn't!"

"Oh," she muttered without turning her head, "it was an awful thing—an awful thing to do to you! . . . I'm *so* ashamed," she muttered. "It was a rotten thing to do!"

"But you did nothing!" he protested. "I'm the one!"

"No, no," she muttered again—"I started it . . . I

on't know why. . . . But I had no right . . . there's
omething you don't understand."

"But what? What is it, Ann?" He didn't know whether
o laugh or cry over this dumb, spinsterly integrity of
New England conscience which, it seemed to him, was
aking the episode so bitterly to heart.

She paused in her long stride below another street
amp, and turning, spoke sternly, desperately, to him:

"Listen!" she said. "You've got to forget everything
hat happened tonight. . . . I never knew you felt that
vay about me. . . . You've got to forget about me. . . .
ou must never think of me that way again!"

"Why?" he said.

"Because," she muttered, "it's wrong . . . wrong."

"Why is it wrong?"

She did not answer for a moment, and then, turning,
ooked him straight in the eye:

"Because," she said, with quiet bluntness, "nothing
an come of it. . . . I don't feel that way about you."

He could not answer for a moment, and it seemed to
im that a thin film of ice had suddenly hardened round
is heart.

"Oh," he said presently; and, after a moment, added,
and don't you think you ever could?"

She did not answer, but began to walk rapidly ahead.
Ie caught up with her again, took her by the arm and
ulled her around to face him. He said sharply:

"Answer me! Don't you think you ever could?"

Her face was full of dumb, sullen misery; she mut-
ered:

"There's something you don't understand—something
ou don't know about."

"That's not what I asked you. Answer me."

"No," she muttered sullenly. "I can't feel that way
bout you. . . . I never will." She turned with a miser-

able look in her face and began to walk again. The ring
of ice kept hardening round his heart all the time; he
caught up with her again, and again stopped her.

"Listen, Ann. You've got to tell me why. I've got to
know." She shook her head miserably and turned away,
but he caught her, and pulled her back, saying in a
sharper, more peremptory tone:

"No, now—I've got to know. Is it because—you just
never could feel that way about a fellow like me—
because you could never think about me in that
way——?"

She didn't answer for a moment; she just stood looking
at him dumbly and miserably; and finally she shook her
head in a movement of denial:

"No," she said. "It's not that."

The ring of ice kept getting thicker all the time, it
seemed he would not be able to speak the words, but in a
moment he said:

"Well, then, is it—is it someone else?"

She made a sudden tormented movement of anguish
and despair, and turning, tried to walk away. He seized
her, and jerked her back to him, and said:

"Answer me, God-damn it! Is that the reason why?"

He waited a long moment before the answer came,
and then she muttered it out so low he could scarcely
hear it.

"Yes," she said, and wrenched her arm free. "Let me
go."

He caught her again, and pulled her back. The ring of
ice seemed to have frozen solid, and in that cold block he
could feel his heart throbbing like a trip-hammer.

"Who is it?" he said.

She did not answer, and he shook her roughly. "You
answer me. . . . Is it someone you knew back
home——?"

"Let me go," she muttered. "I won't tell you."

"By God, you will," he said thickly, and held her. Who is it? Is it someone you met back home, or not?"

"No!" she shouted, and wrenched free with a kind of stifled sob, and started ahead, almost running: "Leave me alone now! I won't tell you!"

A sudden flash of intuition, an instant flash of recognition and horror went through him like a knife. His heart seemed to have frozen solid, his breath to have stopped: he jumped for her like a cat, and whisking her around towards him, said:

"Ann! Look at me a moment!" He put his fingers underneath her chin and jerked her face up roughly: "Are you in love with Starwick?"

A long wailing note of dumb anguish and despair was torn from her; she tried to break from his grasp, and as he wrenched to get free, cried pitiably, in a terror-stricken voice:

"Leave me alone! Leave me alone!"

"Answer, God-damn you!" he snarled. "Is it Starwick or not?"

With a last frenzied effort, she wrenched free, and screamed like a wounded animal:

"*Yes! Yes!* . . . I've told you now! Are you satisfied? Will you leave me alone?" And with a sobbing breath, she began to run blindly.

He ran after her again, and caught up with her and took her in his arms, but not to embrace her, but just to hold her, stop her, somehow quiet, if he could, the wild, dumb, pitiable anguish of that big creature, which tore through the ventricles of his heart like a knife. He himself was sick with horror, and a kind of utter, paralyzing terror he had never felt before; he scarcely knew what he was doing, what he was saying, but the sight of that great, dumb creature's anguish, that locked and

inarticulate agony of grief, was more than he could bear
And cold with terror, he began to mumble with
thickened tongue: "Oh, but Ann, Ann!—Starwick, Star
wick!—it's no use! It's no use!—Christ, what a shame
What a shame!" For suddenly he knew what Starwic
was, what he had never allowed himself to admit tha
Starwick had become, and he kept mumbling thickly
"Christ! Christ! What a pity! What a shame!" not know
ing what he was saying, conscious only, with a kind o
sickening horror, of the evil mischance which had wit
such a cruel and deliberate perversity set their live
awry, and of the horrible waste and loss which ha
warped forever this grand and fertile creature's life an
which now would bring all her strength, her love, th
noble integrity of her spirit, to barren sterile nothing.

At the moment he had only one feeling, overwhelmin
and intolerable, somehow to quiet her, to stop, to hea
this horrible wound of grief and love, to bring peace t
her tormented spirit somehow, to do anything, use hi
life in any way that would give her a little peace an
comfort.

And he kept holding her, patting her on the shoulders
saying foolishly over and over again, and not knowin
what he said:

"Oh, it's all right! . . . It's all right, Ann! . . . Yo
mustn't look like this, you mustn't act this way . . . it'
going to be all right!" And knowing miserably, horribly
that it was not all right, that the whole design and fabri
of their lives were ruinously awry, that there was a hur
too deep ever to heal, a wrong too cruel, fatal, and per
verse ever to be righted.

She stayed there in his arms, she turned her face int
his shoulder, she put her slender, strong and lovely hand
upon his arms and held on to him desperately, and there
in the frozen, sleeping stillness of that street in a littl

French town, she wept hoarsely, bitterly, dreadfully, like some great creature horribly wounded; and all he could do was hold on to her until the last torn cry of pain had been racked and wrenched out of her.

When it was all over, and she had grown quiet, she dried her eyes, and looking at him with a dumb, pleading expression, she whispered miserably:

"You won't tell them? You won't say anything to Frank about this, will you? You'll never let him know?"

And stabbed again by wild, rending pity, sick with horror at her devastating terror, he told her he would not.

They walked home in silence through the frozen, sleeping streets. It was after midnight when they got back to the pension: the whole house was long ago asleep. As they went up the stairs a clock began to strike.

XII

He did not see her the next morning until it was time for lunch. She had gone out early with the big Alsatian dog, and had spent the morning walking in the forest. During the morning he told Elinor and Starwick that he was going back to Paris. Starwick said nothing at all, but Elinor, after a moment's silence, said coldly, and with a trace of sarcasm:

"Very well, my dear. You're the doctor. If the lure of the great city has proved too much for you, go you must." She was silent for a moment, and then said ironically, "Does this mean that we are not to have the honor of your distinguished company on our trip? . . . Really," she said curtly, "I wish you'd try to make up your mind what you're going to do. . . . The suspense, darling, is growing *quite* unbearable. If you're trying to break it to us gently," she went on poisonously, "I beg of you to let the blow fall now, and not to spare us any longer. After all," she said with a kind of evil drollery, "we may manage to survive the shock. . . . Really, I should like to know," she said sharply, as he did not answer. "If you're not going, we'll get someone else to take your place—we wanted a fourth party to help share in the expenses," she added venomously, "and I'd like to know at once what your intentions are."

He stared at her with a smoldering face and with a swelter of hot and ugly anger in his heart, but as usual her envenomed attack was too quick and sudden for him. Before he could answer, even as his tongue was blundering at a hot reply, she turned swiftly away, and with an air of resignation, said to Starwick:

"Will you try to find out what his intentions are? I can't find out what he wants to do. *Apparently*," she concluded in a rich, astounded voice, "apparently, you young friend is tongue-tied." She walked away, contained and beautifully self-possessed as ever, save for two angry spots of color in her face.

When she had gone, Starwick turned to him, and said with quiet reproof:

"You ought to let her know. You really ought, you know."

"All right!" he said quickly and hotly, "I'm letting you know right now. I'm not going."

Starwick said nothing for a moment, then with a quiet, weary, and sorrowful resignation, he said:

"I'm sorry, Gene."

The other said nothing, but just stood looking at Starwick with eyes which were cold and hard and ugly with their hate. Starwick's quiet words, the almost Christlike humility with which he uttered them, now seemed to him to be nothing but the mask of a sneering arrogance of pride and contemptuous assurance, the badge of his immeasurable good fortune. With cold, measuring eyes of hate he looked at Starwick's soft and graceful throat, the languid indolence of his soft, voluptuously graceful figure, and with murderous calculation he thought: "How easy it would be for me to twist that damned, soft neck of yours off your shoulders! How easy it would be to take that damned, soft body in my hands and break it like a rotten stick across my knees! Oh, you damned, soft, pampered makeshift of a human being—you thing of cunning tricks and words and accents—you synthetic imitation of a living artist—you dear, damned darling of aesthetic females—you Boston woman's lap-dog, you——"

The foul words thickened to a swelter of blind hate and murder in his heart, and would not give him ease, or phrase the choking and intolerable burden of his hate; the light of hate and murder burned in his naked eye, curled his hands into two rending paws of savage power in which he seemed to feel the substance of that warm, soft throat between the strangling grip of his long fingers; and all the time he felt hopelessly tricked, out-witted, beaten by the very nakedness of his surrender to his hate, beaten by something too subtle, soft and cunning for him ever to grasp, by something which, for so it now seemed, would always beat him, by something whose impossible good fortune it would always be to take from him the thing he wanted most.

A thousand times he had foreseen this thing. A thousand times, he had foreseen, as young men will foresee, the coming of the enemy—and always he had pictured him in a definite form and guise. Always he had come, armed in insolence and power, badged with the open menace of the jeering word, the sneering tongue, the brandished fist. Always he had come to strike terror to the heart with naked threat and open brag, to try to break the heart and courage of another man, to win his jeering domination of another's life, by violence and brutal courage. He had never come by stealth but always by the frontal attack, and the youth, like every youth alive, had sworn that he would be ready for him when he came, would meet him fiercely and without retreat, and would either conquer him or most desperately lie dead before he yielded to the inexpiable shame of foul dishonor.

And now the enemy had come, but in no way that he had ever known, in no guise that he had ever pictured. The enemy had come, not armed in brutal might and open brag and from the front, but subtle, soft, and infinitely cunning, and from a place, and in a way that he had never foreseen. The enemy had come behind the mask of friendship, he had come with words of praise, with avowals of proud belief and noble confidence in an attitude of admiration and humility—had come in such a way, and even as he spoke the words of praise and proud belief in him, had taken from him what he wanted most in life, and had not seemed to take it, or to want it, or to care.

Starwick and Elinor had quarreled again: this time it was because he too had decided to go back to Paris that afternoon. No one but Elinor knew the purpose of his going; and that purpose, whatever it was, did not please her. When Eugene entered the dining room for his last meal with them, they were at it hammer and tongs, totally oblivious of the sensation they were causing among the whispering and conspiring old men and women all about them. Or, if not oblivious, they were indifferent to it: even in their quarrels they kept their grand and rare and special manner—a manner which more and more conceived the universe as an appropriate

backdrop for the subtle and romantic complications of
their own lives, and which, in its remote and lofty detachment from the common run of man, said that here
was an intercourse of souls that was far too deep and
rare for the dull conscience of the world to apprehend.

Elinor was talking earnestly, positively, an accent
rich, yet sharp, cultivated, yet formidably assured, a
well-mannered authority, positive with denial and the
conviction of experience.

"You cannot do it! I tell you that you cannot *do* it!
You will come a cropper if you do!"

Starwick's face was flushed deeply with anger; he
answered quietly in a mannered tone filled with a sense
of outrage and indignation:

"I resent that *very* much," he said. "It is *very* wrong,
and *very* unfair of you to speak that way! I *resent* it!" he
said quietly, but with stern reproof.

"Sorry!" she clipped the word out curt and brusque,
the way the English say it. "If you resent it, you resent
it—and that's *that!* But after *all*, my dear, what else do
you expect? If you insist on bringing any little cut-throat
you pick up in a Montmartre bistro along with you
everywhere you go, your friends are going to complain
about it! And they've a right to!"

"I *resent* that *very* much!" he said again, in his mannered tone.

"Sorry!" she said crisply, curtly, as before. "But that's
the way I feel about it!" She looked at him for a moment,
and then, suddenly shaking her head in a short and
powerful movement, she said in a whispering shudder
of revulsion and disgust:

"No good, Frank! . . . I'm willing to make all the
allowances I can . . . but the man's no good—no good!
. . . He just won't do!" Her tone was the tone of a
powerful New Englander, of "fiber," character and

breeding, putting the final dogma of his judgment upon
an inferior person who "just won't do."

And again, Starwick, two spots of bright color burning in his cheeks, said coldly, quietly, and with an inflexible obstinacy:

"I resent that *very* much!"

He had apparently decided that Alec, the Frenchman
they had met in a Montmartre bar one night, and who
had accompanied them on most of their expeditions
since, should be their guest in their forthcoming travels
over France. Moreover, with that arrogant secretiveness
that was characteristic of him, Frank had made an appointment to meet the Frenchman in Paris that evening,
and had not until that morning informed anyone of his
intentions. This was the cause of the quarrel.

As Eugene entered, they looked up at him indifferently, and resumed their quarrel; Ann came in a little
later, sat down without speaking, and began to eat in
sullen silence. It was an unpleasant meal. Elinor as-
sumed her customary manner of gay, light raillery, but
this time, in powerful contrast to her hilarious good
spirits of the night before, she was full of spite and
malice—the angry desire of her tormented spirit to
sting and wound as if, by causing pain to others, she
could in some measure assuage her own.

"Darling," she said to Eugene, in her deft, malicious
way, "I do hope you're not going to forget all about me
now that you're deserting me? . . . Won't you write me
now and then to cheer me up? . . . Or is this going to
be good-by forever! . . . Because, darling, if it is, I
want you to say so right out . . . no matter how it
hurts, I'd rather know the worst right now, so that I can
go out in the garden and eat worms, or howl, or beat my
head against the wall, or something," she said drolly,
but with a glint of spiteful motive in her eyes and in her

smooth tone that left no doubt of her intention. "Won't you say it ain't so, darling? . . . I mean, won't you remember me long enough sometime just to write a letter to me . . . I don't care how short it is if you'll just write and let me know that you still *care*," she said maliciously. "Come on, darling," she added coaxingly, leaning towards him, "say you will. . . . Promise to write me just a little letter . . . just a *teeny-weeny* little one like that," she measured drolly between two fingers, and then, while he glared at her with a hot face and angry eyes, she got in the instant, deft, decisive stroke before he could think up an answer; and so concluded it:

"Good!" she said swiftly, and patted him quickly, decisively, on the arm: "God bless you, darling! I knew you would!"

They finished lunch in a sullen and unhappy silence. After lunch, Eugene went upstairs, packed and closed his valise and came down and paid his bill. When he got outside, Elinor was sitting in the car, waiting for him. Starwick had not yet come down.

"Put your suitcase in behind," she said curtly, "and do tell Frank to hurry if he's coming. There's not much time."

"Where's Ann?" he said. "Is she coming with us to the station?"

"My dear," she said coldly, "I haven't the remotest idea. Why don't you ask her yourself if you want to know?"

He flushed again; and then with a feeling of painful embarrassment and constraint, said:

"Elinor—if you don't mind—that is—I'd like——"

"What?" she said curtly, impatiently, and sharply, turning in her seat and looking at him. "You'd like *what?*"

"If you don't mind," he said, gulping with embarrassment, and at the same moment enraged that he should feel so——

"My money!" he blurted out.

"What? . . . What?" she demanded again, in a brusque, puzzled tone. "*Oh!*" she cried with a sudden air of enlightenment. "Your *money! . . .* You mean those express checks you gave me to keep for you?"

"Yes," he said miserably, feeling an inexplicable shame and embarrassment at having to ask for his own money, and inwardly cursing the folly which, in the rush of affection that followed their recent reconciliation, had caused him to give every cent he had into her keeping. "If you don't mind—that is——"

"But of *course*, my child!" cried Elinor, with a fine air of astonishment. "You shall have it at once!"—and opening her purse she took out the thin little, black folder that contained all the money he had left—three express checks of twenty-dollar denomination. "Here you are, sir!" she said, and gave it to him in such a way that he felt again a sense of guilt and shame as if he were acting meanly towards her, or were taking something that did not belong to him.

"I'm sorry," he stammered apologetically, "sorry to have to ask you for it, Elinor—but you see it's all I've got left."

"It is?" she said curtly. "What did you do with all the rest that you had when we met you?"

"I—I guess I spent it," he stammered.

The answer came, and buried itself in his heart, as quick, as cold, as poisonous as a striking snake:

"You did?" she said curtly. "I wonder where. I'm sure you didn't spend any of it while you were with *us*."

He could have strangled her. The veins stood out upon his forehead like cords, his face was brick-red, and for a moment he went blind with the rush of hot, choking blood to his head. He tried to speak, his throat worked convulsively, but no words came: he just stood there goggling at her stupidly with an inflamed face, uttering a few incoherent croaks. Before he could think of anything to say, she had escaped again: Starwick and Ann were coming out of the pension, and she was speaking to them swiftly, telling them to make haste.

No one spoke during the ride to the station. He sat on the back seat beside Ann and the big Alsatian dog; Starwick and Elinor were in front. When they got to the station, the clock still lacked more than five minutes to traintime. He and Starwick bought third-class fares, and went outside where the women were still waiting for them. Starwick and Elinor walked away a few yards and began their quarrel again; Ann said nothing, but looked at him dumbly, miserably, a look that tore at him with pity and wild regret, and that made him weak and hollow with his blind, impossible desire.

They looked at each other with angry, sullen eyes, tormented with the perverse and headstrong pride of youth, unwilling to make concessions or relent, even when each desperately wanted the other to do so.

"Good-by," he said, and held out his hand. "Good-by, Ann."

"What do you mean?" she began angrily. "What are you going to do?"

"I'm saying good-by," he said doggedly.

"You mean you're not coming with us?"

For a moment he did not answer and then, nodding towards Elinor, he said bitterly:

"Your lady friend there doesn't seem to want me very much. She doesn't seem to think I bear my fair share of the expense."

"What did she say to you?" the girl asked.

"Oh, nothing," he said in a quiet, choking tone of fury. "Nothing in particular. Just one of those friendly little things I've come to look for. She just said she didn't know what I'd done with my money—that I hadn't spent any of it while I was with you."

Her face got brick-red with a heavy, smoldering flush, she looked towards Elinor with angry eyes, and then muttered:

"It was a rotten thing to say!" Turning towards him again, she said in a low tone:

"Do you mean then that you've given up the trip? You're not coming with us?"

"That's what I've told you, isn't it?" he said harshly. "What else do you expect?"

She looked at him sullenly, angrily, a moment longer; and suddenly her eyes were wet with tears.

"It's going to be a fine trip for me, isn't it?" she muttered. "I've got a lot to look forward to, haven't I?"

"Oh, you'll get along, I guess," he jeered. "I don't think you're going to miss *my* company very much." And felt a desperate hope that she would.

"Oh, it's going to be charming, charming, isn't it!" she said bitterly. "Nothing to do but hold down the back seat alone with the dog—while *they*," she nodded towards Elinor and Starwick—"are up there having their wonderful talks together—leaving me alone to watch the dog while they stay out all night together—oh, it's going to be simply wonderful, isn't it!" she said with an infuriated sarcasm.

"So that's the reason I was wanted?" he said. "To keep you company on the back seat! To take the place of the dog! To make it look good, eh—to make the party look a little more respectable back in Boston when they hear of Mr. Starwick and his two lady friends! That's why you wanted me, is it? To fill in extra space—to be a kind of damned male nurse and chaperon to you and Elinor and Frank Starwick——"

She took a step towards him and stopped, her hands clenched beside her, her eyes shot with tears, her big body trembling for a moment with baffled anger and despair:

"God-damn you!" she said in a small, choked voice; and, her hands still clenched, she turned away abruptly to hide her tears.

At this moment Starwick approached and, his ruddy face flushing as he spoke, he said quietly, casually:

"Ann, look! Will you let me have a thousand francs?"

She turned around, glared at Starwick for a moment with angry, reddened eyes and then, to his astonishment and her own, boomed out comically, and in an enraged tone:

"No—o!"

His face went crimson with embarrassment, but after looking at her steadily for a moment, he turned, and walked back to Elinor. In a moment she could be heard saying coldly, positively:

". . . I am sorry, Francis, but I cannot! . . . You should have thought about all that before! . . . If you won't stay out here and go in with us tomorrow, you'll have to do the best you can by yourself. . . . No, sir, I cannot . . . if you want to put it that way, yes; I *won't*, then! . . . I do not *like* the man. . . . I *thoroughly* disapprove of what you're doing. . . . I *will* not help you!"

Some low, excited words passed between them, and in a moment Starwick said:

"You have no right to say that! I *resent* that *very* much!"

His ruddy face was deeply flushed with anger and humiliation; he turned abruptly on his heel and walked away without farewell. At this moment the guards could be heard calling, "En voiture! En voiture, messieurs!" and Elinor, glancing towards Ann and Eugene, said curtly:

"If you're going to catch that train, you'll have to hurry!"

Eugene turned to say good-by to Ann; she paid no attention to his outstretched hand but stood, her hands clenched, glaring angrily at him with wet eyes.

"Good-by!" he said roughly. "Aren't you going to say good-by?"

She made no answer, but just stood glaring at him, and then turned away.

"All right," he said angrily. "Do as you like!"

Without a word to Elinor, he picked up his valise, ran into the station and got through the gates just as the little suburban train began to move. Starwick was climbing up into a compartment, Eugene followed him, flung his valise inside, and clambered in, breathless, just as a guard with a remonstrant face slammed the door behind him.

XIII

During the journey back to Paris, Eugene and Starwick said little. The two young men were the sole occupants of the compartment, they sat facing each other, looking out through the windows with gloomy eyes. The grey light of the short, winter's day was fading rapidly: when they entered Paris dusk had come; as the train rattled over the switchpoints in the yard-approaches to the Gare St. Lazare, they could see lights and life and sometimes faces in the windows of the high, faded buildings near the tracks. Through one window, in a moment's glimpse, Eugene saw a room with a round table with a dark cloth upon it, and with the light of a shaded chandelier falling on it, and a dark-haired boy of ten or twelve leaning on the table, reading a book, with his face propped in his hands, and a woman moving busily about the table, laying it with plates and knives and forks. And as the train slackened speed, he saw, high up in the topmost floor of an old house that rose straight up from the tracks, a woman come to the window, look for a moment at a canary-bird cage which was hanging in the window, reach up and take it from its hook. She had the rough, blowsy, and somewhat old-fashioned look of a whore of the Renoir period; and yet she was like someone he had known all his life.

They passed long strings of silent, darkened railway compartments, and as they neared the station, several suburban trains steamed past them, loaded with people going home. Some of the trains were the queer little double-deckers that one sees in France: Eugene felt like laughing every time he saw them and yet, with their loads of Frenchmen going home, they too were like something he had always known. As the train came into the station, and slowed down to its halt, he could see a boat-train ready for departure on another track. Sleek as a panther, groomed, opulent, ready, purring softly as a cat, the train waited there like a luxurious projectile, evoking perfectly, and at once, the whole structure of the world of power and wealth and pleasure that had created it. Beyond it one saw the whole universe of pleasure—a world of great hotels, and famed resorts, the thrilling structure of the huge, white-breasted liners, and the slanting race and drive of their terrific stacks. One saw behind it the dark coast of France, the flash of beacons, the grey, fortressed harbor walls, the bracelet of their hard, spare lights, and beyond, beyond, one saw the infinite beat and swell of stormy seas, the huge nocturnal slant and blaze of liners racing through immensity, and forever beyond, beyond, one saw the faint, pale coasts of morning and America, and then the spires and ramparts of the enfabled isle, the legendary and aerial smoke, the stone and steel, of the terrific city.

Now their own train had come to a full stop, and he and Starwick were walking up the quay among the buzzing crowd of people.

Starwick turned and, flushing painfully, said in a constrained and mannered tone:

"Look! Shall I be seeing you again?"

Eugene answered curtly: "I don't know. If you want to find me, I suppose I shall be at the same place, for a time."

"And after that?—Where will you go?"

"I don't know," he answered brusquely again. "I haven't thought about it yet. I've got to wait until I get money to go away on."

The flush in Starwick's ruddy face deepened perceptibly, and, after another pause, and with obvious embarrassment, he continued as before:

"Look! Where are you going now?"

"I don't know, Francis," he said curtly. "To the hotel, I suppose, to leave my suitcase and see if they've still got a room for me. If I don't see you again, I'll say good-by to you now."

Starwick's embarrassment had become painful to watch; he did not speak for another moment, then said:

"Look! Do you mind if I come along with you?"

He did mind; he wanted to be alone; to get away as soon as he could from Starwick's presence and all the hateful memories it evoked, but he said shortly:

"You can come along if you like, of course, but I see no reason why you should. If you're going to the studio we can take a taxi and you can let me off at the hotel.

But if you're meeting somebody over on this side later on, why don't you wait over here for him?"

Starwick's face was flaming with shame and humiliation; he seemed to have difficulty in pronouncing his words and when he finally turned to speak, the other youth was shocked to see in his eyes a kind of frantic, naked desperation.

"Then, look!" he said, and moistened his dry lips. "Could you let me have some—some money, please?"

Something strangely like terror and entreaty looked out of his eyes:

"I've *got* to have it," he said desperately.

"How much do you want?"

Starwick was silent, and then muttered:

"I could get along with 500 francs."

The other calculated swiftly: the sum amounted at the time to about thirty dollars. It was almost half his total remaining funds but—one look at the desperate humiliation and entreaty of Starwick's face, and a surge of savage, vindictive joy swept through him—it would be worth it.

"All right," he nodded briefly, and started to walk forward again.

"You come with me while I leave this stuff at the hotel and later on we'll see if we can't get these checks cashed."

Starwick consented eagerly. From that time on, Eugene played with him as a cat plays with a mouse. They got a taxi and were driven across the Seine to his little hotel, he left Starwick below while he went upstairs with his valise, promising to "be down in a minute, after I've washed up a bit," and took a full and leisurely three-quarters of an hour. When he got downstairs, Starwick's restless manner had increased perceptibly: he was pacing up and down, smoking one cigarette after another. In the same leisurely and maddening manner, they left the hotel. Starwick asked where they were going: Eugene replied cheerfully that they were going to dinner at a modest little restaurant across the Seine. By the time they had walked across the bridge, and through the enormous arches of the Louvre, Starwick was gnawing his lips with chagrin. In the restaurant, Eugene ordered dinner and a bottle of wine; Starwick refused to eat, Eugene expressed regret and pursued his meal deliberately. By the time he had finished, and was cracking nuts, Starwick was almost frantic. He demanded impatiently to know where they were going, and the other answered chidingly:

"Now, Frank, what's the hurry? You've got the whole night ahead of you: there's no rush at all. . . . Besides, why not stay here a while? It's a good place. Don't you think so? I discovered it all by myself!"

Starwick looked about him, and said:

"Yes, the place is all right, I suppose, the food looks good—it really does, you know—but *God!*" he snarled bitterly, "how dull! how dull!"

"*Dull?*" Eugene said chidingly, and with an air of fine astonishment. "Frank, Frank, such language—and from *you!* Is this the poet and the artist, the man of feeling and of understanding, the lover of humanity? Is this *grand*, is this *fine*, is this *swell?*" he jeered. "Is this the lover of the French—the man who's more at home here than he is at home? Why, Frank, this is unworthy of you: I thought that every breath you drew was saturated with the love of France. I thought that every pulse-beat of your artist's soul beat in sympathy with the people of this noble country. I thought that you would love this place—find it *simply swell*," he sneered, "and *very* grand and *most* amusing—and here you turn your nose up at the people and call them dull—as if they were a lot of damned Americans! *Dull!* How can they be *dull*, Frank? Don't you see they're *French?* . . . Now this boy here, for example," he pointed to a bus-boy of eighteen years who was noisily busy piling dishes from a table onto a tray. "Isn't he a *sweet* person, Frank?" he went on with an evil, jeering mimicry. "And there's something *very* grand and *enormously* moving about the way he piles those dishes on a tray," he continued with a deliberate parody of Starwick's mannered accent. "I *mean*, the whole thing's there—it really is, you know—it's like that painting by Cimabue in the Louvre that we both like so much—you know the one of the Madonna with the little madonnas all around her. I mean the way he uses his hands—Look!" he crooned rapturously as the bus-boy took a thick, blunt finger and vigorously wiped his rheumy nose with it. "Now where, *where,* Frank," he said ecstatically, "could you find anything like that in America? I *mean*, the *grace*, the *dignity*, the complete unself-consciousness with which that boy just wiped his nose across his finger—or his finger across his nose—Hah! hah! hah!—I get all confused, Frank— *really!*—the movement is so beautiful and fluid—it's hard to say just which is which—which does the *wiping* —nose or finger—I mean, the whole thing's *quite* incredible—and *most* astonishing—the way it comes back on itself: it's like a *fugue,* you know," and looking at the other earnestly, he said deeply: "You see what I mean, don't you?"

Starwick's face had flamed crimson during the course of this jeering parody: he returned the other's look with hard eyes, and said with cold succinctness:

"Quite! . . . If you don't mind, could we go along now and"—his flush deepened and he concluded with painful difficulty, ". . . and . . . and do what you said you would!"

"But of *course!*" the other cried, with another parody of Starwick's tone and manner. "At once! Immediately! *Tout de suite!* . . . as we say over here! . . . Now, *there* you are!" he said enthusiastically. "*There* you are, Frank! . . . *Tout de suite!*" he murmured rapturously. "*Tout de suite!* . . . Not 'at once!' Not 'right away!' Not 'immediately!' But *tout de suite!* . . . Ah, Frank, how different from our own coarse tongue! Quel charme! Quelle musique! Quelle originalité! . . . I *mean*, the whole thing's there! . . . It really is, you know!"

"Quite," said Starwick as before, and looked at him with hard, embittered eyes. "Could we go now?"

"Mais oui, mais oui, mon ami! . . . But first, I want you to meet yon noble youth who wipes his nose with such a simple unaffected dignity, and is, withal, so *French* about it! . . . I know him well, we artists have the common touch, n'est-ce pas? Many a time and oft have we talked together. . . . Why, Frank, you're going to love him like a brother . . . the whole, great heart of France is beating underneath that waiter's jacket . . . and, ah! such grace, such flashing rapier-work of Gallic wit, such quick intelligence and humor. . . . Ecoutez, garçon!" he called; the boy turned, startled, and then, seeing the young men, his thick lips slowly wreathed themselves in a smile of amiable stupidity. He came towards them smiling eagerly, a clumsy boy of eighteen years with the thick features, the dry, thick lips, the blunted, meaty hands and encrusted nails of the peasant. It was a face of slow, wondering intelligence, thick-witted, unperceptive, flushed with strong, dark color, full of patient earnestness, and animal good-nature.

"Bonsoir, monsieur," he said, as he came up. "Vous

désirez quelquechose?" And he grinned at them slowly, with a puzzled, trustful stare.

"But yes, my boy! . . . I have been telling my friend about you, and he wants to meet you. He is, like me, an American . . . but a true friend of France. And so I told him how you loved America!"

"But yes, but yes!" the boy cried earnestly, clutching eagerly at the suggestion. "La France and l'Amérique are of the true friends, n'est-ce pas, monsieur?"

"You have reason! It's as you say!"

"Vashingtawn!" the boy cried suddenly, with a burst of happy inspiration.

"But yes! But yes! . . . Lafayette!" the other yelled enthusiastically.

"Pair-*shing!*" the boy cried rapturously. "La France et l'Amérique!" he passionately proclaimed, and he turned slowly to Starwick, joined his thick, blunt fingers together, and thrusting them under Starwick's nose, nodded his thick head vigorously and cried: "C'est comme ça! . . . La France et l'Amérique!"—he shook his thick, joined fingers vigorously under Starwick's nose again, and said: "Mais oui! Mais oui! . . . C'est toujours comme ça!"

"O my God!" groaned Starwick, turning away, "how dull! How utterly, *unspeakably* dreary!"

"Monsieur?" the boy spoke inquiringly, and turned blunt, puzzled features at Starwick's dejected back.

Starwick's only answer was another groan: flinging a limp arm over the back of his chair, he slumped in an attitude of exhausted weariness. The boy turned a patient, troubled face to the other youth, who said, in an explanatory way:

"He is profoundly moved. . . . What you have said has touched him deeply!"

"Ah-h!" the boy cried, with an air of sudden, happy enlightenment, and thus inspired, began with renewed ardor, and many a vigorous wag of his thick and earnest beak, to proclaim:

"Mais c'est vrai! C'est comme je dis! . . . La France et l'Amérique—" he intoned anew.

"O God!" groaned Starwick without turning, and waved a feeble and defeated arm. "Tell him to go away!"

"He is deeply moved! He says he can stand no more!"

The boy cast an earnest and immensely gratified look at Starwick's dejected back, and was on the point of pushing his triumph farther, when the proprietor angrily called to him, bidding him be about his work and leave the gentlemen in peace.

He departed with obvious reluctance, but not without vigorously nodding his thick head again, proclaiming that "La France et l'Amérique sont comme ça!" and shaking his thick, clasped fingers earnestly in a farewell gesture of racial amity.

When he had gone, Starwick looked around wearily, and in a dispirited tone said:

"God! What a place! How did you ever find it! . . . And how do you manage to stand it!"

"But look at him, Frank . . . I mean, don't you just *lo-o-ve* it?" he jibed. "I mean, there's something so *grand* and so *simple* and so *unaffected* about the way he did it! It's really *quite* astonishing! It really is, you know!"

The poor bus-boy, indeed, had been intoxicated by his sudden and unaccustomed success. Now, as he continued his work of clearing tables and stacking dishes on a tray, he could be seen nodding his thick head vigorously and muttering to himself: "Mais oui, mais oui, monsieur! . . . La France et l'Amérique. . . . Nous sommes de vrais amis!" and from time to time he would even pause in his work, to clasp his thick fingers together illustrating this, and to mutter: "C'est toujours comme ça!"

This preoccupied elation soon proved the poor boy's undoing. For even as he lifted his loaded tray and balanced it on one thick palm, he muttered "C'est comme ça," again, making a recklessly inclusive gesture with his free hand; the mountainously balanced tray was thrown off balance, he made a desperate effort to retrieve it, and as it crashed upon the floor, he pawed frantically and sprawled after it, in one general ruinous smash of broken crockery.

There was a maddened scream from the proprietor. He came running clumsily, a squat, thick figure of a bourgeois Frenchman, clothed in black, and screaming imprecations. His mustaches bristled like the quills of an enraged porcupine, and his ruddy face was swollen and suffused, an apoplectic red:

"Brute! Fool! Imbecile!" he screamed as the frightened boy clambered to his feet and stood staring at him with a face full of foolish and helpless bewilderment. ". . . Salaud! . . . Pig! . . . Architect!" he screamed out this meaningless curse in a strangling voice, and rushing at the boy, cuffed him clumsily on the side of the face, and began to thrust and drive him before him in staggering lunges.

"—And what grace, Frank!" Eugene now said cruelly. "How *grand* and *simple* and how *unself-conscious* they are in everything they do! I *mean*, the way they use their hands!" he said ironically, as the maddened proprietor gave the unfortunate boy another ugly, clumsy shove that sent him headlong. "I *mean*, it's like a fugue—like Cimabue or an early primitive—it really is, you know——"

"Assassin! Criminal!" the proprietor screamed at this moment, and gave the weeping boy a brutal shove that sent him sprawling forward upon his hands and knees:

"Traitor! Misérable scélérat!" he screamed, and kicked clumsily at the prostrate boy with one fat leg.

"Now where?—where?" Eugene said maliciously, as the wretched boy clambered to his feet, weeping bitterly, "—where, Francis, could you see anything like that in America?"

"God!" said Starwick, getting up. "It's unspeakable!" And desperately: "Let's go!"

They paid the bill and went out. As they went down the stairs, they could still hear the hoarse, choked sobs of the bus-boy, his thick face covered with his thick, blunt fingers, crying bitterly.

He didn't know what Starwick wanted the money for, but it was plain he wanted it for something, badly. His agitation was pitiable:—the bitter exasperation and open flare of temper he had displayed once or twice in the restaurant was so unnatural to him that it was evident his nerves were being badly rasped by the long delay. Now, he kept consulting his watch nervously: he turned, and looking at Eugene with a quiet but deep resentment in his eyes, he said:

"Look. If you're going to let me have the money, I wish you'd let me have it now—please. Otherwise, I shall not need it."

And Eugene, touched with a feeling of guilt at the deep and quiet resentment in his companion's face, knowing he had promised him the money, and feeling that this taunting procrastination was ungenerous and mean, said roughly:

"All right, come on. You can have it right away."

They turned into the rue St. Honoré, turned again, and walked to the Place Vendôme, where there was a small exchange office—or "all-night bank"—where travelers' checks were cashed. They entered, he cashed his three remaining checks: the amount was something over 900 francs. He counted the money, kept out 500 francs for Starwick, stuffed the rest into his pocket, and, turning, thrust the little sheaf of banknotes into Starwick's hand, saying brutally:

"There's your money, Frank. And now, good-by to you. I needn't detain you any longer."

He turned to go, but the implication of his sneer had not gone unnoticed:

"Just a minute," Starwick's quiet voice halted him. "What did you mean by that?"

He paused, with a slow thick anger beating in his veins:

"By what?"

"By saying you needn't detain me any longer?"

"You got what you wanted, didn't you?"

"You mean the money?"

"Yes."

Starwick looked quietly at him a moment longer, then thrust the little roll of banknotes back into his hand:

"Take it," he said.

For a moment the other could not speak. A murderous fury choked him: he ground his teeth together, and clenched his fist, he felt a moment's almost insane desire to grip that soft throat with his strangling hand, and beat the face into a bloody jelly with his fist.

"Why, God-damn you," he grated between clenched teeth. "God-damn you for a——!" He turned away, saying harshly: "To hell with you! . . . I'm through!"

He began to walk away across the Square at a savage stride. He heard footsteps following him: near the corner of the rue St. Honoré, Starwick caught up with him, and said doggedly:

"No, but I'm going with you! . . . I really *must*, you know!" His voice rose and became high, almost woman-ish, with his passionate declaration: "If there's anything between you and me that has to be settled before you go away, you can't leave it like this . . . we've got to have it out, you know . . . we really must!"

The other youth stood stock still for a moment. Every atom of him—blood, bone, the beating of his heart, the substance of his flesh—seemed to congeal in a paralysis of cold murder. He licked his dry lips, and said thickly:

"Have it out!" The blood swarmed through him in a choking flood, it seemed instantly to rush down through his hands and to fill him with a savage, rending strength, the curse was torn from him in a bestial cry and snarling:

"Have it out! Why, you damned rascal, we'll have it out, all right! We'll have it out, you dirty little fairy ——" The foul word was out at last, in one blind ex-pletive of murderous hate, and suddenly that tortured, impossibly tangled web of hatred, failure, and despair found its release. He reached out, caught Starwick by the throat and collar of his shirt, and endowed with that immense, incalculable strength which hatred and the sudden lust to kill can give a man, he lifted the slight figure from the ground as if it were a bundle of rags and sticks, and slammed it back against the façade of a building with such brutal violence that Starwick's head bounced and rattled on the stone. The blow knocked Starwick senseless: his hat went flying from his head, his cane fell from his grasp and rattled on the pavement with a hard, lean clatter. For a moment, his eyes rolled back and forth with the wooden, weighted movement of a doll's. Then, as Eugene released his grip, his legs buckled at the knees, his eyes closed and his head sagged, and he began to slump down towards the pavement, his back sliding all the time against the wall.

He would have fallen if Eugene had not caught him, held him, propped him up against the wall, until he could recover. And at that moment, Eugene felt an instant, overwhelming revulsion of shame, despair, and sick horror, such as he had never known before. For a moment all the blood seemed to have drained out of his heart and left it a dead shell. He thought he had killed Starwick—broken his neck or fractured his skull: even in death—or unconsciousness—Starwick's frail body retained its languorous dignity and grace. His head dropped heavily to one side, the buckling weight of the unconscious figure slumped in a movement of terrible and beautiful repose—the same movement that one sees in a great painting of Christ lowered from the cross, as if, indeed, the whole rhythm, balance and design of that art which Starwick had observed with such impassioned mimicry had left its image indelibly upon his own life, so that, even in death or senselessness, his body would portray it.

At that moment, the measure of ruin and defeat which the other young man felt was overwhelming. It seemed to him that if he had deliberately contrived to crown a ruinous career by the most shameful and calamitous act of all, he could not have been guilty of a worse crime than the one he had just committed. It was not merely the desperate, sickening terror in his heart when he thought that Starwick might be dead— that he had killed him. It was even more than this, a sense of profanation, a sense of having done something so foul and abominable that he could never recover from it, never wash its taint out of his blood. There are some people who possess such a natural dignity of person—

such a strange and rare inviolability of flesh and spirit—
that any familiarity, any insult, above all any act of
violence upon them, is unthinkable. If such an insult
be intended, if such violence be done, the act returns a
thousandfold upon the one who does it: his own blow
returns to deal a terrible revenge; he will relive his crime
a thousand times in all the shame and terror of inexpiable memory.

Starwick was such a person: he had this quality of
personal inviolability more than anyone the other youth
had ever known. And now, as he stood there holding
Starwick propped against the wall, calling him by name,
shaking him and pleading with him to recover consciousness, his feeling of shame, despair, and bitter
ruinous defeat was abysmal, irremediable. It seemed to
him that he could have done nothing which would more
have emphasized his enemy's superiority and his own
defeat than this thing which he had done. And the feeling that Starwick would always beat him, always take
from him the thing he wanted most, that by no means
could he ever match the other youth in any way, gain
even the most trifling victory, was now overpowering in
its horror. With a sick and bitter heart of misery, he
cursed the wretched folly of his act. He would willingly
have cut off his hand—the hand that gave the blow—if
by so doing he could undo his act, but he knew that it
was now too late, and with a feeling of blind terror he
reflected that this knowledge of his defeat and fear was
now Starwick's also, and that as long as Starwick lived,
he would always know about it, and realize from this
alone the full measure of his victory. And this feeling of
shame, horror, and abysmal, inexpiable regret persisted
even after, with a feeling of sick relief, he saw Starwick's eyes flutter, open, and after a moment of vague,

confused bewilderment, look at him with a quiet consciousness.

Nevertheless, his feeling of relief was unspeakable. He bent, picked up Starwick's hat and cane, and gave them to him, saying quietly:

"I'm sorry, Frank."

Starwick put on his hat, and took the cane in his hand.

"It doesn't matter. If that's the way you felt, you had to do it," he said in a quiet, toneless and inflexible voice. "But now, before we leave each other, we must see this through. We've got to bring this thing into the open, find out what it is. That *must* be done, you know!" His voice had risen with an accent of inflexible resolve, an accent which the other had heard before, and which he knew no fear of death or violence or any desperate consequence could ever alter by a jot. "I've got to understand what this thing is before I leave you," Starwick said. "That must be done."

"All right!" Eugene said blindly, desperately. "Come on, then!"

And together, they strode along in silence, along the empty pavements of the rue St. Honoré, past shuttered shops, and old, silent buildings which seemed to abide there and attend upon the anguish of tormented youth with all the infinite, cruel, and impassive silence of dark time, the unspeakable chronicle of foredone centuries, the unspeakable anguish, grief, and desperation of a million vanished, nameless, and forgotten lives.

And thus, in bitter shame and silence and despair, the demented, drunken, carnal, and kaleidoscopic circuit of the night began.

XIV

About ten o'clock the next morning someone knocked at Eugene's door, and Starwick walked in. Without re-

ferring to the night before Starwick immediately, in his
casual and abrupt way, said:

"Look. Elinor and Ann are here: they came in this
morning."

"Where are they?" Excitement, sharp and sudden as
an electric shock, shot through him. "Here? Downstairs?"

"No: they've gone shopping. I'm meeting them at
Prunier's for lunch. Ann said she might come by to see
you later on."

"Before lunch?"

"Ace," said Starwick. "Look," he said again, in his
casual, mannered tone, "I don't suppose you'd care to
come to lunch with us?"

"Thanks," Eugene answered stiffly, "but I can't. I've
got another engagement."

Starwick's face flushed crimson with the agonizing
shyness and embarrassment which the effort cost him.
He leaned upon his cane and looked out the window as
he spoke.

"Then, look," he said, "Elinor asks to be remembered
to you." He was silent a moment, and then continued
with painful difficulty, "We're all going to the Louvre
after lunch: I want to see the Cimabue once more before we leave."

"When are you leaving?"

"Tomorrow," Starwick said. "Look!" he spoke carefully, looking out the window, "we're leaving the Louvre
at four o'clock. . . . I thought . . . if you were going
to be over that way. . . . I think Elinor would like to
see you before she goes. . . . We'll be there at the
main entrance." The anguish which the effort had cost
him was apparent: he kept looking away out the window, leaning on his cane, and for a moment his ruddy
face was contorted by the old, bestial grimace of inarticulate pain and grief which the other had noticed

the first time they had met, in Cambridge, years before. Then Starwick, without glancing at Eugene, turned towards the door. For a moment he stood, back turned, idly tapping with his cane against the wall.

"It would be nice if you could meet us there. If not——"

He turned, and for the last time in life the two young men looked squarely at one another, and each let the other see, without evasion or constraint, the image of his soul. Henceforth, each might glimpse from time to time some shadow-flicker of the other's life, the destiny of each would curiously be interwoven through twinings of dark chance and tragic circumstance, but they would never see each other face to face again.

Now, looking steadily at him before he spoke, and with the deep conviction of his spirit, the true image of his life, apparent in his face, his eyes, his tone and manner, Starwick said:

"If I don't see you again, good-by, Eugene." He was silent for a moment and, the color flaming in his face from the depth and earnestness of his feeling, he said quietly: "It was good to have known you. I shall never forget you."

"Nor I, you, Frank," the other said. "No matter what has happened—how we feel about each other now— you had a place in my life that no one else has ever had."

"And what was that?" said Starwick.

"I think it was that you were young—my own age— and that you were my friend. Last night after—after that thing happened," he went on, his own face flushing with the pain of memory, "I thought back over all the time since I have known you. And for the first time I realized that you were the first and only person of my own age that I could call my friend. You were my one true friend—the one I always turned to, believed in with unquestioning devotion. You were the only real friend that I ever had. Now something else has happened. You have taken from me something that I wanted, you have taken it without knowing that you took it, and it will always be like this. You were my brother and my friend——"

"And now?" said Starwick quietly.

"You are my mortal enemy. Good-by."

"Good-by, Eugene," said Starwick sadly. "But let me tell you this before I go. Whatever it was I took from you, it was something that I did not want or wish to take. And I would give it back again if I could."

"Oh, fortunate and favored Starwick," the other jeered. "To be so rich—to have such gifts and not to know he has them—to be forever victorious, and to be so meek and mild."

"And I will tell you this as well," Starwick continued. "Whatever anguish and suffering this mad hunger, this impossible desire, has caused you, however fortunate or favored you may think I am, I would give my whole life if I could change places with you for an hour— know for an hour an atom of your anguish and your hunger and your hope. . . . Oh, to feel so, suffer so, and live so!—however mistaken you may be! . . . To have come lusty, young, and living into this world . . . not to have come, like me, still-born from your mother's womb—never to know the dead heart and the passionless passion—the cold brain and the cold hopelessness of hope—to be wild, mad, furious, and tormented—but to have belief, to live in anguish, but to live—and not to die." . . . He turned and opened the door. "I would give all I have and all you think I have, for just one hour of it. You call me fortunate and happy. *You* are the most fortunate and happy man I ever knew. Good-by, Eugene."

"Good-by, Frank. Good-by, my enemy."

"And good-by, my friend," said Starwick. He went out and the door closed behind him.

Eugene was waiting for them at four o'clock that afternoon when they came out from the Louvre. As he saw them coming down the steps together he felt a sudden blind rush of affection for all of them, and saw that all of them were fine people. Elinor came towards him instantly, and spoke to him warmly, kindly, and sincerely, without a trace of mannerism or affectation or concealed spitefulness. Starwick stood by quietly, while he talked to Elinor: Ann looked on sullenly and dumbly and thrust her hands in the pockets of her fur jacket. In the dull, grey light they looked like handsome, first-rate, dignified people, who had nothing mean or petty in them and with whom nothing but a spacious, high, and generous kind of life was possible. By comparison, the Frenchmen coming from the museum and streaming past them looked squalid and provincial; and the Americans and other foreigners had a shabby, dull, inferior look. For a moment the bitter and passionate enigma of life pierced him with desperation and wild hope. What was wrong with life? What got into people such as these to taint their essential quality, to twist and warp and mutilate their genuine and higher purposes? What were these perverse and evil demons of cruelty and destructiveness, of anguish, error, and confusion that got into them, that seemed to goad them on, with a wicked and ruinous obstinacy, deliberately to do the things they did not want to do—the things that were so shamefully unworthy of their true character and their real desire?

It was maddening because it was so ruinous, so wasteful and so useless; and because it was inexplicable. As these three wonderful, rare, and even beautiful people stood there telling him good-by, every movement, look, and word they uttered was eloquent with the quiet but passionate and impregnable conviction of the human faith. Their quiet, serious, and affectionate eyes, their gestures, their plain, clear, and yet affectionate speech, even the instinctive tenderness that they felt towards one another which seemed to join them with a unity of living warmth and was evident in the way they stood, glanced at each other, or in swift, instinctive gestures—all this with a radiant, clear, and naked loveliness seemed to speak out of them in words no one could misunderstand, to say:

"Always there comes a moment such as this when, poised here upon the ledge of furious strife, we stand and look; the marsh-veil shifts from the enfevered swamp, the phantoms are dispersed like painted smoke, and standing here together, friend, we all see clear again, our souls are tranquil and our hearts are quiet—and we have what we have, we know what we know, we are what we are."

It seemed to him that all these people now had come to such a moment, that this clear peace and knowledge rested in their hearts, and spoke out of their eyes; it seemed to him that all his life, for years, since he had first gone to the dark North and known cities—since he had first known Starwick—was now a phantasmal nightmare—a kaleidoscope of blind, furious days, and drunken and diverted nights, the measureless sea-depth of incalculable memory, an atom lost and battered in a world of monstrous shapes, and deafened in a world of senseless, stupefying war and movement and blind fury. And it seemed to him now that for the first time he—and all of them—had come to a moment of clarity and repose, and that for the first time their hearts saw and spoke the truth that lies buried in all men, that all men know.

Elinor had taken him by the hand, and was saying quietly:

"I am sorry that you will not go with us. We have had a strange and hard and desperate time together, but that is over now, Eugene: we have all been full of pain and trouble, and all of us are sorry for the things we've done. I want you to know that we all love you, and will always think of you with friendship, as our friend, and will hope that you are happy, and will rejoice in your success as if it were our own. . . . And now, good-by, my dear; try to think of us always as we think of you—with love and kindness. Do not forget us; always remember us with a good memory, the way we shall remember you. . . . Perhaps—" for a moment her face was touched with her gay, rueful smile—"perhaps when I'm an old Boston lady with a cat, a parrot, and a canary, you will come to see me. I will be a nice old lady, then— but also I will be a ruined old lady—for they don't forget —not in a lifetime, not in Boston—and this time, darling, I have gone too far. So I shan't have many callers, I shall leave them all alone—and if you're not too rich, too famous, and too proper by that time, perhaps you'll come to see me. . . . Now, good-by."

"Good-by, Elinor," he said. "And good luck to you."

"Look," said Starwick quietly, "we're going on— Elinor and I . . . I thought . . . if you're not doing anything else . . . perhaps you and Ann might have dinner together."

"I'm—I'm not," he stammered, looking at Ann, "but maybe you . . ."

"No," she muttered, staring sullenly and miserably at the ground. "I'm not either."

"Then," Starwick said, "we'll see you later, Ann. . . . And good-by, Eugene."

"Good-by, Frank."

They shook hands together for the last time, and Starwick and Elinor turned and walked away. Thus, with such brief and casual words, the bond of friendship—all of the faith, belief, and passionate avowal of their youth—was forever broken. They saw each other once thereafter; by chance their lives would have strange crossings; but they never spoke to each other again.

They waited in awkward silence for a moment until they saw Starwick and Elinor get into a taxi and drive off. Then they walked away together across the great quadrangle of the Louvre. A haze of bluish mist, soft, smoky as a veil, hung in the air across the vistaed sweep of the Tuileries and the Place de la Concorde. The little taxis drilled across the great space between the vast wings of the Louvre and through the arches, filling the air with wasplike drone and menace, the shrill excitement of their tootling horns. And through that veil of bluish haze, the vast mysterious voice of Paris reached their ears: it was a sound immense and murmurous as time, fused of the strident clamors of its four million subjects, and yet, strangely muted, seductive, sensuous, cruel and thrilling, filled with life and death. The mysterious fragrance of that life filled Eugene with the potent intoxication of its magic. He drew the pungent smoky air into his lungs, and it seemed freighted with the subtle incense of the great city's hope and secret promise, with grief and joy and terror, with a wild and nameless hunger, with intolerable desire. It numbed his entrails and his loins with sensual prescience, and it made his heart beat hard and fast; his breath came quickly: it was mixed into the pulses of his blood and gave to grief and joy and sorrow, the wild mixed anguish beating in his heart, its single magic, its impalpable desire.

They walked slowly across the great Louvre court and through the gigantic masonries of the arch into the rue de Rivoli. The street was swarming with its dense web of afternoon: the sensuous complications of its life and traffic, the vast honeycomb of business and desire; the street was jammed with its brilliant snarl of motors, with shout and horn and cry, and with the throbbing menace of machinery, and on the other side, beneath arched colonnades, the crowd was swarming in unceasing flow.

They crossed the street and made their way through a thronging maze into the Place de la Comédie Française, and found a table on the terrace of La Régence. The pleasant old café was gay with all its chattering groups of afternoon, and yet, after the great boil and fury of the streets, it was strangely calm, detached, and pleasant, too. The little separate verandas of its terrace, the tables and the old settees and walls, gave the café an incredibly familiar and intimate quality, as if one were seated in a pleasant booth that looked out on life, a box in an old theater whose stage was the whole world.

In one of the friendly boothlike verandas of this pleasant old café, they found a table in a corner, seats against the wall, and sat down and gave their order to the waiter. Then, for some time, as they drank their brandy, they looked out at the flashing pulsations of the street, and did not speak.

Presently Ann, without looking at him, in her level, curt, and almost grimly toneless speech, said:

"What did you and Frank do last night?"

Excitement caught him; his pulse beat faster; he glanced quickly at her, and said:

"Oh—nothing. We went out to eat—walked around a bit—that was all."

"Out all night?" she said curtly.

"No. I turned in early. I was home by twelve o'clock."

"What happened to Frank?"

He looked at her sharply, startled. "Happened? What do you mean—'what happened to him?' "

"What did he do when you went home?"

"How should I know? He went back to the studio, I suppose. Why do you want to know?"

She made no answer for a moment, but sat looking sullenly into the street. When she spoke again, she did not look at him, her voice was level, hard, and cold, quietly, grimly inflectionless.

"Do you think it's a very manly thing for a big hulking fellow like you to jump on a boy Frank's size?"

Hot fury choked him, passed before his vision in a blinding flood. He ground his teeth, rocked gently back and forth, and said in a small, stopped voice:

"Oh, so he told you, did he? He had to come whining to you about it, did he? The damned little . . . !"

"He told us nothing," she said curtly. "Frank's not that kind; he doesn't whine. Only, we couldn't help noticing a lump on the back of his head the size of a goose egg, and it didn't take me long to figure out the rest." She turned and looked at him with a straight, unrelenting stare, and then said harshly:

"It was a wonderful thing to do, wasn't it? I suppose you think that settles everything. You can be proud of yourself, now, can't you?"

The thin fine blade of cruel jealousy pierced him suddenly, and was twisted in his heart. In a voice trembling with all the sweltering anguish and defeat that packed his overladen heart, he sneered in bitter parody:

"Come now, Frankie, dear!—Did bad naughty mans crack little Frankie's precious head?—There, there, dearie!—Mamma kiss and make it well . . . let nice big nursey-worsey kiss-um and make-um well!—Next time Frankie-pankie goes for a walk, big Boston nursey Ann will go wiv-ems, won't she, pet, to see that wuff, wuff man leave poor little Frankie be."

She reddened angrily, and said:

"No one's trying to be Frankie's nurse. He doesn't need it, and he doesn't want it. Only, I think it's a rotten shame that a big hulking lout like you should have no more decency than to maul around as fine a person as Frank is. You ought to be ashamed of yourself; it was a rotten thing to do!"

"Why, you bitch!" he said slowly, in a low, strangled tone. "You nice, neat, eighteen-caret jewel of a snobby Boston bitch!—Go back to Boston where you came from!" he snarled. "That's where you belong; that's all you're worth. . . . So I'm a big, hulking lout, am I? And that damned little affected aesthete's the finest person that you ever knew!—Why, God-damn the lot of you for the cheap, lying, fakey Boston bitches that you are! —with your 'he's a *swell* person, he really is, you know,' —'Oh, *grand!* Oh, *swell!* Oh, *fine!*'" he jeered incoherently. "Why, damn you, who do you think you are, anyway?—that you think I'm going to stand for any more of your snobby Boston backwash!—So I'm a big, hulking lout, am I?"—the words rankled bitterly in his memory. "And dear, darling little Francis is too fine, too fine—oh, dearie me, now, yes—to have his precious little head cracked up against a wall by the likes of me. . . . Why, damn you, Ann!" he said in a grating voice, "what are you, anyway, but a damned dull lummox of a girl from Boston? Who the hell do you think you are, anyway, that I should sit here and take your snobby backwash and play second fiddle while two cheap Boston women praise Starwick up to the skies all day long, and tell me what a great genius he is and how much finer than anyone else that ever lived? By God, it is to laugh!" he raved incoherently, blind with pain and passion, hindering his own progress by his foolish words of wounded pride. "To see the damned affected aesthete get it all! You're not worth it! You're not worth it!" he cried bitterly. "You call me a big hulking lout—and I feel more, know more, see more, have more life and power and understanding in me in a minute than the whole crowd of you will ever have—why, I'm so much better than the rest of you that—that—that—there's no comparison!" he said lamely; and concluded, "Oh, you're not worth it! You're not worth it, Ann! Why should I get down on my knees to you this way, and worship you, and beg you for just one word of love and mercy—when you call me a big, hulking lout—and you are nothing but a rich, dull Boston snob—and you're not worth it!" he cried desperately. "Why has it got to be like this, when you're not worth it, Ann?"

Her face flushed, and in a moment, laughing her short and angry laugh, she said:

"God! I can see this is going to be a pleasant evening, with you raving like a crazy man and passing out your compliments already." She looked at him with bitter eyes, and said sarcastically, "You say such nice things to people, don't you? Oh, charming! Charming! Simply delightful!" She laughed her sudden angry laugh again. "God! I'll never forget some of the nice things that you said to me!"

And already tortured by remorse and shame, the huge, indefinable swelter of anguish in his heart, he caught her hand, and pleaded miserably, humbly.

"Oh, I know! I know!—I'm sorry, Ann, and I'll do better—so help me God, I will!"

"Then why must you carry on like this?" she said. "Why do you curse and revile me and say such things about Francis, who is one of the finest people that ever lived, and who has never said a word against you?"

"Oh, I know!" he groaned miserably, and smote his brow. "I don't mean to—it just gets the best of me—Ann, Ann! I love you so!"

"Yes," she muttered, "a funny kind of love, when you can say such things to me!"

"And when I hear you praise up Starwick, it all comes back to me—and Christ! Christ!—why did it have to be this way? Why did it have to be Starwick that you——?"

She got up, her face flaring with anger and resentment.

"Come on!" she said curtly. "If you can't behave yourself—if you're starting in on that—I'm not going to stay——"

"Don't go! Don't go!" he whispered, grabbing her hand and holding it in a kind of dumb anguish. "You said you'd stay! It's just for a few hours longer—oh, don't go and leave me, Ann! I'm sorry! I promise I'll do better. It's only when I think of it—oh, don't go, Ann! Please don't go! I try not to talk about it but it gets the best of me! I'll be all right now. I'll not talk about it any more—if you won't go. If you'll just stay with me a little longer—it will be all right. I swear that everything will be all right if you don't go."

She stood straight and rigid, her hands clenched convulsively at her sides, her eyes shot with tears of anger and bewilderment. She made a sudden baffled movement of frustration and despair, and cried bitterly:

"God! What is it all about? Why can't people be happy, anyway?"

They made a furious circuit of the night. They went
back to all the old places—to the places they had been
to with Elinor and Starwick. They went to Le Rat Mort,
to Le Coq et l'Ane, to Le Moulin Rouge, to Le Bal
Tabarin, to La Bolée, to the Jockey Club, to the Dome
and the Rotonde—even to the Bal Bullier. They went to
the big night resorts and to the little ones, to great cafés
and little bars, to dive and stew and joint and hole, to
places frequented exclusively by the rich and fashionable—the foreigners, the wealthy French, the tourists,
the expatriates—and to other places where the rich and
fashionable went to peer down into the caldrons of the
lower depths of all those creatures who inhabited the
great swamp of the night—the thieves, the whores, the
rogues, the pimps, the lesbians, and the pederasts—
the human excrement, the damned and evil swarm of
sourceless evil that crawled outward from the rat-holes
of the dark, lived for a period in the night's huge blaze
of livid radiance, and then were gone, vanished, melted
away as by an evil magic into that trackless labyrinth
from which they came.

Where had it gone? That other world of just six weeks
before, with all its nocturnal and unholy magic, now
seemed farther off and stranger than a dream. It was
impossible to believe that these shabby places of garish
light, and tarnished gold, and tawdry mirrors, were the
same resorts that had glowed in all their hot and close
perfumes just six weeks before, had burned there in the
train of night like some evil, secret and unholy temple of
desire. It was all worn off now: cheap as Coney Island,
tawdry, tarnished as the last year's trappings of a circus,
bedraggled, shabby as a harlot's painted face at noon.
All of its sinister and intoxicating magic had turned dull
and pitiably sordid: its people were pathetic, and its
music dead—serving only to recall the splendid evil

people and the haunting music of six weeks before.

And they saw now that this was just the way it was, the way it had always been. Places, people, music—they were just the same. All that had changed had been themselves. And all through the night they went from place to place, drinking, watching, dancing, doing just the things they had always done, but it was no good—it had all gone stale—it would never be any good again. They sat there sullenly, like people at a waning carnival, haunted by the ghosts of memory and departure. The memory of Elinor and Starwick—and particularly of Starwick—haunted each place they went to like a deathshead at a feast. And again Eugene was filled with the old, choking, baffled, and inchoate anger, the sense of irretrievable and certain defeat: Starwick in absence was even more triumphantly alive than if he had been there—he alone, by the strange, rare quality in him, had been able to give magic to this sordid carnival, and now that he was gone, the magic had gone, too.

The night passed in a kaleidoscope of baffled fury, of frenzied search and frustrate desire. All night they hurtled back and forth between the two blazing poles of Montmartre and Montparnasse: later he was to remember everything like the exploded fragments of a nightmare—a vision of dark, silent streets, old shuttered houses, the straight slant and downward plunge out of Montmartre—the sudden blaze of lights at crossings, boulevards, in cafés, night-clubs, bars and avenues, the cool plunge and shock of air along dark streets again, the taxis' shrill horns tootling at space, empty reckless corners, the planted stems of light across the Seine, the bridges and the sounding arches and dark streets, the steep slant of the hill, the livid glare of night and all the night's scarred faces over again.

They did not know why they stayed, why they hung

on, why they continued grimly at this barren hunt. But something held them there together: they could not say good-by and part. Ann hung on sullenly, angrily, in a kind of stubborn silence, saying little, ordering brandy at the bars and cafés, champagnes in the night resorts, drinking little herself, sitting by him in a sullen, angry silence while he drank.

He was like a maddened animal: he raved, stormed, shouted, cursed, implored, entreated, reviled her, and made love to her at once—there was no sense, or reason, or coherence in anything he said: it came out of him in one tortured expletive, the urge of the baffled touch, that conflict of blind love and hate and speechless agony, in his tormented spirit:

"Oh, Ann! . . . You lovely bitch! . . . You big, dark, dumb, lovely, sullen Boston bitch! . . . Oh, you whore! You whore!" he groaned, and seizing her hand, he caught it to him, and said desperately, "Ann, Ann, I love you! . . . You're the greatest . . . grandest . . . best . . . most beautiful girl that ever lived . . . Ann! Look at me—you big, ox-dumb brute. . . . Oh, you bitch. . . . You Boston bitch. . . . Will it never come out of you? . . . Won't you ever let it come? . . . Can't it be thawed, melted, shaken loose? . . . Oh, you dumb, dark, sullen, lovely bitch . . . is there nothing there? . . . is this all you are? . . . Oh, Ann, you sweet, dumb whore, if you only knew how much I love you——"

"God!" she cried, with her quick, short, and angry laugh that gave her face its sudden, radiant tenderness, its indescribable loveliness and purity, "God! But you're the gallant lover, aren't you? First you love me, then you hate me, then I'm a dumb, sullen Boston bitch, and then a whore, and then the grandest and most beautiful girl that ever lived! God, you're wonderful, you are!" She aughed bitterly. "You say such charming things."

"Oh, you bitch!" he groaned miserably. "You big, sweet, dumb, and lovely bitch—Ann, Ann, for God's sake, speak to me, talk to me!" He seized her hand and shook it frantically. "Say just one word to show me you're alive—that you've got one, single atom of life and love and beauty in you. Ann, Ann—look at me! In God's name, tell me, what are you? Is there nothing there? Have you nothing in you? For Christ's sake, try to say a single, living word—for Christ's sake, try to show me that you're worth it, that it's not all death and codfish, Boston, Back Bay, and cold fishes' blood"—he raved on incoherently:

"Oh! Boston and cold fishes' blood, my eye!" she muttered, with an angry flush in her face.

"And you?—What are you?" he jeered. "For God's sake, what kind of woman are you? I never heard you speak a word that a child of ten could not have spoken. I never heard you say a thing that ought to be remembered. The only things I know about you are that you are a Boston spinstress—thirty—no longer very young—a few grey hairs already on your head—comfortably secure on dead investments—over here on a spree—away from father and the family and the *Boston Evening Transcript*—but never losing them: always knowing that you will return to them—in God's name, woman, is that all you are?"

She laughed her sudden, short and angry laugh, and yet there was no rancor in it.

"That's what Frank would call a brief but masterly description, isn't it? I suppose I should be grateful." She looked at him with quiet eyes, and said simply: "What of it? Even if what you say is true, what of it? As you say, I'm just a dull, ordinary kind of person, and until you and Francis came along, no one thought me anything else, or thought any the less of me for being like that. Listen," her voice was hard and straight and sullen, "what do you expect people to be, anyway? Do you think it's fair and decent to talk about how beautiful I am, when I'm not beautiful, and then to turn and curse me because I'm just an ordinary girl?" She was silent a moment, with an angry flush upon her face, and then she said: "As for my intellect, I went to Bryn Mawr, and I got through without flunking, with a C average. That's about the kind of brain I've got." She turned and looked at him with straight, angry eyes, now shut a little with tears:

"What of it?" she said. "You say that I am dull and dumb and ordinary—well, I never pretended to be anything else. You know, we all can't be great geniuses, like you and Francis," she said, and suddenly her eyes were wet, and tears began to trickle down across her flushed face. "I'm just what I am, I've never pretended to be any different—if you think I'm dull and stupid and ordinary, you have no right to insult me like this.—Come on, I'm going home." She started to get up, he seized her pulled her to him:

"Oh, you bitch! . . . You big, dumb, lovely bitch . . . Oh, Ann, Ann, you sweet whore, how I love you— I can never let you go—oh, God-damn you, Ann——"

It ended at last, at daybreak in a bistro near Les Halles, where they had often gone at dawn with Elinor and Starwick for rolls and chocolate or coffee. Outside they could hear the nightly roar and rumble of the market, the cries of the venders, and smell all the sweet smells of earth and morning, of first light, health, and joy, and day beginning.

When they left the bistro full light had come, and they at length had fallen silent. They realized that it was useless, hopeless, and impossible, that nothing could be said.

He left her at the gate outside the studio. She pressed the bell, the gate swung open, and for a moment before she left him she stood looking at him with a flushed, angry face, wet angry eyes—a look of dumb, sullen misery that tore at his heart, and for which he had no word.

"Good-by," she said. "If I don't see you again——"
She paused and clenched her fists together at her side, closed her eyes, tears spurted out, and in a choking voice she cried out:

"Oh, this will be a fine thing for me, all right! This trip has just been wonderful. God! I'm sorry that I ever saw any of you——"

"Ann! Ann!"

"If you need money—if you're broke——"

"Ann!"

"God!" she cried again. "Why did I ever come!"

She was weeping bitterly, and with a blind, infuriated movement she rushed through the gate and slammed it behind her.

The Web and the Rock

LOVE'S BITTER MYSTERY

Editor's Preface

AT THIS point the hero changes his name—Eugene Gant becomes George Webber. And also his appearance: while Gant had long dangling arms, Webber's legs are too short.

In one respect it is probably a somewhat specious change. In temperamental terms this is almost the same hero, and in factual terms it is the same story. Whereas Eugene Gant steps on the boat for America at the close of *Of Time and the River,* George Webber steps off it. The central sections of *The Web and the Rock* deal with Webber's early struggles in New York City, his first meetings with Mrs. Jack, the Great Lady of his provincial aspirations, and, through her, his introduction to metropolitan society.

Yet the change in the hero actually does represent a change in Wolfe's work. "This is a book of discovery," Wolfe wrote to his later editor, "hence of union with life; not a book of personal revolt, hence of separation from life." In his prefatory note to *The Web and the Rock* he adds that the novel has a strong element of satiric exaggeration: "not only because it belongs to the nature of the story—'the innocent man' discovering life —but because satiric exaggeration also belongs to the nature of life, and particularly American life." And it is just this realization of the farcical element in the highest human affairs—and of a nevertheless essential humanity—that tempers Wolfe's final rejection of the Enfabled Rock itself.

For "Monk" Webber gives up Esther Jack—and Mrs. Jack *is* the city. This was Gant-Webber's crucial experience, his coming of age. All the earlier spiritual advances are crystallized in the intensity of this love affair, and, with its overtones of cultural conflict as well as its central depiction of the pain and cruelty that mark the tender passion, it is all in all a fascinating episode.

The selection that is printed here is the whole of Book VI in *The Web and the Rock*. It traces the conclusion of the love story. I have also included Wolfe's summary of the novel to this point and the chapter headings he used in the later novels.

THE WEB AND THE ROCK

Love's Bitter Mystery

A Vision of Death in April

THAT spring—in the green sorcery of that final, fatal, and ruinous April—a madness which was compounded of many elements took possession of him and began to exert completely its mastery of death, damnation, and horror over the whole domain of his body, mind, and spirit. He thought that he was lost, and he looked on life with the eye, not of a dead man, but of a man who had died against his will, who had been torn bitterly out of the glorious music of the day, and who, out of the shades of death, revisits all the glory he has lost and feeds upon it with a heart of fire, a tongueless cry, a passion of soundless grief, an agony of regret and loss.

And in the tortured, twisted crevices of his brain, he felt, with a wave of desolating self-pity and despair, that Esther had contrived this ruin against him. He saw her at the center of a corrupt and infamous world, inhabited by rich, powerful, and cynical people—great, proud, and potent beak-nosed Jews, their smooth-skinned wives who made a fashion and a cult of books and plays and nigger carvings, the so-called leaders in the arts themselves, the painters, writers, poets, actors, critics, sly and crafty in their knowingness and in their hate and jealousy of each other—and in this picture of her world, the only thing, he thought, that gave joy to these dead, sterile, and hateful lives in their conspiracy of death was the castration of the spirit of a living man. They had used Esther as a bait to snare the yokel. And it seemed to him that they had succeeded. It seemed that he was fairly caught at last in the trap which they had laid, and into which his own folly had led him, that his ruin was complete and incurable, that he was shorn of his strength forever, and that for him there was no hope of recovery or salvation.

He was now twenty-seven years old, and like a man who has waited too long before the approaching hoof beats of disaster, who has watched with too dull, too careless, or too assured an eye the coming of a flood, the approach of the enemy, or like an ignorant young fighter who, having never been hurt, having never tested the full strength of an immense and merciless power, having never been stung by the bitter asp of defeat, having never been made wary by a blow of incredible, unrealizable force, and who thinks in his insolence and pride that he is the measure of all things and will be triumphant in every conflict, so, now, it seemed to him he had been overtaken by disaster, and was fairly, fatally engulfed in an abyss of ruin he had not foreseen.

And yet he thought that no spring ever came more sweetly or more gloriously to any man than that one came to him. The sense of ruin, the conviction that he was lost, the horrible fear that all the power and music in his life, like the flying remnants of a routed army, had been blown apart into the fragments of a ghastly dissolution so that they would never come back to him, never again the good times, the golden times, the nights his spirit prowled with the vast stealth and joy of a tiger across the fields of sleep, and the days when his power leaped on from strength to strength, from dream to dream, to the inevitable and sustained accomplishment of a great, exultant labor—the sense of having lost all this forever, so far from making him hate the spring and the life he saw around him, made him love it more dearly and more passionately than he had ever done before.

In the back yard of the old brick house in which he lived, one of those small, fenced back yards of a New York house, a minute part in the checkered pattern of a block, there was, out of the old and worn earth, a patch of tender grass, and a single tree was growing there. That April, day by day, he watched the swift coming of that tree into its glory of young leaf again. And then one day he looked into its heart of sudden and magical green and saw the trembling lights that came and went into it, the hues that deepened, shifted, changed before one's eye to every subtle change of light, each delicate and impalpable breeze, and it was so real, so vivid, so intense that it made a magic and a mystery, evoking the whole poignant dream of time and of man's life upon the earth, and instantly, it seemed to Monk, the tree became coherent with his destiny, and his life was one with all its brevity from birth to death.

The peculiar power and property of spring for evoking the whole sense of man's unity with all the elusive and passionate enigmas of life came, Monk felt, from the effect of the color green upon his memory and his sense of time. The first green of the year, and particularly the first green in the city, had a power not only of drawing all the swarming chaos and confusion of the city into one great lyrical harmony of life, it had also such a magical power over all his memories that the life that moved and passed around him became an instant part of all the moments of his life. So, too, the past became as real as the present, and he lived in the events of twenty years ago with as much intensity and as great a sense of actuality as if they had just occurred. He felt that there was no temporal past or present, no *now* more living than any reality of *then;* the fiction of temporal continuity was destroyed, and his whole life became one piece with the indestructible unity of time and destiny.

Thus over his whole mind that spring there hung the sorcery of this enchanted green, and for this reason his life that spring attained the focal intensity of a vision. And it was a vision of death and dissolution, ever present in a thousand images that swarmed incredibly in his brain. He saw the world in the hues of death, not because he was trying to fly from reality, but because he was trying to embrace it, not because he wanted to escape out of a life that he had found unendurable into some pleasing fable of his own devising, but because for years the hunger that had driven him with a desire for knowledge so insatiate that he wanted to pluck the final core and essence out of every object still moved him forward towards an escape *into* life. But now it seemed to him that life itself had played him false.

Save for those hours each day when Esther stayed with him, and the hours when he had to go to the school to meet his classes, he spent his time either in a mad and furious walking of the streets from night to morning, or at home in a contemplation of complete solitude. For hours at a time he would sit immovable in a chair, or lie extended on his cot with his hands folded beneath his head, apparently sunk in senseless apathy, but in reality, although he did not stir a muscle, every faculty was engaged in the most furious activity he had ever known. The images of the past and present swept through his mind in a stream of blinding light.

As he thought of Esther, of her world, and of the ruin in which he felt she had involved him, suddenly he would be roused by the sound of deathless birdsong in the tree. Then he would start up from his cot and go to the window, and as he looked into the magic heart of the green tree, the moments of lost time awoke with all their tragic memories, as actual as the room in which he stood.

Suddenly he thought of the time in his childhood when he had seen a man shaken like a rat, slapped in the face, retreating and cringing before his enemy while his wife and young son looked on with white and staring faces. And he knew that from that moment that man's spirit and his life were broken. He remembered the day, the time, the ghastly and unnatural silence of the neighborhood which heard and saw it all. And for months thereafter the man had walked by all the curious, staring, and quietly contemptuous faces of the town with a lowered head, and when he spoke to anyone, when he tried to smile, his smile was horrible—a pitiful grimace, an ingratiating and servile smirk rather than a smile. And his wife and his son went silently and alone thereafter, with furtive glances, frightened, stricken, and ashamed.

Again, when he was twelve years old, he had seen a man publicly whipped and slapped by his wife's lover. The man was a shabby little creature, the husband of a bold and sensual woman, whose lover, a strong, handsome, brutal-looking man of wealth and authority, came to fetch her in his motor every evening after dinner. When this happened, the husband, who at this time would be watering the lawn before the house, would keep his pallid face fixed on the ground before him, never speaking to the lover, or to his own wife as she passed by him on the walk.

One night, however, when the lover came and halted his car before the house and signaled for the woman to come out, the husband had suddenly thrown down his hose, rushed across the lawn and down the cement steps to the place where the car was halted, and begun to speak to the other man in a high, trembling, and excited voice. In a moment there was a low roar of anger and surprise from the big man in the car, he had thrown open the door so violently that the husband was hurled back, and then he had seized the husband, shaken, mauled, and slapped him, cursing him foully and savagely, and with a deliberate arrogance publishing his relations with the man's wife to the neighborhood and to the whole audience of the silent, staring street.

It was a sight unutterable in its naked shame, and the most shameful thing was the hideous fear of the husband, who, after his first wild impulse of courage, was now squeaking like a rat with terror, pleading to be let go and not to be slapped again. Finally, in his frenzy, he had wrenched free from the other man, and scrambled and stumbled backward up the steps in horrible retreat, his thin hands held out in a protesting and pleading manner before him as the other man followed him heavily, cursing him and mauling at him with clumsy blows that somehow seemed more shameful because of their clumsiness, the man's heavy panting breath, and the wet and naked silence of the air.

Then the woman had come swiftly from the house, assailed her cowering husband furiously, saying he had disgraced her and himself by "acting like a fool," and then ordered him into the house like a beaten child. And the man had gone, he had taken it all with a cringing and whimpering apology, and then had half-run, half-stumbled into the merciful concealment of the house, his head lowered and tears streaming down the reddened flanks of his thin, slapped face. Then the woman had got into the car with her cursing and boastfully threatening lover, and had talked to him in a low, earnest, and persuasive voice until he was pacified.

The car drove off, and as it turned the corner at the foot of the hill, Monk could hear the woman's sudden, rich, and sensual burst of laughter. Then darkness had come, and all the far sounds and brooding mystery of the night, the great stars had flashed into the sky again, and on the porches up and down the street he could hear once more the voices of the neighbors, quiet, sly, and immensely greedy, breaking from time to time into coarse, sudden shouts of laughter. And he had hated that night forever, and it seemed to him there was no darkness in it deep enough to cover his own shame.

These memories and many others now came back to him, and the result was a nightmare vision of man's cruelty, vileness, defeat, and cowardice so unendurable that he writhed upon his cot, ripping the sheets between convulsive hands, and cursing with a twisted mouth, and finally smashing his bloody knuckles at the wall as the black horror of man's cruelty and fear writhed like a nest of vipers in his brain.

These things he had seen and known in his childhood, and he had sworn, as every other boy has sworn, that he would die or be beaten to a senseless pulp before he let them happen to him. And he had steeled his heart and set his teeth against the coming of the enemy, and he had sworn he would be ready for him when he came.

But now, at the beginning of that fatal April, it seemed to him that the enemy had come, but not as he expected him, not from the direction where he looked for him, not in the fierce shape and manner he had visioned him. For it seemed to him that the enemy had come on him from an unknown quarter, and that he had not known him when he came, and that he had wrought upon him a defeat, a humiliation, a ruin more horrible and irrevocable than had happened to either of these two men.

And yet, like a man who has been overpowered by his enemies and had the organs of his virility torn from him, he still knew every furious desire, every soaring hope of creation and fulfillment that he ever had. The plans and projects for a dozen books, a hundred stories, worked in his brain like madness: the whole form and body of a book, complete from start to finish, would blaze suddenly and entire within him, and he would hurl himself into it with savage and complete absorption. And this surge of new creation might continue for a week.

At such a time, in the intervals between his furious bursts of writing, he would walk the streets again with something like a return of the joy he once had felt in all the life around him. And just as his whole complex of bitter and confused feelings about Esther had become entwined and interwoven with everything he thought or felt or said that spring, so, too, he looked now with an eye of wild desire at every other woman that he saw.

One day he saw a handsome, strong, and brawny Irish girl, with the coarse, wild beauty of her race as she came round an ugly corner beneath the brutal rust and slamming racket of the elevated structure. And as she turned the corner a gust of wind drove suddenly at her, thrusting her dress back through her legs, and in a minute her whole figure was stamped and printed nakedly against the wind—broad, potent belly, heavy breasts, and great columnar thighs coming forward with a driving sensual energy. And instantly a feeling of such power rose up in him that he felt he could tear the buildings up by the roots like onions from the earth. The blazing image of the brawny, lusty beauty of the woman was stamped into his brain forever, giving its savage memory of joy to the hideous clamor of the ugly street and all the crowds of grey-faced people that swarmed round her.

Again, in one of the narrow, crowded little streets near lower Broadway, full of the old, rusty, and gloomy-looking buildings of another time, but also filled with the sensuous and basic substances of life and commerce—with bales and crates and powerful machinery, with a smell of coffee, leather, turpentine, and rope, and with the clopping sound and the movement of great, slow-footed horses, the rumble of wheels upon the cobbles, the oaths, cries, and orders of drivers, packers, movers, and bosses—a young woman passed him as he stood before a leather store.

She was tall and slender, yet her figure was tremendously seductive, and she walked with a proud and sensual stride. Her face was thin and delicate, her eyes were clear and radiant, yet a vague and tender look dwelt in them, and her hair was carrot-colored, blown, spun like silk, escaping with a kind of witchcraft from the edges of her hat. She walked past him with a slow and undulant step, her mouth touched faintly with a smile at once innocent and corrupt, benignant and yet filled with a compassionate and seductive tenderness, and he watched her go with a feeling of wild joy and lust, a sense of unutterable loss and pain.

He knew that she was gone forever, that he would never see her again, and at the same moment he was certain he would find her and possess her. It was like magic, and the magic came not only from the lovely girl, but from the old and narrow street with its rich, dingy, and thrilling compost of the past, with its strong, clean odors of sensuous materials, and raw and honest substances, and especially the clean and glorious smell of leather from the leather shop—the smell of the big valises, bags, and cases piled before the shop which came to him strongly as the woman passed—all of this, together with the delicate, strange, and lovely light of April, made a scene of joy and magic which he thought would last forever.

He never forgot the girl, the street, the odor of the leather. It was part of the intolerable joy and pain of all that spring. And somehow the thought of her, though for what reason he never knew, was joined forever with the thought of ships, the smell of the sea, the slant and drive and frontal breast of a great racing liner, and the wild prophecy of a voyage.

So it was with him in the brief intervals when, for no apparent reason, his spirits rose again and swept him upward for a day or two with new impulses back to life, to love, and to creation. And then, suddenly, out of the heart of joy, and the magical gold and glory and exultant music of the earth, the white blind horror of his madness would return again to stun him and to shatter the sequence of his energy into a thousand pieces.

Sometimes the wave of death and horror came upon the insane impulses of a half-heard word, a rumor of laughter in the street at night, the raucous shout and gibe of young Italian thugs as they passed by below his window in the darkness, or a look of mockery, amusement, curiosity from some insolent face at a restaurant table, some whispered, unheard communication. And sometimes it came from sourceless depths, from no visible or tangible cause whatever. It would come as he sat quietly in a chair at home, as he stared at the ceiling from his cot, from a word in a poem, from a line in a book, or simply as he looked out of the window at that one green tree. But whenever it came, and for whatever cause, the result was always the same: work, power, hope, joy, and all creative energy were instantly engulfed and obliterated in its drowning and overwhelming tide. He would rise with it inside him and hurl himself insanely against the world like a man maddened by an agony of physical pain, like a man stamping and stumbling blindly about a room in an insanity of pain, with every tissue of his life drawn and fed into the maw of a cancerous tumor, or clutching between his frantic hands a whole horrible hell of abscessed and aching teeth.

And always now, when the convulsion of pain and horror drove him mad, he sought again the spurious remedy of the bottle. The raw gin gurgled down his tilted throat like water down a gully drain, numbing and deadening the mad particles of the brain, the raging tumults of blood, heart, and leaping nerves with its temporary illusions of power, deliberation, and control. Then it would begin to burn and seethe like a slow oil in his blood. His brain burned slowly and literally like a dull fire smoldering in a blackened, rusty brazier, and he would sit numbed and silent in the sullen darkness of a slowly mounting and murderous rage until he went out in the street to find the enemy, to curse and brawl and seek out death and hatred in dive and stew, among the swarms of the rats of the flesh, the livid, glittering dead men of the night.

And then from night to morning, like a creature destined to live forever in a hideous nightmare, seeing all things and persons of the earth in kaleidoscopic shapes of madness, he would prowl again the huge and obscene avenue of night, shone upon forever with its immense and livid wink. He would go along rat's alley where the dead men were, while the street, the earth, the people, even the immense and cruel architectures, reeled about him in a demented and gigantic dance, and all the cruel and livid faces of its creatures seemed to burn up at him suddenly with the features of snakes, foxes, vultures, rats, and apes—while he looked forever for a living man.

And morning would come again, but with no light and singing. He would recover out of madness and see with sane, untroubled eyes once more, but out of weary and fathomless depths of the spirit, into the heart of a life which he thought he had lost forever.

When Esther came again at noon, sometimes she seemed to him the fatal root of all his madness, which now could be plucked out of him no more than the fibrous roots of a crawling cancer from the red courses of the blood. At other times the green of that first April of their life together would come back again, and then she was united to the heart of joy, to all that he loved in life, to all the gold and singing of the earth.

But then at night when she had gone, he could remember her no longer as she had looked at noon. The dark and fatal light of absence, the immense and velvet night, menaced with its thousand intangible treacheries, fell upon her, and the radiant face of noon, the light of certitude, possession, and health, had vanished utterly. Fixed in an arrogant power, her face as he saw it then flamed like a strange and opulent jewel; in his feverish imagination it smoldered drowsily with all the slumberous and insatiate passions of the East, it spoke of a desire illimitable as the ocean, a body to be taken by all men, and never to be possessed by any.

Again and again, a mad, distorted picture blazed within his mind. He saw a dark regiment of Jewish women in their lavish beauty, their faces melting into honey, their eyes glowing, their breasts like melons. Seated in power and wealth, and fitly walled by the arrogant and stupendous towers of the city, he saw their proud bodies opulently gowned and flashing with the somber fires of ancient jewels as they paced with the velvet undulance of an intolerable sensuality the proud and splendid chambers of the night. They were the living rack on which the trembling backs of all their Christian lovers had been broken, the living cross on which the flesh and marrow of Christian men had been crucified. And they were more lost than all the men whom they had drowned within the sea-gulf of their passion, their flesh more tormented than the flesh of all the men whose lives had been nailed upon their lust, and whose wrung loins hung dry and lifeless like a withered stalk from the living wall of their desire. And behind them always in the splendor of the night were the dark faces of great, beak-nosed Jews, filled with insolence and scorn, with dark pride and an unutterable patience, with endurance and humility and an ancient and unspeakable irony as they saw their daughters and their wives yield their bodies into the embraces of their Gentile lovers.

Thus when Esther left him, the madness passed into him instantly, and instantly he knew that he was mad and yet was powerless to check it. He stood there looking at the tree and watched that black abomination of death and hatred sweep upon him like a wave. It soaked first into the deep folds and convolutions of his brain its damnable slime of poison, and then it channeled out its blackened tongues along the veins and arteries of his flesh. It heated and inflamed his brain with a dull, sweltering fire that was like a smear of blood and murder, but all else within the house of the flesh it chilled, froze, and constricted with a reptile's fangs. It shriveled up his heart in a ring of poisonous ice, it deadened the feeling in his fingers, his flesh withered and turned numb, dead, and sallow-looking, his cheeks were tinged with a greenish hue, his mouth got dry, the tongue was thick and pulpy, the edges of the lips had an acrid and bitter taste, the thighs and buttocks felt weak and flabby, the sockets of the knee bent down beneath the body's weight and felt watery and feeble, the feet and toes grew cold, white, phthisic, the guts got sick, numb, and nauseously queasy, and the loins which once had leaped and quivered with a music of joy and life, under the poisonous and constricting fury grew sterile, sour, and dry.

And in the seizures of his madness he felt that there was no remedy, no relief, and no revenge for the falseness of women, their tender cruelty, and their corrupt innocence. The frenzied curses, oaths, and prayers of the lover could not prevail over the merciless necessity of a woman's nature. Nor could all a woman's tears, protests, and passionate avowals change it. Nothing could stop or control a woman's insatiate desires as she faced her hated doom of old age and death. For all the good it would do, the lover might as well shout at a wall, spit off the bridge into the river, attempt to tie a rope around a hurricane, or build a picket fence upon the middle of the ocean as expect to make a woman faithful.

Could women not lie, and lie, and lie, and yet still think that they had spoken truth? Could they not beat their breasts and tear their hair, smash their accusing lovers in the face, and scream that such purity, fidelity, steadfastness as theirs had never been known since the beginning of time? Yes! Could they not sweat nobility at every pore and with every moan and sob of protest until they lay blear-eyed, bedraggled, red-faced, blown and panting on the bed, exhausted with these ardors of their pure, innocent, and womanly natures—and yet could they not lie, betray, and cheat you in the flick of an eye, the turn of a corner, in any one of the million blind, undiscoverable, and unknowable cells of the trackless jungle of the city, where your rivals lay coiled like snakes to poison faith and spread corruption at the heart of love?

The evil splinter of a shameful memory passed like a poisoned arrow through his brain. He remembered suddenly the vile and cunning words that one of Esther's friends in the theatrical world had spoken to him almost three years before, the only open words of accusation and indictment that anyone had ever spoken, that anyone had ever dared to speak, to him against Esther. And as the hateful words came back to him, he remembered also the time, the place, the street, the very hand's breadth of grey, rootless city pavement where they had been spoken.

He had been walking with this girl along the street where she lived, at about eleven o'clock in the evening. And as she spoke the words, they were passing below the striped sidewalk awning of a new apartment house. And even as the words struck numbly their envenomed fangs into his heart, he looked up into the loose, tough, pustulate face of a young flunkey in the door of the building, he saw the heavy braid upon his uniform, his brass buttons, his insolent grin, and the man's face had been fixed forever in his memory with a sense of hatred and of loathing.

The girl, looking at him with a sly and secret malice in her starved and ugly little face, had warned him of the woman he had met only a month before, saying, in a careful and regretful tone that ended with a sudden burst of venom and of bitterness:

"She *likes* young men. I'm sorry, but that's what they say about her. I'm afraid that's the way it is, I really am, you know."

And now, in an instant of black horror, the words returned to him with all their poisonous and rankling connotations. In the hot anger that surged up in him when he first heard them, he had regarded what the girl had said as an act of ugly malice, the jealous hatred of the grey, fleshless dead for the beautiful, warm, and glorious living. But he could not forget them. Again and again the words returned to fester at the roots of his heart like foul, cureless sores.

They evoked a picture of the whole horrible world of the theater, the livid, glittering, nighttime world of Broadway, a world of weariness, of death, hatred, and a sterile prostitution, eager to slime all living things with its own filth. And as he thought of this great rat's alley where the dead men were, the great street of the night lit with its obscene winks of sterile light and swarming with a million foul, corrupt, and evil faces—the faces of rats, snakes, vultures, all the slimy crawls and sucks and eyeless reptiles of the night, the false and shoddy faces of the accursed actors, with all the sly communication of their obscene whispering—he was driven mad again with horror, doubt, and unbelief. It seemed incredible that this vital, beautiful, and wholesome-looking woman with her fresh, jolly, noonday face of flowerful health and purity and joy could be joined in any way, could be connected by any filament, however small, to this evil nighttime world of shoddy, filth, and death.

And now, in one stunned instant of his madness, the foul and rankling memory of the unforgettable words had passed across his brain, evoking a poisonous breed of viper thoughts and insane fabrications. He saw again some casual glance upon her face, remembered a hundred casual words and acts and intonations, and, however trivial and momentary, they all seemed blackly pregnant now with revelations of falseness, treachery, and evil. Now for the first time, in the darkness of his tortured mind, he thought he understood them at their true and shameful value.

And suddenly a dozen images of betrayal blazed through his mind with stabbing intensities of hatred and despair, no less torturing to his spirit for being pictures projected out of nothing but the madness of his own enfevered brain. He saw her secure against detection in all the swarming immensity of the city, guarded and protected by the power of the arrogant, insolent wealth that surrounded her. Or again he saw her buried safely in the cruel loveliness of spring somewhere in the country, at the homes and estates of rich and sensual Jewish women, who aided and abetted her.

He saw her quilted in the silken tapestries of wealth and lust, and melting into tenderness in the embrace of some accursed boy. Sometimes it was a stripling with blond hair and downy apple-cheeks. Sometimes it was some sensitively obscure and artistic youth who pined above the teacups of æsthetic women, expiring with pale languor the limp lily of his energy into an embrace of jade earrings and exquisite yearnings. And sometimes it was some accursed actor in the theater, some youth with a thin, poisonous face and hateful sideburns, some insolent darling of erotic theatrical females—"one of our best young actors," who did the youthful lover in some merry jest of bawdry in Budapest, some light-hearted chronicle of whoredom in Vienna, or some pleasant little squib of native fornication in the suave purlieus of Newport's Younger Set, almost as good, if you please, in the "civilized" refinements of its humor as the merry urbanities of plays about the European whores and cuckolds.

As his maddened brain invented these images of self-torture, tongueless words of hate and scorn twisted his features in a writhing and convulsive snarl. Oh, was she merry, was she gay, was she witty and quick and light, in these delicate engagements of love and treason? Did she carry it off with the celebrated "light touch" of the fashionable art-theater comedy? Tell me, was it light and delicate, sweet sirs, was it with a hey, now, noble dames, with a hey and a ho and a hi-nonny-neigh, my gentles all? Deary me, now! Could she sit on her delicate tail and banter away about the light refinements of adultery? Was it all done gracefully to the tune of jolly jokes about the fairies and the lesbians?

Oh, tell me, tell me, now! Were she and her friends, the rich and sensual Jewish women he had seen at her apartment—were they merry about adultery, pale green toilet paper, cellophane, Cal Coolidge, the talkies, the Shubert brothers, prohibition, and the culinary patios of Alice Foote McDougall? Were they impressed, as they ought to be, by the plays of Pirandello? Were they sealed, as was most fit and fashionable, of the tribe of Lawrence? Had they read all the latest books, sweet friends? Had they looked with sneering smiles of intellectual arrogation upon the faces of their fellow subscribers in those delightful mid-act promenades that gave the final touch of triumph and disdain to those evenings of ripe culture at the Guild? Did they know "Lynn and Alfred," good my lord? Had they seen this, had they read that, and was it "swell" or "grand" or "lousy," son of man?

Did they know all the words and remember all the answers, know all the places for the painting of a laugh, all of the touchstones of a sneer, as well as all the proper things for reverence and worship? Oh, were they all, sweet friends, wise, witty, brave, and modern, the last latest miracle of time and better than their fathers ever were, too good, too fine, and too enlightened for the common grief and agony of such base clay as his, too rare for all the sorrow of such men as ever once had drawn in below immense and timeless skies the burden of their grief and agony? Were they not released by the miracle of the age and science from all the blights of hatred, love, and jealousy, of passion and belief, which had been rooted in the structure of man's life and soul for twenty thousand years? Oh, could they not tell you who were made of baser earth the place where you might take your packed and overladen hearts (if only you were rich enough!), the physician who could analyze your error, medicine your woe in forty stylish treatments, instruct you in deep damnation of an ancient grief three times a week, mend and repair your sorrowful and overladen spirits out of the chaos of their grief and folly in an eight months' alchemy of fashionable redemption?

Yes! Had she not herself been saved and freed forever from all the fears and phantoms flesh is heir to by this same magic, grown sublimely healthy, sane, and knowing on this same medicine? And now did she not sob, pray, plead, and entreat, threaten suicide and vengeance, show jealousy, rage, pain, sorrow, indignation, swear she was the noblest and most unfortunate woman that ever walked the earth, that such sorrow, tragedy, and love as hers had never before been known—all with as much unreason, passion, intemperance, and confusion as if she were only some ignorant and suffering child of Eve who wore a bloody clout twelve times a year, and whose tumultuous, unenlightened soul had never known the healing light at all?

Yes! They were a rare and subtle breed, the liberated princelings of the age, beyond the bloody imperfections of his own base, sweating, stinking earth of toil and agony. And suddenly he wondered if he was going to strangle to death like a mad dog in the darkness, hurl his strength against a world of bloodless phantoms, madden and die desperately of grief among the corrupt and passionless dead, a horrible race of rootless ciphers who *felt* that they felt, *thought* that they thought, *believed* that they believed, but who were able to feel, think, and believe nothing. Had he loved a woman who never had loved him, and had he now gone mad, was he ruined, lost, and broken because of the frailties of a toy, the inconstancies of dough and tallow, the airy frolics of butterflies and sparrows?

Or was the treason consummated darkly, without the gay and lightsome touch of delicate banter? Did she in some green and cruel loveliness of spring melt with a poppied tenderness into the arms of some fleshly and swarthy youth, some actor with full lips and the flowing volutes of a sensual nostril, some dark, moist creature with a full, white, hairless body and a thick, spermatic neck?

Or was it some dark and sullen youth who irritably tapped on tables and had "lived in Paris," and who scowled with a febrile discontent at the images of his misprized talents? Did she look at him with an eye of glowing tenderness, gently stroke his thin, dark features, and say in tones of wonder that his face was "lovely," "so delicate," and "like an angel's"? Did she tell him that "no one could ever know how beautiful you are"? Did she say: "You have the greatest and most beautiful quality in you of anyone I have ever known, the greatest power, the greatest genius. No one could ever know how grand and rich and beautiful your spirit is the way I do."

And then did she speak of the tragic difference in the years that divided them and made true happiness impossible? Did she speak of the sorrows of her life, and weep as she spoke of them, and swear this was "the great love of her life," that all the love and living that had gone before were nothing when compared to it, that she had never dreamed, had never been able to believe it possible, that such a glory of love as this could exist on earth, and that in all the history of the world there had never before been anything to equal it? Did she use the big words, the grand words, and yield herself into easy surrender as she spoke nobly of high love and holy purity, eternal faithfulness, physical and spiritual consecration?

The accursed images streamed through his maddened mind their black processional of death and shame as he stared blindly into the heart of the pulsing and magical green. He was caught in a trap of folly, ruin, and madness, hating his life and the abomination of shame in which his life lay drowned, stripped to his naked woe before the staring and merciless eye of the earth, and nowhere able to avoid it or hide himself out of its sight, and in no way able to utter to any man the weight of evil and horror that lay upon his heart.

Sometimes at noon, in the presence of Esther's rosy, healthful face of love, all the gold and singing of the past came back to him with exultant joy and sanity, but always, always, when she had gone, this cruel and sinister vision of Esther at night and in absence, the potent and evil flower of a corrupt and infamous world, would awake in him again with a searing vividness of horror. The madness would swarm into him again, poisoning his bone, brain, and blood with its malignant taint.

Then he would call Esther on the phone, and if he found her in her room he would curse and taunt her foully, ask her where her lover was, and if she had him by her at that moment, and believe he heard him whispering and snickering behind her even as she swore no one was there. And then, cursing her again, he would tell her never to come back to him, and rip the phone out of its moorings in the wall, hurl it on the floor, and smash and trample it underneath his feet, as if the instrument itself had been the evil and malignant agent of his ruin.

But if he could not find her when he called for her, if her Irish maid should answer and tell him she was out, his despair and madness knew no bounds. He would ask the woman a hundred furious questions. Where had her mistress gone? When would she return? How could he find her at once? Who was with her? What message had she left for him? And if the maid could not answer all these questions exactly and at once, he was convinced he was being duped and mocked at with a jeering contempt and arrogance. He would read into the rich and rather unctuously respectful tone of the Irish maid an undernote of mockery, the evil amusement of the hireling, lewd and confident, her own life bribed, tainted, and polluted with the wage of silence and collusion.

And he would leave the phone to drain the bottle to its last raw drop, then rush out in the streets to curse and fight with people, with the city, with all life, in tunnel, street, saloon, or restaurant, while the whole earth reeled about him its gigantic and demented dance.

And then, in the crowded century of darkness that stretched from light to light, from sunset until morning, he would prowl a hundred streets and look into a million livid faces seeing death in all of them, and feeling death everywhere he went. He would be hurled through tunnels to some hideous outpost of the mighty city, the ragged edge of Brooklyn, and come out in the pale grey light of morning in a wasteland horror of bare lots and rust and rubbish; of dismal little houses flung rawly down upon the barren earth, joined each to each in blocks that duplicated one another with an idiot repetition.

Sometimes, in such a place, the madness and the

shapes of death would leave him as suddenly and mysteriously as they had come, and he would come back in the morning, come back from death to morning, walking on the Bridge. He would feel below him its living and dynamic tremble, its vast winglike sweep and flight. Then he would smell the fresh, half-rotten river smell, the glorious spermy sea-wrack with its exultant prophecy of the sea and voyages, and the sultry fragrance of the roasted coffee. He could see below him the great harbor with its flashing tides, its traffic of proud ships, and before him he could see the great frontal cliff of the terrific city, with morning, bright, shining morning, blazing again upon its thousand spires and ramparts.

So it was with him in the green sorcery of that final, fatal, and ruinous April. He was a hater of living men who saw nothing but death and cold corruption in everything and everyone around him, and who yet loved life with so furious and intolerable a desire that each night he seemed to revisit the shores of this great earth like a ghost, an alien, and a stranger, his brain filled with its wild regret of memory, and with insatiable thirst for all the joy and glory of a life that he thought he had lost forever.

II. THE QUARREL

Underlying all the madness of his life that April, central to it, touching it at every point, was his love for Esther, a love which now, through self-inflicted jealousy, his loathing of the world she moved in, his sense of ruin and lost hope, had been converted into bitter hate. It had been almost three years since he first met Esther and since he had begun to love her, and now, like a man who emerges from the blind rout and fury of a battle and, looking back across the field, sees clearly for the first time that he is party to a broken force, sees legible at last the news of his own defeat, so now it was possible for Monk to see all of the emergent and consecutive stages through which his love for her had run.

There had been the time, in the beginning, when he had felt a young man's exultant pride and vainglory in what he thought of as a brilliant personal conquest—the possession of the love of a beautiful and talented woman —a tribute to his vanity.

Then his vanity and joy of sensual conquest gave way to the humility and adoration of love, until every pulse, energy, and passion of his life became obsessed by her.

And then, before he knew it, the trapper was trapped, the conqueror conquered, the proud and the insolent laid low, and she was entombed in his flesh, fatally absorbed in his blood until it seemed that he would never get her out of him again, never look out on life again with his own proper vision, never recover again the exultant solitudes of his youth, never again distill out of his flesh and spirit the terrible invasions of love which rob men of their unshared secrecy, their deep-walled loneliness, the soaring music of their isolation. And when he first began to realize the deep exclusiveness of love, the extent to which it was absorbing all his thoughts and energies, he felt the price he paid for it was too exorbitant, and he began to fret and chafe against the shackles which his heart had forged.

And now, finally, all the proud, triumphant music of this love which had possessed and conquered him was being broken, corrupted, made dissonant and harsh by these recurring waves of doubt, suspicion, hate, and madness which had at last exerted a final and ruinous dominance over all his life.

In the furious chronicle of this passion, with its in-

umerable memories of things done, its countless inter-
wisted shades and moments, thoughts and feelings,
ach of which was so alive with a wordless fabric of pain,
oy, tenderness, love, cruelty, and despair that it seemed
o feed itself with the whole packed pageant of the earth,
he reality of measured and recorded time had been exploded and these three years were really longer than
any ten that Monk had ever known before. All that he
had seen, done, felt, read, thought, or dreamed in all
his former life seemed but the food and substance of
his present time.

And as Monk's thoughts made all this clear to him,
the full and conscious knowledge of her invasion of his
life and his subjection to her conquest seemed intolerable. The conviction of his ruin and defeat was now
rooted in his heart, and he swore that he would free
himself, and draw his breath alone as he had once, or die.

These thoughts and resolutions Monk had formed one
night as he lay the long dark hours through upon his
cot, staring up at the ceiling of his room. The next day
when Esther came to him as usual, the sight of her jolly,
rosy face was like a challenge to him. It seemed to him
a suspicious circumstance that she should be so radiant
when he was so depressed, and instantly the worm was
eating at his heart again. As she came in and greeted
him in her usual cheerful way, all the images of betrayal
that his madness had ever fashioned now flashed in his
brain once more; he passed his hand blindly and clumsily
before his eyes, his vision reeled with swimming motes,
and he began to speak in a voice grown hoarse with
rending hate.

"So!" he said, with exaggerated emphasis. "You've
come back to me, have you? You've come back, now that
day is here, to spend an hour or two with me! I suppose

I ought to be grateful that you haven't forgotten me al
together!"

"Why, what on earth?" she said. "In God's name
what is it now?"

"You know damn well what it is!" he flung bac
brutally. "You can't go on forever playing me for a foo
I may be just a country yokel, but I do catch on after
while!"

"Oh, come now, George," she said soothingly, "don'
be such a fool just because I wasn't in when you tele
phoned last night. Katy told me you called, and I'm sorry
I wasn't there. But, good heavens! Anybody would thin
from the way you talk that I was carrying on with othe
men."

"Think!" he said in a thick tone, and suddenly he be
gan to snarl with brutal laughter. "Think! Why, God
damn you, I don't *think, I know!* . . . Yes! Every time
my back is turned!"

"So help me God, I never have," she said in a trem
bling voice, "and you know it! I have been good and
faithful to you since the first moment that I met you
No one has come near me, no one has touched me, and
in your evil, lying heart you know it!"

"God, how can you say it!" he said, shaking his head
with a kind of sullen wonder. "How can you stand there
and look at me and say the words! It's a wonder you
don't choke to death on them!"

"It's the living truth!" she said. "And if your mind
wasn't poisoned by evil and vile suspicions, you'd know
it! You mistrust everyone because you think everyone is
as vile and base as you are!"

"Don't you worry about that!" he shouted furiously.
"I'll trust anyone that's worth it! I know when people
can be trusted, all right!"

"Oh, you *know*, you *know*," she said bitterly. "God,

you know nothing! You wouldn't know the truth if it stopped you on the street!"

"I know *you*, all right!" he shouted. "And I know that damned crowd you run around with, too!"

"Listen to me!" she cried warningly. "You may not like the people I work with——"

"You're damned right I don't like the people you work with!" he shouted. "Nor any of their crowd—those fine Jewish ladies on Park Avenue with their million-dollar soul yearnings and their fancy fornications!" Then, quietly, dangerously, he turned to her and said: "I should like to ask you a single question." He stood facing her. "Tell me, Esther, do you know what a whore is?"

"Wh-a-a-t?" she said, in a faltering and uncertain voice that ended on a high note of hysteria. "What did you sa-a-y?"

He leaped savagely upon her, gripping her arms, pinning her and thrusting her back against the wall.

"Answer me!" he snarled insanely. "You heard me! You're good enough at using words like faith, and truth, and love, and loyalty! But you don't even know what I'm saying, do you, when I ask you if you know what a whore is! That's not a word to use about those fine ladies on Park Avenue, is it? That doesn't apply to the like of them, does it? You're God-damned right it doesn't!" he whispered slowly, with all the choking passion of his hate.

"Let me go!" she said. "Take your hands off me!"

"Oh, no—not yet! You're not going yet. You're not going till I instruct your pure, sweet innocence!"

"Oh, I have no doubt that you can tell me," she said bitterly. "I have no doubt that you're an authority on the subject! That's the trouble with you now! That's the reason that your mind's so full of filth and evil when

you speak of decent women! You never knew a decent
woman till you met me. You've gone with dirty, rotten
women all your life—and that's the only kind of woman
that you know about. That's the only kind you understand!"

"Yes, I know about them, Esther, and I understand
them better than I do all the fancy soul yearnings of
your million-dollar friends. I've known two hundred of
the other kind—the common street and house and gutter
whore—I've known them in a dozen countries, and there
never was one yet like these fine Park Avenue ladies!"

"You can bet your life they weren't!" she said quietly.

"They didn't have a million dollars, and they didn't
live in twenty-room apartments. And they didn't whine
and whimper about their souls, and say their lovers
were too coarse and low to understand them. They were
not fine and dainty in whatever light you saw them, but
they knew that they were whores. Some were fat, worn-
out old rips with pot bellies and no upper teeth, and a
snuff stick dripping from the edges of their mouth."

"You can save your precious knowledge for those
who want to hear it," Esther said. "But it only sickens
me! I don't want to know any more about this great
wisdom you've dug out of the gutter."

"Oh, come, now!" he jeered quietly. "Is this the fine
artist who sees life clearly and who sees it whole? Is
this the woman who finds truth and beauty everywhere?
Since when have you begun to turn your nose up at the
gutter? But maybe you don't like my kind of gutter?
Now, if it were only a fine art-theater gutter—if it were
only a fine old gutter from Vienna or Berlin—that would
be a different matter, wouldn't it? Or a nice, juicy, running sewer of a gutter in Marseilles? That's the real
stuff, isn't it? In fact, you made designs one time for a
fine gutter in Marseilles, didn't you? The one about

the whore who was the mother of all men living, and who mothered the waifs and outcasts of the earth into her all-engulfing belly—Madame Demeter! I could have told you something of that gutter, too, because I have been there on my travels, pet, although I never happened to run into that particular lady! And of course my vile, low nature could not appreciate the deep, symbolic beauty of the play," he snarled, "although it might have given you a few pointers about the stinks and smells of the Old Quarter and the bits of rotten fish and fruit and excrement in the alleyways! But you didn't ask me, did you? I have a good eye and a splendid nose, and the memory of an elephant—but I lack the deeper vision, don't I, darling? And besides, my base soul could never rise to the high beauties of a fine old gutter in Marseilles or Budapest—it could not rise above the gutter of a Southern Niggertown! And, of course, that's only common, native clay—that is not *art!*" he said in a strangling voice.

"Now, quiet, quiet, quiet!" she said gently. "Don't lash yourself into a frenzy. You're out of your head and you don't know what you're saying." For a moment she stroked his hand tenderly and looked sorrowfully at him. "In God's name, what is it? What is all this wild talk about gutters and alleyways and theaters? What has it got to do with you and me? What has it got to do with how I love you?"

His lips were blue and trembled stiffly, and his face had grown livid and was twisted in a convulsion of mad, mindless fury, and it was true that he was no longer fully conscious of what he said.

Suddenly she grasped him by the arms and shook him fiercely. Then she seized him by the hair and furiously pulled his stunned, drugged stare around to her.

"Listen to me!" she said sharply. "Listen to what I'm

going to tell you!" He stared at her sullenly, and for a moment she paused, her eyes shot angrily with tears and her small figure trembling with the energy of a dogged and indomitable will.

"George, if you hate the people that I work with and the work I do—I'm sorry for it. If the actors and the other people working in the theater are as vile and rotten as you say they are, I am sorry for that, too. But I did not make them what they are, and I have never found them that way. I have found many of them vain and pitiful and shabby, poor things without a grain of talent or of understanding, but not vile and evil as you say they are. And I have known them all my life. My father was an actor, and he was as wild and mad as you are, but he had as glorious and beautiful a spirit as anyone that ever lived."

Her voice trembled, and the tears began to flow from her eyes. "You say we are all base and vile and have no faithfulness! Oh, you fool! I heard him crying for me in the middle of the night—I rushed in and found him lying on the floor and the blood was pouring from his mouth! I felt the strength of ten people and I lifted him up and put him across my back and carried him to his bed." She paused, her voice was trembling so she could not continue for a moment. "His blood soaked through my nightgown on my shoulders—I can feel it yet—he could not speak—he died there holding to my hand and looking at me with his great grey eyes—and that was almost thirty years ago. You say we are all base and vile and have no love for anyone except ourselves. Do you think I could ever forget him? No, never, never, never!"

She closed her eyes, raising her flushed face slightly, and tightly pressing her lips together. In a moment she went on, more quietly:

"I'm sorry if you do not like my work, or the people

that I have to work with. But it's the only work I know
—the work I like the best—and, George, no matter what
you say, I am proud of the work I do. I am a fine artist
and I know my value. I know how cheap and trashy
most plays are—yes! and some of the people who play in
them, too! But I know the glory and the magic is there
just the same, and that nothing in this world can beat it
when you find it!"

"Ah! The glory and the magic—rot!" he muttered.
All of them talk their bilge about the glory and the
magic! It's the glory and magic of bitches in heat! All of
them looking for some easy love affairs! With our best
young actors, hey?" he said savagely, seizing her by the
arm. "With our would-be Ibsens under twenty-five! Is
that it? With our young scene designers, carpenters,
electricians—and all the other geniuses with their boyish
apple-cheeks!" he said chokingly. "Is that the glory and
the magic that you talk of? Yes! the glory and the magic
of erotic women!"

She wrenched herself away from his hard grasp, and
suddenly she held her small, strong hands up before his
face.

"Look at these hands," she said quietly and proudly.
"You poor fool, look at them! Are those the hands of an
erotic woman? They have done more work than any
man's you ever knew. There's strength and power in
them. They have learned how to sew and paint and
design and create—and they can do things now that no
one else on earth can do. And they cooked for you! They
cooked the finest meals for you that you have ever
eaten." She seized him fiercely by the arms again and
drew him to her, and looked up at him with a flaming
face. "Oh, you poor, mad fool," she whispered in the
rapt tone of a woman in a trance. "You tried to throw me
over—but I stuck to you. I stuck to you," she whispered

in an exultant and triumphant chant. "You tried to drive
me away from you, you cursed me and reviled me—but
I stuck to you, I stuck to you! You've tortured and abused
me and made me go through things that no one else on
earth would have endured—but you couldn't drive me
off," she cried with an exultant laugh, "you couldn't get
rid of me because I love you more than anything on earth
and it will never change. Oh, I've stuck to you! I've stuck
to you! You poor, mad creature, I have stuck to you because I love you, and there's more beauty and more glory
in your mad, tormented spirit than in anyone I ever
knew! You are the best, the best," she whispered. "You
are mad and evil, but you are the best, and that's the
reason that I've stuck to you! And I'm going to get the
best, the highest out of you if I have to kill myself in doing it! I'll give my strength and knowledge to you. I'll
teach you how to use the best in you. Oh, you'll not go
wrong!" she said with almost gleeful triumph. "I'll not
let you go wrong or mad or false or cheap, or lower than
the best on earth. In God's name, tell me what it is," she
cried out as she shook him desperately. "Tell me what
there is that I can do about it—and I'll help you. I'll
show you the clear design, the thread of gold, and you
must always stick to it! I'll show you how to get it out of
you. I'll not let you lose the pure gold that you have in
you below a mass of false and evil things. I'll not let you
throw your life away on drunkenness and wandering and
cheap women and low brothels. Tell me what it is and I
will help you." She shook him fiercely. "Tell me! Tell
me!"

He stared thickly at her through the blind, swimming
glaze of madness, and as it passed and he saw her face
before him once again, his mind picked up wearily and
obscurely, and with a stunned, uncertain consciousness,
the broken thread of what he had been saying, and he

proceeded in the dull, dead, toneless recitation of an automaton:

"They live in little houses in the nigger districts of a Southern town, or they live across the railroad tracks, and they have chains upon their blinds—that is their trade-mark—and they have a lattice all around the house. Sometimes you went there in the hot afternoon, and your shoes were covered with white dust, and everything was hot and quiet and raw and foul and ugly in the sun, and you wondered why you had come and felt that everyone you knew was looking at you. And sometimes you went there in the middle of the night in winter. You could hear the niggers shouting and singing in their shacks and see their smoky little lights behind old dingy yellow shades, but everything was closed and secret and all the sounds were shut away from you, and you thought a thousand eyes were looking at you. And now and then a Negro would prowl by. You would wait and listen in the dark, and when you tried to light a cigarette your fingers trembled so the light went out. You could see the street lamp at the corner wink and shutter with its hard, cold light, and the stiff, swinging shadows of bare branches on the ground, and the cold, raw clay of Niggertown below the light. You prowled around a dozen corners in the dark and went back and forth before the house a dozen times before you rang the bell. And inside the house, it was always hot and close and smelled of shiny furniture and horsehair and varnish and strong antiseptics. And you could hear a door that opened and shut quietly and someone going out. One time there were two of them who were sitting cross-legged on a bed and playing cards. They told me to choose between them, and they kept on playing cards. And when I left, they grinned and showed their toothless gums at me and called me 'son.'"

She turned away with a burning face and a bitter and contracted mouth.

"Oh, it must have been charming . . . charming!" she said quietly.

"And sometimes you were sitting all night long on a rickety bed in a little cheap hotel. You gave a dollar to the nigger and you waited till the night clerk went to sleep, and the nigger brought the woman to you or took you to her room. They came in on one train and they went out on another in the middle of the night, and the cops were always after them. You could hear the engines shifting in the train yards all night long, and you could hear doors opening and closing all along the hall, and footsteps creaking by as easy as they could, and the rattling of the bed casters in cheap rooms. And everything smelled foul and dank and musty in the room. Your lips got dry, and your heart was pounding in you like a hammer, and every time you heard someone creaking down the hall your guts got numb and you held your breath. You stared at the doorknob and waited for the door to open, and you thought it was your time."

"A fine life! A fine life!" she cried bitterly.

"I wanted more than that," he said. "But I was seventeen, away from home, at college. I took what I could get."

"Away from home!" she cried in her bitter tone. "As if that was any excuse!" And then, irrationally and bitterly: "Yes! And a fine home it was, wasn't it? They let you go away like that and never gave you another thought! Oh, a fine lot they were, those relatives of yours, those Christian Baptists! A fine lot! A fine life! And you dare to curse me and my people!"

"You . . . your people," he repeated slowly in his drugged monotone; and then, as the meaning of her words penetrated his consciousness, a black fury of hate

and rage surged up in him instantly, and he turned upon
her savagely. "Your people!" he shouted. "What about
your people!"

"Now you're beginning again!" she cried warningly,
with a flushed, excited face. "I've told you now——"

"Yes, you've told me, all right! You can say anything
you God-damn please, but if I open my mouth——"

"I didn't say anything! You're the one!"

His anger dropped away as suddenly as it had flared
up, and he shrugged his shoulders in a gesture of weary
and exasperated consent.

"All right, all right, all right!" he said impatiently.
"Let's forget about it! Let's drop the subject!" He made a
dismissing gesture and his face smoldered sullenly and
morosely.

"It's not me! I didn't start it! You're the one!" she said
again in a protesting tone.

"All right, all *right!*" he cried irritably. "It's all over,
I tell you! For God's sake let it drop!"

Then, almost immediately, in a voice that crooned
and lilted gently with a savage and infuriated contempt,
he continued:

"*So*—I mustn't say a word about your precious people!
They're all too fine and grand for me to talk about! I
wouldn't understand them, would I, dear? I'm too low
and vile to appreciate the rich Jews who live on Park
Avenue! Oh, yes! And as for your own family——"

"You leave my family alone!" she cried in a high,
warning voice. "Don't you open your dirty mouth about
them!"

"Oh, no. No indeed. I mustn't open my dirty mouth. I
suppose it wouldn't do at all for me to say——"

"I'm warning you!" she cried in a sobbing voice. "I'll
smash you in your face if you say a word about my
family! We're too good for you, that's the trouble! You've

never been used to meeting decent people before, you've never known any nice people in your life till you met me, and you think everyone is as vile as your low corner-drugstore mind makes them out to be!"

She was trembling violently, she bit her lips furiously, tears were streaming from her eyes, and for a moment she stood rigid in a kind of shuddering silence while she clenched and unclenched her hands convulsively at her sides in order to control herself. Then she continued more calmly, almost inaudibly at first, in a voice of passionate and trembling indignation:

"Wench! Hussy! Jew! These are some of the vile names you have called me, and I have been decent and faithful all my life! God! What a pure, sweet mind you've got! I suppose those are some more of the lovely and elegant expressions you learned down there in Old Catawba where you came from! You're a wonder, you are! It must have been a fine lot you grew up with! God! What a nerve you've got to open your mouth about *me!* Your family——"

"You shut up about my family!" he shouted. "You know nothing about them! They're a damned sight better than this poisonous, life-hating set of theatrical rats you go with!"

"Oh, yes! they must be simply wonderful!" she said, with bitter sarcasm. "They've done a hell of a lot for you, haven't they? Turning you loose upon the world at sixteen, and then washing their hands of you! God! You Christians are a charming lot! You talk about the Jews! Just try to find a Jew that would treat his sister's children in that way! Your mother's people kicked you out when you were sixteen years old, and now you can go to hell as far as any of them are concerned. Do they ever think of you? How often do you hear from one of them? How often does your aunt or uncle write to you?

Oh, you needn't speak—I know!" she said bitterly, with a deliberate intent to wound him. "You've told me of this grand family of yours for three years now. You've reviled and hated all my people—and now, I ask you, who's stuck by you, who's been your friend? Be honest, now. Do you think that crowd you came from give a damn about you? Do you think they'd ever understand or value anything you do? Do you think one of them cares if you live or die?" She laughed ironically. "Don't make me laugh!" she said. "Don't make me laugh!"

Her words had bitten deep into his pride, and she felt a fierce joy when she saw that they had rankled deep. His face had grown white with pain and fury, and his lips moved numbly, but she was unable to control herself because her own resentment and her hurt had been so great.

"And what did this wonderful father you're always talking about do for you?" she went on. "What did he ever do for you but let you go to hell?"

"That's a lie!" he said thickly. "It's . . . a . . . dirty . . . lie! Don't you dare open your mouth about him! He was a great man, and everyone who ever knew him said the same!"

"Yes, a great bum!" she jeered. "A great whisky drinker! A great woman chaser! That's what he was! He gave you a fine home, didn't he? He left you a large fortune, didn't he? You ought to thank him for all he's done for you! Thank him for making you an outcast and a wanderer! Thank him for filling your heart with hate and poison against the people who have loved you! Thank him for your black, twisted soul and all the hate in your mad brain! Thank him for making you hate yourself and your own life! Thank him for making a monster of you who stabs his friends to the heart and then deserts them! And then see if you can't be as much like him as you can! Since that's what you want, follow in his foot-steps, and see if you can't be as vile a man as he was!"

She could not stop herself from saying it, her heart was full of hate and bitterness for a moment and she wanted to say the most cruel and wounding thing she could to him. She wanted to hurt him as he had hurt her, and as she looked at him she felt a horrible joy be-cause she saw she had hurt him terribly. His face was the color of chalk, his lips were numb and blue, and his eyes glittered. When he tried to speak he could not, and when he did, his lips moved stiffly and she could scarcely hear at first what he was saying.

"Get out of here!" he said. "Get out of my place and never come back to it!"

She did not move, she could not move, and suddenly he screamed at her:

"Get out, God-damn you, or I'll drag you out into the street by the hair of your head!"

"All right," she said, in a trembling voice, "all right, I'll go. This is the end. But some day I hope to God some power will make you know what I am like. Some day I hope you will be made to suffer as you have made me suffer. Some day I hope you will see what you have done to me."

"Done to you!" he said. "Why, God-damn you, I've given my life to you! That's what I've done to you! You've grown fat and prosperous on my life and energy. You've sapped and gutted me; you've renewed your youth at my expense—yes! and given it back again into that old painted whore-house of a theater. 'Oh, deary me, now!'" he sneered, with an insane and mincing parody of her complaint. "'What have you done to me, you cruel brute?' What have you done to this nice, sweet, female American maid who hardly knows the difference between sodomy and rape, she is so pure and innocent!

What did you mean, you depraved scoundrel, by seduc-
ing this pure, sweet girl of forty when you were all of
twenty-four at the time, and should have been ashamed
to rob this Broadway milkmaid of her fair virginity?
Shame on you, you big country slicker, for coming here
among these simple, trusting city bastards and wreaking
your guilty passion upon this innocent, blushing bride
before she had had scarcely twenty-five years' experience
in the ways of love! Shame on you, you bloated plutocrat
of a two-thousand-dollar-a-year instructor, for enticing
her with your glittering gold, and luring her away from
the simple joys she had always been accustomed to!
When you met her she had scarcely three Pierce Arrows
she could call her own—but she was happy in her innocent poverty," he sneered, "and content with the simple
pleasures of the Jewish millionaires and the innocent
adulteries of their wives!"

"You know I have never been like that," she said, with
quivering indignation. "You know I've never gone with
any of those people. George, I know what I am like,"
she said proudly, "and your vile words and accusations
cannot make me any different. I've worked hard, and
been a decent person, and I have cared for what is good
and beautiful all my life. I am a fine artist and I know
my value," she said, in a proud and trembling voice,
"and nothing that you say can change it."

"Done to you!" he said again, as though he had not
heard her words. "You've wrecked my life and driven
me mad, that's what I've done to you! You've sold me out
to my enemies, and now they are sniggering at me behind my back!"

The foul words thickened in his throat and poured
from his mouth in a flood of obscenity, his voice grew
hoarse with violence and hate.

Outside, people were going along the street and he

could hear them as they passed below his room. Suddenly someone laughed, the mirthless, harsh, and raucous laughter of the streets. The sound smote savagely upon his ears.

"Listen to them!" he cried insanely. "By God, they're laughing at me now!" He rushed to the window and shouted out: "Laugh! Laugh! Go on and laugh, you dirty swine! To hell with all of you! I'm free from you! No one can hurt me now!"

"No one is trying to hurt you, George," Esther said. "No one is your enemy but yourself. You are destroying yourself. There's something mad and evil in your brain. You must get it out or you are lost."

"Lost? Lost?" he repeated stupidly and numbly for a moment. Then: "Get out of here!" he screamed suddenly. "I know you now for what you are, and I hate you!"

"You don't know me and you have never known me," she said. "You want to hate me, you want to make me out a rotten woman, and you think you can make it so by speaking lying words. But I know what I am like and I am not ashamed of anything but that I should hear such words from you. I have been a good and decent person all my life, I have loved you more dearly than anyone in the world, I have been faithful to you, I have been your dear and loving friend, and now you are throwing away the best thing you have ever had. George, for God's sake, try to get this madness out of you. You have the greatest strength and the greatest beauty in your spirit of anyone I have ever known, and you have this mad and evil thing in you that is destroying you."

She paused, and for a moment he felt within his maddened brain a dim glow of returning reason, a dull, foul, depthless shame, a numb sense of hopeless regret, inexpiable guilt, irrevocable loss.

"What do you think it is?" he muttered.

"I don't know. I did not put it there. You've always had it since I met you. You are dashing yourself to pieces on it."

And suddenly she could control her trembling lips no longer, a cry of wild despair and grief burst from her throat, she smote herself fiercely with her clenched fist and burst into tears.

"O God! This thing has beaten me! I used to be so strong and brave! I was sure I could do anything, I was sure I could get this black thing out of you, but now I know I can't! I used to love life so, I saw glory and richness everywhere, it kept getting better all the time. Now, when I wake up I wonder how I can get through one more day. I hate my life, I have come to the end of things, I want to die."

He looked at her with a dull, lost stare. He passed his hand stupidly across his face, and for a moment it seemed that light and sanity were coming back into his eyes.

"Die?" he said dully. Then the flood of hate and darkness swept across his brain again. "Die! Then, die, die, *die!*" he said savagely.

"George," she said, in a tone of trembling and passionate entreaty, "we must not die. We were made to live. You must get this evil darkness from your soul. You must love life and hate this living death. George!" she cried again, her voice rising in a note of powerful conviction, "I tell you life is good and beautiful. George, believe what I say to you, because I have lived so much, I have known so many things, there is so much beauty and richness in me, and I will give it all to you. George, for God's sake help me, stretch out your hand to help me, and I will help you, and we will both be saved."

"Lies! Lies! Lies!" he muttered. "Everything I hear is lies."

"It is the living truth!" she cried. "So help me God, it's true!"

He paused, staring stupidly and dully for a moment. Then, with a flaring of mad hate again, he screamed at her:

"Why are you standing there? Get out of here! Get out! You have lied to me and cheated me, and you are trying to trick me now with words!"

She did not move.

"Get out! Get out!" he panted hoarsely.

She did not move.

"Get out, I say! Get out!" he whispered. He seized her savagely by the arm and began to pull her towards the door.

"George!" she said, "is this the end? Is all our love going to end like this? Don't you want ever to see me again?"

"Get out! Get out, I tell you! And never come back again!"

A long wailing note of despair and defeat broke from her lips.

"O God! I want to die!" she cried. Then she cast her arm back across her face and wept bitterly, hopelessly.

"Die! Die! Die, then!" he yelled, and, thrusting her brutally through the door, he slammed it after her.

III. The Years that the Locust Hath Eaten

Outside in the hall it was dark, and there was nothing but the sound of living silence in the house. Esther went down the old stairs that sagged and creaked, and she heard the sound of silence and of time. It spoke no words that she could hear, but it brooded from old, dark walls and mellow woods and the quiet depth and fullness of an ancient, structural, and liberal space. Its face was dark and imperturbable, and its heart, as the heart of the king, inscrutable, and in it was all the knowledge of countless obscure lives and forty thousand days, and all of the years that the locust hath eaten.

She stopped upon the stairs and waited and looked back at the closed door, and she hoped that it would open. But it did not open, and she went out into the street.

The street was full of young and tender sunlight. It fell like spring and youth upon the old brick of the dingy buildings, and on all the hard violence of the city's life, and it gave life and joy and tenderness to everything. The streets were filled with their hard, untidy life, so swift, electric, and so angular, and so endless, rich, and various.

Some men with naked tattooed arms were loading boxes on a truck: they dug steel hooks into the clean white wood, and their muscles stood out like whipcord. Some children with dark faces and black Latin hair were playing baseball in the street. They nimbly snatched their game amid the thick flood of the traffic, they dodged among the wheels on strong, hard legs, they called and shouted hoarsely to one another, and the trucks and motors roared past in a single direction. And the people passed along the street in an unbroken stream, each driven to some known end, some prized or wished-for consummation. Their flesh was dried and hardened by the city's shocks, their faces were dark and meager, believing in unbelief, and most unwise.

And suddenly Esther wanted to cry out to them, to speak to them, to tell them not to hurry, not to worry, not to care, and not to be afraid, that all their ugly labor, their hard thrust and push and violence, their bitter calculations for mean gains and victories, their petty certitudes and false assurances, were of no profit in the end. The rivers would run forever, and April would come as sweetly and as fairly and with as sharp a cry when all their strident tongues were stopped with dust. Yes! For all their bicker and the fever of their fierce uneasiness, she wanted to tell them that their cries would go unheard, their love would be misprized, their pain unnoticed, that the glory of the spring would still shine calmly and with joy when all their flesh was rotten, and that other men some day on other pavements would think of them, of all their efforts and endurances, even of all their crimes and boasts of power, with pity and with condescension.

In the living light of April an old woman, a demented hag, poked, muttering, with a skinny finger into the rotting vegetation of a garbage can. Suddenly, she turned her withered face up to the sun, and bared her yellowed fangs of teeth, and shook her scrawny fist at heaven, and returned to her garbage can, and left it once again, holding her wrists together while tears streamed from her rheumy eyes, and she cried, "Misery! O Misery!" Then, the old hag stopped again, she drew her foul skirts up around her buttocks, she bared her flabby yellow thighs, and she danced, mincing and turning in a horrible parody of joy, cackling from the rag-end of an obscene memory. And still nobody noticed her except a slovenly policeman, who idly twirled his club as he surveyed her with hard eyes, above the brutal rumination of his gum-filled jaw, and a few young toughs who mocked at her. They smiled loose, brutal smiles, and smote each other in their merriment, and they cried out, "Jesus!"

And the people passed around her, some with a moment's look of shame and loathing, some with the bitter, puckered mouth of outraged decency, but for the most part with impatient brusqueness, their hard eyes fixed upon their moment's destiny. Then the old woman dropped her skirts, turned back again, returned, and shook her fist at passers-by, and no one noticed her, and she went back to her garbage can. The crone wept weakly, and the soft, living light of April fell upon her.

Esther passed before a hospital where an ambulance was waiting at the curb. The driver, his lean face tallowy, tough, and juiceless, stunned and dried, was bent above his wheel as his hard, drugged stare ate ravenously the contents of a tabloid newspaper:

"Love Pirates Make Whoopee in Love Nest"

"'Heart-broken, Loved Him!' Helen Cries"

"'Bigamy,' Sobs Dancer—Asks for Balm"

The brutal and sterile words leaped from the page to smite her as she passed with their foul, leering cheapness, evoking pictures of a life that was black, barren, idiot, and criminal in its empty violence, in which the name of love was mocked by lurid posturings, and in which even the act of murder had no horror.

Over all was the smell of blood and cheap perfumery. Here were the visages of all the human emotions:

Of passion—a vacant doll face and two fat, erotic calves.

Of crime—the flashlit stare of brutal faces and grey hats in the camera, the roadside motor car, the shattered glass.

Of love—"Honest, girlie, if I don't see you soon I'm goin' nuts. I'm mad about you, kid. I just can't get my lovin' baby off my mind. I see that sweet face of yours in my dreams, kid. Those lovin' kisses burn me up. Honest, kid, if I thought some other guy was goin' with you, I'd croak the both of you."

Of grief—a mother weeping for the photographer three hours after her child had burned to death.

She's dead.

"All right, Mrs. Moiphy, we want a shot of you now lookin' at the baby's shoes."

But she's dead.

"That's the stuff, momma. A little more expression, Mrs. Moiphy. Let's have the mother-love look, momma. Hold it!"

But she's dead.

"They'll be readin' about you tonight, momma. They'll be eatin' it up. We'll spread your map all over the front page, momma."

She's dead. She's dead.

Could it be true, then, that under the living and glorious light of these great skies, upon this proud, glittering, sea-flung isle, loaded to its lips with swarming life, the mistress of mighty ships and founded imperially among the flashing tides, among these furious streets and on this crowded rock which she had loved so well, and where she had found as much beauty, joy, and rich magnificence as any spot on earth could offer, that a monstrous race of living dead had grown up, so hateful, sterile, brutal in their senseless inhumanity that a man yet living could view them only with disgust and horror, and hope for their merciful and sudden extinction, with all the hideous life they had created, beneath the clean salt tides that swept around them? Had the city suckled at its iron breast a race of brute automatons, a stony, asphalt compost of inhuman manswarm ciphers, snarling their way to ungrieved deaths with the harsh expletives of sterile words, repeated endlessly, and as rootless of the earth, and all the blood and passion of a living man, as the great beetles of machinery they hurled at insane speed through the furious chaos of the streets?

No. She could not think that it was true. Upon this rock of life, and in these stupendous streets, there was as good earth as any that the foot could find to walk upon, as much passion, beauty, warmth, and living richness as any place on earth could show.

A young intern, jacketed in white, came out of the hospital, threw his bag loosely into the ambulance, spoke briefly to the driver, clambered up and sat down carelessly with his legs stretched out upon the other seat, and the car slid off smoothly through the traffic with a clangor of electric bells. The intern looked back lazily at the crowded street, and she knew that they would return with a dead or wounded man, one mangled atom or one pulsebeat less in the unnumbered desolations of the swarm, and the intern would go in to his interrupted lunch, and the driver would return with hunger to his paper.

Meanwhile and forever the bright tides of the rivers flowed about the isle of life. In the windows of wide-sheeted glass upon the first floor of the hospital, the babies sat up in their sunlit cots, the crisp, starched nurses bent above them, and the children stared into the furious streets with innocence and wonder, with delight and with no memory.

And upon the balconies above the street the men who had been sick and afraid of death now sat in sunlight, knowing they would live. They had recovered life and hope, and on their faces was the proud and foolish look of sick men who have felt the hand of death upon the bridles of their hearts, and who now, with a passive and uncertain faith, renew themselves. Their bodies looked shrunken in their dressing gowns, upon their starved, pale cheeks a furze of beard was growing, the young wind fanned their lank, unvital hair, their jaws hung open, and with foolish, happy smiles they turned their faces towards the light. One smoked a cheap cigar, his thin hand took it slowly and unsteadily to his lips, he looked about and grinned. Another walked a few steps back and forth uncertainly. They were like children who have been born again, and there was something foolish, puzzled, and full of happiness in their look. They drew the air and light into them with a thin, fond greed, their enfeebled flesh, reft of the coarseness of its work and struggle, soaked in the solar energy. And sometimes the brisk nurses came and went, sometimes their kinsmen stood beside them awkwardly, dressed clumsily in the hard and decent clothes they saved for Sundays, holidays, and hospitals.

And between the old red brick of two blank walls a slender tree, leaved with the poignant, piercing green of late April, looked over the boarding of a fence, and its loveliness among all the violence of the street, the mortared harshness of its steel and stone, was like a song, a triumph, and a prophecy—proud, lovely, slender, sudden, trembling—and like a cry with its strange music of man's bitter brevity upon the everlasting and immortal earth.

Esther saw these things and people in the street, and everything and all mistaken persons cried exultantly and fiercely for life; and in this she knew from her profoundest heart that they were not mistaken, and the tears were flowing down her face, because she loved life dearly, and because all the triumphant music, the power, the glory, and the singing of proud love grew old and came to dust.

IV. REMORSE

When Esther had gone, when Monk had thrust her through the door and slammed it after her, his spirit was torn by a rending pity and a wild regret. And for a

moment he stood in the bare center of the room, stunned
with shame and hatred for his act and life.

He heard her pause upon the stairs, and he knew that
she was waiting for him to come and grasp her by the
hand and speak one word of love or friendship to her,
and lead her back into the room again. And suddenly he
felt an intolerable desire to go and get her, crush her in
his embrace, lock her into his heart and life again, to
take the glory and the grief together and to tell her, come
what might, and be she fifteen, twenty, thirty years beyond his age, and grown grey and wrinkled as the witch
of Endor, that she was sealed into his brain and heart
so that he could love no one but her forever, and in this
faith to live and die with a single and unfaltering affirma-
tion. Then his pride fought stubbornly and wretchedly
with regret and shame, he made no move to go to her,
and presently he heard the street door close, and he
knew that he had driven her into the street again.

And at the moment she had left the house, the aching,
silent solitude of loneliness, for so many years before he
met her the habit of his life, but now, so had she stolen
his fierce secrecy away from him, a hateful and abhor-
rent enemy, settled upon his soul the palpable and chill-
ing vacancy of isolation. It inhabited the walls, the
timbers, and the profound and lonely silence of the
ancient house. He knew that she had gone from him and
left him in the house alone, and her absence filled his
heart and filled the room like a living spirit.

He craned convulsively at his neck like a struggling
animal, his mouth contracted in a grimace of twisted
pain, and his foot was lifted sharply from the floor as if
he had been struck hard upon the kidneys: the images
of wild and wordless pity and regret passed like a thin
blade through his heart, a bestial cry was torn from his
lips, he flung his arms out in a gesture of bewilderment

and agony. Suddenly he began to snarl like a maddened animal, and savagely to smash his fist into the wall.

He could not find a tongue for his bewilderment, but he now felt with unutterable certitude the presence of a demon of perverse denial which was, and was everywhere, abroad throughout the universe, and at work forever in the hearts of men. It was the cunning, subtle cheat, the mocker of life, the scourger of time; and man, with the full glory and the tragic briefness of his days before him in his sight, bowed like a dull slave before the thief that looted him of all his joy, and held him sullen but submissive to its evil wizardry. He had seen and known its dark face everywhere. About him in the streets the legions of the living dead were swarming constantly: they stuffed themselves on straw and looked on glorious food with famished eyes of hunger and desire, and saw it ready to their touch, bursting from the great plantation of the earth the abundance of its golden harvest, and none would stretch forth his hand to take what had been given him, and all were stuffed with straw, and none would eat.

Oh, there would have been a solace for their foul defeat if they had striven fatally with an invincible and fatal destiny which tore life bleeding from their grip, and before whom now they desperately lay dead. But they were dying like a race of dull, stunned slaves, cringing upon a crust of bread before great trestles groaning with the food they wanted, and had not the courage to take. It was incredible, incredible, and it seemed to him as if there really was above these swarming hordes of men a malignant and ironic governor who moved them like the puppets in a ghastly comedy, mocking their impotence with vast illusions of a sterile power.

Did he belong, then, to this damned race of famished half-men who wanted food and had not courage to go

beyond the husks, who sought for pleasure constantly
and stained the night with the obscene glitter of a thousand weary amusements, who longed for joy and com-
radeship and yet, with dull, deliberate intent, fouled
their parties with horror, shame, and loathing every time
they met? Did he belong to an accursed race which
spoke of its defeat, and yet had never fought, which used
its wealth to cultivate a jaded boredom, and yet had
never had the strength or energy to earn satiety, and
had not the courage to die?

Did he belong, then, to this set of meager slaves who
feebly snarled their sterile way to death without the consummation of a single moment of hunger, grief, or love?
Must he belong, then, to a fearful, fumbling race that
twiddled its desire between its pallid fingers and furtively took its love round corners or in uneasy spasms on
the distressful edges of a couch or, trembling, upon the
rattling casters of a bed in a cheap hotel?

Must he be like them, forever furtive and forever
cautious, in all things dull and trembling, and for what,
for what? That youth might sicken and go sour, and turn
with bitter discontent to grey and flabby middle age, and
hate joy and love because it wanted them and was not
brave enough to have them, and still be cautious, halfway, and withholding.

And for what? To save themselves for what? To save
their wretched lives that they might lose them, to starve
their wretched flesh that they might lie dead and rotten
in their graves, to cheat, deny, and dupe themselves until
the end.

He remembered the bitter and despairing accusation
of Esther's cry: "You fool! You poor, mad fool! This is the
finest thing that you will ever have, and you are throwing it away!"

And instantly the conviction came to him that she had

told the truth. He had walked the streets by night, by day, in hundreds of hours long past and furiously accomplished, searching the faces of a million people to see if there was one who was as jolly, fresh, and fair as she, to see if there was one who had an atom of her loveliness, a glimmer of the glorious richness, joy, and noble beauty that showed in every act and visage of her life, and there was no one he had ever seen who could compare with her: they were all stale and lifeless by comparison.

Now the savage hatred he had felt when he had cursed her in their bitter quarrel was turned tenfold against himself, and against these people in the streets. For he felt that he had betrayed her love, turned on her, sold her out to the dull, timorous slaves, and in so doing, that he had betrayed life and sold it out to barren death.

She had said to him with passionate indignation and entreaty: "What do you think it's been about if I don't love you? Why do you think I've come here day by day, cooked for you, cleaned up after you, listened to your insults and vile abuse, left my work, given up my friends, kept after you and wouldn't let you go when you tried to throw me over, if it wasn't because I love you?"

Oh, she had told the truth, the naked, literal truth. For what purpose, what crafty, deep, and scheming purpose, had this woman poured upon him for three years the lavish bounty of her love and tenderness? Why had she lived ten thousand hours alone with him, leaving the luxury and the beauty of her home for the cyclonic chaos of his poor dwelling?

He looked about him. Why had she come daily into the mad confusion of this big room in which it always seemed, no matter what patient efforts she made to keep it tidy, that the tumult and fury of his spirit had struck all things like lightning, so that everything—books, shirts, collars, neckties, socks, stained coffee cups half-filled

with sodden butts, postcards, letters five years old and
laundry bills, student themes and tottering piles of his
own manuscript, notebooks, a ragged hat, the leg of a
pair of drawers, a pair of shoes with dried, cracked
leather, no heels, and two gaping holes upon their
bottoms, the Bible, Burton, Coleridge, Donne, Catullus,
Heine, Spenser, Joyce, and Swift, a dozen fat anthologies
of every kind, plays, poems, essays, stories, and the old,
worn, battered face of *Webster's Dictionary*, piled up
precariously or strewn in a pell-mell circle round his cot,
covered with ashes, hurled face downward on the floor
before he slept—was a cyclonic compost of the dust and
lumber of the last ten years. Here were scraps, fragments, and mementoes of his wandering in many countries, none of which he could destroy, most of which
filled him with weariness when he looked at it, and all of
which seemed to have been hurled in this incredible confusion with the force of an explosion.

Why had this elegant and dainty woman come daily
into the wild disorder of this mad place? What had she
hoped to get from him that she had clung to him, loved
him, lavished her inexhaustible tenderness upon him,
stuck to him in the face of all the rebuffs, injuries, and
insults he had heaped upon her, with all the energy of
her indomitable will?

Yes—why, why? With a cold, mounting fury of self-
loathing, he asked himself the questions. What was her
deep and scheming plot? Where was the cunning treachery that had maddened him with a thousand poisonous
suspicions? Where was the subtle trap that she had laid
for him? What was the treasure that she coveted, the
priceless possession which she planned to steal away
from him, and which was the end and purpose of all
these snares of love?

What was it now? Was it his great wealth and high

position in society? Was it his proud title as instructor in an immense and swarming factory of the brain, the noble honor he shared with eighteen hundred fearful, embittered, and sterile little men? Was it his rare culture, the distinguished ability required to speak to jaded typists and swart, ill-smelling youths with raucous voices of "the larger values," "the liberal outlook," "the saner, deeper, and more comprehensive point of view"? Was it the delicate and sympathetic perception required to see the true beauty of their sullen, stunned, and inert minds, the jewels buried in the dreary illiteracy of their compositions, the thrills and ardors pulsing in "The Most Exciting Moment of My Life," or the simple, rich, and moving truths of "My Last Year at Erasmus High"?

Or was it, now, the elegance of his person, the fastidiousness of his costume, the tender and winning charm of his address, the rare beauty of his form and countenance, that had enchanted her? Was it the graceful and yet nonchalant dignity with which his knees and buttocks dignified these fine old kangaroo bags, through which, 'twas true, his hindward charms gleamed an unearthly white, but which he wore, withal, with what fashionable distinction, with what assured and easy poise? Was it the stylish ease with which he wore his coat, the elegant "three button sack," of which the lower two were missing, and which was dashingly festooned with remnants of last year's steak and gravy? Or was it the ungainly body that urchins gibed at in the streets, the bounding and lunging stride, the heavy, slouching shoulders, the gangling arms, the shock of unkempt hair, the face too small and the legs too short for the barrel-like structure of the body, the out-thrust head, the bulging underlip, the dark and upward-peering scowl? Were these the charms that had caught the lady's fancy?

Or was it something else she prized—something finer,

obler, deeper? Was it for the great beauty of his soul,
he power and richness of his "talent"? Was it because
e was a "writer"? The word blazed in his consciousness
or a moment, making him writhe with a convulsive
hame and evoking a cruel picture of futility, despair,
nd shoddy pretense. And suddenly he saw himself as
. member of the whole vast shabby army he despised:
he pale, futile yearners of the arts, the obscure and
ensitive youths who thought their souls too fine, their
eelings too delicate and subtle, their talents too rare
nd exquisite for the coarse and vulgar apprehension of
he earth.

For ten years he had known them, he had heard their
vords, and seen their puny arrogance, and become
amiliar with all their feeble attitudes and mimicries, and
hey had sickened his bowels with hopeless impotence,
tunned his heart with a grey horror of unbelief and
lesolate futility. And now, in a single moment of blind-
ng shame, they returned to mock him with appalling
evelation. Pale, sterile, feeble, and embittered, they
:ame—a myriad horde—gnawing the nail of rankling
liscontent, scowling the venom of their misprized
alents, sneering with envious contempt against the
bilities and accomplishments of stronger and more
;ifted men than they, and unconfidently solaced by a
vague belief in talents which they did not own, drugged
eebly by cloudy designs for a work which they would
1ever consummate. He saw them all—the enervate
hapsodists of jazz, the comic strip, and primitive
\pollos, Wastelanders, Humanists, Expressionists, Sur-
ealists, Neo-primitives, and Literary Communists.

The words of fraudulent pretense that he had heard
hem speak a thousand times came back to him, and
suddenly it seemed to him they uttered a final judgment
on his own life, too. Had he not scowled and glowered

gloomily, whined at the lack of this, the want of that, the
intrusion of some shackling obstacle that kept his genius
from its full fruition? Had he not bewailed the absence
of some earthly heaven in whose unpolluted ethers his
rare soul could wing its way triumphantly to great
labors? Was not the sun of this base, stinking earth too
hot, the wind too cold, the shifting weathers of the
seasons too rude and variable for the tender uses of his
sweet, fair hide? Were not the bitter world he lived in
and the men he knew given to base gain and sordid purposes? Was it not a barren, sordid, ugly world in which
the artist's spirit withered and went dead, and if he
changed his skies—oh! if he could only change his skies!
—would he not change his soul, as well? Would he not
flower and blossom in the living light of Italy, grow great
in Germany, bloom like the rose in gentle France, find
roots and richness in old England, and utterly fulfill his
purposes if he, too, like an aesthetic exile from Kansas
whom he had met in Paris, could only "go to Spain to do
a little writing"?

For months and years had he not fumbled, fiddled,
faltered, and pretended, just as they? Had he not cursed
at a world that paid no tribute to his unsuspected talents,
eaten his flesh in bitterness, sneered and mocked at the
work of better men, looked out the window, fumbled
and scowled, and fiddled—and what had he done?
Written a book that nobody would publish!

And she, who was the fine, rare artist, the rich
delicate, and certain talent, the person who knew and
was sure and had power, the one who worked, created,
and produced, had endured it all, cared for him, excused
his indolence, and believed in him. During all this time
while he had cursed and grumbled at the hardship of his
life, coddled his whims, whined that he could do no writing for himself because of his exhausting labors at the

chool, the woman had done the labor of a titan. She had
un her household, governed her family, planned and
uilt a new house in the country, been chief designer for
 clothing manufacturer, and constantly improved and
trengthened herself in her art, making designs and
ostumes for thirty plays, doing a day's work in the morn-
ng while he slept, and yet having energy and time left
ver to come to his place and cook, and spend eight
ours a day together with him.

This sudden perception of Esther's indomitable cour-
ge and energy, her power to work, and her balanced
ontrol over all the decisive acts and moments of her
fe, in contrast to the waste, confusion, and uncertainty
f his own, smote him a hammer-blow of shame and self-
ontempt. And, as if in mute evidence of the contrast,
he divided character of the room was suddenly revealed
 him. While the part that he inhabited was struck with
 cyclonic chaos, the corner by the window where Esther
orked and had her table was trim, spare, certain, alert
nd orderly, and ready instantly for work. Upon the
hite, clean boards of the table were fastened the crisp
heets of drawing paper covered with the designs that
he had made for costumes, each of which was so alive
ith a brave and jaunty energy, with a delicate and
cisive certainty, that they lived instantly, not only with
ll her own sure talent, but with the lives of all the
haracters they were designed to clothe. And, right and
ft, the instruments and materials she loved so well and
ould use with such sure magic were arranged and ready
r her instant touch. There were the tubes and boxes of
aint, the fine brushes, the sliding rule, the gleaming
ompass, and the long, neatly-sharpened pencils, and
ehind the table, hanging from nails driven in the
alls, were the T-square, the yard measure, and the
iangle.

And now each thing that she had touched and owned
each vestige of her life within that room, cried ou
against him with passionate tongue the judgment of a
intolerable regret. In their living stillness these thing
were more inexorable and swift than the black rout o
the avenging furies that ever once through dark and fata
skies impended on the driven figure of a man, mor
eloquent than the trumpet blast of an accusing venge
ance. And their mute and scattered presence ther
evoked a picture of her life more whole and final tha
the minute chronicle of twenty thousand days, for it ra
like a thread of gold back through the furious confusion
of time and cities, and bound her to the strange los
world that he had never known.

His mind, now goaded by an intolerable desire t
know her, see her, have and own her, to mine her lif
up bit by bit out of the depthless pit of time and th
furious oblivion of the city's life, and to join it, root an
branch with all the fibrous tendrils of everything tha
she had seen and known and touched, to his own
prowled beastwise back across the jungle of the pas
scenting the final limits and last implications of ever
casual word, each story, scene, or moment, each sigh
or sound or odor he had torn from her in three years wit
his tireless and insatiate hunger. He wove the web lik
a terrific spider until two earths, two lives, two destinie
as far and separate as any under sun could be, wer
woven to their jointure by the dark miracle of chanc

Hers, the streets of life, the manswarm passing in i
furious weft, the tumult of great cities, the thunder of th
hooves and wheels upon the cobbles, and the soli
façades of dark, lavish brown.

His, the lives of secret men who lived alone, and wh
had seen cloud shadows passing in the massed green o
the wilderness for two hundred years, and whose burie

bones were pointing ninety ways across the continent.

For her, the memory of great names and faces, the flashing stir and thrust of crowds, the shout of noonday in exultant cities, the stamp of the marching men and great parades, the hard cry of the children playing in the streets, and men who leaned at evenings quietly on the sills of old dark brown.

For him, the great winds howling in the hills at night, the creaking of stiff boughs in winter wind, and the great empurpled hills that faded faint and far into the edges of a limitless desire, the sound of a bell, wind-broken, the whistle cry that wailed away into blue gates and passes of the North and West.

For her, forgotten fume-flaws of bright smoke above Manhattan, and the proud cleavages of ships, and the sea-flung city masted to its lips with trade and voyages. For her, suave silks and creamy linens, old dark woods, the wink of mellow wines and heavy, ancient silvers, the dainty succulence of rare foods and cookery, the velvet backs and proud-groomed undulance of luxurious beauty, the ornate masks and gestures of the actors' faces, and the lost burial of their eyes.

For him, the lamplight in a close and shuttered winter room, the smell of camphor and of apples, the flare and crumble of the ash there in the grate, and the ash of time in Aunt Maw's voice, that death-triumphant Joyner voice, drawling of death and sorrow, the sin and shame of his father's life, and phantoms of lost Joyner kinsmen back in the hills a hundred years ago.

Even while all those elements of fire and earth of which he was compacted coursed unresolved in the wild blood from which he sprang, she paced, a child, along the city streets. Even while he stared within his mother's flesh, she was an adolescent girl, orphaned of love, knowledged in grief and loss and bitterness, and strong in hopeful fortitude. Even while he, a boy of twelve, lay on the grass before his uncle's house and dreamed his dreams, she lay, a woman ripe in love and loveliness, in the embraces of a husband. And even while, a youth, he saw afar the glorious towers of the fabled city, and felt along his loins the joy and certitude of all the glory, love, and power that he would win there, she was a woman seated at the heart of power, freed from confusion, and certain of her talent and her strength.

Thus did his memory shuttle back and forth across the skeins of chance until it wove the jointure of their lives together.

And, finally, he saw this brave and faithful spirit which was so certain of its strength, so sure of its power to make its life prevail, faced for the first time by the thing it could not meet or conquer, and fighting wildly, with a desperate and pitiable fury, as if against some intolerable personal injustice, against the common and invincible enemy of mankind—the passing of youth, the loss of love, the coming of old age and weariness and completion. This final, brutal necessity that put the mark of its possession upon the lives of all men living was the thing she would not accept, and that could nowhere be escaped or denied. She was dashing her life against its iron face. Inexorable and wordless, it was present in all the desperate and ugly war that had been waged between them, it stood outside them, waiting while they fought, and it bore the terrible judgment of the clock, the stayless doom of time. It was silent before their words of bitter injury and reproach, silent before love, hatred, faith, and unbelief alike, and its face was grim, immovable, and final.

She would not yield to it, nor admit the justice of the

fate it spoke. She shook her fist into the face of iron destiny. And as he saw the desperate and useless struggle, his heart was torn with a wild regret and pity for her, for he knew that she was right, no matter how inexorable or general the fate she shared with all the earth. He knew that she was right, and would be right if she went to her grave with a curse of wild denial on her lips, because such beauty, courage, love, and youth, and strength as she had known should not grow old, and should never die, and that truth was with her, no matter how inevitable the triumph of this all-devouring, all-victorious enemy.

And as he saw the way it was, there came to him an image of man's whole life upon the earth. It seemed to him that all man's life was like a tiny spurt of flame that blazed out briefly in an illimitable and terrifying darkness, and that all man's grandeur, tragic dignity, his heroic glory came from the brevity and smallness of this flame, and that he knew his light was little and would be extinguished, and that only darkness was immense and everlasting, and that he died with defiance on his lips, and that the shout of his hatred and denial rang with the last pulsing of his heart into the maw of all-engulfing night.

And now again the foul, intolerable shame returned to sicken him with hatred of his life, for it seemed to him that he had betrayed the only faithful, strong, and certain thing that he had ever known. And in betraying it, it seemed to him that he had not only dishonored life, spat in the face of love, and sold out the person who had loved him to the hateful legions of rat's alley where the dead men lived, but that he had also betrayed himself and bargained with the dead for his own ruin and defeat. For, if his heart was poisoned at its sources, his

brain warped and twisted by its madness, his life polluted and brought to naught, what enemy had worked
this evil on him but himself?

Men have their visions from afar and in a lonely place,
and the great vision of this earth and all her power and
glory has ever had the city at its end. So it had been with
him. He had come to the city as young men come, with
joy and hope, with certain faith, and with the conviction
he had power to make his life prevail. He had possessed
the strength, the faith, the talent to do all things if he
had played the man and kept the same heart, the same
courage and belief, that he had had within him as a
child. And had he used his life well and bravely to this
purpose? No. Instead, he had spat upon the glory that
was given him, betrayed love, and like a whining slave
had miserably sold his life into the hands of other slaves,
until now, like them, he jeered at his own vision as the
daydream of a yokel, and gave to the passion and belief
of youth the fool's mockery of a false, inept, and mirthless laughter.

And for what? For what? He had spoken to her of the
"shame" he felt because of her. For what other thing
should he feel a second's shame save for the foul insult
and injury he had heaped upon the one who loved him,
whom he loved? Feel shame! Great God! Before what—
or whom? Must he then bow his head and hurry past
below the stare of all the grey-faced ciphers in the street?

They say! *They* say! *They! They! They!* And who were
they that he should strain his ears to hear them in the
streets or care the tail-end of a tinker's curse for all their
bastardly gentility? *They! They!* Who were *they* that he
should sell out the grand woman, the fine artist, and the
true aristocrat to any vulgar little slut or snob that aped
or swanked its way through the cheap perfumery of a

fraudulent society? Feel shame! Apologize! To whom! Good God, must he slink by below the thoroughbred disdain of fine old country-club Princetonians, cringe below the scornful nostrils of high-mettled Junior Leaguers, endure with flaming face the amused, distasteful glances of young princelings of the Harvard Club, cringe and slink it when he faced the noble-blooded heirs of Hayes and Garfield scoundrels who scarcely yet had breathed the sweat and horse-p—s knavery of their fathers from their nostrils? Or squirm, great God, before the amused, ironic glances of a Saturday Reviewer, the fine old culture of the Dekes and Betas, or the snickering whispers and sly nudges of the pale sucks and crawling worms at the School for Utility Cultures?

They! They! And who were *they?* The apes and rats and parrots of the earth without the courage of their own disbelief, the puny pavement cynics who winked and leered with knowing smirk their little hearsay filth. *They!* The feeble little city yokels who sneered and mocked and jingled in their pockets the cheap coin of their stale pick-me-up scurrilities. *They!* The wretched and impotent little instructors at the School for Utility Cultures, the tenth-rate literary triflers who had no heart or courage for avowal, for any living passion, mercy, love, or strong belief whatever, whose mouths were filled with ugly slanders, and who could be gay and gaudy on a thimble's measure of bad gin, snickering and whispering over some rag of gossip about a lesbic actress, a pederastic poet, or the unclean rumor that hovered about a celebrity they would have swallowed dung to meet.

They! They! Why, how was he any better than any damned dull slave who winked and nodded it with knowing leer and ravenously gulped down the lies and slop a shrewder knave had thrown together for him, saying:

"Sure, I know! I know! You're telling me! . . . I know! You know how it is, don't you? . . . Nah-h!"—when the poor fool had been blind and ignorant from his birth?

Yes, he had winced and faltered in the stare of men like these, and yet his fathers were great men, and had known the wilderness, and had winced and faltered in the stare of no one. And had their spirit died upon the earth? Suddenly he knew that it had not. He saw that it lived in the very air around him, and he knew it still belonged to the fabric of man's life, as real and living as it ever was.

Had not ten million men before him brought their strength and talents and all the golden legendry of their youth into the city? Had they not heard the accursed clatter of their feet upon the metal stairs, the entrance tilings, and seen the hard, dead eyes and heard the cold and loveless greetings of the men from whom they bought the refuge of their little cells? Had they not with hearts of fire, with the burning hunger of their savage loneliness, hurled themselves out of these little cells into the streets again? Wild-eyed and desperate, mad of brain, had they not coursed the terrible streets in which there was neither curve nor pause nor any place that they might enter, and searched the myriad faces with a desperate hope, and then returned into their little cells mocked by the city's terrible illusions of abundance and variety, and by the cruel enigma of man's loneliness among eight million, his poverty and desolation at the seat of a stupendous power and wealth?

Had they not cursed in the darkness of their little rooms at night, and ripped the sheets between convulsive fingers, beat their fists against the wall? Had they not seen a thousand insults to the living in the streets of night, and smelled the foul stench of a brutal privilege, seen the leer of a criminal authority, the smirk of a cor rupt and indifferent power, and had they not grown mad with shame and horror?

And yet all did not grow grey of heart or dead of eye, or wearily ape the gabble of the dead. All did not madden desperately to defeat. For some had seen the city's stupefying and unnumbered cruelty, and lived upon their hate of it, and not grown cruel. Some had drawn mercy from the cobblestones, found love within a little room, and all the living richness of the earth and April in the furious clamors of a street. And some had struck the city's stony heart and brought forth lucent water, and wrung out of her iron breast the grandest music that the earth has known. They had bloodily learned the secret of her stern soul, and with the power and passion of their lives won from her what they sought in youth.

Were there not still men who strode with confidence the streets of life, knew fortitude and danger and endurance in their daily work, and yet leaned with calm eyes at evening on their window sills? Were there not men who in the rush and glare of furious noon thickened the air with strong, hoarse curses from the seats of trucks, sat with gloved hands of cunning on the throttle, looked with a glint of demon hawk-eyes on the rails, lifted their voices in command to swarthy, sweating laborers, men who drank, fought, whored, and fed stupendously, and yet were brave and gentle in their hearts, filled with the warm blood and the liberal passion of living men?

And as he thought of them, the earth was living with the brave presences of men and women who had torn joy and passion strongly from the earth, just as now the whole of his big room was living with the life of Esther. The memory of her small and bitterly wounded face, stricken with the surprise and grief of a child whose gaiety and affection has been killed suddenly by a blow, returned to twist into his heart its merciless and avenging blade.

But now his life was so caught up and whirled about in this wild dance of madness and despair, of love, hatred, faith, and disbelief, of a savage jealousy and a despairing penitence, that he no longer knew what justice or what falseness rested in his curse or prayer or self-reproach, or whether he was mad or sane, or if his life and sinew had been seduced and rotted by an evil thing, or fed and nourished by a good one. At the end he only knew that, true, false, fair, foul, young, old, good, evil, or anything he thought whatever, she was rooted in the fabric of his life and he must have her.

He struck his fist into his face, a wild and wordless cry was torn from his throat, and he rushed from his room and from the house, out in the street to find her.

V. Pursuit and Capture

All at once she saw his apelike shadow moving on the pavement. In firm young sunlight it came bounding after her, the body and the long arms prowling, the legs leaping high in their strange stride, and her heart was twisted suddenly and beat hard with pain and joy. But she did not turn to look at him, she lowered her face stubbornly and went on faster as if she did not see him, and the shadow bounded after her, came up beside her, walked abreast of her, and still she did not look at him, and he did not speak.

At length he seized her by the arm and, in a voice surly with shame and obstinacy, said:

"What's wrong with you now? Where are you going? What the hell's the trouble now?"

"You told me to go," she said with offended dignity,

and she tried to pull her arm away. "You told me to leave you and never to come back again. You drove me out. You're the one."

"Come back," he said with sullen shame, and stood still as though to turn her around and head her back down the street.

She jerked her arm away from him and walked on. Her lip was trembling and she did not speak.

He stood a moment looking at her retreating figure, and in his mounting shame and baffled rage the old black fury rose up in him suddenly and he bounded after her, yelling frantically:

"Come back! Come back, God-damn it! Don't disgrace me in the streets!" He seized her arm again and roared: "Don't bawl! I beg and beseech you not to bawl!" he shouted.

"I'm not bawling!" she said. "I'm not disgracing you! You're the one!"

Some people had stopped to stare at them, and when he noticed them, he turned on them savagely and snarled:

"It's no business of yours, you leering swine! What are you looking at?"

Then, turning towards her small form menacingly, he said in a hoarse voice and with a contorted face:

"You see, don't you? You see what you've done! They're looking at us! Great God, they're lapping it up —you can see them lick their filthy chops about it! And you enjoy it!" he shouted. "You love it! Anything, by God, so long as you attract attention! Anything to degrade, ruin, and humiliate me!"

He had her by the arm, and he now began to pull her back along the street so fast she had to run to keep up with him.

"Come on!" he said in a frantic and entreating tone.

"Come on, for God's sake! You're ruining me! Please come on!"

"I'm coming. I'm coming," she said, and the tears were running down her face. "You said you didn't want me any more."

"That's right"—he said—"cry! Boo-hoo! Weep your glycerine tears!"

"No. They are real tears," she said with dignity.

"Oh, glub-glub! Oh, gul-lup, gul-lup! Woe is me! Oi yoi yoi! Play to the crowd! Get their sympathy!"

Suddenly he burst into a wild, mad laugh, and, turning, shouted into the street loudly, waving his arms meanwhile in beckoning gestures:

"All right, boys! Step right up! We will now witness a very high-class performance by one of our best art-theater actresses, only a nickel, five cents, the twentieth part of a dollar!"

He paused, glancing at her for a moment, and then he cried out bitterly:

"All right! You win! I'm no match for you!"

"I'm not playing to any crowd," she said. "You're the one!"

"With her nice, damned, delicate little rosy face! Is this another of your tricks? Out here on the street, and letting the tears trickle down your pure, sweet, womanly face!"

"You're the one!" she said. She stopped suddenly and looked at him, her face flushed, her rosy lip curling, and then said in a quiet and scornful voice, as if pronouncing the most insulting judgment she knew: "Do you know what you're acting like? Well, I'll tell you. You're acting like a Christian, that's what you're acting like!"

"And you're acting like a Jew! A damned, crafty Jezebel of a Jew! That's what you're acting like!"

"That's all right about the Jews," she said. "We're too

good for you, that's all. You know nothing about us, and you will never be able in your vile, low soul to understand what we are like as long as you live."

"Understand!" he cried. "Oh, I understand enough! You're not so damned wonderful and mysterious as you think! So we're too vile and low to understand how noble and great you are, are we? Tell me, then," he cried in an excited and combative tone, "if we're so low as you say we are, why don't you stick to your own race? Why is it that every damned one of you is out to get a Christian if you can? Will you tell me that? Hey?"

In the excitement of a fresh dispute they had paused again, and now faced each other in the middle of the sidewalk with red, angry faces, oblivious of all the people who passed around them.

"No. No," she said strongly, in a protesting tone. "You can't say that. That's not true, and you know it's not!"

"Not true," he cried, with a wild, exasperated laugh as he struck his forehead with his palm and made a gesture of imploring supplication heavenward. "Not true! My God, woman, how can you stand there and look me in the face when you say it? You know it's true! Why, every God-damned one of you, man or woman, will crawl upon your hands and knees—yes!—creep and crawl and contrive until you have a Gentile in your clutches! . . . Jesus God! That it should come to this!" and he laughed bitterly and madly.

"That it should come to what?" she said, with an angry laugh. "God, but you're crazy! You don't know what you're saying half the time. You open your mouth and it just comes out!"

"Answer me!" he said hoarsely. "Isn't it the truth? You know God-damn well it's the truth!"

"I'm going now!" she cried, in a high, excited voice. "You're beginning again! I told you I wouldn't listen to

your vileness any longer!" And she wrenched her arm
out of his grasp and began to walk away, with a flaming,
angry face.

He followed her instantly, and stopped her, clasping
her hand warmly and firmly between his own, and speaking to her in a low, entreating voice.

"Oh, come on!" he said, ashamed of himself and trying to laugh it off. "Come on back with me! I didn't
mean it. Don't you see I didn't mean it? Don't you know
I was only joking? Don't you see that was all it was?"
he said urgently, and again he tried to pass it off with
a hearty laugh that rang hollowly in the street.

"Yes! A fine joker you are!" she said scornfully. "Your
idea of a joke would be to see somebody break his neck!
That's the kind of joke you'd like! . . . I know! I know!"
she continued, almost hysterical in her excitement. "You
don't need to tell me. You're always reviling us. You
couldn't see the truth about us anyway, you hate us so!"

He stared thickly and blindly at her for a moment with
bloodshot eyes, in which the fires of love and hate, of
conviction and mistrust, of sanity and madness, flared
instantly together in one joined flame, and behind which
his spirit looked out silently, like something trapped and
baffled, desperate, haggard, and bewildered. Suddenly
her face shone clearly in his vision, and he saw it, small
and flushed and wounded bitterly, at the same instant
that he heard her words of resentful indignation.

And then, with a returning sense of his unforgivable
injustice, he realized that she had spoken the truth, and
that in the furious excess of his exasperation and vitu-
perative bitterness he had said things he had not meant
to say, used words the way one uses a murderous
weapon, with the sole intent to wound her, words which
he could not now unsay or ever atone for. And again a
wave of intolerable shame overwhelmed him, and the

desperation of defeat now filled his heart. It seemed he was so entirely in the grip of this madness that he could not for five minutes control a sure and certain impulse. The very impulse which had driven him into the streets to find her, the impulse of passionate regret and faith and strong conviction, had been forgotten with the first words that he spoke to her, and again he had fouled himself and her with a vile, choking glut of filthy insult and abuse.

And now, ashamed to look into her face, he looked instead into the street, and saw it plainly as it was—harsh and angular with its chaotic architectures, the raw, prognathous fronts of its new buildings, the grimed dinginess of its old ones, the lumpy copings, the rusty fire escapes, the grimy warehouses, and the occasional glow and richness of old red brick and calmer time. It was simply an American street, he had seen its like a thousand times, and it had no curve nor stay nor pause in it, nor any planned coherence.

They had paused beneath a slender tree, one of the few along the street; it grew up from a lonely scrap of earth wedged in between an old brick house and the grey pavement; and through young boughs, now leaved with the first smoky green of the year, the sun cast a net of dancing spangles on the wide brim of Esther's hat and the rich green of the dress she wore, swarming in moths of golden light upon her straight, small shoulders. Her face, now flaming with her hurt, looked out like a strange and lovely flower below her hat, and it had the mingled looks he had seen in it ten thousand times—the straight, proud, faithful look of children, and their grieved, bewildered innocence; and all the dark opulence of the women of her race.

And as he looked at her, his entrails stirred with tenderness, with the desire to hold her gently and caress her.

Slowly he moved his hand until he touched hers with his fingertips, and softly said:

"No, Esther, I don't hate you. I love you better than my life."

Then, arm in arm, they turned and went back to his room again. And everything was with them as it always was.

VI. The Weaver at Work Again

Monk leaned stiffly, legs apart, and with his back to Esther. His weight was supported on his extended arms and the palms of his hands, which rested on the ledge of sun-warm stone outside the window. With his head outthrust, half-sunken in his shoulder blades, he glowered right and left along the street. The delicate lights of April passed over his head and shoulders, a breeze fanned past him from the street, and behind him, on the wall, the sheets of tracing paper rattled crisply. It was another day.

Frowning, and slipping her finger rapidly in and out of the old ring she wore—a gesture habitual to her in moments of nervousness, impatience, and serious meditation or decision—Esther looked at him with a faint, bitter smile, a feeling of tenderness and anger and a scornful humor.

"Now," she thought, "I know exactly what he's thinking. There are still a few things in the universe which have not been arranged to suit his pleasure, so he wants to see them changed. And his desires are modest, aren't they? *Very!*" she thought bitterly. "All he wants is to eat his cake and keep on having it forever. He's tired of me and he wishes I would go away and leave him here alone to contemplate his navel. He also wishes I would stay here with him. I am the one he loves, his jolly little

Jew that he adores and could devour, and I am also the evil wench who lies in wait for unsuspecting country boys. I am the joy and glory of his life, and I am also the sinister and corrupt harpy who has been employed by the forces of darkness to kill and destroy his life. And why? Why, because he is so innocent and pure—God! Could anyone believe it if they heard it!—and all the rotten people who hate life are staying up at night plotting how to wreck and ruin him. The Jews hate the Christians, and they also love them. The Jewish women seduce the pure young Christian boys because they love them and want to destroy them, and the Jewish men, cynical and resigned, look on and rub their hands in glee because they hate the Christians and also love them, too, and want to destroy them because they love to see them suffer, but really adore them because they feel such sympathy and pity for them, and yet say nothing because they get an obscene sexual satisfaction from the spectacle, and because their souls are old and patient, and they have known that their women were unfaithful for seven thousand years, and they must suffer and endure it! Weave! Weave! Weave! He weaves it day and night out of his crazy and tormented brain until not even Einstein could make head or tail of it—and yet he thinks it all as plain and clear as day! The Jews are the most generous and liberal people on earth, and have the most wonderful food upon their tables, but when they invite you to eat it, they wait until it gets halfway down your throat and you have a look of pleasure on your face, and then they say something cruel and cunning to you in order to make you lose your appetite."

And touched again by the old and worldly humor of her race, she smiled with an ironic expression as she thought: "Lose your appetite! It's just too bad the way you lose *your* appetite! I've been cooking for you three years now, young fellow, and the only time I've ever seen you lose your appetite was when you couldn't lift another forkful to your mouth! Lose his appetite! God! The nerve of that fellow! When I've seen him eat until his eyes were glazed and stuck out of his head, and all he could do for three hours after when I spoke to him was grunt like a pig! Yes! And even when you came to see us all—these horrible people that you say we are— you lost your appetite, didn't you? God, will I ever forget the night he came in when we were at dinner and he said: 'No, not a thing! Not a thing! I just finished a big dinner at the Blue Ribbon and I couldn't touch a bite. . . . Well,' he says, 'I think I will take just a cup of coffee, if you don't mind. I'll drink it while the rest of you are eating.' A cup of *coffee!* It is to laugh! Three heaping plates full of my meat balls, a whole dish of asparagus, a bowl of salad—you cleaned out all that was left in the big salad bowl—you can't deny it—two helpings of Cookie's apple dumplings—and *coffee!* My God, he never thought of coffee till he'd finished! A bottle of Fritz's best St. Julien, that's what you had, my boy, as well you know—'I don't mind if I do take a glass, Fritz' —and one of his best cigars, and two glasses of his oldest brandy! A cup of *coffee!* That was your cup of coffee! God! We all laughed our heads off at what Alma said when he had gone. 'Mother, if that's his notion of a cup of coffee, I'm glad he didn't feel like having a ham sandwich, too.' And even Fritz said, 'Yes, it's lucky for us that he wasn't hungry. I understand the crops are not so good this year as they were last.' We simply roared about that cup of coffee! Not that any of us begrudged it to you! As cruel and unjust as you have been, you can't say that about us. That kind of smallness and meanness is the thing you Christians do."

She looked at him, the trace of an ironic smile upon her lips.

"Your cup of coffee! Oh, don't worry about that, my lad! You'll get your cup of coffee, sure enough! Just wait till you are married to some anemic little Christian girl —she'll get your cup of coffee for you. Christian coffee! Two grains of coffee in a bucketful of stale dish water! That's the kind of coffee that you'll get! Yes! Who'll feed you then? Who'll cook for you?"

She pondered with a faint, bitter smile.

"Some little goy with a hank of yellow hair, the hips of a washboard, and the eyes of a drowned cat. . . . I know now what she'll give you. I can see it! Oxtail soup out of a can with all the ox left out of it, picked-up cod-fish with a gob of that horrible, white, gooey, Christian sauce, a slice of gluten bread, acidophilus milk, and a piece of stale angel cake that the little wench picked up at a bakery on her way home from the movies. 'Come, Georgie, darling! Be a nice boy now. You haven't eaten any of your good boiled spinach, dear. It's good for you, pet, it's full of nice, healthy iron. (Healthy iron, your granny! In three months' time he'll turn green with belly-ache and dyspepsia. . . . You'll think of me every time you take another bite!) No, you bad boy! You can't have any more creamed chipped beef. You've already had meat three times this month, you've had six and three-eighths ounces of meat in the last three weeks, dear, and it's very bad for you. You'll be getting uric acid the first thing you know. If you're a good boy, pet, I'll let you have a nice, burned-up lamb chop week after next. I've got the most delicious menu all fixed up for the next two weeks. I read all about it in Molly Messmore's Food Hints in *The Daily Curse*. Oh, yum! yum! yum! Your mouth will water, all right, when you see what I've prepared for you, dear. (Yes, and if I know anything about him, his eyes will water, too!) Next week is going to be Fish Week, darling. We're going to have nothing but fish, pet, won't that be nice? (Oh, yes! That will be just too nice for words.) Molly says fish is good for you, lamb, the body needs lots of fish, it's Brain Food, pet, and if my big boy is going to use that great big wonderful brain of his and think all those beautiful thoughts, he's got to be a good boy and eat lots of fish like his momma tells him to. Monday, darling, we are going to have imported Hungarian catfish with henhouse noodles, and Tuesday, pet, we are going to have roast Long Island suckers with gastric juice, and Wednesday, love, we are going to have stewed, milkfed bloaters à la Gorgonzola with stinkweed salad, and Thursday, sweet, we are going to have creamed cod with chitling gravy, and Friday—Friday is really Fish Day, lamb, Friday we are going— You bad boy! You take that ugly *fwown* wight off your face! I don't like to see my big boy's beautiful face all *winkled* up by that ugly *fwown*. Open your moufy now, and swallow down this nice big spoonful of stewed prune juice. There! Now doesn't he feel better? It's good for my darling's bow-wels. You'll wake up in the morning feeling wonderful!'"

Proud, somber, darkly flushed, slipping her finger in and out of the ring, she looked at him with a faint, brooding smile and an exultant sense of triumph.

"Oh, you'll think of me! You'll think of me, all right! You think you can forget me, but you can't! If you forget all the rest of it, you'll have to think of me each time you put a bite of Christian food into your mouth!"

"Weave, weave, weave!" she thought. "Weave, you crazy and tormented weaver, until you are caught up and tangled hopelessly in your own web! Use nothing that you have. Go crazy wanting what you haven't got. And what is it that you want? Do you know? Could you say? Have you the glimmer of a notion what it is you want? To be here and not to be here. To be in Vienna, London, Frankfort, and the Austrian Tyrol at the same moment. To be in your room and out in the street at the same time. To live in the city and know a million people, and to live on a mountain top and know only three or four. To have one woman, one house, one horse, one cow, one little piece of earth, one place, one country, and one of everything, and to have a thousand women, to live in a dozen countries, to travel on a hundred ships, to try ten thousand kinds of food and drink, and to live five hundred different lives—all at one and the same time! To look through walls of brick into a million rooms and see the lives of all the people, and to look into my heart, to tear me open, to ask me a million questions, to think about me all the time, to grow mad thinking of me, to imagine a thousand filthy and insane things about me and then to believe them right away, to chew me up and devour me until there's nothing left of me— and then to forget about me. To have a hundred plans and ideas for the work you are going to do, the books and stories you are going to write, to begin a dozen things and to finish nothing. To want to work like a madman and then to sprawl upon your rump and gaze dreamily at the ceiling and wish there was some way that it would all come out of you like ectoplasm, and that the pencil would just walk across the paper by itself and do all that ugly work for you of putting down and working out, of revising, writing, getting stumped, cursing, stamping around and beating its head against the wall, sweating blood and crying, 'Christ! I'm going mad!'—getting tired and desperate, and swearing off forever, and then sitting down to sweat and curse and work like hell again! Oh, wouldn't life be simply glorious if all that part of it could be cut out! Wouldn't it be fine if glory, reputation, love were ready at our beck and call, and if the work we want to do, the satisfaction that we hope to get, would just walk in on us when we wished for it, and go away and leave us when we were tired of it!"

Her eyes flashed with impatience as she looked at him.

"Here he is, lashing about and beating himself to pieces everywhere! Sure of his purpose, and letting himself be taken from it every time the phone rings, every time someone offers him a drink, every time some fool comes knocking at the door! Burning with desire for everything except the thing he has, and tired of anything he has the moment that he has it! Hoping to save himself by getting on a ship and going to another country, to find himself by getting lost, to change himself by changing his address, to get a new life by finding a new sky! Always believing he will find something strange and rich and glorious somewhere else, when all the glory and the richness in the world is here before him, and the only hope he has of finding, doing, saving anything is in himself, and by himself!"

With the hatred which she had for failure, her abhorrence of indecision and confusion, and the almost material value which she set upon success—on a life and talent wisely used, and on a knowledge always guided by a clear design—she clenched and unclenched her fists, trembling in a fury of indomitable determination as she looked at him, thinking:

"God! If I could only give him a part of my power to work and get things done! If I could only set him on the track and keep him there until he does it! If I could only teach him how to collect his strength and use it to some good end, and get the pure gold out of him—yes, the best! the best! for that's the only thing that's good enough!—and not to let it all be wasted, frittered away, and buried below a mass of false and worthless things! If I could only show him how to do it—and, by God!" she thought, doubling her fists together at her sides, "I will!"

VII. The Parting

April passed, and May came on, and there was neither change nor hope of change in Monk. In a thousand darts and flicks and fancies of his swarming brain, his life was buffeted in a mad devil's dance like a bird hurled seaward on the wind, and, ever in his sight, always within his touch, forever to be captured and yet never caught, the ever-shifting visages of that mercurial atom, truth, melted from his furious attempt like images of painted smoke and left him baffled and bewildered, a maddened animal that beat its knuckles bloody against the strong wall of the earth.

Sometimes a memory, an evocation of classic purities, swept calmly through his mind and left it for a moment untainted and undistressed. And then he longed no more for rich Cockaigne, for amorous flesh and lips empurpled with ripe grapes, but for even and eternal skies, a parapet of untortured stone, and calm eyes that looked out upon an untumultuous and unchanging sea that feathered with remote and punctual sighings on the rocks. There time went by on unrelenting beat; the even sky hung tragically above the heads of men who thought of living but who calmly knew that they must die. The grief of time, the sorrowful hauntings of brief days, rested upon them, and they never wept. They lived their lives out like the seasons, giving to each its due:

To spring, all of the leaping and the dancing, the flashing of young forms in silver pools, the hunt, the capture, and the race.

To summer, battle, the swift thud of mighty flesh, victory without pity or injustice, defeat with resignation.

Then to October they brought all their grain of wisdom, their ripe deliberation. Their calm eyes saw a few things that endured—the sea, the mountain, and the sky—and they walked together, talking with grave gestures of the fate of man. Their feast was truth and beauty, and they lay together on unyielding mats, tasting the wine, the olive, and a crust of bread.

When December came, without lamentings in the room, but by the wall and quietly, they turned their grey heads tranquilly below their robes, and died.

Was this, then, the answer? He shook his head and wiped the image from his eyes. No, no. There was no answer. If such men had lived, they had been touched by all our woes, by all the madness, grief, and fury flesh can know. Torture and maddening of the brain were theirs as well as ours, and through all time, through the brief tickings of all human lives, the river flowed, dark, unceasing, and inscrutable.

And now the worm was feeding at his life again, a knife was driven through his heart and twisted there, and suddenly he went blank and empty and his flesh turned rotten.

So it was that Esther found him when she came that day at noon.

He sat upon his cot in sullen, sodden, leaden apathy and would not rouse to talk to her. And when she saw him so, she thought to draw him out by telling in her bright and jolly way about a play that she had seen the night before. She told him all about it, who the actors

were, and how they did, and how the audience responded, and as she brought to instant life the scene
there in the theater, she burst forth in her jaunty way
and said how fine, how grand, how swell it was.

These simple-seeming words from her sophisticated
mouth now goaded Monk into a sudden fury.

"Oh, *fine!* Oh, *grand!* Oh, *swell!*" he snarled, with
savage parody. "God! You people make me sick! The
way you talk!" and lapsed again into a moody silence.

Esther had been pacing lightly round the room, but
now she spun about and faced him, her rosy cheeks
turned crimson with a sudden anger.

"You people! You people!" she cried, in a high, excited voice. "In heaven's name, what is it now? What
people are you talking about? I'm no people! I'm no
people!" she said with a stammering resentment. "I don't
know who you're talking about!"

"Oh, yes you do!" he muttered sullenly and wearily.
"The whole damned lot of you! You're all alike! You're
one of them!"

"One of whom?" said Esther furiously. "I'm one of
nobody—I'm myself, that's who I am! There's no sense
to anything you say any more! You hate the whole
world and you curse and revile everybody! You don't
know what you're saying half the time! You people!
You're always calling me 'you people,'" she said bitterly, "when you don't know what people you're talking
about!"

"Oh, yes I do!" he said gloomily. "The whole damned
lot of you—that's who!"

"Of whom? Of whom?" she cried, with an agonized,
exasperated laugh. "God! You just keep muttering the
same thing over and over, and it makes no sense!"

"The whole damned crowd of million-dollar Jew and
Gentile aesthetes—that's who I mean! With your

twaddle about 'Have you seen this?' and 'Have you read that?'—with your bilge about books and plays and pictures, moaning about art and beauty and how it is the thing you all are living for, when none of you care a good God-damn for anything but keeping in the swim! Ah, you make me sick!—the whole damned crowd of you, with your jokes about the fairies and the lesbians, and your books and plays and nigger carvings!" he said with choking incoherence. "Yes. You know a lot about it, don't you? When you've got to read the magazines to see what you should like—and you'll go back on your word, you'll change your mind, you'll betray a thing you said was good in thirty seconds, if you find your dirty crowd's against you! . . . The friends and patrons of the arts!" he said with an infuriated yell of unsure laughter. "Jesus God! That it should come to this!"

"Oh, that it should come to this! That it should come to what? You poor fool, you're raving like a crazy man."

"That the good man—the real artist—the true poet—should be done to death——"

"Oh, done to death, my eye!"

"—by the malice and venom of these million-dollar apes and bastards of the arts and their erotic wives! 'Oh, how we do love art!'" he sneered. "'I'm so much interested in the work you're doing! I know you have so much to offer—and we *ne-e-d* you so-o,'" he whispered, almost speechlessly, "'and won't you co-o-me to tea on Thursday? I'm all al-o-o-ne—' . . . The bitches! The dirty bitches!" he bellowed suddenly like a maddened bull, and then, reverting to a tone of whining and seductive invitation, "'—and we can have a *nice*, long talk together! I so much want to talk to you! I feel you have so much to gi-i-ve me.' Ah, the filthy swine! And you, you, *you!*" he gasped. "That's *your crowd!* And is that your game, too?" His voice threaded away to a whisper of exhausted hatred, and his breath labored heavily in the silence.

She made no answer for a moment. She looked at him quietly, sorrowfully, shaking her head slightly in a movement of scorn and pity.

"Listen!" she said at length. He turned sullenly away from her, but she seized him by the arm, pulled him back to her, and spoke to him sharply in a commanding tone. "Listen, you poor fool! I'm going to tell you something! I'm going to tell you now what's wrong with you! You curse and revile everybody and you think that everyone is down on you and wants to do you harm. You think that everyone is against you and is staying awake at night thinking how to get the best of you. You think everyone is plotting how to keep you down. Well, let me tell you something," she said quietly. "This thing which you have made up in your mind does not exist. This is a monster of your own creating. George, look at me!" she spoke sharply to him. "I am a truthful person, no matter what you say, and I swear to you that this ugly thing has no existence anywhere except in your own mind. These people that you curse and rail at have never hated you and do not wish to do you any injury."

"Oh," he said with savage sarcasm, "I suppose then that they love me! I suppose they spend their time in planning how they can do me good!"

"No," she said. "They neither love nor hate you. Most of them have never heard of you. They wish to do you neither harm nor good. They never think of you." She paused, looking sadly at him for a moment. Then she said: "But I can tell you this—even if they knew you, it would not be the way you think it is. People are not that way at all. For God's sake," she cried with strong feeling, "don't blacken your mind and warp your life with all these vile and ugly thoughts that are not so!

Try to have a little faith and wisdom when you think of people! They are not the way you think they are! No one wants to do you any harm!"

He stared at her stupidly and sullenly for a moment. The madness had flared out of him again and now he looked at her wearily with the old sense of shame and foul disgust.

"I know they're not," he said dully. "I know what they are like. I curse at them because I know I am no good. . . . Oh, I can't tell you!" he said with a sudden, desperate, and baffled movement, "I can't tell you what it is! It's not the way you think it is, either. I don't hate everyone the way you think—in spite of all I say. I hate no one but myself. Esther, in God's name, what's gone wrong with me? What's the matter with my life? I used to have the strength of twenty people. I loved life and had the power and courage to do anything. I worked and read and traveled with the energy of a great dynamo. I wanted to eat the earth, and feed myself with all the books and men and countries in the world. I wanted to know about the lives of all the people, to be everywhere, to see and know everything like a great poet, and I walked and roamed about the streets feeding on everything that the people did or said with a furious hunger that was never satisfied. Everything sang out for me with glory and with triumph, and I was sure I had the power and talent to do everything I wanted. I wanted fame and love and glory, and I was sure that I could get them. And I wanted to do fine work, to make my life prevail, and to grow and come to good and strengthen in my work forever. I wanted to be a great man. Why should I be ashamed to say I wanted to be a great man, and not a little, ugly, sterile fellow? . . . And now all that has gone. I hate my life and everything I see around me. Good God! if I had lived my life—if I were old and worn-out and had never got anything from life I wanted, I could see the reason for it!" he burst out furiously. "But I'm only twenty-seven—and I'm worn-out already! By God! an old and worn-out old man at twenty-seven!" he yelled, and began to beat his fist into the wall.

"Oh, worn-out! Worn-out, my eye!" she said with a short and angry laugh. "You act as if you're worn-out! You've worn me out, you mean. You wear out everybody else the way you lash around. You wear yourself out beating your head against a wall! But—worn-out! You're worn-out about the same way that the Hudson River is."

"Oh—don't—for God's sake—don't!" he said in a choked and furious tone, sticking his arm out in a movement of baffled, exasperated impatience. "Don't give me any more of that soft soap. Listen! I'm telling you the truth! It's not the same with me as it used to be. I've lost the hope and confidence I had. I haven't the same energy and strength I had. God-damn it, woman, don't you understand?" he said furiously. "Haven't you seen it for yourself? Don't you understand I've lost my squeal?" he shouted, beating himself upon the breast and glaring at her with an insane fury. "Don't you know it's been six months since I made my squeal?"

As absurd and comical as these last words were, as incredible as they might have sounded to a hidden listener, neither of them laughed. Instead, they stood, earnest, combative, and passionately serious, opposing hot, excited faces to each other. She understood him.

This "squeal" to which he had referred, and which, curiously, in the midst of all the tortured madness and dark fury of these recent months had seemed a thing of moment to him, was simply a cry of animal exuberance. Since his earliest childhood this tongueless expletive had risen in him in a surge of swelling joy, had collected in his throat and then been torn from his lips in a wild goat-cry of pain and joy and ecstasy.

Sometimes it came in some moment of triumph or achievement, and sometimes it came for no tangible reason, and from inscrutable and nameless sources. He had known it ten thousand times in childhood, and it had come to him upon the lights and hues of a million evanescent things; and the whole intolerable good and glory of the immortal earth, the whole intolerable sense of pain and joy, the whole intolerable knowledge of man's briefness on the earth, had been packed, though in what way he did not know, and in what words he could not say, into each moment that the great cry came.

Sometimes it had come simply in a brief and incommunicable moment—in the sultry and exultant odors of ground coffee, or in the smell of frying steaks across the neighborhood in the first frosty evenings of October. Sometimes it was in the full, thick swells of the rivers after heavy rain, with their alluvial glut; or in the swell of melons bedded in the sweet, ripe hay of country wagons; it was in the odors of hot tar and oil upon the heated pavements of a street in summer.

Again, it was in all the spicy odors of the old-time grocery stores—and suddenly he remembered a forgotten moment in his childhood when he had stood in such a store and seen a summer storm collect into black-crested clouds of inky and empurpled light, and then watched for ten minutes the deluge of torrential rain as it had sluiced and spurted on the old, dejected head, the gaunt, grey buttocks, and the steaming flanks of the grocery horse, hitched to the wagon, haltered to a paving block, and waiting at the curb with dolorous patience.

This obscure and forgotten moment returned to him again with all the old and inscrutable exulting the scene had brought to him. And he remembered as well all things and persons in the store—the aproned clerks, with cuffs of straw and armbands catching up their sleeves, with pencils behind their ears and a straight part in the middle of their hair, the ingratiating unction of their tone and manner as they took the orders of reflective housewives, as well as all the rich and spicy odors that rose upward from great bins and barrels in the store. He remembered the smell of pickles brined in Atlantean casks, and the mellow, grainy odors of the floors and counter plankings which seemed to have been seasoned in all the spicy savors of a dozen years.

There were the smells of rich and bitter chocolate and of tea; of new, ground coffee pouring from the mill; of butter, lard, and honey, and sliced bacon; of smoked ham, and yellow cheese, cut in thick wedges from a ponderous chunk; as well as all the earthy smells of fresh garden vegetables and orchard fruits—of crisp, podded peas, tomatoes, and string beans, of fresh corn and new potatoes, and of apples, peaches, plums, and the solid plunk and promise, the strange, sultry thrill of big green watermelons.

And this whole scene that day—sights, sounds, and odors, sultry air and inky light and spurting and torrential rain sweeping in gusty sheets along the gleaming and deserted pavements, as well as the steaming flanks of the old grey grocery horse, and a lovely young woman, newly wed, biting her tender lips with a delicious incertitude as she gave her orders to the clerk who waited prayerfully before her—had awakened in his young boy's heart a powerful sensation of joy, abundance, and proud, welling triumph, a sensation of personal victory and fulfillment that was overwhelming, though in what way, by what coherent and connecting agency, he did not know.

But most often, more obscurely, from more hidden sources of immense and fathomless exulting the great cry had been torn from him as a child in moments when the picture of abundance was not so clearly painted and where the connecting influences, the limitless evocations of triumph and fulfillment, were not apparent or articulate, but in which the full conviction of his joy had been as strong as when the picture was complete and definite.

Sometimes the cry was packed into the passing of a cloud upon the massed green of a hill, and sometimes, with the most intolerable ecstasy that he had ever known, it was in the green light of the woods, the lyric tangle of the wilderness, the cool, bare spaces underneath a canopy of trees, and the gold spangles of the sun that swarmed with a strange, enchanted light in the magic sorcery of cool, depthless green. There would be a dip, a slope, a glade in all this magic, a spring cupped in a cushion of green moss, the great bole of a rotted oak across the path, and over there was the crystal clarity of forest water falling over rock and in the pool a woman with bare legs and swelling thighs and kilted skirts, and all about her the strange lights of magic gold and depthless green, the rock, the fern, the springy carpet of the forest earth, and all the countless voices of high afternoon that, with dart and sudden thrum, or stitch and call or furious drummings in the wood, passed all about her to uncounted deaths and were lost and came again.

And the cry had come upon the faint and broken ringing of a bell in afternoon, over the dusky warmth of meadows, and the strong, hot fragrance of the clove, and upon the raining of the acorns to the earth at night, and on the high and distant roaring of the wind in autumn. It was in the strong, free shout of children playing in the streets at dusk, and in quiet voices at the summer's end, and in a woman's voice and laughter in the street at night, and in the tugging of a leaf upon a bough.

In frost and starlight and far-broken sounds at night, in living leaves, in sudden rain, and in the menace of impending snow, and in the soft, numb spitting of the snow against the window glass. In first light, dawn, and circuses, the dance and swing of lanterns in the dark, the green, winking lights of semaphores, and the sounds of shifting engines, the crash and jar of freight cars in the dark, the shouts and oaths of circus men, the rhythm of the driven stake, the smells of canvas, sawdust, and strong boiling coffee, and the lion reek, the black and yellow of the tigers, strong, tawny camel smells, and all strange sounds and sights and odors that they brought to little towns.

And in the solemn joy of quiet fields from which the heat and fury of the day had passed, and in the great body of the earth collecting into coolness and to night, respiring quietly in the last light of the day. In hoof and wheel that broke the silence of a street at dawn, and in the birdsong breaking into light, and in the hard and cloven trot of cattle coming from the fields into the road at dusk, and the late red sun that faded without violence or heat across hill pastures to the wood; in evening and stillness on the land, and the sharp thought and ache and joy of distant towns.

The wild cry had risen to his lips with all these things and with all movements of arrival and departure, with the thought of new lands, cities, ships, and women; with wheel and flange and rail that bent across the earth like space and a triumphant music, with men and voyages, and the immortal sound of time that murmured constantly about the walls of mighty stations; and with the rush, the glare, the pistoned drive, the might and power of the locomotive, and with great flares and steamings that passed instantly upon the rails at night. It was in the acrid dinginess of enormous station platforms thick with the smoke of forty trains, and it was in the hot green snore of pullman cars at night, in the heart of the youth who listened from his berth exultantly to the slow stir and velvet rustle of a woman as she languorously stretched her thighs in darkness, and as he saw the immense dark structure of the earth wheel calmly past his vision with an even stroke, and heard more strange and more familiar than a dream, in silence and the pauses of the night, the voices of unknown men upon a little platform in Virginia.

The cry had risen from all thoughts that he had had of voyages and distances, of the immense and lonely earth, and of great rivers that from the depths of midnight and lost sources in the hills drew slowly with mined and secret droppings of the earth in darkness their alluvial glut across the continent, and in his thoughts of the lonely, dark, encrusted earth, and of America at night with dark corn steady in the night and the cool rustling of the blades. It was in his thought of all the rivers, mountains, plains, and deserts, and in his thought of all the little sleeping towns across the continent, of great flares flashing on the rails and briefly on great fields of wheat, and of all his dreams and visions of women in the West who stood at evening in the doors and looked with quiet eyes into green, depthless fields of corn or golden wheat or straight into the blazing hues of desert suns.

Thus, in this whole picture of the earth, which, in many years long past and furiously accomplished, and in the constant travail of his mind and heart had been

continued, not only out of all that he had seen and
known and remembered, but also out of all that his
hunger and desire had drawn from the earth which it
had never seen, the wild goat-cry of joy and triumph
had its life. It had been in his whole design and pattern
of the earth which had grown so complete and radiant in
his mind that sometimes in the night he thought he saw
it all stretched out upon the canvas of his vision—hills,
mountains, plains, and deserts, fields printed in the
moonlight and great sleeping woods, as well as all its
groaning weight of towns and cities. It was in his vision
of immense, mysterious rivers flowing in the dark, and
in the eighteen thousand miles of coast at which the
sea forever was working in the moon's light wink, with
glut and coil, with hissing surge, with lapse and reluc-
ation of its breath, feathering eternally at the million
pockets of the land.

And the cry was torn from his thoughts of tropic darkness and the jungles of the night, and all things dark
and evil and unknown; it rose with demoniac joy out of
the sleeping wildness, and from lush, jungle depths
where the snake's cold eye lay bedded on a bank of
fern; it was torn also from his vision of strange, tropic
plants on which the tarantula, the adder, and the asp
had fed themselves asleep on their own poisons, and
where, green-golden, gloosy blue, and bitter red, the
tufted parrakeets awoke the dark with their proud,
brainless scream.

And the cry had come, most fiercely and with the
wildest joy when it was torn from the heart of darkness
and the fields of sleep. In many a silent night, and from
the prison of a city room, his spirit had swept out across
the fields of sleep and he had heard the heartbeats of ten
million men around him, and the wild and wordless cry
was torn from him. From those dark tides and waters of

men's sleep on which a few stars sparely looked, the cry
had called to all great fish that swam in night's dark
glades and waters; and to all blind crawls and sucks and
grope-things of the brain, to all subtlest, unseen stirs
all half-heard, half-articulated whisperings, all things
that swam or stirred or crawled within the fields of sleep
to all the forested and far, it had sent forth its cry of
triumph and return.

And finally, in the city streets and at a thousand times
this tongueless expletive of passion and of triumph had
been torn from his throat. Sometimes it came with all
the warm, hot odors of the pavements in late spring
and the spermy fragrance of the earth that seemed to
burst in waves of rich fecundity through all the steel
and stone; and it came with savage joy out of the
sorcery of April, the magic of first green in city streets
the pageantry of glorious women who seemed them
selves to have burst out of the earth overnight and to be
blooming in the streets one day like splendid flowers.

It had come to him when he had smelled the sea
wrack of the harbor, the clean, salt fragrance of the
tides, and it was in cool, flowing tides of evening water
and in deserted piers and in the sliding lights of little
tugs. And it had risen to his lips when he had heard the
great ships blowing in the gulf of night, or heard exult
antly the shattering *baugh* of their departure as they
slid into line and pointed for the sea at noon on Saturday
And it had come to him each time he saw the proud
white breasts of mighty ships, the racing slant and drive
of the departing liners, and watched them dwindle and
converge into their shape away from piers, black with
crowds of cheering people.

So had it come to him ten thousand times, and in ten
thousand places, this wild goat-cry of tongueless tri

umph, pain, and ecstasy. And in it was the memory of all things far and fleeting and forever lost, which had gone the moment he had seen them, and which, with a heart of fire and an intolerable wild regret, he had wished to hold and fix forever in his life. In other springs it had risen to the mighty pulsations of energy and joy which swept above all the city's million-footed life, in the winglike sweep and soar of the great bridges, and in all the thousand potent smells of wharves and markets. But now, this cruel spring, he had ranged the city furiously, had felt as keenly and as piercingly as ever the sorcery and the magic of its vernal tides—and yet no single thing had torn the goat-cry from his lips.

And now that he no longer felt the impulse of this savage and uncontrollable cry, it really seemed to him that he had lost out of his life and spirit something precious and incalculable. For he had always known that it was something more than the animal vitality of a boy.

For the cry had come from no fictitious imagery, no dream or romance of his fancy, no false hallucination of desire. The cry had welled up from the earth with a relentless certitude, and all the gold and glory of the earth was in it. It had been for him a kind of touchstone to reality, for it had never played him false. It had always come as a response to an actual and indubitable glory, and to a reality as tangible as minted gold. Knowledge, power, and truth had been in that wild cry. It had united him to the whole family of the earth, for he had always known that men in every age and history had felt the same wild cry of triumph, pain, and passion on their lips, and that it had come to them from the same movements, seasons, and unchanging certitudes of joy as it had come to him.

This was the true gold of the earth, and now he felt,

with a sense of his own ruin and defeat, that he had lost
something priceless, irrecoverable, forever.

"And you know it, don't you?" he said bitterly. "You
admit it. You know yourself that I have lost it, don't
you?"

"Oh, you've lost nothing," she said quietly. "Listen
to me! You haven't lost your energy or strength. You'll
see you've got it just as much as you ever had. You
haven't lost your joy or interest in life. You've only lost
something that didn't matter, anyway."

"That's what *you* say," he muttered sullenly. "That's
all *you* know about it."

"Listen to me! I know all about it. I know exactly
what you've lost. You've lost a way you had of letting off
steam. And that has happened to us all. Good heavens!
We can't be twenty-one forever!" she said angrily. "But
you'll see that you've lost nothing valuable or essential.
You've got all the strength and power you always had.
Yes—and more! For you'll learn to use it better. You'll
keep getting stronger all the time. George, I swear to
you that this is so! That's the way it was with me, and
it will be the same with you."

She paused, flushed and frowning for a moment.

"Lost your squeal!" she muttered. "God! How you
talk!" Her lip curled slightly and for a moment her
voice was touched with the cynical humor of old Jewish
scorn. "Don't you worry about losing your squeal," she
said quietly. "You worry about getting a little sense into
your head—that's what you need, young fellow, a great
deal more than any squeal you had. . . . Lost his
squeal!" she muttered over again.

For a moment more she surveyed him with a serious
and angry frown, snapping the ring on and off her finger with a rapid movement of her hand. Then her
expression softened, her warm throat trembled, her jolly

face began to bloom with new flowers of red, and suddenly she burst into a rich, choking, woman's laugh:

"Lost your squeal! God, but you're wonderful! Would anyone ever believe the things you say!"

He stared at her sullenly for a moment, and then, wildly and suddenly, he laughed, smiting himself upon the forehead with the heel of his palm and crying, "Haw!"

Then, scowling gloomily, he turned to her and muttered obscurely and incoherently, as if someone else had been guilty of an offense which he would pass over with a kind of disgusted charity:

"I know! I know! Don't say anything about it," and he turned away and began to stare moodily out of the window.

During all this cruel month of May, below pain, below his moods of sodden, dull despair, below the close-spun, thick-wrought fabric of their life together, below all the intense and shifting weathers of their hearts in which at times, for fleeting intervals, their love flared up as warm and tender as it had ever done, an ugly, grim, and desperate struggle was being waged between them.

Day by day, the stubborn, brutal fight went on—the man snarling, raging about among his walls like an infuriated animal, hurling foul curses, taunts, and accusations at her, the woman weeping, sobbing, screaming denials, and finally departing tragically, her face swollen by tears, saying that the end had come, that she was telling him good-by forever, and that she would never see him again.

And yet, within two hours, she would call him on the telephone again, or a messenger would appear bearing a telegram or a brief, swiftly worded letter, which he would rip open instantly and read rigidly, with a livid and contorted face and trembling fingers, his features twisted with a sneer of cursing disbelief as he snarled mockery at his own folly, and his heart stabbed fiercely against his will with wild pity and regret by these swift simple words that cried with truth, honesty, and passion and winged their way straight and sure between his armor.

And then, next day, she would be there at his side once more, her small, sad face serious and resolved, fixed in a solemn look of final renunciation. Sometimes she said she had come for one last word of parting and farewell, in friendship; and sometimes she said she had come to gather materials and belongings which she needed for her work. But she was always there, as certain as a destiny, and he now began to comprehend what he had never been able to understand before, what he could never have believed possible in his earlier youth—that, packed into this delicate figure, behind this flowerlike and rose-lipped face, were stored the energies of an indomitable will, that this exquisite and lovely little creature who could weep bitterly, renounce sorrowfully, and day by day depart tragically and for ever, was beyond comparison the most determined, resolute, and formidable antagonist he had ever known.

"All right!" she would say fatally, with an air of somber and tragic consent at the end of one of these brutal scenes of the will. "All right! Leave me if you like. You've thrown me over. You've gone back on me. You've deserted the best friend you ever had." And then, shrugging her shoulders in a little gesture of bitter acquiescence, and speaking in a sing-song voice: "You've done for me! I'm dead! You've killed me!"

"Haw, haw! Whee! Fine! Go on!" He laughed crazily, applauding with his hands. "Give us some more of it! Tomorrow night, *East Lynn!*"

"She's dead! She's done for!" she continued in the
same brooding and fatal monotone. "Your darling's dead!
She loved you and you killed her! Your Jew's dead! No
more! No more!" She smiled a bitter, puckered, turned-
down smile and made again the motion of tragic content. "It's all over. Finished. Done for. . . . You'll be
sorry!" she cried, with a sudden change in tone and
manner.

He staggered about the room, smiting his forehead
savagely with his clenched fist, and reeling with wild,
infuriated laughter:

"*Camille*, by God!" he shouted. "That's right! Cry!
Weep! Yell out so everyone can hear it! Fine! Great! I
love it! It's music to my ears!"

"You'll get no rest!" she cried out in a warning tone.
I'll haunt you. You think you can forget me, but you
can't. I'll come back from the grave to haunt you. You'll
see! You'll see! I'll bring Azrael and Beelzebub back to
haunt you—yes! I'll bring the spirits of great rabbis back
who know the cabala! Oh, you'll get no rest! I'll bring the
spirits of my people back to haunt you! I'll bring the
spirits of my Christian blood back to haunt you, too!
. . . God!" she cried suddenly, with a scornful humor,
I'll bet that they're a trashy, lifeless lot of ghosts compared to all the Jews—like these little anemic Christian
wenches that you go with!" She paused, her small face
was knotted suddenly with a surge of jealous fury, tears
spurted from her eyes, she doubled her fists, drew them
up to her sides, and held them tightly clenched for a
moment, trembling rigidly with speechless rage.

"Don't you bring any more of them up here!" she
said in a small, choked, trembling voice.

"Oh, so that's it, is it?" he said heavily, with an ugly,
grating sneer. "That's where the shoe pinches, is it?
That's what galls her, eh?" He made a sudden gesture

of brutal contempt. "To hell with you!" he said coarsely "I'll do as I damn well please—and you can't stop me!"

"You'll not bring any more of those girls up here!" she cried, in a high, shaking voice. "This is our place. This place is mine as well as yours. You'll not bring them to my place!" She turned away to hide her tears, biting her trembling lip, and in a moment she said in a tone of bitter reproach, "What would you think if I carried on that way with men? I never have, but if I really did it how would you feel? God, you couldn't stand it! You'd go crazy!"

Then he cursed and stormed and thought up new accusations to fling at her, bitter, groundless, and unreasoning, and she wept, denied, assailed him as before And in the end he beat her down till there was no more resistance left in her, and she said with a bitter smile making a slight gesture of acquiescence with her shoulders:

"All right! Go with your little pick-ups! Do as you please! I'm through!"

And then she left him, saying once more as she had said a dozen times, that he would never see her face again.

He was determined now, by some single and brutal violence, to wrench their lives asunder in a final act of parting, and thus, he hoped, to free himself from the sense of ruin, desolation, and loss unutterable which had possessed and conquered him, and of which he had grown desperately afraid. And the woman was determined that he should not leave her.

But after May slid into June there came a desperate day on which at last Monk forced the issue. He told her he was through with her forever, their life was finished he wanted to forget her utterly, to tear and strip her very memory from his blood, his brain, his heart, and go away somewhere, away from this accursed city, where he could gather up the shattered fragments of his life and build it back anew to a single integrity of purpose and design. He'd go to Europe—that's what he'd do!—put a wide ocean there between them, and let its raging waters wash away the last remaining vestiges of all their life together, and it would then be just as though the two of them had never met and loved and lived and cursed and fought!

In the white-hot fury of his resolve, he gathered up his books, his clothes, and everything he owned, flung them together, and stormed out of the house, knowing as he stepped upon the pavement that he never would again set foot across that threshold.

VIII. Esther's Farewell

It was the end of the academic year at the School for Utility Cultures, so there was nothing to keep Monk in New York. He wanted desperately to get away, and, hating the thought of cutting short his trip abroad at the end of the summer, he obtained a leave of absence for the fall term. Then, with a lighter heart than he had known in many months, he booked his passage for Southampton.

When he went aboard the boat at midnight, he found a letter from Esther waiting for him. As the purser handed it to him and he saw her handwriting on the envelope, he cursed beneath his breath, and was angry with himself because at sight of it his heart had pounded furiously with joy and hope in spite of all his high resolve.

"God-damn it!" he muttered. "Can't she let me go in

peace?"—and clutched the letter in his trembling hand as he went to find his room where he could be alone to read it.

He ripped it open nervously, and this is what he read:

MY DEAR,

The boat will not sail until dawn, but I hope you will get this when you go aboard so you can read it before you go to bed.

I thought for a moment of going to the boat to see you off, but then I decided not to. It would have been too much. It's a good thing you're going away now—I don't think I could have stood it another week. This spring has been the worst time I've ever gone through. It has been worse than hell—I never knew there was any torture like it. My heart feels all sore and bloody as if it had a sword stuck through it. I cried all last night, and I have cried for the last hour and a half—I thought there were no more tears in me, but they keep coming. I never used to cry, and now it seems since I met you I cry all the time. You say I only talk like this to torture you, but I am only telling the truth—I have never wanted to torture you. I have only wanted to love you and do what's good for you.

I am worn-out and heart-broken. Once I thought I was so strong I could do anything—but this thing has beaten me. Last night I did something I haven't done since I was a little child—I got down and prayed to God, if there is a God, to do something to help me. But I know there is no God. You have taken the finest thing you ever had and thrown it away. I have always told you the truth about myself—I have been good and faithful and true to you ever since I first met you, and you haven't got sense enough to see it. Some day you may know what I'm really like, but then it will be too late. There is no wrong or evil in me—it is all in your dark and terrible mind. You think a thing, and then immediately you make it so.

For God's sake, don't let yourself go on like this. Don't throw away the great thing that is in you. Don't let your great mind, your great talent, go to pieces because of these other things inside you that tear you apart. I love you, I believe in your genius, I always shall—no matter what anyone says. ["No matter what anyone says, eh? Oh, the evil-hearted and malignant swine! So that's what they're saying to her! That's it! Their envy and ratlike jealousy squalling with triumph now because they think they have finally done me to death. Meanwhile, what have *you* been doing? Talking up for me, eh? Defending me, eh? Saying how good and fine I am, and that they don't know me. For what? To satisfy your hunger and martyrdom, to appear grand and noble and forgiving, to show how great and good and noble you are, and how mean and low and unworthy I am! I know you!" With livid and contorted face he smoothed out the letter he had crumpled in his trembling fingers, and went on.]

No matter what has happened, no matter what has passed between us, I love you now, with all my heart and soul, and I always shall. No one will ever touch me again. I shall go to my grave with you in my heart. I know you will sneer when you read this, and have evil thoughts about me, but I have told you the truth and nothing else. You have caused me the greatest pain of anyone I have ever known, but you have also given me the greatest joy and happiness. No matter what dark and terrible thoughts are in your mind, you have the rarest and grandest quality of anyone I have ever known. You have made a great music in me. I can't imagine now what life would have been like if I had never known you.

I get so worried thinking about you and wondering what you are doing. Promise me that you won't drink too much. Alcohol seems to have a bad effect on you—instead of making you happy and cheerful it gets you so depressed, and sometimes you get into one of your crazy fits. You simply can't afford to waste the precious thing that is in you.

And please, please, don't go around having trouble with other people. I know I'll get nervous wondering what new scrapes you've got into. For heaven's sake, have a little sense about things. No one's laughing at you—no one's trying to insult you—no one hates you and wants to injure you. These things exist only in your imagination. You have absolutely no idea what effect you have on other people—you do not look like anyone else on earth, and when they stare at you in a restaurant that does not mean they are laughing at you. Please try to be gentle and kind to people—you can do anything you like with them when you are lovely—instead of hating you, they adore you, and will do anything you want them to.

Todd has promised me she'll go around to Waverly Place and put the room in order. I have told her what to do with my paints and drawing materials—I could not bear to go back there if you were not there, and if you do not come back, I shall never go there again.

I wonder if you'll ever miss me, and think about your little Esther. I'm sure of one thing—you'll never again find a cook like her. She knew what her George liked best. Maybe when you've had to eat Christian food again you'll want me back. I can see your sensitive nose now turning up in disgust at the smell of it. When they give you what they call a salad—a leaf of wilted lettuce on a plate with three drops of vinegar on it—just remember the salads I used to make for you. ["By God, and she's right, too," he thought with a tortured grin. "I'll never taste food like that again."]

I hope you are feeling better and are going to bed at night. Don't drink so much coffee—you drank gallons at a time this year. I think that's one reason you got so nervous. You need a rest, too. Getting the book done was a tremendous job and enough to wear anyone out.

Now please, dear, don't get mad at me for what I'm going to say—I know how excited and angry you get when anyone talks to you about the book. But don't lose heart because one publisher has turned it down—you get mad at me when I talk about it, but I am sure someone will take it yet. After all, it is a big piece of work, and some people might be afraid to publish it. Miss Scudder told me it was about five times as long as the average novel, and would have to be cut. Perhaps when you write the next one you can make it shorter. ["I might have expected this!" he muttered, grinding his teeth. "She has given up hope for this one already. I can see that. That's what she means by this talk about the next one! Well, there'll be no next one. No more, no more! Let the rats die now in their own venom!"]

Now please be patient with me, dear—I am sure you can do something with this one if you will only make a few concessions. I was talking again to Seamus Malone the other night. He said that parts of the book were "simply magnificent!" ["God, what a lie!" he thought. "What he probably said was 'Not bad,' or 'Rather interesting,' delivered in a tone of impatience or heavy indifference, as if to say, 'Oh, what the hell!'"] But he said it was much too long and would have to be cut. ["They can go to hell before I will!"] It would have to be published in two big volumes as it stands, and you know, dear, that's not possible. ["It's not, eh? And why? They've been printing Proust for the last five years, book by book. And whether it's two or four volumes, whose business is it but my own? They'll read it, they will, damn them, as I wrote it, if I have to cram it down their lofty throats!"]

I keep telling myself it's all over between us. You have thrown me over—left me flat. But when I think of you going with those common women you always pick up anywhere, I go crazy. [He smiled with bitter joy, then with heavy, scowling face read on.]

You would not tell me what you meant to do, and I don't know where to reach you. I'll try American Express in London, and will keep on writing you although I don't know if you will ever answer me. Will you be coming home later this summer? And if you do come, would you like to see me? If you aren't coming back that soon, and you really cared to see me, I could come to you in August. I think of all the beautiful places we could see together, and my heart aches at the thought of your going to Munich and Vienna without me. ["So! You dare to suggest that! You would come to me, would you? By God, they can wind my guts around a drum before you will!"] But I don't suppose you'd want me to, would you?

I don't know what I'm saying. I'm half crazy with this thing. For God's sake, do something to help me. I am sinking, drowning—please, please put out your hand. Save me. I love you. I am yours till death.

God bless you.

ESTHER

For several minutes he sat there, silent, tense, and still, the last page of her letter open in his hand. Then slowly, with set jaw, he put the pages all together, folded them with great deliberation, slowly tore them once across, and then again, and slowly rose, walked to the open porthole and thrust his hand through, and let the fragments of the letter slowly sift between his fingers into darkness and the river.

You Can't Go Home Again

THE QUEST OF THE
FAIR MEDUSA

Editor's Preface

IN A WAY, says Wolfe, the phrase summed up everything George Webber had ever learned.

"You can't go back home to your family, back home to your childhood, back home to romantic love, back home to a young man's dreams of glory and of fame." Nor back home, as he says, to the father you have lost, to someone who can help you and save you; nor back home to the old forms and systems of things which once seemed everlasting but which are changing all the time; nor back home to the escapes of time and memory—to that dark ancestral cave, the womb from which mankind emerged and which forever pulls one back.

Just as *The Web and the Rock* marked Webber's renunciation of the city and of romantic love, here he gives up the last treasured illusion of his youth: artistic success and fame. In two memorable episodes—Piggy Logan's "Circus" and the Fire on Park Avenue—*You Can't Go Home Again* also traces the end of Mrs. Jack's world. And it is here that Webber watches the finale of his childhood home, too. For Libya Hill—the Altamont of the later novels—has been caught up equally in the boom and the bust: the grass roots have turned sour.

So Brooklyn is all that Webber has: the Brooklyn of Mr. Marple, Frenchy and C. Green himself—the Brooklyn of "Sunday in duh mont' of March"—of the "aliens" and the "mob"—of the poor and the anonymous—and also the Brooklyn of Wolfe's American Promise and even, before his last illness, his salute to Death itself. "To lose the earth you know, for greater knowing; to lose the life you have, for greater life; to leave the friends you loved, for greater loving; to find a land more kind than home, more large than earth—"

It is probable that Wolfe, if he had lived, would have revised *You Can't Go Home Again.* Some of the episodes are loose; the writing is uneven. Yet the sections I have mentioned and others—those on Lloyd McHarg, Randy Shepperton and Mr. Jack at Morn—are brilliant examples of social satire. In terms of vitality and warmth probably nothing better has been done in current writing; at the moment nothing like this is even being attempted.

The selection that is printed here is from Book IV of *You Cant Go Home Again.* It is the opening section of George Webber's Brooklyn experiences. I have again included Wolfe's summary of the story to this point, and also the final "statement of belief" which closes the volume and the series.

YOU CAN'T GO HOME AGAIN

The Quest of the Fair Medusa

George took Randy's advice and moved. He did not know where to go. All he wanted was to get away as far as possible from Park Avenue, from the aesthetic jungles of the lion hunters, from the half-life of wealth and fashion that had grown like a parasite upon the sound body of America. He went to live in Brooklyn.

He had made a little money from his book, so now he paid his debts and quit the job he held as a teacher at the School for Utility Cultures. From this time on, he earned his precarious living solely by what he wrote.

For four years he lived in Brooklyn, and four years in Brooklyn are a geologic age—a single stratum of grey time. They were years of poverty, of desperation, of loneliness unutterable. All about him were the poor, the outcast, the neglected and forsaken people of America, and he was one of them. But life is strong, and year after year it went on around him in all its manifold complexity, rich with its unnoticed and unrecorded little happenings. He saw it all, he took it all in hungrily as part of his experience, he recorded much of it, and in the end he squeezed it dry as he tried to extract its hidden meanings.

And what was he like inside while these grey years were slipping by? What was he up to, what was he doing, what did he want?

That's rather hard to tell, because he wanted so many things, but the thing he wanted most was Fame. Those

*were the years of his concentrated quest of that fair
Medusa. He had had his little taste of glory, and it was
bitter in his mouth. He thought the reason was that he
had not been good enough—and he had not been good
enough. Therefore he thought that what he had had was
not Fame at all, but only a moment's notoriety. He had
been a seven-day wonder—that was all.*

*Well, he had learned some things since he wrote his
first book. He would try again.*

*So he lived and wrote, and wrote and lived, and lived
there by himself in Brooklyn. And when he had worked
for hours at a stretch, forgetting food and sleep and
everything, he would rise from his desk at last and stag-
ger forth into the nighttime streets, reeling like a drunkard with his weariness. He would eat his supper at a
restaurant, and then, because his mind was feverish and
he knew he could not sleep, he would walk to Brooklyn
Bridge and cross it to Manhattan, and ferret out the
secret heart of darkness in all the city's ways, and then
at dawn come back across the Bridge once more, and so
to bed in Brooklyn.*

*And in these nightly wanderings the old refusals
dropped away, the old avowals stood. For then, somehow, it seemed to him that he who had been dead was
risen, he who had been lost was found again, and he who
in his brief day of glory had sold the talent, the passion,
and the belief of youth into the keeping of the fleshless
dead, until his heart was corrupted and all hope gone,
would win his life back bloodily, in solitude and darkness. And he felt then that things would be for him once
more as they had been, and he saw again, as he had
once seen, the image of the shining city. Far-flung, and
blazing into tiers of jeweled light, it burned forever in
his vision as he walked the Bridge, and strong tides were*

bound around it, and the great ships called. So he walked the Bridge, always he walked the Bridge.

And by his side was that stern friend, the only one to whom he spoke what in his secret heart he most desired. To Loneliness he whispered, "Fame!"—and Loneliness replied, "Aye, brother, wait and see."

THE LOCUSTS HAVE NO KING

THE tragic light of evening falls upon the huge and rusty jungle of South Brooklyn. It falls without glare or warmth upon the faces of all the men with dead eyes and flesh of tallow-grey as they lean upon their window sills at the sad, hushed end of day.

If at such a time you walk down this narrow street, between the mean and shabby houses, past the eyes of all the men who lean there quietly at their open windows in their shirt-sleeves, and turn in at the alley here and follow the two-foot strip of broken concrete pavement that skirts the alley on one side, and go to the very last shabby house down at the end, and climb up the flight of worn steps to the front entrance, and knock loudly at the door with your bare knuckles (the bell is out of order), and then wait patiently until someone comes, and ask whether Mr. George Webber lives here, you will be informed that he most certainly does, and that if you will just come in and go down this stairway to the basement and knock at the door there on your right, you will probably find him in. So you go down the stairway to the damp and gloomy basement hall, thread your way between the dusty old boxes, derelict furniture, and other lumber stored there in the passage, rap on the door that has been indicated to you, and Mr. Webber himself will open it and usher you right into his room, his home, his castle.

The place may seem to you more like a dungeon than a room that a man would voluntarily elect to live in. It is long and narrow, running parallel to the hall from front to rear, and the only natural light that enters it comes through two small windows rather high up in the wall, facing each other at the opposite ends, and these are heavily guarded with iron bars, placed there by some past owner of the house to keep the South Brooklyn thugs from breaking in.

The room is furnished adequately but not so luxuriously as to deprive it of a certain functional and Spartan simplicity. In the back half there is an iron bed with sagging springs, a broken-down dresser with a cracked mirror above it, two kitchen chairs, and a steamer trunk and some old suitcases that have seen much use. At the front end, under the yellow glow of an electric light suspended from the ceiling by a cord, there is a large desk, very much scarred and battered, with the handles missing on most of the drawers, and in front of it there is a straight-backed chair made out of some old, dark wood. In the center, ranged against the walls, where they serve to draw the two ends of the room together into aesthetic unity, stand an ancient gate-legged table, so much of its dark green paint flaked off that the dainty pink complexion of its forgotten youth shows through all over, a tier of bookshelves, unpainted, and two large crates or packing cases, their thick top boards pried off to reveal great stacks of ledgers and of white and yellow manuscript within. On top of the desk, on the table, on the bookshelves, and all over the floor are scattered, like fallen leaves in autumn woods, immense masses of loose paper with writing on every sheet, and everywhere are books, piled up on their sides or leaning crazily against each other.

This dark cellar is George Webber's abode and working quarters. Here, in winter, the walls, which sink four feet below the level of the ground, sweat continuously with clammy drops of water. Here, in summer, it is he who does the sweating.

His neighbors, he will tell you, are for the most part Armenians, Italians, Spaniards, Irishmen, and Jews—in short, Americans. They live in all the shacks, tenements, and slums in all the raw, rusty streets and alleys of South Brooklyn.

And what is that you smell?

Oh, that! Well, you see, he shares impartially with his neighbors a piece of public property in the vicinity; it belongs to all of them in common, and it gives to South Brooklyn its own distinctive atmosphere. It is the old Gowanus Canal, and that aroma you speak of is nothing but the huge symphonic stink of it, cunningly compacted of unnumbered separate putrefactions. It is interesting sometimes to try to count them. There is in it not only the noisome stenches of a stagnant sewer, but also the smells of melted glue, burned rubber, and smoldering rags, the odors of a boneyard horse, long dead, the incense of putrefying offal, the fragrance of deceased, decaying cats, old tomatoes, rotten cabbage, and prehistoric eggs.

And how does he stand it?

Well, one gets used to it. One can get used to anything, just as all these other people do. They never think of the smell, they never speak of it, they'd probably miss it if they moved away.

To this place, then, George Webber has come, and here "holed in" with a kind of dogged stubbornness touched with desperation. And you will not be far wrong if you surmise that he has come here deliberately, driven by a resolution to seek out the most forlorn and isolated hiding spot that he could find.

Mr. Marple, a gentleman who has a room on the second floor, comes stumbling down the darkened basement stairway with a bottle in his hand and knocks upon George Webber's door.

"Come in!"

Mr. Marple comes in, introduces himself, does the right thing with the bottle, sits down, and begins to make talk.

"Well, now, Mr. Webber, how d'yah like that drink I mixed for yah?"

"Oh, I like it, I like it."

"Well, now, if yah don't, I want yah t'come right out an' say so."

"Oh, I would, I would."

"I mean I'd like to know. I'd appreciate yah tellin' me. What I mean is, I made that stuff myself from a little private formuler I got—I wouldn't buy no stuff from a bootlegger—I wouldn't take no chance wit' the bastards. I buy the alcohol that goes into that drink from a place I know, an' I always know what I'm gettin'—d'yah know what I mean?"

"Yes, I certainly do."

"But I'd like to know what yah think of it, I'd appreciate yah tellin' me."

"Oh, it's fine, it couldn't be better."

"I'm glad yah like it, an' you're sure I didn't disturb yah?"

"Oh, no, not at all."

"Because I was on my way in when I sees your light there in the winder, so I says to myself, now that guy may think I've got an orful nerve buttin' in like this but I'm gonna stop an' get acquainted an' ast him if he'd like a little drink."

"I'm glad you did."

"But if I disturbed yah I wantcha t'say so."

"Oh, no, not at all."

"Because here's the way it is wit' me. I'm interested in youman nature—I'm a great student of psychology—I can read faces the minute I look at a guy—it's somethin' that I always had—I guess that's why I'm in the insurance game. So when I sees a guy that interests me I wanta get acquainted wit' him an' get his reactions to things. So when I sees your light I says to myself, he may tell me to get the hell outa there but there ain't no harm in tryin'."

"I'm glad you did."

"Now, Mr. Webber, I think I'm a pretty good judge of character——"

"Oh, I'm sure you are."

"—an' I been lookin' at yah an' sorta sizin' yah up while yah been sittin' there. Yah didn't know I was sizin' yah up but that's what I been doin' all the time yah been sittin' there because I'm a great student of youman nature, Mr. Webber, an' I gotta size up all grades an' classes every day in my business—*you* know—I'm in the insurance game. An' I wanna ast yah a question. Now if it's too personal I wantcha t'come right out an' say so, but if yah don't mind answerin' I'm gonna ast it to yah."

"Not at all. What is it?"

"Well, Mr. Webber, I already reached my own conclusions, but I'm gonna ast it to yah just t'see if it don't bear me out. Now what I'm gonna ast yah—an' yah don't have to answer if yah don't want to—is—What's your line?—What business are yah in? Now yah don't need to tell me if it's too personal."

"Not at all. I'm a writer."

"A *what?*"

"A writer. I wrote a book once. I'm trying to write another one now."

"Well, now, it may surprise yah but that's just what I

figgered out myself. I says to myself, now there's a guy, I says, that's in some kind of intelleckshul work where he's got t'use his head. He's a writer or a newspaperman or in the advertisin' business. Y'see I've always been a great judge of youman nature—that's *my* line."

"Yes, I see."

"An' now I wanna tell yah somethin' else, Mr. Webber. You're doin' the thing yah was cut out for, you're doin' the thing yah was born to do, it's what yah been pre-parin' to do all your life sinct yah was a kid—am I right or wrong?"

"Oh, I guess you're right."

"An' that's the reason you're gonna be a big success at it. Stick to writin', Mr. Webber. I'm a great judge of youman nature an' I know what I'm talkin' about. Just stick to the thing yah always wanted to be an' yah'll get there. Now some guys never find theirselves. Some guys never know what they wanna be. That's the trouble wit' some guys. Now wit' me it's different. I didn't find myself till I was a grown man. You'd have t'laugh, Mr. Webber, if I told yah what it was I wanted t'be when I was a kid."

"What was it, Mr. Marple?"

"Say, Mr. Webber—y'know it's funny—yah won't believe me—but up to the time I was about twenty years old, a grown man, I was crazy to be a railroad en-gineer. No kiddin'. I was nuts about it. An' I'd a-been just crazy enough to've gone ahead an' got a job on the railroad if the old man hadn't yanked me by the collar an' told me t'snap out of it. Yah know I'm a Down-Easter by birth—don't talk like it any more—I been here too long—but that's where I grew up. My old man was a plumber in Augusta, Maine. So when I tells him I'm gonna be a locomotive engineer he boots me one in the seat of the pants an' tells me I ain't no such thing. 'I've sent yah to school,' he says, 'you've had ten times the

choolin' that I had, an' now yah tell me that you're
onna be a railroad hogger. Well, you're not,' the old
nan says, 'you're gonna be one member of the fambly
hat's comin' home at night wit' clean hands an' a white
ollar. Now you get the hell outa here an' hunt yah up a
ob in some decent high-class business where yah'll
ave a chanct t'advance an' associate wit' your social
kals.' Jesus! It was a lucky thing for me he took that
tand or I'd never a-got where I am today. But I was
ood an' sore about it at the time. An' say, Mr. Webber
—you're gonna laugh when I tell yah this one—I ain't
ctually over the darn thing yet. No kiddin'. When I see
ne of these big engines bargin' down the track I still
et that funny crawly feelin' I usta have when I was a
id an' looked at 'em. The guys at the office had t'laugh
bout it when I told 'em, an' now when I come in they
all me Casey Jones.—Well, what d'yah say yah have
nother little snifter before I go?"

"Thanks, I'd like to, but maybe I'd better not. I've still
ot a little work I ought to do before I turn in."

"Well, now, Mr. Webber, I know just how it is. An'
hat's the way I had yah sized up from the first. That
uy's a writer, I says, or in some sort of intelleckshul
ccupation where he's got to use his head—was I right
r wrong?"

"Oh, you were right."

"Well, I'm glad to've metcha, Mr. Webber. Don't
nake yourself a stranger around here. Yah know, a guy
ets sorta lonely sometimes. My wife died four years ago
o I been livin' upstairs here ever sinct—sorta figgered
hat a single guy didn't need no more room than I got
ere. Come up to see me. I'm interested in youman na-
ure an' I like to talk to people an' get their different
eactions. So any time yah feel like chewin' the rag a bit,
rop in."

"Oh, I will, I will."

"Good night, Mr. Webber."

"Good night, Mr. Marple."

Good night. Good night. Good night.

Across the basement hall, in another room similar to George Webber's, lived an old man by the name of Wakefield. He had a son somewhere in New York who paid his rent, but Mr. Wakefield rarely saw his son. He was a brisk and birdy little man with a chirping, cheerful voice; and, although he was almost ninety, he always seemed to be in good health and was still immensely active. His son had provided him with a room to live in, and he had a little money of his own—a few dollars a month from a pension—enough to supply his meagre wants; but he lived a life of utter loneliness, seeing his son only on the occasion of a holiday or a rare visit, and the rest of the time living all by himself in his basement room.

Yet he had as brave and proud a spirit as any man on earth. He longed desperately for companionship, but he would have died rather than admit he was lonely. So independent was he, and so sensitive, that, while he was always courteous and cheerful, his tone when he responded to a greeting was a little cold and distant, lest anyone should think he was too forward and eager. But once satisfied of one's friendliness, no one could respond more warmly or more cordially than old man Wakefield.

George grew fond of him and liked to talk with him, and the old man would invite him eagerly into his part of the basement and proudly display his room, which he kept with a soldierlike neatness. He was a veteran of the Union Army in the Civil War, and his room was filled with books, records, papers, and old clippings bearing on the war and on the part his regiment had

played in it. Although he was alert and eager toward
the life around him, and much too brave and hopeful a
spirit to live mournfully in the past, the Civil War had
been the great and central event in old man Wakefield's
life. Like many of the men of his generation, both North
and South, it had never occurred to him that the war was
not the central event in everyone's life. Because it was
so with him, he believed that people everywhere still
lived and thought and talked about the war all the time.

He was a leading figure in the activities of his Grand
Army Post, and was always bustling about with plans
and projects for the coming year. It seemed to him that
the Grand Army organization, whose thinning ranks of
old and feeble men he still saw with the proud eyes of
forty or fifty years before, was the most powerful society
in the nation, and that its word of warning or stern reproof was enough to make all the kings of the earth
quake and tremble in their boots. He was bitterly scornful and would bristle up immediately at mention of the
American Legion: he fancied slights and cunning
trickery on the part of this body all the time, and he
would ruffle up like a rooster when he spoke of the
Legionnaires, and say in an angry, chirping tone:

"It's jealousy! Nothing in the world but sheer tar-
nation *jealousy*—that's what it is!"

"But why, Mr. Wakefield? Why should they be jealous
of you?"

"Because we reely did some soldierin'—that's why!"
he chirped angrily. "Because they know we fit the Rebels
—yes! and *fit* 'em good—and *licked* 'em, too!" he cackled
triumphantly—"in a war that *was* a war! . . . Pshaw!"
he said scornfully, in a lowered voice, looking out the
window with a bitter smile and with eyes that had suddenly grown misty. "What do these fellows know about
a war?—Some *bob-tail—raggedy—two-by-two*—little

jackleg feller—of a *Legionnary!*" He spat the words out with malignant satisfaction, breaking at the end into a vindictive cackle. "Standin' to their necks all day in some old trench and never gettin' within ten miles of the enemy!" he sneered. "If they ever saw a troop of cavalry, I don't know what they'd make of it! I reckon they'd think it was the circus come to town!" he cackled. "A war! A *war!* Hell-fire, that warn't no war!" he cried derisively. "If they wanted to see a war, they should've been with us at the Bloody Angle! But, pshaw!" he said. "They'd a-run like rabbits if they'd been there! The only way you could a-kept 'em would've been to tie 'em to a tree!"

"Don't you think they could have beaten the Rebels, Mr. Wakefield?"

"Beat 'em?" he shrilled. *"Beat* 'em! Why, boy, what are you talkin' about? . . . Hell! If Stonewall Jackson ever started for that gang, he'd run 'em ragged! Yes, sir! They'd light out so fast they'd straighten out all the bends of the road as they went by!" cried old man Wakefield, cackling. "Pshaw!" he said quietly and scornfully again. "They couldn't do it! It ain't in 'em! . . . But I'll tell you this much!" he cried suddenly in an excited voice. "We're not goin' to put up with it much longer! The boys have had just about as much of it as they can stand. If they try to do us like they done last year— pshaw!" he broke off again, and looked out the window shaking his head—"Why, it's all as plain as the nose on your face! It's jealousy—just plain, confounded *jealousy* —that's all in the world it is!"

"What is, Mr. Wakefield?"

"Why, the way they done us last year!" he cried. "Puttin' us way back there at the tail-end of the *pee*-rade, when by all the rights—as everybody knows—we should've come first! But we'll fix 'em!" he cried warn-ingly. "We've got a way to fix 'em!" he said with a triumphant shake of the head. "I know the thing we're goin' to do *this* year," he cried, "if they try another trick like that on us!"

"What are you going to do, Mr. Wakefield?"

"Why," he cackled, "we won't *pee*-rade! We simply won't *pee*-rade! We'll tell 'em they can hold their derned *pee*-rade without us!" he chirped exultantly. "And I reckon that'll fix 'em! Oh, yes! That'll bring 'em round, or I miss *my* guess!" he crowed.

"It ought to, Mr. Wakefield."

"Why, boy," he said solemnly, "if we ever did a thing like that, there would be a wave of protest—a *wave* of protest—" he cried with a sweeping gesture of the arm, as his voice rose strongly—"from here to Californy! . . . The people wouldn't *stand* for it!" he cried. "They'd make *those* fellers back down in a hurry!"

And, as George left him, the old man would come with him to the door, shake his hand warmly, and, with an eager and lonely look in his old eyes, say:

"Come again, boy! I'm always glad to see you! . . . I got stuff in here—photygraphs, an' books, an' such as that about the war—that you ain't seen yet. No, nor no one else!" he cackled. "For no one else has got 'em! . . . Just let me know when you're comin' an' I'll be here."

Slowly the years crept by and George lived alone in Brooklyn. They were hard years, desperate years, lonely years, years of interminable writing and experimentation, years of exploration and discovery, years of grey time-lessness, weariness, exhaustion, and self-doubt. He had reached the wilderness period of his life and was hacking his way though the jungles of experience. He had stripped himself down to the brutal facts of self and work. These were all he had.

He saw himself more clearly now than he had ever done before, and, in spite of living thus alone, he no longer thought of himself as a rare and special person who was doomed to isolation, but as a man who worked and who, like other men, was a part of life. He was concerned passionately with reality. He wanted to see things whole, to find out everything he could, and then to create out of what he knew the fruit of his own vision.

One criticism that had been made of his first book still rankled in his mind. An unsuccessful scribbler turned critic had simply dismissed the whole book as a "barbaric yawp," accusing Webber of getting at things with his emotions rather than with his brains, and of being hostile toward the processes of the intellect and "the intellectual point of view." These charges, if they had any truth in them, seemed to George to be the kind of lifeless half-truth that was worse than no truth at all. The trouble with the so-called "intellectuals" was that they were not intellectual enough, and their point of view more often than not had no point, but was disparate, arbitrary, sporadic, and confused.

To be an "intellectual" was, it seemed, a vastly different thing from being intelligent. A dog's nose would usually lead him towards what he wished to find, or away from what he wished to avoid: this was intelligent. That is, the dog had the sense of reality in his nose. But the "intellectual" usually had no nose, and was lacking in the sense of reality. The most striking difference between Webber's mind and the mind of the average "intellectual" was that Webber absorbed experience like a sponge, and made use of everything that he absorbed. He really learned constantly from experience. But the "intellectuals" of his acquaintance seemed to learn noth-

ng. They had no capacity for rumination and digestion.
They could not reflect.

He thought over a few of them that he had known:

There was Haythorpe, who when George first knew
him was an aesthete of the late baroque in painting,
writing, all the arts, author of one-act costume plays—
"Gesmonder! Thy hands pale chalices of hot desire!"
Later he became an aesthete of the primitives—the
Greek, Italian, and the German; then aesthete of the
nigger cults—the wood sculptures, coon songs, hymnals,
dances, and the rest; still later, aesthete of the comics—
of cartoons, Chaplin, and the Brothers Marx; then of
Expressionism; then of the Mass; then of Russia and the
Revolution; at length, aesthete of homosexuality; and
finally, death's aesthete—suicide in a graveyard in Connecticut.

There was Collingswood, who, fresh out of Harvard,
was not so much the aesthete of the arts as of the mind.
First, a Bolshevik from Beacon Hill, practitioner of promiscuous, communal love as the necessary answer to
"bourgeois morality"; then back to Cambridge for post-
graduate study at the feet of Irving Babbitt—Collingswood is now a Humanist, the bitter enemy of Rousseau,
romanticism, and of Russia (which is, he now thinks,
Rousseau in modern form); the playwright, next—New
Jersey, Beacon Hill, or Central Park seen in the classic
unities of the Greek drama; at length, disgusted realist—
all that's good in modern art or letters is to be found in
advertisements"; then a job as a scenario writer and two
years in Hollywood—all now is the moving picture, with
easy money, easy love affairs, and drunkenness; and
finally, back to Russia, but with his first love lacking—
"no sex triflings now, my comrades—we who serve the
cause and wait upon the day lead lives of Spartan
abstinence—what was the free life, free love, en-

lightened pleasure of the proletariat ten years ago is now despised as the contemptible debauchery of "bourgeois decadence."

There was Spurgeon from the teaching days at the School for Utility Cultures—good Spurgeon—Chester Spurgeon of the Ph.D.—Spurgeon of "the great tradition"—thin-lipped Spurgeon, ex-student of Professor Stuart Sherman, and bearer-onward of the Master's Torch. Noble-hearted Spurgeon, who wrote honeyed flatteries of Thornton Wilder and his *Bridge*—"The tradition of the Bridge is Love, just as the tradition of America and of Democracy is Love. Hence—" Spurgeon hences—Love grows Wilder as the years Bridge on across America. Oh, where now, good Spurgeon, "intellectual" Spurgeon—Spurgeon whose thin lips and narrowed eyes were always so glacial prim on Definitions! Where now, brave intellect, by passion uninflamed? Spurgeon of the flashing mind, by emotion unimpulsed, is now a devoted leader of the intellectual Communists (See Spurgeon's article entitled, "Mr. Wilder's Piffle," in the *New Masses*).—So, Comrade Spurgeon, hail! Hail, Comrade Spurgeon—and most heartily, my bright-eyed Intellectual, farewell!

Whatever George Webber was, he knew he was not an "intellectual." He was just an American who was looking hard at the life around him, and sorting carefully through all the life he had ever seen and known, and trying to extract some essential truth out of this welter of his whole experience. But, as he said to his friend and editor, Fox Edwards:

"What *is* truth? No wonder jesting Pilate turned away! The truth, it has a thousand faces—show only one of them, and the *whole* truth flies away! But how to show the whole? That's the question. . . .

"Discovery in itself is not enough. It's not enough to

find out what things are. You've also got to find out where they come from, where each brick fits in the wall."

He always came back to the wall.

"I think it's like this," he said. "You see a wall, you look at it so much and so hard that one day you see clear through it. Then, of course, it's not just one wall any longer. It's every wall that ever was."

He was still spiritually fighting out the battle of his first book, and all the problems it had raised. He was still searching for a way. At times he felt that his first book had taught him nothing—not even confidence. His feelings of hollow desperation and self-doubt seemed to grow worse instead of better, for he had now torn himself free from almost every personal tie which had ever bound him, and which formerly had sustained him in some degree with encouragement and faith. He was left, therefore, to rely almost completely on his own resources.

There was also the insistent, gnawing consciousness of work itself, the necessity of turning towards the future and the completion of a new book. He was feeling, now as never before, the inexorable pressure of time. In writing his first book, he had been unknown and obscure, and there had been a certain fortifying strength in that, for no one had expected anything of him. But now the spotlight of publication had been turned upon him, and he felt it beating down with merciless intensity. He was pinned beneath the light—he could not crawl out of it. Though he had not won fame, still he was known now. He had been examined, probed, and talked about. He felt that the world was looking at him with a critic eye.

It had been easy in his dreams to envision a long and fluent sequence of big books, but now he was finding it a different matter to accomplish them. His first book had been more an act of utterance than an act of labor. It was an impassioned expletive of youth—something that had been pent up in him, something felt and seen and imagined and put down at white-hot heat. The writing of it had been a process of spiritual and emotional evacuation. But that was behind him now, and he knew he should never try to repeat it. Henceforth his writing would have to come from unending labor and preparation.

In his effort to explore his experience, to extract the whole, essential truth of it, and to find a way to write about it, he sought to recapture every particle of the life he knew down to its minutest details. He spent weeks and months trying to put down on paper the exactitudes of countless fragments—what he called "the dry, caked colors of America"—how the entrance to a subway looked, the design and webbing of the elevated structure, the look and feel of an iron rail, the particular shade of rusty green with which so many things are painted in America. Then he tried to pin down the foggy color of the brick of which so much of London is constructed, the look of an English doorway, of a French window, of the roofs and chimney pots of Paris, of a whole street in Munich—and each of these foreign things he then examined in contrast to its American equivalent.

It was a process of discovery in its most naked, literal, and primitive terms. He was just beginning really to see thousands of things for the first time, to see the relations between them, to see here and there whole series and systems of relations. He was like a scientist in some new field of chemistry who for the first time realizes that he has stumbled upon a vast new world, and who will then pick out identities, establish affiliations, define here and there the outlines of sub-systems in crystalline union, without yet being aware what the structure of the whole is like, or what the final end will be.

The same processes now began to inform his direct

observation of the life around him. Thus, on his nocturnal ramblings about New York, he would observe the
homeless men who prowled in the vicinity of restaurants,
lifting the lids of garbage cans and searching around
inside for morsels of rotten food. He saw them everywhere, and noticed how their numbers increased during
the hard and desperate days of 1932. He knew what
kind of men they were, for he talked to many of them;
he knew what they had been, where they had come from,
and even what kind of scraps they could expect to dig
out of the garbage cans. He found out the various places
all over the city where such men slept at night. A favorite
rendezvous was a corridor of the subway station at
Thirty-third Street and Park Avenue in Manhattan.
There one night he counted thirty-four huddled together
on the cold concrete, wrapped up in sheathings of old
newspaper.

It was his custom almost every night, at one o'clock or
later, to walk across the Brooklyn Bridge, and night after
night, with a horrible fascination, he used to go to the
public latrine or "comfort station" which was directly
in front of the New York City Hall. One descended to
this place down a steep flight of stairs from the street,
and on bitter nights he would find the place crowded
with homeless men who had sought refuge there. Some
were those shambling hulks that one sees everywhere, in
Paris as well as New York, in good times as well as bad—
old men, all rags and bags and long white hair and bushy
beards stained dirty yellow, wearing tattered overcoats in
the cavernous pockets of which they carefully stored away
all the little rubbish they lived on and spent their days
collecting in the streets—crusts of bread, old bones with
rancid shreds of meat still clinging to them, and dozens
of cigarette butts. Some were the "stumble bums" from
the Bowery, criminal, fumed with drink or drugs, or half-

insane with "smoke." But most of them were just flotsam of the general ruin of the time—honest, decent, middle aged men with faces seamed by toil and want, and young men, many of them mere boys in their teens, with thick unkempt hair. These were the wanderers from town to town, the riders of freight trains, the thumbers of rides on highways, the uprooted, unwanted male population of America. They drifted across the land and gathered in the big cities when winter came, hungry, defeated, empty, hopeless, restless, driven by they knew not what, always on the move, looking everywhere for work, for the bare crumbs to support their miserable lives, and finding neither work nor crumbs. Here in New York, to this obscene meeting place, these derelicts came, drawn into a common stew of rest and warmth and a little surcease from their desperation.

George had never before witnessed anything to equal the indignity and sheer animal horror of the scene. There was even a kind of devil's comedy in the sight of all these filthy men squatting upon those open, doorless stools. Arguments and savage disputes and fights would sometimes break out among them over the possession of these stools, which all of them wanted more for rest than for necessity. The sight was revolting, disgusting, enough to render a man forever speechless with very pity.

He would talk to the men and find out all he could about them, and when he could stand it no more he would come out of this hole of filth and suffering, and there, twenty feet above it, he would see the giant hackles of Manhattan shining coldly in the cruel brightness of the winter night. The Woolworth Building was not fifty yards away, and a little farther down were the silvery spires and needles of Wall Street, great fortresses of stone and steel that housed enormous banks. The blind injustice of this contrast seemed the most brutal part of the whole experience, for there, all around him in the cold moonlight, only a few blocks away from this abyss of human wretchedness and misery, blazed the pinnacles of power where a large portion of the entire world's wealth was locked in mighty vaults.

They were now closing up the restaurant. The tired waitresses were racking the chairs upon the tables, completing the last formalities of their hard day's work in preparation for departure. At the cash register the proprietor was totting up the figures of the day's take, and one of the male waiters hovered watchfully near the table, in a manner politely indicating that while he was not in a hurry he would be glad if his last customer would pay his bill and leave.

George called for his check and gave the man some money. He took it and in a moment returned with the change. He pocketed his tip and said, "Thank you, sir." Then as George said good night and started to get up and leave, the waiter hesitated and hung around uncertainly as if there was something he wanted to say but scarcely knew whether he ought to say it or not.

George looked at him inquiringly, and then, in a rather embarrassed tone, the waiter said:

"Mr. Webber . . . there's . . . something I'd like to talk over with you sometime. . . . I—I'd like to get your advice about something—that is, if you have time," he added hastily and almost apologetically.

George regarded the waiter with another inquiring look, in which the man evidently read encouragement, for now he went on quickly, in a manner of almost beseeching entreaty:

"It's—it's about a story."

The familiar phrase awakened countless weary echoes in Webber's memory. It also resolved that hard and honest patience with which any man who ever sweated to write a living line and to earn his bread by the hard uncertain labor of his pen will listen, as an act of duty and understanding, to any other man who says he has a tale to tell. His mind and will wearily composed themselves, his face set in a strained smile of mechanical anticipation, and the poor waiter, thus encouraged, went on eagerly:

"It's—it's a story a guy told me several years ago. I've been thinking about it ever since. The guy was a foreigner," said the waiter impressively, as if this fact was enough to guarantee the rare color and fascinating interest of what he was about to reveal. "He was an Armenian," said the waiter very earnestly. "Sure! He came from over there!" He nodded his head emphatically. "And this story that he told me was an *Armenian* story," said the waiter with solemn emphasis, and then paused to let this impressive fact sink in. "It was a story that he knew about—he told it to me—and I'm the only other guy that knows about it," said the waiter, and paused again, looking at his patron with a very bright and feverish eye.

George continued to smile with wan encouragement, and in a moment the waiter, after an obvious struggle with his soul, a conflict between his desire to keep his secret and to tell it, too, went on:

"Gee! You're a writer, Mr. Webber, and you know about these things. I'm just a dumb guy working in a restaurant—but if I could put it into words—if I could get a guy like you who knows how it's done to tell the story for me—why—why—" he struggled with himself, then burst out enthusiastically—"there'd be a fortune in it for the both of us!"

George felt his heart sink still lower. It was turning out just as he knew it would. But he still continued to smile pallidly. He cleared his throat in an undecided fashion, but then said nothing. And the waiter, taking silence for consent, now pressed on impetuously:

"Honest, Mr. Webber—if I could get somebody like you to help me with this story—to write it down for me the way it ought to be—I'd—I'd—" for a moment the waiter struggled with his lower nature, then magnanimity got the better of him and he cried out with the decided air of a man who is willing to make a generous bargain and stick to it—"I'd go fifty-fifty with him! I'd —I'd be willing to give him half! . . . And there's a fortune in it!" he cried. "I go to the movies and I read *True Story Magazine*—and I never seen a story like it! It's got 'em all beat! I've thought about it for years, ever since the guy told it to me—and I know I've got a gold mine here if I could only write it down! . . . It's— it's——"

Now, indeed, the waiter's struggle with his sense of caution became painful to watch. He was evidently burning with a passionate desire to reveal his secret, but he was also obviously tormented by doubts and misgivings lest he should recklessly give away to a comparative stranger a treasure which the other might appropriate to his own use. His manner was very much that of a man who has sailed strange seas and seen, in some unknown coral island, the fabulous buried cache of forgotten pirate's plundering, and who is now being torn between two desperate needs—his need of partnership, of outward help, and his imperative need of secrecy and caution. The fierce interplay of these two powers discrete was waged there on the open battlefield of the waiter's countenance. And in the end he took the obvious way out. Like an explorer who will take from his pocket an uncut gem of tremedous size and value and cunningly hint that in a certain place he knows of there are many more like it, the waiter decided to tell a little part of his story without revealing all.

"I—I can't tell you the whole thing tonight," he said apologetically. "Some other night, maybe, when you've got more time. But just to give you an idea of what's in it—" he looked around stealthily to make sure he was in no danger of being overheard, then bent over and lowered his voice to an impressive whisper—"just to give you an idea, now—there's one scene in the story where a woman puts an advertisement in the paper that she will give a ten-dollar gold piece and as much liquor as he can drink to any man who comes around to see her the next day!" After imparting this sensational bit of information, the waiter regarded his patron with glittering eyes. "Now!" said the waiter, straightening up with a gesture of finality. "You never heard of anything like *that*, did you? You ain't never seen *that* in a story!"

George, after a baffled pause, admitted feebly that he had not. Then, when the waiter continued to regard him feverishly, with a look that made it plain that he was supposed to say something more, he inquired doubtfully whether this interesting event had really happened in Armenia.

"Sure!" cried the waiter, nodding vigorously. "That's what I'm telling you! The whole thing happens in Armenia!" He paused again, torn fiercely between his caution and his desire to go on, his feverish eyes almost burning holes through his questioner. "It's—it's—" he struggled for a moment more, then surrendered abjectly —"well, I'll tell you," he said quietly, leaning forward, with his hands resting on the table in an attitude of confidential intimacy. "The idea of the story runs like this. You got this rich dame to begin with, see?"

He paused and looked at George inquiringly. George did not know what was expected of him, so he nodded to show that his mind had grasped this important fact, and said hesitantly:

"In Armenia?"

"Sure! Sure!" The waiter nodded. "This dame comes from over there—she's got a big pile of dough—I guess she's the richest dame in Armenia. And then she falls for this guy, see?" he went on. "He's nuts about her, and he comes to see her every night. The way the guy told it to me, she lives up at the top of this big house—so every night the guy comes and climbs up there to see her—oh, a hell of a long ways up—" the waiter said—"thirty floors or more!"

"In Armenia?" George asked feebly.

"Sure!" cried the waiter, a little irritably. "That's where it all takes place! That's what I'm telling you!"

He paused and looked searchingly at George, who finally asked, with just the proper note of hesitant thoughtfulness, why the lover had had to climb up so far.

"Why," said the waiter impatiently, "because the dame's old man wouldn't let him in! That was the only way the guy could get to her! The old man shut her up way up there at the top of the house because he didn't want the dame to get married! . . . But then," he went on triumphantly, "the old man dies, see? He dies and leaves all his dough to this dame—and then she ups and marries this guy!"

Dramatically, with triumph written in his face, the waiter paused to let this startling news soak into the consciousness of his listener. Then he continued:

"They lived together for a while—the dame's in love with him—and for a year or two they're sitting pretty. But then the guy begins to drink—he's a booze hound, see?—only she don't know it—she's been able to hold him down for a year or two after they get married. . . .

Then he begins to step out again. . . . The first thing you know he's staying out all night and running around with a lot of hot blondes, see? . . . Well, then, you see what's coming now, don't you?" said the waiter quickly and eagerly.

George had no notion, but he nodded his head wisely.

"Well, that's what happens," said the waiter. "The first thing you know the guy ups and leaves the dame and takes with him a lot of her dough and joolry. . . . He just disappears—just like the earth had opened and swallowed him up!" the waiter declared, evidently pleased with his poetic simile. "He leaves her cold, and the poor dame's almost out of her head. She does everything—she hires detectives—she offers rewards—she puts ads in the paper begging him to come back. . . . But it's no use—she can't find him—the guy's lost. . . . Well, then," the waiter continued, "three years go by while the poor dame sits and eats her heart out about this guy. . . . And then—" here he paused impressively, and it was evident that he was now approaching the crisis—"then she has an idea!" He paused again, briefly, to allow this extraordinary accomplishment on the part of his heroine to be given due consideration, and in a moment, very simply and quietly, he concluded: "She opens up a night club."

The waiter fell silent now, and stood at ease with his hands clasped quietly before him, with the modest air of a man who has given his all and is reasonably assured it is enough. It now became compellingly apparent that his listener was supposed to make some appropriate comment, and that the narrator could not continue with his tale until this word had been given. So George mustered his failing strength, moistened his dry lips with the end of his tongue, and finally said in a halting voice:

"In—in Armenia?"

The waiter now took the question, and the manner of its utterance, as signs of his listener's paralyzed surprise. He nodded his head victoriously and cried:

"Sure! You see, the dame's idea is this—she knows the guy's a booze hound and that sooner or later he'll come to a place where there's lots of bar-flies and fast women. That kind always hang together—sure they do! . . . So she opens up this joint—she sinks a lot of dough in it—it's the swellest joint they got over there. And then she puts this ad in the paper."

George was not sure that he had heard aright, but the waiter was looking at him with an expression of such exuberant elation that he took a chance and said:

"What ad?"

"Why," said the waiter, "this come-on ad that I was telling you about. You see, that's the big idea—that's the plan the dame dopes out to get him back. So she puts this ad in the paper saying that any man who comes to her joint the next day will be given a ten-dollar gold piece and all the liquor he can drink. She figures that will bring him. She knows the guy is probably down and out by this time and when he reads this ad he'll show up. . . . And that's just what happens. When she comes down next morning she finds a line twelve blocks long outside, and sure enough, here's this guy the first one in the line. Well, she pulls him out of the line and tells the cashier to give all the rest of 'em their booze and their ten bucks, but she tells this guy he ain't gonna get nothing. 'What's the reason I ain't?' he says—you see, the dame is wearing a heavy veil so he don't recognize her. Well, she tells him she thinks there's something phony about him—gives him the old line, you know—tells him to come upstairs with her so she can talk to him and find out if he's O.K. . . . Do you get it?"

George nodded vaguely. "And then what?" he said.

"Why," the waiter cried, "she gets him up there—and then—" he leaned forward again with fingers resting on the table, and his voice sank to an awed whisper—"*she—takes—off—her—veil!*"

There was a reverential silence as the waiter, still leaning forward with his fingers arched upon the table, regarded his listener with bright eyes and a strange little smile. Then he straightened up slowly, stood erect, still smiling quietly, and a long, low sigh like the coming on of evening came from his lips, and he was still. The silence drew itself out until it became painful, and at length George squirmed wretchedly in his chair and asked:

"And then—then what?"

The waiter was plainly taken aback. He stared in frank astonishment, stunned speechless by the realization that anybody could be so stupid.

"Why—" he finally managed to say with an expression of utter disillusion—"that's *all!* Don't you see? That's all there is! The dame takes off her veil—he recognizes her—and there you are! . . . She's found him! . . . She's got him back! . . . They're together again! . . . *That's* the story!" He was hurt, impatient, almost angry as he went on: "Why, anybody ought to be able to see——"

"Good night, Joe."

The last waitress was just going out and had spoken to the waiter as she passed the table. She was a blonde, slender girl, neatly dressed. Her voice was quiet and full of the casual familiarity of her daily work and association; it was a pleasant voice, and it was a little tired. Her face, as she paused a moment, was etched in light and shadow, and there were little pools of violet beneath her clear grey eyes. Her face had the masklike fragility and loveliness, the almost hair-drawn fineness, that one often sees in young people who have lived in the great city and who have never had wholly enough of anything except work and their own hard youth. One felt instantly sorry for the girl, because one knew that her face would not long be what it was now.

The waiter, interrupted in the flood of his impassioned argument, had been a little startled by the casual intrusion of the girl's low voice, and turned toward her. When he saw who it was, his manner changed at once, and his own seamed face softened a little with instinctive and unconscious friendliness.

"Oh, hello, Billie. Good night, kid."

She went out, and the sound of her brisk little heels clacked away on the hard pavement. For a moment more the waiter continued to look after her, and then, turning back to his sole remaining customer with a queer, indefinable little smile hovering in the hard lines about his mouth, he said very quietly and casually, in the tone men use to speak of things done and known and irrecoverable:

"Did you see that kid? . . . She came in here about two years ago and got a job. I don't know where she came from, but it was some little hick town somewhere. She'd been a chorus girl—a hoofer in some cheap road show—until her legs gave out. . . . You find a lot of 'em in this game—the business is full of 'em. . . . Well, she worked here for about a year, and then she began going with a cheap gigolo who used to come in here. You know the kind—you can smell 'em a mile off—they stink. I could've told her! But, hell, what's the use? They won't listen to you—you only get yourself in dutch all around—they got to find out for themselves—you can't teach 'em. So I left it alone—that's the only way. . . . Well, six or eight months ago, some of the girls found out she was pregnant. The boss let her out. He's not a bad guy—but, hell, what can you expect? You can't keep 'em around a place like this when they're in that condition, can you? . . . She had the kid three months ago, and then she got her job back. I understand she's put the kid in a home somewhere. I've never seen it, but they say it's a swell kid, and Billie's crazy about it—goes out there to see it every Sunday. . . . She's a swell kid, too."

The waiter was silent for a moment, and there was a far-off look of tragic but tranquil contemplation in his eyes. Then, quietly, wearily, he said:

"Hell, if I could tell you what goes on here every day —the things you see and hear—the people you meet and all that happens. Jesus, I get sick and tired of it. Sometimes I'm so fed up with the whole thing that I don't care if I never see the joint again. Sometimes I get to thinking how swell it would be not to have to spend your whole life waiting on a lot of mugs—just standing around and waiting on 'em and watching 'em come in and out . . . and feeling sorry for some little kid who's fallen for some dope you wouldn't wipe your feet on . . . and wondering just how long it'll be before she gets the works. . . . Jesus, I'm fed up with it!"

Again he was silent. His eyes looked off into the distance, and his face was set in that expression of mildly cynical regret and acceptance that one often notices in people who have seen much of life, and experienced its hard and seamy side, and who know that there is very little they can do or say. At last he sighed deeply, shook himself, threw off the mood, and resumed his normal manner.

"Gee, Mr. Webber," he said with a return of his former eagerness, "it must be great to be able to write books and stories—to have the gift of gab—all that flow of language—to go anywhere you like—to work when you want to! Now, take that story I was telling you about," he said earnestly. "I never had no education—but if I could only get some guy like you to help me—to write it down the way it ought to be—honest, Mr. Webber, it's a great chance for somebody—there's a fortune in it—I'd go fifty-fifty!" His voice was pleading now. "A guy I knew one time, he told it to me—and me and him are the only two that knows it. This guy was an Armenian, like I said, and the whole thing happened over there. . . . There'd be a gold mine in it if I only knew how to do it."

It was long after midnight, and the round disk of the moon was sinking westward over the cold, deserted streets of slumbering Manhattan.

The party was in full swing now.

The gold and marble ballroom of the great hotel had been converted into a sylvan fairyland. In the center a fountain of classic nymphs and fauns sent up its lighted sprays of water, and here and there about the floor were rustic arbors with climbing roses trailing over them, heavy with scented blossoms. Flowering hothouse trees in tubs were banked around the walls, the shining marble pillars were wreathed about with vines and garlands, and overhead gay lanterns had been strung to illuminate the scene with their gentle glow. The whole effect was that of an open clearing in a forest glade upon Midsummer Night where Queen Titania had come to hold her court and revels.

It was a rare, exotic spectacle, a proper setting for the wealthy, care-free youth for whom it had been planned. The air was heavy with the fragrance of rich perfumes, and vibrant with throbbing, pulsing rhythms of sensuous music. Upon the polished floor a hundred lovely girls in brilliant evening gowns danced languidly in the close embrace of pink-cheeked boys from Yale and

Harvard, their lithe young figures accentuated smartly by the black and white of faultless tailoring.

This was the coming-out party of a fabulously rich young lady, and the like of it had not been seen since the days before the market crashed. The papers had been full of it for weeks. It was said that her father had lost millions in the debacle, but it was apparent that he still had a few paltry dollars left. So now he was doing the right thing, the expected thing, the necessary and inescapable thing, for his beautiful young daughter, who would one day inherit all that these ruinous times had left him of his hard-earned savings. Tonight she was being "presented to Society" (whose members had known her since her birth), and all "Society" was there.

And from this night on, the girl's smiling face would turn up with monotonous regularity in all the rotogravure sections of the Sunday papers, and daily the nation would be kept posted on all the momentous trivia of her life—what she ate, what she wore, where she went, who went with her, what night clubs had been honored by her presence, what fortunate young gentleman had been seen accompanying her to what race track, and what benefits she had sponsored and poured tea for. For one whole year, from now until another beautiful and rich young lady from next season's crop of beautiful and rich young ladies was chosen by the newspaper photographers to succeed her as America's leading debutante, this gay and care-free creature would be for Americans very much what a royal princess is for Englishmen, and for very much the same reason—because she was her father's daughter, and because her father was one of the rulers of America. Millions would read about her every move and envy her, and thousands would copy her as far as their means would let them. They would buy cheap imitations of her costly dresses, hats, and underclothes, would smoke the same cigarettes, use the same lipstick, eat the same soups, sleep on the same mattresses that she had allowed herself to be pictured wearing, smoking, using, eating, and sleeping on in the handsome colored advertisements on the back covers of magazines —and they would do it, knowing full well that the rich young lady had set these fashions for a price—was she not her father's daughter?—all, of course, for the sake of sweet charity and commerce.

Outside the great hotel, on the Avenue in front of it and on all the side streets in the near vicinity, sleek black limousines were parked. In some of them the chauffeurs slouched dozing behind their wheels. Others had turned on their inside lights and sat there reading the pages of the tabloids. But most of them had left their cars and were knotted together in little groups, smoking, talking, idling the time away until their services should be needed again.

On the pavement near the entrance of the hotel, beside the huge marquee which offered shelter from the wind, the largest group of them, neat in their liveried uniforms, had gathered in debate. They were discussing politics and theories of international economy, and the chief disputants were a plump Frenchman with a waxed mustache, whose sentiments were decidedly revolutionary, and an American, a little man with corky legs, a tough, seamed face, the beady eyes of a bird, and the quick, impatient movements of the city. As George Webber came abreast of them, brought thither by the simple chance of his nightly wanderings, the argument had reached its furious climax, and he stopped a while to listen.

The scene, the situation, and the contrast between the two principal debaters made the whole affair seem utterly grotesque. The plump Frenchman, his cheeks glowing with the cold and his own excitement, was dancing about in a frenzy, talking and gesticulating volubly. He would lean forward with thumb and forefinger uplifted and closed daintily in a descriptive circle —a gesture that eloquently expressed the man's conviction that the case he had been presenting for immediate and bloody world revolution was complete, logical, unshakable, and beyond appeal. When any of the others interposed an objection, he would only grow more violent and inflamed.

At last his little English began to break down under the strain imposed upon it. The air about him fairly rang with objurgations, expletives, impassioned cries of *"Mais oui! . . . Absolument! . . . C'est la vérité!"* —and with laughs of maddened exasperation, as if the knowledge that anyone could be so obtuse as not to see it as he saw it was more than he could endure.

"Mais non! Mais non!" he would shout. *"Vous avez tort! . . . Mais c'est stupide!"* he would cry, throwing his plump arms up in a gesture of defeat, and turning away as if he could stand it no longer and was departing —only to return immediately and begin all over again.

Meanwhile, the chief target of this deluge, the little American with the corky legs and the birdy eyes, let him go on. He just leaned up against the building, took an occasional puff at his cigarette, and gave the Frenchman a steady look of cynical impassivity. At last he broke in to say:

"O.K. . . . O.K., Frenchy. . . . When you get through spoutin', maybe *I'll* have somethin' to say."

"Seulement un mot!" replied the Frenchman, out of breath. "One vord!" he cried impressively, drawing himself up to his full five feet three and holding one finger in the air as if he were about to deliver Holy Writ—"I 'ave to say one vord more!"

"O.K.! O.K.!" said the corky little American with cynical weariness. "Only don't take more than an hour and a half to say it!"

Just then another chauffeur, obviously a German, with bright blue eyes and a nut-cracker face, rejoined the group with an air of elated discovery.

"Noos! I got noos for you!" he said. "I haf been mit a drifer who hass in Rooshia liffed, and he says that conditions there far *worser* are——"

"*Non! Non!*" the Frenchman shouted, red in the face with anger and protest. "*Pas vrai! . . . Ce n'est pas possible!*"

"Oh, for Christ's sake," the American said, tossing his cigarette away with a gesture of impatience and disgust. "Why don't you guys wake up? This ain't Russia! You're in America! The trouble with you guys," he went on, "is that you've been over there all your life where you ain't been used to nothin'—and just as soon as you get over here where you can live like a human bein' you want to tear it all down."

At this, others broke in, and the heated and confused dialogue became more furious than ever. But the talk just went round and round in circles.

George walked away into the night.

The lives of men who have to live in our great cities are often tragically lonely. In many more ways than one, these dwellers in the hive are modern counterparts of Tantalus. They are starving to death in the midst of abundance. The crystal stream flows near their lips but always falls away when they try to drink of it. The vine, rich-weighted with its golden fruit, bends down, comes near, but springs back when they reach to touch it.

Melville, at the beginning of his great fable, *Moby Dick,* tells how the city people of his time would, on every occasion that was afforded them, go down to the dock, to the very edges of the wharf, and stand there looking out to sea. In the great city of today, however, there is no sea to look out to, or, if there is, it is so far away, so inaccessible, walled in behind such infinite ramifications of stone and steel, that the effort to get to it is disheartening. So now, when the city man looks out, he looks out on nothing but crowded vacancy.

Does this explain, perhaps, the desolate emptiness of city youth—those straggling bands of boys of sixteen or eighteen that one can always see at night or on a holiday, going along a street, filling the air with raucous jargon and senseless cries, each trying to outdo the others with joyless catcalls and mirthless quips and jokes which are so feeble, so stupidly inane, that one hears them with strong mixed feelings of pity and of shame? Where here, among these lads, is all the merriment, high spirits, and spontaneous gaiety of youth? These creatures, millions of them, seem to have been born but half made up, without innocence, born old and stale and dull and empty.

Who can wonder at it? For what a world it is that most of them were born into! They were suckled on darkness, and weaned on violence and noise. They had to try to draw out moisture from the cobblestones, their true parent was a city street, and in that barren universe no urgent sails swelled out and leaned against the wind, they rarely knew the feel of earth beneath their feet and no birds sang, their youthful eyes grew hard, unseeing, from being stopped forever by a wall of masonry.

In other times, when painters tried to paint a scene of awful desolation, they chose the desert or a heath of barren rocks, and there would try to picture man in his great loneliness—the prophet in the desert, Elijah being fed by ravens on the rocks. But for a modern painter, the

most desolate scene would be a street in almost any one
of our great cities on a Sunday afternoon.

Suppose a rather drab and shabby street in Brooklyn,
not quite tenement perhaps, and lacking therefore even
the gaunt savagery of poverty, but a street of cheap brick
buildings, warehouses, and garages, with a cigar store or
a fruit stand or a barber shop on the corner. Suppose a
Sunday afternoon in March—bleak, empty, slaty grey.
And suppose a group of men, Americans of the working
class, dressed in their "good" Sunday clothes—the cheap
machine-made suits, the new cheap shoes, the cheap
felt hats stamped out of universal grey. Just suppose this,
and nothing more. The men hang around the corner
before the cigar store or the closed barber shop, and now
and then, through the bleak and empty street, a motor
car goes flashing past, and in the distance they hear
the cold rumble of an elevated train. For hours they
hang around the corner, waiting—waiting—waiting——

For what?

Nothing. Nothing at all. And that is what gives the
scene its special quality of tragic loneliness, awful emptiness, and utter desolation. Every modern city man is
familiar with it.

And yet—and yet——

It is also true—and this is a curious paradox about
America—that these same men who stand upon the
corner and wait around on Sunday afternoons for nothing
are filled at the same time with an almost quenchless
hope, an almost boundless optimism, an almost indestructible belief that something is bound to turn up,
something is sure to happen. This is a peculiar quality of
the American soul, and it contributes largely to the
strange enigma of our life, which is so incredibly mixed
of harshness and of tenderness, of innocence and of
crime, of loneliness and of good fellowship, of desolation

and of exultant hope, of terror and of courage, of nameless fear and of soaring conviction, of brutal, empty, naked, bleak, corrosive ugliness, and of beauty so lovely and so overwhelming that the tongue is stopped by it, and the language for it has not yet been uttered.

How explain this nameless hope that seems to lack all reasonable foundation? I cannot. But if you were to go up to this fairly intelligent-looking truck driver who stands and waits there with his crowd, and if you put to him your question, and if he understood what you were talking about (he wouldn't), and if he were articulate enough to frame in words the feelings that are in him (he isn't)—he might answer you with something such as this:

"Now is duh mont' of March, duh mont' of March—now it is Sunday afternoon in Brooklyn in duh mont' of March, an' we stand upon cold corners of duh day. It's funny dat dere are so many corners in duh mont' of March, here in Brooklyn where no corners are. Jesus! On Sunday in duh mont' of March we sleep late in duh mornin', den we get up an' read duh papers—duh funnies an' duh sportin' news. We eat some chow. An' den we dress up in duh afternoon, we leave our wives, we leave duh funnies littered on duh floor, an' go outside in Brooklyn in duh mont' of March an' stand around upon ten t'ousand corners of duh day. We need a corner in duh mont' of March, a wall to stand to, a shelter an' a door. Dere must be *some* place inside in duh mont' of March, but we never found it. So we stand around on corners where duh sky is cold an' ragged still wit' winter, in our good clothes we stand around wit' a lot of udder guys we know, before duh barber shop, just lookin' for a door."

Ah, yes, for in summer:

It is so cool and sweet tonight, a million feet are walking here across the jungle web of Brooklyn in the dark, and it's so hard now to remember that it ever was the month of March in Brooklyn and that we couldn't find a door. There are so many million doors tonight. There's a door for everyone tonight, all's open to the air, all's interfused tonight: remote the thunder of the elevated trains on Fulton Street, the rattling of the cars along Atlantic Avenue, the glare of Coney Island seven miles away, the mob, the racket, and the barkers shouting, the cars swift-shuttling through the quiet streets, the people swarming in the web, lit here and there with livid blurs of light, the voices of the neighbors leaning at their windows, harsh, soft, all interfused. All's illusive in the liquid air tonight, all mixed in with the radios that blare from open windows. And there is something over all tonight, something fused, remote, and trembling, made of all of this, and yet not of it, upon the huge and weaving ocean of the night in Brooklyn—something that we had almost quite forgotten in the month of March. What's this?—a sash raised gently?—a window?—a near voice on the air?—something swift and passing, almost captured, there below?—there in the gulf of night the mournful and yet thrilling voices of the tugs?—the liner's blare? Here—there—some otherwhere—was it a whisper?—a woman's call?—a sound of people talking behind the screens and doors in Flatbush? It trembles in the air throughout the giant web tonight, as fleeting as a step—near—as soft and sudden as a woman's laugh. The liquid air is living with the very whisper of the thing that we are looking for tonight throughout America— the very thing that seemed so bleak, so vast, so cold, so hopeless, and so lost as we waited in our good clothes on ten thousand corners of the day in Brooklyn in the month of March.

If George Webber had never gone beyond the limits

of the neighborhood in which he lived, the whole chronicle of the earth would have been there for him just the same. South Brooklyn was a universe.

The people in the houses all around him, whose lives in the cold, raw days of winter always seemed hermetic, sterile, and remote, as shut out from him as though they were something sealed up in a tin, became in spring and summer so real to him it seemed that he had known them from his birth. For, as the days and nights grew warmer, everybody kept their windows open, and all the dwellers in these houses conducted their most intimate affairs in loud and raucous voices which carried to the street and made the casual passer-by a confidant of every family secret.

God knows he saw squalor and filth and misery and despair enough, violence and cruelty and hate enough, to crust his lips forever with the hard and acrid taste of desolation. He found a sinister and demented Italian grocer whose thin mouth writhed in a servile smile as he cringed before his customers, and the next moment was twisted in a savage snarl as he dug his clawlike fingers into the arm of his wretched little son. And on Saturdays the Irishmen would come home drunk, and then would beat their wives and cut one another's throats, and the whole course and progress of their murderous rages would be published nakedly from their open windows with laugh, shout, scream, and curse.

But he found beauty in South Brooklyn, too. There was a tree that leaned over into the narrow alley where he lived, and George could stand at his basement window and look up at it and watch it day by day as it came into its moment's glory of young and magic green. And then towards sunset, if he was tired, he could lie down to rest a while upon his iron bed and listen to the dying birdsong in the tree. Thus, each spring, in that one tree, he found all April and the earth. He also found devotion, love, and wisdom in a shabby little Jewish tailor and his wife, whose dirty children were always tumbling in and out of the dingy suffocation of his shop.

In the infinite variety of such common, accidental, oft-unheeded things one can see the web of life as it is spun. Whether we wake at morning in the city, or lie at night in darkness in the country towns, or walk the streets of furious noon in all the dusty, homely, and en-during lights of present time, the universe around us is the same. Evil lives forever—so does good. Man alone has knowledge of these two, and he is such a little thing.

For what is man?

First, a child, soft-boned, unable to support itself on its rubbery legs, befouled with its excrement, that howls and laughs by turns, cries for the moon but hushes when it gets its mother's teat; a sleeper, eater, guzzler, howler, laugher, idiot, and a chewer of its toe; a little tender thing all blubbered with its spit, a reacher into fires, a beloved fool.

After that, a boy, hoarse and loud before his com-panions, but afraid of the dark; will beat the weaker and avoid the stronger; worships strength and savagery, loves tales of war and murder, and violence done to others; joins gangs and hates to be alone; makes heroes out of soldiers, sailors, prize fighters, football players, cowboys, gunmen, and detectives; would rather die than not out-try and out-dare his companions, wants to beat them and always to win, shows his muscle and demands that it be felt, boasts of his victories and will never own defeat.

Then the youth: goes after girls, is foul behind their backs among the drugstore boys, hints at a hundred seductions, but gets pimples on his face; begins to think about his clothes, becomes a fop, greases his hair, smokes cigarettes with a dissipated air, reads novels, and writes poetry on the sly. He sees the world now as a pair of legs and breasts; he knows hate, love, and jealousy; he is cowardly and foolish, he cannot endure to be alone; he lives in a crowd, thinks with the crowd, is afraid to be marked off from his fellows by an eccentricity. He joins clubs and is afraid of ridicule; he is bored and unhappy and wretched most of the time. There is a great cavity in him, he is dull.

Then the man: he is busy, he is full of plans and reasons, he has work. He gets children, buys and sells small packets of everlasting earth, intrigues against his rivals, is exultant when he cheats them. He wastes his little three-score years and ten in spendthrift and inglorious living; from his cradle to his grave he scarcely sees the sun or moon or stars; he is unconscious of the immortal sea and earth; he talks of the future and he wastes it as it comes. If he is lucky, he saves money. At the end his fat purse buys him flunkeys to carry him where his shanks no longer can; he consumes rich food and golden wine that his wretched stomach has no hunger for; his weary and lifeless eyes look out upon the scenery of strange lands for which in youth his heart was panting. Then the slow death, prolonged by costly doctors, and finally the graduate undertakers, the perfumed carrion, the suave ushers with palms outspread to leftwards, the fast motor hearses, and the earth again.

This is man: a writer of books, a putter-down of words, a painter of pictures, a maker of ten thousand philosophies. He grows passionate over ideas, he hurls scorn and mockery at another's work, he finds the one way, the true way, for himself, and calls all others false —yet in the billion books upon the shelves there is not one that can tell him how to draw a single fleeting breath in peace and comfort. He makes histories of the universe, he directs the destiny of nations, but he does not know his own history, and he cannot direct his own destiny with dignity or wisdom for ten consecutive minutes.

This is man: for the most part a foul, wretched, abominable creature, a packet of decay, a bundle of degenerating tissues, a creature that gets old and hairless and has a foul breath, a hater of his kind, a cheater, a scorner, a mocker, a reviler, a thing that kills and murders in a mob or in the dark, loud and full of brag surrounded by his fellows, but without the courage of a rat alone. He will cringe for a coin, and show his snarling fangs behind the giver's back; he will cheat for two sous, and kill for forty dollars, and weep copiously in court to keep another scoundrel out of jail.

This is man, who will steal his friend's woman, feel the leg of his host's wife below the tablecloth, dump fortunes on his whores, bow down in worship before charlatans, and let his poets die. This is man, who swears he will live only for beauty, for art, for the spirit, but will live only for fashion, and will change his faith and his convictions as soon as fashion changes. This is man, the great warrior with the flaccid gut, the great romantic with the barren loins, the eternal knave devouring the eternal fool, the most glorious of all the animals, who uses his brain for the most part to make himself a stench in the nostrils of the Bull, the Fox, the Dog, the Tiger, and the Goat.

Yes, this is man, and it is impossible to say the worst of him, for the record of his obscene existence, his baseness, lust, cruelty, and treachery, is illimitable. His life is also full of toil, tumult, and suffering. His days are mainly composed of a million idiot repetitions—in goings and comings along hot streets, in sweatings and freezings, in the senseless accumulation of fruitless tasks, in decaying and being patched, in grinding out his life so that he may buy bad food, in eating bad food so that he may grind his life out in distressful defecations. He is the dweller in that ruined tenement who, from one moment's breathing to another, can hardly forget the bitter weight of his uneasy flesh, the thousand diseases and distresses of his body, the growing incubus of his corruption. This is man, who, if he can remember ten golden moments of joy and happiness out of all his years, ten moments unmarked by care, unseamed by aches or itches, has power to lift himself with his expiring breath and say: "I have lived upon this earth and known glory!"

This is man, and one wonders why he wants to live at all. A third of his life is lost and deadened under sleep; another third is given to a sterile labor; a sixth is spent in all his goings and his comings, in the moil and shuffle of the streets, in thrusting, shoving, pawing. How much of him is left, then, for a vision of the tragic stars? How much of him is left to look upon the everlasting earth? How much of him is left for glory and the making of great songs? A few snatched moments only from the barren glut and suck of living.

Here, then, is man, this moth of time, this dupe of brevity and numbered hours, this travesty of waste and sterile breath. Yet if the gods could come here to a desolate, deserted earth where only the ruin of man's cities remained, where only a few marks and carvings of his hand were legible upon his broken tablets, where only a wheel lay rusting in the desert sand, a cry would burst out of their hearts and they would say: "He lived, and he was here!"

Behold his works:

He needed speech to ask for bread—and he had Christ! He needed songs to sing in battle—and he had Homer! He needed words to curse his enemies—and he had Dante, he had Voltaire, he had Swift! He needed cloth to cover up his hairless, puny flesh against the seasons—and he wove the robes of Solomon, he made the garments of great kings, he made the samite for the young knights! He needed walls and a roof to shelter him—and he made Blois! He needed a temple to propitiate his God—and he made Chartres and Fountains Abbey! He was born to creep upon the earth—and he made great wheels, he sent great engines thundering down the rails, he launched great wings into the air, he put great ships upon the angry sea!

Plagues wasted him, and cruel wars destroyed his strongest sons, but fire, flood, and famine could not quench him. No, nor the inexorable grave—his sons leaped shouting from his dying loins. The shaggy bison with his thews of thunder died upon the plains; the fabled mammoths of the unrecorded ages are vast scaffoldings of dry, insensate loam; the panthers have learned caution and move carefully among tall grasses to the water hole; and man lives on amid the senseless nihilism of the universe.

For there is one belief, one faith, that is man's glory, his triumph, his immortality—and that is his belief in life. Man loves life, and, loving life, hates death, and because of this he is great, he is glorious, he is beautiful, and his beauty is everlasting. He lives below the senseless stars and writes his meanings in them. He lives in fear, in toil, in agony, and in unending tumult, but if the blood foamed bubbling from his wounded lungs at every breath he drew, he would still love life more dearly than an end of breathing. Dying, his eyes burn beautifully, and the old hunger shines more fiercely in them— he has endured all the hard and purposeless suffering, and still he wants to live.

Thus it is impossible to scorn this creature. For out of

his strong belief in life, this puny man made love. At his best, he *is* love. Without him there can be no love, no hunger, no desire.

So this is man—the worst and best of him—this frail and petty thing who lives his day and dies like all the other animals, and is forgotten. And yet, he is immortal, too, for both the good and evil that he does live after him. Why, then, should any living man ally himself with death, and, in his greed and blindness, batten on his brother's blood? . . .

CREDO

I have never before made a statement of belief [George wrote in his conclusion to Fox], although I have believed in many things and said that I believed in them. But I have never stated my belief in concrete terms because almost every element of my nature has been opposed to the hard framework, the finality, of formulation.

Just as you are the rock of life, I am the web; just as you are Time's granite, so, I think, am I Time's plant. My life, more than that of anyone I know, has taken on the form of growth. No man that I have known was ever more deeply rooted in the soil of Time and Memory, the weather of his individual universe, than was I. You followed me through the course of that whole herculean conflict. For four years, as I lived and worked and explored the jungle depths of Brooklyn—jungle depths coincident with those of my own soul—you were beside me, you followed, and you stuck.

You never had a doubt that I would finish—make an end—round out the cycle—come to the whole of it. The only doubt was mine, enhanced, tormented by my own fatigue and desperation, and by the clacking of the feeble and malicious little tongues which, knowing nothing, whispered that I would never make an end again because I could not begin. We both knew how grotesquely false this was—so false and so grotesque that it was sometimes the subject of an anguished and exasperated laugh. The truth was so far different that my own fears were just the opposite: that I might never make an end to anything again because I could never get through telling what I knew, what I felt and thought and *had* to say about it.

That was a giant web in which I was caught, the product of my huge inheritance—the torrential recollectiveness, derived out of my mother's stock, which became a living, million-fibered integument that bound me to the past, not only of my own life, but of the very earth from which I came, so that nothing in the end escaped from its in-rooted and all-feeling explorativeness. The way the sunlight came and went upon a certain day, the way grass felt between bare toes, the immediacy of noon, the slamming of an iron gate, the halting skreak upon the corner of a streetcar, the liquid sound of shoe leather on the pavements as men came home to lunch, the smell of turnip greens, the clang of ice tongs, and the clucking of a hen—and then Time fading like a dream, Time melting to oblivion, when I was two years old. Not only this, but all lost sounds and voices, forgotten memories exhumed with a constant pulsing of the brain's great ventricle, until I lived them in my dreams, carrying the stupendous and unceasing burden of them through the unresting passages of sleep. Nothing that had ever been was lost. It all came back in an endless flow, even the blisters of the paint upon the mantelpiece in my father's house, the smell of the old leather sofa with my father's print upon it, the smell of dusty bottles and of cobwebs in the cellar, the casual stomping of a slow, gaunt hoof

upon the pulpy lumber of a livery stable floor, the prou
lift and flourish of a whisking tail, and the oaty drop
pings. I lived again through all times and weathers I ha
known—through the fag-ends of wintry desolation in th
month of March and the cold, bleak miseries of ragge
red at sunset, the magic of young green in April, th
blind horror and suffocation of concrete places in mid
summer sun where no limits were, and October with th
smell of fallen leaves and wood smoke in the air. Th
forgotten moments and unnumbered hours came back t
me with all the enormous cargo of my memory, togethe
with lost voices in the mountains long ago, the voice
of the kinsmen dead and never seen, and the house
they had built and died in, and the rutted roads the
trod upon, and every unrecorded moment that Aun
Maw had told me of the lost and obscure lives they le
long, long ago. So did it all revive in the ceaseless puls
ings of the giant ventricle, so did the plant go back
stem by stem, root by root, and filament by filament
until it was complete and whole, compacted of the ver
earth that had produced it, and of which it was itself th
last and living part.

You stayed beside me like the rock you are until
unearthed the plant, followed it back through every fibe
of its pattern to its last and tiniest enrootment in th
blind, dumb earth. And now that it is finished, and th
circle come full swing—we, too, are finished, and I hav
a thing to say:

I believe that we are lost here in America, but I be
lieve we shall be found. And this belief, which mount
now to the catharsis of knowledge and conviction, is fo
me—and I think for all of us—not only our own hope
but America's everlasting, living dream. I think the lif
which we have fashioned in America, and which ha

fashioned us—the forms we made, the cells that grew, the honeycomb that was created—was self-destructive in its nature, and must be destroyed. I think these forms are dying, and must die, just as I know that America and the people in it are deathless, undiscovered, and immortal, and must live.

I think the true discovery of America is before us. I think the true fulfillment of our spirit, of our people, of our mighty and immortal land, is yet to come. I think the true discovery of our own democracy is still before us. And I think that all these things are certain as the morning, as inevitable as noon. I think I speak for most men living when I say that our America is Here, is Now, and beckons on before us, and that this glorious assurance is not only our living hope, but our dream to be accomplished.

I think the enemy is here before us, too. But I think we know the forms and faces of the enemy, and in the knowledge that we know him, and shall meet him, and eventually must conquer him is also our living hope. I think the enemy is here before us with a thousand faces, but I think we know that all his faces wear one mask. I think the enemy is single selfishness and compulsive greed. I think the enemy is blind, but has the brutal power of his blind grab. I do not think the enemy was born yesterday, or that he grew to manhood forty years ago, or that he suffered sickness and collapse in 1929, or that we began without the enemy, and that our vision faltered, that we lost the way, and suddenly were in his camp. I think the enemy is old as Time, and evil as Hell, and that he has been here with us from the beginning. I think he stole our earth from us, destroyed our wealth, and ravaged and despoiled our land. I think he took our people and enslaved them, that he polluted the fountains of our life, took unto himself the rarest treasures of our own possession, took our bread and left us with a crust, and, not content, for the nature of the enemy is insatiate —tried finally to take from us the crust.

I think the enemy comes to us with the face of innocence and says to us:

"I am your friend."

I think the enemy deceives us with false words and lying phrases, saying:

"See, I am one of you—I am one of your children, your son, your brother, and your friend. Behold how sleek and fat I have become—and all because I am just one of you, and your friend. Behold how rich and powerful I am—and all because I am one of you—shaped in your way of life, of thinking, of accomplishment. What I am, I am because I am one of you, your humble brother and your friend. Behold," cries Enemy, "the man I am, the man I have become, the thing I have accomplished —and reflect. Will you destroy this thing? I assure you that it is the most precious thing you have. It is yourselves, the projection of each of you, the triumph of your individual lives, the thing that is rooted in your blood, and native to your stock, and inherent in the traditions of America. It is the thing that all of you may hope to be," says Enemy, "for—" humbly—"am I not just one of you? Am I not just your brother and your son? Am I not the living image of what each of you may hope to be, would wish to be, would desire for his own son? Would you destroy this glorious incarnation of your own heroic self? If you do, then," says Enemy, "you destroy yourselves—you kill the thing that is most gloriously American, and in so killing, kill yourselves."

He lies! And now we know he lies! He is not gloriously or in any other way, ourselves. He is not our friend, our son, our brother. And he is not American! For, although he has a thousand familiar and convenient faces, his own true face is old as Hell.

Look about you and see what he has done.

Dear Fox, old friend, thus we have come to the end of the road that we were to go together. My tale is finished—and so farewell.

But before I go, I have just one more thing to tell you:

Something has spoken to me in the night, burning the tapers of the waning year; something has spoken in the night, and told me I shall die, I know not where. Saying:

"To lose the earth you know, for greater knowing; to lose the life you have, for greater life; to leave the friends you loved, for greater loving; to find a land more kind than home, more large than earth——

"—Whereon the pillars of this earth are founded, towards which the conscience of the world is tending— a wind is rising, and the rivers flow."

CRITICISM AND
AUTOBIOGRAPHY

The Story of a Novel

Editor's Preface

TH E Story of a Novel (1936) is Wolfe's own account of his literary methods and habits. In a way his four big books are also the four parts of a novel about a novelist writing a novel, and this is the epilogue.

In terms of the local literary scene *The Story of a Novel* is much more than this. It has already been discussed in the Introduction, however, and all I can add here is that it is printed complete and is worth reading complete.

THE STORY OF A NOVEL

A N EDITOR, who is also a good friend of mine, told me about a year ago that he was sorry he had not kept a diary about the work that both of us were doing, the whole stroke, catch, flow, stop, and ending, the ten thousand fittings, changings, triumphs, and surrenders that went into the making of a book. This editor remarked that some of it was fantastic, much incredible, all astonishing, and he was also kind enough to say that the whole experience was the most interesting he had known during the twenty-five years he had been a member of the publishing business.

I propose to tell about this experience. I cannot tell anyone how to write books; I cannot attempt to give anyone rules whereby he will be enabled to get his books published by publishers or his stories accepted by high-paying magazines. I am not a professional writer; I am not even a skilled writer; I am just a writer who is on the way to learning his profession and to discovering the line, the structure, and the articulation of the language which I must discover if I do the work I want to do. It is for just this reason, because I blunder, because every energy of my life and talent is still involved in this process of discovery, that I am speaking as I speak here. I am going to tell the way in which I wrote a book. It will be intensely personal. It was the most intense part of my life for several years. There is nothing very literary about it. It is a story of sweat and pain and despair and partial achievement. I don't know how to write a story yet. I don't know how to write a novel yet. But I have learned something about myself and about the work of writing, and if I can, I am going to try to tell what it is.

I don't know when it occurred to me first that I would be a writer. I suppose that like a great many other children in this country of my generation, I may have thought that it would be a fine thing because a writer was a man like Lord Byron or Lord Tennyson or Long-fellow or Percy Bysshe Shelley. A writer was a man who was far away like these people I have mentioned, and since I was myself an American and an American not of the wealthy or university-going sort of people, it seemed to me that a writer was a man from a kind of remote people that I could never approach.

I think this has happened to us all—or almost all of us here in America. We're still more perturbed by the strangeness of the writing profession than any other people I have known on the earth. It is for this reason, I think, that one finds among a great number of our people, I mean the laboring, farming sort of people from which I came, a kind of great wonder and doubt and romantic feeling about writers so that it is hard for them to understand that a writer may be one of them and not a man far away like Lord Byron or Tennyson or Percy Bysshe Shelley. Then there is another kind of American who has come from the more educated, university-going kind of people, and these people also become fascinated with the glamour and difficulty of writing, but in a different way. They get more involved or fancy than the most involved and fancy European people of this sort. They become more "Flauberty" than Flaubert. They establish little magazines that not only split a hair with the best of them, but they split more hairs than Europeans think of splitting. The Europeans say: "Oh, God, where did these people, these aesthetic Americans, ever come from?" Well, we have known it all. I think all of us who have tried to write in this country may have fallen in between these two groups of well-meaning and misguided people, and if we become writers finally, it is in spite of each of them.

I don't know how I became a writer, but I think it was because of a certain force in me that had to write and that finally burst through and found a channel. My people were of the working class of people. My father, a stonecutter, was a man with a great respect and veneration for literature. He had a tremendous memory, and he loved poetry, and the poetry that he loved best was naturally of the rhetorical kind that such a man would like. Nevertheless it was good poetry, Hamlet's Soliloquy, *Macbeth*, Mark Antony's Funeral Oration, Grey's "Elegy," and all the rest of it. I heard it all as a child; I memorized and learned it all.

He sent me to college to the state university. The desire to write, which had been strong during all my days in high school, grew stronger still. I was editor of the college paper, the college magazine, etc., and in my last year or two I was a member of a course in playwriting which had just been established there. I wrote several little one-act plays, still thinking I would become a lawyer or a newspaperman, never daring to believe I could seriously become a writer. Then I went to Harvard, wrote some more plays there, became obsessed with the idea that I had to be a playwright, left Harvard, had my plays rejected, and finally in the autumn of 1926, how, why, or in what manner I have never exactly been able to determine, but probably because the force in me that had to write at length sought out its channel, I began to write my first book in London. I was living all alone at that time. I had two rooms—a bedroom and a sitting room—in a little square in Chelsea in which all the houses had that familiar, smoked brick and cream-yellow-plaster look of London houses. They looked exactly alike.

As I say, I was living alone at that time and in a foreign country. I did not know why I was there or what the direction of my life should be, and that was the way I began to write my book. I think that is one of the hardest times a writer goes through. There is no standard, no outward judgment, by which he can measure what he has done. By day I would write for hours in big ledgers which I had bought for the purpose; then at night I would lie in bed and fold my hands behind my head and think of what I had done that day and hear the solid, leather footbeat of the London bobby as he came by my window, and remember that I was born in North Carolina and wonder why the hell I was now in London lying in the darkened bed, and thinking about words I had that day put down on paper. I would get a great, hollow, utterly futile feeling inside me, and then I would get up and switch on the light and read the words I had written that day, and then I would wonder: why am I here now? why have I come?

By day there would be the great, dull roar of London, the gold, yellow, foggy light you have there in October. The manswarmed and old, weblike, smoky London! And I loved the place, and I loathed it and abhorred it. I knew no one there, and I had been a child in North Carolina long ago, and I was living there in two rooms in the huge octopal and illimitable web of that overwhelming city. I did not know why I had come, why I was there.

I worked there every day with such feelings as I have described, and came back to America in the winter and worked here. I would teach all day and write all night, and finally about two and a half years after I had begun the book in London, I finished it in New York.

I should like to tell about this, too. I was very young

at the time, and I had the kind of wild, exultant vigor which a man has at that period of his life. The book took hold of me and possessed me. In a way, I think it shaped itself. Like every young man, I was strongly under the influence of writers I admired. One of the chief writers at that time was Mr. James Joyce with his book *Ulysses*. The book that I was writing was much influenced, I believe, by his own book, and yet the powerful energy and fire of my own youth played over and, I think, possessed it all. Like Mr. Joyce, I wrote about things that I had known, the immediate life and experience that had been familiar to me in my childhood. Unlike Mr. Joyce, I had no literary experience. I had never had anything published before. My feeling towards writers, publishers, books, that whole fabulous far-away world, was almost as romantically unreal as when I was a child. And yet my book, the characters with which I had peopled it, the color and the weather of the universe which I had created, had possessed me, and so I wrote and wrote with that bright flame with which a young man writes who never has been published, and who yet is sure all will be good and must go well. This is a curious thing and hard to tell about, yet easy to understand in every writer's mind. I wanted fame, as every youth who ever wrote must want it, and yet fame was a shining, bright, and most uncertain thing.

The book was finished in my twenty-eighth year. I knew no publishers and no writers. A friend of mine took the huge manuscript—it was about 350,000 words long—and sent it to a publisher whom she knew. In a few days, a week or two, I received an answer from this man saying that the book could not be published. The gist of what he said was that his house had published several books like it the year before, that all of them had failed, and that, further, the book in its present form was so amateurish, autobiographical, and unskillful that a publisher could not risk a chance on it. I was, myself, so depressed and weary by this time, the illusion of creation which had sustained me for two and a half years had so far worn off, that I believed what the man said. At that time I was a teacher in one of New York's great universities, and when the year came to a close, I went abroad. It was only after I had been abroad almost six months that news came to me from another publisher in America that he had read my manuscript and would like to talk to me about it as soon as I came home.

I came home on New Year's Day that year. The next day I called up the publisher who had written me. He asked me if I would come to his office and talk to him. I went at once, and before I had left his office that morning, I had signed a contract and had a check for five hundred dollars in my hand.

It was the first time, so far as I can remember, that anyone had concretely suggested to me that anything I had written was worth as much as fifteen cents, and I know that I left the publisher's office that day and entered into the great swarm of men and women who passed constantly along Fifth Avenue at Forty-eighth Street and presently I found myself at 110th Street, and from that day to this I have never known how I got there.

For the next six or eight months I taught at the university and worked upon the manuscript of my book with this editor. The book appeared in the month of October, 1929. The whole experience still had elements of that dreamlike terror and unreality that writing had had for me when I had first begun it seriously and had lain in my room in London with my hands below my head and thought: Why am I here? The awful, utter nakedness of print, that thing which is for all of us so namelessly akin to shame, came closer day by day. That

I had wanted this exposure, I could not believe. It seemed to me that I had shamelessly exposed myself and yet that subtle drug of my desire and my creating held me with a serpent's eye, and I could do no other. I turned at last to this editor who had worked with me and found me, and I asked him if he could foretell the end and verdict of my labor. He said that he would rather tell me nothing, that he could not prophesy or know what profit I would have. He said, "All that I know is that they cannot let it go, they cannot ignore it. The book will find its way."

And that fairly describes what happened. I have read in recent months that this first book was received with what is called a "storm of critical applause," but this really did not happen. It got some wonderful reviews in some places; it got some unfavorable reviews in others, but it unquestionably did have a good reception for a first book, and, what was best of all, as time went on it continued to make friends among people who read books. It continued to sell over a period of four or five years in the publisher's edition, and later in a cheaper edition, the Modern Library, it renewed its life and began to sell again. The upshot of it was that after the publication of this book in the autumn of 1929, I found myself with a position as a writer. And here one of the first of my great lessons as a writer began.

Up to this time I had been a young man who wanted to be a writer more than anything on earth and who had created his first book in the great blaze of illusion which a young writer must feel when he has no evidence except his hope to drive him on. Now, in a certain measure, this had changed. I had been a writer in hope and in desire before and now I was a writer in fact. I would read about myself, for example, as one of the "younger American writers." I was a person who, some of the critics said, was to be watched. They were looking forward to my future book with interest and with a certain amount of apprehension. Here, too, my education as a writer was increasing all the time. Now, indeed, I could hear myself discussed, and somehow the fact was far more formidable than I had dreamed that it could be. It worried me, confused me, gave me a strange feeling of guilt and responsibility. I was a young American writer, and they had hopes and fears about my future, and what would I do, or would it be anything, nothing, much or little? Would the faults which they had found in my work grow worse or would I conquer them? Was I another flash in the pan? Would I come through? What would happen to me?

I let it worry me. I would go home at night and look around my room and see that morning's coffeecup still unwashed and books on the floor and a shirt where I had thrown it the night before and great stacks of manuscript and everything so common and familiar-looking and so disorderly, and then I would think that I was now "a young American writer"; that somehow I was practising an imposture on my readers and my critics because my shirt looked the way it did and my books and my bed—not, you understand, because they were disorderly, common, familiar, but just because they looked the way they did.

But now another fact began to gnaw a way into my consciousness.

The critics had begun to ask questions about the second book, and so now I had to think about the second one as well. I had always wanted to think about the second one and the thirty-second one and the fifty-second one. I had been sure that I had a hundred books in me, that all of them would be good, that each of them would make me famous. But here again was a strange and jolting transition from wild hope and exultant conviction; and plain, blazing fact remained. Now that I had actually written one book and *they*, the actual readers and critics who had read it, were looking for a second, I was up against it. I was not up against it the way I dreaded, I was just up against it cold and hard as one comes up against a wall. I was a writer. I had made the writer's life my life; there was no going back; I had to go on. What could I do? After the first book there had to be a second book. What was the second book to be about? Where would it come from?

This inexorable fact, although it became more and more pressing, did not bother me so much at first. Rather I was concerned with many other things that had to do with the publication of that first book, and as before, I had foreseen none of them. In the first place, I had not foreseen one fact which becomes absolutely plain after a man has written a book, but which he cannot foresee until he has written one. This fact is that one writes a book not in order to remember it, but in order to forget it, and now this fact was evident. As soon as the book was in print, I began to forget about it, I wanted to forget about it, I didn't want people to talk to me or question me about it. I just wanted them to leave me alone and shut up about it. And yet I longed desperately for my book's success. I wanted it to have the position of proud esteem and honor in the world that I longed for it to have—I wanted, in short, to be a successful and a famous man, and I wanted to lead the same kind of obscure and private life I'd always had and not to be told about my fame and success.

From this problem, another painful and difficult situation was produced. I had written my book, more or less, directly from the experience of my own life, and, furthermore, I now think that I may have written it with a cer-

tain naked intensity of spirit which is likely to charac-
terize the earliest work of a young writer. At any rate, I
can honestly say that I did not foresee what was to happen. I was surprised not only by the kind of response my
book had with the critics and the general public, I was
most of all surprised with the response it had in my
native town. I had thought there might be a hundred
people in that town who would read the book, but if
there were a hundred outside of the Negro population,
the blind, and the positively illiterate who did not read
it, I do not know where they are. For months the town
seethed with a fury of resentment which I had not believed possible. The book was denounced from the pulpit
by the ministers of the leading churches. Men collected
on street corners to denounce it. For weeks the women's
clubs, bridge parties, teas, receptions, book clubs, the
whole complex fabric of a small town's social life was
absorbed by an outraged clamor. I received anonymous
letters full of vilification and abuse, one which threatened to kill me if I came back home, others which were
merely obscene. One venerable old lady, whom I had
known all my life, wrote me that although she had never
believed in lynch law, she would do nothing to prevent
a mob from dragging my "big overgroan karkus" across
the public square. She informed me further, that my
mother had taken to her bed "as white as a ghost" and
would "never rise from it again."

There were many other venomous attacks from my
home town and for the first time I learned another lesson
which every young writer has got to learn. And that
lesson is the naked, blazing power of print. At that time
it was for me a bewildering and almost overwhelming
situation. My joy at the success my book had won was
mixed with bitter chagrin at its reception in my native
town. And yet I think I learned something from that

experience, too. For the first time I was forced to consider squarely this problem: Where does the material of an artist come from? What are the proper uses of that material, and how far must his freedom in the use of that material be controlled by his responsibility as a member of society? This is a difficult problem, and I have by no means come to the bottom of it yet. Perhaps I never shall, but as a result of all the distress which I suffered at that time and which others may have suffered on account of me, I have done much thinking and arrived at certain conclusions.

My book was what is often referred to as an autobiographical novel. I protested against this term in a preface to the book upon the grounds that any serious work of creation is of necessity autobiographical and that few more autobiographical works than *Gulliver's Travels* have ever been written. I added that Dr. Johnson had remarked that a man might turn over half the volumes in his library to make a single book, and that in a similar way, a novelist might turn over half the characters in his native town to make a single figure for his novel. In spite of this the people in my native town were not persuaded or appeased, and the charge of autobiography was brought against me in many other places.

As I have said, my conviction is that all serious creative work must be at bottom autobiographical, and that a man must use the material and experience of his own life if he is to create anything that has substantial value. But I also believe now that the young writer is often led through inexperience to a use of the materials of life which are, perhaps, somewhat too naked and direct for the purpose of a work of art. The thing a young writer is likely to do is to confuse the limits between actuality and reality. He tends unconsciously to describe an event in such a way because it actually happened that way, and from an artistic point of view, I can now see that this is wrong. It is not, for example, important that one remembers a beautiful woman of easy virtue as having come from the state of Kentucky in the year 1907. She could perfectly well have come from Idaho or Texas or Nova Scotia. The important thing really is only to express as well as possible the character and quality of the beautiful woman of easy virtue. But the young writer, chained to fact and to his own inexperience, as yet unliberated by maturity, is likely to argue, "she must be described as coming from Kentucky because that is where she actually did come from."

In spite of this, it is impossible for a man who has the stuff of creation in him to make a literal transcription of his own experience. Everything in a work of art is changed and transfigured by the personality of the artist. And as far as my own first book is concerned, I can truthfully say that I do not believe that there is a single page of it that is true to fact. And from this circumstance, also, I learned another curious thing about writing. For although my book was not true to fact, it was true to the general experience of the town I came from and I hope, of course, to the general experience of all men living. The best way I can describe the situation is this: it was as if I were a sculptor who had found a certain kind of clay with which to model. Now a farmer who knew well the neighborhood from which this clay had come might pass by and find the sculptor at his work and say to him, "I know the farm from which you got that clay." But it would be unfair of him to say, "I know the figure, too." Now I think what happened in my native town is that having seen the clay, they became immediately convinced that they recognized the figure, too, and the results of this misconception were so painful and ludicrous that the telling of it is almost past belief.

It was my experience to be assured by people from my native town not only that they remembered incidents and characters in my first book, which may have had some basis in actuality, but also that they remembered incidents which so far as I know had no historical basis whatever. For example, there was one scene in the book in which a stonecutter is represented as selling to a notorious woman of the town a statue of a marble angel which he has treasured for many years. So far as I know, there was no basis in fact for this story, and yet I was informed by several people later that they not only remembered the incident perfectly, but had actually been witnesses to the transaction. Nor was this the end of the story. I heard that one of the newspapers sent a reporter and a photographer to the cemetery and a photograph was printed in the paper with a statement to the effect that the angel was the now famous angel which had stood upon the stonecutter's porch for so many years and had given the title to my book. The unfortunate part of this proceeding was that I had never seen or heard of this angel before, and that this angel was, in fact, erected over the grave of a well-known Methodist lady who had died a few years before and that her indignant family had immediately written the paper to demand a retraction of its story, saying that their mother had been in no way connected with the infamous book or the infamous angel which had given the infamous book its name. Such, then, were some of the unforeseen difficulties with which I was confronted after the publication of my first book.

Month was passing into month; I had had a success. The way was opened to me. There was only one thing for me to do and that was work, and I was spending my time consuming myself with anger, grief, and useless passion about the reception the book had had in my native town, or wasting myself again in exuberant elation because of the critics and the readers' praise, or in anguish and bitterness because of their ridicule. For the first time, I realized the nature of one of the artist's greatest conflicts, and was faced with the need of meeting it. For the first time I saw not only that the artist must live and sweat and love and suffer and enjoy as other men, but that the artist must also work as other men and that, furthermore, he must work even while these common events of life are going on. It seems a simple and banal assertion, but I learned it hardly, and in one of the worst moments of my life. There is no such thing as an artistic vacuum; there is no such thing as a time when the artist may work in a delightful atmosphere, free of agony that other men must know, or if the artist ever does find such a time, it is something not to be hoped for, something not to be sought for indefinitely.

At any rate, while my life and energy were absorbed in the emotional vortex which my first book had created, I was getting almost no work done on the second. And now I was faced with another fundamental problem which every young writer must meet squarely if he is to continue. How is a man to get his writing done? How long should he work at writing, and how often? What kind of method, if any, must he find in following his work? I suddenly found myself face to face with the grim necessity of constant, daily work. And as simple as this discovery may seem to everyone, I was not prepared for it. A young writer without a public does not feel the sense of necessity, the pressure of time, as does a writer who has been published and who must now begin to think of time schedules, publishing seasons, the completion of his next book. I realized suddenly with a sense of definite shock that I had let six months go by since the publication of my first book and that, save for a great many notes and fragments, I had done nothing. Meanwhile, the book continued to sell slowly but steadily, and in February, 1930, about five months after its publication, I found it possible to resign from the faculty of New York University and devote my full time to the preparation of a second book. That spring I was also fortunate enough to be awarded the Guggenheim Fellowship which would enable me to live and work abroad for a year. And accordingly at the beginning of May, I went abroad again.

I was in Paris for a couple of months, until the middle of July, and although I now compelled myself to work for four or five hours a day, my effort at composition was still confused and broken, and there was nothing yet that had the structural form and unity of a book. The life of the great city fascinated me as it had always done, but also aroused all the old feelings of naked homelessness, rootlessness, and loneliness which I have always felt there. It was, and has always remained for me, at least, the most homesick city in the world; the place where I have felt mostly an alien and a stranger, and certainly for me as fascinating and seductive as the city is, it has never been a good place to work. But here I would like to say something about places to work because that is another problem which causes young writers a great deal of doubt, uncertainty, and confusion, and, I think, uselessly.

I had gone through the whole experience and now I was almost done with it. I had come to Paris first six years before, a youth of twenty-four, filled with all the romantic faith and foolishness which many young men at that time felt when they saw Paris. I had come there that first time, so I told myself, to work, and so glamorous was the magic name of Paris at that time, that I really thought one could work far better there than anywhere on earth; that it was a place where the very air was impregnated with the energies of art; where the artist was bound to find a more fortunate and happy life than he could possibly find in America. Now I had come to see that this was wrong. I had come to understand very plainly that what many of us were doing in those years when we fled from our own country and sought refuge abroad was not really looking for a place to work, but looking for a place where we could escape from work; that what we were really fleeing from in those years was not the Philistinism, the materialism, and ugliness in American life which we said we were fleeing from, but from the necessity of grappling squarely with ourselves and the necessity of finding in ourselves, somehow, the stuff to live by, to get from our own lives and our own experience the substance of our art which every man who ever wrote a living thing has had to get out of himself and without which he is lost.

The place to work! Yes, the place to work *was* Paris; it *was* Spain; it *was* Italy and Capri and Majorca, but, great God, it was also Keokuk, and Portland, Maine, and Denver, Colorado, and Yancey County, North Carolina, and wherever we might be, if work was there within us at the time. If this was all that I had learned from these voyages to Europe, if the price of all this wandering had been just this simple lesson, it would have been worth the price, but that was not all. I had found out during these years that the way to discover one's own country was to leave it; that the way to find America was to find it in one's heart, one's memory, and one's spirit, and in a foreign land.

I think I may say that I discovered America during these years abroad out of my very need of her. The huge gain of this discovery seemed to come directly from my sense of loss. I had been to Europe five times now; each time I had come with delight, with maddening eagerness to return, and each time how, where, and in what way I did not know, I had felt the bitter ache of homelessness, a desperate longing for America, an overwhelming desire to return.

During that summer in Paris, I think I felt this great homesickness more than ever before, and I really believe that from this emotion, this constant and almost intolerable effort of memory and desire, the material and the structure of the books I now began to write were derived.

The quality of my memory is characterized, I believe, in a more than ordinary degree by the intensity of its sense impressions, its power to evoke and bring back the odors, sounds, colors, shapes, and feel of things with concrete vividness. Now my memory was at work night and day, in a way that I could at first neither check nor control and that swarmed unbidden in a stream of blazing pageantry across my mind, with the million forms and substances of the life that I had left, which was my own, America. I would be sitting, for example, on the terrace of a café watching the flash and play of life before me on the Avenue de l'Opéra, and suddenly I would remember the iron railing that goes along the boardwalk at Atlantic City. I could see it instantly just the way it was, the heavy iron pipe; its raw, galvanized look; the way the joints were fitted together. It was all so vivid and concrete that I could feel my hand upon it and know the exact dimensions, its size and weight and shape. And suddenly I would realize that I had never seen any railing that looked like this in Europe. And this utterly familiar, common thing would suddenly be revealed to me with all the wonder with which we discover a thing which we have seen all our life and yet have never known before. Or again, it would be a bridge, the look of an old iron bridge across an American river, the sound the train makes as it goes across it; the spoke-and-hollow rumble of the ties below; the look of the muddy banks; the slow, thick, yellow wash of an American river; an old flat-bottomed boat half-filled with water stogged in the muddy bank; or it would be, most lonely and haunting of all the sounds I know, the sound of a milk wagon as it entered an American street just at the first grey of the morning, the slow and lonely clopping of the hoof upon the street, the jink of bottles, the sudden rattle of a battered old milk can, the swift and hurried footsteps of the milkman, and again the jink of bottles, a low word spoken to his horse, and then the great, slow, clopping hoof receding into silence, and then quietness and a bird song rising in the street again. Or it would be a little wooden shed out in the country two miles from my home town where people waited for the streetcar, and I could see and feel again the dull and rusty color of the old green paint and see and feel all of the initials that had been carved out with jackknives on the planks and benches within the shed, and smell the warm and sultry smell so resinous and so thrilling, so filled with a strange and nameless excitement of an unknown joy, a coming prophecy, and hear the streetcar as it came to a stop, the moment of brooding, drowsing silence; a hot thrum and drowsy stitch at three o'clock; the smell of grass and hot sweet clover; and then the sudden sense of absence, loneliness, and departure when the streetcar had gone and there was nothing but the hot and drowsy stitch at three o'clock again.

Or again, it would be an American street with all its jumble of a thousand ugly architectures. It would be Montague Street or Fulton Street in Brooklyn, or Eleventh Street in New York, or other streets where I had lived; and suddenly I would see the gaunt and savage webbing of the elevated structure along Fulton Street, and how the light swarmed through in dusty, broken bars, and I could remember the old, familiar rusty color, that incomparable rusty color that gets into so many things here in America. And this also would be like something I had seen a million times and lived with all my life.

I would sit there, looking out upon the Avenue de l'Opéra, and my life would ache with the whole memory of it; the desire to see it again; somehow to find a word for it; a language that would tell its shape, its color, the way we have all known and felt and seen it. And when I understood this thing, I saw that I must find for myself the tongue to utter what I knew but could not say. And from the moment of that discovery, the line and purpose of my life was shaped. The end towards which every energy of my life and talent would be henceforth directed was in such a way as this defined. It was as if I had discovered a whole new universe of chemical elements and had begun to see certain relations between some of them but had by no means begun to organize the whole series into a harmonious and coherent union. From this time on, I think my efforts might be described as the effort to complete that organization, to discover that articulation for which I strove, to bring about that final coherent union. I know that I have failed thus far in doing so, but I believe I understand pretty thoroughly just where the nature of my failure lies, and of course my deepest and most earnest hope is that the time will come when I shall not fail.

At any rate, from this time on the general progress of the three books which I was to write in the next four and a half years could be fairly described in somewhat this way. It was a progress that began in a whirling vortex and a creative chaos and that proceeded slowly at the expense of infinite confusion, toil, and error toward clariication and the articulation of an ordered and formal structure. An extraordinary image remains to me from that year, the year I spent abroad when the material of these books first began to take on an articulate form. It seemed that I had inside me, swelling and gathering all the time, a huge black cloud, and that this cloud was loaded with electricity, pregnant, crested, with a kind of hurricane violence that could not be held in check much longer; that the moment was approaching fast when it must break. Well, all I can say is that the storm did break. It broke that summer while I was in Switzerland. It came in torrents, and it is not over yet.

I cannot really say the book was written. It was something that took hold of me and possessed me, and before I was done with it—that is, before I finally emerged with the first completed part—it seemed to me that it had done for me. It was exactly as if this great black storm cloud I have spoken of had opened up and, mid flashes of lightning, was pouring from its depth a torential and ungovernable flood. Upon that flood everything was swept and borne along as by a great river. And I was borne along with it.

There was nothing at first which could be called a novel. I wrote about night and darkness in America, and the faces of the sleepers in ten thousand little towns; and of the tides of sleep and how the rivers flowed forever in the darkness. I wrote about the hissing glut of tides upon ten thousand miles of coast; of how the moonlight blazed down on the wilderness and filled the cat's cold eye with blazing yellow. I wrote about death and sleep, and of that enfabled rock of life we call the city. I wrote about October, of great trains that thundered through the night, of ships and stations in the morning; of men in harbors and the traffic of the ships.

I spent the winter of that year in England from

October until March, and here perhaps because of the homely familiarity of the English life, the sense of order and repose which such a life can give one, my work moved forward still another step from this flood-tide chaos of creation. For the first time the work began to take on the lineaments of design. These lineaments were still confused and broken, sometimes utterly lost, but now I really did get the sense at last that I was working on a great block of marble, shaping a figure which no one but its maker could as yet define, but which was emerging more and more into the sinewy lines of composition.

From the beginning—and this was one fact that in all my times of hopelessness returned to fortify my faith in my conviction—the idea, the central legend that I wished my book to express had not changed. And this central idea was this: The deepest search in life, it seemed to me, the thing that in one way or another was central to all living was man's search to find a father, not merely the father of his flesh, not merely the lost father of his youth, but the image of a strength and wisdom external to his need and superior to his hunger, to which the belief and power of his own life could be united.

Yet I was terribly far away from the actual accomplishment of a book—how far away I could not at that time foresee. But four more years would have to pass before the first of a series of books on which I was now embarked would be ready for the press, and if I could have known that in those next four years there would be packed a hundred lives of birth and death, despair, defeat and triumph, and the sheer exhaustion of a brute fatigue, I do not know whether or not I could have found the power within myself to continue. But I was still sustained by the exuberant optimism of youth. My temperament, which is pessimistic about many things, has always been a curiously sanguine one concerning time, and although more than a year had now gone by and I had done no more than write great chants on death and sleep, prepare countless notes and trace here and there the first dim outlines of a formal pattern, I was confident that by the spring or the fall of the next year my book would somehow miraculously be ready.

So far as I can describe with any accuracy, the progress of that winter's work in England was not along the lines of planned design, but along this line that I have mentioned—writing some of the sections which I knew would have to be in the book. Meanwhile what was really going on in my whole creative consciousness, during all this time, although I did not realize it at the moment, was this: What I was really doing, what I had been doing all the time since my discovery of my America in Paris the summer before, was to explore day by day and month by month with a fantatical intensity, the whole material domain of my resources as a man and as a writer. This exploration went on for a period which I can estimate conservatively as two years and a half. It is still going on, although not with the same all-absorbing concentration, because the work it led to, the work that after infinite waste and labor it helped me wonderfully to define, that work has reached such a state of final definition that the immediate task of finishing it is the one that now occupies the energy and interest of my life.

In a way, during that period of my life, I think I was like the Ancient Mariner who told the Wedding Guest that his frame was wrenched by the woeful agony which forced him to begin his tale before it left him free. In my own experience, my wedding guests were the great ledgers in which I wrote, and the tale which I told to them would have seemed, I am afraid, completely incoherent, as meaningless as Chinese characters, had any reader seen them. I could by no means hope to give a comprehensive idea of the whole extent of this labor because three years of work and perhaps a million and a half words went into these books. It included everything from gigantic and staggering lists of the towns, cities, counties, states, and countries I had been in, to minutely thorough, desperately evocative descriptions of the undercarriage, the springs, wheels, flanges, axle rods, color, weight, and quality of the day coach of an American railway train. There were lists of the rooms and houses in which I had lived or in which I had slept for at least a night, together with the most accurate and evocative descriptions of those rooms that I could write —their size, their shape, the color and design of the wallpaper, the way a towel hung down, the way a chair creaked, a streak of water rust upon the ceiling. There were countless charts, catalogues, descriptions that I can only classify here under the general heading of Amount and Number. What were the total combined populations of all the countries in Europe and America? In how many of those countries had I had some personal and vital experience? In the course of my twenty-nine or thirty years of living, how many people had I seen? How many had I passed by on the streets? How many had I seen on trains and subways, in theaters, at baseball or football games? With how many had I actually had some vital and illuminating experience, whether of joy, pain, anger, pity, love, or simple casual companionship, however brief?

In addition, one might come upon other sections under some such cryptic heading as "Where now?" Under such a heading as this, there would be brief notations of those thousands of things which all of us have seen for just a flash, a moment in our lives, which seem to be of no consequence whatever at the moment that we see them, and which live in our minds and hearts forever, which are somehow pregnant with all the joy and sorrow of the human destiny, and which we know, somehow, are therefore more important than many things of more apparent consequence. "Where now?" Some quiet steps that came and passed along a leafy nighttime street in summer in a little town down South long years ago; a woman's voice, her sudden burst of low and tender laughter; then the voices and the footsteps going, silence, the leafy rustle of the trees. "Where now?" Two trains that met and paused at a little station at some little town at some unknown moment upon the huge body of the continent; a girl who looked and smiled from the window of the other train; another passing in a motor car on the streets of Norfolk; the winter boarders in a little board-inghouse down South twenty years ago; Miss Florrie Mangle, the trained nurse; Miss Jessie Rimmer, the cashier at Reed's drugstore; Doctor Richards, the clair-voyant; the pretty girl who cracked the whip and thrust her head into the lion's mouth with Johnny J. Jones Carnival and Combined Shows.

"Where now?" It went beyond the limits of man's actual memory. It went back to the farthest adyt of his childhood before conscious memory had begun, the way he thought he must have felt the sun one day and heard Peagram's cow next door wrenching the coarse grass against the fence, or heard the streetcar stop upon the hill above his father's house at noon; and Earnest Pea-gram coming home to lunch, his hearty voice in midday greeting; and then the streetcar going, the sudden lonely green-gold silence of the streetcar's absence and an iron gate slamming, then the light of that lost day fades out. "Where now?" He can recall no more and does not know if what he has recalled is fact or fable or a fusion of the two. Where now—in these great ledger books, month after month, I wrote such things as this, not only the concrete, material record of man's ordered memory, but all the things he scarcely dares to think he has remembered; all the flicks and darts and haunting lights that flash across the mind of man that will return unbidden at an unexpected moment: a voice once heard; a face that vanished; the way the sunlight came and went; the rustling of a leaf upon a bough; a stone, a leaf, a door.

It may be objected, it has been objected already by certain critics, that in such research as I have here attempted to describe there is a quality of intemperate excess, an almost insane hunger to devour the entire body of human experience, to attempt to include more, experience more, than the measure of one life can hold, or than the limits of a single work of art can well define. I readily admit the validity of this criticism. I think I realize as well as any one the fatal dangers that are consequent to such a ravenous desire, the damage it may wreak upon one's life and on one's work. But having had this thing within me, it was in no way possible for me to reason it out of me, no matter how cogently my reason worked against it. The only way I could meet it was to meet it squarely, not with reason but with life.

It was part of my life; for many years it was my life; and the only way I could get it out of me was to live it out of me. And that is what I did. I have not wholly succeeded in that purpose yet, but I have succeeded better than I at one time dared to hope. And now I really believe that so far as the artist is concerned, the unlimited extent of human experience is not so important for him as the depth and intensity with which he experiences things. I also know now that it is a great deal more important to have known one hundred living men and women in New York, to have understood their lives, to have got, somehow, at the root and source from which their natures came than to have seen or passed or talked with 7,000,000 people upon the city streets. And what finally I should most like to say about this research which I have attempted to describe is this: That foolish and mistaken as much of it may seem, the total quality, end, and impact of that whole experience was not useless or excessive. And from my own point of view, at least, it is in its whole implication the one thing I may have to tell about my experience as a writer which may be of some concrete value to other people. I consider this experience on the whole the most valuable and practical in my whole writing life thus far. With all the waste and error and confusion it led me into, it brought me closer to a concrete definition of my resources, a true estimate of my talents at this period of my life, and, most of all, toward a rudimentary, a just-beginning, but a living apprehension of the articulation I am looking for, the language I have got to have if, as an artist, my life is to proceed and grow, than any other thing that has ever happened to me.

I know the door is not yet open. I know the tongue, the speech, the language that I seek is not yet found, but I believe with all my heart that I have found the way, have made a channel, am started on my first beginning. And I believe with all my heart, also, that each man for himself and in his own way, each man who ever hopes to make a living thing out of the substances of his one life, must find that way, that language, and that door—must find it for himself as I have tried to do.

When I returned to America in the spring of 1931, although I had three or four hundred thousand words of material, I had nothing that could be published as a novel. Almost a year and a half had elapsed since the publication of my first book and already people had begun to ask that question which is so well meant, but which as year followed year was to become more intolerable to my ears than the most deliberate mockery: "Have you finished your next book yet?" "When is it going to be published?"

At this time I was sure that a few months of steady work would bring the book to completion. I found a place, a little basement flat in the Assyrian quarter in South Brooklyn, and there I went about my task.

The spring passed into the summer; the summer, into autumn. I was working hard, day after day, and still nothing that had the unity and design of a single work appeared. October came and with it a second full year since the publication of my first book. And now, for the first time, I was irrevocably committed so far as the publication of my book was concerned. I began to feel the sensation of pressure, and of naked desperation, which was to become almost maddeningly intolerable in the next three years. For the first time I began to realize that my project was much larger than I thought it would be. I had still believed at the time of my return from Europe that I was writing a single book, which would be comprised within the limits of about 200,000 words. Now as scene followed scene, as character after character came into being, as my understanding of my material became more comprehensive, I discovered that it would be impossible to write the book I had planned within the limits I had thought would be sufficient.

All of this time I was being baffled by a certain time element in the book, by a time relation which could not be escaped, and for which I was now desperately seeking some structural channel. There were three time elements inherent in the material. The first and most obvious was an element of actual present time, an element which carried the narrative forward, which represented characters and events as living in the present and moving forward into an immediate future. The second time element was of past time, one which represented these same characters as acting and as being acted upon by all the accumulated impact of man's experience so that each moment of their lives was conditioned not only by what they experienced in that moment, but by all that they had experienced up to that moment. In addition to these two time elements, there was a third which I conceived as being time immutable, the time of rivers, mountains, oceans, and the earth; a kind of eternal and unchanging universe of time against which would be projected the transience of man's life, the bitter briefness of his day. It was the tremendous problem of these three time elements that almost defeated me and that cost me countless hours of anguish in the years that were to follow.

As I began to realize the true nature of the task I had set for myself, the image of the river began to haunt my mind. I actually felt that I had a great river thrusting for release inside of me and that I had to find a channel into which its flood-like power could pour. I knew I had to find it or I would be destroyed in the flood of my own creation, and I am sure that every artist who ever lived has had the same experience.

Meanwhile, I was being baffled by a fixed and impossible idea whose error at the time I did not fully apprehend. I was convinced at that time that this whole gigantic plan had to be realized within the limits of a single book which would be called "The October Fair." It was not until more than a year had passed, when I realized finally that what I had to deal with was material which covered almost 150 years in history, demanded the action of more than 2000 characters, and would in its final design include almost every racial type and social class of American life, that I realized that even the pages of a book of 200,000 words were wholly inadequate for the purpose.

How did I finally arrive at this conclusion? I think it is not too much to say that I simply wrote myself into it. During all that year, I was writing furiously, feeling now the full pressure of inexorable time, the need to finish something. I wrote like mad; I finished scene after scene, chapter after chapter. The characters began to come to life, to grow and multiply until they were numbered by the hundreds, but so huge was the extent of my design, as I now desperately realized, that I can liken these chapters only to a row of lights which one sometimes sees at night from the windows of a speeding train, strung out across the dark and lonely countryside.

I would work furiously day after day until my creative energies were utterly exhausted, and although at the end of such a period I would have written perhaps as much as 200,000 words, enough in itself to make a very long book, I would realize with a feeling of horrible despair that what I had completed was only one small section of a single book.

During this time I reached that state of naked need and utter isolation which every artist has got to meet and conquer if he is to survive at all. Before this I had been sustained by that delightful illusion of success which we all have when we dream about the books we are going to write instead of actually doing them. Now I was face to face with it, and suddenly I realized that I had committed my life and my integrity so irrevocably to this struggle that I must conquer now or be destroyed. I was alone with my own work, and now I knew that I had to be alone with it, that no one could help me with it now no matter how anyone might wish to help. For the first time I realized another naked fact which every artist must know, and that is that in a man's work there are contained not only the seeds of life, but the seeds of death, and that that power of creation which sustains us will also destroy us like a leprosy if we let it rot stillborn in our vitals. I had to get it out of me somehow. I saw that now. And now for the first time a terrible doubt began to creep into my mind that I might not live long enough to get it out of me, that I had created a labor so large and so impossible that the energy of a dozen life-times would not suffice for its accomplishment.

During this time, however, I was sustained by one piece of inestimable good fortune. I had for a friend a man of immense and patient wisdom and a gentle but unyielding fortitude. I think that if I was not destroyed at this time by the sense of hopelessness which these gigantic labors had awakened in me, it was largely be-cause of the courage and patience of this man. I did not give in because he would not let me give in, and I think it is also true that at this particular time he had the ad-vantage of being in the position of a skilled observer at a battle. I was myself engaged in that battle, covered by its dust and sweat and exhausted by its struggle, and I understood far less clearly than my friend the nature and the progress of the struggle in which I was engaged. At this time there was little that this man could do except observe, and in one way or another keep me at my task, and in many quiet and marvelous ways he succeeded in doing this.

I was now at the place where I must produce, and even the greatest editor can do little for a writer until he has brought from the secret darkness of his own spirit into the common light of day the completed concrete accomplishment of his imagining. My friend, the editor, has likened his own function at this painful time to that of a man who is trying to hang onto the fin of a plunging whale, but hang on he did, and it is to his tenacity that I owe my final release.

Meanwhile, my creative power was functioning at the

highest intensity it had ever known. I wrote at times without belief that I would ever finish, with nothing in me but black despair, and yet I wrote and wrote and could not give up writing. And it seemed that despair itself was the very goad that urged me on, that made me write even when I had no belief that I would ever finish. It seemed to me that my life in Brooklyn, although I had been there only two and a half years, went back through centuries of time, through ocean depths of black and bottomless experience which no ordinary scale of hours would ever measure. People have sometimes asked me what happened to my life during these years. They have asked me how I ever found time to know anything that was going on in the world about me when my life was so completely absorbed by this world of writing. Well, it may seem to be an extraordinary fact, but the truth is that never in my whole life have I lived so fully, have I shared so richly in the common life of man as I did during these three years when I was struggling with the giant problem of my own work.

For one thing, my whole sensory and creative equipment, my powers of feeling and reflection—even the sense of hearing, and above all my powers of memory, had reached the greatest degree of sharpness that they had ever known. At the end of the day of savage labor, my mind was still blazing with its effort, could by no opiate of reading, poetry, music, alcohol, or any other pleasure, be put at rest. I was unable to sleep, unable to subdue the tumult of these creative energies, and as a result of this condition, for three years I prowled the streets, explored the swarming web of the million-footed city and came to know it as I had never done before. It was a black time in the history of the nation, a black time in my own life and, I suppose, it is but natural that my own memory of it now should be a pretty grim and painful one.

Everywhere around me, during these years, I saw the evidence of an incalculable ruin and suffering. My own people, the members of my own family, had been ruined, had lost all the material wealth and accumulation of a lifetime in what was called the "depression." And that universal calamity had somehow struck the life of almost every one I knew. Moreover, in this endless quest and prowling of the night through the great web and jungle of the city, I saw, lived, felt, and experienced the full weight of that horrible human calamity.

I saw a man whose life had subsided into a mass of shapeless and filthy rags, devoured by vermin; wretches huddled together for a little warmth in freezing cold squatting in doorless closets upon the foul seat of a public latrine within the very shadow, the cold shelter of palatial and stupendous monuments of wealth. I saw acts of sickening violence and cruelty, the menace of brute privilege, a cruel and corrupt authority trampling ruthlessly below its feet the lives of the poor, the weak, the wretched, and defenseless of the earth.

And the staggering impact of this black picture of man's inhumanity to his fellow man, the unending repercussions of these scenes of suffering, violence, oppression, hunger, cold, and filth and poverty going on unheeded in a world in which the rich were still rotten with their wealth left a scar upon my life, a conviction in my soul which I shall never lose.

And from it all, there has come as the final deposit, a burning memory, a certain evidence of the fortitude of man, his ability to suffer and somehow to survive. And it is for this reason now that I think I shall always remember this black period with a kind of joy that I could not at that time have believed possible, for it was during this time that I lived my life through to a first completion, and through the suffering and labor of my own life came to share those qualities in the lives of people all around me. And that is another thing which the making of a book has done for me. It has given my life that kind of growth which I think the fulfillment of each work does give the artist's life, and insofar as I have known these things, I think that they have added to my stature.

The early winter of 1933 arrived and with it, it seemed to me, the final doom of an abysmal failure. I still wrote and wrote, but blindly, hopelessly, like an old horse who trots around in the unending circle of a treadmill and knows no other end nor purpose for his life than this. If I slept at night, it was to sleep an unceasing nightmare of blazing visions that swept across my fevered and unresting mind. And when I woke, it was to wake exhausted, not knowing anything but work, lashing myself on into a hopeless labor, and so furiously at it through the day; and then night again, a frenzied prowling of a thousand streets, and so to bed and sleepless sleep again, the nightmare pageantry to which my consciousness lay chained a spectator.

There was a kind of dream which I can only summarize as dreams of Guilt and Time. Chameleonlike in all their damnable and unending fecundities, they restored to me the whole huge world that I had known, the billion faces and the million tongues, and they restored it to me with the malevolent triumph of a passive and unwanted ease. My daily conflict with Amount and Number, the huge accumulations of my years of struggle with the forms of life, my brutal and unending efforts to record upon my memory each brick and paving stone of every street that I had ever walked upon, each face of every thronging crowd in every city, every country with which my spirit had contested its savage and uneven struggle for supremacy—they all returned now—each stone, each street, each town, each country—yes, even every book in the library whose loaded shelves I had tried vainly to devour at college—they returned upon the wings of these mighty, sad, and somehow quietly demented dreams—I saw and heard and knew them all at once, was instantly without pain or anguish, with the calm consciousness of God, master of the whole universe of life against whose elements I had contended vainly for all-knowledge for so many years. And the fruit of that enormous triumph, the calm and instant passivity of that inhuman and demented immortality, was somehow sadder and more bitter than the most galling bitterness of defeat in my contention with the multitudes of life had ever been.

For above that universe of dreams there shone forever a tranquil, muted, and unchanging light of time. And through the traffic of those thronging crowds—whose faces, whose whole united and divided life was now instantly and without an effort of the will, my *own*— there rose forever the sad unceasing murmurs of the body of this life, the vast recessive fadings of the shadow of man's death that breathes forever with its dirgelike sigh around the huge shores of the world.

And *beyond, beyond*—forever *above, around, behind* the vast and tranquil consciousness of my spirit that now held the earth and all her elements in the huge clasp of its effortless subjection—there dwelt forever the fatal knowledge of my own inexpiable *guilt*.

I did not know what I had done—I only knew that I had ruinously forgotten time, and by so doing had betrayed my brother men. I had been long from home— why, how, or in what way, I could not know—but drugged there in the drowsy fumes of some green country of the witches' magic, with something in me dark and full of grief I could not quite remember. And suddenly I was home again—walking alone beneath that light of tranquil, quiet, and unchanging brown, walking the roads, the hill-slopes, and the streets of my familiar country—sometimes the *exact* and *actual* lineaments of home, my childhood, and my native town, so that not only all that I had known and remembered—each familiar street and face and house and every cobblestone upon the pavement—but countless things I never knew that I had seen, or had forgotten that I ever knew—a rusty hinge upon the cellar door, the way a stair creaked, or an old cracked blister of brown paint upon the woodwork by the grate, an oak tree trunk upon the hill all hollowed out upon one side by a knotted hole, the glazed pattern of the glass in the front door, the brass handle of a streetcar brake-control, quite rubbed to silver on one side by the hard grip of the motorman, and covered by a cloth tobacco sack—such things as these, together with a million others, returned now to torment my sleep.

And even more than these, more, more familiar even than these scenes of memory and inheritance, were those landscapes that somehow had been *derived* from them— the streets, the towns, the houses, and the faces that I saw and imagined not the way they *were*, but the way they *should* be in the unfathomed, strange, and unsuspected logics of man's brain and heart—and that were, on this account, more real than realness, and more true than home.

I had been long from home—I had grown old in some evil and enchanted place, I had allowed my life to waste and rot in the slothful and degrading surfeits of Circean time. And now my life was lost—my work undone—I had betrayed my home, my friends, my people in the duties of some solemn and inviolable trust—and suddenly I was home again, and *silence* was my answer!

They did not look at me with looks of bitterness and hate, they did not lash me with the fierce opprobrium of scorn, or curse me with the menaces of vengeance and reprisal—oh, if they had, what balm of anguish and of judgment even curses would have had!—but instead their look was silence, and their tongue was mute. And again, again, I walked the streets of that familiar town, and after years of absence saw again the features of familiar faces, and heard familiar words, the sounds of well-known voices once again, and with a still and deep amazement saw the shift and interplay of action, the common familiarity of day, the traffic of the streets, and saw that it was all as it had always been, I had forgotten nothing—until I passed them, and death fell.

I walked among them, and their movements ceased, I walked among them, and their tongues were still, I walked among them, and they neither moved nor spoke until I passed, and if they looked at me, their eyes were blank with silence and no memory; there was no reproach, no grief, and no contempt, there was no bitterness and scorn—if I had died, there should at least have been the ghost of memory, but it was as if I never had been born. And so I passed them by, and everywhere I trod was death, and when I had gone by, behind me I could hear their voices start again; the clamors of the street, and all the traffic of bright day awoke—but only after I had passed them by!

And so the whole town flowed around me, was behind me, and at once, without a bridge or instant of transition, I was walking on a barren road, across the huge sweep of a treeless waste and barren vacancy and that tranquil, sad, and fatal light shone on me from the horror of a planetary vacancy, the lidless and remorseless eye of an unperturbed sky that ate into my naked spirit constantly the acid of unuttered shame.

Another and more pertinent variety of these dreams of Guilt and Time would take this form: It seemed to me that I had gone abroad, was living there, and yet was conscious that I was still employed as an instructor at the university. Remote from all the violence and turmoil of America, the harsh impact of its daily life, remote too from the rasping jargon of the university, its corridors packed with swarthy faces, loud with strident tongues, away from all the jar and rush and hurly-burly of its fevered life, its unwholesome tensions and its straining nerves, I lived my life in foreign luxuries of green and gold. I dreamed my life away in ancient Gothic towns, or in the pleasant romance of a château country, my spirit slid from land to land, from one enchantment to another, my life was passing by in spells of drowsy magic—and yet I was forever haunted by a consciousness of Time and Guilt, the obscure gnawing of forsaken trust. And suddenly I would seem to wake into a full and frenzied consciousness: I had been gone from home a year—my classes at the university had been waiting on me—and instantly I was there again, rushing through those swarming corridors, hurrying frantically from one class-room to another, trying desperately to find the classes I had so forgotten. There was a grotesque and horrible quality of humor in these dreams, which unfortunately I could not appreciate: I was somehow convinced my forlorn classes had been seeking for me for a year, I saw them searching through the mazes of the corridors, prowling among the swarming myriads of their 30,000 fellow students, sitting in patient dejection at the hours appointed for our meetings in classrooms where their absent teacher never entered. And finally—and most

horrible of all—I saw the mounting pile of unmarked
student themes—those accursed themes that grew in
number week by week—that piled up in mountainous
and hopeless accumulations—whose white backs were
hideously innocent of the scrawled comment with which
I had once—tormented by twin agonies of boredom and
conscience—covered every scrap of their surface. And
now it was too late! Even a month, two weeks, a week—
some miracle of time and frenzied labor—might have
served somehow to retrieve myself—but now it was the
last day of the term, the last class ended, the last irrevocable moment of salvation had gone by. I found myself
suddenly standing there in the offices of the English
faculty, struck dumb with horror, confronted by the
great white mountain of those unmarked themes. I
turned, a ring of silent forms encircled me, not staring,
not harsh with scorn or anger, and not thrusting close,
but just looking at me with the still surveyal of their
condemnation. My little Jews stood first, their dark eyes
fixed on me with a dejected but unwavering reproach,
and behind them stood the jury of my peers, the outer
circle of instructors.

They were all there—students, instructors, friends,
enemies, and the huge damnation of that pile of unmarked themes—there was no word spoken, nothing but
their quiet look of inflexible and unpardoning accusal.

This dream returned to torture sleep a hundred times:
Each time I would awake from it in a cold sweat of
anguish and of horror, and so strong was the impression
of the dream, so real and terrible the spell of its conviction, that sometimes I would wake out of this dream and
lie for minutes in cold terror while my mind fought with
the phantoms of my sleep to argue me back into reality.

Nor were these dreams of Guilt and Time the only
ones: my mind and memory in sleep blazed with a fiery

river of unending images: the whole vast reservoirs of memory were exhumed and poured into the torrents of this fiery flood, a million things, once seen and long forgotten, were restored and blazed across my vision in this stream of light—and a million million things unseen, the faces, cities, streets, and landscapes yet unseen and long imagined—the unknown faces yet more real than these that I had known, the unheard voices more familiar than the voices I had heard forever, the unseen patterns, masses, shapes, and landscapes in their essence far more real than any actual or substantial fact that I had ever known—all streamed across my fevered and unresting mind the flood of their unending pageantry—and suddenly I knew that it would never end.

For sleep was dead forever, the merciful, dark, and sweet oblivions of childhood sleep. The worm had entered at my heart, the worm lay coiled and feeding at my brain, my spirit, and my memory—I knew that finally I had been caught in my own fire, consumed by my own hungers, impaled on the hook of that furious and insatiate desire that had absorbed my life for years. I knew, in short, that one bright cell in the brain or heart or memory would now blaze on forever—by night, by day, through every waking, sleeping moment of my life, the worm would feed and the light be lit—that no anodyne of food or drink, or friendship, travel, sport or women could ever quench it, and that nevermore until death put its total and conclusive darkness on my life, could I escape.

I knew at last I had become a writer: I knew at last what happens to a man who makes the writer's life his own.

Such was the state my life had come to in the early winter of 1933, and even at that moment, although I could not see it, the end of my huge labor was in sight.

In the middle of December of that year the editor, of whom I have spoken, and who, during all this tormented period, had kept a quiet watch upon me, called me to his home and calmly informed me that my book was finished. I could only look at him with stunned surprise, and finally I only could tell him out of the depth of my own hopelessness, that he was mistaken, that the book was not finished, that it could never be completed, that I could write no more. He answered with the same quiet finality that the book was finished whether I knew it or not, and then he told me to go to my room and spend the next week in collecting in its proper order the manuscript which had accumulated during the last two years.

I followed his instructions, still without hope and without belief. I worked for six days sitting in the middle of the floor surrounded by mountainous stacks of typed manuscript on every side. At the end of a week I had the first part of it together, and just two days before Christmas, 1933, I delivered to him the manuscript of "The October Fair," and a few days later, the manuscript of "The Hills Beyond Pentland." The manuscript of "The Fair" was, at that time, something over 1,000,000 words in length. He had seen most of it in its dismembered fragments during the three preceding years, but now, for the first time, he was seeing it in its sequential order, and once again his intuition was right; he had told me the truth when he said that I had finished the book.

It was not finished in any way that was publishable or readable. It was really not a book so much as it was the skeleton of a book, but for the first time in four years the skeleton was all there. An enormous labor of revision, weaving together, shaping, and, above all, cutting remained, but I had the book now so that nothing, not even the despair of my own spirit, could take it from me. He told me so, and suddenly I saw that he was right.

I was like a man who is drowning and who suddenly, at the last gasp of his dying effort, feels earth beneath his feet again. My spirit was borne upward by the greatest triumph it had ever known, and although my mind was tired, my body exhausted, from that moment on I felt equal to anything on earth.

It was evident that many problems were before us, but now we had the thing, and we welcomed the labor before us with happy confidence. In the first place there was the problem of the book's gigantic length. Even in this skeletonized form the manuscript of "The October Fair" was about twelve times the length of the average novel or twice the length of *War and Peace*. It was manifest, therefore, that it would not only be utterly impossible to publish such a manuscript in a single volume, but that even if it were published in several volumes, the tremendous length of such a manuscript would practically annihilate its chances of ever finding a public which would read it.

This problem now faced us, and the editor grappled with it immediately. As his examination of the manuscript of "The October Fair" proceeded, he found that the book did describe two complete and separate cycles. The first of these was a movement which described the period of wandering and hunger in a man's youth. The second cycle described the period of greater certitude, and was dominated by the unity of a single passion. It was obvious, therefore, that what we had in the two cyclic movements of this book was really the material of two completely different chronicles, and although the second of the two was by far the more finished, the first cycle, of course, was the one which logically we ought to complete and publish first, and we decided on this course.

We took the first part first. I immediately prepared a

minutely thorough synopsis which described not only the course of the book from first to last, but which also included an analysis of those chapters which had been completed in their entirety, of those which were completed only in part, and of those which had not been written at all, and with this synopsis before us, we set to work immediately to prepare the book for press. This work occupied me throughout the whole of the year 1934. The book was completed at the beginning of 1935, and was published in March of that year under the title of *Of Time and the River.*

In the first place, the manuscript, even in its unfinished form, called for the most radical cutting, and because of the way in which the book had been written, as well as the fatigue which I now felt, I was not well prepared to do by myself the task that lay ahead of us.

Cutting had always been the most difficult and distasteful part of writing to me; my tendency had always been to write rather than to cut. Moreover, whatever critical faculty I may have had concerning my own work had been seriously impaired, for the time being at least, by the frenzied labor of the past four years. When a man's work has poured from him for almost five years like burning lava from a volcano; when all of it, however superfluous, has been given fire and passion by the white heat of his own creative energy, it is very difficult suddenly to become coldly surgical, ruthlessly detached.

To give a few concrete illustrations of the difficulties that now confronted us: The opening section of the book describes the journey of a train across the State of Virginia at night. Its function in the book is simply to introduce some of the chief characters, to indicate a central situation, to give something of the background from which the book proceeds, and perhaps through the movement of the train across the stillness of the earth to establish a certain beat, evoke a certain emotion which is inherent to the nature of the book. Such a section, therefore, undoubtedly serves an important function, but in proportion to the whole purport of the book, its function is a secondary one and must be related to the whole book in a proportionate way.

Now in the original version, the manuscript which described the journey of the train across Virginia at night was considerably longer than the average novel. What was needed was just an introductory chapter or two, and what I had written was over 100,000 words in length, and this same difficulty, this lack of proportion, was also evident in other parts of the manuscript.

What I had written about the great train was really good. But what I had to face, the very bitter lesson that everyone who wants to write has got to learn, was that a thing may in itself be the finest piece of writing one has ever done, and yet have absolutely no place in the manuscript one hopes to publish. This is a hard thing, but it must be faced, and so we faced it.

My spirit quivered at the bloody execution. My soul recoiled before the carnage of so many lovely things cut out upon which my heart was set. But it had to be done, and we did it.

The first chapter in the original manuscript, a chapter which the editor, himself, admitted was as good a single piece of writing as I had ever done, was relentlessly kicked out, and the reason it was kicked out was that it was really not a true beginning for the book but merely something which led up to the true beginning; therefore it had to go. And so it went all up and down the line. Chapters 50,000 words long were reduced to ten or fifteen thousand words, and having faced this inevitable necessity, I finally acquired a kind of ruthlessness of my own, and once or twice, myself, did more cutting than my editor was willing to allow.

Another fault that has always troubled me in writing is that I have often attempted to reproduce in its entirety the full flood and fabric of a scene in life itself. Thus, in another section of the book, four people were represented as talking to each other for four hours without a break or intermission. All were good talkers; often all talked, or tried to talk, at the same time. The talk was wonderful and living talk because I knew the life and character and the vocabulary of all these people from its living source, and I had forgotten nothing. Yet all the time, all that was actually happening in this scene was that a young woman had got out of her husband's motor car and gone into her mother's house and kept calling to the impatient man outside every time he honked his horn, "All right. All right. I'll be with you in five minutes." These five minutes really lengthened into four hours, while the unfortunate man outside honked upon his horn, and while the two women and two young men of the same family inside carried on a torrential discourse and discussed exhaustively the lives and histories of almost everyone in town, their memories of the past, adventures of the present, and speculations of the future. I put it all down in the original manuscript just as I had seen and known and lived it a thousand times, and even if I do say so myself, the nature of the talk, the living vitality and character of the language, the utter naturalness, the flood-tide river of it all was wonderful, but I had made four people talk 80,000 words—200 printed pages of close type in a minor scene of an enormous book, and of course, good as it was, it was all wrong and had to go.

Such, then, were some of our major difficulties with

the manuscript we had in hand, and although since its publication there have been many declarations to the effect that the book would have benefited by a much more radical cutting, the cutting we did do was much more drastic than I had dreamed was possible.

Meanwhile I was proceeding at full speed with the work of completing my design, finishing the unfinished parts and filling in the transition links which were essential.

This in itself was an enormous job and kept me writing all day long as hard as I could go for a full year. Here again the nature of my chief fault was manifest. I wrote too much again. I not only wrote what was essential, but time and time again my enthusiasm for a good scene, one of those enchanting vistas which can open up so magically to a man in the full flow of his creation, would overpower me, and I would write thousands of words upon a scene which contributed nothing of vital importance to a book whose greatest need already was ruthless condensation.

During the course of this year, I must have written well over a half million words of additional manuscript, of which, of course, only a small part was finally used.

The nature of my method, the desire fully to explore my material, had led me into another error. The whole effect of those five years of incessant writing had been to make me feel not only that everything had to be used, but that everything had to be told, that nothing could be implied. Therefore, at the end, there were at least a dozen additional chapters which I felt had to be completed to give the book its final value. A thousand times I debated this question desperately with my editor. I told him that these chapters had to go in simply because I felt the book would not be complete without them, and with every argument he had, he tried to show me that I was wrong. I see now that on the whole he was right about it, but at the time I was so inextricably involved in my work, that I did not have the detachment necessary for a true appraisal.

The end came suddenly—the end of those five years of torment and incessant productivity. In October I took a trip to Chicago, a two weeks' vacation, my first in over a year. When I returned I found that my editor had quietly and decisively sent the manuscript to the press, the printers were already at work on it, the proof was beginning to come in. I had not foreseen it; I was desperate, bewildered. "You can't do it," I told him, "the book is not yet finished. I must have six months more on it."

To this he answered that the book was not only finished, but that if I took six months more on it, I would then demand another six months and six months more beyond that, and that I might very well become so obsessed with this one work that I would never get it published. He went on to say, and I think with complete justice, that such a course was wrong for me. I was not, he said, a Flaubert kind of writer. I was not a perfectionist. I had twenty, thirty, almost any number of books in me, and the important thing was to get them produced and not to spend the rest of my life in perfecting one book. He agreed that with six months' additional work upon the book, I might achieve a certain finish and completeness, but he did not think that the benefit would be nearly as great as I thought it would be, and his own deep conviction was that the book should be published at once without further delay, that I should get it out of me, forget about it, turn my life to the final completion of the work which was already prepared and ready, waiting for me. He told me, furthermore, exactly what the nature of the criticism would be, the criticism of its length, its adjectives, its overabundance, but he told me not to despair.

He told me finally that I would go on and do better work, that I would learn to work without so much confusion, waste, and useless torment, that my future books would more and more achieve the unity, sureness, and finality that every artist wants his work to have, but that I had to learn in the way I had learned, groping, struggling, finding my own way for myself, that this was the only way to learn.

In January, 1935, I finished the last of my revisions on the proof; the first printed copies came from the press in February. The book was released for final publication early in March. I was not here when it came out. I had taken a ship for Europe the week before, and as the ship got farther and farther from the American shores, my spirits sank lower and lower, reaching, I think, the lowest state of hopeless depression they had ever known. This, I believe, was largely a physical reaction, the inevitable effect of relaxation upon a human organism which had for five years been strained to its utmost limit. My life seemed to me to be like a great spring which had been taut for years and which was now slowly uncoiling from its tension. I had the most extraordinary sense of desolation I had ever known when I thought about my book. I had never realized until now how close I had been to it, how much a part of me it had become, and now that it had been taken away from me, my life felt utterly futile, hollow as a shell. And now that the book was gone, now that there was nothing more that I could do about it, I felt the most abysmal sensation of failure. I have always been somewhat afraid of print, although print is a thing I have tried so hard to achieve. Yet it is literally true that with everything I have ever written, I have felt when the hour of naked print drew nigh a kind of desperation and have even entreated my publisher not only to defer the publication of my book until another season, but have asked the editors of magazines to put off the publication of a story for another month or two until I had a chance to work on it some more, do something to it, I was not always sure what.

Now I had an overwhelming sense of shame greater than any I had felt before. I felt as if I had ruinously exposed myself as a pitiable fool who had no talent and who once and for all had completely vindicated the prophecies of the critics who had felt the first book was just a flash in the pan. It was in this frame of mind that I arrived in Paris on March 8, the day the book was to be published in America. I had come away to forget about it, and yet I thought about it all the time. I walked the streets from dawn to dark, from night to morning, at least a dozen times in two short weeks I heard the celebration of mass at Sacré Cœur, and then would walk the streets again and come back to my hotel at ten o'clock and lie upon the bed, and still I could not sleep.

After several days of this, I steeled myself to go to the office of the travel agency where a message might be waiting for me. I found a cablegram there. It was from my publisher, and it said simply: "Magnificent reviews somewhat critical in ways expected, full of greatest praise." I read it the first time with a feeling of almost intolerable joy but as I continued to read and reread it, the old dark doubt began to creep across my mind and by the time night had come I was convinced that this wonderful cable was just a sentence of doom, and that my editor, out of the infinite compassion of his spirit, had taken this means of breaking the news to me that my book was a colossal failure.

Three days passed in which I prowled the streets of Paris like a maddened animal, and of those three days

I could later remember almost nothing. At the end of that time I sent a frenzied cablegram to that editor in which I told him I could stand anything better than this state of damnable uncertainty and pleaded with him to give me the blunt truth no matter how bitter it might be. His answer to this cable was such that I could no longer doubt him or the reception which the book had had at home.

This completes, as far as I can remember it, the story of the making of a book and what happened to its maker. I know it is too long a story; I know, also, that it must seem to be a story filled with the record of a man's blunders and ludicrous mistakes, but simply because it is that kind of story, I hope that it may have some value. It is a story of the artist as a man and as a worker. It is a story of the artist as a man who is derived out of the common family of earth and who knows all the anguish, error, and frustration that any man alive can know.

The life of the artist at any epoch of man's history has not been an easy one. And here in America, it has often seemed to me, it may well be the hardest life that man has ever known. I am not speaking of some frustration in our native life, some barrenness of spirit, some arid Philistinism which contends against the artist's life and which prevents his growth. I do not speak of these things because I do not put the same belief in them that I once did. I am speaking as I have tried to speak from first to last in the concrete terms of the artist's actual experience, of the nature of the physical task before him. It seems to me that the task is one whose physical proportions are vaster and more difficult here than in any other nation on the earth. It is not merely that in the cultures of Europe and of the Orient the American artist can find no antecedent scheme, no structural plan, no body of tradition that can give his own work the validity and truth that it must have. It is not merely that he must make somehow a new tradition for himself, derived from his own life and from the enormous space and energy of American life, the structure of his own design; it is not merely that he is confronted by these problems; it is even more than this, that the labor of a complete and whole articulation, the discovery of an entire universe and of a complete language, is the task that lies before him.

Such is the nature of the struggle to which henceforth our lives must be devoted. Out of the billion forms of America, out of the savage violence and the dense complexity of all its swarming life; from the unique and single substance of this land and life of ours, must we draw the power and energy of our own life, the articulation of our speech, the substance of our art.

For here it seems to me in hard and honest ways like these we may find the tongue, the language, and the conscience that as men and artists we have got to have. Here, too, perhaps, must we who have no more than what we have, who know no more than what we know, who are no more than what we are, find our America. Here, at this present hour and moment of my life, I seek for mine.

reliable and true, that it must have it; and we attach

it to a chief of the topographical tradition for long

... derived from his candidate and from the century is

... sense and example of Virgilian life, the structure of his

... distinguish life that merely that he is comforted. An

... these problems it is even occur, that time that the labor

of a variable and much intellectual, the discovery of

... an entire universe and of a complete harmony, is all

that that he claims, and

Such is the meaning of the struggle to which he would

... him must must be devoted. Out of the future known of

... America, out of the same science and the doctrine of

... philosophy of all its community, from that instinct and

... single substance of his head and life of comfort must go

... that the power and universal not even take the struggle

... in of our world, the substance of time and

For here, it for us to see in hand and honor a radiant

... those we may find the tongue, the language, and the

... substance that as men and authors we have you to have

Here, too, perhaps, may we, who have no more than

... fulfilling we have who have no tune, than what we know,

... we are no more than that we be, that for now in

... the at this present hour and moment of the first time

... in time.

THE SHORT STORIES

The Short Stories

Editor's Preface

WOLFE is not commonly thought of as a short story writer—or anyhow a *short* story writer—and it is true that most of the tales in *From Death to Morning* (1935) and *The Hills Beyond* (1941) were written in connection with or came out of the novels. Yet the first of these volumes is also a first-rate collection, and the second could stand on "Chickamauga" alone.

What you notice again as you go through these stories—and you may notice it even more sharply in the short ones—is the range of Wolfe's interests: his curiosity about and receptivity to the different areas of human experience. And not merely—for this most autobiographical of writers—the areas of his own personal and lived experience.

Among the stories that are printed here, for instance, "The Face of the War" deals with the general Southern scene in 1918. "Dark in the Forest" is the portrait of a dying Jew whom Wolfe met in a German railway coach in the early 1930's. "Chickamauga" is the account of the Confederate "victory" near Chattanooga, Tennessee, in September 1863. "In the Park" is an episode from Mrs. Jack's youth in the 1900's.

In that last story, in fact—so accurately has Wolfe caught the accents and the tones of Mrs. Jack's per-

sonality—is the seed of a perfect artistic plagiarism: fo
the test of an artist is how much he *can* borrow fron
the common fund of human experience, and at hi
best he is the impenitent thief of life. And yet the not
of pure exaltation on which the story ends—the "littl
brainless cries" of the birds in the park at sunrise—i
something only Wolfe could have done.

So he refreshed the whole tradition of realism in ou
literature. And, in terms of our larger literary current
today, in a tradition that has been marked psycholog
cally by an increasing reluctance to deal with ordinar
matters, and technically by an increasing refraction c
experience until you might almost think that breathing
too, is mostly a matter of mirrors—in these terms, Wolf
also reminded us that life—even life in America—wa
still livable.

FROM DEATH TO MORNING

The Face of the War

HEAT-BRUTAL August the year the war ended: here are four moments from the face of the war. One—at Langley Field: a Negro retreating warily out of one of the rude shedlike offices of the contracting company on the flying field, the white teeth bared in a horrible grimace of fear and hatred, the powerful figure half-crouched, apelike, ready to leap or run, the arms, the great black paws, held outward defensively as he retreats under the merciless glazed brutality of the August sun, over the barren, grassless horror of hard dry clay, the white eyeballs fixed with an expression of mute unfathomable hatred, fear, and loathing upon the slouchy, shambling figure of a Southern white —a gang boss or an overseer—who advances upon him brandishing a club in his meaty hand, screaming the high thick throat-scream of blood-lust and murder: "I'll stomp the guts out of you, you God-damned black bastard! I'll beat his God-damn brains out!"—and smashing brutally with his club, coming down across the Negro's skull with the sickening resilient thud, heard clear across the field, of wood on living bone. Behind the paunch-gut white, an office clerk, the little meager yes-man of the earth, a rat in shirt-sleeves, quick as a rat to scamper to its hiding, quick as a rat to come in to the kill when all is safe, with rat's teeth bared—advancing in the shambling wake of his protector, fear's servile seconder, murder's cringing aide, coming in behind with rat's teeth bared, the face white as a sheet, convulsed with fear and with the coward's lust to kill without mercy or reprisal, the merciless sun blazing hot upon the arm-band buckles on the crisp shirt-sleeve, and with a dull metallic glint upon the barrel of the squat blue automatic that he clutches with a trembling hand, offering it to his blood-mad master, whispering frantically—"Here! . . . Here, Mister Bartlett! . . . Shoot the bastard if he tries to hit you!"

Meanwhile, the Negro retreating slowly all the time, his terrible white stare of fear and hatred no longer fixed upon his enemy, but on the evil glint of that cylinder of blue steel behind him, his arms thrust blindly, futilely before him as his hated foe comes on, his black face, rilled and channeled first with lacings of bright red, then beaten to a bloody pulp as the club keeps smashing down with its sickening and resilient crack:

"You . . . God-damn . . . black . . . son-of-a-bitch!" the voice, thick, high, phlegmy, choked with murder. "I'll teach ye—" Smash! the cartilage of the thick black nose crunches and is ground to powder by the blow "—if a God-damned nigger can talk back to a white man!"— Smash. A flailing, horribly clumsy blow across the mouth which instantly melts into a bloody smear through which the Negro, eyes unmoving from the blue glint of the steel, mechanically spits the shattered fragments of his solid teeth—"I'll bash in his God-damned head—the damned black bastard—I'll show him if he can—" Smash! Across the woolly center of the skull and now, the scalp ripped open to the base of the low forehead, the powerful black figure staggering drunkenly, bending at the knees, the black head sagging, going down beneath the blows, the arms still blindly thrust before him, upon one knee now on the barren clay-baked earth, the head sunk down completely on the breast, blood over all, the kneeling figure blindly rocking, swaying with the blows, the arms still out until he crashes forward on the earth, his arms outspread, face to one side, and then the final nausea of horror—the murderous kick of the shoe into the blood-pulp of the unconscious face, and then silence, nothing to see or hear now but the heavy, choked, and labored breathing of the paunch-gut man, the white rat-face behind him with the bared rat's fangs of terror, and the dull blue wink of the envenomed steel.

Again, the coward's heart of fear and hate, the coward's lust for one-way killing, murder without danger to himself, the rat's salvation from the shipwreck of his self-esteem—armed with a gun now, clothed in khaki, riding the horse of his authority, as here. Three boys, all employed by the contracting company, are walking after supper on the borders of the flying field in the waning light of evening, coming dark. They are walking down near the water's edge, across the flat marshy land, they are talking about their homes, the towns and cities they have known and come from, their colleges and schools, their plans for an excursion to the beach at the week end, when they draw their pay. Without knowing it, they have approached a hangar where one of the new war planes with which the government is experimenting has been housed. Suddenly, the soldier who is there on guard has seen them, advances on them now, one hand upon the revolver in his holster, his little furtive eyes narrowed into slits. Face of the city rat, dry, grey, furtive, pustulate, the tallowy lips, the rasping voice, the scrabble of a few harsh oaths, the stony gravel of a sterile, lifeless speech:

"What are ya doin' here ya f—— little bastards!— Who told ya t'come f—— round duh hangah?"

One of the boys, a chubby red-cheeked youngster from

the lower South, fair-haired, blue-eyed, friendly and slow
of speech, attempts to answer:

"Why, mister, we just thought——"

Quick as a flash, the rat has slapped the boy across the
mouth, the filthy fingertips have left their mottled print
upon the boy's red cheek, have left their loathsome, foul
and ineradicable print upon the visage of his soul forever:

"I don't give a f—— what ya t'ought, ya little p——!
Annuddeh woid out a ya f—— trap an' I'll shoot the
s—— outa ya!" He has the gun out of its holster now,
ready in his hand; the eyes of the three boys are riveted
on the dull wink of its blue barrel with a single focal intensity of numb horror, fascinated disbelief.

"Now get t' f—— hell outa here!" the hero cries, giving the boy he has just slapped a violent shove with his
free hand. "Get t' f—— hell away from heah, all t'ree of
youse! Don't f—— aroun' wit me, ya little p——," the
great man snarls now, eyes a-glitter, narrow as a snake's,
as he comes forward with deadly menace written in his
face. "Annuddeh woid outa ya f—— traps, an' I'll shoot
t' s—— outa youse! On yuh way, now, ya p——! Get t'
hell away from me befoeh I plug yah!"

And the three boys, stunned, bewildered, filled with
shame, and sickened out of all the joy and hope with
which they had been speaking of their projects just a
moment before, have turned, and are walking silently
away with the dull shame, the brutal and corrosive
hatred which the war has caused, aching and rankling
in their hearts.

Again, an image of man's naked desire, brutal and
imperative, stripped down to his raw need, savage and
incurious as the harsh pang of a starved hunger which
takes and rends whatever food it finds—as here: Over

the bridge, across the railway track, down in the Negro settlement of Newport News—among the dives and stews and rusty tenements of that grimy, dreary, and abominable section, a rude shack of unpainted pine boards, thrown together with the savage haste which war engenders, to pander to a need as savage and insatiate as hunger, as old as life, the need of friendless, unhoused men the world over.

The front part of this rawly new, yet squalid place, has been partitioned off by rude pine boards to form the semblance of a lunchroom and soft-drink parlor. Within are several tables, furnished with a few fly-specked menu cards, on which half a dozen items are recorded, and at which none of the patrons ever look, and a wooden counter, with its dreary stage property of lukewarm soda pop, a few packages of cigarettes and a box of cheap cigars beneath a dingy little glass case; and beneath a greasy glass humidor, a few stale ham and cheese sandwiches, which have been there since the place was opened, which will be there till the war is done.

Meanwhile, all through the room, the whores, in their thin and meager mummers, act as waitresses, move patiently about among the crowded tables and ply their trade. The men who are seated at the tables belong for the most part to that great group of unclassed creatures who drift and float, work, drift, and starve, are now in jail, now out again, now foul, filthy, wretched, hungry, out of luck, riding the rods, the rusty boxcars of a freight, snatching their food at night from the boiling slum of hoboes' jungle, now swaggering with funds and brief prosperity—the floaters, drifters, and half-bums, that huge nameless, houseless, rootless, and anomalous class that swarm across the nation.

They are the human cinders of the earth. Hard, shabby, scarred and lined of face, common, dull and meager of visage as they are, they have the look of having crawled that morning from the boxcar in the train yard of another city or of having dropped off a day coach in the morning, looking casually and indifferently about them, carrying a cardboard suitcase with a shirt, two collars, and a tie. Yet a legend of great distances is written on them—a kind of atomic desolation. Each is a human spot of moving rust naked before the desolation of the skies that bend above him, unsheltered on the huge and savage wilderness of the earth, across which he is hurled—a spot of grimy grey and dingy brown, clinging to the brake-rods of a loaded freight.

He is a kind of human cinder hurled through space, naked, rootless, nameless, with all that was personal and unique in its one life almost emptied out into that huge vacancy of rust and iron and waste, and lonely and incommunicable distances, in which it lives, through which it has so often been bombarded.

And this atom finds its end at length, perhaps, at some unknown place upon the savage visage of the continent, exploded, a smear of blood on the rock ballast, a scream lost in the roar of pounding wheels, a winding of entrails round the axle rods, a brief indecipherable bobbing of blood and bone and brains upon the wooden ties, or just a shapeless bundle of old soiled brown and grey slumped down at morning in a shabby doorway, on a city street, beneath the elevated structure, a bundle of rags and bone, now cold and lifeless, to be carted out of sight by the police, nameless and forgotten in its death as in its life.

Such, for the most part, were the men who now sat at the tables in this rude house of pleasure, looking about them furtively, warily, with an air of waiting calculation, or indecision, and sometimes glancing at one another with sly, furtive, rather sheepish smiles.

As for the women who attended them, they were prostitutes recruited, for the most part, from the great cities of the North and Middle West, brutally greedy, rapacious, weary of eye, hard of visage, overdriven, harried and exhausted in their mechanical performance of a profession from which their only hope was to grasp and clutch as much as they could in as short a time as possible. They had the harsh, rasping, and strident voices, the almost deliberately exaggerated and inept extravagance of profanity and obscenity, the calculated and overemphasized style of toughness which one often finds among poor people in the tenement sections of great cities—which one observes even in small children —the constant oath, curse, jeer, threat, menace, and truculent abuse, which really comes from the terrible fear in which they live, as if, in that world of savage aggression and brute rapacity, from which they have somehow to wrest their bitter living, they are afraid that any betrayal of themselves into a gentler, warmer, and more tolerant kind of speech and gesture, will make them suspect to their fellows, and lay them open to the assaults, threats, tyrannies, and dominations they fear.

So was it with these women now: one could hear their rasping voices everywhere throughout the smoke-filled room, their harsh jeering laughter, and the extravagant exaggeration and profusion with which they constantly interlarded their strident speech with a few oaths and cries repeated with a brutal monotony—such phrases as "Christ!"—"Jesus!"—"What t' God-damn hell do I care?" —"Come on! Whatcha goin' t' do now! I got no time t' —— around wit' yuh! If ya want t' —— come on an' pay me—if ya don't, get t' God-damn hell outa here"— being among the expressions one heard most frequently.

Yet, even among these poor, brutally exhausted, and fear-ridden women, there was really left, like something pitiably living and indestructible out of life, a kind of buried tenderness, a fearful, almost timid desire to find some friendship, gentleness, even love among the rabble-rout of lost and ruined men to whom they ministered.

And this timid, yet inherent desire for some warmer and more tender relation even in the practice of their profession, was sometimes almost ludicrously apparent as they moved warily about among the tables soliciting patronage from the men they served. Thus, if a man addressed them harshly, brutally, savagely, with an oath—which was a customary form of greeting—they would answer him in kind. But if he spoke to them more quietly, or regarded them with a more kindly smiling look, they might respond to him with a pathetic and ridiculous attempt at coquetry, subduing their rasping voices to a kind of husky, tinny whisper, pressing against him intimately, bending their bedaubed and painted faces close to his, and cajoling him with a pitiable pretense at seductiveness, somewhat in this manner:

"Hello there, big boy! . . . Yuh look lonesome sittin' there all by yourself. . . . Whatcha doin' all alone? . . . Yuh want some company? Huh?"—whispered hoarsely, with a ghastly leer of the smeared lips, and pressing closer—"Wanta have some fun, darling? . . . Come on!"—coaxingly, imperatively, taking the patron by the hand—"I'll show yuh a big time."

It was in response to some such blandishment as this that the boy had got up from his table, left the smoke-filled room accompanied by the woman, and gone out through a door at one side into the corridor that led back to the little partitioned board compartments of the brothel.

Here, it was at once evident that there was nothing to do but wait. A long line of men and women that stretched from one end of the hallway to another stood waiting for their brief occupancies of the little compartments at the other end, all of which were now obviously and audibly occupied.

As they came out into the hall, the woman with the boy called out to another woman at the front end of the line: "Hello, May! . . . Have ya seen Grace?"

"Aah!" said the woman thus addressed, letting cigarette smoke coil from her nostrils as she spoke, and speaking with the rasping, exaggerated, and brutal toughness that has been described: "I t'ink she's in number Seven here havin' a ——."

And having conveyed the information in this delicate manner, she then turned to her companion, a brawny, grinning seaman in the uniform of the United States Navy, and with a brisk, yet rather bantering humor, demanded:

"Well, whatcha say, big boy? . . . Gettin' tired of waitin'? . . . Well, it won't be long now . . . Dey'll be troo in dere in a minute an' we're next."

"Dey better had be!" the sailor replied with a kind of jocular savagery. "If dey ain't, I'll tear down duh —— joint! . . . Christ!" he cried in an astounded tone, after listening attentively for a moment. "Holy Jeez!" he said with a dumfounded laugh. "What t' hell are dey doin' in deh all dis time? Who is dat guy, anyway?—A whole regiment of duh Marines, duh way it sounds t' me! Holy *Je-sus!*" he cried with an astounded laugh, listening again —"Christ!"

"Ah, c'mon, Jack!" the woman said with a kind of brutal, husky tenderness, snuggling close to his brawny arm meanwhile, and lewdly proposing her heavy body against his. "Yuh ain't gonna get impatient on me now, are yuh? . . . Just hold on a minute moeh an' I'll give ya somet'ing ya neveh had befoeh!——"

"If yuh do," the gallant tar said tenderly, drawing his

mighty fist back now in a gesture of savage endearment that somehow seemed to please her, "I'll come back here and smack yuh right in duh puss, yuh son-of-a-bitch!" he amorously whispered, and pulled her to him.

Similar conversations and actions were to be observed all up and down the line: there were lewd jests, ribald laughter, and impatiently shouted demands on the noisy occupants of the little compartments to "come on out an' give some of duh rest of us a chanct, f'r Chris' sake!" and other expressions of a similar nature.

It was a brutally hot night in the middle of August: in the hallway the air was stifling, weary, greasily humid. The place was thick, dense, stale and foul with tobacco smoke, the stench of the men, the powder and cheap perfume of the women, and over all, unforgettable, over-powering, pungent, resinous, rude and raw as savage nature and man's naked lust, was the odor of the new, unpainted, white-pine lumber of which the whole shambling and haphazard place had been constructed.

Finally, after a long and weary wait in that stifling place, during which time the doors of the compartments had opened many times, and many men and women had come out, and many more gone in, the boy and the woman with him had advanced to the head of the line, and were next in the succession of that unending and vociferous column.

Presently, the door of the room for which they waited opened, a man came out, shut the door behind him, and then went quickly down the hall. Then for a moment there was silence, impatient mutters in the line behind them, and at length the woman with the boy, muttering:

"I wondeh what t' hell she's doin' all dis time!— Hey!" she cried harshly, and hammered on the door, "Who's in dere? . . . Come on out, f'r Chris' sake! . . . Yuh're holding up duh line!"

In a moment, a woman's voice answered wearily:

"All right, Fay! . . . Just a moment, dear. . . . I'll be there."

"Oh," the woman with the boy said, in a suddenly quiet, strangely tender kind of voice. "It's Margaret. . . . I guess she's worn out, poor kid." And knocking at the door again, but this time gently, almost timidly, she said in a quiet voice:

"How are yuh, kid? . . . D'ya need any help?"

"No, it's all right, Fay," the girl inside said in the same tired and utterly exhausted tone. "I'll be out in a moment. . . . Come on in, honey."

The woman opened the door softly and entered the room. The only furnishings of the hot, raw, and hideous little place, besides a chair, an untidy and rumpled looking bed, and a table, was a cheap dresser on which was a doll girdled with a soiled ribbon of pink silk, tied in a big bow, a photograph of a young sailor inscribed with the words, "To Margaret, the best pal I ever had—Ed"—and a package of cigarettes. An electric fan, revolving slowly from left to right, droned incessantly, and fanned the close stale air with a kind of sporadic and sweltering breeze.

And from moment to moment, as it swung in its half-orbit, the fan would play full upon the face and head of the girl, who was lying on the bed in an attitude of utter pitiable weariness. When this happened, a single strand of her shining hair, which was straight, lank, fine-spun as silk, and of a lovely red-bronze texture, would be disturbed by the movement of the fan and would be blown gently back and forth across her temple.

The girl, who was tall, slender, and very lovely was, save for her shoes and stockings, naked, and she lay extended at full length on the untidy bed, with one arm thrust out in a gesture of complete exhaustion, the other folded underneath her shining hair, and her face, which had a fragile, transparent, almost starved delicacy, turned to one side and resting on her arm, the eyelids closed. And the eyelids also had this delicacy of texture, were violet with weariness, and so transparent that the fine network of the veins was plainly visible.

The other woman went softly over to the bed, sat down beside her, and began to speak to her in a low and tender tone. In a moment the girl turned her head towards the woman, opened her eyes, and smiled, in a faint and distant way, as of someone who is just emerging from the drugged spell of an opiate:

"What? . . . What did you say, darling? . . . No, I'm all right," she said faintly, and sitting up, with the other woman's help, she swiftly pulled on over her head the cheap one-piece garment she was wearing, which had been flung back over the chair beside the bed. Then, smiling, she stood up, took a cigarette out of the package on the dresser, lighted it, and turning to the boy, who was standing in the door, said ironically, with something of the rasping accent which the other women used, beneath which, however, her pleasant rather husky tone was plainly evident.

"All right, 'Georgia'! Come on in!"

He went in slowly, still looking at her with an astounded stare. He had known her the first moment he had looked at her. She was a girl from the little town where the state university, at which he was a student, was situated, a member of a family of humble decent people, well known in the town: she had disappeared almost two years before, there had been rumor at the time that one of the students had "got her in trouble," and since that time he had neither seen nor heard of her.

"How are all the folks down home?" she said. "How's everyone in Hopewell?"

Her luminous smoke-grey eyes were hard and bright as she spoke, her mouth, in her thin young face, was hard and bitter as a blade, and her voice was almost deliberately hard and mocking. And yet, beneath this defiant scornfulness, the strange, husky tenderness of the girl's tone persisted, and as she spoke, she put her slender hand lightly on his arm, with the swift, unconscious tenderness of people in a world of strangers who suddenly meet someone they know from home.

"They're all right," he stammered in a confused and bewildered tone, his face beginning to smolder with embarrassment as he spoke.

"Well, if you see anyone I know," she said in the same ironic tone, "say hello for me. . . . Tell 'em that I sent my love."

"All right," he blurted out stupidly. "I—I—certainly will."

"And I'm mad at you, 'Georgia,'" she said with a kind of mocking reproachfulness, "I'm mad at you for not telling me you were here. . . . The next time you come here you'd better ask for me—or I'll be mad! . . . We homefolks have got to stick together. . . . So you ask for Margaret—or I'll be mad at you—do you hear?"

"All right!" he stammered confusedly again, "I certainly will."

She looked at him a moment longer with her hard bright stare, her bitter, strangely tender smile. Then, thrusting her fingers swiftly through his hair, she turned to the other woman and said:

"Be nice to him, Fay. . . . He's one of the folks from down my way. . . . Good-by, 'Georgia.' . . . When you come back again you ask for Margaret."

"Good-by," he said, and she was gone, out the door and down that stifling little hall of brutal, crowding, and imperative desire, into the market-place again, where for the thousandth time she would offer the sale of her young slender body to whoever would be there to buy; to solicit, take, accept the patronage of any of the thousand nameless and unknown men that the huge cylinder of chance and of the night might bring to her.

He never saw her after that. She was engulfed into the great vortex of the war, the huge dark abyss and thronging chaos of America, the immense, the cruel, the indifferent and the magic land, where all of us have lived and walked as strangers, where all of us have been so small, so lonely, and forsaken, which has engulfed us all at length, and in whose dark and lonely breast so many lost and nameless men are buried and forgotten.

This, then, was the third visage of calamity, the image of desire, the face of war.

Again, the speed, haste, violence, savage humor, and the instant decisiveness of war:—A sweltering noon on one of the great munition piers at Newport News where now the boy is working as material checker. Inside the great shed of the pier, a silent, suffocating heat of one hundred ten degrees, a grimy, mote-filled air, pollenated with the golden dust of oats which feed through a gigantic chute into the pier in an unending river, and which are sacked and piled in tremendous barricades all up and down the length of that enormous shed.

Elsewhere upon the pier, the towering geometries of war munitions: the white hard cleanliness of crated woods containing food and shot provender of every sort —canned goods, meat, beans, dried fruits, and small arms ammunitions—the enormous victualing of life and death fed ceaselessly into the insatiate and receiving maw of distant war.

The sweltering air is impregnated with the smells of all these things—with smell of oats and coarse brown sacking, with the clean fresh pungency of crated boxes, and with the huge, drowsy, and nostalgic compact of a pier—the single blend of a thousand multiform and mixed aromas, the compacted fragrance of the past, sharp, musty, thrilling, unforgettable, as if the savor of the whole huge earth's abundance had slowly stained, and worn through, and soaked its mellow saturation into the massive and encrusted timbers.

But now all work has ceased: all of the usual sounds of work—the unceasing rumble of the trucks, the rattling of winches and the hard, sudden labor of the donkey engines on the decks of ships, the great nets swinging up and over with their freight of boxes, the sudden rattling fall, and rise again, the shouts and cries of the black sweating stevedores, the sharp commands of the gang bosses, overseers, and loading men—all this has stopped, has for the moment given over to the measured stamp of marching men, the endless streams of men in khaki uniforms who have all morning long, since early light, been tramping through the pier and filing up a gangplank into the side of a great transport which waits there to engulf them.

The Negro stevedores sprawl lazily on loaded oat sacks round the grain chute, the checkers doze upon the great walled pile of grain or, kneeling in a circle down behind some oaty barricade, they gamble feverishly with dice.

Meanwhile, the troops come through. The sweltering brown columns tramp in, pause, are given rest, wearily shift the brutal impediment of the loaded knapsacks on their shoulders, take off their caps, wipe their sleeves across their red sweating faces, curse quietly among themselves, and then wait patiently for the lines to move again.

Down by the shipside, at the gangplank's end, a group

of officers are seated at a table as the troops file by them, examining each man's papers as he comes to them, passing them on from hand to hand, scrawling signatures, filing, recording, putting the stamp of their approval finally on the documents that will release each little khaki figure to its long-awaited triumph of the ship, the voyage, the new land, to all the joy and glory it is panting for, and to the unconsidered perils of battle, war, and death, disease or mutilation, and the unknown terror, horror, and disgust.

But now a column of black troops is coming by. They are a portion of a Negro regiment from Texas, powerful big men, naïve and wondering as children, incorrigibly unsuited to the military discipline. Something, in fact, is missing, wrong, forgotten, out of place, with everyone's equipment: one has lost his cap, another is without a belt, another is shy two buttons on his jacket, still another has mislaid his canteen, one is shy a good part of his knapsack equipment, and dumbly, ignorantly bewildered at his loss—everyone has lost something, left something behind, done something wrong, now misses something which he has to have.

And now, in one of the pauses of their march along the pier, each one of them pours out the burden of his complaint; into the sweltering misery of the heated air, the babel of black voices mounts. And the target of their bewilderment, the object on whom this whole burden of mischance and error is now heaped, the overburdened and exhausted ruler to whom each now turns in his distress, and, with the naïve and confident faith of a child, asks for an instant solution of the tangled web of error in which he is enmeshed—is an infuriated little bullock of a white man, a first lieutenant, their commander, who during the mountainous accumulations of that catastrophic morning has been driven completely out of his head.

Now he stamps up and down the pier like a maddened animal, the white eyeballs, and the black, sweat-rilled faces follow him back and forth on his stamping and infuriated lunges with the patient, dutiful, and all-confiding trustfulness of children.

His red solid little face is swollen with choked fury and exasperation: as the unending chronicle of their woes mounts up he laughs insanely, clutches violently at the neck-band of his coat as if he is strangling, and stamps drunkenly and blindly about like a man maddened with the toothache.

And still they petition him, with the confident hope and certitude of trusting children that one word from their infallible governor will settle everything:—one tells about his missing belt, another of his forgotten canteen, another of his lost cap, his depleted and half-furnished knapsack—affectionately, incorrigibly, they address him as "Boss!" in spite of his curses, threats, entreaties, his final maddened screams that they must address him in a military manner, and the man stamps up and down, out of his wits with choking and unutterable exasperation, cursing vilely:

"You God-damned black bone-headed gang of sausage-brained gorillas!" he yells chokingly, and clutches at his throat—"Oh, you damned thick-skulled solid-ivory idiot brothers of a one-eyed mule! You sweet stinking set of ape-faced sons-of-bitches, you! If your brains were made of dynamite you wouldn't have enough to blow your nose, you poor dumb suffering second cousins of an owl! . . . Oh, you just wait, you ink-complected bastards, you!" he now shouts with a kind of fiendish and anticipatory pleasure. "Just wait until I get

you in the front-line trenches—I'll line you up there till
those German bastards shoot you full of daylight if it's
the last thing I ever live to do, you . . . damned . . .
ignorant . . . misbegotten . . . cross . . . between a
. . . a . . . a . . . wall-eyed possum and a camel's
hump—why, you low-down, ignorant bunch of . . .
of——"

"Boss?"

"Don't call me Boss!" in a high, choking, almost
strangled gurgle. "You dumb son-of-a-bitch, how often
have I got to tell you not to call me BOSS!" he yells.

"I know, Boss—" in a plaintive tone—"but my belt-
buckle's busted. Is you got a piece of string?"

"A *piece of string!*" he chokes. "Why, you damned—
you—you—a piece of string!" he squeaks, and finally
defeated, he takes off his cap, throws it on the floor and,
sobbing, stamps upon it.

But an even greater affliction is in store for this unhappy man. Down at the shipside now, where the examining officers are sitting at the table, there has come a
sudden pause, a disturbing interruption in the swift and
mechanical dispatch with which the troops have been
filing in before them. Six of the big black soldiers in a
group have been stopped, sharply questioned, and then
brusquely motioned out of line.

The officer picks up his cap, yells, "What in Christ's
name is the matter now?" and rushes down to where they
stand, in an attitude of crushed dejection, with tears
rolling down their ebony cheeks. A moment's excited
interrogation of the officers seated at the table informs
him of the trouble: the six Negroes, all of whom are
members of his command, have been under treatment
for venereal diseases, but have somehow managed to
sneak away from camp without a clean bill of health.
Now their delinquency and stratagem of escape has been

discovered, they have been denied their embarkation papers, and weeping and begging, with the pitiable confidence which all these blacks put in their commanding officer, they are fairly groveling before him, pleading with him that they be allowed to take ship with the rest of their companions.

"We ain't done nothin', Boss!" their leader, a huge ape of a man, black as ebony, is sniffling, pawing at the officer's sleeve. "Dey ain't nothin' wrong with us!"—"We don't want to stay heah in dis Gawd-damn hole, Boss!" another sniffles. "We want to go to France wheah you is! . . . Don't leave us behind, Boss! . . . We'll do any-t'ing you say if you'll jest take us along wid you!——"

"Why, you black clappy bastards!" he snarls—"I wish you were in hell, the lot of you! . . . How the hell do you expect *me* to do anything now at the last moment?" he yells, and filled with a frenzy that can find no stay or answer he goes stamping back and forth like a man gone mad with the very anguish of exasperation and despair. He charges into the midst of that small group of tainted and dejected blacks like a maddened little bull. He raves at them, he reviles them and curses them most foully, for a moment it seems that he is going to assault them physically. And they gather around him, weeping, entreating, crying, begging him for rescue and release, until at length, as if driven frantic by their clamor, he claps both hands to his ears and screaming, "All right, all right, all right!—I'll try—but if they let you go I hope they kill every clappy son-of-a-bitch in the first attack"—he rushes away to the table where the examining officers are seated at their work, engages them long and earnestly in a passionate and persuasive debate and finally wins them over to his argument.

It is decided that the infected Negroes shall be given a physical examination here and now upon the pier, and a tall medical officer, delegated for this task, rises from the table, signs briefly to the rejected men, and, accompanied by their red-faced little officer, marches them away behind the concealing barrier of the great wall of sacked oats.

They are gone perhaps ten minutes: when they return the Negroes are cavorting with glee, their black faces split by enormous ivory grins, and they are scraping around their little officer like frantic children. They fairly fawn upon him, they try to kiss his hands, they pat his shoulders with their great black paws—the story of their triumphant restoration to the fold is legible in every move they make, in everything they do.

The tall medical officer marches sternly ahead, but with a faint grin playing round the corners of his mouth, and the little red-faced officer is still cursing bitterly, but in his curses now there is a gentler note, the suggestion almost of a lewd tenderness.

And at length that brown, enormous, apparently interminable column has filed into the ship's great side, and there is nothing on the pier now but far lost sounds and silence, the breath of coolness, evening, the on-coming, undulant stride of all-enfolding and deep-breasted night.

Only the Dead Know Brooklyn

DERE'S no guy livin' dat knows Brooklyn t'roo an' t'roo, because it'd take a guy a lifetime just to find his way aroun' duh f—— town.

So like I say, I'm waitin' for my train t' come when I sees dis big guy standin' deh—dis is duh foist I eveh see of him. Well, he's lookin' wild, y'know, an' I can see dat he's had plenty, but still he's holdin' it; he talks good an' is walkin' straight enough. So den, dis big guy steps up to a little guy dat's standin' deh, an' says, "How d'yuh get t' Eighteent' Avenoo an' Sixty-sevent' Street?" he says.

"Jesus! Yuh got me, chief," duh little guy says to him. "I ain't been heah long myself. Where is duh place?" he says. "Out in duh Flatbush section somewhere?"

"Nah," duh big guy says. "It's out in Bensonhoist. But I was neveh deh befoeh. How d'yuh get deh?"

"Jesus," duh little guy says, scratchin' his head, y'know —yuh could see duh little guy didn't know his way about —"yuh got me, chief. I neveh hoid of it. Do any of youse guys know where it is?" he says to me.

"Sure," I says. "It's out in Bensonhoist. Yuh take duh Fourt' Avenoo express, get off at Fifty-nint' Street, change to a Sea Beach local deh, get off at Eighteent' Avenoo an' Sixty-toid, an' den walk down foeh blocks. Dat's all yuh got to do," I says.

"G'wan!" some wise guy dat I neveh seen befoeh pipes up. "Whatcha talkin' about?" he says—oh, he was wise, y'know. "Duh guy is crazy! I tell yuh what yuh do," he says to duh big guy. "Yuh change to duh West End line at Toity-sixt'," he tells him. "Get off at Noo Utrecht an' Sixteent' Avenoo," he says. "Walk two blocks oveh, foeh blocks up," he says, "an' you'll be right deh." Oh, a *wise* guy, y'know.

"Oh, yeah?" I says. "Who told *you* so much?" He got me sore because he was so wise about it. "How long you been livin' heah?" I says.

"All my life," he says. "I was bawn in Williamsboig," he says. "An' I can tell you t'ings about dis town you neveh hoid of," he says.

"Yeah?" I says.

"Yeah," he says.

"Well, den, you can tell me t'ings about dis town dat nobody else has eveh hoid of, either. Maybe you make it all up yoehself at night," I says, "befoeh you go to sleep —like cuttin' out papeh dolls, or somp'n."

"Oh, yeah?" he says. "You're pretty wise, ain't yuh?"

"Oh, I don't know," I says. "Duh boids ain't usin' my head for Lincoln's statue yet," I says. "But I'm wise enough to know a phony when I see one."

"Yeah?" he says. "A wise guy, huh? Well, you're so wise dat some one's goin' t'bust yuh one right on duh snoot some day," he says. "Dat's how wise *you* are."

Well, my train was comin', or I'da smacked him den and dere, but when I seen duh train was comin', all I said was, "All right, mugg! I'm sorry I can't stay to take keh of you, but I'll be seein' yuh sometime, I hope, out in duh cemetery." So den I says to duh big guy, who'd been standin' deh all duh time, "You come wit me," I says. So when we gets onto duh train I says to him, "Where yuh goin' out in Bensonhoist?" I says. "What numbeh are yuh lookin' for?" I says. *You* know—I t'ought if he told me duh address I might be able to help him out.

"Oh," he says, "I'm not lookin' for no one. I don't know no one out deh."

"Then whatcha goin' out deh for?" I says.

"Oh," duh guy says, "I'm just goin' out to see duh place," he says. "I like duh sound of duh name—Bensonhoist, y'know—so I t'ought I'd go out an' have a look at it."

"Whatcha tryin' t'hand me?" I says. "Whatcha tryin' t'do—kid me?" *You* know, I t'ought duh guy was bein' wise wit me.

"No," he says, "I'm tellin' yuh duh troot. I like to go

out an' take a look at places wit nice names like dat. I like to go out an' look at all kinds of places," he says.

"How'd yuh know deh was such a place," I says, "if yuh neveh been deh befoeh?"

"Oh," he says, "I got a map."

"A *map?*" I says.

"Sure," he says, "I got a map dat tells me about all dese places. I take it wit me every time I come out heah," he says.

And Jesus! Wit dat, he pulls it out of his pocket, an' so help me, but he's *got* it—he's tellin' duh troot—a big map of duh whole f—— place with all duh different pahts mahked out. You know—Canarsie an' East Noo Yawk an' Flatbush, Bensonhoist, Sout' Brooklyn, duh Heights, Bay Ridge, Greenpernt—duh whole goddam layout, he's got it right deh on duh map.

"You been to any of dose places?" I says.

"Sure," he says, "I been to most of 'em. I was down in Red Hook just last night," he says.

"Jesus! Red Hook!" I says. "Whatcha do down deh?"

"Oh," he says, "nuttin' much. I just walked aroun'. I went into a coupla places an' had a drink," he says, "but most of the time I just walked aroun'."

"Just walked aroun'?" I says.

"Sure," he says, "just lookin' at t'ings, y'know."

"Where'd yuh go?" I asts him.

"Oh," he says, "I don't know duh name of duh place, but I could find it on my map," he says. "One time I was walkin' across some big fields where deh ain't no houses," he says, "but I could see ships oveh deh all lighted up. Dey was loadin'. So I walks across duh fields," he says, "to where duh ships are."

"Sure," I says, "I know where you was. You was down to duh Erie Basin."

"Yeah," he says, "I guess dat was it. Dey had some of dose big elevators an' cranes an' dey was loadin' ships, an' I could see some ships in drydock all lighted up, so I walks across duh fields to where dey are," he says.

"Den what did yuh do?" I says.

"Oh," he says, "nuttin' much. I came on back across duh fields after a while an' went into a coupla places an' had a drink."

"Didn't nuttin' happen while yuh was in dere?" I says.

"No," he says. "Nuttin' much. A coupla guys was drunk in one of duh places an' started a fight, but dey bounced 'em out," he says, "an' den one of duh guys stahted to come back again, but duh bartender gets his baseball bat out from under duh counteh, so duh guy goes on."

"Jesus!" I said. "Red Hook!"

"Sure," he says. "Dat's where it was, all right."

"Well, you keep outa deh," I says. "You stay away from deh."

"Why?" he says. "What's wrong wit it?"

"Oh," I says, "it's a good place to stay away from, dat's all. It's a good place to keep out of."

"Why?" he says. "Why is it?"

Jesus! Whatcha gonna do wit a guy as dumb as dat? I saw it wasn't no use to try to tell him nuttin', he wouldn't know what I was talkin' about, so I just says to him, "Oh, nuttin'. Yuh might get lost down deh, dat's all."

"Lost?" he says. "No, I wouldn't get lost. I got a map," he says.

A map! Red Hook! Jesus!

So den duh guy begins to ast me all kinds of nutty questions: how big was Brooklyn an' could I find my way

aroun' in it, an' how long would it take a guy to know
duh place.

"Listen!" I says. "You get dat idea outa yoeh head
right now," I says. "You ain't neveh gonna get to know
Brooklyn," I says. "Not in a hundred yeahs. I been livin'
heah all my life," I says, "an' I don't even know all deh is
to know about it, so how do you expect to know duh
town," I says, "when you don't even live heah?"

"Yes," he says, "but I got a map to help me find my
vay about."

"Map or no map," I says, "yuh ain't gonna get to know
Brooklyn wit no map," I says.

"Can you swim?" he says, just like dat. Jesus! By dat
time, y'know, I begun to see dat duh guy was some
kind of nut. He'd had plenty to drink, of course, but he
had dat crazy look in his eye I didn't like. "Can you
swim?" he says.

"Sure," I says. "Can't you?"

"No," he says. "Not more'n a stroke or two. I neveh
loined good."

"Well, it's easy," I says. "All yuh need is a little con-
idence. Duh way I loined, me older bruddeh pitched me
off duh dock one day when I was eight yeahs old, cloes
an' all. 'You'll swim,' he says. 'You'll swim all right—
or drown.' An', believe me, I *swam!* When yuh know
yuh got to, you'll do it. Duh only t'ing yuh need is con-
idence. An' once you've loined," I says, "you've got nut-
in' else to worry about. You'll neveh forget it. It's somp'n
dat stays wit yuh as long as yuh live."

"Can yuh swim good?" he says.

"Like a fish," I tells him. "I'm a regulah fish in duh
vateh," I says. "I loined to swim right off duh docks wit
all duh oddeh kids," I says.

"What would you do if yuh saw a man drownin'?" duh
guy says.

"Do? Why, I'd jump in an' pull him out," I says. "Dat's what I'd do."

"Did yuh eveh see a man drown?" he says.

"Sure," I says. "I see two guys—bot' times at Coney Island. Dey got out too far, an' neider one could swim. Dey drowned befoeh any one could get to 'em."

"What becomes of people after dey've drowned out heah?" he says.

"Drowned out where?" I says.

"Out heah in Brooklyn."

"I don't know whatcha mean," I says. "Neveh hoid of no one drownin' heah in Brooklyn, unless you mean a swimmin' pool. Yuh can't drown in Brooklyn," I says. "Yuh gotta drown somewhere else—in duh ocean, where dere's wateh."

"Drownin'," duh guy says, lookin' at his map. "Drownin'." Jesus! I could see by den he was some kind of nut, he had dat crazy expression in his eyes when he looked at you, an' I didn't know what he might do. So we was comin' to a station, an' it wasn't my stop, but I got off anyway, an' waited for duh next train.

"Well, so long, chief," I says. "Take it easy, now."

"Drownin'," duh guy says, lookin' at his map. "Drownin'."

Jesus! I've t'ought about dat guy a t'ousand times since den an' wondered what eveh happened to 'm goin' out to look at Bensonhoist because he liked duh name! Walkin' aroun' t'roo Red Hook by himself at night an' lookin' at his map! How many people did I see get drowned out heah in Brooklyn! How long would it take a guy wit a good map to know all deh was to know about Brooklyn!

Jesus! What a nut *he* was! I wondeh what eveh happened to 'im, anyway! I wondeh if someone knocked him on duh head, or if he's still wanderin' aroun' in duh subway in duh middle of duh night wit his little map! Duh poor guy! Say, I've got to laugh, at dat, when I t'ink about him! Maybe he's found out by now dat he'll neveh live long enough to know duh whole of Brooklyn. It'd take a guy a lifetime to know Brooklyn t'roo an' t'roo. An' even den, yuh wouldn't know it all.

Dark in the Forest, Strange as Time

SOME years ago, among the people standing on one of the platforms of the Munich railway station, beside the Swiss express, which was almost ready to depart, there were a woman and a man—a woman so lovely that the memory of her would forever haunt the mind of him who saw her, and a man on whose dark face the legend of a strange and fatal meeting was already visible.

The woman was at the flawless summit of a mature and radiant beauty, packed to the last red ripeness of her lip with life and health, a miracle of loveliness in whom all the elements of beauty had combined with such exquisite proportion and so rhythmical a balance that even as one looked at her he could scarcely believe the evidence of his eyes.

Thus, although not over tall, she seemed at times to command a superb and queenly height, then to be almost demurely small and cosy as she pressed close to her companion. Again, her lovely figure seemed never to have lost the lithe slenderness of girlhood, yet it was ripe, lavish, undulant with all the voluptuous maturity of womanhood, and every movement she made was full of seductive grace.

The woman was fashionably dressed; her little toque-like hat fitted snugly down over a crown of coppery reddish hair and shaded her eyes which had a smoke-blue and depthless quality that could darken almost into black, and change with every swiftest shade of feeling that passed across her face. She was talking to the man in low and tender tones, smiling a vague voluptuous smile as she looked at him. She spoke eagerly, earnestly, gleefully to him, and from time to time burst into a little laugh that came welling low, rich, sensual, and tender from her throat.

As they walked up and down the platform talking, the woman thrust her small gloved hand through the arm of his heavy overcoat and snuggled close to him, sometimes nestling her lovely head, which was as proud and graceful as a flower, against his arm. Again they would pause, and look steadfastly at each other for a moment. Now she spoke to him with playful reproof, chided him, shook him tenderly by the arms, pulled the heavy furred lapels of his overcoat together, and wagged a small gloved finger at him warningly.

And all the time the man looked at her, saying little, but devouring her with large dark eyes that were burning steadily with the fires of death, and that seemed to feed on her physically, with an insatiate and voracious tenderness of love. He was a Jew, his figure immensely tall, cadaverous, and so wasted by disease that it was lost, engulfed, forgotten in the heavy and expensive garments that he wore.

His thin white face, which was wasted almost to a fleshless integument of bone and skin, converged to an immense hooked nose, so that his face was not so much a face as a great beak of death, lit by two blazing and voracious eyes and colored on the flanks with two burning flags of red. Yet, with all its ugliness of disease and emaciation it was a curiously memorable and moving face, a visage somehow nobly tragic with the badge of death.

But now the time had come for parting. The guards were shouting warnings to the passengers, all up and down the platform there were swift serried movements, hurried eddyings among the groups of friends. One saw people embracing, kissing, clasping hands, crying, laughing, shouting, going back for one hard swift kiss, and then mounting hastily into their compartments. And one heard in a strange tongue the vows, oaths, promises, the jests and swift allusions, that were secret and precious to each group and that sent them off at once in roars of laughter, the words of farewell that are the same the whole world over:

"Otto! Otto! . . . Have you got what I gave you? . . . Feel! Is it still there?" He felt, it was still there: fits of laughter.

"Will you see Else?"

"How's that? Can't hear"—shouting, cupping hand to ear, and turning head sideways with a puzzled look.

"I—say—will—you—see—Else?" fairly roared out between cupped palms above the tumult of the crowd.

"Yes. I think so. We expect to meet them at St. Moritz."

"Tell her she's got to write."

"Hey? I can't hear you." Same pantomime as before.

"I—say—tell—her—she's got—to write"—another roar.

"Oh, yes! Yes!" Nodding quickly, smiling, "I'll tell her."

"—or I'll be mad at her!"

"What? Can't hear you for all this noise"—same business as before.

"I—say—tell—her—I'll—be—mad—if she—doesn't

—write," roared out again deliberately at the top of his lungs.

Here, a man who had been whispering slyly to a woman, who was trembling with smothered laughter, now turned with grinning face to shout something at the departing friend, but was checked by the woman who seized him by the arm and with a face reddened by laughter, gasped hysterically.

"No! No!"

But the man, still grinning, cupped his hands around his mouth and roared:

"Tell Uncle Walter he has got to wear his——"

"How's that? Can't hear!"—cupping ear and turning head to one side as before.

"I—say," the man began to roar deliberately.

"No! No! No! Sh-h!" the woman gasped frantically, tugging at his arm.

"—to—tell—Uncle Walter—he—must—wear—his woolen——"

"No! No! No!—Heinrich! . . . Sh-h!" the woman shrieked.

"—The—heavy—ones—Aunt—Bertha embroidered with his—initials!" the man went on relentlessly.

Here the whole crowd roared, and the women screamed with laughter, shrieking protests, and saying:

"Sh-h! Sh-h!" loudly.

"Ja—I'll tell him!" the grinning passenger yelled back at him as soon as they had grown somewhat quieter. "Maybe—he hasn't—got—'em—any—more," he shouted as a happy afterthought. "Maybe—one—of —the—Fräuleins—down—there—" he gasped and choked with laughter.

"Otto!" the women shrieked. "Sh-h!"

"Maybe—one—of—the—Fräuleins—got them—away—from"—he began to gasp with laughter.

"O-o-o-t-to! . . . Shame on you—Sh-h!" the women screamed.

"Souvenir—from—old—München," roared back his fellow wit, and the whole group was convulsed again. When they had recovered somewhat, one of the men began in a wheezing and faltering tone, as he wiped at his streaming eyes:

"Tell—Else"—here his voice broke off in a feeble squeak, and he had to pause to wipe his eyes again.

"What?"—the grinning passenger yelled back at him.

"Tell—Else," he began again more strongly, "that Aunt—Bertha—oh! my God!" he groaned weakly again, faltered, wiped at his streaming eyes, and was reduced to palsied silence.

"What?—What?" shouted the grinning passenger sharply, clapping his hand to his attentive ear. "Tell Else what?"

"Tell—Else—Aunt—Bertha—is—sending—her—rec-ipe—for—layer—cake," the man fairly screamed now as if he would get it out at any cost before his impend-ing and total collapse. The effect of that apparently meaningless reference to Aunt Bertha's layer cake was astonishing: nothing that had gone before could ap-proach the spasmodic effect it had upon this little group of friends. They were instantly reduced to a shudder-ing paralysis of laughter, they staggered drunkenly about, clasped one another feebly for support, tears streamed in torrents from their swollen eyes, and from their wide-open mouths there came occasionally feeble wisps of sound, strangled gasps, faint screams from the women, a panting palsied fit of mirth from which they finally emerged into a kind of hiccoughing recovery.

What it was—the total implication of that apparently banal reference which had thrown them all into such a convulsive fit of merriment—no stranger could ever know, but its effect upon the other people was infectious; they looked towards the group of friends, and grinned, laughed, and shook their heads at one another. And so it went all up and down the line. Here were people grave, gay, sad, serious, young, old, calm, casual, and excited; here were people bent on business and people bent on pleasure; here people sharing by every act, word, and gesture the excitement, joy, and hope which the voyage wakened in them, and people who looked wearily and indifferently about them, settled themselves in their seats and took no further interest in the events of the departure—but everywhere it was the same.

People were speaking the universal language of departure, that varies not at all the whole world over—that language which is often banal, trivial, and even useless, but on this account curiously moving, since it serves to hide a deeper emotion in the hearts of men, to fill the vacancy that is in their hearts at the thought of parting, to act as a shield, a concealing mask to their true feeling.

And because of this there was for the youth, the stranger, and the alien who saw and heard these things, a thrilling and poignant quality in the ceremony of the train's departure. As he saw and heard these familiar words and actions—words and actions that beneath the guise of an alien tongue were identical to those he had seen and known all his life, among his own people—he felt suddenly, as he had never felt before, the overwhelming loneliness of familiarity, the sense of the human identity that so strangely unites all the people in the world, and that is rooted in the structure of man's life, far below the tongue he speaks, the race of which he is a member.

But now that the time had come for parting, the woman and the dying man said nothing. Clasped arm to arm they looked at each other with a stare of burning and voracious tenderness. They embraced, her arms clasped him, her living and voluptuous body drew towards him, her red lips clung to his mouth as if she could never let him go. Finally, she fairly tore herself away from him, gave him a desperate little push with her hands, and said, "Go, go! It's time!"

Then the scarecrow turned and swiftly climbed into the train, a guard came by and brutally slammed the door behind him, the train began to move slowly out of the station. And all the time the man was leaning from a window in the corridor looking at her, and the woman was walking along beside the train, trying to keep him in sight as long as she could. Now the train gathered motion, the woman's pace slowed, she stopped, her eyes wet, her lips murmuring words no one could hear, and as he vanished from her sight she cried, "*Auf Wiedersehen!*" and put her hand up to her lips and kissed it to him.

For a moment longer the younger man, who was to be this specter's brief companion of the journey, stood looking out the corridor window down the platform toward the great arched station sheds, seeming to look after the group of people departing up the platform, but really seeing nothing but the tall, lovely figure of the woman as she walked slowly away, head bent, with a long, deliberate stride of incomparable grace, voluptuous undulance. Once she paused to look back again, then turned and walked on slowly as before.

Suddenly she stopped. Someone out of the throng of people on the platform had approached her. It was a young man. The woman paused in a startled manner, lifted one gloved hand in protest, started to go on, and the next moment they were locked in a savage embrace, devouring each other with passionate kisses.

When the traveler returned to his seat, the dying man who had already come into the compartment from the corridor and had fallen back into the cushions of his seat, breathing hoarsely, was growing calmer, less exhausted. For a moment the younger man looked intently at the beaklike face, the closed weary eyes, wondering if this dying man had seen that meeting on the station platform, and what knowledge such as this could now mean to him. But that mask of death was enigmatic, unrevealing; the youth found nothing there that he could read. A faint and strangely luminous smile was playing at the edges of the man's thin mouth, and his burning eyes were now open, but far and sunken and seemed to be looking from an unspeakable depth at something that was far away. In a moment, in a profound and tender tone, he said:

"Zat vas my vife. Now in ze vinter I must go alone, for zat iss best. But in ze spring ven I am better she vill come to me."

All through the wintry afternoon the great train rushed down across Bavaria. Swiftly and powerfully it gathered motion, it left the last scattered outposts of the city behind it, and swift as dreams the train was rushing out across the level plain surrounding Munich.

The day was grey, the sky impenetrable and somewhat heavy, and yet filled with a strong, clean Alpine vigor, with that odorless and yet exultant energy of cold mountain air. Within an hour the train had entered Alpine country, now there were hills, valleys, the immediate sense of soaring ranges, and the dark enchantment of the forests of Germany, those forests which are something more than trees—which are a spell, a magic, and a sorcery, filling the hearts of men, and particularly those strangers who have some racial kinship with that land, with a dark music, a haunting memory, never wholly to be captured.

It is an overwhelming feeling of immediate and impending discovery, such as men might have who come for the first time to their father's country. It is like coming to that unknown land for which our spirits long so passionately in youth, which is the dark side of our soul, the strange brother and the complement of the land we have known in our childhood. And it is revealed to us instantly the moment that we see it with a powerful emotion of perfect recognition and disbelief, with that dreamlike reality of strangeness and familiarity which dreams and all enchantment have.

What is it? What is this wild fierce joy and sorrow swelling in our hearts? What is this memory that we cannot phrase, this instant recognition for which we have no words? We cannot say. We have no way to give it utterance, no ordered evidence to give it proof, and scornful pride can mock us for a superstitious folly. Yet we will know the dark land at the very moment that we come to it, and though we have no tongue, no proof, no utterance for what we feel, we have what we have, we know what we know, we are what we are.

And what are we? We are the naked men, the lost Americans. Immense and lonely skies bend over us, ten thousand men are marching in our blood. Where does it come from—the sense of strangeness, instant recognition, the dream-haunted, almost captured memory? Where does it come from, the constant hunger and the rending lust, and the music, dark and solemn, elfish, magic, sounding through the wood? How is it that this boy, who is American, has known this strange land from the first moment that he saw it?

How is it that from his first night in a German town he has understood the tongue he never heard before, has spoken instantly, saying all he wished to say, in a strange language which he could not speak, speaking a weird argot which was neither his nor theirs, of which he was not even conscious, so much did it seem to be the spirit of a language, not the words, he spoke, and instantly, in this fashion, understood by every one with whom he talked?

No. He could not prove it, yet he knew that it was there, buried deep in the brain and blood of man, the utter knowledge of this land and of his father's people. He had felt it all, the tragic and insoluble admixture of the race. He knew the terrible fusion of the brute and of the spirit. He knew the nameless fear of the old barbaric forest, the circle of barbaric figures gathered round him in their somber and unearthly ring, the sense of drowning in the blind forest horrors of barbaric time. He carried all within himself, the slow gluttony and lust of the unsated swine, as well as the strange and powerful music of the soul.

He knew the hatred and revulsion from the never-sated beast—the beast with the swine-face and the quenchless thirst, the never-ending hunger, the thick, slow, rending hand that fumbled with a smoldering and unsated lust. And he hated the great beast with the hate of hell and murder because he felt and knew it in himself and was himself the prey of its rending, quenchless, and obscene desires. Rivers of wine to drink, whole roast oxen turning on the spit, and through the forest murk, the roaring wall of huge beast-bodies and barbaric sound about him, the lavish flesh of the great blonde women, in brutal orgy of the all-devouring, never-sated maw of the huge belly, without end or surfeit—all was mixed into his blood, his spirit, and his life.

It had been given to him somehow from the dark time-horror of the ancient forest together with all that was magical, glorious, strange, and beautiful: the husky horn-notes sounding faint and elfin through the forests, the infinite strange weavings, dense mutations of the old Germanic soul of man. How cruel, baffling, strange, and sorrowful was the enigma of the race: the power and strength of the incorruptible and soaring spirit rising from the huge corrupted beast with such a radiant purity, and the powerful enchantments of grand music, noble poetry, so sorrowfully and unalterably woven and inwrought with all the blind brute hunger of the belly and the beast of man.

It was all his, and all contained in his one life. And it could, he knew, never be distilled out of him, no more than one can secrete from his flesh his father's blood, the ancient and immutable weavings of dark time. And for this reason, as he now looked out the window of the train at that lonely Alpine land of snow and dark enchanted forest he felt the sense of familiar recognition instantly, the feeling that he had always known this place, that it was home. And something dark, wild, jubilant, and strange was exulting, swelling in his spirit like a grand and haunting music heard in dreams.

And now, a friendly acquaintance having been established, the specter, with the insatiate, possessive curiosity of his race, began to ply his companion with innumerable questions concerning his life, his home, his profession, the journey he was making, the reason for that journey. The young man answered readily, and without annoyance. He knew that he was being pumped unmercifully, but the dying man's whispering voice was so persuasive, friendly, gentle, his manner so courteous, kind, and insinuating, his smile so luminous and winning, touched with a faint and yet agreeable expression of weariness, that the questions almost seemed to answer themselves.

The young man was an American, was he not? . . .

Yes. And how long had he been abroad—two months? Three months? No? Almost a year! So long as that! Then he liked Europe, yes? It was his first trip? No? His fourth?—The specter lifted his eyebrows in expressive astonishment, and yet his sensitive thin mouth was touched all the time by his faint, wearily cynical smile.

Finally, the boy was pumped dry: the specter knew all about him. Then for a moment he sat staring at the youth with his faint, luminous, subtly mocking, and yet kindly smile. At last, wearily, patiently, and with the calm finality of experience and death, he said:

"You are very young. Yes. Now you vant to see it all, to haf it all—but you haf nothing. Zat iss right—yes?" he said with his persuasive smile. "Zat vill all change. Some day you vill vant only a little—maybe, den, you *haf* a little—" and he flashed his luminous, winning smile again. "Und zat iss better—Yes?" He smiled again, and then said wearily, "I know. I know. Myself I haf gone eferyvere like you. I haf tried to see eferyt'ing—und I haf had nothing. Now I go no more. Eferyvere it iss ze same," he said wearily, looking out the window, with a dismissing gesture of his thin white hand. "Fields, hills, mountains, riffers, cities, peoples—you vish to know about zem all. Vun field, vun hill, vun riffer," the man whispered, "zat iss enough!"

He closed his eyes for a moment: when he spoke again his whisper was almost inaudible—"Vun life, vun place, vun time."

Darkness came, and the lights in the compartment were turned on. Again that whisper of waning life made its insistent, gentle, and implacable demand upon the youth. This time it asked that the light in the compartment be extinguished, while the specter stretched himself out upon the seat to rest. The younger man consented willingly and even gladly: his own journey was near its end and outside, the moon, which had risen early, was shining down upon the Alpine forests and snows with a strange, brilliant, and haunting magic which gave to the darkness in the compartment some of its own ghostly and mysterious light.

The specter lay quietly stretched out on the cushions of the seat, his eyes closed, his wasted face, on which the two bright flags of burning red now shone with vermilion hue, strange and ghastly in the magic light as the beak of some great bird. The man scarcely seemed to breathe: no sound or movement of life was perceptible in the compartment except the pounding of the wheels, the leathery stretching and creaking sound of the car, and all that strange-familiar and evocative symphony of sounds a train makes—that huge symphonic monotone which is itself the sound of silence and forever.

For some time held in that spell of magic light and time, the youth sat staring out the window at the enchanted world of white and black that swept grandly and strangely past in the phantasmal radiance of the moon. Finally he got up, went out into the corridor, closing the door carefully behind him, and walked back down the narrow passageway through car after car of the rocketing train until he came to the dining car.

Here all was brilliance, movement, luxury, sensual warmth and gaiety. All the life of the train now seemed to be concentrated in this place. The waiters, surefooted and deft, were moving swiftly down the aisle of the rocketing car, pausing at each table to serve people from the great platters of well-cooked food which they carried on trays. Behind them the *sommelier* was pulling corks from tall frosty bottles of Rhine wine: he would hold the bottle between his knees as he pulled, the cork would come out with an exhilarating pop, and he would drop the cork then into a little basket.

At one table a seductive and beautiful woman was eating with a jaded-looking old man. At another a huge and powerful-looking German, with a wing collar, a shaven skull, a great swine face, and a forehead of noble and lonely thought, was staring with a concentrated look of bestial gluttony at the tray of meat from which the waiter served him. He was speaking in a guttural and lustful tone, saying, *"Ja! . . . Gut! . . . und etwas von diesem hier auch. . . ."*

The scene was one of richness, power, and luxury, evoking as it did the feeling of travel in a crack European express, which is different from the feeling one has when he rides on an American train. In America, the train gives one a feeling of wild and lonely joy, a sense of the savage, unfenced, and illimitable wilderness of the country through which the train is rushing, a wordless and unutterable hope as one thinks of the enchanted city towards which he is speeding; the unknown and fabulous promise of the life he is to find there.

In Europe, the feeling of joy and pleasure is more actual, ever present. The luxurious trains, the rich furnishings, the deep maroons, dark blues, the fresh, well-groomed vivid colors of the cars, the good food and the sparkling, heady wine, and the worldly, wealthy, cosmopolitan look of the travelers—all of this fills one with a powerful sensual joy, a sense of expectancy about to be realized. In a few hours' time one goes from country to country, through centuries of history, a world of crowded culture and whole nations swarming with people, from one famous pleasure-city to another.

And, instead of the wild joy and nameless hope one feels as he looks out the window of an American train, one feels here (in Europe) an incredible joy of realization, an immediate sensual gratification, a feeling that there is nothing on earth but wealth, power, luxury, and love, and that one can live and enjoy this life, in all the infinite varieties of pleasure, forever.

When the young man had finished eating, and paid his bill, he began to walk back again through corridor after corridor along the length of the rocketing train. When he got back to his compartment, he saw the specter lying there as he had left him, stretched out upon the seat, with the brilliant moonlight still blazing on the great beak of his face.

The man had not changed his position by an inch, and yet at once the boy was conscious of some subtle, fatal change he could not define. What was it? He took his seat again and for some time stared fixedly at the silent ghostly figure opposite him. Did he not breathe? He thought, he was almost sure, he saw the motion of his breathing, the rise and fall of the emaciated breast, and yet he was not sure. But what he plainly saw now was that a line, vermilion in its moon-dark hue, had run out of the corner of the firm set mouth and that there was a large vermilion stain upon the floor.

What should he do? What could be done? The haunted light of the fatal moon seemed to have steeped his soul in its dark sorcery, in the enchantment of a measureless and inert calmness. Already, too, the train was slackening its speed, the first lights of the town appeared, it was his journey's end.

And now the train was slowing to a halt. There were the flare of rails, the switch-lights of the yard, small, bright, and hard, green, red, and yellow, poignant in the dark, and on other tracks he could see the little goods cars and the strings of darkened trains, all empty, dark, and waiting with their strange attentiveness of recent life. Then the long station quays began to slide slowly past the windows of the train, and the sturdy goatlike porters were coming on the run, eagerly saluting, speaking, calling to the people in the train who had already begun to pass their baggage through the window.

Softly the boy took his overcoat and suitcase from the rack above his head and stepped out into the narrow corridor. Quietly he slid the door of the compartment shut behind him. Then, for a moment, still unsure, he stood there looking back. In the semidarkness of the compartment the spectral figure of the cadaver lay upon the cushions, did not move.

Was it not well to leave all things as he had found them, in silence, at the end? Might it not be that in this great dream of time in which we live and are the moving figures, there is no greater certitude than this: that, having met, spoken, known each other for a moment, as somewhere on this earth we were hurled onward through the darkness between two points of time, it is well to be content with this, to leave each other as we met, letting each one go alone to his appointed destination, sure of this only, needing only this—that there will be silence for us all and silence only, nothing but silence, at the end?

Already the train had come to a full stop. The boy went down the corridor to the end, and in a moment, feeling the bracing shock of the cold air upon his flesh, breathing the vital and snow-laden air into his lungs, he was going down the quay with a hundred other people, all moving in the same direction, some towards certitude and home, some towards a new land, hope, and hunger, the swelling prescience of joy, the promise of a shining city. He knew that he was going home again.

Circus at Dawn

THERE were times in early autumn—in September —when the greater circuses would come to town —the Ringling Brothers, Robinson's, and Barnum and Bailey shows, and when I was a route-boy on the morning paper, on those mornings when the circus would be coming in I would rush madly through my route in the cool and thrilling darkness that comes just before break of day, and then I would go back home and get my brother out of bed.

Talking in low excited voices we would walk rapidly back towards town under the rustle of September leaves, in cool streets just greyed now with that still, that unearthly and magical first light of day which seems suddenly to rediscover the great earth out of darkness, so that the earth emerges with an awful, a glorious sculptural stillness, and one looks out with a feeling of joy and disbelief, as the first men on this earth must have done, for to see this happen is one of the things that men will remember out of life forever and think of as they die.

At the sculptural still square where at one corner, just emerging into light, my father's shabby little marble shop stood with a ghostly strangeness and familiarity, my brother and I would "catch" the first streetcar of the day bound for the "depot" where the circus was—or sometimes we would meet someone we knew, who would give us a lift in his automobile.

Then, having reached the dingy, grimy, and rickety

659

depot section, we would get out and walk rapidly across the tracks of the station yard, where we could see great flares and steamings from the engines, and hear the crash and bump of shifting freight cars, the swift sporadic thunders of a shifting engine, the tolling of bells, the sounds of great trains on the rails.

And to all these familiar sounds, filled with their exultant prophecies of flight, the voyage, morning, and the shining cities—to all the sharp and thrilling odors of the trains—the smell of cinders, acrid smoke, of musty, rusty freight cars, the clean pine board of crated produce, and the smells of fresh stored food—oranges, coffee, tangerines, and bacon, ham and flour and beef—there would be added now, with an unforgettable magic and familiarity, all the strange sounds and smells of the coming circus.

The gay yellow sumptuous-looking cars in which the star performers lived and slept, still dark and silent, heavily and powerfully still, would be drawn up in long strings upon the tracks. And all around them the sounds of the unloading circus would go on furiously in the darkness. The receding gulf of lilac and departing night would be filled with the savage roar of the lions, the murderously sudden snarling of great jungle cats, the trumpeting of the elephants, the stamp of the horses, and with the musty, pungent, unfamiliar odor of the jungle animals: the tawny camel smells, and the smells of panthers, zebras, tigers, elephants, and bears.

Then, along the tracks, beside the circus trains, there would be the sharp cries and oaths of the circus men, the magical swinging dance of lanterns in the darkness, the sudden heavy rumble of the loaded vans and wagons as they were pulled along the flats and gondolas, and down the runways to the ground. And everywhere, in the thrilling mystery of darkness and awakening light, there would be the tremendous conflict of a confused, hurried, and yet orderly movement.

The great iron-grey horses, four and six to a team, would be plodding along the road of thick white dust to a rattling of chains and traces and the harsh cries of their drivers. The men would drive the animals to the river which flowed by beyond the tracks, and water them; and as first light came one could see the elephants wallowing in the familiar river and the big horses going slowly and carefully down to drink.

Then, on the circus grounds, the tents were going up already with the magic speed of dreams. All over the place (which was near the tracks and the only space of flat land in the town that was big enough to hold a circus) there would be this fierce, savagely hurried, and yet orderly confusion. Great flares of gaseous circus light would blaze down on the seared and battered faces of the circus toughs as, with the rhythmic precision of a single animal—a human riveting machine—they swung their sledges at the stakes, driving a stake into the earth with the incredible instancy of accelerated figures in a motion picture. And everywhere, as light came, and the sun appeared, there would be a scene of magic, order, and of violence. The drivers would curse and talk their special language to their teams, there would be the loud, gasping, and uneven labor of a gasoline engine, the shouts and curses of the bosses, the wooden riveting of driven stakes, and the rattle of heavy chains.

Already in an immense cleared space of dusty beaten earth, the stakes were being driven for the main exhibition tent. And an elephant would lurch ponderously to the field, slowly lower his great swinging head at the command of a man who sat perched upon his skull, flourish his grey wrinkled snout a time or two, and then solemnly wrap it around a tent pole big as the mast of a racing schooner. Then the elephant would back slowly away, dragging the great pole with him as if it were a stick of matchwood.

And when this happened, my brother would break into his great *whah-whah* of exuberant laughter, and prod me in the ribs with his clumsy fingers. And farther on, two town darkeys, who had watched the elephant's performance with bulging eyes, would turn to each other with apelike grins, bend double as they slapped their knees and howled with swart rich nigger-laughter, saying to each other in a kind of rhythmical chorus of question and reply:

"He don't play with it, do he?"

"No, *suh!* He don't send no boy!"

"He don't say, 'Wait a minute,' do he?"

"No, suh! He say, 'Come with me!' That's what he say!"

"He go *boogety—boogety!*" said one, suiting the words with a prowling movement of his black face towards the earth.

"He go rootin' faw it!" said the other, making a rooting movement with his head.

"He say, 'Ar-rumpf!'" said one.

"He say, 'Big boy, we is on ouah way'!" the other answered.

"Har! Har! Har! Har! Har!"—and they choked and screamed with their rich laughter, slapping their thighs with a solid smack as they described to each other the elephant's prowess.

Meanwhile, the circus food-tent—a huge canvas top without concealing sides—had already been put up, and now we could see the performers seated at long trestled tables underneath the tent, as they ate breakfast. And the savor of the food they ate—mixed as it was with our strong excitement, with the powerful but wholesome smells of the animals, and with all the joy, sweetness, mystery, jubilant magic, and glory of the morning and the coming of the circus—seemed to us to be of the most maddening and appetizing succulence of any food that we had ever known or eaten.

We could see the circus performers eating tremendous breakfasts, with all the savage relish of their power and strength: they ate big fried steaks, pork chops, rashers of bacon, a half-dozen eggs, great slabs of fried ham, and great stacks of wheat-cakes which a cook kept flipping in the air with the skill of a juggler, and which a husky-looking waitress kept rushing to their tables on loaded trays held high and balanced marvelously on the fingers of a brawny hand. And above all the maddening odors of the wholesome and succulent food, there brooded forever the sultry and delicious fragrance—that somehow seemed to add a zest and sharpness to all the powerful and thrilling life of morning—of strong boiling coffee, which we could see sending off clouds of steam from an enormous polished urn, and which the circus performers gulped down, cup after cup.

And the circus men and women themselves—these star performers—were such fine-looking people, strong and handsome, yet speaking and moving with an almost stern dignity and decorum, that their lives seemed to us to be as splendid and wonderful as any lives on earth could be. There was never anything loose, rowdy, or tough in their comportment, nor did the circus women look like painted whores, or behave indecently with the men.

Rather, these people in an astonishing way seemed to have created an established community which lived an ordered existence on wheels, and to observe with a stern fidelity unknown in towns and cities the decencies of family life. There would be a powerful young man, a handsome and magnificent young woman with blonde hair and the figure of an Amazon, and a powerfully built, thick-set man of middle age, who had a stern, lined, responsible-looking face and a bald head. They were probably the members of a trapeze team—the young man and woman would leap through space like projectiles, meeting the grip of the older man and hurling back again upon their narrow perches, catching the swing of their trapeze in midair, and whirling thrice before they caught it, in a perilous and beautiful exhibition of human balance and precision.

But when they came into the breakfast tent, they would speak gravely yet courteously to other performers, and seat themselves in a family group at one of the long tables, eating their tremendous breakfasts with an earnest concentration, seldom speaking to one another, and then gravely, seriously, and briefly.

And my brother and I would look at them with fascinated eyes: my brother would watch the man with the bald head for a while and then turn towards me, whispering:

"D-d-do you see that f-f-fellow there with the bald head? W-w-well he's the heavy man," he whispered knowingly. "He's the one that c-c-c-catches them! That f-f-fellow's got to know his business! You know what happens if he m-m-misses, don't you?" said my brother.

"What?" I would say in a fascinated tone.

My brother snapped his fingers in the air.

"Over!" he said. "D-d-done for! W-w-why, they'd be d-d-d-dead before they knew what happened. Sure!" he said, nodding vigorously. "It's a f-f-f-fact! If he ever m-m-m-misses it's all over! That boy has g-g-g-got to know his s-s-s-stuff!" my brother said. "W-w-w-why," he went on in a low tone of solemn conviction, "it w-w-w-wouldn't surprise me at all if they p-p-p-pay him s-s-seventy-five or a hundred dollars a week! It's a fact!" my brother cried vigorously.

And we would turn our fascinated stares again upon these splendid and romantic creatures, whose lives were so different from our own, and whom we seemed to know with such familiar and affectionate intimacy. And at length, reluctantly, with full light come and the sun up, we would leave the circus grounds and start for home.

And somehow the memory of all we had seen and heard that glorious morning, and the memory of the food-tent with its wonderful smells, would waken in us the pangs of such a ravenous hunger that we could not wait until we got home to eat. We would stop off in town at lunchrooms and, seated on tall stools before the counter, we would devour ham-and-egg sandwiches, hot hamburgers red and pungent at their cores with coarse spicy sanguinary beef, coffee, glasses of foaming milk and doughnuts, and then go home to eat up everything in sight upon the breakfast table.

In the Park

THAT year I think we were living with Bella; no, we weren't, I guess we were living with Auntie Kate— well, maybe we were staying with Bella: I don't know, we moved around so much, and it's so long ago. It gets all confused in my mind now; when Daddy was acting he was always on the go, he couldn't be still a minute; sometimes he was playing in New York, and sometimes he went off on a tour with Mr. Mansfield and was gone for months.

Anyway, that night when the show was over we went out onto the street and turned up Broadway. We were both so happy and excited that we fairly bounded along, and that was the way it was that night. It was one of the first fine days in spring, the air was cool and delicate and yet soft, and the sky was of a velvety lilac texture, and it was glittering with great stars. The streets outside the theater were swarming with hansoms, four-wheelers, private carriages and victorias; they kept driving up in front of the theater all the time and people kept getting into them.

All of the men looked handsome, and all of the women were beautiful: everyone seemed to be as happy and elated as we were, it seemed as if a new world and new people had burst out of the earth with the coming of spring—everything ugly, dull, sour, and harsh had vanished—the streets were flashing with life and sparkle. I saw all of it, I felt myself a part of it all, I wanted to possess it all, and there was something I wanted to say so much it made my throat ache, and yet I could not say it because I could not find the words I wanted. I could not think of anything else to say—it sounded foolish, but suddenly I seized my father's arm and cried: "Oh, to be in April, now that England's there."

"Yes!" he shouted, "Also in Paris, Naples, Rome, and Dresden! Oh, to be in Budapest!" cried Daddy, "now that April's here and the frost is on the pumpkin, and the dawn comes up like thunder out of the night that covers me."

He seemed to have grown young again; he was the way he used to be when I was a little girl and I would knock at his study door and he would call out in a wonderful actor's voice, "Enter, Daughter of Des-o-la-tion, into this abode of mis-er-ee."

His eyes sparkled, and he threw back his head and laughed his wild and happy laugh.

I think that must have been the year before he died; I was about eighteen: I was a beauty—I was like peaches and cream——

In those days when he was acting I used to meet him after the theater and we would go somewhere to eat. *There* was a fellow after your heart: the very best was *just* about good enough for him. New York was awfully nice in those days. They had such nice places to go to— I don't know, they didn't have all this noise and confusion; it seems like another world sometimes. You could go to White's or Martin's or Delmonico's—there were a lot of nice places. There was also a place called Mock's; I never went there, but one of the first things I remember as a child was hearing Daddy come home late at night and say he'd been to Mock's. When he came home, I would listen at the grating of the heater in my room and I could hear him and the other actors talking to my mother: it was fascinating; and sometimes it was all about Mock's. "Oh, have you been to Mock's?" I thought I heard my mother say. "Oh, yes! I have been to Mock's," my father said. "And what did you have at Mock's?" my mother said. "Oh, I had some oysters and a glass of beer and some mock-turtle soup at Mock's," my father said.

We used to go to White's almost every night after the show, with two priests who were friends of Daddy's: Father Dolan and Father Chris O'Rourke. Father Dolan was a big man with the bluest eyes I ever saw, and Father Chris O'Rourke was a little man with a swarthy and greasy face: it was all full of black marks, it was one of the strangest faces I ever saw; but there was something very powerful and sweet about it. Father

Dolan was a very fine, high sort of man: he was very kind
and jolly, but he also had a fine mind and he was very
outspoken and honest. He loved the theater, he knew
a great many actors, a great many of them went to his
Church, and he loved my father. He was a great scholar,
he knew the plays of Shakespeare almost by heart—
he and Daddy used to tag each other's lines, to see who
knew the most. I never knew my father to catch him up
but once, and that was on a line from *King Lear*, "The
prince of darkness is a gentleman"—Father Dolan said
it came from *As You Like It*."

How those fellows loved to eat and drink: if one of
them had to say Mass the next day we had to hurry,
because you can't eat or drink after midnight if you are
saying Mass the next day. Because of this, both these
priests would immediately take out their watches and
lay them on the table before them when they sat down.
Father Chris O'Rourke drank nothing but beer and as
soon as he sat down a waiter would bring him a half-
dozen glasses which he would drink at once. But if these
two priests had a glass of beer on the table before them
when midnight came, they left it: no matter what it was,
no matter whether they'd finished eating or drinking or
not, when the stroke of midnight came these fellows quit,
if they were going to say Mass the morning after.

Father Chris O'Rourke would eat and drink for almost
an hour as if his life depended on it: he was very near-
sighted, he wore thick glasses, and from time to time
he would seize his watch and bring it right under his
nose while he peered and squinted at it. Because of his
own hurry to get through before twelve o'clock, he
thought everyone else must be the same way: he was
afraid someone would not get fed, and he was always
urging and belaboring people to hurry up and eat. Father Dolan loved to eat, too, but he was a great talker:

sometimes he would get to talking to Daddy and forget to eat: when he did this Father Chris O'Rourke would almost go out of his head, he would keep nudging and poking at Father Dolan and pointing at his watch with a look of agony on his face, leaning over and muttering at him in an ominous sort of way, "You're going to be *late!* It's almost *twelve!*"

"Bedad, then!" said Father Dolan, "I'll be late!" He was a big man, but he had a funny little Irish voice; it was very crisp and jolly and had a little chuckling lilt in it, and it seemed to come from a long way off. "I never saw a man like ye, Chris, to be always thinkin' of his belly! Did the great Saints of the Church spend their time guzzlin' and crammin', or did they spend it in meditatin' and prayin' an' mortifyin' their flesh? Did ye never hear of the sin of gluttony?"

"Yis," said Father Chris O'Rourke, "that I have, an' I've also heard of the wicked sin of wanton waste. Shame on ye, Dan Dolan, wit yer talk about the great Saints of the Church: there was niver a great Saint yit that would praise a man fer wastin' what the Lord had set before him. Do ye think I'll sit here an' see good food go to waste whin there's poor people all over the world tonight that's goin' witout?"

"Well," said Father Dolan, "I've read most of the argyments of the learned reasoners of the Church, as well as the damnable heresies of the infidels, all the way from St. Thomas Aquinas to Spinozey, an' in me young days I could split a hair meself wit the best of them, but in all me life I niver heard the beat of that one: it makes Aristotle look like Wordsworth's Idiot Boy. Bedad, if ye can prove that what ye're doin' wit yer gorgin' is feedin' the poor all over the earth, I won't put anything past yer powers of reasonin', Chris—ye could show the Pope that Darwin was a Jesuit, an' he'd believe ye!"

Well, as I say, when we got to the restaurant the first thing Father Chris O'Rourke would do was to lay his watch upon the table, and the first thing Daddy would do was to order two or three bottles of champagne: they used to know we were coming and it would be waiting for us in great silver buckets full of ice. Then Daddy would pick up the menu—it was a great big card simply covered with the most delicious things to eat, and he would frown and look serious and clear his throat, and say to Father Dolan, "What does the pontifical palate crave, Dan?"

After the play, that night, we went to White's and these two priests were waiting for us when we got there. A little later Mr. Gates came in—he's still alive, I saw him on the street the other day, he's getting quite old. He was married to one of the most beautiful women you ever saw, and she was burned to death in an automobile accident. He saw the thing happen right under his eyes: isn't that the most horrible thing you ever heard of? Well, you could tell by the way Mr. Gates walked that he was awfully excited about something: he was another of these great fat fellows, and you could see his old jowls quivering as he came.

"Good God!" said Daddy, "here comes Bunny with a full head of steam on!"

Mr. Gates began to speak to Daddy half across the room, all of the people stopped and stared at him.

"Joe! Joe!" he said—he had a funny hoarse kind of voice, one of those foggy whisky voices; I think he drank a good deal. "Joe, do you know what I've done? I've just bought a horseless carriage. Come on! You're going for a ride with me!"

"Now, wait! Wait! Wait!" said Daddy, holding up his hand just like an actor. "Not so fast, Bunny! Sit down and have a bite to eat first, and tell us about it. When did you do this desperate deed?"

"Today," Mr. Gates said in a sort of hoarse whisper. "Do you suppose I've done right?"

He looked around at us with his old eyes simply bulging out of his head and with a sort of scared look on his face. Oh! We laughed so much about it: Father Dolan began to laugh, and Daddy had to pound him on the back, he got to coughing so!

Mr. Gates was an awfully nice man: he was a great fat fellow, but he was so handsome; there was something so delicate about him, his mouth kept trembling and twitching so when he was excited and wanted to say something. I think that was why they called him Bunny.

So Daddy said, "Sit down and have something to eat and then we'll see."

Mr. Gates said, "Say, Joe, I've got the mechanic outside here, and I don't know what to do with him."

"You mean you hired him for keeps?" Daddy said.

"Yes," Mr. Gates said, "and I'm damned if I'm not embarrassed! I don't know what to do with him. I mean, what is his social standing?"

"Does he wash?" Daddy said.

"Well," said Mr. Gates, looking at Father Dolan, "I think he uses holy water."

"Oh, Mr. Gates!" I said. "How awful! Right before Father Dolan, too!"

But Father Dolan laughed just as I knew he would: he was another great fat fellow, he was an awfully nice man. Father Chris O'Rourke laughed, too, but I don't think he liked it so much.

"I mean," Mr. Gates said, "I don't know how to treat the man. Is he above me, or below me, or what?"

"It looks to me," Daddy said, "as if he were on top of

you. I think you've gone and got yourself saddled with a black elephant."

Daddy was so wonderful like that, everybody loved him. Mr. Gates was so worried about the driver: it all seems so funny now to think back on it—he didn't know whether the man was to eat at the table with his family, and be treated like one of them, or what. There was something so delicate about Mr. Gates: he was big and fat, but a very sensitive, fine person.

"It looks like a neat little problem in social etiquette, Bunny," Daddy said. "Well, let's have him in here for a bite to eat. We'll see what he looks like."

So Mr. Gates went out and got him, and pretty soon he came back with him, and he was really an awfully nice young fellow: he had a little mustache, and he wore a Norfolk jacket and a flat cap, and everybody stared so, and nudged each other, he was awfully embarrassed. But Daddy was wonderful with people, he made him feel right at home. He said, "Sit down, young fellow. If we're going to run an engine we've got to feed the driver."

So he sat down, and we had a wonderful meal: you'd get great juicy chops in that place, cooked in butter, and steaks an inch thick, and the most marvelous oysters and sea food.

I know it was pretty late in the season, but we started off with oysters and champagne: I don't think the young fellow was used to drinking. Daddy kept filling up the young fellow's glass, and he got quite drunk. He was awfully funny, he kept talking about his responsibility.

"It's a terrible responsibility to know that all these lives are dependent on you," he said; then Daddy would fill up his glass again.

"A moment's hesitation in a crisis," he said, "and all is lost."

"A truer word was never spoken," said Daddy, and he filled his glass up again.

"A man must have a clear brain and a steady hand," he said.

"Right you are," said Daddy. "This will make you so steady, son, that you will get practically paralyzed."

Mr. Gates and Father Dolan laughed so much that the tears began to trickle down their cheeks. Oh, we had an awfully good time in those days, there was something so innocent about everything.

Then we all got up to go, and I was really quite nervous: the poor kid could hardly stand up, and I didn't know what was going to happen. Daddy was so happy and excited, there was something so wild about him, his eyes danced like devils, and he threw back his head and laughed, and you could hear him all over the place.

Father Chris O'Rourke had to hold Mass the next morning, and he left us, but Father Dolan came along. We all went outside, with the young man being helped along by Daddy and Mr. Gates, and everyone in the restaurant followed us outside, and Mr. Gates told me to sit up front beside the driver. God, I was proud! And Daddy and Mr. Gates and Father Dolan got in behind; how they ever did it I don't know, it must have been awfully small—I think Daddy must have sat on Father Dolan's lap. Oh, yes! I know he did.

And everybody cheered as we started off: the actors followed us out of the restaurant and stood looking after us as we drove off into the lilac and velvet darkness, and I can still remember how I looked back and saw their smiling and unnatural faces, their bright masks, their lonely and haunted eyes. They kept shouting funny things at Daddy and asking if he had any last messages, and De Wolfe Hopper was there and he ran around pretending to be a horse and neighing, and trying to climb up a lamppost. Oh, it was thrilling!

So Mr. Gates said, "Whither away, Joe?"

And Daddy said, "To the Golden Gate and may she never stop!"

Then Daddy said to the young fellow who was driving, "How fast can she go, son?" and the young fellow said, "She can do twenty miles an hour without any trouble."

"Downhill, you mean," said Daddy just to tease him, so we started to go, and God! I was thrilled! It seemed to me we were flying. I suppose he did go twenty miles an hour, but it seemed like a hundred would now and we passed a policeman on a horse and the horse got frightened and tried to run away and God! the cop was so mad: he came galloping after us and shouted for us to stop, and Daddy laughed just like a crazy man and said, "Go on, son! Go on! There's not a horse in the world can catch you!"

But the young fellow was scared and he slowed down and then the cop came up and said what did we mean, and where did we think we were, and he'd a good mind to put us all under arrest for disturbing the peace at that hour of night, with "that thing"; he kept calling it "that thing" in such a scornful way, and I got so angry at him, I thought it was so beautiful, it was painted the richest kind of winy red, it looked good enough to eat, and I was so mad to think the man should talk that way.

I don't know why it made me mad, but I think the reason must have been that the car didn't seem to me like a thing at all. It's hard to tell you how it was, but it was almost as if the car were some strange and beautiful and living creature which we had never known before but which now gave to all our lives a kind of added joy and warmth and wonder. And I believe that was the way it was with those first motor cars. Somehow each one of them seemed different from all the others, each one seemed to have a different name, a separate life and personality; and although I know they would look crude and funny and old-fashioned now, it was all different then. We had never seen or known them in the world before, we had only dreamed or heard they could exist, and now that I was riding in one, it all seemed unbelievable and yet gloriously real and strange, as every beautiful thing is when it first happens to you. The car was as magical to me as if it had come out of some other world like Mars, and yet the very moment that I saw it I seemed to have known about it always, and it seemed to belong to that day, that hour, that year, somehow to be a part of all that happened that night; to belong to Daddy and the priests and Mr. Gates, the young mechanic and all the haunted faces of the actors, and to all the songs we sang that year, the things we did and said, and something strange and innocent and lost and long ago.

I can remember now the way the old car looked, so well that I could close my eyes and draw it for you. I can remember its rich wine-color, its great polished lamps of brass, the door that opened in its round, fat back, and all its wonderful and exciting smells—the strong and comforting smell of its deep leather, and the smells of gasoline and oil and grease that were so strong and warm and pungent that they seemed to give a kind of thrilling life and ecstasy to everything in the whole world. They seemed to hold the unknown promise of something wonderful and strange that was about to happen and that belonged to the night, and to the mystery and joy of life, the ecstasy of the lilac dark, as all the smells of flowers and leaf and grass and earth belonged to them.

So I guess that was the reason that I got so mad when I heard the policeman call the car "that thing," although I did not know the reason then. It looked as if the cop were going to run us in, but then Daddy got up out of Father Dolan's lap, and when the cop saw Father Dolan of course he got very nice to us: and Mr. Gates talked to him and gave him some money, and Daddy joked with him and made him laugh, and then Daddy showed him his police badge and asked him if he knew Big Jake Dietz at police headquarters, and told him he was one of Jake's best friends, and then I was so proud to see the way the cop came round.

And the cop said for us all to go into Central Park and we could ride all we damn pleased for all he cared, but you wouldn't catch him in one of those things, they'd blow up on you at any moment and then where'd you all be? And Daddy said he hoped we'd all be in Heaven, and what's more we'd take our own priest with us, so there'd be no hitch in any of the formalities, and we all got so tickled and began to laugh and the cop did too, and then he began to brag about his horse, and God! it *was* a beautiful horse, and he said give him a horse always, that they'd never make one of those things that could go faster than a horse. The poor fellow! I wonder what he'd say now!

And Daddy teased him and said the time would come when you'd have to go to the zoo to see a horse, and the policeman said by that time you'd have to go to a junkshop to see a motor car, and Daddy said, "The trouble with us is that we're anachronisms." And the policeman said, well, he didn't know about that, but he wished us luck and hoped we all got out of it alive.

So he rode off and we drove into Central Park and started off as hard as we could go and began to climb a hill, when sure enough, we broke down just as the policeman said we would. I guess the young fellow may have had too much to drink, he seemed wild and excited, but anyway we saw a hansom halfway up the hill in front of us and he cried out, "Watch me pass them," and did something to the car, and just as we got up even with them and were trying to go by, the car coughed and spluttered and stood still. Well, we could hear the people in the hansom laughing, and one of them shouted something back to us about the tortoise and the hare. And I felt so mad at them and so humiliated and so sorry for our driver, and Daddy said, "Never mind, son, the race may not always be to the swift, but even the hare will sometimes have his day."

But our young fellow felt so bad he couldn't say a word. He got out of the car and walked round and round it, and finally he began to explain to us the way it happened and how it could never happen again in a hundred years. And well, you see it was this way, and well, you see it was that. And we didn't understand a word of what he was saying, but we felt so sorry for him that we told him he was right. So he began to poke around inside of it, and then he would turn something here and twist something there, and grab the crank and whirl it round and round until I was afraid he was going to wring his arm off. Then he would get down on his back and crawl in under it and bang and hammer at something underneath. And nothing happened. Then he would get up and walk round and round the car again and mutter to

678   FROM DEATH TO MORNING

himself. Finally, he gave up and said he was afraid we'd
have to get out of the car and take a hansom if we
wanted to get home without walking. So we started to
get out, and the mechanic was so mad and so embarrassed at the way his car had acted that he grabbed it
and shook it as if it were a brat. And nothing happened.

He gave it one last try. He grabbed the crank like a
crazy man and began to whirl it round and round until
he was exhausted. And when nothing happened he suddenly shouted out, "Oh, damn that thing," kicked it in
the tire as hard as he could, and collapsed across the
radiator, sobbing as if his heart would break. And I don't
know what that did to it or how it happened, but suddenly the car began to chug and wheeze again, and there
we were ready to go, and the young fellow with a grin
that stretched from ear to ear.

So we went on up that hill and coasted down the next,
and now we really seemed to fly. It was like soaring
through the air, or finding wings you never knew you
had before. It was like something we had always known
about and dreamed of finding, and now we had it like a
dream come true. And I suppose we must have gone the
whole way round the park from one end to another, but
none of us really knew how far we went or where we
were going. It was like that kind of flight you make in
dreams, and sure enough, just like something you are
waiting for in a dream, we came tearing around a curve
in the road and there before us we could see the same
hansom we had tried to pass upon the hill. And the
minute that I saw it I knew that it was bound to happen,
it seemed too good to be true, and yet I had felt sure all
the time that it was going to turn out just this way. And
that was the way it was with all of us, we threw back
our heads and roared with laughter, we yelled and waved

our hands at all the people in the cab, we went tearing by them as if they were rooted to the earth, and as we passed them Daddy turned and shouted back at them, "Cheer up, my friends, they also serve who only stand and wait."

So we passed them by and left them far behind us and they were lost; and now there was nothing all around us but the night, the blazing stars, the lilac darkness in the park, and God! but it was beautiful. It was just the beginning of May and all the leaves and buds were coming out, they had that tender feathery look, and there was just a little delicate shaving of moon in the sky, and it was so cool and lovely, with the smell of the leaves, and the new grass, and all the flowers bursting from the earth till you could hear them grow: it seemed to me the loveliest thing that I had ever known, and when I looked at my father, his eyes were full of tears and he cried out, "Glory! Oh, glory! Glory!" and then he began in his magnificent voice, "What a piece of work is a man! how noble in reason! how infinite in faculty! in form and moving how express and admirable! in action how like an angel! in apprehension how like a god!"

And the words were so lovely, the music was so grand, that somehow it made me want to cry, and when he had finished he cried out, "Glory!" once again, and I saw his wild and beautiful brow there in the darkness, and I turned my eyes up towards the sky and there were the tragic and magnificent stars, and a kind of fate was on his head and in his eyes, and suddenly as I looked at him I knew that he was going to die.

And he cried, "Glory! Glory!" and we rode all through the night, and round and round the park, and then dawn came, and all of the birds began to sing. And now the birdsong broke in the first light, and suddenly I heard each sound the birdsong made. It came to me like music I had always heard, it came to me like music I had always known, the sounds of which I never yet had spoken, and now I heard the music of each sound as clear and bright as gold, and the music of each sound was this: at first it rose above me like a flight of shot, and then I heard the sharp, fast skaps of sound the birdsong made. And now they were smooth drops and nuggets of bright gold, and now with chittering bicker and fast-fluttering skirrs of sound the palmy, honied bird cries came. And now the bird-tree sang, all filled with lutings in bright air; the thrum, the lark's wing, and tongue-trilling *chirrs* arose. And now the little brainless cries arose, with liquorous, liquefied lutings, with lirruping chirp, plumbellied smoothness, sweet lucidity. And now I heard the rapid *kweet-kweet-kweet-kweet-kweet* of homely birds, and then their *pwee-pwee-pwee:* others had thin metallic tongues, a sharp cricketing stitch, and high shrew's caws, with eery rasp, with harsh, far calls—these were the sounds the bird cries made. All birds that are awoke in the park's woodland tangles; and above them passed the whirr of hidden wings, the strange lost cry of the unknown birds in full light now in the park, the sweet confusion of their cries was mingled. "Sweet is the breath of morn, her rising sweet with charm of earliest birds," and it was just like that, and the sun came up, and it was like the first day of the world, and that was the year before he died and I think we were staying at Bella's then, but maybe we were staying at the old hotel, or perhaps we had already moved to Auntie Kate's: we moved around so much, we lived so many places, it seems so long ago, that when I try to think about it now it gets confused and I cannot remember.

THE HILLS BEYOND

Chickamauga

ON THE seventh day of August, 1861, I was nine-teen years of age. If I live to the seventh day of August this year I'll be ninety-five years old. And the way I feel this mornin' I intend to live. Now I guess you'll have to admit that that's goin' a good ways back.

I was born up at the Forks of the Toe River in 1842. Your grandpaw, boy, was born at the same place in 1828. His father, and mine too, Bill Pentland—*your* great-grandfather, boy—moved into that region way back right after the Revolutionary War and settled at the Forks of Toe. The real Indian name fer hit was Estatoe, but the white men shortened hit to Toe, and hit's been known as Toe River ever since.

Of course hit was all Indian country in those days. I've heared that the Cherokees helped Bill Pentland's father build the first house he lived in, where some of us was born. I've heared, too, that Bill Pentland's grand-father came from Scotland back before the Revolution, and that thar was three brothers. That's all the Pent-lands that I ever heared of in this country. If you ever meet a Pentland anywheres you can rest assured he's descended from one of those three.

Well, now, as I was tellin' you, upon the seventh day of August, 1861, I was nineteen years of age. At seven-thirty in the mornin' of that day I started out from home and walked the whole way in to Clingman. Jim Weaver had come over from Big Hickory where he lived the night before and stayed with me. And now he went along with me. He was the best friend I had. We had growed up alongside of each other: now we was to march alongside of each other fer many a long and weary mile—how many neither of us knowed that mornin' when we started out.

Hit was a good twenty mile away from where we lived to Clingman, and I reckon young folks nowadays would consider twenty mile a right smart walk. But fer people in those days hit wasn't anything at all. All of us was good walkers. Why, Jim Weaver could keep goin' without stoppin' all day long.

Jim was big and I was little, about the way you see me now, except that I've shrunk up a bit, but I could keep up with him anywheres he went. We made hit into Clingman before twelve o'clock—hit was a hot day, too—and by three o'clock that afternoon we had both joined up with the Twenty-ninth. That was my regiment from then on, right on to the end of the war. Anyways, I was an enlisted man that night, the day that I was nineteen years of age, and I didn't see my home again fer four long years.

Your Uncle Bacchus, boy, was already in Virginny: we knowed he was thar because we'd had a letter from him. He joined up right at the start with the Fourteenth. He'd already been at First Manassas and I reckon from then on he didn't miss a big fight in Virginny fer the next four years, except after Antietam where he got wounded and was laid up fer four months.

Even way back in those days your Uncle Bacchus had those queer religious notions that you've heared about. The Pentlands are good people, but everyone who ever knowed 'em knows they can go queer on religion now and then. That's the reputation that they've always had. And that's the way Back was. He was a Russellite even in those days: accordin' to his notions the world was comin' to an end and he was goin' to be right in on hit when hit happened. That was the way he had hit figgered out. He was always prophesyin' and predictin' even back before the war, and when the war came, why, Back just knowed that this was hit.

Why, law! He wouldn't have missed that war fer anything. Back didn't go to war because he wanted to kill Yankees. He didn't want to kill nobody. He was as tender-hearted as a baby and as brave as a lion. Some fellers told hit on him later how they'd come on him at Gettysburg, shootin' over a stone wall, and his rifle bar'l had got so hot he had to put hit down and rub his hands on the seat of his pants because they got so blistered. He was singin' hymns, they said, with tears a-streamin' down his face—that's the way they told hit, anyway—and every time he fired he'd sing another verse. And I reckon he killed plenty because when Back had a rifle in his hands he didn't miss.

But he was a good man. He didn't want to hurt a fly. And I reckon the reason that he went to war was because he thought he'd be at Armageddon. That's the way he had hit figgered out, you know. When the war came, Back said: "Well, this is hit, and I'm a-goin' to be thar. The hour has come," he said, "when the Lord is goin' to set up His kingdom here on earth and separate the sheep upon the right hand and the goats upon the left— jest like hit was predicted long ago—and I'm a-goin' to be thar when hit happens."

Well, we didn't ask him which side *he* was goin' to be on, but we all knowed which side without havin' to ask. Back was goin' to be on the *sheep* side—that's the way *he* had hit figgered out. And that's the way he had hit figgered out right up to the day of his death ten years ago. He kept prophesyin' and predictin' right up to the end. No matter what happened, no matter what mistakes he made, he kept right on predictin'. First he said the war was goin' to be the Armageddon day. And when that didn't happen he said hit was goin' to come along in the eighties. And when hit didn't happen then he moved hit up to the nineties. And when the war broke out in 1914 and the whole world had to go, why Bacchus knowed that *that* was hit.

And no matter how hit all turned out, Back never would give in or own up he was wrong. He'd say he'd made a mistake in his figgers somers, but that he'd found out what hit was and that next time he'd be right. And that's the way he was up to the time he died.

I had to laugh when I heared the news of his death, because of course, accordin' to Back's belief, after you die nothin' happens to you fer a thousand years. You jest lay in your grave and sleep until Christ comes and wakes you up. So that's why I had to laugh. I'd a-give anything to've been there the next mornin' when Back woke up and found himself in heaven. I'd've give anything just to've seen the expression on his face. I may have to wait a bit but I'm goin' to have some fun with him when I see him. But I'll bet you even then he won't give in. He'll have some reason fer hit, he'll try to argue he was right but that he made a little mistake about hit somers in his figgers.

But Back was a good man—a better man than Bacchus Pentland never lived. His only failin' was the failin' that so many Pentlands have—he went and got queer religious notions and he wouldn't give them up.

Well, like I say then, Back was in the Fourteenth. Your Uncle Sam and Uncle George was with the Seventeenth, and all three of them was in Lee's Army in Virginny. I never seed nor heared from either Back or Sam fer the next four years. I never knowed what had happened to them or whether they was dead or livin' until I got back home in '65. And of course I never heared from George again until they wrote me after Chancellorsville. And then I knowed that he was dead. They told hit later when I came back home that hit took seven men to take him. They asked him to surrender. And then they had to kill him because he wouldn't be taken. That's the way he was. He never would give up. When they got to his dead body they told how they had to crawl over a whole heap of dead Yankees before they found him. And then they knowed hit was George. That's the way he was, all right. He never would give in.

He is buried in the Confederate cemetery at Richmond, Virginny. Bacchus went through thar more than twenty years ago on his way to the big reunion up at Gettysburg. He hunted up his grave and found out where he was.

That's where Jim and me thought that we'd be too. I mean with Lee's men, in Virginny. That's where we thought that we was goin' when we joined. But, like I'm goin' to tell you now, hit turned out different from the way we thought.

Bob Saunders was our captain; L. C. McIntyre our major; and Leander Briggs the colonel of our regiment. They kept us thar at Clingman fer two weeks. Then they marched us into Altamont and drilled us fer the next two months. Our drillin' ground was right up and down where Parker Street now is. In those days thar was nothing thar but open fields. Hit's all built up now. To look at hit today you'd never know thar'd ever been an open field thar. But that's where hit was, all right.

Late in October we was ready and they moved us on. The day they marched us out, Martha Patton came in all the way from Zebulon to see Jim Weaver before we went away. He'd known her fer jest two months; he'd met her the very week we joined up and I was with him when he met her. She came from out along Cane River. Thar was a camp revival meetin' goin' on outside of Clingman at the time, and she was visitin' this other gal in Clingman while the revival lasted; and that was how Jim Weaver met her. We was walkin' along one evenin' towards sunset and we passed this house where she was stayin' with this other gal. And both of them was settin' on the porch as we went past. The other gal was fair, and she was dark: she had black hair and eyes, and she was plump and sort of little, and she had the pertiest complexion, and the pertiest white skin and teeth you ever seed; and when she smiled there was a dimple in her cheeks.

Well, neither of us knowed these gals, and so we couldn't stop and talk to them, but when Jim saw the little 'un he stopped short in his track like he was shot, and then he looked at her so hard she had to turn her face. Well, then, we walked on down the road a piece and then Jim stopped and turned and looked again, and when he did, why, sure enough, he caught *her* lookin' at him too. And then her face got red—she looked away again.

Well, that was where she landed him. He didn't say a word, but Lord! I felt him jerk there like a trout upon the line—and I knowed right then and thar she had him hooked. We turned and walked on down the road a ways, and then he stopped and looked at me and said:

"Did you see that gal back thar?"

"Do you mean the light one or the dark one?"

"You know damn good and well which one I mean," said Jim.

"Yes, I seed her—what about her?" I said.

"Well, nothin'—only I'm a-goin' to marry her," he said.

I knowed then that she had him hooked. And yet I never believed at first that hit would last. Fer Jim had had so many gals—I'd never had a gal in my whole life up to that time, but Lord! Jim would have him a new gal every other week. We had some fine-lookin' fellers in our company, but Jim Weaver was the handsomest feller that you ever seed. He was tall and lean and built just right, and he carried himself as straight as a rod: he had black hair and coal-black eyes, and when he looked at you he could burn a hole through you. And I reckon he'd burned a hole right through the heart of many a gal before he first saw Martha Patton. He could have had his pick of the whole lot—a born lady-killer if you ever seed one—and that was why I never thought that hit'd last.

And maybe hit was a pity that hit did. Fer Jim Weaver until the day that he met Martha Patton had been the most happy-go-lucky feller that you ever seed. He didn't have a care in the whole world—full of fun—ready fer anything and into every kind of devilment and foolishness. But from that moment on he was a different man. And I've always thought that maybe hit was a pity that hit hit him when hit did—that hit had to come jest at that time. If hit had only come a few years later—if hit could only have waited till the war was over! He'd wanted to go so much—he'd looked at the whole thing as a big lark—but now! Well, she had him, and he had her: the day they marched us out of town he had her promise, and in his watch he had her picture and a little lock of her black hair, and as they marched us out, and him beside me, we passed her, and she looked at him, and I felt him jerk again and knowed the look she gave him had gone through him like a knife.

From that time on he was a different man; from that time on he was like a man in hell. Hit's funny how hit all turns out—how none of hit is like what we expect. Hit's funny how war and a little black-haired gal will change a man—but that's the story that I'm goin' to tell you now.

The nearest rail head in those days was eighty mile away at Locust Gap. They marched us out of town right up the Fairfield Road along the river up past Crestville, and right across the Blue Ridge there, and down the mountain. We made Old Stockade the first day's march and camped thar fer the night. Hit was twenty-four miles of marchin' right across the mountain, with the roads the way they was in those days, too. And let me tell you, fer new men with only two months' trainin' that was doin' good.

We made Locust Gap in three days and a half, and I wish you'd seed the welcome that they gave us! People were hollerin' and shoutin' the whole way. All the women folk and childern were lined up along the road, bands a-playin', boys runnin' along beside us, good shoes, new uniforms, the finest-lookin' set of fellers that you *ever* seed—Lord! you'd a-thought we was goin' to a picnic from the way hit looked. And I reckon that was the way most of us felt about hit, too. We thought we was goin' off to have a lot of fun. If anyone had knowed what he was in fer or could a-seed the passel o' scarecrows that came limpin' back barefoot and half naked four years later, I reckon he'd a-thought twice before he 'listed up.

Lord, when I think of hit! When I try to tell about hit thar jest ain't words enough to tell what hit was like. And when I think of the way I was when I joined up— and the way I was when I came back four years later! When I went away I was an ignorant country boy, so tender-hearted that I wouldn't harm a rabbit. And when I came back after the war was over I could a-stood by and seed a man murdered right before my eyes with no more feelin' than I'd have had fer a stuck hog. I had no more feelin' about human life than I had fer the life of a sparrer. I'd seed a ten-acre field so thick with dead men that you could have walked all over hit without steppin' on the ground a single time.

And that was where I made my big mistake. If I'd only knowed a little more, if I'd only waited jest a little longer after I got home, things would have been all right. That's been the big regret of my whole life. I never had no education. I never had a chance to git one before I went away. And when I came back I could a-had my schoolin' but I didn't take hit. The reason was I never knowed no better: I'd seed so much fightin' and killin' that I didn't care fer nothin'. I jest felt dead and numb like all the brains had been shot out of me. I jest wanted to git me a little patch of land somewheres and settle down and fergit about the world.

That's where I made my big mistake. I didn't wait long enough. I got married too soon, and after that the childern came and hit was root, hawg, or die: I had to grub fer hit. But if I'd only waited jest a little while hit would have been all right. In less'n a year hit all cleared up. I got my health back, pulled myself together and got my feet back on the ground, and had more mercy and understandin' in me, jest on account of all the sufferin' I'd seen, than I ever had. And as fer my head, why hit was better than hit ever was: with all I'd seen and knowed I could a-got a schoolin' in no time. But you see I wouldn't wait. I didn't think that hit'd ever come back. I was jest sick of livin'.

But as I say—they marched us down to Locust Gap in less'n four days' time, and then they put us on the cars fer Richmond. We got to Richmond on the mornin' of one day, and up to that very moment we had thought that they was sendin' us to join Lee's Army in the north.

But the next mornin' we got our orders—and they was sendin' us out west. They had been fightin' in Kentucky: we was in trouble thar; they sent us out to stop the Army of the Cumberland. And that was the last I ever saw of old Virginny. From that time on we fought it out thar in the west and south. That's where we was, the Twenty-ninth, from then on to the end.

We had no real big fights until the spring of '62. And hit takes a fight to make a soldier of a man. Before that, thar was skirmishin' and raids in Tennessee and in Kentucky. That winter we seed hard marchin' in the cold and wind and rain. We learned to know what hunger was, and what hit was to have to draw your belly in to fit your rations. I reckon by that time we knowed hit wasn't goin' to be a picnic like we thought that hit would be. We was a-learnin' all the time, but we wasn't soldiers yet. It takes a good big fight to make a soldier, and we hadn't had one yet. Early in '62 we almost had one. They marched us to the relief of Donelson—but, law! They had taken her before we got thar—and I'm goin' to tell you a good story about that.

U. S. Grant was thar to take her, and we was marchin' to relieve her before old Butcher could git in. We was seven mile away, and hit was comin' on to sundown— we'd been marchin' hard. We got the order to fall out and rest. And that was when I heared the gun and knowed that Donelson had fallen. Thar was no sound of fightin'. Everything was still as Sunday. We was settin' thar aside the road and then I heared a cannon boom. Hit boomed five times, real slow like—Boom!—Boom! —Boom!—Boom!—Boom! And the moment that I heared hit, I had a premonition. I turned to Jim and I said: "Well, thar you are! That's Donelson—and she's surrendered!"

Cap'n Bob Saunders heared me, but he wouldn't believe me and he said: "You're wrong!"

"Well," said Jim, "I hope to God he's right. I wouldn't care if the whole damn war had fallen through. I'm ready to go home."

"Well, he's wrong," said Captain Bob, "and I'll bet money on hit that he is."

Well, I tell you, that jest suited me. That was the way I was in those days—right from the beginnin' of the war to the very end. If thar was any fun or devilment goin' on, any card playin' or gamblin', or any other kind of foolishness, I was right in on hit. I'd a-bet a man that red was green or that day was night, and if a gal had looked at me from a persimmon tree, why, law! I reckon I'd a-clumb the tree to git her. That's jest the way hit was with me all through the war. I never made a bet or played a game of cards in my life before the war or after hit was over, but while the war was goin' on I was ready fer anything.

"How much will you bet?" I said.

"I'll bet you a hundred dollars even money," said Bob Saunders, and no sooner got the words out of his mouth than the bet was on.

We planked the money down right thar and gave hit to Jim to hold the stakes. Well, sir, we didn't have to wait half an hour before a feller on a horse came ridin' up and told us hit was no use goin' any farther—Fort Donelson had fallen.

"What did I tell you?" I said to Cap'n Saunders, and I put the money in my pocket.

Well, the laugh was on him then. I wish you could a-seen the expression on his face—he looked mighty sheepish, I tell you. But he admitted hit, you know, he had to own up.

"You were right," he said. "You won the bet. But—I'll tell you what I'll do!" He put his hand into his pocket and pulled out a roll of bills. "I've got a hundred dollars left—and with me hit's all or nothin'! We'll draw cards fer this last hundred, mine against yorn—high card wins!"

Well, I was ready fer him. I pulled out my hundred, and I said, "Git out the deck!"

So they brought the deck out then and Jim Weaver shuffled hit and held hit while we drew. Bob Saunders drawed first and he drawed the eight of spades. When I turned my card up I had one of the queens.

Well, sir, you should have seen the look upon Bob Saunders' face. I tell you what, the fellers whooped and hollered till he looked like he was ready to crawl through a hole in the floor. We all had some fun with him, and then, of course, I gave the money back. I never kept a penny in my life I made from gamblin'.

But that's the way hit was with me in those days—I was ready fer hit—fer anything. If any kind of devilment or foolishness came up I was right in on hit with the ringleaders.

Well, then, Fort Donelson was the funniest fight that I was ever in because hit was all fun fer me without no fightin'. And that jest suited me. And Stone Mountain was the most peculiar fight that I was in because—well, I'll tell you a strange story and you can figger fer yourself if you ever heared about a fight like *that* before.

Did you ever hear of a battle in which one side never fired a shot and yet won the fight and did more damage and more destruction to the other side than all the guns and cannon in the world could do? Well, that was the battle of Stone Mountain. Now, I was in a lot of battles.

But the battle of Stone Mountain was the queerest one of the whole war.

I'll tell you how hit was.

We was up on top of the mountain and the Yankees was below us tryin' to drive us out and take the mountain. We couldn't git our guns up thar, we didn't try to —we didn't *have* to git our guns up thar. The only gun I ever seed up thar was a little brass howitzer that we pulled up with ropes, but we never fired a shot with hit. We didn't git a chance to use hit. We no more'n got hit in position before a shell exploded right on top of hit and split that little howitzer plumb in two. Hit jest fell into two parts: you couldn't have made a neater job of hit if you'd cut hit down the middle with a saw. I'll never fergit that little howitzer and the way they split hit plumb in two.

As for the rest of the fightin' on our side, hit was done with rocks and stones. We gathered together a great pile of rocks and stones and boulders all along the top of the mountain, and when they attacked we waited and let 'em have hit.

The Yankees attacked in three lines, one after the other. We waited until the first line was no more'n thirty feet below us—until we could see the whites of their eyes, as the sayin' goes—and then we let 'em have hit. We jest rolled those boulders down on 'em, and I tell you what, hit was an awful thing to watch. I never saw no worse destruction than *that* with guns and cannon during the whole war.

You could hear 'em screamin' and hollerin' until hit made your blood run cold. They kept comin' on and we mowed 'em down by the hundreds. We mowed 'em down without firin' a single shot. We crushed them, wiped them out—jest by rollin' those big rocks and boulders down on them.

There was bigger battles in the war, but Stone Mountain was the queerest one I ever seed.

Fort Donelson came early in the war, and Stone Mountain came later towards the end. And one was funny and the other was peculiar, but thar was fightin' in between that wasn't neither one. I'm goin' to tell you about that.

Fort Donelson was the first big fight that we was in—and as I say, we wasn't really in hit because we couldn't git to her in time. And after Donelson that spring, in April, thar was Shiloh. Well—all that I can tell you is, we was thar on time at Shiloh. O Lord, I reckon that we was! Perhaps we had been country boys before, perhaps some of us still made a joke of hit before—but after Shiloh we wasn't country boys no longer. We didn't make a joke about hit after Shiloh. They wiped the smile off of our faces at Shiloh. And after Shiloh we was boys no longer: we was vet'ran men.

From then on hit was fightin' to the end. That's where we learned what hit was like—at Shiloh. From then on we knowed what hit would be until the end.

Jim got wounded thar at Shiloh. Hit wasn't bad—not bad enough to suit him, anyways—fer he wanted to go home fer good. Hit was a flesh wound in the leg, but hit was some time before they could git to him, and he was layin' out thar on the field and I reckon that he lost some blood. Anyways, he was unconscious when they picked him up. They carried him back and dressed his wound right thar upon the field. They cleaned hit out, I reckon, and they bandaged hit—thar was so many of 'em they couldn't do much more than that. Oh, I tell you what, in those days thar wasn't much that they could do. I've seed the surgeons workin' underneath an open shed with meat-saws, choppin' off the arms and legs and throwin' 'em out thar in a pile like they was sticks of wood, some-

times without no chloroform or nothin', and the screamin'
and the hollerin' of the men was enough to make your
head turn grey. And that was as much as anyone could
do. Hit was live or die and take your chance—and thar
was so many of 'em wounded so much worse than Jim
that I reckon he was lucky they did anything fer him
at all.

I heared 'em tell about hit later, how he come to,
a-layin' stretched out thar on an old dirty blanket on the
bare floor, and an army surgeon seed him lookin' at his
leg all bandaged up and I reckon thought he'd cheer
him up and said: "Oh, that ain't nothin'—you'll be up
and fightin' Yanks again in two weeks' time."

Well, with that, they said, Jim got to cursin' and
a-takin' on something terrible. They said the language
he used was enough to make your hair stand up on end.
They said he screamed and raved and reached down
thar and jerked that bandage off and said—"Like hell I
will!" They said the blood spouted up thar like a fountain, and they said that army doctor was so mad he
throwed Jim down upon his back and sat on him and he
took that bandage, all bloody as hit was, and he tied hit
back around his leg again and he said: "Goddam you,
if you pull that bandage off again, I'll let you bleed to
death."

And Jim, they said, came ragin' back at him until you
could have heared him fer a mile, and said: "Well, by
God, I don't care if I do; I'd rather die than stay here any
longer."

They say they had hit back and forth thar until Jim
got so weak he couldn't talk no more. I know that when
I come to see him a day or two later he was settin' up
and I asked him: "Jim, how is your leg? Are you hurt
bad?"

And he answered: "Not bad enough. They can take

the whole damn leg off," he said, "as far as I'm concerned, and bury hit here at Shiloh if they'll only let me
go back home and not come back again. Me and Martha
will git along somehow," he said. "I'd rather be a cripple
the rest of my life than have to come back and fight in
this damn war."

Well, I knowed he meant hit too. I looked at him and
seed how much he meant hit, and I knowed thar wasn't
anything that I could do. When a man begins to talk
that way, thar hain't much you can say to him. Well,
sure enough, in a week or two, they let him go upon a
two months' furlough and he went limpin' away upon a
crutch. He was the happiest man I ever seed. "They gave
me two months' leave," he said, "but if they jest let me
git back home old Bragg'll have to send his whole damn
army before he gits me out of thar again."

Well, he was gone two months or more, and I never
knowed what happened—whether he got ashamed of
himself when his wound healed up all right, or whether
Martha talked him out of hit. But he was back with us
again by late July—the grimmest, bitterest-lookin' man
you ever seed. He wouldn't talk to me about hit, he
wouldn't tell me what had happened, but I knowed from
that time on he'd never draw his breath in peace until
he left the Army and got back home fer good.

Well, that was Shiloh, that was the time we didn't
miss, that was where we lost our grin, where we knowed
at last what hit would be until the end.

I've told you of three battles now, and one was funny,
one was strange, and one was—well, one showed us
what war and fightin' could be like. But I'll tell you of a
fourth one now. And the fourth one was the greatest of
the lot.

We seed some big fights in the war. And we was in
some bloody battles. But the biggest fight we fought was

Chickamauga. The bloodiest fight I ever seed was Chickamauga. Thar was big battles in the war, but thar never
was a fight before, thar'll never be a fight again, like
Chickamauga. I'm goin' to tell you how hit was at
Chickamauga.

All through the spring and summer of that year Old
Rosey follered us through Tennessee.

We had him stopped the year before, the time we
whupped him at Stone's River at the end of '62. We
tard him out so bad he had to wait. He waited thar six
months at Murfreesboro. But we knowed he was a-comin'
all the time. Old Rosey started at the end of June and
drove us out of Shelbyville. We fell back on Tullahoma
in rains the like of which you never seed. The rains that
fell the last week in June that year was terrible. But
Rosey kept a-comin' on.

He drove us out of Tullahoma too. We fell back across
the Cumberland, we pulled back behind the mountain,
but he follered us.

I reckon thar was fellers that was quicker when a fight
was on, and when they'd seed just what hit was they had
to do. But when it came to plannin' and a-figgerin', Old
Rosey Rosecrans took the cake. Old Rosey was a fox. Fer
sheer natural cunnin' I never knowed the beat of him.

While Bragg was watchin' him at Chattanooga to
keep him from gittin' across the Tennessee, he sent
some fellers forty mile upstream. And then he'd march
'em back and forth and round the hill and back in front
of us again where we could look at 'em, until you'd
a-thought that every Yankee in the world was there.
But, law! All that was just a dodge! He had fellers
a-sawin' and a-hammerin', a-buildin' boats, a-blowin'
bugles and a-beatin' drums, makin' all the noise they
could—you could hear 'em over yonder gittin' ready—

and all the time Old Rosey was fifty mile or more down-stream, ten mile *past* Chattanooga, a-fixin' to git over way down thar. That was the kind of feller Rosey was.

We reached Chattanooga early in July and waited fer two months. Old Rosey hadn't caught up with us yet. He still had to cross the Cumberland, push his men and pull his trains across the ridges and through the gaps before he got to us. July went by, we had no news of him. "O Lord!" said Jim, "perhaps he ain't a-comin'!" I knowed he was a-comin', but I let Jim have his way.

Some of the fellers would git used to hit. A feller'd git into a frame of mind where he wouldn't let hit worry him. He'd let termorrer look out fer hitself. That was the way hit was with me.

With Jim hit was the other way around. Now that he knowed Martha Patton he was a different man. I think he hated the war and army life from the moment that he met her. From that time he was livin' only fer one thing —to go back home and marry that gal. When mail would come and some of us was gittin' letters he'd be the first in line; and if she wrote him why he'd walk away like someone in a dream. And if she failed to write he'd jest go off somers and set down by himself: he'd be in such a state of misery he didn't want to talk to no one. He got the reputation with the fellers fer bein' queer—unso-ciable—always a-broodin' and a-frettin' about somethin' and a-wantin' to be left alone. And so, after a time, they let him be. He wasn't popular with most of them—but they never knowed what was wrong, they never knowed that he wasn't really the way they thought he was at all. Hit was jest that he was hit so desperate hard, the worst-in-love man that I ever seed. But, law! I knowed! I knowed what was the trouble from the start.

Hit's funny how war took a feller. Before the war I was the serious one, and Jim had been the one to play.

I reckon that I'd had to work too hard. We was so poor. Before the war hit almost seemed I never knowed the time I didn't have to work. And when the war came, why, I only thought of all the fun and frolic I was goin' to have; and then at last, when I knowed what hit was like, why, I was used to hit and didn't care.

I always could git used to things. And I reckon maybe that's the reason that I'm here. I wasn't one to worry much, and no matter how rough the goin' got I always figgered *I* could hold out if the others could. I let termorrer look out fer hitself. I reckon that you'd have to say I was an optimist. If things got bad, well, I always figgered that they could be worse; and if they got so bad they couldn't be no worse, why, then I'd figger that they couldn't last this way ferever, they'd have to git some better sometime later on.

I reckon towards the end thar, when they got so bad we didn't think they'd ever git no better, I'd reached the place where I jest didn't care. I could still lay down and go to sleep and not worry over what was goin' to come termorrer, because I never *knowed* what was to come and so I didn't let hit worry me. I reckon you'd have to say that was the Pentland in me—our belief in what we call predestination.

Now, Jim was jest the other way. Before the war he was happy as a lark and thought of nothin' except havin' fun. But then the war came and hit changed him so you wouldn't a-knowed he was the same man.

And, as I say, hit didn't happen all at once. Jim was the happiest man I ever seed that mornin' that we started out from home. I reckon he thought of the war as we all did, as a big frolic. We gave hit jest about six months. We figgered we'd be back by then, and of course all that jest suited Jim. I reckon that suited all of us. It would give us all a chance to wear a uniform and to see the world, to shoot some Yankees and to run 'em north,. and then to come back home and lord it over those who hadn't been and be a hero and court the gals.

That was the way hit looked to us when we set out from Zebulon. We never thought about the winter. We never thought about the mud and cold and rain. We never knowed what hit would be to have to march on an empty belly, to have to march barefoot with frozen feet and with no coat upon your back, to have to lay down on bare ground and try to sleep with no coverin' above you, and thankful half the time if you could find dry ground to sleep upon, and too tard the rest of hit to care. We never knowed or thought about such things as these. We never knowed how hit would be there in the cedar thickets beside Chickamauga Creek. And if we had a-knowed, if someone had a-told us, why, I reckon that none of us would a-cared. We was too young and ignorant to care. And as fer *knowin'*—law! The only trouble about *knowin'* is that you've got to know what knowin's *like* before you know what knowin' *is*. Thar's no one that can tell you. You've got to know hit fer yourself.

Well, like I say, we'd been fightin' all this time and still thar was no sign of the war endin'. Old Rosey jest kept a-follerin' us and— "Lord!" Jim would say, "will it never end?"

I never knowed myself. We'd been fightin' fer two years, and I'd given over knowin' long ago. With Jim hit was different. He'd been a-prayin' and a-hopin' from the first that soon hit would be over and that he could go back and get that gal. And at first, fer a year or more, I tried to cheer him up. I told him that hit couldn't last ferever. But after a while hit wasn't no use to tell him that. He wouldn't believe me any longer.

Because Old Rosey kept a-comin' on. We'd whup him and we'd stop him fer a while, but then he'd git his

wind, he'd be on our trail again, he'd drive us back.—
"O Lord!" said Jim, "will hit never stop?"

That summer I been tellin' you about, he drove us
down through Tennessee. He drove us out of Shelbyville,
and we fell back on Tullahoma, to the passes of the hills.
When we pulled back across the Cumberland I said to
Jim: "Now we've got him. He'll have to cross the mountains now to git at us. And when he does, we'll have him.
That's all that Bragg's been waitin' fer. We'll whup the
daylights out of him this time," I said, "and after that
thar'll be nothin' left of him. We'll be home by Christmas, Jim—you wait and see."

And Jim just looked at me and shook his head and
said: "Lord, Lord, I don't believe this war'll ever end!"

Hit wasn't that he was afraid—or, if he was, hit made
a wildcat of him in the fightin'. Jim could get fightin'
mad like no one else I ever seed. He could do things,
take chances no one else I ever knowed would take. But
I reckon hit was jest because he was so desperate. He
hated hit so much. He couldn't git used to hit the way
the others could. He couldn't take hit as hit came. Hit
wasn't so much that he was afraid to die. I guess hit was
that he was still so full of livin'. He didn't want to die
because he wanted to live so much. And he wanted to
live so much because he was in love.

. . . So, like I say, Old Rosey finally pushed us back
across the Cumberland. We was in Chattanooga in July,
and fer a few weeks hit was quiet thar. But all the time I
knowed that Rosey would keep comin' on. We got wind
of him again along in August. He had started after us
again. He pushed his trains across the Cumberland, with
the roads so bad, what with the rains, his wagons sunk
down to the axle hubs. But he got 'em over, came down
in the valley, then across the ridge, and early in September he was on our heels again.

We cleared out of Chattanooga on the eighth. And our tail end was pullin' out at one end of the town as Rosey came in through the other. We dropped down around the mountain south of town and Rosey thought he had us on the run again.

But this time he was fooled. We was ready fer him now, a-pickin' out our spot and layin' low. Old Rosey follered us. He sent McCook around down towards the south to head us off. He thought he had us in retreat but when McCook got thar we wasn't thar at all. We'd come down south of town and taken our positions along Chickamauga Creek. McCook had gone too far. Thomas was follerin' us from the north and when McCook tried to git back to join Thomas, he couldn't pass us, fer we blocked the way. They had to fight us or be cut in two.

We was in position on the Chickamauga on the seventeenth. The Yankees streamed in on the eighteenth, and took their position in the woods a-facin' us. We had our backs to Lookout Mountain and the Chickamauga Creek. The Yankees had their line thar in the woods before us on a rise, with Missionary Ridge behind them to the east.

The Battle of Chickamauga was fought in a cedar thicket. That cedar thicket, from what I knowed of hit, was about three miles long and one mile wide. We fought fer two days all up and down that thicket and to and fro across hit. When the fight started that cedar thicket was so thick and dense you could a-took a butcher knife and drove hit in thar anywheres and hit would a-stuck. And when that fight was over that cedar thicket had been so destroyed by shot and shell you could a-looked in thar anywheres with your naked eye and seed a black snake run a hundred yards away. If you'd a-looked at that cedar thicket the day after that fight was over you'd a-wondered how a hummin' bird the size of your thumbnail could a-flown through thar without bein' torn into

pieces by the fire. And yet more than half of us who
went into that thicket came out of hit alive and told the
tale. You wouldn't have thought that hit was possible.
But I was thar and seed hit, and hit was.

A little after midnight—hit may have been about two
o'clock that mornin', while we lay there waitin' for the
fight we knowed was bound to come next day—Jim woke
me up. I woke up like a flash—you got used to hit in
those days—and though hit was so dark you could
hardly see your hand a foot away, I knowed his face at
once. He was white as a ghost and he had got thin as a
rail in that last year's campaign. In the dark his face
looked white as paper. He dug his hand into my arm so
hard hit hurt. I roused up sharp like; then I seed him and
knowed who hit was.

"John!" he said—"John!"—and he dug his fingers in
my arm so hard he made hit ache—"John! I've seed him!
He was here again!"

I tell you what, the way he said hit made my blood
run cold. They say we Pentlands are a superstitious
people, and perhaps we are. They told hit how they saw
my brother George a-comin' up the hill one day at sunset,
how they all went out upon the porch and waited fer
him, how everyone, the childern and the grownups alike,
all seed him as he clumb the hill, and how he passed
behind a tree and disappeared as if the ground had
swallered him—and how they got the news ten days
later that he'd been killed at Chancellorsville on that
very day and hour. I've heared these stories and I know
the others all believe them, but I never put no stock in
them myself. And yet, I tell you what! The sight of that
white face and those black eyes a-burnin' at me in the
dark—the way he said hit and the way hit was—fer
I could feel the men around me and hear somethin'

movin' in the wood—I heared a trace chain rattle and hit was enough to make your blood run cold! I grabbed hold of him—I shook him by the arm—I didn't want the rest of 'em to hear—I told him to hush up——

"John, he was here!" he said.

I never asked him what he meant—I knowed too well to ask. It was the third time he'd seed hit in a month—a man upon a horse. I didn't want to hear no more—I told him that hit was a dream and I told him to go back to sleep.

"I tell you, John, hit was no dream!" he said. "Oh, John, I heared hit—and I heared his horse—and I seed him sittin' thar as plain as day—and he never said a word to me—he jest sat thar lookin' down, and then he turned and rode away into the woods. . . . John, John, I heared him and I don't know what hit means!"

Well, whether he seed hit or imagined hit or dreamed hit, I don't know. But the sight of his black eyes a-burnin' holes through me in the dark made me feel almost as if I'd seed hit too. I told him to lay down by me—and still I seed his eyes a-blazin' thar. I know he didn't sleep a wink the rest of that whole night. I closed my eyes and tried to make him think that I was sleepin' but hit was no use—we lay thar wide awake. And both of us was glad when mornin' came.

The fight began upon our right at ten o'clock. We couldn't find out what was happenin': the woods thar was so close and thick we never knowed fer two days what had happened, and we didn't know for certain then. We never knowed how many we was fightin' or how many we had lost. I've heard them say that even Old Rosey himself didn't know jest what had happened when he rode back into town next day, and didn't know that Thomas was still standin' like a rock. And if Old Rosey didn't know no more than this about hit, what could a common soldier know? We fought back and forth across that cedar thicket fer two days, and thar was times when you would be right up on top of them before you even knowed that they was thar. And that's the way the fightin' went—the bloodiest fightin' that was ever knowed, until that cedar thicket was soaked red with blood, and thar was hardly a place left in thar where a sparrer could have perched.

And as I say, we heared 'em fightin' out upon our right at ten o'clock, and then the fightin' came our way. I heared later that this fightin' started when the Yanks come down to the Creek and run into a bunch of Forrest's men and drove 'em back. And then they had hit back and forth until they got drove back themselves, and that's the way we had hit all day long. We'd attack and then they'd throw us back, then they'd attack and we'd beat them off. And that was the way hit went from mornin' till night. We piled up there upon their left: they mowed us down with canister and grape until the very grass was soakin' with our blood, but we kept comin' on. We must have charged a dozen times that day—I was in four of 'em myself. We fought back and forth across that wood until there wasn't a piece of hit as big as the palm of your hand we hadn't fought on. We busted through their right at two-thirty in the afternoon and got way over past the Widder Glenn's, where Rosey had his quarters, and beat 'em back until we got the whole way cross the Lafayette Road and took possession of the road. And then they drove us out again. And we kept comin' on, and both sides were still at hit after darkness fell.

We fought back and forth across that road all day with first one side and then the tother holdin' hit until that road hitself was soaked in blood. They called that road the Bloody Lane, and that was jest the name fer hit.

We kept fightin' fer an hour or more after hit had gotten dark, and you could see the rifles flashin' in the woods, but then hit all died down. I tell you what, that night was somethin' to remember and to marvel at as long as you live. The fight had set the wood afire in places, and you could see the smoke and flames and hear the screamin' and the hollerin' of the wounded until hit made your blood run cold. We got as many as we could —but some we didn't even try to git—we jest let 'em lay. It was an awful thing to hear. I reckon many a wounded man was jest left to die or burn to death because we couldn't git 'em out.

You could see the nurses and the stretcher-bearers movin' through the woods, and each side huntin' fer hits dead. You could see them movin' in the smoke an' flames, an' you could see the dead men layin' there as thick as wheat, with their corpselike faces an' black powder on their lips, an' a little bit of moonlight comin' through the trees, and all of hit more like a nightmare out of hell than anything I ever knowed before.

But we had other work to do. All through the night we could hear the Yanks a-choppin' and a-thrashin' round, and we knowed that they was fellin' trees to block us when we went fer them next mornin'. Fer we knowed the fight was only jest begun. We figgered that we'd had the best of hit, but we knowed no one had won the battle yet. We knowed the second day would beat the first.

Jim knowed hit too. Poor Jim, he didn't sleep that night—he never seed the man upon the horse that night —he jest sat there, a-grippin' his knees and starin', and a-sayin': "Lord God, Lord God, when will hit ever end?"

Then mornin' came at last. This time we knowed jest where we was and what hit was we had to do. Our line was fixed by that time. Bragg knowed at last where

Rosey had his line, and Rosey knowed where we was. So we waited there, both sides, till mornin' came. Hit was a foggy mornin' with mist upon the ground. Around ten o'clock when the mist began to rise, we got the order and we went chargin' through the wood again.

We knowed the fight was goin' to be upon the right— upon our right, that is—on Rosey's left. And we knowed that Thomas was in charge of Rosey's left. And we all knowed that hit was easier to crack a flint rock with your teeth than to make old Thomas budge. But we went after him, and I tell you what, that was a fight! The first day's fight had been like playin' marbles when compared to this.

We hit old Thomas on his left at half-past ten, and Breckenridge came sweepin' round and turned old Thomas's flank and came in at his back, and then we had hit hot and heavy. Old Thomas whupped his men around like he would crack a rawhide whup and drove Breckenridge back around the flank again, but we was back on top of him before you knowed the first attack was over.

The fight went ragin' down the flank, down to the center of Old Rosey's army and back and forth across the left, and all up and down old Thomas's line. We'd hit him right and left and in the middle, and he'd come back at us and throw us back again. And we went ragin' back and forth thar like two bloody lions with that cedar thicket so tore up, so bloody and so thick with dead by that time, that hit looked as if all hell had broken loose in thar.

Rosey kept a-whuppin' men around off of his right, to help old Thomas on the left to stave us off. And then we'd hit old Thomas left of center and we'd bang him in the middle and we'd hit him on his left again, and he'd whup those Yankees back and forth off of the right into

his flanks and middle as we went fer him, until we run
those Yankees ragged. We had them gallopin' back and
forth like kangaroos, and in the end that was the thing
that cooked their goose.

The worst fightin' had been on the left, on Thomas's
line, but to hold us thar they'd thinned their right out
and had failed to close in on the center of their line. And
at two o'clock that afternoon when Longstreet seed the
gap in Wood's position on the right, he took five brigades
of us and poured us through. That whupped them. That
broke their line and smashed their whole right all to
smithereens. We went after them like a pack of ragin'
devils. We killed 'em and we took 'em by the thousands,
and those we didn't kill and take right thar went
streamin' back across the Ridge as if all hell was at their
heels.

That was a rout if ever I heared tell of one! They went
streamin' back across the Ridge—hit was each man fer
himself and the devil take the hindmost. They caught
Rosey comin' up—he rode into them—he tried to check
'em, face 'em round, and get 'em to come on again—hit
was like tryin' to swim the Mississippi upstream on a
boneyard mule! They swept him back with them as if
he'd been a wooden chip. They went streamin' into Rossville like the rag-tag of creation—the worst-whupped
army that you ever seed, and Old Rosey was along with
all the rest!

He knowed hit was all up with him, or thought he
knowed hit, for everybody told him the Army of the
Cumberland had been blowed to smithereens and that
hit was a general rout. And Old Rosey turned and rode
to Chattanooga, and he was a beaten man. I've heard tell
that when he rode up to his headquarters thar in Chattanooga they had to help him from his horse, and that he
walked into the house all dazed and fuddled like, like

he never knowed what had happened to him—and that he jest sat thar struck dumb and never spoke.

This was at four o'clock of that same afternoon. And then the news was brought to him that Thomas was still thar upon the field and wouldn't budge. Old Thomas stayed thar like a rock. We'd smashed the right, we'd sent it flyin' back across the Ridge, the whole Yankee right was broken into bits and streamin' back to Rossville for dear life. Then we bent old Thomas back upon his left. We thought we had him, he'd have to leave the field or else surrender. But old Thomas turned and fell back along the Ridge and put his back against the wall thar, and he wouldn't budge.

Longstreet pulled us back at three o'clock when we had broken up the right and sent them streamin' back across the Ridge. We thought that hit was over then. We moved back stumblin' like men walkin' in a dream. And I turned to Jim—I put my arm around him, and I said: "Jim, what did I say? I knowed hit, we've licked 'em and this is the end!" I never even knowed if he heard me. He went stumblin' on beside me with his face as white as paper and his lips black with the powder of the cartridge bite, mumblin' and mutterin' to himself like someone talkin' in a dream. And we fell back to position, and they told us all to rest. And we leaned thar on our rifles like men who hardly knowed if they had come out of that hell alive or dead.

"Oh, Jim, we've got 'em and this is the end!" I said.

He leaned thar swayin' on his rifle, starin' through the wood. He jest leaned and swayed thar, and he never said a word, and those great eyes of his a-burnin' through the wood.

"Jim, don't you hear me?"—and I shook him by the arm. "Hit's over, man! We've licked 'em and the fight is over!—Can't you understand?"

And then I heared them shoutin' on the right, the word came down the line again, and Jim—poor Jim!—he raised his head and listened, and "O God!" he said, "we've got to go again!"

Well, hit was true. The word had come that Thomas had lined up upon the Ridge, and we had to go fer him again. After that I never exactly knowed what happened. Hit was like fightin' in a bloody dream—like doin' somethin' in a nightmare—only the nightmare was like death and hell. Longstreet threw us up that hill five times, I think, before darkness came. We'd charge up to the very muzzles of their guns, and they'd mow us down like grass, and we'd come stumblin' back—or what was left of us—and form again at the foot of the hill, and then come on again. We'd charge right up the Ridge and drive 'em through the gap and fight 'em with cold steel, and they'd come back again and we'd brain each other with the butt end of our guns. Then they'd throw us back and we'd re-form and come on after 'em again.

The last charge happened jest at dark. We came along and stripped the ammunition off the dead—we took hit from the wounded—we had nothin' left ourselves. Then we hit the first line—and we drove them back. We hit the second and swept over them. We were goin' up to take the third and last—they waited till they saw the color of our eyes before they let us have hit. Hit was like a river of red-hot lead had poured down on us: the line melted thar like snow. Jim stumbled and spun round as if somethin' had whupped him like a top. He fell right towards me, with his eyes wide open and the blood a-pourin' from his mouth. I took one look at him and then stepped over him like he was a log. Thar was no more to see or think of now—no more to reach—except that line. We reached hit and they let us have hit—and we stumbled back.

And yet we knowed that we had won a victory. That's what they told us later—and we knowed hit must be so because when daybreak came next mornin' the Yankees was all gone. They had all retreated into town, and we was left there by the Creek at Chickamauga in possession of the field.

I don't know how many men got killed. I don't know which side lost the most. I only know you could have walked across the dead men without settin' foot upon the ground. I only know that cedar thicket which had been so dense and thick two days before you could've drove a knife into hit and hit would of stuck, had been so shot to pieces that you could've looked in thar on Monday mornin' with your naked eye and seed a black snake run a hundred yards away.

I don't know how many men we lost or how many of the Yankees we may have killed. The generals on both sides can figger all that out to suit themselves. But I know that when that fight was over you could have looked in thar and wondered how a hummin' bird could've flown through that cedar thicket and come out alive. And yet that happened, yes, and something more than hummin' birds—fer men came out, alive.

And on that Monday mornin', when I went back up the Ridge to where Jim lay, thar just beside him on a little torn piece of bough, I heard a redbird sing. I turned Jim over and got his watch, his pocket-knife, and what few papers and belongin's that he had, and some letters that he'd had from Martha Patton. And I put them in my pocket.

And then I got up and looked around. It all seemed funny after hit had happened, like something that had happened in a dream. Fer Jim had wanted so desperate hard to live, and hit had never mattered half so much to me, and now I was a-standin' thar with Jim's watch and

Martha Patton's letters in my pocket and a-listenin' to that little redbird sing.

And I would go all through the war and go back home and marry Martha later on, and fellers like poor Jim was layin' thar at Chickamauga Creek.

Hit's all so strange now when you think of hit. Hit all turned out so different·from the way we thought. And that was long ago, and I'll be ninety-five years old if I am livin' on the seventh day of August, of this present year. Now that's goin' back a long ways, hain't hit? And yet hit all comes back to me as clear as if hit happened yesterday. And then hit all will go away and be as strange as if hit happened in a dream.

But I have been in some big battles, I can tell you. I've seen strange things and been in bloody fights. But the biggest fight that I was ever in——the bloodiest battle anyone has ever fought——was at Chickamauga in that cedar thicket——at Chickamauga Creek in that great war.

THE VIKING PORTABLE LIBRARY

(LIST CONTINUED ON FOLLOWING PAGE)

THE VIKING PORTABLE LIBRARY